RICHA GOYAL SIKRI

NO STONE UNTURNED

THE HUNT FOR AFRICAN GEMS: TRUE SHORT STORIES

AUSTIN MACAULEY PUBLISHERS™

LONDON • CAMBRIDGE • NEW YORK • SHARJAH

The book title *No Stone Unturned* was coined by Rachel Beitsch-Feldman.

A CIP catalogue record for this title is available from the British Library.

ISBN 9781035867844 (Paperback)
ISBN 9781035867851 (ePub e-book)

www.austinmacauley.com

First Published 2024
Austin Macauley Publishers Ltd®
1 Canada Square
Canary Wharf
London
E14 5AA

For my son, Ranvir, my most precious gem.

This book is dedicated to:
Geologists and miners, artisanal and institutional, who converse with Mother Earth to find her rare treasures.
The lapidary workers who take pebbles and rocks and transform them into gems.
Gem merchants, the original storytellers.
And coloured stones, the mineral creatures that have become my addiction, my IKIGAI.

CONTENTS

Beginnings

WRITING A book on coloured gems was never part of my life's plan. I had been serving as an executive director for one of Asia's leading aviation and tourism companies for two decades. But ten years ago, three distinct events catapulted me into an unimaginable journey, which had me thinking about a book in the middle of a global pandemic.

The first occurred in 2010 when I was trying to buy a ruby necklace. The seller claimed the rubies were untreated, but I later learnt they were glass-filled, worth a fraction of what I would have paid had I purchased the jewel.

To avoid other such fraudulent encounters, I enrolled in a private gemmology course. Seeing the microcosm of inclusions inside a gem recalibrated my perception of these rare works of mineral art, aka gemstones. In 2014, encouraged by my gemmology teacher, I created a travel experience to the sapphire mines in Sri Lanka. The second trigger was watching Sri Lankan miners extract rough gems using age-old methods, a humbling experience that made me question my past behaviour in carelessly dismissing the purchase of a jewel. But it also left many unanswered questions that led to new sojourns. Each gem adventure fuelled an insatiable desire to continue learning.

The third event was making my Instagram account public in 2017. The platform was my gem diary where I had been documenting my learnings on coloured stones. My writing style resonated with gem and jewellery lovers, industry stakeholders, and members of the press. Their attention offered opportunities to write articles, speak at conferences, and execute storytelling campaigns. In March 2018, I left my corporate career to pursue this madness that had infected my soul.

On 15th May 2020, Gemfields, the world's leading gem-mining and marketing firm announced their latest book project, a collection of adventure stories based on African gemstones with each tale modelled on actual events. They invited interested storytellers to apply.

I knew the company well, having visited their emerald mine in Zambia and their rough ruby and emerald auctions on more than one occasion. The book seemed like a gift from the gem gods, blending my love of storytelling with my coloured stone obsession. I contacted Gemfields, and by June 2020, began working on *No Stone Unturned*. Gemfields had only two conditions when they commissioned this book: 'no diamonds, and only Africa.' Outside of this, I was free to shape the content as I deemed fit.

Introduction

IF I ask you, what are the primary sources of rubies, emeralds, and sapphires? You'll probably say, Colombia, Burma (Myanmar), or Sri Lanka. The truth? About 80 per cent of coloured stones come from the incredibly diverse, spectacularly beautiful continent of Africa, most unearthed as recently as in the last 15 to 60 years.

African gem deposits are among the oldest in the world. Take emeralds, which formed ~2.7 billion years ago in South Africa, ~2.6 billion years ago in Zimbabwe, and ~500 million years ago in Zambia. Most of these deposits remained undiscovered until the 20th century. Meanwhile, the geologically younger Colombian emeralds (formed ~30-65 million years ago) attained fame courtesy of the colonial conquests and trade routes of the 16th century, which introduced the world to their exceptional beauty.

Gems have been mined through artisanal methods in Africa since the pharaohs ruled the deserts. Nonetheless, it was because of three exploration waves that the world finally learnt of their existence. The first was during the modern colonial expansion, or the 'Scramble for Africa' in the late 19th century, which brought geologists, miners, and explorers from the West to aid the search for minerals. After World War II, as African nations became independent, a combination of factors - infrastructure development, population expansion, and the need for income - fuelled a second wave of discovery. We are now in the midst of the third wave and there will be many more, as the African mineral story has only just begun.

Since time immemorial, coloured gems have been reservoirs of wealth, communicators of status, culture, taste, and time capsules. Most were first valued for their functional capabilities, as exemplified by ancient tools like the 385,000-year-old quartz blades found in Southern India, and a 7,000-year-old wooden axe with a nephrite (jade) blade from China. Lapis lazuli, agate, chalcedony, and garnets were inscribed with symbols to create seals and signatures in Egypt, the Indus Valley, Mesopotamia, Greece, and Rome.

I can go on about how gems were carved into artefacts and jewels, playing a vital role in denoting rank and healing, how they started and ended wars, killed, and saved lives. But even if I acknowledge every single way gems have served humans, I can't do justice to these wondrous mineral creatures. Why? Because the one aspect about a gem you won't learn in an academic course, museum, or jewellery store is their intangible power to hypnotise, enchant, and cast a spell. The interaction of light with their colourful hearts impacts us at a visceral level that can't be explained in words and must only be experienced. I believe it's because the elements found in gemstones like chromium, iron, and manganese (to name three), are also found in humans.

This book is an attempt to shine a light on the world's most notable gem deposits that happen to be in Africa, and the incredible individuals connected with their stories, while demystifying the secrets of the Earth, and the gem and jewellery industry. Use each story as a portal to travel to a colourful world where you will learn new things, laugh, smile, fall in love, and hopefully, like me, never leave. So, grab that popcorn, coffee, or something stronger, as we embark on a fantastical journey into a colourful realm like no other.

T for Tourmaline

April 1968
Madagascar

'DON'T MOVE, don't think, just go back to sleep,' Julius told himself sternly. He lay restless in the dark, listening to the rhythmic hum of the ceiling fan. His mind refused to rest, replaying his journey from Germany to Madagascar. The night's shadows turned into worrisome thoughts.

I hope that shipment of rough emeralds reached the lapidary. The order deadline for the necklace layout is only two months away. Taking a deep breath, he turned, provoking a groan from the sofa as it struggled to contain his six-foot frame. *That last glass of red wine with dinner was not a good idea after the long flight.*

Parched, Julius reached for the water jug and almost knocked over the vase on the crowded side table, unlocking a memory he was cursed to repeatedly recall. That fateful Wednesday he'd asked his mother to lay dinner earlier than usual so he could catch a movie with his friends.

As Julius's eyes adjusted to the darkness of the room, he pictured the dinner scene from eight years ago at his home in Idar-Oberstein, Germany. His father, with whom he shared a strong bond, was seated to his right. Julius was enthusiastically sharing with him details of his recent gem-cutting internship at Master Wilhelm Dreher's lapidary.

The aroma of roast chicken infused the room as his mother placed the platter on the table. But before she could sit down, Julius, gesturing animatedly, accidentally knocked over her red wine glass. She shrieked. His father quickly stood up to help.

'Let's focus on dinner now, Julius. We'll discuss business tomorrow,' he said.

The memory of that night embedded its hooks, dragging Julius into a past he didn't wish to revisit. He recalled making mental notes while walking home after the movie; he wanted to continue the dinnertime discussion with his father. Turning the corner towards his house, he was surprised to bump into their family doctor.

'Julius! Where have you been?' the doctor exclaimed. 'Go home now; your father is dying. He's had a heart attack.'

And just like that, at age 19, Julius's life changed. That conversation with his father, forever incomplete.

Shaking himself from the cold clutches of dark reflections, Julius fumbled for the lamp switch. He squinted as the light jolted him back to reality: he was in Antananarivo, Madagascar, to acquire rough gems for his family's lapidary business in Idar-Oberstein. The lone hotel in the country's capital was sold out, prompting his gem supplier, Professor Liandrat, to offer Julius a sofa-bed in his study. It was luxurious compared to what he had endured during his gem-hunting trips to Brazil.

Unable to relax, his mind continued wandering. During the drive from the airport that morning, the cheerfully chatty taxi driver updated him on local politics. Philibert Tsiranana had been the president of Madagascar for almost ten years since he had been elected in 1959, presiding over a tumultuous period in the country's history. Critics of the government claimed the country was independent only in name since the economy was still tethered to France, and in a state of decline.

The driver said an uprising was imminent, especially from young citizens who were frustrated at the lack of job opportunities. Political complications aside, the afternoon had been productive for Julius. He'd gotten straight to work, making his first purchase—a parcel of rough aquamarine crystals—within hours of arriving in the capital.

Colour's perfect for the European market, he'd mused, taking in the icy blue hue of the crystals. But this was an easy win—he needed more to make this trip worthwhile. Perhaps he'd get lucky again, like last time when he stumbled upon a rough emerald alongside a pile of potatoes at the local market. That emerald had not only covered the expenses of his last visit but yielded a handsome profit.

The wall clock reminded him it was 3.30 am. Abandoning sleep, Julius got out of his makeshift bed and sauntered towards the bookshelves behind the sofa. The floor felt cool beneath his bare feet. He wasn't looking for anything, but when surrounded by books, courtesy demanded an exploratory browse. A light breeze carried the perfume of jasmine flowers from outside the window that intermingled with the smell of ageing print as Julius approached the bookcase.

The faint glow of the lamp directed him towards a familiar name: Lacroix. *Minéralogie de Madagascar* by Alfred Lacroix. A celebrated French mineralogist from the late 19th century, Lacroix had dedicated 25 years to studying minerals found in Madagascar. The three leather-bound volumes in the study were a compilation of his formidable research.

Grateful for his fluency in French, Julius brought the books closer to the lamp. After perusing descriptions of rock formations in volume one, he casually started flipping through the pages of volume two. *Hang on a minute; what was that?* He'd spotted something peculiar and slowly turned back the pages. There it was: a series of black and white photographs of flat gem slices with geometric patterns that Lacroix described as tourmaline.

Julius's family had been buying, cutting, and selling gem-quality tourmalines for generations, but he'd never seen anything like the specimens in the book. Are these really tourmalines? The photo caption described colour combinations of fuchsia pink with olive green, electric blue triangles encircled by purple and green bands. The design patterns on these exotic tourmalines resembled views from a child's kaleidoscope rather than a natural mineral formed millions of years ago.

Shaking his head in disbelief, Julius turned another page and stopped short. A magnified photograph of a tourmaline slice stared back at him. It showed three sharp symmetrical lines converging towards a central point from the outer rims of the slice. The closest visual reference Julius could think of was the distinctive three-pointed star of Mercedes-Benz. The star formation was surrounded by a perfect triangle, which was further encased within borders of varying colour. Mesmerised, he continued reading. Thirty minutes later, he found what would become his mission for this trip: a map showing a likely location for these alien-like mineral creations.

As the sun rose, illuminating the study two hours later, it caught Julius pacing up and down in deep thought. There was a mad glint in his eyes, a smile on his lips, and a renewed sense of purpose in his brisk stride.

'Did you sleep well?' Professor Liandrat asked Julius at breakfast.

'I did. But awoke early. I found something in your study.' Getting straight to the point was Julius's style.

The professor took the book from Julius and exchanged a smile with his wife. 'Ah! A detailed account of minerals on our island,' he said, flipping through the pages.

Julius continued, 'Professor, the author describes a unique variety of tourmaline I've never seen before. He explains that it's only found in Anjanabonoina where a gentleman called Leon Krafft was extensively mining the material. Do you know if this mine is still active? Have you heard of this Leon Krafft?'

'You are asking the wrong person, Julius,' he said, placing the book on a nearby stool. 'Speak to Mrs Liandrat,' he gestured towards her as she spread marmalade on her toast. 'You see, Leon Krafft was my father-in-law.'

* * *

The next day, Julius sat with Professor Liandrat in his garden, assessing gems. He savoured the creamy texture of his coffee, reminding himself to drink it slowly to avoid ordering another cup. The sun was high in the sky, and he stole a quick glance towards the main gate of the house. His mind struggled to stay focused on the fresh parcels of uncut gems Professor Liandrat presented for possible purchase.

During breakfast, the trio had agreed for Mrs Liandrat to visit a family friend to enquire about an old prospector called Rasimone who had mined with her father for several years at Anjanabonoina. They were waiting for her to return.

'If there's anyone who can help you find this obscure location on the map, Julius, it's probably Rasimone,' Mrs Liandrat had explained.

The light's perfect to inspect gems right now. I should make the most of it, he thought, forcing himself to return to the task at hand. Balancing a cylindrical tourmaline between his forefinger and thumb, he raised it towards the sun. In the afternoon light, the stone looked more like a crystallised rose sherbet, garnished with exotic herbs and spices, than a precious gem extracted from the depths of the Earth.

'Isn't it something?' the professor remarked, observing every micro-movement on Julius's face.

Following his mother's advice to control his facial expressions, Julius nonchalantly continued inspecting the gem. After making mistakes in the years after his father had passed, he'd developed a stricter criterion for assessing rough material. As he was looking down the length of the crystal from the top (also known as the 'C axis'), his eye caught a flash of bright yellow in the distance. It was Mrs Liandrat's dress.

'I have news!' she exclaimed, settling down in the empty lounge chair next to her husband. 'I found someone who knows Rasimone's whereabouts.' Placing the crystal on the table, Julius leaned forward. She continued, 'He now lives in Antsirabe, which is around three-and-a-half to maybe four hour's drive from here.'

'Can we go see him?' asked Julius, a smile escaping his cool demeanour.

'Of course, Julius,' she said. 'I already sent word that we'll wait for him at the Antsirabe guesthouse tomorrow at 11 am, which means we need to leave before sunrise.'

When Rasimone arrived at the guesthouse the following day, both Julius and Mrs Liandrat were there to meet him. An elderly, heavyset man, he was wearing brown pants and a faded cream-coloured shirt with beige stripes. Rasimone belonged to the Merina[1] community that dominated the region, his Malay-Indonesian ancestry reflected in his facial features. The years spent working under the sun as a prospector showed in the wrinkles around his almond-shaped eyes. Thrilled to see each other again, Mrs Liandrat and Rasimone spent the first 15 minutes reminiscing about times gone by and remembering her late father.

After initial pleasantries were exchanged, Mrs Liandrat asked the question scorching Julius's mind. 'Rasimone, can you help Mr Petsch find the location on this map where my father was mining for tourmalines with you. Do you remember how to get there?'

Scratching his balding head, Rasimone replied, 'Yes, I can do that, Madame Liandrat, but it's not so easy to find, you see.' Turning to Julius, he said, 'We'll have to walk a great distance to reach the mine. There are no roads and no bridges over rivers—just never-ending stretches of grassland and hills. I hope you're willing to pay me for my troubles, Mr Petsch?' he asked, with a twinkle in his eye.

'Yes, of course! What did you have in mind?'

'Very easy, Mr Petsch!' said Rasimone, straightening his back. 'I would like to have a small barrel of red wine. If you give this to me now, I will return tomorrow morning and take you both to the location.' Smiling, the duo agreed and sealed the deal with a handshake.

* * *

It was close to noon the next day and Julius could no longer hide his anxiety. 'Do you think he'll show?' he asked Mrs Liandrat, pacing up and down the front patio of the guest house.

'I'm not sure, Julius. We've been waiting for five hours now. It seems this old gentleman has had fun at our expense. Why don't we go inside and have

---

1 The Merina represent the dominant ethnic group in Madagascar (one of around 20). The name Merina is said to mean "elevated people" since they are from the central plateau of the country. Historians believe the Merina people entered Madagascar in the fifteenth century. Although their origins are uncertain, many believe their lineage is derived from Austronesians.

lunch?' she suggested. 'If he's still not here by the time we finish, we'll head back home.'

Julius nodded. He was disappointed but too polite to express his sentiments.

After polishing off a local fish delicacy with rice and cold beer, Julius and Mrs Liandrat decided to skip the fried banana for dessert and head home. As they stepped into the main living room with their bags, they spotted Rasimone standing by the door, crumpling his hat in his hand while cleaning his dusty shoes on the back of his trousers. On seeing them, his face lit up.

'Madame Liandrat, please excuse me for being so late. The delicious wine you gave me yesterday—I started drinking it with my friends. Then we had too much, and I overslept, but I'm here now, so let's go today!'

His forthright confession made it impossible not to smile. After deciding to stay another night at the guest house, the trio spent the rest of the afternoon organising supplies for the long drive to the mine. They agreed to leave before sunrise in Mrs Liandrat's old Land Rover, keeping a suitable buffer for delays.

* * *

It was only 6.30 in the morning, but they'd been driving for almost two hours, rattling like pebbles in a can over broken roads, when Rasimone asked the driver to stop.

'Mr Petsch, this is the end of the road,' he said.

Puzzled, Julius asked, 'So, have we reached the location?'

'No, no, we must walk now. The jeep won't go farther,' said Rasimone, as he jumped out of the Land Rover, chuckling at Julius's question.

Mrs Liandrat asked, 'Rasimone, what about all the supplies? How many hours will we have to walk? How will we carry everything?'

'Madame Liandrat, we will make an expedition. Don't worry; let's first go meet the village chief.'

They had reached the hamlet of Ambohimanambola. As the sun stretched over the horizon, a cluster of rectangular-shaped huts came into view. Their traditional earthen walls were covered with sloping thatched roofs that extended to protect the foundation from rainwater erosion. The simplicity of the structure against the lush green vegetation reminded Julius of crayon drawings from his childhood.

Surrounded by curious villagers, Rasimone explained their quest to the chief, seeking his guidance.

'Rasimone, there is no problem,' said the chief. 'To reach this location, you will have to make a safari for which you need people to help carry all your equipment and guide you on the journey. You pay me for my people's time, and I will provide you with however many you require. This is the only way.'

After settling for a then generous sum of five dollars per day, per person, to the chief's distinct satisfaction, the walking expedition was underway. Rasimone and a guide from the village were in the lead, followed by Mrs Liandrat, Julius, and ten villagers carrying food, camping equipment, tools, and water. A cool breeze kept them company, along with intermittent singing by their crew as they walked past farms and vast expanses of open land. Their first obstacle, a river, arrived within four hours of their departure.

'We need to find a narrow section to cross and also to keep a lookout for crocodiles,' Rasimone coolly explained as he guided them along the riverbank. Fifteen minutes later, the group nervously entered the flowing waters. The river surged towards them, inching closer to their waists. The villagers, accustomed to river crossings and long journeys by foot, moved briskly, carrying the supplies over their heads. Although 50 years old, Mrs Liandrat and the elderly Rasimone were both as sturdy as the Land Rover they'd left behind and kept good pace with the younger lot in the group.

As they progressed towards the opposite riverbank, Julius, more confident of his footing, jumped ahead to take a photograph of the motley crew. After an uneventful passage, they stopped by the river for a quick lunch of rice cakes, cheese, bread, and fruit. Refreshed and recharged, the group continued their march, navigating two more rivers, an encounter with a snake, and dodging scorpions and mosquitoes while armed only with bamboo sticks to clear the now dense shrub.

As the day advanced and the light dimmed, Rasimone urged them to move faster. Using the sun as his guide, he was eager to begin the final part of their journey before it set. In the twilight, the ground seemed to rise beneath their feet, increasing the pressure on their already aching calves. After an entire day navigating through the grasslands, with the last three hours a strenuous hike by moonlight, they finally reached a clearing, which Rasimone declared as their destination.

There was no time to rest. The displeasure of the rumbling clouds motivated them to swiftly set up a rudimentary camp under the ominous sky. They had barely gotten the shelters up before a severe thunderstorm descended on their base, washing away any plans for a restful night.

The fragrance of rain-drenched soil greeted Julius the next morning. He lay listening to the sounds of the camp. Feeling relieved to have endured the stormy night, Julius emerged from his tent seeking his companions. He spotted Rasimone supervising the coffee preparation nearby. A few feet away, one of their crew was boiling rice. Julius made eye contact with Mrs Liandrat. Puzzled by her expression, he turned, noticing several outcrops of rocks in the vicinity. Worried they may be in the wrong location, and not at the tourmaline mine, he hurried over to examine the nearest formation.

The ground was damp and sticky underfoot. Wedged next to the rock was a rough, cylindrical tourmaline crystal. Julius gave it a powerful tug and released the stone. He hurriedly cleaned it with his damp shirt. Like a pirate searching for land through his spyglass, Julius held the cylindrical crystal against the early morning light, seeking the kaleidoscope effect he'd seen in Lacroix's book.

Spotting the geometric colour patterns, he smiled. But, alas, there was no three-pointed Mercedes-Benz star. Disappointed, Julius turned towards the camp, feeling the heat of the rising sun on his back. He stopped short.

Staring back at him was a shimmering array of crystals strewn around the campsite. The torrential rain he'd been cursing all night had, by some act of providence, washed away the topsoil of the mound they'd found refuge on, revealing innumerable gem-quality tourmalines. Some were still embedded in their host rock while others lay scattered around them on the surface. The intrepid group had camped on top of a hill,[1] made of unprocessed tourmaline-rich gravel, which the original miners had created 44 years ago.

As the Madagascan sun continued to climb, the gems started twinkling in the morning light. Elated and nervous, Julius turned towards his companions for some validation.

'Eat up, Mr Petsch. We have many stones to collect,' said Rasimone, as he handed Julius a mug of hot coffee with a big smile across his face. Reaching for the mug and accompanying plate of Mokary rice cake, Julius noticed a stubbier tourmaline crystal tucked behind the cake on the metal plate.

He grabbed it like a greedy child in a candy shop, raising it once again to the sun. Gleaming back at him were three sharp lines converging in the centre of the tourmaline slice, surrounded by kaleidoscopic bands of mineral colour.

---

1   Gravel hill: full of mineral ore that may not have been processed.

Author's Note

This story is based on several interviews conducted in 2020 with Mr Julius Petsch. After this important discovery, Mr Petsch set about acquiring the surrounding land and pegging his claim. He registered the German-Madagascar Company, investing one million Deutsche marks from his family's personal savings to establish a mechanised mine. His core team was a Malagasy mining engineer who was the local director of the firm, and an old friend, Professor Hugo Strunz, a famous German mineralogist and geologist. They purchased their mining equipment from army surplus auctions in Germany, spending considerable funds to ship the heavy machinery to Madagascar.

To get access to the mine, the team deployed their imported equipment to build a road, taking a few weeks to bring the first shipment to the mine. Instead of hiring mine workers as casual day labour (as was the norm), Mr Petsch legally employed the workers at the mine, paying them a market salary. He built traditional homes for the mine workers and their families, along with a school for their children, a medical dispensary, and an agricultural farm for the supply of fruit and vegetables to the mine and the families.

At its peak, the German-Madagascar Company employed approximately 200 citizens. In 1976, with the advent of communism in Madagascar, Mr Petsch was overnight declared an 'imperialist exploiter'. His entire operation was seized by the government of Madagascar. He lost his investment and his stock of gemstones at the mine. The key government players at that time burned the mine's equipment, along with the geological and gemmological research.

Ten years later, after a regime change, government officials offered to return everything (or what was left) to Mr Petsch, requesting that he rebuild the operation. He declined. Mr Petsch moved on to play a pivotal role in the professional development of gemstone deposits across Africa. In the decades that followed, he worked in both advisory and corporate roles (consultant to the Zambian government for emeralds and CEO of the famous Sandawana Emerald Mine in Zimbabwe, to name just two).

In 1977, the Gemological Institute of America (GIA) recognised the tourmaline species re-discovered by Julius Petsch as a calcium-rich lithium tourmaline and named it in honour of Richard T. Liddicoat, former President of GIA.

The gem business Mr Petsch's grandfather established in 1901 is today counted among the top gem-manufacturing and distribution firms in the world. Mr Petsch is also one of the founders of the International Coloured Gemstone Association (ICA) and served as its president for two years. He is succeeded in the business by his son. Now in his eighties, Mr Petsch has retired. He lives in Germany, in a picturesque location, surrounded by mountains, with a beautiful garden, encircled by colour, and life.

Slices of Liddicoatite tourmaline featuring the Mercedes Benz-like inclusion. The patterns differ depending on the conditions during formation for each rough tourmaline crystal. Photo credit: Richa Goyal Sikri.

For a Good Life

1976
Kenya

JOSEPH WALKED behind his brother and stepsister as the group made their way through Tsavo National Park. It was the dead of night, and his heart skipped a beat each time the male lion roared in the distance. The symphonic notes of insect chirps enveloped them, punctuated by the high-pitched calls of the golden palm weaver birds and the percussion of owls. A calm breeze caressed the Kenyan savannah and Joseph worried it was more foe than friend, offering up their human scent to the predators of Tsavo. They made their way in single file, mindful to stay light on their feet, alert to every movement, sound, and smell that may suggest danger.

The park closed at six, but Joseph's brother knew the gate warden who got them in after sunset. With a total area of nearly 22,000 square kilometres, Tsavo National Park was the most extensive protected zone in Kenya, and one of the largest in the world, home to vast herds of mammals such as rhinos, lions, elephants, leopards and more. You'd have to be desperate—willing to risk your life—to trek in Tsavo after dark.

Joseph's thoughts drifted towards home as he trudged behind his siblings, remembering how only a few days ago he'd bid his parents goodbye and boarded a train to Nairobi from his village. Given limited prospects after school, they'd encouraged him to join his successful brother in the city. The feeling of excitement as he'd jumped onto the railway platform to hug his brother had been replaced with disillusionment when Joseph discovered his sibling's alcohol-drenched lifestyle. Despondent thoughts were gripping his heart. He felt trapped.

'Joseph! That's a snake; jump!' his stepsister snapped.

Joseph's reflexes kicked in, jolting him back to reality. He leapt, hopping over a rock python, which slithered away. Leading the trek through the bush was Joseph's elder brother, who operated on the fringes of the law as a rough gem broker. No longer using their family name, Mbiriri, his brother now called himself Jeff Wamugosi. Since foreign buyers could not buy directly at the mine, dealers like him had mushroomed near the gem deposits, serving as essential links in the informal supply chain. Jeff's trusted circle included two siblings (a stepbrother and sister) from their father's second wife and, now, Joseph.

They were on their way to a location inside the reserve where people traded rough coloured stones. Three years ago, in 1973, the discovery of rubies within Tsavo had sparked a gem rush, bringing prospectors and dealers to the park. John Saul along with his geologist Elliot W Miller were credited with the discovery and Saul had been the first to establish a ruby mine in the Mangari Swamp at Tsavo. Poor understanding of geology and mining procedures, and a lack of funds, limited professional mining to the informed and affluent. This heightened unregulated activity in the area, resulting in theft and pilferage from formal operations.

As they reached their destination, they saw trading had begun. Small groups of miners and brokers were huddled together, checking rough stones. Upon entering the arena, sellers started approaching them with their wares. Since Joseph was a newcomer, he remained on the side-lines. Jeff and his team got to work, placing their torches underneath ruby crystals to check their colour, which made the crystals glow like hot embers in their hands. The atmosphere was festive, with twinkling flashlights, muted chatter, and an air of hope and enterprise. Yet the threat of becoming a late-night snack for a lion or a leopard motivated the dealers to proceed at a brisk pace.

Joseph watched as his siblings selected rubies displaying red or intense pink colours. When his stepbrother and sister were unsure about a stone, they would pass it to Jeff, who would take the final decision. Jeff also took care of payments, drawing notes from a hidden pocket sewn inside the lining of his trousers. Bright stars shone like diamonds in the midnight sky as the group continued working by the light of the moon, their torches flitting like fireflies.

By 2 am, they had finished buying and were safely back in the tent, their shelter in the forest for the next seven days. Other buyers were not as lucky. They slept in trenches dug in the ground, risking the wrath of Tsavo's permanent inhabitants.

The following day, the siblings spent a few hours checking the stones for any fakes and sorting them in parcels made by folding strips of newspaper. It was a technique Jeff had learnt packing spices for an Indian dukawalla (shopkeeper). By noon, the boys would start drinking their country liquor and retire to separate tents with girls they had picked up on their drive from the nearby town of Voi.

For the past few years, Joseph had been working with troubled youth groups back home. The misery he'd seen caused by excessive alcohol and related vices motivated him to stay away from the bottle. Instead, he killed time examining their purchases, memorising the colour of the rubies, their shape, and other virtues so he'd know what to look for next time.

It took them eight days to finish their cash. Satisfied with what they'd bought, the group returned to Voi, eager to sell their rubies to merchants with export permits and access to international markets. It was in Voi that Joseph realised the value of the small pebbles they carried, as the money changed hands. The trip to Tsavo had generated more cash than Joseph had seen in his life; he was hooked.

The following day, after bidding goodbye to their stepsiblings, the two brothers left for Nairobi, where Jeff's wife and children were awaiting their arrival. A trip that should have taken two to three days became a month-long roller-coaster ride as Jeff stopped at every drinking hole and brothel on his way home. He had outstanding bills to settle. Flush with cash, Jeff behaved like a rich man who deserved enjoyment. Halfway to Nairobi, he'd drunk away his earnings and had no alternative but to return to Tsavo, accumulating more debt on his way back to the mines.

Joseph felt helpless seeing his brother live inside a never-ending cycle of poor choices, that carried him down a treacherous path. When Jeff had money, his so-called friends circled him like sharks, ravenous for a bite, swimming away as the cash ran dry and his debts piled up. This was not the life Joseph had imagined when he'd left home. But there was no turning back. He decided to lie low, learn whatever he could, and think of a way out.

* * *

1977
Nairobi

Joseph was sipping his sugarcane juice under the shady palm tree, which provided a brief respite from the merciless Kenyan sun as noon approached. He was watching men in suits and ladies in dresses step in and out of the bank building. After working with his siblings for a year, he'd parted ways on good terms by promising them a commission from his gem trades for the next six months.

That morning he'd closed his first independent sale—a rough ruby from the Mangari area near the John Saul Mine in Tsavo. Joseph had taken the ruby to a licenced dealer in Nairobi whose clients were gem cutters from Thailand. Once the man saw the neon glow radiating from the stone as he placed it under the blue UV light, he didn't take long to close the deal. Eager

23

to buy more of the same quality, he taught Joseph how to distinguish the best from the good.

'Rubies that glow like this have very little iron inside and more chromium, which gives them their colour. When you bring them in the sunlight from the shadow, the good ones become brighter like they've been lit from inside. Gemmologists call this fluorescence,' he explained.

Taking a final swig of his drink, Joseph licked his lips, savouring its sweet taste. *Next time I'll charge more*, he thought, handing the glass back to the juice cart. He tucked his faded shirt into his pants and started walking towards the bank's imposing entrance.

The elderly clerk frowned at Joseph as he placed his tattered notes on the counter. 'What do you want to do with this money?' he said.

Wondering why the man was asking a silly question, Joseph said, 'I want to bank it.'

The clerk directed him to a nearby desk to fill a deposit slip. A few minutes later, Joseph returned, handing over the paperwork and his weathered bundle of 2,000 Kenyan shillings.

The old man looked at the slip, then at Joseph. His demeanour softened. He took off his glasses, smiled, and said, 'Young man, do you want to lose all your money? Where did you get this account number from?'

Joseph explained how he'd opened an account in the town of Voi at the Kenya Commercial Bank (KCB) branch. To avoid the risk of theft on his return journey from Nairobi to Voi, he wanted to deposit the cash in the Nairobi branch.

After praising him for his sensible thinking, the cashier replied, 'Son, you're in the wrong place. This is Barclays Bank, not Kenya Commercial Bank. You must deposit your earnings in the same bank where you opened your account. If you want us to take your cash, then you have to open a new account with us. Do you understand?'

Joseph's shoulders slumped as he realised his foolishness. The teller gave Joseph the address of Kenya Commercial Bank's Nairobi branch, instructing him to take his money only to that location. A few hours later, he had managed to deposit his funds in his account.

On the return journey to Voi, Joseph leaned his head against the window of the bus, thinking about his day. Although depositing his money had reminded him of his inadequacies, he also felt a sense of achievement. He smiled to himself as he closed his eyes. Learning how to safeguard his earnings was another small step towards a more secure future.

After reaching Voi, restless to reconfirm the money transfer, Joseph visited his local Kenya Commercial Bank branch. The staff informed him his money hadn't arrived and he should come back in a few days. Thinking nothing of it, he left, returning a week later. Despite the wait, he was told the money hadn't been transferred from the Nairobi branch. The drama of the missing 2,000 Kenyan shillings went on for weeks. Joseph could sense something was wrong but couldn't verify the bank's claims.

On one of his visits, as luck would have it, someone called the teller away while he was checking Joseph's account details. The staff's momentary absence was all Joseph needed to lean across the table and take a quick peek at the bank book. Tracing his finger along the line in front of his name, he saw 2,600 Kenyan shillings, which was the total amount. The bank clerk had been lying to Joseph. He had less than a minute to control his desire to punch the man and think of a solution.

The clerk came back and sat in his seat with a conciliatory smile. Before he could continue with his charade, Joseph leaned closer and said, 'I know you've been lying to me; I've seen the book entry. Should I call your supervisor now, or are you ready to confess?'

As Joseph's threat settled in, the gummy grin faded from the clerk's face. He started trembling, muttering an explanation. Worried he may lose his job, he offered to close the account and hand over the entire balance, which Joseph accepted. An important lesson learnt, Joseph deposited his funds in another bank, making sure to double check the paperwork. A year later, courtesy of his prudent financial planning, he was able to save enough to build a small house for his mother in Nairobi.

* * *

1984
6.30 pm
Tsavo National Park, Kenya

Seven years of hard work had elevated Joseph's status in the gem brokerage business, and he was now the proud owner of a pickup truck. Independent wheels provided greater mobility, security, and shelter. Since his first visit eight years ago, gem-mining had grown inside Tsavo. There were six to seven official mines and hundreds of informal diggers and brokers trading rough gems. Regulars like Joseph had built small mud huts for shelter and provision shacks called canteens had sprung up, selling tea, biscuits, local cigarettes, and drinks.

The usual group of mine-workers, diggers and dealers had gathered by the canteen outside Tsavo National Park, shaking the dust and day from their clothes. A pinkish-orange hue was spreading across the evening sky, echoing the colour of Joseph's soft drink. After a gruelling day of mining, the men regaled each other with daredevil tales and pinched a moment's pleasure through a smoke or a snack. Joseph sat on a plastic, yellow-coloured barrel listening to the victim of a recent snake bite who was showing him the marks on his leg as proof.

The mindless chatter dimmed as the group of men noted the arrival of a Kenyan mine owner. He was looking for Joseph, and pulling him away, said, 'I have work for you. Bring some men and wait for me near your hut around 11 tonight. I'll show you where to go, OK?'

Joseph nodded his assent. Only two mines from the official count of six were presently producing rubies. The inactive mines sponsored informal diggers to find them stones or purchased rough gems in the open market, which they resold under their licence. This intensified competition for dealers like Joseph. The same mine owners would also hire brokers, who in turn funded diggers to infiltrate a competitor's concession under cover of darkness for mineral-rich ore.

It was an assignment Joseph didn't enjoy taking because if he got caught during the theft, he knew he couldn't reveal his client's identity. Everyday dealings of this sort created a messy interdependence between legal mine owners, brokers, and diggers working inside and near the gem concessions.

Joseph waited at the appointed hour with two diggers he'd found for the still-to-be-determined job. Smoke from the evening fires hung above the cluster of mud huts. To kill time, the trio started discussing likely scenarios for their nocturnal assignment. One of them speculated that it may involve slipping into the John Saul ruby mine as the mine's geologist who ran the operation, Elliot Miller, was in hospital because of an accident.

'They tunnelled into the John Saul Mine from the one next door, Joseph,' the digger explained. 'Because of the double tunnel, one under the other, the floor collapsed. Elliot Miller's hip was crushed, and his dog Rocky also died.' Joseph had heard about the accident but kept listening to this version. 'Now Miller's in hospital, Joseph, so all buyers go to buy rubies cheap from the mine's staff. You know the tsavorite (green grossular garnet) miner Campbell Bridges? He went to complain to the police and asked them to stop the mine staff from selling the rubies but the police didn't do anything.'

An hour later, having run out of things to discuss, they lay down to rest. The crackle of the fire prompted Joseph to grab a few twigs to feed its grumbling, ember-filled belly. The delayed arrival of the mine owner was giving Joseph a sense of unease.

The owner finally showed up around one in the morning, two hours after the appointed hour. Six security men ambled behind him, carrying pickaxes and shovels. Joseph stood up and approached them, smiling, eager to get going. To his surprise, the mine chief rushed past him towards the cluster of huts, shouting, 'Demolish! Demolish!' The noise awoke the community of dealers and diggers who started congregating near Joseph's hut.

Once the mine owner had everyone's attention, he accused Joseph of being a double agent who had alerted the intended target of their planned heist. 'You try to double-cross me?!' he shouted at him. 'Now you spoil things for everyone here. I'll see how you continue to work in Tsavo!'

Baffled at the owner's behaviour, since he was still awaiting details of the assignment, Joseph pleaded his innocence. Confusion and worry were etched on the faces of his friends as they wondered how this development might impact their future prospects. One of Joseph's fiercest competitors joined the attack against him, ingratiating himself to the mine owner, hoping to eliminate his competition and secure his position. As a last-ditch attempt to salvage his reputation, Joseph brought his pickup truck from behind his hut.

Parking the vehicle so the headlights faced his shelter, he said, 'I've done nothing wrong, but if you don't believe me, use this light so it's easier for your men to see when they destroy my hut, but please, spare the others.'

His efforts were in vain. The mine's security guards continued the demolition of the community cluster. Deeply upset by the turn of events, Joseph collected his belongings and left for the nearby village of Kasigau.

The next day, he was summoned to a meeting, organised by the mine owners, near the canteen where a cluster of huts were still untouched. A few hundred people had arrived, all individuals who lived inside the mining concessions. The mine owner's group started to speak, labelling the diggers and dealers present as Zaruras (nomadic gem diggers), and gave them all 24 hours to clear out of the concession. Interestingly, the eviction included Joseph's arch-rival, who thought he was bulletproof as he had supported the first demolition.

As the cold dagger of betrayal dug its teeth into the hearts of the gem community, murmurs of dissent started radiating through the crowd. Then, the bulldozers arrived, along with reinforcements. Joseph stood leaning against the door of his truck, watching the drama unfold from a distance. His rival fell into a rage, assaulting the men tasked to raze everything to the ground. As they forcefully pushed against him, he stumbled, accidentally knocking over a pot of boiling water, resulting in severe burns.

Joseph had seen enough. He got into his pickup to escape his rival's painful wail echoing through the air. As he drove away, he glanced in the rear-view mirror. The men and their machines were turning the mud huts into dust. The unpleasantness of the incident reminded Joseph of his fragile position in the industry. Living in the shadows of informality to eke out a living, forever dependant on someone's mercy, was no way to build the better life he so desperately desired. He vowed to find another way, maybe by prospecting for gems on his own, which meant he'd have to leave Tsavo. It would be tough, but deep in his heart he knew the only way to a secure future was to start mining via a registered claim.

* * *

1986
Kuranze

This time I won't hide, thought Joseph as he drove towards the estate-owner's house on the hill in Kuranze. Two years had passed since the incident in Tsavo, but it still haunted him. He'd continued working as a gem trader, spending even less than before on himself, and managed to save enough money for an entrepreneurial leap. As he approached the main gate, a security guard stopped him.

'I'm here to see Major Eggers; I have some business with him,' said Joseph.

'Is he expecting you?' asked the man, looking sceptical.

Pretending to be irritated, Joseph said, 'No, but I have an important matter I need to discuss with him, so please open the gate.' A few seconds later, Joseph was driving his truck up the steep path on his way to the mansion on top of the hill.

'Wait here, the major will join you in a few minutes,' said the butler ushering Joseph to a seat on a veranda that overlooked the vast estate. He brought him a glass of iced lemonade and a plate of warm home-baked biscuits.

As Joseph bit into the cinnamon-flavoured treat, gazing at the expanse before him, he recalled his last visit to the area six years ago with his cousin. They'd been following a trail of breadcrumbs left by rough-gem dealers who spoke of a location near the Kenya-Tanzania border where people could extract gems from the topsoil with minimal digging. Joseph remembered how his cousin had taken a circuitous route to avoid detection by the mzungu (the white man, in this case, Major Eggers) who owned the ranch.

Upon reaching the deposit, they'd collected some samples and Joseph had noticed bands of light and dark mineral streaks within rock formations mirroring the ones near the mines in Tsavo.

As the sweet and sour flavour of the lemonade hit the back of Joseph's throat he smiled thinking how much had changed since that clandestine visit. He was now in the house of the very man they had feared six years ago, hoping to strike a deal.

'Good afternoon,' said Major Eggers, interrupting Joseph's reflections. He promptly stood up to shake the extended hand. Despite his 63-year-old frame, Major Eggers was an imposing Irishman who exuded self-confidence. Having retired from the Kenyan army, he now lived a quiet life with his wife in a mansion overlooking their lands in Kuranze. 'My staff inform me we have some business to discuss. Do we know each other?' he asked, gesturing for Joseph to take a seat.

It's now or never, thought Joseph, forcing his shoulders back to make eye contact. He explained how he was a gem prospector and wanted to explore a section of the major's estate with his permission. As was customary, Joseph proposed to compensate the major via a yearly payment of 60,000 Kenyan shillings on the proviso that any gems Joseph found he would keep for himself.

After hearing him out, the major warned about the growing nuisance of poachers in the area, who were becoming a security headache. He further cautioned Joseph that irrespective of whether any gems were found or not, he would owe the major the committed amount—60,000 Kenyan shillings— at the end of the year. Twenty minutes later, the men shook hands and Joseph left the estate, excited to have a chance to prospect without looking over his shoulder.

In the years that followed, Joseph's explorations led him to register multiple concessions in the region with the Ministry of Mines and begin formal mining operations. Most of his production during this initial period was of the lesser-valued rhodolite garnet. Trading as a merchant, however, helped him cross-subsidise his mining operations. Joseph was keen to repay his community, who had supported him during his years in Tsavo, so he invited others to prospect with him and established three villages in Kuranze: Ziwa, Klbanda and Uwanja.

Despite his best efforts, the brokerage business remained his mainstay as individuals invited by him found more valuable gems like tsavorite and tourmaline and developed their independent mining operations. Undeterred, Joseph continued investing, hoping for a lucrative discovery, like a gambler unwilling to get up from the casino table long after his luck has run out.

* * *

2005
Nairobi

'I'm home!' shouted Joseph, walking through the front door of his house in Nairobi. Almost two decades had passed since he'd made a deal with Major Eggers. He was now a family man living in Nairobi but still toiling away at his mining operation.

His wife responded, 'Wash up and come to the table—I'm putting out dinner.'

A few minutes later, Joseph was sitting at the dining table with his wife, son, and three daughters. It had been a hard day negotiating with the bank to extend the working capital loan for his company.

'Did you hear what I said, Daddy?' asked his eldest daughter.

'No, my dear, sorry. I was thinking about something else. Tell me again, I'm listening now,' he said. His daughter started talking about her teacher's advice on how she may be well suited for a possible career in human resources.

Once dinner was over, Joseph ambled into the kitchen to speak with his wife. Seeing her washing dishes in the sink, he went over and put his arms around her waist, leaning his head on her shoulders.

She started laughing and said, 'Joseph Mbiriri, what's wrong with you? The children could come in any minute and my hands are full of soap.'

Giving her a quick kiss on the shoulder, he moved alongside her and started helping.

'Is everything OK, Joe?' she asked. Pondering whether he should share his burdens, he kept quiet for a few seconds. 'Joe?' she prompted again.

Looking at her, he said, 'I don't know. The meeting today with the bank was tough. It's been almost 20 years and the mining operation still hasn't produced anything of serious value. I managed another extension on the loan, but don't know how long we can carry on. I hate to say it, but maybe I should think about selling.'

Before his wife could reply, they both heard a hurried knock on their front door, followed by the ringing of the doorbell. Walking towards the entrance, Joseph called out, 'Who is it?'

A voice replied, 'Boss, it's me, Peter.'

I hope there hasn't been an accident at the mine, thought Joseph as he opened the door. 'Peter! What are you doing here? All OK at the mine?'

Rushing past Joseph, Peter opened the canvas satchel he was carrying and started placing rocks in varying sizes on the dining table. He turned to face Joseph with a big grin. 'We did it, boss! We found nice pockets of good tsavorite. I brought you samples.'

Still absorbing what Peter had just said, Joseph picked up the first rock and took it towards the lamp by the sofa. As he turned the stone under the light, it started sparkling as if someone had sprinkled glitter on its surface.

'Is that shiny stuff gold, boss?' Peter asked, crouching next to Joseph.

'No, it's pyrite, which people also call fool's gold, because only foolish people think it's gold,' explained Joseph chuckling at Peter, who grinned back. The electric green tsavorite was peeking from one side of the dull grey rock. Joseph brought it closer to the light. 'See this deep green colour on top?' he said, pointing towards the tsavorite. 'This is what we've been seeking.'

'What are all these black bits, boss?' Peter was enjoying his learning moment with Joseph.

'Good question, Peter. They call this graphite. This is a metamorphic rock, you see?'

Scratching his head, Peter asked, 'Because of all these different-coloured materials inside the rock?'

'Yes, but the bits you see here, like the black graphite, the green tsavorite, the pyrite; they're in the rock because millions of years ago when this rock was deep within the Earth, it experienced extreme heat and pressure, which changed its personality. Elements like chromium and vanadium entered the rock. When the rock cooled down, all these liquids became hard crystal. For us, the most important part is the green part, which scientists call green grossular garnet, and we call tsavorite,' said Joseph.

The duo were so engrossed with the rock in their hands, they failed to notice Mrs Mbiriri walk into the living room from the kitchen. 'Joseph Mbiriri! What is this mess on my table? I just finished cleaning up!'

Joseph walked over to her, placed the rock in her hand and said, 'My dear, this mess is my life's work. Sit down please, I have good news to share.'

Author's Note

This story is based on actual events as relayed by Joseph Mbiriri. After almost 20 years of exploration and mining, Joseph found tsavorite in the Kuranze area in southern Kenya. Subsequently, his exploration yielded other gemstones such as tourmaline, enabling him to expand his mining operation. He enjoyed a good relationship with Major Eggers and his wife, who came to depend on him. Before leaving to buy supplies in Nairobi, Joseph would check in with Mrs Eggers who would provide him with her shopping list, including bread from her favourite baker.

A few years after Joseph had been mining in the area, Major Eggers was shot by a gang of poachers and passed away due to complications from the wound. Left alone, Mrs Eggers moved with her staff to Mombasa, and Joseph lost contact with her.

Joseph's brother Jeff passed away due to deteriorating health. Because of Joseph's success, he was able to take his brother to Germany to enjoy an overseas trip before his passing.

Although the story is based on Joseph's personal experiences, minor fictional elements have been incorporated in each segment to aid narration.

Joseph is a respected member of the gem and mining community in Kenya. He has four children: three daughters and one son. The eldest daughter works in human resources and the second is pursuing a career in project management. His third daughter studied gemmology with the Gemological Institute of America (GIA) and has a degree in fashion and jewellery design. His son is a geologist and has joined him in the mining company and gem-trading business. Joseph is now the proud owner of various mineral concessions and is seeking investment for his latest venture: a spinel mine.

Scorpions and Raiders

Early 1980s
Kenya

'CAPTAIN, ARE you sure we should fly into the storm?' asked Richie, the co-pilot.

'Don't know, but there's no choice now, so tighten your seatbelt and follow my lead. I promise, this'll not be our last adventure.'

The brave pilot, Captain Fonz, took a deep breath and propelled the plane forward.

'Naushad!' Daudi Osman's voice pierced the tepid afternoon air, snapping the 12-year-old back to reality. 'Stop daydreaming about aeroplanes and get down from that bloody rock! If you fall and break your neck, your mother will kill me!' said his father.

Disappointed at being interrupted before he could save his imaginary passengers, Naushad started climbing down from the tall stone formation, his secret hiding spot. He loved lying on the cool surface of the hard rock, observing the activities at his father's aquamarine mine in Kenya. To Naushad, the miners from the Samburu tribe, clad in their colourful robes with bright red ochre in their hair, resembled supernatural beings against the arid, craggy landscape. He would concoct stories setting characters from his favourite television show, *Happy Days*, on an alien planet, with the tribesmen as the indigenous inhabitants.

Naushad's family were merchants. His great-grandfather, Sidi Hamir, had immigrated to Kenya in the early 1900s from Jamnagar, a town in the western state of Gujarat in India. He established a convenience store in Nairobi, settling into the life of a tradesperson, known in Kenya as 'duka-wallas', a colloquial term derived from the Urdu word 'dukaan' for shop and 'wallas' for keepers. Naushad's father, however, wasn't interested in the monotonous life of a shopkeeper. After finishing his formal education, Daudi Osman began working in a printing press in the capital and spent his weekends hunting in the surrounding lands. A few years later, a random excursion brought him to a local herdsman who sold him a handful of soito (precious stones).

Daudi was unsure of their value, so it surprised him when the stones turned out to be rough aquamarines, which he sold for a handsome profit. Spurred by this initial success, he started experimenting with the gem trade, spending weekends exploring the countryside, away from his wife and children. His deep interest led him to an aquamarine deposit in the remote Samburu District of Kenya, where his son, Naushad, was visiting him during his school holidays.

Naushad breathed a sigh of relief seeing Clement waiting for him instead of his father. Although Clement's official title was driver/mechanic, he was Daudi's right-hand man, and Naushad's best friend at the mine. Hailing from the Turkana tribe, Clement knew a lot about gemstones and was always telling Naushad stories he'd heard from village elders. Most importantly for Naushad, Clement wore an open shirt tied loosely with a knot at his waist, oozing rugged street style and swag, which reminded the boy of his favourite Bollywood character, 'Vijay', played by the legend of Indian cinema, Amitabh Bachchan.

'Why you go climb that rock all the while, Twiga?' Clement asked, using the Swahili word for giraffe as a term of endearment. 'You got a dame up there or what?' He winked.

The boy responded by engaging Clement in a playful boxing match.

'OK, OK, I give up, Muhammad Ali,' said Clement, raising his hands in surrender. 'C'mon. Wash up and go eat your khichee.'

'It's khich-ree, Clement,' said Naushad, correcting his pronunciation of the Indian-style savoury rice and lentil porridge. 'And it's so boring. Why do I have to eat it every day?'

'You know why,' said Clement, pacifying the child. 'All them Indian people don't eat meat and it's easier to keep dry food like rice and lentils for a long time at the mine.'

'I know.' Naushad sighed, resigning to his fate.

'Cheer up, Twiga. In the evening, we'll go to Father Peter's home for some goat stew, OK? Stop your whining now and have your khich-reeee.'

Sitting across from his dad and the general manager of the mine, Kishore[1], Naushad was feigning interest in his lunch so he could listen in on the grown-ups' conversation. Kishore was responsible for various functions, including the vital task of sorting and classifying the mine's aquamarine production. As the trio worked through their modest meal, Kishore leaned over and whispered to Naushad's father, Daudi, in Hindi.

---

1   This name has been changed.

'Bhai-Saab, dekha? [Big brother, did you see?]' he said. 'Simba[1] didn't show up for work today.'

Naushad's ears perked up at the mention of Simba, the notorious mine worker about whom he'd heard many stories. His father grunted in response.

Kishore continued, 'How will we continue like this?'

'Let it go; pilferage is part and parcel of any mining operation.'

'There are also rumours that bandits are roaming in the area. We don't have any security, you know.'

Naushad could see his father was getting irritated. 'We are in the middle of nowhere, there are only cattle rustlers around, and they're harmless. The aqua production is good; please focus on grading all the rocks fast so we can make some money from their sale. That should be your priority.'

Naushad made a mental note to ask Clement about the raiders. He'd heard his dad complain before about missing mine workers, which usually meant pilferage of stones. Simba was a well-known serial offender. After selling the stolen goods to a rogue broker in town, he would make his way to the local bar and insist the owner build a tower of beer crates to match his height (five feet three inches). Then, with one shove, he would topple the structure, roaring in laughter to cheers and applause from jealous onlookers who egged him on. It was his moment in the sun. When Simba's money finished, he would return to the mine, a diligent worker, until the next episode, which coincided with increased production at the mine.

'Finished your lunch, Naushad?' Daudi asked his son. 'Good boy; now wash up and stay with Kishore-bhai [brother] and Clement in the sort house.'

'Daddy, where are you going to be?' Naushad asked, hoping for another geology lesson.

'We found a quartz vein, and, as I explained to you before, where we find quartz, there's a solid chance of discovering aqua, as quartz is the host rock, remember?'

Naushad nodded, enjoying this private moment with his father.

'Chalo, batao [C'mon, say] which mineral family does aquamarine belong to?'

Chewing his lower lip, Naushad replied, 'Beryl?'

'Is that a question or a statement?' Daudi enquired, giving his son a stern look.

'S-s-statement, sir, just like emerald and morganite—also beryl.'

---

1   This name has been changed.

Smiling at his son, Daudi said, 'Well done. You know the answer, so don't be nervous. Speak up, OK? Now, let's get back to our duties.'

Naushad ran off, elated at extracting a word of encouragement from his dad instead of the usual scolding.

The sort house was a simple brick building with large square windows. Tables and chairs were placed next to the windows to maximise natural light, ideal for inspecting crystals. Naushad entered the space and stood by the door, watching the scene for a few minutes. Despite his unfamiliarity with his father's new venture, he sensed that valuable work was being done in the room. The worker at the first table was examining extracted chunks of hard rock, looking for traces of aquamarine. He placed promising ones in a basket, which the supervisor would check before moving them to the second station.

Naushad remembered his father explaining how the selected rocks would undergo a delicate process called cobbing, where the workers freed the aquamarine crystal from the host rock using pliers and a small pickaxe, being careful not to damage the precious gem. Naushad saw Clement waving him over to where he was sitting with Kishore, sorting piles of rough aquamarine. Resembling frozen chunks that had broken off an iceberg, the pale blue stones glistened in the afternoon sun, making Naushad thirsty for a drink. *I'll ask Clement to get me a cold Tree Top juice when we go out in the evening for dinner*, he thought, licking his lips.

'Naushad, beta [son], come, let me show you how we do the sorting and grading,' said Kishore, directing the child to sit on the stool next to him. 'See, we have three sections here: the nice ones, the average, and the cloudy stones, because they all fetch different prices. Then, in each category, we further divide them. Now, look at this one. You tell me, where should it go?'

Gulping, Naushad took the rough hexagonal crystal from Kishore and raised it against the light, comparing its appearance to the sorted lot on the table.

'Bolo? [Say?]' Kishore enquired.

Naushad placed the stone in the average section.

'Shabash! [Well done!] Why don't you sort this pile with me?'

Before Naushad could respond, a terrible howl from outside the sort house trumped the tinkering of the tools inside. Exchanging a look of alarm with Kishore, Clement said, 'That sound like boss. I check?'

Nodding his assent, Kishore said, 'Go fast. I'll lock the stones and bring the first-aid kit.'

Asking no one for permission, Naushad leapt from the stool and ran out after Clement.

The duo spotted Daudi sitting on the ground clutching his foot. The Samburu tribesmen had stopped working and were arguing about the next course of action. Clement was by Daudi's side in seconds.

'What happen, boss?'

Unable to form a sentence because of the stinging sensation coursing through his body, Daudi only said, 'Scorpion', pointing to the vile creature a mine worker was smashing with a rock, just as a concerned Kishore arrived holding a small medical box.

After hearing about the scorpion, a panic-stricken Kishore started tearing apart the first-aid box, lamenting, 'Lord help us, what will we do? I have nothing in this kit that will work.' Kishore's agitated state added to Daudi's growing irritation and pain.

Clement jumped up. 'I got an idea, boss; wait here.' He returned a minute later, driving their rickety Land Rover.

Kishore slapped his forehead, admonishing Clement, 'You fool, there's no clinic in the nearest town. Why have you brought the Landy?'

'No, boss, you don't understand,' said Clement while opening the hood of the running Land Rover. 'The only way to fix the sting is to give an electric shock to the big boss,' he declared with a sense of urgency. 'I'll pull out the spark-plug cable and zap boss with it. This will kill the poison.' Clement explained how he'd seen something similar done to a white guy. Two mine workers also jumped in, claiming they'd heard the story at a bar. The trio couldn't remember if the man had survived the high-voltage remedy.

'This is insane!' exclaimed Kishore, looking at Daudi for a reaction.

As the pain continued to rise, Daudi grunted, 'OK, let's do it.'

With his eyes as wide as saucers, Kishore started reasoning with Daudi. 'Bhai-Saab [Big brother], what madness is this? We'll think of something else. What if the shock kills you?!'

Ignoring Kishore's escalated state of alarm, Daudi looked Clement dead in the eye. 'You sure about this?'

'Boss, I know what I do,' said Clement. 'You relax, it all be over soon, then you give me a big reward, OK?'

Time seemed to slow down as Clement pulled out the spark-plug cable and took a firm stand with his feet apart, ready to electrocute Daudi. The onlookers became silent, the only audible sound being the low growl of the electric current. Sweat was dripping down Daudi's forehead as he brought the index finger of his left hand towards the cables. The rest of his body moved further away, resembling the Leaning Tower of Pisa, as if trying to talk him out of this mad act he was about to commit.

Kishore started praying out loud. The Samburu workers inched closer, some whispering, others grinning, entertained by the outcome of the afternoon, placing wagers, and giving odds on the suffering man's chances of survival. The Indian staff inside the sort house watched with their noses pressed against the windows, along with the security personnel.

Naushad stood petrified, glancing from Clement to his dad and then back to Clement. To Naushad, his father looked more like a child headed for a vaccination than the formidable man he knew.

Taking a step closer to Daudi, Clement asked, 'Ready, boss? You come near the cables now.'

Daudi took a deep breath and moved in for the shock.

It was over in the blink of an eye. As soon as Daudi's finger touched the live wire, his body convulsed for a split second. He yelped and pulled back.

Signalling with the cable for Daudi to return for another hit, Clement said, 'Not enough, boss. I think you need one more.'

Daudi considered Clement's suggestion for a second before he exclaimed, 'That's it! I don't care what your white man did. I'm done. Return the Landy to the shade. I'm going for my afternoon nap. Naushad, stay away from the rock. Everyone, show over, back to work. You too, Kishore.' With that, he spun around and walked off towards his tent, a mild limp in his left leg the only sign of the deadly scorpion sting.

Watching Daudi limping away to the safety of his tent, a relieved Kishore turned around, only to stop short at the scene before his eyes. A young Samburu lad was being challenged by the remaining onlookers to repeat the electric shock experience. Kishore intervened in time, ushering everyone back to work and instructing Clement to take the deadly jeep away. Disappointed by the lack of fireworks, the miners picked up their tools and headed towards the quartz vein. An ash-faced Kishore made his way to the sort house, taking deep breaths and gesturing to the spectators by the windows to return to their sorting stations.

As the crowd dispersed, Naushad remained rooted, unable to move, still unsure of what had transpired. He felt a hand on his shoulder. It was Clement. 'You OK, Twiga?'

'Will Daddy be fine, Clement?'

'Oh yes! Don't you worry now, I fix him good. Come, let's get back to work. You help me sort them aqua, OK? And then we go for a nice dinner at Father Peter's house.'

A few hours later, Naushad and Clement were bouncing down the bumpy road in the life-saving jeep, headed towards the nearby town, a two-hour drive from the mine. Before leaving, Naushad went to see his dad and was relieved to find him in good spirits and pain-free, unruffled by the events of the afternoon.

By the time they reached Father Peter's cottage, the sky had turned an ethereal shade of pink and orange, mirroring the bright colours of the bougainvillea flowers encircling the pillars on the front porch. Father Peter came out to greet them with a wave and a warm smile. Within the first few months of commencing work at the deposit, Clement had sought out the small church in the nearby town and befriended the Kenyan priest. Daudi and Clement would help Father Peter by carting his parcels to and from Nairobi. Naushad benefitted from the friendship by tucking into a few meaty dinners when he was visiting his father at the mine.

'Welcome back, young man. I hope you're hungry?' Father Peter asked as he shook hands with Naushad.

Two hours later, stuffed with a generous helping of delicious nyama choma[1], irio[2], sukuma wiki[3], and ugali[4], Naushad lay curled in a cosy hammock hanging in the living room's corner.

The boy fell asleep to the sound of Father Peter and Clement's laughter, his mind drifting between the day's adventures and his 12-year-old imagination.

Naushad was in the middle of rescuing an alien race from a giant scorpion when a thunderous bang awoke him. What was that? Someone was pounding on the front door of the cottage. The room fell silent. Father Peter walked over to check the source of the disturbance. A local tribesman rushed in, looking worried.

'Come in, Alami,' said Father Peter. 'What brings you here at this late hour?'

Alami was too distressed to sit down. 'Sorry to disturb you, Father,' he said, 'but my friends and I heard there may be some armed bandits around. I just wanted to warn you.'

Reaching for the rosary hanging from his neck, Father Peter replied, 'That is disturbing news. Are you sure? We have nothing of value to offer them.'

'I don't know, Father,' Alami continued, while wiping the sweat off his brow with his shirtsleeve. 'My friend saw them, apparently two hours away. I'm going home now, but maybe tomorrow we can gather everyone to discuss and prepare?'

---

1   Traditional grilled meat.
2   Kenyan mashed potatoes with peas and corn.
3   Collard greens cooked with spices and tomatoes.
4   Maize flour porridge.

Feeling the weight of leadership, Father Peter stated, 'Yes, that's a good idea. Don't fret; God will protect us.'

Turning to face the room after seeing Alami off, Father Peter suggested, 'Clement, perhaps you and Naushad should stay here tonight.'

Rubbing his forehead in thought, Clement replied, 'Can't do that, Father. I promised the boss we'd return straight after dinner. He'll worry if we don't. It's only eight o'clock. We'll leave now. I'll drive fast, and we'll make good time.'

The jeep's headlights provided limited visibility through the thick veil of the night on the way back to the mine. Out of the corner of his eye, Naushad could see Clement's tense profile, deep in thought, eyes sharp, forehead wrinkled, and focused on driving as the vehicle rattled and rumbled over potholes and jagged stretches. Feeling confused and worried, Naushad asked, 'Clement, are these bandits dangerous?'

Clement sighed. 'They are wicked men, Twiga. They carry guns and steal food and other belongings. Big headache for everyone.'

Clement looked over at Naushad and could see him nibbling his lower lip. He looked concerned.

'Will they catch us on the way home?' Naushad asked.

Ruffling Naushad's hair, Clement replied, 'Don't you worry, I not let anything bad happen to you, OK?'

Yawning in response, Naushad leaned back and closed his eyes as Clement returned to concentrating on the journey ahead.

'Wake up, Twiga,' Clement whispered, shaking Naushad's shoulder, two hours later.

'Have we reached the mine?' asked Naushad.

'Yes, but we must be silent now, Twiga.'

Still dazed from his nap, and having momentarily forgotten the circumstances of their departure from Father Peter's cottage, Naushad asked, 'Why?'

Without breaking his concentrated gaze towards the mine, Clement replied, 'Something's wrong.'

The hair on the back of Naushad's neck stood up as he straightened himself and started looking around. He noticed Clement had parked the jeep behind a large clump of bushes with the headlights off. He recognised the dim lights of the sort house in the distance. Naushad could feel the tension in Clement's manner. 'What's going on, Clement? Why are we hiding here?'

'Something not right,' said Clement, squinting into the darkness. 'You see them donkeys? Where they come from? And look like gas lanterns lit in the sort house. Only the big bosses have those lanterns in their tents and why they go to sort house at night?'

Naushad kept quiet. He couldn't understand why these details were important but didn't want to question Clement's judgement. 'Should we go there and check?'

'Maybe I have a look, Twiga; you stay here.'

Feeling his heart sink at the thought of being left behind, Naushad said, 'I don't want to stay in the jeep alone, Clement. Please take me with you.'

Clement looked at Naushad. The situation was impossible. After weighing the pros and cons of leaving Naushad, Clement agreed to bring him along on the condition that the boy stay close to him and remain quiet.

The duo dashed towards the sort house, crouching to stay out of sight. They hunkered down beneath the main window as they reached the building. Clement raised his head, peering inside the room. Naushad sat on his haunches, searching for clues in Clement's face. He heard a man's voice shouting, 'Nobody move, or we kill everyone!'

In a split second, Clement ducked. He placed his finger on his lips, reminding Naushad to stay silent, and pointed towards the jeep. As they made their way back to the safety of the vehicle, tears in Naushad's eyes blurred his vision. His animal instinct for self-preservation overruled his desire to run to his father's arms.

After five minutes, which felt more like 15, the duo made it to the Land Rover.

As soon as Clement closed the door, a teary-eyed Naushad asked, 'What's happening, Clement? Is Daddy safe? Are those the robbers with the guns?'

Clement stared at Naushad, considering what he should say. He'd seen the backs of at least four men standing and pointing rifles at the mine workers who were lying face down on the floor of the sort house, naked. Daudi and Kishore were in the same state as the staff. He remembered seeing three other men helping themselves to the flour, rice, and sugar from the secure store in the room's corner. A fourth raider stuffed fistfuls of the mine's rough aquamarine crystals in a jute bag.

Clement felt helpless. He knew the bandits wouldn't hesitate to kidnap Naushad if they were discovered, and he swore to himself that he would protect the boy at all costs. 'Twiga, the boss is fine. They only want the rice and sugar as they hungry,' said Clement, hoping his response would reassure Naushad. 'You don't worry; they will leave soon, but we need to stay quiet and hide till then, OK? I not let anything bad happen to you, I promise. I be now like Ameetaab Bochan, and you be Fonzie.'

Naushad nodded. He lowered himself in the jeep's seat, and said, 'Clement, it's Amitabh Bachchan, not Ameetaab Bochan.'

Clement smiled in response and returned to observing the scene from a safe distance. They sat in silence. The looting by the bandits intermittently disturbed the sounds of the wilderness. A visceral sense of self-preservation kept them imprisoned in the Land Rover as they waited for the bandits to leave. After what felt like forever, they spotted a few gang members emerge from the sort house. Clement pushed Naushad to the floor of the jeep and sank lower in the driver's seat while monitoring the men. He'd counted eight before but could now only see six. They were loading their haul on the donkeys, getting ready to leave.

The last two emerged from the building walking backwards, their rifles pointed towards the open door. Without warning, they fired inside the sort house, then bolted the entrance door. Securing their cargo in less than a minute, they disappeared into the night, leaving little trace of their incursion.

After he was sure the raiders were not returning, Clement looked down at Naushad. Curled up on the floor of the jeep, the boy was shaking like a leaf. Tears were rolling down his cheeks. Clement pulled him up and put his arms around Naushad, rocking him back and forth. 'They've left, Twiga. It's over. Shhh, it's all over now.'

Naushad was crying into Clement's shoulder. Not knowing what awaited them at the sort house, Clement said, 'Come, let's go help everyone at the mine. OK, Fonzie?'

Pulling away from Clement's drenched shirt sleeve, Naushad nodded as he wiped away his tears.

Author's Note

This story is based on actual events as gathered during several interviews with Naushad Osman. Fictional elements have been included to aid narration.

Daudi Osman and his crew survived the attack by the armed bandits. The incident occurred in the early eighties when Daudi was operating an aquamarine mine in the Samburu District of Kenya.

Because of the remote location, Naushad never visited his father at the aquamarine mine, and his role in that segment of the story with the bandits is fictitious. Other than the occasional cattle rustlers, the area was safe, and the bandit attack took Daudi and his crew by surprise. After the raid, fearing for their lives, the Indian crew at the mine refused to continue working and Daudi soon closed the operation, relinquishing the licence. He lost most of the aquamarine production to the raiders.

During the late seventies and early eighties, attacks by armed raiders were a common occurrence in Kenya. The home guards were ill-equipped to fight back. Government forces only reached the mine well after the bandits had left. As the severity of the menace increased, the Kenyan government acted, increasing resources and security personnel in the troubled areas. By the mid-eighties, state forces had brought the situation under control.

Daudi's next stint was with tsavorite mining in the Taita Taveta area. Although safe from armed bandits, his problem here was continuous theft by the local Zarura gangs. The Zaruras were known for being natural geologists. They travelled in small groups looking for mining operations with weak security, which they infiltrated, selling their spoils to informal gem brokers, who moved on motorbikes from one deposit to the next. The brokers further sold to agents responsible for finding buyers, either by exporting the rough gems through registered traders or smuggling them to cutting centres outside of Kenya.

Simba used to work at Daudi's tsavorite mine. As is typical with grass-roots-level mining operations, a percentage of production (20 to 30) is shared with the mine workers. Despite this, pilferage is a common occurrence in all gemstone mines. When workers get their hands on a valuable stone, after selling, some seek intoxicants and the company of women.

The scorpion incident occurred at a tsavorite mine belonging to Daudi two years after the aquamarine raid. Naushad was visiting his father at the mine and witnessed the incident first-hand. Clement was a beloved figure in Naushad's life at the mine, and they were close. Although Clement did take Naushad to get meat for dinner, the character of the Kenyan priest (Father Peter) is fictitious.

Naushad wanted to become a pilot, but their family lacked the resources. Because of the mercurial nature of gem-mining, combined with security and socio-political challenges, Daudi's career mirrored the twists and turns of a roller-coaster ride. Financial difficulties led him to leave mining and join his cousin's transportation business. Daudi returned to gem-mining in 1993, establishing the Davis Mining company with his friend Visram when Kenya was witnessing a robust production of tsavorite.

Meanwhile, Naushad worked in a restaurant after graduating from college before his big break with Pan Am airlines as a flight steward. After his stint in civil aviation, Naushad joined the family mining firm in 2015, taking over the company's active licences for tsavorite, coinciding with other family members retiring from the industry.

Clement and Simba are no longer alive. Daudi Osman is now 77 years old and working with his son in the mining industry. He never saw a doctor for the scorpion sting, and his foot is fine.

Young Naushad (seated) with the mine workers from his father's mine.
Photo taken around 1979-1981.

Daudi Osman standing next to the door of his pickup truck with Clement sitting on top of the infamous land rover. This photo was taken when the jeep broke down enroute to Osman's mine. Photo from 1980.

Naushad Osman sitting in the foreground with Clement sitting behind him. Others in the photo include Daudi Osman's business partners at that time. Photo from 1980.

Gem Gods in Zaire

2014
Guy Clutterbuck's office
International Financial Services Centre (IFSC)
Dublin, Ireland

GUY CLUTTERBUCK had a wry smile on his face as he placed his teacup back on the saucer. 'The pivotal moment in my career, when I knew I was on the right track,' he said, 'was when I bought emeralds from a Pathan dealer in Peshawar, Pakistan, sold them to a Gujarati merchant in India, and made a profit.'

He was expecting Vivienne[1] to laugh. Most people usually did at this point. But being a journalist, she innocently looked back at him and asked, 'Why is that important?'

'Individuals from both communities have a stellar reputation for being superb negotiators. Their knowledge on gems and their tenacity to extract the best possible price is legendary in our industry. I'd been in the business for only six years when I did that deal. As an Englishman, to buy emeralds from a Pathan, sell it to a Gujarati, and make a profit told me I would be alright.'

Vivienne chuckled.

She gets it now, thought Guy.

'I think we have enough for the article, Mr Clutterbuck. I'm going to stop the recording.'

'Please call me Guy. Mr Clutterbuck sounds old and formal. May I ask when this article will be published?'

'Next month. I'll give you a heads-up,' replied Vivienne.

'I don't think anything I've ever done in my career impressed my wife more than learning I was going to be in your newspaper. She's an avid reader, especially on Sunday!'

'Thank you. That's very kind of you to say. We try,' said Vivienne, while peering out of the office window. A terrible thunderstorm was raging

---

1   This name has been changed.

outside. She glanced at her watch and was relieved to note she still had time to make her next appointment.

'It's pouring outside. If you're not in a hurry, why not wait until you can at least step out with an umbrella without getting drenched?' suggested Guy.

'Thank you. I have some time to spare.'

'I'll get us some fresh tea,' Guy said as he grabbed the tray and left the room.

Vivienne took the opportunity to stretch, walking over to a collection of framed photographs arranged on a sleek wooden console. She spotted a familiar face, as Guy returned with a refreshed tea tray and a new assortment of biscuits.

'Is that Ahmad Shah Massoud?' asked Vivienne, pointing at a photo of Guy with the Afghan military commander.

'Well spotted! It is, indeed,' said Guy. 'He was known as the "Lion of Panjshir valley" in Afghanistan for his resistance against Soviet troops from 1979 until 1989, and his defence against the Taliban.'

'When was this photo taken?' asked Vivienne, returning to her seat across from Guy.

'1988,' said Guy, as he poured Vivienne a fresh cup of tea. 'I had taken an influential gem dealer to meet Commander Massoud. You know, Panjshir Valley is home to some of the finest emeralds in the world. Some would say the top-quality gems of Panjshir could take on any Colombian emerald in existence.'

Vivienne took a chocolate Hobnob biscuit from the plate Guy was holding out. 'How was he?' she asked.

'One of the most incredible human beings I have ever met. The man radiated this energy when he walked into a room. A phenomenal person. I was so upset when I learnt he'd been killed, interestingly, three days before the September 11th attacks on the World Trade Centre in New York.'

'You'd already been to Africa before Afghanistan?'

'Correct. I am in this business because of Africa.'

'How's that?' Vivienne asked.

'I had a friend. Oliver Chiponda. He was from Malawi but lived in Zambia because his father was a political refugee. He went to school in England, which is where we became friends. After his education, he returned to Zambia. One day, he called me out of the blue and invited me to visit Zambia. "They're digging emeralds in the bush," he'd said. I sold my flat in London, took the money from that, and flew on Aeroflot to Lusaka, a 28-hour flight via Helsinki, Moscow, Odessa, Cairo, Entebbe, Luanda. I arrived feeling like death.'

'Which year was this?'

'Mmm, around 1985, I think. I was 23 years old.'

'That sounds like a lot for a 23-year-old to do? What was Lusaka like back then?'

'Very dangerous. To make matters worse, Ollie fell out of favour with his father who had traded his mother for a younger lady. While his dad was living in a palatial residence on the north road of the city, Oliver and his mother were living in a township called Chilenge South, which was a pretty rough neighbourhood at that time. Their home was a humble brick structure with an asbestos roof. Hardly any sanitation. At night, you couldn't step out because of a curfew in the city. Couldn't even open a window because thieves would use fishing rods to steal anything of value they could extract from a home.'

'Really? That's crazy.'

'It was crazy. I was living in this impoverished neighbourhood with five thousand pounds in cash.'

'Was your family in the gemstone business? Did you know something about emeralds when you went to Zambia?' asked Vivienne. She felt as if she was missing a piece of the puzzle and couldn't understand why a 23-year-old would sell his home and fly to Africa because of a phone call.

'Not really. My father had a printing business but from the start I was keen to be independent. Economically speaking, England was not an exciting place to be in at that time. I was working as a roadie for Pink Floyd. In a way, being close to the entertainment industry energised me. When Oliver invited me to Zambia, I was straight away drawn to exploring the art of the possible.

'My only source of any gem knowledge was Robert Webster's book on gems. Once it became clear that Ollie didn't have any emerald connections, based on what I'd read in the book, I decided to try my luck with diamonds in Zaire[1].'

'Oh my! What did Ollie say when you told him?'

'He thought I was insane and tried to stop me. I must have been mad to think I could just troop into the heart of Zaire as a white guy, buy diamonds, and leave in one piece. In those days, Zaire was really dangerous. It was not long after the Kolwezi massacre[2] of 1978. Zaire was very much the heart of

[1]   Zaire changed its name to Democratic Republic of Congo (DRC) in 1997. Also known as Congo.

[2]   Ottaway, D. B. (1978). "Death and Destruction in a Terrorized City in Zaire." The Washington Post.

darkness. I was an enthusiast for Joseph Conrad[1] anyway, so I thought I'd go and discover my own heart of darkness visiting the diamond mines.'

'Was there even a flight in those days?'

'Don't recall. Even if there was, I couldn't afford to spend more money on a plane ticket,' said Guy. 'My destination inside Zaire was a place called Ilebo, which was a good 1,700-plus kilometres from Lubumbashi, a small town in southern Zaire across the Zambian border from a place call Chililabombwe[2], in Zambia. To get there, I took a bus from Lusaka to Kitwe. That in itself was a risk because highway robbery was rampant. Don't forget, there was a lot of weaponry and ordnance leftover from the days when Joshua Nkomo, the revolutionary freedom fighter, was living in exile in Zambia, from where he led an armed battle against the white minority rule of southern Rhodesia, now Zimbabwe.'

'Isn't Kitwe near the Kafubu emerald deposit?'

'Yes. I'm surprised you know,' said Guy.

'I recently wrote an article on the Gemfields Emerald Mine in Zambia. I believe it's near Kitwe.'

'It is indeed, but they didn't own the mine in 1985. It was controlled by the government with a group of investors from the industry,' explained Guy.

'Did you visit the mine?'

'No way! When I reached Kitwe, I heard there was a large emerald mine nearby, but the concession was heavily guarded, and paramilitary forces were known to be quite trigger-happy to keep intruders out.'

'Who told you?' asked Vivienne.

'This man I was staying with in Kitwe. I went to a public school in England and there were a lot of boys who had connections in India, Africa, Pakistan. One of my schoolmates had arranged for me to spend a few nights with an acquaintance of his, an undertaker from Lancaster.'

'An undertaker? A white man from Lancashire working as an undertaker in Kitwe?'

'Sounds bizarre when you say it out loud. Plan was to stay for a few days with him and his English wife at their home in Kitwe, find my way to the Zambian border town of Chililabombwe, and then cross over to reach Lubumbashi in Zaire from where I was going to take a train to Ilebo.'

---

1   Joseph Conrad (1857–1924): English writer of Polish descent, whose works include the novella, *Heart of Darkness* (1899).

2   A Zambian town located near the border with Zaire (now DRC). The name means "the croaking of the frogs" in the Bemba language.

'Fascinating. So, you reached Kitwe, safe and sound, and this undertaker you are staying with advises you to stay away from the Kafubu emerald fields,' said Vivienne, as she prompted Guy to resume his account.

'Yes. I'm not sharing his name because the next part of the story is a bit macabre. You're not recording this, I hope?'

'I would never record without your permission.'

'Good. Good. You see, the Senegalese were the main controllers of the illicit emerald business. They would travel to the Kafubu emerald region in small groups with a village idiot, a scapegoat. Once they had acquired whatever emeralds they needed to make the trip worthwhile, they'd kill him and deposit the body with this undertaker. He would leave them alone with the corpse to do what they pleased with the body.'

'Oh my gosh! You mean they stuffed the body with the rough emeralds?' said Vivienne. The story had taken a dark turn, which she hadn't expected.

'That's what this undertaker explained probably happened. It was a way of transporting the emeralds in a lead-lined coffin across various borders. I was a naïve 23-year-old who'd thrown myself into this world that I barely understood. And I found these stories the undertaker was telling me quite disturbing. By morning, I had decided to abandon my plans of staying with them and continue my journey to Zaire.'

'The stories didn't deter you from your mission?' Vivienne asked.

'Not at all. I'd sold my apartment, come all this way, so I wasn't going to go back empty-handed. I got a lift from some expats till Chililabombwe and there I met some Portuguese Angolans.'

'Portuguese Angolans,' Vivienne repeated. 'Sounds odd.'

'As I am sure you know, Angola was under Portuguese colonial rule until November 1975 when the Portuguese left. This couple had left during that period and set up shop in Zambia. There were quite a few nefarious characters in Lubumbashi, almost a "Casablanca in the forties" feel, but in Zaire. I was grateful to cross under their protection to the safety of their house in Lubumbashi. They were very kind and hospitable towards me and thought I was insane to travel on a train from Lubumbashi to Ilebo. It was a time of complete chaos, but I took my chances and set off.'

A knock on the door interrupted their conversation. It was Guy's assistant informing him that the parcel he'd been waiting for had arrived. 'Vivienne, you're in for a special treat today,' said Guy, as he pulled out a penknife from his desk drawer. Vivienne and the assistant watched in silence as he took his time to open the FedEx package, removing each layer slowly until he reached a bubble-wrapped box the size of his fist.

He instructed his assistant to clear the papers from his desk, so the only thing left was a large leather pad with crisp white sheets of paper on top that were neatly tucked in the corners. The deliberate clearing of space and careful handling of the package increased the tension in the room. Vivienne sent a brief message to her office, cancelling her next appointment.

As Guy pulled back the final layer of bubble wrap and opened the box, Vivienne let out a gasp. Nestled within a creamy velvet cushion was a large pear-shaped emerald displaying a medium tone, richly saturated, slightly bluish-green. 'It's 15.32 carats,' said Guy, as he gently took the precious stone in his hand.

'I've never seen such a beautiful emerald,' said Vivienne. 'The crystal quality is exceptional! The way it glimmers, mesmerising. Is it Zambian?'

'The finest Zambian emerald ever discovered. This beauty has a very interesting story. The original rough it was cut from weighed 323 grams. It was a perfect hexagonal crystal, covered in dark mica schist. When I moved the rough in my hand using the light to try to see inside, the emerald changed colour from bluish-green to a pure green. I remember telling my two African suppliers, "I can't see it. This is a casino for me. A gamble. I have no idea what's inside".'

'What did they say?'

'They said I should trust them because they were aquamarine specialists,' said Guy.

'I am afraid I don't understand,' said Vivienne.

'Because aquamarine and emerald are both part of the beryl mineral family, their crystal structure is the same. Hexagonal. Trace elements in the stone impact its colour. The blue colour of an aqua comes from iron, whereas emerald get its green from chromium,' explained Guy.

'Doesn't an emerald also contain iron?' asked Vivienne. She had working gemmological knowledge, given her specialisation in the gem and jewellery sector.

'Very good. Yes, Zambian emeralds also have iron but the key element that is responsible for the green is chromium. Interestingly, higher iron increases the bluish tinge in an emerald. It can also make the stone darker. My suppliers explained that when they see a crystal behaving in this manner, it contains something special inside.'

'Sorry, Guy. I'm not following. What do you mean by "behaving in this manner"? You mean the colour appearing blue-green in one section and green in another?' asked Vivienne.

'Yes. But it was more than that. When I examined the rough emerald, I could see certain segments of the crystal were clearer than the rest, which seemed cloudy. As per my Zambian suppliers, the cloudy bits were almost protecting something spectacular inside.'

'What a romantic way of explaining the gemmological characteristics of the emerald,' said Vivienne. 'Is this why you were you saying it's like a casino?'

'Exactly. You may have decades of experience and knowledge, but there's an element of magic that's difficult to explain. After I extracted this 15.32-carat emerald from the rough, I was giving a lecture at the Gem-A[1], and one of the experts said, "Hang on a second. There's something not quite right about this stone. There are no inclusions in it; it's completely clean." And I had kittens when I heard this because I had already started selling the less important, smaller emeralds I'd cut from the same rough.'

'Oh no. Then?'

'I called my suppliers and asked them if the stone could be a clever synthetic. They confirmed it was a natural emerald, but then they said, "We have another problem. We've been in a car accident and are sitting in jail so can you send us some cash?" I sent cash by Western Union so they could get a lawyer and get out.'

'Hilarious. But what about this emerald? What's the verdict?' asked Vivienne.

'I just got it back from the SSEF[2] gem lab, and they said it is highly unusual in its clarity, but it's a natural emerald. I'm off the hook!' said Guy.

'Incredible,' whispered Vivienne, as she gazed at the breathtaking emerald. She found it hard to look away. Guy broke the spell by placing the stone back in its case.

'What was the weight of the rough, again?' asked Vivienne.

'It was 323 grams, and I managed to get 400-carats' worth of good-quality emeralds out of it. A yield of 20 per cent.'

'Eighty per cent wastage!'

'Yield from the general quality, what we call run-of-mine, can be as low as only 18 per cent. A skilled gem cutter may extract 35 per cent to 40 per cent from a high-quality rough emerald.'

'High quality meaning an emerald that doesn't contain too many fractures and surface-reaching fissures?' asked Vivienne.

'Exactly. Very good. You know a lot about gemstones,' said Guy.

'Still a lot to learn.'

1 The Gemmological Association of Great Britain.
2 Swiss Gemmological Institute.

'But this is the best way. By asking questions. Most emeralds contain fissures and fractures, which impact the clarity, and get in the way of light performance of an emerald. A lapidary will take care of it either by removing the included parts of the rough emerald or treating it with oils and resins to improve the clarity—or both.'

'Thank you for showing me the emerald. That was indeed a special treat,' said Vivienne. 'Should we get back to your story?'

Guy laughed. 'Aren't you late for your meeting?'

'I've cancelled it. Where were we? You boarded the train from Lubumbashi to Ilebo. And then?'

'I was in premier class deluxe. The train was moving at 10 to 20 miles an hour and I was sharing the compartment with three big African women who were travelling with live chickens in the compartment. We would go to the dining car together, which would serve vast quantities of rice and nshima (ground corn). Honestly, I could have gotten off and walked beside the train. Anyway, after four days of this excruciatingly slow train journey, one afternoon, we heard a mighty bang. The train was derailed.

'Here's the funny part. No one was upset or surprised. It was almost as if they were expecting the derailment to happen. Passengers peacefully got out. There were no paths or roads, the Belgians had really left a mess in Zaire. Once everyone had gathered their belongings, we all started walking along the railway track.'

'How long was the walk?' asked Vivienne.

'I think we walked for around 100 miles. There was an unsaid code that we were united in our hardship. At night we would sleep by the side of the rail track. I had purification tablets to disinfect my water.'

'And this is where the live chickens came in handy for the women?'

'You got it. It took us five days to reach a small town where I found a truck to bring me to Ilebo.'

'A truck? Why didn't you take a bus?'

'The circumstances in underdeveloped countries are different from what we take for granted in a first-world nation. There is no official public transport system. You have these trucks and private bus services that operate in certain areas. Most people just walk for hours, days, weeks, months till they reach their destination. I got to Ilebo but was stuck there for a week because of heavy rains. I'd been told a steamer would take me down the Kasai River. This was the only way to reach the diamond mining areas of Tshikapa or Mbuji-Mayi.'

'You'd been on the road for how long by now?'

'More than two weeks, I think. To cut a long story short, I got on the steamer. After two days, the main propeller fell off and, again, I was stranded, this time in the middle of the jungle in Zaire.'

'What terrible luck!' said Vivienne.

'Not a question of luck. These vehicles have been left over from the colonial era. There are no spare parts or workshops where equipment could be fixed. There is nothing except the grit and spirit of the local people, and what nature has given them.'

'How did you get out of the jungle?' Vivienne prompted.

'We walked until we found a trail that led us to another small hamlet. The residents informed us a truck would be along in a few days. The internal part of the jungle was serviced by these very robust trucks that would take forever to get from A to B but that was the only way any commodities could get through. The trucks were the arteries of life in Zaire. But I had another problem: malaria. These huge mosquitoes in the jungle had bitten me and despite the anti-malaria pills, I was running a high fever by the time the truck arrived.'

'Weren't you carrying any medication?'

'I guess Western medicine was created keeping in mind normal mosquitoes. The ones I encountered must have been a special variety or something. I was sick as a dog. How I survived, I don't know. The truck got us as far as Kikwit.'

'Hold on. Isn't Kikwit where the Ebola outbreak started?'

'Correct. By the time I reached Kikwit, I had lost all sense of colour. Everything was black and white. In fact, I passed out on the truck. My fellow African travellers were very kind. They knew I was bound for Kikwit, and once we arrived at my destination, they helped me off and handed me over to another local family that was living in a mud hut by the side of the road. They knew I was dying. They gave me food. Eventually, I gained enough strength to catch another truck to Kinshasa.'

'Why Kinshasa? What about the diamond mines?'

'I was in no condition to continue my quest. At this stage, I was just looking to get to Kinshasa where I had a reliable friend—Greg Kronsten— who was the chairman of Zaire's HQ of Grindlays Bank. My other friend from England, his father was the British ambassador in Kinshasa. I needed food, shelter, medicines. When I eventually got back to England, I spent the best part of a year going in and out of the hospital of tropical diseases.'

'It was just one thing after another, wasn't it. Sounds unbelievable,' said Vivienne.

'It was, and I'd forgotten a lot of it. Funny, when you start sharing a story, it all comes back. I was totally mad to undertake that journey,' said Guy.

'Your friend must have been shocked to see you,' said Vivienne.

'He was, but I had another encounter before Kinshasa where I was held up at gunpoint by the Zaire police. They were armed with these very rusty old automatic weapons called G3s. I had managed a seat in the front of the truck with the driver, and they stuffed their guns through the windows. A lot of them had never seen a white guy. I was wearing old combat trousers, which I got from an army surplus. And they said, "Pantalons militaires. Vous êtes mercenaire [Your pants are from the military. You are a mercenary]." White guy wearing army trousers was not a good combination. They butted me with their rifle. As I keeled over, one of them spotted my cloth belt full of cash around my waist, which he tore off.'

'Oh God, they took your money?!' Vivienne was sitting on the edge of her seat.

'Luckily for me, it was in local currency, which was virtually worthless. You needed a big bundle of local money in those days to buy a loaf of bread. My pounds[1] were in my boots, which were saved. But just imagine, I'm on my knees by the side of the road with my hands behind my head. These guys are towering above me and shouting, "You're a mercenary" with their guns pointed in my direction.'

'What did you say?'

'I said, "Je suis l'ami de l'ambassadeur britannique Mr Snodgrass [I am a friend of the British ambassador, Mr Snodgrass]." The minute I said his name, they all burst out laughing. It was a funny name. And that immediately diffused the situation. People are nearer the knuckle in Africa and running on instinct. They let me go. I somehow made it to Kinshasa, where Greg looked after me. I stayed with him for two weeks to get some flesh back on my bones.

'During that time he kept saying, "You're the first European to travel from Lubumbashi to Kinshasa since the Kolwezi massacre." He couldn't get over the fact that I'd spent six weeks in the jungles of Zaire and lived to tell the tale. As it turns out, the only way for me to get back to Lusaka and catch my return flight to England was to cross the border again from Lubumbashi to Chililabombwe. Greg got me a lift on an American supply plane to Lubumbashi.'

'Why couldn't you just fly out from Kinshasa? Why go back?' asked Vivienne.

1   Great British Pounds – UK currency.

'I'd left some of my possessions with Ollie. And I had already purchased a return ticket to London from Lusaka. I couldn't afford to buy another airline ticket from Kinshasa to London. It's not like now where we have so many choices. In those days, not even the capital cities were well connected.'

'Did the same family help you cross the border again?'

'I didn't connect with them. After everything I'd gone through in the last month, I felt confident to cross on my own. I purchased a bus ticket from Lubumbashi to Chililabombwe. I was the only mzungu on this bus.'

'Mzungu? What is that?' asked Vivienne.

'A white person. We were bobbing along this rough path towards our destination when our bus was stopped. This chap in a dirty white coat boarded and said, "In fact, I am the minister of health. There has been an outbreak of cholera in Lubumbashi, so everyone must get off the bus for inoculation".'

'How bizarre!'

'That's not the crazy part. He injected the entire bus with the same needle, except for me because I paid a hundred dollars to avoid getting inoculated.'

'What?! These people just let themselves be jabbed by a stranger. Why?'

'Because he claimed that he was the minister. God knows whether he was injecting or drawing blood or what? I didn't want to find out.'

'Wasn't this around the time the HIV virus was exploding across the African continent?' asked Vivienne.

'It was. Researchers were finding HIV-positive patients across many African nations,' said Guy. 'They used to call it the "slim disease" in certain countries before the terms HIV and AIDS were coined by the medical community. Terrible times.'

'Hearing your story, one can understand how it spread so quickly.'

'Indeed. After escaping the inoculation, I got a lift with some locals who were driving to Zambia in an old beat-up Mercedes. We got to a roadblock after crossing the border, and it was armed by the paramilitary. I was pulled out of the vehicle. This was not long after the Rhodesian and Zimbabwean war of independence. Apartheid was in full swing in South Africa. As a white guy, I was not particularly welcome and rightfully so from their perspective.'

'They pulled you out because you were white?' asked Vivienne.

'They were searching for undeclared currency. Being a foreigner, the probability of finding it on me was high. I had a declaration form, which they checked but also ignored and said, "No, no you have not declared this money." They commandeered our vehicle and drove us to the police station in Chililabombwe and threw me in a jail cell. After some back and forth, they let the locals leave. I was frightened because at that time a foreigner could easily go missing. In the last month, I'd heard enough stories about travellers being fed to crocodiles for their possessions to realise that it could happen to me.'

'Instead of tea you should be serving tequila with this story, Guy,' said Vivienne.

Guy's assistant had come in twice in the last 30 minutes to enquire about some pending errands he was supposed to finish. He'd shooed her away.

'Stay with me now; we're almost home,' said Guy. 'The police called me in for interrogation and stripped me. They laid out all my possessions on the floor. Given my travel plans, I was carrying maps and a notebook in which I was documenting details related to my experiences. They started accusing me of being a spy for South Africa. I was standing there, naked, professing my innocence, and scared out of my brains. One of them picked up a small cassette player I was carrying. Among my tapes was one of Jimmy Cliff.'

'The Jamaican musician?' asked Vivienne.

'The same. "Many Rivers to Cross" is a song I can hear over and over. I'll never tire of that one. Everything changed once they found his cassette. They became quite affable, returned my clothes, possessions, and drove me in the police Land Rover back to the main highway where they flagged down a charcoal truck and got me a ride to Lusaka.'

'Because of Jimmy Cliff? Why?'

'That's what I was wondering. I finally reached Ollie's house in Chilenge South. He opened the door, and for a few seconds he's just stood there, staring at me like he'd seen a ghost. I was trembling, pumping adrenalin, because I'd managed to survive. I began speaking, and I couldn't construct a proper sentence. It was like my brain was broken or something. Ollie finally got me to calm down and tell him everything that had happened to me in the last two months. He explained that when the police officers saw Jimmy Cliff's tape, they felt I couldn't be a spy because he was a cultural hero in Zambia.'

'Incredible. You were saved by Jimmy Cliff.'

'Yeah. Would love to meet Jimmy Cliff one day, shake his hand and thank him.'

'Did you at least find a fabulous emerald after almost dying in Zaire?'

'I'm afraid not. I phoned my sister from the main post office on Cairo Road in Lusaka. I'd spoken to my family from Kinshasa to let them know I was alive and promised I'd call her from Lusaka. She informed me there had been a tragedy in the family, and I needed to fly back to London.'

'Oh no. After everything, you returned empty-handed?'

'I felt like such a failure. Couldn't leave things the way they were. Next year, I worked on building sites for cash. Lived on four pounds a week, and dhal[1] and rice for a year. After saving every single penny obsessively for 12 months, I had three thousand pounds, enough to return to Zambia and try again. With Ollie's help I purchased a superb rough emerald. A friend of mine in London was a gemmologist who'd promised that he'd evaluate and buy whatever I brought back. Guess what?'

'You sold it for a lot of money?'

'It was fake. A beautiful fake with a hexagonal prism and a mica coating. They'd done a great job disguising it. Seventy pounds. That's how much it cost me in 1986. For three years, I kept going to Africa and got nothing. On my third trip, I remember kneeling down and praying before my flight. I was desperate to turn this thing around. My friends and family thought I was losing my mind. They would constantly ask, "Why are you going back to Africa?" And I had no answer for them.'

'Please tell me you found an emerald this time. I'm going to need something stronger than tea if you didn't,' said Vivienne.

'Something did happen this time. Ollie and I stumbled upon a chap with an oil drum by the side of the road. His name was Mr Bandra. When we looked inside the drum, it was full to the brim with rough, deep blue aquamarine crystals. You don't see that quality today. Very rare. From a game park in Lukusuzi in Eastern Zambia.'

'It wasn't what you were looking for though? They weren't emeralds?'

'They weren't, but I couldn't afford to be fussed. I bought them and, on my return, sold the first batch to Mr Petsch[2], a renowned gem cutter and merchant based in Idar-Oberstein, Germany. But it was a small amount. I knew if I wanted to make it in the industry, I would have to target the US, which was a fast-growing market at that time. I travelled to New York and sold the remaining aqua to a gem merchant there for US$30,000. That vindicated what I was doing. It was a huge, effervescent moment.'

'What an amazing story. I wish I'd recorded your account, Guy,' said Vivienne. They both looked out of the window. The rain had stopped. It was time to get back to work.

'Honestly, I haven't narrated the story from start to finish to anyone before. It's always been segments of the tale. It truly is a miracle I survived.'

'The gem gods protected you,' said Vivienne, as she stood up.

---

1   Lentils flavoured with Indian spices.
2   Julius Petsch (Story 1).

'Anyone who knows Africa knows it can go right or wrong on a knife's edge. I was young enough to be protected by my naivety. From what I had observed during my travels, the patina of white South Africans at that time could be pretty arrogant. All those people I encountered in the Democratic Republic of Congo (DRC) and Zambia, they could see I didn't have that; I think it's what protected me.'

'Interesting. Thank you again for this wonderful account, and for showing me that very special emerald.' She looked at her watch. It would be a late night working in the office to make up for the time she lost listening to Guy's story, but she had no regrets.

'I'm sorry I was unable to show you the 60-carat Mozambican aquamarine, but it will be available for the photo shoot for your article.'

'Excellent. And may I just say I think it's very generous of you to donate the aquamarine. I'm sure it will fetch a good price at the auction.'

'It's for a worthy cause. I've been an admirer of Fine Cell Work for a long time. The work they do in teaching embroidery to incarcerated individuals, which enables them to not only learn a new skill but also earn from the sale of their creations, fantastic. My contribution is nothing in comparison to what they are achieving.'

Vivienne smiled. As she stepped out of Guy's office, she turned around and said, 'Donating a gemstone worth 40 thousand pounds is not nothing. Hope we meet again, Guy Clutterbuck.'

Author's Note

This story is based on actual events as experienced by Guy Clutterbuck. The information presented was gathered by the author through a series of interviews with Guy in 2021. In 2014, Guy donated a 60-carat Mozambican aquamarine for a charity auction benefitting Fine Cell Work. Although his donation received coverage by various media platforms including BBC Four Radio, the character of Vivienne and the interaction in Guy's office is fictional. All other elements as outlined in the story are true. Political references are based on conversations with Guy Clutterbuck and various media reports.

Soon after Guy's success with Zambian aquamarine, the Senegalese community of gem merchants learnt of the stone's value and moved from the Kafubu emerald fields (where they controlled the illicit emerald business), to the eastern province. Their increased presence led to an escalation of violence and Guy decided to visit Thailand instead where he learnt how to cut gemstones with the Asian Institute of Gemmological Studies (AIGS), followed by a course with the Gemological Institute of America (GIA) in Santa Monica, USA.

In Bangkok, he met an American dealer who offered to teach him about lapis lazuli from Afghanistan in exchange for Guy teaching him about Zambian aquamarine (which the dealer was currently buying from Gilgit, Pakistan). Guy was introduced to key players in the lapis industry and started travelling to Afghanistan. In 1998, he took an influential American gem dealer to meet Commander Massoud in Panjshir Valley, Afghanistan, and a few years later, he organised and accompanied BBC *Newsnight* correspondent John Simpson for a documentary on the lapis mines of Afghanistan. In 2015, Guy was commissioned by National Geographic to front an eight-part documentary series titled Mine Kings.

Since 1988 (three years after he began on the gem trail), Guy Clutterbuck has been working in the industry as a merchant, acquiring rough and cut gemstones in Ethiopia, Greenland, Colombia, Zambia, Zimbabwe, Mozambique, Tanzania, South Africa, Madagascar, Pakistan, Afghanistan, Myanmar, Thailand, and Sri Lanka. His clients reside in Europe, the US, and the Far East. He believes that the hard knocks he experienced in his early years in the industry cemented his interest in gemstones.

To quote Guy, 'Having invested as much as I had, I couldn't walk away. The trials are an essential rite of passage for any newcomer. If you don't stick around, you are not supposed to be dealing in stones. There is a magic around them. It's the most extraordinary privilege to be able to handle stones and make a living out of them.'

In addition to his work as a gem merchant, Guy is also sponsoring mining projects in Mozambique, Zambia, and Sri Lanka.

A Gun, a Dinner and a Flight

13th June 1990
Antananarivo, Madagascar

'YOU KNOW Ernie Bisonio?' Abe Nassi asked Sanjay[1]. 'The man almost got me killed once in South Africa.'

Nassi was driving to a farm 40 minutes outside of Antananarivo to see a few kilos of rough emeralds. He was conversing with Sanjay, an Indian gem broker from Johannesburg who had arranged the meeting with the Malagasy mine owner. They were both sitting in the back of a Land Rover, which Sanjay had arranged, accompanied by their driver and an escort the mine owner had sent to help direct them to the remote location.

'I've heard of him, but I don't know him personally,' said Sanjay.

'Ernie called me one day and said he could arrange rough emeralds for me. I asked him, "How? From where?" He claimed to know a bunch of guys in Rhodesia[2] and he was talking about this region called Sandawana and said, "You wanna buy the emeralds, you gotta come down to Jo'burg. It's two or maybe three kilos of good-quality rough emeralds, available to buy for US$250,000".'

'When was this?' asked Sanjay.

'Mmm around 1978, I think. Yeah, '78,' said Nassi. 'Of course, I knew about the Sandawana emeralds because I'd bought two small parcels of the stuff from a couple in Geneva a year earlier. Small sizes, but intense, bright green colour.'

'Geneva?'

'Yeah. The sellers owned a farm in Rhodesia. Middle-aged couple, blue eyed, fair skinned. I met them through a broker. When I asked them about the origin of the emeralds, they named a place called Bulawayo, which is near the Sandawana emerald deposit. Twelve months later, Ernie offered me an opportunity to buy two or three kilos of those intense green emeralds. I

---

1   This name has been changed.
2   Zimbabwe. The country gained independence in 1980.

was hooked. But US$250,000 is a lot of money, especially in 1978. I roped in my longtime friend in the business, Reg Miller.'

'Miller. Never heard of him,' said Sanjay.

'Reg and I, we go way back. He's got his own lapidary and gem business, but we collaborate on large purchases and consult each other. Good friend. Anyway, I called Reg and told him what's what and we decided to travel to Jo'burg to see these Sandawana stones.'

'What about the money?'

'We wired the 250K to Chase Manhattan Bank's affiliate bank in Jo'burg. Got there on a Thursday and called Ernie. He told us the viewing would be over the weekend so we should get the cash ready. We go to the bank in Jo'burg. I can't remember the exact exchange rate, but by the time we finished converting the US dollars into South African rand, we had a large suitcase full of cash on our hands. I still remember the look on the bank manager's face. They had to close the branch early to handle the transaction. We took our bag of money and went back to the hotel, only to discover they didn't have a secure room to store our money. Now this was turning into a thing because we had to hire a guard. Anyway, we did all this and waited for Ernie's call.'

'And then?'

'Friday, no phone call. Saturday morning, after breakfast, we were sitting and wondering what was going on. We'd come all this way, got the cash, and no emeralds. Finally, Ernie called. He said, "Abe, it's all set. We're going to take a helicopter around 11 pm to this location near the border. There, in the middle of this dry riverbed, we can see the emeralds. It's a full moon, so it won't be a problem. And we must pay them, so bring the cash with you." I heard this, and I said to him, "Ernie, I have one question for you. Does it say moron on my face?"'

Sanjay burst out laughing. 'The thing is, Abe,' he said, 'I can imagine you saying it.'

'I gave Ernie hell,' said Abe. 'I said, "I will not go to some bloody riverbed in the middle of the night to look at emeralds by moonlight! What do you take me for?!"'

'What about all the money you'd changed?'

'We had to go back to the bank Monday morning and change all the rand back into dollars. A complete administrative nightmare. Waste of time and money.'

'You were smart. I've heard terrible stories of people disappearing trying to buy stones like this,' said Sanjay.

'So how much more time till we reach this farm?' asked Abe, switching Sanjay's attention to the task ahead. 'We've been on the road for more than an hour.'

'Almost there. I think that's the gate. Antoine[1], the guy who owns the mine, is waiting for us inside.'

The sentry at the entrance had been expecting them and didn't waste any time opening the main gate. Abe noticed an armed guard standing on top of the farmhouse. *I'd have security too if I had a stash of emeralds in the middle of nowhere*, he thought.

As they stepped out of the vehicle, Abe looked around. It was all green as far as the eye could see. The land was being used for terraced rice farming, and he spotted some structures, one of which looked like a stable. Antoine had set up seating in the garden in front of the main double-storey building: a wooden table with a white sheet on top, and two weather-beaten wooden chairs on either side.

'Welcome, Mr Nassi,' said Antoine, walking towards them with his arms outstretched.

The man had an interesting look. During the drive, Sanjay told Abe that Antoine was half French and half Malagasy. *I hope he's not the hugging type*, thought Abe. The man clasped Abe's outstretched hand, shaking it vigorously. As the party walked towards the table, Abe observed the miner from the corner of his eye. The man was well-groomed. He wore a white linen shirt, khaki pants, and his hair was slick. His manner was deferential, and he was oozing charm. Abe wasn't sure whether that was a good thing or bad.

'Would you like some coffee to freshen you up after your drive?' Antoine asked.

'Thank you, but I had a late breakfast,' said Abe.

He had rushed through the meal and hadn't had time for his morning coffee, but for some reason he wanted to get on with the emerald viewing despite the dull ache that was settling in the back of his caffeine-deprived head.

After a few minutes of idle conversation around Abe's business and Antoine's French lineage, the rough emeralds arrived. The stones had been packed in five jute bags. Antoine stood up, picked up the first jute bag, and started pouring the rocks on the table.

Halfway through his pour, Abe said, 'Stop.'

'What's wrong?'

'Is the rest of the material the same quality?' asked Abe.

---

1   Name changed.

Antoine straightened. He placed the bag on the table with a loud thud. 'Yes. All are more or less the same quality. Six kilos of rough emeralds for three million US dollars.'

'I'm not interested,' said Abe.

'Make me an offer,' said Antoine.

'This material's not for me.'

'No problem. What's your counter?'

'I don't think you understand. I don't cut or deal in this quality. It's not for me.'

'What do you mean, it's not for you? You cut emeralds; you sell them. This may not be top grade, but it's still emerald. Give me your best price, and I'll consider it.'

'I don't think you understand the gem business, my friend. I specialise in a particular quality. I don't have the time or the customers for this grade of emeralds. For the last time, this material is not for me,' said Abe emphatically.

Antoine reached behind his back and pulled out a revolver. He placed it on the table next to the emeralds. 'And like I said before, make me an offer.'

Without a moment's hesitation, Abe said, 'Oh, you wanna use a gun? Better use it fast before I kill you.'

He stood up, turned his back to Antoine, and started walking towards his jeep. Sanjay, who'd been sitting next to Abe at the table, jumped up and followed.

Antoine burst out laughing. 'No hard feelings, Mr Nassi,' he shouted. 'I look forward to seeing you again.'

Abe didn't stop to acknowledge him. He knew he wasn't safe till their jeep had made it out of the compound. It took all his willpower to control the urge to walk fast. *Don't let them sense your fear*, he told himself. Once they'd been on the road for ten minutes and made sure no one was following, Abe let out a sigh of relief. Sanjay was shaking like a leaf and kept apologising profusely.

As they pulled up on the front porch of Abe's hotel, Sanjay asked him, 'Abe, were you prepared to shoot him?'

'I was, but I couldn't.'

'Why?'

'Because I don't have a gun,' said Abe. He closed the door of the Land Rover and walked inside the hotel.

* * *

After yesterday's debacle, Abe needed a normal day of trading. The situation had been too close for comfort, and he wanted to do a few deals and get back to New York. He called his friend and local contact, Ray Ferguson. Ray had spent the better part of the seventies as CEO of the Gravelotte Emerald Mine in South Africa. He'd run into trouble with the authorities, and, after a stint in Zambia, settled as a gem and mineral specimen dealer in Madagascar.

'Hello? Ray?' said Abe.

'Abe! Are you in Tana? When did you arrive?' said Ray.

'Two days ago. Did you find good morganite for me?'

'I've been on the job since you called last week. Everything's ready for you. And I also found this amazing dinosaur egg and two tonnes of optic-quality quartz,' said Ray.

'Ray! I'm not interested in all this exotic stuff. Haven't you learnt your lesson? Got any other nice gems you think I should see?

'Ya. Got parcels of emeralds and tourmalines.'

'OK, I'll come over after breakfast,' said Abe.

He then called a government minister he had met a year ago. Beyond trading, Abe was keen on acquiring a mining concession in Madagascar. His last mining venture in Tanzania a few years ago had failed because of a fraudulent partner who Abe discovered was selling their sapphire production off the books. The experience had left a bitter taste in his mouth, which he wanted to correct.

The minister had promised to dig out old colonial maps from the ministry's archives for Abe to study. Given his unpleasant exchange with Antoine, Abe figured it couldn't hurt to reconnect with a government official in case he needed extra protection. The minister was delighted to hear from Abe and extended an invitation for dinner at his home. After making a final call to change his airline ticket to leave a day later for New York, Abe made his way to the breakfast room of the hotel.

By noon Abe was sitting in Ray's office, drinking his second cup of coffee, and inspecting a collection of rough gemstones.

'What did you get up to yesterday?' asked Ray.

'This and that. Some bozo took me to a farm to see rough emeralds,' said Abe.

'Oh. How were they?'

'Junk. I call that quality, "fish tank stones", 'cause that's all they're good for. He wanted three million US dollars for six kilos of crap.'

'This is the problem. They think just because it's an emerald it's worth millions. You gotta see the stuff that comes into my office,' said Ray. 'What are your travel plans after this trip?'

'I was planning to see my friend, Campbell Bridges. Did I tell you about him?' said Abe.

'He's the tsavorite miner in Kenya, right?' said Ray.

'Not just a miner, he's a highly respected geologist. Interesting story. He discovered tsavorite in Zimbabwe in 1961 when he was working as a geologist, had nothing to do with the gem business, got transferred to Tanzania, discovered tsavorite there in 1967. Had to ship out because of a regime change. Get this, for the third time, he finds tsavorite in Kenya in 1970. Crazy, huh? That's where he lives now. He's the one who named the stone tsavorite after Tsavo National Park.'

'I didn't realise he'd discovered tsavorite. I've seen a few stones in Madagascar but the colour is dark. Would love to meet him someday,' said Ray.

'He's something else,' said Abe. 'But I worry about him.'

'Why?'

Abe paused, looked up from the gems he was inspecting, and let out a long sigh. 'He's a man of principles mining gemstones in a country that's dealing with issues like corruption and poverty. A man like that who wants to do everything by the book will keep hitting walls he must either work around or punch through. And those walls are only getting thicker and higher.'

'Yeah,' said Ray. 'Sounds like a tough situation. But, like you said, that's his home. I'm sure he'll be fine. If he's a member of the community there; they'll help and protect him.'

'I don't know. When the shit hits the fan, my friend, everyone disappears.'

Abe spent the rest of the day with Ray shortlisting rough-gem parcels for purchase. By 5.30 pm, he'd finalised two parcels of aquamarine, a kilo of morganite, 500 grams of tourmaline, and five rough emeralds, which he was hoping would yield at least three-carat sizes after cutting. The minister had informed Abe that his car would pick him up around 7 pm, which left enough time for him to have a shower and make a few work calls.

By 10 pm, Abe was done with dinner at the minister's residence. Besides the minister's family, Abe's dinner company included two other government officials.

'Thank you for this feast, madame,' said Abe, addressing the minister's wife. 'I'll have to skip breakfast tomorrow.'

The woman laughed, pleased with Abe's compliment. 'You're welcome to come over and enjoy a home-cooked meal anytime.'

'You better be careful because I'll take you up on your offer,' said Abe. 'And please give me the recipe for that octopus salad; it was superb!'

'I'll write it down for you and leave it in the foyer,' she said. 'You can pick it up after your meeting.'

'Do we have a meeting, your excellency?' asked Abe, making eye contact with the minister.

'Nothing so formal; I just wanted your advice on something. Come. Let's go to the living room.'

Abe followed the minister and the two government officials. *What's this about now?* he wondered. Once inside, the minister closed the curtains, and made sure the doors and windows of the room were sealed. Abe was puzzled by his behaviour but stayed quiet.

'Please sit, Abe,' said the minister, gesturing for Abe to take a seat next to him on the main sofa. The other two officials were seated across from them. The minister started speaking in a low tone. Abe had to lean forward to hear what the man was saying.

'I want to speak with you about something very confidential, Abe,' said the minister.

'Sure. Go ahead.'

'I'm planning a coup to overthrow the government.'

The minister's statement left Abe dumbfounded. After his encounter yesterday with the gun-toting dealer, and now this, he felt like he was in a Hollywood movie where the director kept changing the script on him.

'I need to raise US$50,000, Abe, to get the army on my side. Can you help?' asked the minister.

Be cool, Abe told himself, as he leaned back, sinking into the plush comfort of the sofa, and started caressing his beard, pretending to be deep in thought. The minister, along with the two officials, was leaning forward, waiting with bated breath for Abe's response. After a few seconds, Abe said, 'Can be done, but it'll have to be from the US.'

Relieved to hear an affirmative reply, the minister smiled. 'I knew I could trust you, Abe.' He looked at the officials and with a big grin on his face said something to them in French, which to Abe sounded like, 'See, I told you he'll come through.'

'Let me get back to the US,' said Abe. 'I'll arrange for the funds you need.'

The minister started slapping Abe's back in a friendly gesture of happiness. In anticipation of financial help, the minister opened a fresh bottle of Johnnie Walker Black Label whiskey and insisted Abe stay on till they finish the bottle.

The next morning, it took all of Abe's physical and mental strength to reach the airport for his flight back to New York. He was the last passenger to check in. Luckily, the queue at immigration was not long, and the officer was more amused than irritated that he had to ask Abe to remove his sunglasses. By the time Abe reached the Air France business class lounge, desperate for a cup of coffee, the receptionist informed him that boarding had started, and he should go directly to the gate.

At the gate, four police officers and the Air France staff were checking everyone's boarding cards. Some passengers were being pulled aside for a second security check of their hand luggage. Under normal circumstances, Abe wouldn't have paid any attention to an extra security check, but given the events of the last 24 hours, a million thoughts were racing through his mind as he stood in line waiting for his turn.

Did Antoine bribe someone at the airport to take revenge? Maybe the government found out about the minister planning the military coup and he's been arrested? Or maybe it's a random check, so stay calm. When his turn came, the Air France ground staff glanced at his boarding pass and promptly passed it to the police, who motioned for him to step aside. Abe followed. His heart was racing. *Shit. This is it.*

'We need to search your bag,' said the police officer. Abe handed over his American Tourister duffel bag to the man and stepped aside. The officer started methodically removing every single item from the large bag, stuffed with Abe's clothes, toiletries, and papers. As Abe watched the officer take his time, passengers continued boarding the bus.

After the Air France coach left for the aircraft, a security officer pulled a bottle out of Abe's bag and started shouting, in French, 'Pierres précieuses! [Precious stones].'

The senior officer took the bottle. The objects inside the bottle seemed to glow.

Abe stepped forward, and said, 'Pas de pierre précieuse [Not precious stone].' He opened the cap, pulled out what they thought were gems and bit down on one. He then held the broken shell underneath the nose of the officer. 'Pilules d'ail [garlic pills],' he said.

Once it was established that there were no precious stones in Abe's luggage, he invited the officer to step away from the security check with him, discreetly gave the man a hundred dollar note, and asked him who had tipped them off against him. The man just smiled and apologised. As a goodwill gesture, he drove Abe in his jeep to the plane to make sure he made his flight back to New York.

Author's Note

The above story is based on interviews with Abraham Nassi. All three incidents occurred around the same period, and the account in the story is accurate. Minor fictional elements have been included to aid narration. The three incidents in Madagascar in 1990 were enough to motivate Abe Nassi to never return to the country.

Nassi has been part of the coloured gemstone industry since the age of 19 and has run his own company since 1976. His travels worldwide, visiting mines and markets, seeking exceptional gemstones, has enabled him to train his eye to recognise in the field what many gemmologists need microscopes to discover. He has a worldwide reputation as a leader amongst coloured gemstone dealers and has seen some of the most valuable gemstones come through his office.

Many other experts in the field of coloured gemstones seek Abraham's knowledge and opinion regarding the value and quality of coloured stones.

Grossular Green

'WHAT DO you think?' said Bruce Bridges, walking over to huddle with the lawyer who had been fighting their case for the last five years.

'They have all the evidence, the eyewitness testimony. I'm hopeful,' said the lawyer.

'I wish I shared your positive outlook. I could have never imagined we'd be in this situation.'

'Listen, why don't you and your family get some lunch? It'll be a while. I'll text you as soon as they have a verdict. No point everyone hanging around the courthouse.'

* * *

1987—27 years earlier
2.00 pm
Taita-Taveta County
Tsavo National Park, Kenya

'Bruce, stay in the Rangie,' Campbell Bridges instructed his eight-year-old son as he ran after three men who had cut in front of their Range Rover. The trio carried large sacks, and one had an elephant rifle. Bruce assumed they were the poachers his father had mentioned after hearing gunshots last night.

Bruce and his sister, Laura, were at their family's mining concession outside the Tsavo National Park in Taita, Kenya. Their father, Campbell Bridges, was an eminent geologist, miner, and merchant who had discovered a rare green (grossular) garnet 20 years ago in Tanzania. When the government of Tanzania nationalised his mining operation in 1970, Campbell followed geological indicators and used old colonial maps to trace the mineral strike across the border into Kenya.

His discovery of the rare garnet in Kenya led to the establishment of his second mining operation, on the periphery of the Tsavo National Park, which motivated him to name the stone 'tsavorite' as an homage to his new home. Known as the Scorpion Mine, the camp's location near Tsavo meant that Campbell and his team frequently crossed paths with heavily armed, trigger-happy poachers. Being a staunch environmentalist, Campbell worked closely with the Kenya Wildlife Service (KWS) to help in bringing the perpetrators to justice.

As Bruce's father began chasing the poachers, yelling at them to stop, Amos, the mine's head of security, sprinted after him. Both men were unarmed. Not wanting to be left behind, Bruce followed. It was a sunny day, and the heat was palpable as the boy tried to keep up with his father and Amos. Campbell, an Olympic-calibre runner, started gaining ground.

He's going to catch them, thought Bruce as he kept pace with Amos who was 30 metres ahead of him. Without warning, the man with the elephant rifle turned around and fired a shot towards Campbell. Bruce saw his father move just in the nick of time. His heart jumped in his throat.

After a momentary pause, Campbell resumed the chase after the gang, gaining 20 metres on them. The metallic clickety clack of the brass round being inserted in the elephant rifle pierced the tranquillity of the African bush as the poacher fired a second round at Campbell, who ducked behind a tree. Amos and Bruce also took cover. From their vantage point, they saw Campbell emerge and gain another 30 metres on the poachers. And then they heard it, a third round being racked.

Bruce saw his father dive behind a tree, the bullet barely missing him. They stood still, watching in horror as the poacher managed to rack a fourth round at lightning speed. He stood ten metres from the tree where Campbell was seeking cover. His two companions used the opportunity to escape.

After what seemed an eternity, the poacher with the gun started moving backwards while keeping his weapon trained at Campbell's tree cover. The silence of the savannah amplified the sound of his shoes as he moved away, slow and steady, until he gained ground and escaped.

Amos and Bruce caught up with Campbell. Bruce ran up to his father and gave him a tight hug.

'Bruce! I told you to stay in the Range Rover,' Campbell said, horrified to see his son.

'I didn't want to wait alone.'

'Boss,' said Amos. He was carrying the sacks the poachers had dropped. 'Should we see what's inside?'

'Not now,' Campbell responded. 'Let's go to the Taita Saisal Estate. They have a telephone. We'll call KWS [Kenya Wildlife Service], and I also need to pick up Judy and Laura.'

* * *

3.30 pm
The Taita Sisal Estate
Taita-Taveta

Bruce and his sister Laura were pretending to read their books as they eavesdropped on the telephone conversation their father was having with the KWS. They were all at the Taita Sisal Estate. Campbell had dropped off his wife, Judy, and their daughter, Laura, there before leaving for the bush. The estate manager was a good friend, and Campbell felt at peace knowing his wife and daughter were not alone at their mine camp, which was a few hours' drive away. Upon returning to the estate, they shared details of their encounter with the poachers, causing Judy to become upset about Bruce's close proximity. To calm everyone's nerves, she made hot Milo, which the children were savouring by taking slow sips to make it last as long as possible. Campbell joined the family in the estate manager's quarters after finishing the call.

'Right, that's done,' said Campbell, accepting the mug of hot Milo from Judy. 'They said they'll swing by in the morning to gather the sacks. They've issued an alert for the poachers, and the night shift will be on the lookout for the elephant carcass.'

Campbell leaned back on the sofa, savouring the taste of the warm drink. He patted his wife's hand, silently expressing his gratitude for this moment of comfort.

'Dad,' said Bruce, 'what was in the sacks Amos found?'

'Elephant tusks, animal skin, and bush meat.'

'What were they going to do with them?'

'Bruce, there are people who pay a lot of money to get elephant tusks and rhino horns. They carve them into decorations or make herbal medicines.'

'That's horrible. You almost caught the poachers. Are you sad they escaped?'

Campbell took a deep breath. 'Listen, he had a rifle; I wasn't armed. I've got you two to worry about. I didn't want to risk getting shot. Were you scared, Bruce?'

'Not at all!' said Bruce, puffing his chest out in a show of bravado.

His sister, Laura, rolled her eyes, and their parents chuckled.

Bruce ignored them. 'Dad, will you tell us a story, please?'

'One short story and then we need to return to the Scorpion Mine. I want us to drive back while we still have the light.'

The children nodded, taking another sip of their drink.

'After we moved from Tanzania to Kenya, and first discovered tsavorite—this was in 1970—the entire area was still a hunting block. There were no people, only man-eating lions, leopards, elephants, rhinos, and cape buffalos with their big curvy horns.'

'They call them "black death", right, Dad?' asked Bruce.

'Yes, because of all the people they kill each year. To stay cool during the hot summer months,' Campbell continued, 'and to make sure your mother and I didn't become a lion's lunch, we lived in a tree house for the first five years we were mining.'

'The same one that's outside our house at the Scorpion Mine?' asked Laura.

'No, the old one. It was basic, 25 feet above the ground, flat wooden planks for a floor, and an eight-inch-high perimeter board so we didn't roll out of the tree in our sleep.'

'What about the roof?' said Bruce.

'The roof was just thatch; we still got wet when it rained but it worked. And the tree was this large gamble flame tree. It looked like a flat green wispy umbrella from a distance, except for certain months when it would burst into colour with seasonal flowers. We had the best view from the tree house, looking across the vast expanse of the plains towards Tanzania, the only interruption being the block of Mount Kasigau rising sheer, almost like a monolith, for more than 1,000 metres.'

'What's a monolith?' Bruce asked, interrupting his father.

'It's a single block of rock, which rises upwards like a tower or a large pillar,' said Campbell.

'Oh, OK.'

'Each morning the sun rose in a blaze of glory behind Kasigau, and as the temperature dropped, a little cloud would hover like a flying saucer over the mountain.' Campbell paused for a second. He looked at his wife, Judy, and smiled. They were newly married back then; sharing the story with his children was taking him back to that magical time in their lives.

'We can see Mount Kasigau from the new tree house,' said Bruce.

'Yes, you can. We must go prospecting there again one of these days.'

'How did you shower?' asked Laura.

'The same way we do now. We had a big 45-gallon drum up in a tree and a hose came down from it, which was inserted into a rose.'

'What's a rose?' asked Bruce.

'It's that thing you have at the end of a watering can, the flat metal cover with holes.'

'Oh yeah.'

'And I'd fixed a tap there, which we turned on or off. So, after a few months of building this tree house and mining, we had enough tsavorite for our first sales trip abroad. Your mother and I were gone for maybe two months. When we returned, we were in for a surprise. Our tree house was filthy, animal bones scattered everywhere, we got flea bites, and the place stank!'

'Did it stink like when we saw the lion eat the gazelle?'

'Exactly.'

'Ewww, that's horrible. What did you do?'

'We cleaned it all up and threw out the bones, which took us hours. Exhausted, we fell asleep straight after dinner. Then, in the middle of the night, we heard a noise. It was a deep growling sound.'

'Like a dog?'

'No. Not a dog.'

'What was it?' asked Bruce, his eyes wide open, and a chocolate moustache dripping from his upper lip.

'We looked outside and there was a leopard beneath our home.'

'What?!' said Bruce. 'Were you scared?'

'Somewhat worried because, as you know, leopards are excellent climbers. He could have been in bed with us in a matter of seconds, and that's very close quarters for a fight with a leopard. So we kept watching him from the top. He was pacing around the tree, making these guttural sounds to show that he was angry. After each round of pacing, he would claw at the bark of the tree trunk and resume his growling.'

'Did he climb up?'

'He didn't. He threw a tantrum for a few minutes and then left. And this happened every time we travelled. When we were away, the leopard would drag its kill up the tree, eat it on our bed and take over the tree house. On our return, we would clean his mess, just like we clean up after you two. He would visit for a few nights, growling, pacing, drinking water from our basin beneath the tree, and then go away.'

'Why didn't he climb up?'

'Leopards are very smart. It understood and respected the fact that we had built the treehouse. We got into a rhythm; he enjoyed the facilities when we were away but respected our rights as the original occupants when we returned. He complained a lot for a few days, but never crossed the line.'

The children had finished their hot Milo and were licking the remnants from their lips.

'Does the leopard still visit?' asked Bruce, lowering his voice to almost a whisper.

'He does,' said Campbell, mirroring his son's tone. 'You've actually seen him.'

'We have? When? Where?' asked Laura.

'On leopard hill,' replied their father.

'Oh. Is that why you call it leopard hill?' asked Bruce.

'Yes. Around sunset, the leopard climbs on top of that granitic outcrop to catch the last rays of the setting sun. It's the spot that marks the start of our concession, and he has a 360-degree view of everything.'

'But how do you know it's the same leopard?' asked Bruce.

'That's it, you two. Story time's over. We need to head back to the mine now,' interrupted their mother, breaking the spell. 'You both have an early start tomorrow and many chores to finish today.'

After a few minutes of protests, the children acquiesced. Campbell and his family bid the estate manager goodbye and left for the scorpion camp.

Later that evening, after the family had finished dinner, and Bruce and Laura were in bed, Judy admonished Campbell for the day's incident. 'You took an enormous risk today,' she said folding and putting away the children's clothes. She was meticulous about the chore, always ensuring the kids would be well presented despite being miles from any form of civilisation.

'I know, but we can't let these poachers get away with murder,' said Campbell.

'It's not your responsibility, Campbell. They're armed. You were with your son; anything could have happened.'

'Judy, when we moved to Kenya, the elephant population was well over 300,000. Now, as per KWS, it's down to around 20,000. The men we were chasing today had an elephant rifle, but other groups use weapons like AK-47s to take down elephants. When I go to the top of our GG2 Mine, I can hear and see the rifle-fire at night. They aren't just poaching them for tusks but killing animals, left, right, and centre, for bush meat.'

Judy kept folding clothes in silence against the cricket's incessant drone, and the hooting of the owl. 'I know the statistics, Campbell; I don't want you to become one.'

'You know, poachers move in groups using high-powered torches, to blind the animals at night. While the animal is frozen, a guy or two go around the back with pangas [machetes] and hack the Achilles tendon of the poor creature. That's how they butcher them. These poachers must be stopped. KWS needs help, and I didn't go looking for them. These three guys jumped out of nowhere and ran in front of the Range Rover carrying their loot. I can't ignore it, Judy, but I promise I'll be more careful next time.'

Judy sighed. *Next time.* The words hung over her like a dark cloud.

The next morning, Bruce was busy helping the senior mine manager, Kasiki, having forgotten the previous day's events. Kasiki had been working at the Scorpion Mine for more than ten years. He was a trusted employee and Bruce enjoyed spending time with him.

'How many more do we have to do?' asked Bruce.

Kasiki was placing long sticks in dugout pits across the concession. When Bruce was younger, Kasiki had explained to him that the holes were dug into the ground to check for signs of mineralisation. Before the team could refill them, rats and mice would fall inside, and snakes would go in after them and get stuck inside the pits. One of Kasiki's tasks was to place long sticks inside the holes, which would enable the snakes to slither out. A task Bruce enjoyed.

'We owe a lot to these snakes. Because of them, no one troubles us at the mine these days,' said Kasiki, as they both worked their way through the pits.

'What do you mean?' asked Bruce, passing Kasiki a stick.

'The bandits, they're too scared to steal from us. They say we use snakes to guard the concession. And in Kenya people are terrified of snakes,' said Kasiki, laughing at the ridiculous rumour that he'd egged on in the nearby village.

'What about you? Aren't you scared?' asked Bruce.

'Of course, but I know where the pits are.'

'What about that hole?' asked Bruce, pointing to a prospecting pit in the distance.

'Ah. That one's empty now; it was the home of a 14-foot cobra for the longest time.'

'Isn't that the one who escaped last week?'

'Yes. The same.'

'I heard the askaris [security] shouting for Dad, to tell him about the cobra escaping.'

'They got a good scare that day.'

'Dad said he was the same cobra who'd given him blisters on his cheeks.'

Kasiki laughed, recalling the fun they'd had watching Campbell test the cobra's spitting limits.

'Your father's not scared of anything. He would wear these dark glasses and stand in front of the cobra. The snake would hiss at him. We were all a little afraid of what the cobra may do, but not Mr Bridges. Then the snake would spit his venom and it would land on Mr Bridges' glasses and on his cheeks, making his face all red with—what did you say he got?'

'Blisters. How did the cobra escape? Did you put a stick inside the hole for him?'

'No, no. He fell in the hole and then when we put the stick inside, he didn't want to come out.'

'Why?!'

'Because he was eating all the rats that would fall in the hole, becoming nice and fat. So we stopped putting the stick inside because he was helping us by eating the rats.'

'Then what happened?' asked Bruce, impatient for Kasiki to get to the escape.

'One day, the askaris were on their evening patrol. They turned a corner on one of the dirt tracks and came face to face with the cobra. He'd escaped and was standing tall with his hood spread. Angry. Remember, he was 14-feet long, so when he stood up, he was taller than the askaris and his hood was as big as a large shovel.'

'Then?'

'They ran for their lives, went straight to Mr Bridges, but by the time boss went with them to the location, cobra was gone.'

'How did he get out?'

'I show you,' said Kasiki, walking towards the hole with Bruce. 'You see that opening inside the hole?'

'Yes.'

'It seems there were too many rats falling in the hole for the cobra to eat. And these rats started digging a tunnel to get out. He followed them down the tunnel and that's how he got out.'

'He was a smart cobra,' said Bruce.

Kasiki laughed out loud. 'Very smart, like you!'

'Hey! Are you calling me a cobra?'

'You don't want to be smart?' said Kasiki, giving Bruce a playful shove. 'C'mon, let's go back to the camp. I want to see if boss needs any help.'

They walked towards the house and en route found Campbell with his head under the open hood of the Range Rover.

'Dad! I helped Kasiki put all the sticks in the holes for the snakes,' said Bruce as he ran over to the vehicle.

'Good boy.' Campbell stopped his tinkering for a moment to give Bruce a smile and said, 'Kasiki, can you please get me a spanner from the tool chest?'

'Which one, boss?'

'There's a small spanner I keep in the toolbox under the shed. It's the box in which we stored yesterday's production.'

Bruce watched Kasiki head towards the tool shed to retrieve the spanner. He joined his father, watching him turn and prod various sections of the Range Rover's engine.

'So,' said Campbell as he continued working on the vehicle, 'did you see any snakes?'

'No,' said Bruce, shaking his head. 'Kasiki said they take some time to crawl out of the hole. They're not as smart as Patrick.'

Bridges chuckled, hearing his son refer to his pet python, Patrick. Campbell had found the snake several years ago in the bush. He was a little guy, half-dead, and Campbell had nursed him back to health. Patrick grew bigger and became a healthy six-foot rock python who hung around in a basket at the mine. Before they had strongboxes and safe-rooms, Campbell would keep the mine's gem production in Patrick's basket. He never worried about theft, as Patrick took his responsibilities seriously.

'Where is Patrick, Dad?' asked Bruce. 'It's been a few days since I saw him.'

'You know, we lost his basket, so I—'

A scream interrupted their conversation. The sudden and sharp noise piercing through the soft morning made Bruce jump and hit his head on the open bonnet of the vehicle. Both father and son looked towards the sound in time to see Kasiki land 15 feet away from the toolbox he had opened. Kasiki had opened the wrong toolbox, which contained Patrick. The rock python had jumped out of the metal container like a jack-in-the-box. They watched as Kasiki scrambled to his feet and ran full tilt towards the main gate of the concession.

'Kasiki found Patrick,' said Bruce, pointing towards the scene.

'Stay here, Bruce. I'm going to go and fetch that spanner,' said Campbell as he marched towards the tool shed.

Bruce began following Patrick the python, who was slithering away. 'Dad,' he called out, 'I think Patrick's happy he scared Kasiki. Look, he's smiling.'

* * *

78

2005
Scorpion Mine Camp

In the last 25 years, the Scorpion Mine had made a name for itself as the premier source for tsavorite. The concession now had multiple active zones and tunnels.

Despite Bruce's enthusiasm for mining, Campbell had advised his son against studying geology and suggested he explore other avenues.

Bruce earned a business degree in finance and marketing from the University of Arizona. After trying the corporate life for a few years, he returned to Kenya and joined his family's mining operation.

Campbell was regarded as the father of tsavorite in the Kenyan and Tanzanian mining community. International tourist groups and industry delegations were a common sight at the Scorpion Mine, as Campbell freely shared his knowledge on gemstones, particularly tsavorite. He was the only miner in the area who was a trained geologist, and neighbouring mine owners regularly sought his council when they lost their strike line[1].

One such miner was Daudi Osman, who owned a concession nearby with his friends Darshan and Kuldeep Singh. Daudi's mine was experiencing good production, which made them an attractive target for bandits. To protect their mines, Daudi and Campbell continuously applied for firearms licences, only to be told to rely on the Kenyan police force, who were never around when bandits struck.

One morning, Campbell was reviewing geological maps with his son Bruce when Daudi arrived at their camp.

'Campbell, look what I got!' said Daudi, brandishing a shotgun.

'How in the world did you manage that, Daudi?' remarked Campbell. 'Is it effective?'

'Of course, it is!' Daudi handed over the weapon for Campbell to examine.

'But Daudi,' said Campbell as he scratched his beard. 'You've loaded the shotgun with birdshot. I don't know if this will help, my friend.'

'I'll show you! Bring me a piece of mabati [corrugated metal sheet],' said Daudi, exuding confidence.

A few minutes later, a piece of mabati had been placed against a tree and a crowd of onlookers had gathered to watch the show. A few were sniggering

---

1   Strike line: the path of the mineral zone. "Strike" refers to the line formed by the intersection of a horizontal plane and an inclined surface.

at Daudi's confidence, while others were happy to take a break from the mundane tasks of the day. Daudi took aim and fired a shot at close range. To the shock of the audience, the bullet blasted a big hole right through the sheet. The mine workers started clapping and Kasiki, along with a few other staff, rushed over to congratulate Daudi.

'Well done, Daudi, you certainly made an impression on the men,' said Campbell. 'Come and join us for lunch.'

The two men started walking towards one of the main buildings on site where Campbell spent time with his staff and visitors. Bruce followed. Lunch was outdoors, served on a rectangular wooden table that was placed underneath the shade of the roof extending over the veranda. The table had four camp chairs made of wood and canvas, with a few extra ones stacked on the other side of the patio. The large bougainvillea tree in front of the veranda was bursting with bright fuchsia flowers and shielding the diners from the heat of the midday sun.

'I brought some achar [Indian pickle] for you,' said Daudi, placing a glass jar of homemade mango pickle on the table.

'Wonderful, thank you. I love achar; it'll go well with the meat stew,' said Bridges, opening the jar and taking a whiff of the fermented mango fragrance laced with Indian spices. It was impossible to smell anything else once a jar of Indian pickle had been opened.

'Remember, don't double dip in the pickle jar or it'll get spoilt,' Daudi warned. 'Tell me, what were you studying when we arrived?' he asked, pointing towards a square table nearby littered with maps.

'Just trying to read the land. We had a good run in the eighties with the Bonanza Tunnel, and then in the nineties we opened our Number 2 Tunnel, which gave us fantastic tsavorite production.'

'I remember seeing that first lot you mined, amazing material,' said Daudi, helping himself to a slice of bread and dipping it into the curry.

'Two years ago, we hit a barren zone which, as you know, is not uncommon. Three months of nonstop mining, and zero production to show for it. Here's the interesting part. The geology showed that we should continue mining, but we were burning through our cash reserves.'

'What did you do?' asked Daudi.

Bruce jumped in to explain as Campbell concentrated on placing a spoonful of pickle on a dry crust of bread. 'We went back to the Bonanza Tunnel, which we've been mining now for the last two years.'

'How's the production?' asked Daudi.

'It's not what it had been,' said Campbell between mouthfuls of bread dipped in meat stew.

Bruce defensively said, 'It's not too bad.'

'Son, it keeps the lights on, but that's about it. We need good-quality production if this is to remain a serious mining operation.'

They continued their lunch in silence for a few minutes before the conversation moved towards politics and the weather.

'Morning, Dad,' said Bruce, the next morning.

'Morning, Bruce. I think we should reopen the Number 2 Tunnel today.'

'I don't know, Dad. We mined there for months, and we got nothing. I think we've missed the reef zone there. We are off strike[1]. We shouldn't go back and waste our money.

'I just have this feeling it's the right time,' said Campbell.

'Dad, you're a scientist. How can you talk about feelings? The evidence is in front of you.'

'I'm also human, and a miner, and we can't always depend on science. We must also follow our instincts.'

'Dad, I understand—'

'Look!' said Campbell, pointing towards the sky. 'It's Skysweeper. That settles it. We're opening the Number 2 Tunnel.' Campbell started marching towards the tunnel. Kasiki and the other mine workers followed.

Flummoxed by the turn of events, Bruce appealed once again to his father's scientific side. 'Dad, I know the bateleur eagle is your good luck charm, but—'

'Just look at him, Bruce, sweeping the sky as he catches the wind currents. Beautiful. Whenever Skysweeper has flown over the mine, we've had fantastic production. Those are the facts. You can't argue with that. And speaking of science, the geological indicators were positive in the Number 2 Tunnel last time—'

'But we had zero production for more than three months,' protested Bruce.

'This time it'll be different. I can feel it. Let's go ahead with Number 2.'

The determined look on Campbell's face was mirrored by the rest of the team. In that moment, Bruce knew he had no choice but to support the decision.

The next hour was spent reopening the tunnel, moving equipment, and making sure the structure was secure for the miners to move in to begin their work. Campbell was giving instructions with a newfound energy. 'We are close to something, Bruce. I can sense it,' he told his son as he observed

---

1   Off strike: off the path of the mineral zone, which in this case is probably across the slope. Another way of saying a miner is off course.

the rock the miners had exposed. After a brief ten-minute lunch break, Campbell returned to the tunnel with Bruce and the mine workers in tow.

They spent the afternoon chiselling away at the rock face inside the mine, exposing the steel grey host rock for tsavorite, which lay hidden within the reef zone. It was hard work, slowly and meticulously removing slabs of the outer rock by hand. Campbell and Bruce were inside the mine supervising every hammer stroke, interpreting the lines of the earth to determine their next move.

Around 650 to 500 million years ago, geological events caused the metamorphosis of black shale in marine basins into graphite gneisses, the host rock of tsavorite. During this period, high pressure and high temperature caused a chemical reaction, forming tsavorite crystals.

The father-son duo, along with their mining team, were following the path of mineral creation as it had occurred hundreds of millions of years ago. The mica particles twinkled against the bands of marble interlayered with dark grey schist as they continued working the deposit. They were not expecting to strike green for weeks, but the gem gods had other plans. After they had cleared less than a metre of hard rock, Campbell moved closer to the miners, and pointed at the rock face, bringing everyone's attention to what they had been seeking.

'Looking like a potato, boss,' said Kasiki.

Because of the stressful geological conditions under which tsavorite forms, most crystals are often found in small sizes. But on rare occasions, Mother Earth gives the hardworking miner the gift of a mineral-rich nodule, also called a potato because of its shape.

'Careful,' said Campbell. He was trying to stay calm while giving instructions to his chisel men who were uncovering a section that seemed to contain probably the largest tsavorite nodule Campbell had ever encountered in his career.

'Skysweeper,' said Bruce, placing his hand on his father's shoulder as they gazed in wonder. It took them a few hours to clear the entire section.

Once they were done, they stood back to take in their discovery. Kasiki looked at Campbell and said, 'Boss, good?'

* * *

It had been a year since the discovery of the large tsavorite pocket in the Number 2 Tunnel at the Scorpion Mine. The rough had yielded more than five kilos of faceted tsavorite gemstones. Most had been cut in their workshop in Nairobi. The weight loss during the faceting process had been 40 to

50 per cent for the medium to large stones, and as high as 80 per cent for the smaller goods. The bulk of the production ranged in the one- to five-carat range. But, despite the loss during processing, Campbell and his team managed to cut many gems above 12 carats and some as large as 20. It was the best single haul they'd had in the history of the mine.

'Bruce, have you checked the paperwork on the shipments due for export?' Campbell asked his son as he dunked another maandazi (triangle-shaped sweet doughnut-style pastry) into his second cup of coffee.

'Yes, Dad, I checked everything. Don't worry,' said Bruce. 'You really need to stop having those maandazi. Mom won't be happy.'

'Then don't tell her,' said Campbell with a big grin on his face as he took another bite and a sip. April was one of Campbell's beloved months in Nairobi. The days were warm, and the evenings cool.

'Dad, I wanted to ask you something. Why didn't you sell that four-carat tsavorite pair?'

'Because it wasn't the right price, Bruce.'

'But if you'd agreed to their offer, we'd have still made a good margin.'

'It's not about the margin, Bruce. The industry must understand and appreciate the stone's value. Tsavorite is a thousand times rarer than emerald, coloured by the same elements: chromium and vanadium. It's more durable, considerably brighter, and the best part: tsavorite doesn't need to be enhanced or treated. It's 100 per cent natural. Most of the gem-quality material yields only small sizes. To find rough material, which would yield pairs in larger sizes, matching colour, shape, and clarity after cutting, it's ridiculously rare.'

'You can't expect buyers to pay the same price as an emerald, Dad?'

'No. They should pay more.'

'Good morning, billionaires!' said Kamandi, a local gem dealer who had known Campbell Bridges since he moved to Kenya in 1970. Over the years, Campbell and Kamandi had become good friends, and Kamandi made it a point to visit Campbell when he was working from the Nairobi office.

'Morning,' said Campbell, laughing at his friend's remark. 'At least wait till you have a cup of coffee before you start pulling my leg?'

'I'm serious, my friend. According to *DRUM* magazine, you are one of the wealthiest people in Kenya,' said Kamandi, placing the latest issue on the table.

'What?!' said Bridges, leaving the pastry and picking up the publication. Bruce left his paperwork and came over to read the article over his dad's shoulder.

'Several billion? Are they crazy?' said Bruce.

'So, you didn't sell some special tsavorite for billions of Kenyan shillings, as the magazine claims?' asked Kamandi.

'Certainly not; that's ridiculous,' said Campbell. 'That's not even our stone. It was offered to us for 800,000 US dollars, but we didn't buy it.'

'Incredible,' said Bruce. 'The entire article is talking about how we sold this huge tsavorite for billions. I don't know if this is good or bad.'

'It's preposterous! A complete misrepresentation, not only of the facts related to this sale but the actual market value of tsavorite right now. It's going to attract the wrong type of attention.'

'Dad, maybe you're being too paranoid. It's an article in a magazine. It'll soon be forgotten.'

'No, it won't, Bruce. This is going to fuel jealousies; politicians are going to look at us and think we're rolling in money. This is bad, very bad.'

* * *

August 2006
10.00 am
Scorpion Mine

Campbell Bridges stepped out on to the patio of his home at the Scorpion Mine. He was holding a plate of Hobnob biscuits in one hand and a mug of tea in the other. It had been four months since the article in *DRUM* magazine. News of the imaginary tsavorite sale travelled far and wide. People never bothered with tsavorite before, but the promise of billions was enough to trigger an illegal encroachment on his 2,400-acre concession. It started small but increased as the months rolled on. They demanded that Campbell transfer his property and the concession to them, alleging that he had no right to the land, as a mzungu, and that they were the rightful indigenous owners.

Campbell suspected the group had support from local politicians given that police wouldn't assist in the removal of the squatters. He tried explaining to the group that he had moved to the country seven years after independence and showed them the mine's paperwork to diffuse the tension, but they were not interested.

Let's see what happens today, he thought as he sat down to finish his tea, awaiting Dr Bernard Rop, the commissioner of mines who had promised to visit that morning to assess the encroachment. Campbell's two tea companions were an African grey parrot called Lucky and a gazelle he had named Friday. Both were rescues. Many years ago, the family had found the gazelle—on a Friday—in her birthing sack in the bush. A pride of lions had chased away her herd, and Campbell had raised her on their concession. She could now jump eight feet vertically and run 40 to 50 miles an hour, and she used her agility and speed to grab her favourite treat from the kitchen: Hobnob biscuits.

The family lived in a house on the mining concession that was fenced off with thorn trees. Friday was an independent and would come and go as she pleased. She always came back to the house at sunset, regardless of whether she spent the day wandering in the bush or following Campbell around the mine.

Lucky, the parrot, had a similar story. He had flown into the Bridges' house in Nairobi one morning to escape a hawk and never left. 'It's as if he knows we saved him from that hawk,' Campbell would tell guests when introducing them to Lucky's vocabulary of more than 100 words in Swahili. He travelled with the family when they were staying at the mine and the miners taught him many colourful words, which Lucky enjoyed using, especially on visitors.

Campbell picked up another biscuit and fed Friday. She showed her affection by nuzzling her nose against his elbow. He took a deep breath, forgetting his troubles and enjoying a moment of peace. The sound of the commissioner's jeep brought him back to reality as he finished his tea.

'Good morning, Dr Rop. Welcome to the Scorpion Mine,' he said, stepping forward to shake the commissioner's hand.

'Good to be out of the office, Mr Bridges,' replied Commissioner Rop.

'Would you like some refreshments?'

'No, thank you. Unfortunately, I must get back to the office for a meeting, perhaps we could visit the area in question first?'

Before Campbell could respond, Lucky the parrot said, 'Wewe ni nani? [Who are you?]'

Worried the commissioner would reply to Lucky leading to a troublesome conversation, Campbell interrupted, 'That's our parrot, Lucky. Best not to start a conversation with him or we'll be here for a while.'

'What a delightful bird,' said Commissioner Rop. 'Yes, let's go.'

Campbell and Commissioner Rop got in the camp's Peugeot pickup while the mine manager Joseph and the commissioner's aide followed in the other vehicle. Not used to being ignored, Lucky asked again, 'Wewe ni nani? Wewe ni nani?'

'I'm afraid I may have offended your parrot, Mr Bridges,' said the commissioner, as Lucky's tone became frantic watching them get in the car.

'Better him than you. We had an incident recently with the DO[1].'

'Oh? What happened?'

'He'd come for his usual inspection. We were sitting at the table having our discussions and Lucky was hanging around. He comes up to the DO and says, "Wewe ni nani? [Who are you?]"' explained Campbell. 'The DO replied, "Mimi ni Bwana DO Wewe ni nani? [I am Mr DO. Who are you?]"'

'That's funny, what did Lucky say?' said Commissioner Rop.

'He said, "Mimi ni paroti; wewe ni nani? [I am a parrot; who are you?]" Hearing this, the DO got a bit irritated and repeated, "Mimi ni Bwana DO [I am Mr DO]".'

The commissioner started laughing. 'I've met the DO. He is not a patient man. Then?'

'Here's the punch line. Lucky said, "Hapana. Wewe ni nyoka. [No. You are a snake]".'

'Ooooo, you have a devil disguised as a parrot, Mr Bridges. I wish I'd been there to see the DO's face. I bet he wasn't happy,' said the commissioner, as he pulled out a cotton handkerchief to wipe away his tears of laughter.

'No, he was definitely not happy, but we rescued the situation.'

'Thank you for saving me from Lucky. I'm afraid to go back now.'

'He keeps us entertained,' said Campbell. 'Thank you again for coming to see us today.'

'Perhaps you can give me a brief update on the situation.'

'Of course, Commissioner. As you know, my family and I have been mining on this concession since 1970. We do everything by the book. The Kenya Revenue Authority has audited us and given us a clean chit. I've trained a team of cutters in Nairobi to cut almost all the rough that we produce.'

'I'm aware of your contributions over the decades to the mining community, Mr Bridges. You're a highly respected member. What's the problem?'

'Four months ago, an article came out publishing false information that we sold a stone for billions of Kenyan shillings, and since then, we've become a target. This illegal encroachment on our land, which I've been told is supported by a group of local politicians, is growing and they're very aggressive. We went to the local authorities and law enforcement; they've done nothing to help. These individuals are mining in our concession, with no regard for their safety, and I'm also worried about the security of our employees and operation.'

---

1   A high-ranking police officer of the region.

'I see. Have you tried speaking with them to understand what they want?' asked Commissioner Rop.

'They say we're mzungu who have stolen their land and they're simply taking back what belongs to them. I came to this country in 1970, after its independence. We consider Kenya our home. I raised my family here. It seems this group, or whoever's behind them, is using my skin colour as an excuse to take what rightfully belongs to me.'

'I understand you're passionate about Kenya and the work you're doing here, Mr Bridges. Let's stay calm and assess the situation before we unnecessarily take any rash steps. Is that the illegal mining operation?' asked the commissioner, pointing towards a cluster of shelters.

'Yes.'

Hearing the approaching vehicles, the illegal diggers stopped their work, watching the visitors approach.

Campbell started walking towards the digs with the commissioner. His driver and Joseph walked close behind. One of the miners stepped forward, raised his hand at the group, and shouted, 'Accha! Huwezi kupita [Stop! You won't pass].'

Ignoring the man, Campbell and the rest of the party continued making their way towards the diggings. The miner came towards them, shouting. Commissioner Rop stopped walking, unsure of what to do. Campbell saw the man approaching from his left side but kept on moving towards the site. The miner got closer and, addressing Campbell, said, 'Nilikuambia, mzungu, hii sio ardhi yako [I told you, white man, this is not your land].'

As he said the words, he pulled out a panga he'd been holding from behind his back and charged at Campbell who instinctively lifted his arm for protection. The machete cut into his left arm, and within seconds the blood soaked Campbell's khaki shirt. Joseph and the driver started shouting and ran towards Campbell. Commissioner Rop stood rooted to the spot, his face grey, shocked at what he had witnessed. The sight of blood and Campbell's undeterred attitude resulted in the hasty retreat of the diggers. The brief respite allowed the group to safely return to their vehicles.

* * *

July 2009
District Commissioner's (DC) House
Wundanyi, Kenya

Three years had gone by since the illegal miner attacked Campbell. Despite Commissioner Rop being an eyewitness to the assault, local authorities didn't lift a finger. Their inaction emboldened the squatters, and incidents of violence increased around the Scorpion Mine and other mining concessions owned by the Bridges family. The latest one involved the kidnapping of two askaris who worked at the mine. They'd been mercilessly beaten by the kidnappers to scare them into leaving the concession. Campbell, along with his son, were sitting in the DC's house to appeal for help.

'Please have some mango juice,' said the district commissioner, placing the glasses in front of them. 'My wife insists on preparing freshly squeezed mango juice during the season.'

'Thank you,' said Campbell, picking up the glass to take a sip. 'Now, what would you suggest we do? The security situation has gone from bad to worse.'

The DC stayed silent, using the glass of mango juice as a shield.

Bruce jumped in. 'As I'm sure you know, there is a local politician, Calist Mwatela, who is going around the community telling people they need to take back what is theirs; he's a partial owner in the company mining illegally on our claims. We're concerned that people may take the law into their own hands. We need protection and a return to the rule of law.'

The DC's mobile phone started ringing. He put down his mango juice and took the call. 'Good morning, ma'am. Regarding? The Bridges?' He put the phone on speaker, increasing the volume as much as he could so the father and son could hear the conversation. It was Naomi Shaban, the MP (member of parliament) for Taveta.

She said, 'I hear the Bridges family have been petitioning your office for help. I want to make this very clear so there's no confusion: don't help them and don't bother my constituents.'

The DC took the phone off speaker and continued speaking with Shaban for a few more seconds before disconnecting. He leaned forward and said, 'Now you understand why I can't help you.'

* * *

11th August 2009
9.00 am
Wundanyi Law Courts
Taita Taveta County, Kenya

'The weather's perfect, isn't it?' said Campbell, as he stepped out of the pickup truck. He was accompanied by his son, Bruce, the two askaris who had been kidnapped and beaten by the illegal miners, and his heads of security, Philip Syengo and Amos Kiamba. They had a court-hearing related to the incident.

'We still have some time,' their lawyer informed them outside. 'Why don't you wait in your vehicle. I'll call you when your turn comes.'

The courthouse was a white single-storey building, which looked more like a local school classroom, with four walls and an upside-down V-shaped slanted roof. It had large windows with grey grilles. Inside, wooden benches were placed in rows facing the judge, in a church-like style. At a short distance from the courthouse, visitors waited outside on another set of benches placed on top of a raised clay floor, underneath a roof of corrugated metal sheets. A tall palm tree swayed in the cool August breeze. Campbell took a deep breath and closed his eyes. He could smell the rain.

'Dad,' said Bruce. 'Your mobile's ringing.'

Bridges pulled out his phone and said, 'Yes. We are at the courthouse. Are you sure? When? I see. Let me call you back.'

'Who was that?' asked Bruce.

'One of the local gem dealers calling to warn us.'

'About what?'

'It seems, after we left the mine, the access road was blocked by the illegal miners. He was saying it's an ambush.'

'What?'

'He was warning me, so we—Wait, another call,' said Campbell as he picked up his phone again.

Bruce's mobile also started ringing. It was his mother, Judy, calling from their home in Nairobi. 'Bruce, where's your father?' she said.

'We're all at the courthouse, Mom.'

'What's this I'm hearing about an ambush? The phone's been ringing nonstop at home.'

'We're trying to find out. I'll call you back. Someone's calling my mobile.'

Father and son spent the next couple of hours fielding calls from their colleagues and friends in the community as word got out about the trouble at the mine. By 1 pm, they were done with the court proceedings, which only involved the judge postponing the date. They reassembled near their pickup truck to assess whether they should risk returning to the mine.

'Are you sure you want to go back to the mine, Dad?' asked Bruce. 'This roadblock sounds serious.'

'Bruce, we have that German tourist group arriving around 3.30. I can't have them walking into a potentially dangerous situation. We must go.'

'Mom's calling again. She wants to talk to you.'

'Give me the phone,' said Campbell. Bruce handed over his mobile. He couldn't hear his mother, but listening to his father's responses, he could guess her reaction.

'Judy? Yes, we're going,' said Campbell. 'We must, Judy. We have that tourist group arriving in two hours. No, I can't contact them.' He locked eyes with his son. Bruce smiled; he knew his father was getting a hard time from his mom, who was worried for their safety. 'The tour leader's mobile is off or he's not getting any signal,' said Campbell. 'Bruce is with me. We have our askaris as well. The district commissioner's office is close to the court-house. We're going there now to request a police escort. Yes, I'll be careful. Don't worry.' He hung up.

'Did you tell Mom about the death threat you received yesterday?' said Bruce.

'No.'

'Dad, the man clearly said that it made no difference if we had the proper papers and legally owned the mine. They told you they will take the mine by force.'

'People say a lot of things. We're losing time.'

The district commissioner point-blank refused to help Campbell. 'As I've told you and your son before, my hands are tied. There's nothing at all I can do to help.' The group made their way to the local police station. The plan was to appeal to the commanding officer, OCPD George Ikiara. But they were disappointed to see the station door locked with no answer to their repeated knocks. Campbell tried calling Ikiara on his mobile, but it seemed to be switched off. The problem was the tour group who were planning to reach the mine by 3.30 pm. They knew from experience that despite the tour leader being incommunicado, he would reach on time. Campbell felt responsible for the group's safety and was confident he could diffuse the situation before their arrival.

The group of six—Campbell, Bruce, two askaris, and the security chiefs, Philip, and Amos—decided to return to the mine. To defend themselves against any possible attack, the six men had belt knives, a few rungus, or clubs, two pangas, and a First World War bayonet. After being on the road for about an hour, they were getting close to their destination. The tour leader's phone was still off. Bruce stopped trying once he lost the signal.

'Cell service is so patchy in these areas,' said Campbell.

'What's the plan when we get there?' asked Bruce.

'If they attack us, we fight, but if they have guns, I want you to run and save yourself.'

'There they are,' said Bruce, pointing towards the large boulders, tree trunks, and trenches that had been used to create the roadblock. When they stopped their Peugeot pickup, getting ready to step out to try and remove the obstacles, Bruce spotted 10 to 12 men rushing towards them carrying spears, daggers, pangas and bows and arrows. They began shouting, 'Toka, mzungu [Get out, white man],' and 'Afrika sio ya mzungu [Africa is not for white people].'

'Dad, at least take a panga!' said Bruce as Campbell opened his door and stepped out of the pickup.

He started walking unarmed towards the rushing assassins. Bruce and the others got out of the vehicle to join him. At that moment, Bruce saw 30 to 40 men charging down the hill. They were surrounded.

* * *

17th December 2014
12.00 pm
Mombasa High Court House

'Bruce, the judge is back. Gather everyone; it's time,' said their lawyer.

As the family took their seats in the courthouse, all eyes were on Judge Maureen Odero as she approached her seat. She began to read her judgement.

'This offence is no doubt a serious one. It's quite clear the attack on Campbell Bridges was premeditated and well-executed. The four men were armed with dangerous and offensive weapons. The deceased was brutally murdered, leaving a widow, daughter, and son. I am therefore minded to give a stiff and deterrent sentence.'

Mohammed Dadi Kokane, Alfred Njuruka Makoko, Samuel Mwagainia, and James Mwita were sentenced to a total of 160 years in prison by Judge Maureen Odero.

Author's Note

This story is based on actual events, as relayed to the author by Bruce Bridges. Facts and names related to the murder of Campbell Bridges, as shared by Bruce Bridges, were taken from court documents and news articles already in the public domain. Fictional elements, such as scene descriptions and snippets of dialogue, have been added to support the narration.

Campbell Bridges was brutally murdered on 11 August 2009.

The following is an excerpt from a 2017 article written by Eric Konigsberg for *Men's Journal*, detailing the attack:

> A spearman ran at Bridges, trying to impale him, but he grabbed the spear, holding off his attacker with an outstretched arm, leaving his chest exposed. In a flash, a bowie knife plunged deep into Bridges' chest, making a wound the coroner would later measure to be eight inches deep.

> Mr Bridges called out, 'Hey, my sons, someone has done me wrong,' Syengo recalled. 'Bruce and I ran and held him, but it was too late. The man who stabbed him lifted his blade to his mouth to taste his blood, victorious. He said, "Fuck off. Bridges is dead."'

Bruce Bridges continues to trade in tsavorite and has the largest collection of gem-quality tsavorite in the world. However, till the time of writing this story, he was not allowed to deal in gems and minerals in Kenya. Since 2016, the Bridges mining licence has been 'in process' as has his mineral dealer's licence. Bruce continues to employ a maintenance and security team on site, keeping on staff every one of his permanent employees, despite not being allowed to conduct business.

In Oct 2019, Judith (Judy) Bridges received a Lifetime Achievement Award for her contributions to the gem industry at the congress held by the International Colored Gemstone Association (ICA), marking ten years since Campbell Bridges received his Lifetime Achievement Award in 2009. Poignantly, they are the only husband and wife team to have individually received the ICA Lifetime Achievement Award; Judith Bridges is also the first woman in the association's history to receive the award.

In March 2022, the head of security at the Scorpion Mine had his arm broken. (A few years earlier, he had been kidnapped and had his life threatened.) A fresh illegal encroachment has been reported on the concession, despite the 45-year sentence given to the convicted perpetrators of the premeditated attack on Campbell Bridges.

Bruce's future goal is to turn the mine into a national heritage site, which would bring attention to Kenya's national gemstone of tsavorite, provide jobs to the employees who have remained with the family for decades, and create an elephant sanctuary, which would protect the local wildlife. The creation of both the heritage site and the elephant sanctuary would be in honour of Campbell Bridges and his legacy. The project is awaiting the approval of the Kenyan government.

Since Campbell Bridges' tragic murder, the price of top-grade tsavorite has appreciated 1,000 per cent.

Photo overlooking Scorpion Workings and airstrip Overhead Labelled. Photo credit: Bruce Bridges.

Campbell Bridges conducting a security meeting with askaris and Friday (1990). Photo credit: Bruce Bridges.

Campbell Bridges sitting on balcony of new treehouse at The Scorpion Mine Camp (2006). Photo credit: Bruce Bridges.

Campbell, Laura and Bruce Bridges Scorpion Mine Swingset (1984). Photo credit: Bruce Bridges.

Campbell Bridges feeding camp mascot Friday at Scorpion Camp. Photo credit: Bruce Bridges.

Right Place, Wrong Time

April 1990
Linanona Beach
Fort Dauphin, Madagascar

JACK MAMPIHAO sat staring at the waves, mesmerised by the rhythmic rise and fall of the warm waters. The churn of the ocean seemed to mirror his thoughts as he, once again, wondered whether studying tourism over medicine had been the right decision. A small crab crawled towards him as he stretched his left leg, the tense muscles a reminder of the polio that had afflicted him when he was just a two-year-old.

'Next time, we'll swim in the afternoon,' said Jack's classmate and friend, Tony. The boys had jumped in for a quick morning swim only to find the water cold. They were now enjoying the warmth of the midday sun. A Koba vendor offered them the sweet and sticky rice cake, a boiled mixture of ground peanuts, brown sugar, and rice flour. They bought a thin slice, which they shared.

At 18 years of age, Jack and Tony had recently graduated from secondary school. But because of the political unrest in Madagascar, universities were closed. To stay occupied and earn some money, Jack was working in a hotel as a trainee, studying tourism by correspondence. He'd taken special permission from the hotel director to work part time as a tourist guide.

Jack's father was an officer with the national police service, or gendarmerie. It was a transferable job that had enabled Jack, unlike his classmates, to experience many regions of Madagascar and learn diverse tribal dialects[1]. This cultural and linguistic understanding provided Jack an advantage over other guides. A few months ago, his father had received a new posting in Southeast Madagascar. This time, the family decided it would be best for Jack to stay back in Fort Dauphin.

---

1   Madagascar has 18 tribes, and each uses a different dialect. Out of 18, four are dominant. The language diversity has been known to cause offence and trigger fights because certain words that may be viewed in a positive light in the northern part of Madagascar could be considered offensive in the south.

Their post-swim hunger satiated, Jack shared his earlier thoughts out loud with Tony. 'Since I was little, I had this dream of becoming a doctor.'

'Why are you working in the hotel then?' asked Tony.

'With tourism, I can earn money now working as a guide. And we don't know when the medical college will open.'

Not sure how to respond, Tony opted to make patterns in the sand with his finger.

'But sometimes I wonder if I should have waited,' said Jack.

Sensing melancholy creep into Jack's words, Tony attempted to shift the conversation towards more cheerful topics.

'What are your plans for Easter?'

'Nothing. My mother wants me to come home, but it's too far. I'll probably stay at the school.'

'Come with me,' said Tony. 'I'm going to visit my family in Tranomaro. My mother is a wonderful cook. We'll explore the area, catch some birds, go fishing.'

The thought of not being alone during the Easter break cheered Jack, and he agreed. A few days later, the two friends boarded a bush taxi, a Mercedes-Benz 911 truck, to begin their journey to Tranomaro. Jack was no stranger to long road journeys. He knew it would be tough. But nothing prepared him for the number of people the driver kept accepting into the truck.

Within a few hours, Jack and Tony were stuffed like sardines in a can with 65 strangers of all shapes and sizes. The truck's floor was covered with almost 40 sacks containing grains, potatoes, and personal items, including live goats. The carriage above balanced cloth bundles, rolled-up straw mats, live chickens, bicycles, and jerry cans. The few who managed to get a seat in the front of the truck could sit, the rest had to stand and hold the rack for support.

Jack tried to sit on the floor but soon realised he might get trampled. A green tarp on top of the carriage offered fleeting protection from the sun. But above the tarp the driver had precariously balanced baskets full of fruits, which would sometimes fall through the torn sections on the heads of the passengers. Jack was struggling to breathe, sandwiched between two individuals whose body odour was stifling.

The path was uneven, with limestone outcrops and deep potholes that made the truck bounce and sway, sometimes tilting almost 30 degrees. Jack gave up on drinking water as most of it would spill because of the constant disruptive motion of the truck as it tumbled towards Tranomaro. The entire drive took ten painfully long hours. There was neither respite from the crush of people nor the rattling of bones, except for a few toilet breaks along the way.

When the boys finally reached their destination and got off, Jack turned to Tony and said, 'Oh God! I don't know how I'm going to do the trip back, Tony.'

'Last time was worse for me,' said Tony, as he stretched his arms from right to left.

'Worse?!' said Jack. 'I can't imagine. My arm still feels like it's holding the rack.'

'My home is a short walk away,' said Tony. 'Let's hurry before it gets dark.'

After Tony's reunion with his family, the boys were treated to a delicious dinner of romazava, a traditional meat and vegetable broth, flavoured with ginger, garlic, tomato, and onions. Tony's mother cooked hers with small eggplants and served it with a generous helping of rice and freshly prepared chilli sakay sauce. The boys ate till they couldn't stuff another morsel in their mouths.

'We'll go fishing tomorrow,' said Tony a few hours later, as they started drifting off into a food-induced coma.

'Sure,' said Jack. 'Please thank your mother again for the food.'

'I will, but she won't give us that every day, you know,' said Tony. He chuckled under his breath. 'Our staple is beans and rice.'

The next morning, the boys started exploring the surrounding area. They borrowed some fishing rods from Tony's father and began navigating the spiny forest. The landscape looked like something out of an alien adventure story: tall green cacti rising skywards from the dusty plains, surrounded by thick thorny bush, and bulbous baobab trees dotting their path. Jack loved baobab trees; there was something human about their strange shapes.

The boys started naming them as they made their way towards the fish-pond. Some looked like fat, stubby monsters, with thorny shrubs growing out of their heads; others were intertwined in a romantic embrace. There was a large one with folds on the trunk, which Tony said reminded him of his grandmother who was always grumpy.

The forest was also full of lemurs, and the boys enjoyed watching their funny antics as they leapt from one tree to the next.

'Look,' said Tony, pointing towards a family of lemurs walking upright ahead of the boys.

'Tony, see how that one jumped over the other,' said Jack, laughing out loud.

The lemurs kept them entertained, hopping sideways on their two hind legs with outstretched arms to balance themselves. The cacti in the forest were now a lush green colour and full of flowers. 'We had a cyclone two months ago,' said Tony. 'That's why you see flowers and all these rocks and pebbles on the ground. Most of the time, this area is parched, so when it rains, it washes all the soil away.'

Jack bent and picked up a tiny rock. 'What's this?' he asked.

'I don't know, never seen a blue rock like this before,' said Tony, as he kept walking towards the pond.

Jack put the pebble in his pocket and followed. When they reached the pond, he was disappointed to see it was dry and covered with green concentrated algae.

'How are we going to catch any fish in this?' said Jack.

Tony started laughing. 'It happens, my friend,' he said. 'Sometimes, you still get a few small ones.'

An hour later, after catching no fish, the friends decided to head deeper into the spiny forest. They'd been walking for around 30 minutes when they heard the rumbling of a truck behind them. They waved at the vehicle to stop and asked the passengers where they were going. The men inside the truck told them they had come to collect rocks to make tiles.

Always looking to make extra cash, Jack asked the men if the boys could join them. 'We'll help you collect the rocks for free. Next time, you just send us a message and we can have them ready for you.' The men agreed, and the boys hopped into the truck, delighted to get a lift.

'What are the names of these rocks you collect?' asked Tony.

'Calcite, agate, jasper, green amazonite, and large sizes of black tourmaline.'

'And how much would you pay us to collect and keep them for you next time?' asked Jack.

'We pay you 50 francs a kilogram [about US$0.001].'

Jack's heart sank when he heard the measly sum, but they were already in the truck. When they reached the location, the boys jumped off and started helping with the rock collection. Each weighed more than a few kilos and Jack struggled with his bad leg under the weight. Frustrated by his body's limitations, he kicked a rock lying on the ground, dislodging it.

What's that? Thought Jack, as he bent to pick up a deep blue stone. He compared it to the one he'd collected earlier and noticed they were similar in their colour and shape. These would be perfect to shoot down birds.

'You find something interesting?' asked Tony, coming up behind Jack. He'd seen his friend walk away and followed.

'See, this stone is like the one I showed you before. I was thinking I'll use it to shoot down some fody birds.'

'Fody? The brown one, which turns a bright red colour when it's time for the rice harvest?' asked Tony.

'Yes, same.'

'But you're a tourist guide; don't you feel bad shooting down birds?'

'I do. They're beautiful, but when the rice is ready for harvest, they come in a large flock and wipe out most of the crop, so I think it's not so bad that I shoot them down,' said Jack.

'C'mon. Let's go find you some fody.'

'First, we need more small stones like this one. See, it's pointy, which is great, and I like the colour.'

'You collect the blue ones, and I'll use these green ones,' said Tony, showing Jack a light green glass-like stone.

The boys spent the rest of their time shooting down birds and picking up stones. The February rains had indeed washed away the topsoil as Tony had explained earlier, and the ground was littered with rocks in all shapes, colours, and sizes. They both had their favourite colours, which they picked. Once the men had finished their work, they offered to drop the boys back at Tony's home.

Their truck was now full of heavy amazonite, jasper, and brown and green calcite. Some of the agates they had collected were already broken in the centre, and the men showed the boys the beautiful patterns inside, explaining how a lapidary would cut and polish them to create decorative objects. Jack in turn took out the small blue stones he'd collected to show the men, hoping they may find them interesting. His pockets were sagging under their weight. He was disappointed when they showed no interest and declared the stones to be too small to be of any value.

Back in Fort Dauphin, Jack couldn't get his experience of the rocks out of his mind. He started searching for sources to learn more about basic geology, but the books he found were complicated and he couldn't connect what he was reading to what he'd seen. The next vacation was four months away and Jack already had plans to learn how to use a new type of pliotra, or slingshot, which was made of leather and could accommodate a larger rock. This time, he had his sights set on guinea fowl.

* * *

June 1990
Fort Dauphin

Jack and Tony were listening to the news on the radio at a food shack in the local market. There was another report about a protest rally by university students in the capital of Antananarivo. The noise from the weekly vegetable market next to the eatery was making it difficult to follow what the reporter was saying on the radio. Seated next to the boys, a group of men were drinking white rum and relishing fried pork sausages while women and children shopped for clothes and vegetables at the market.

Tony tried increasing the radio volume, but the shack owner slapped his hand away with a green fly swatter. 'Eh! No one touches my radio.'

'We can't hear anything, Uncle,' said Tony.

'You boys want to hear the news, eh? Or just waiting for the football score?' said the shack owner. 'You buy nothing. Just loiter around. Useless.'

'I got you those tourists last week for lunch,' said Jack.

'Mm,' grumbled the man under his breath, as he increased the volume on the radio.

'And can we get a small plate of the pork sausage?' said Jack. *This should buy us an hour*, he thought.

'Hey, Jack.' One of his friends from university joined the duo at their table.

'Where were you?' asked Jack. 'I haven't seen you for a while.'

'I took some French tourists to the coast,' the friend said. 'Interested in a guide job? A Chinese man is looking for someone to take him to Tranomaro.'

'Why Tranomaro?' asked Tony.

'He's looking for rocks. He said they have nice ones that he wants to take back home and cut.'

'We saw those rocks,' said Jack. 'They're so heavy. I've still got one month of school before the holidays. Sorry, can't go.'

* * *

July 1990
Fort Dauphin

'Jack,' said Tony. 'More Chinese are looking for a guide to Tranomaro. You interested?'

'It's the same stupid rocks, Tony,' said Jack. 'The hotel director gave me permission to only work part time when I am not in training. I can't leave before the training's finished.'

'I don't think it's the big rocks. Something else is going on, Jack.'

'How do we find out?' asked Jack.

'There's no telephone service. Only way is to write a letter,' said Tony. 'Maybe my father can find out more.'

Tony's letter took two weeks to reach his family, and another two weeks for the boys to receive a reply. Tony's family reported an influx of Chinese men in the area looking for special rocks. Jack's training term had finished, and the boys got on the first taxi-brousse out of Fort Dauphin.

'They must be paying a higher price for the agate and jasper than those construction men we met,' said Jack.

'But father said they were looking for a special stone,' said Tony. 'The ones we saw didn't look very special to me.'

'To us, those stones are not special because we see them lying around, but maybe the Chinese don't have any in their country.'

'But why are they in Tranomaro?' asked Tony. 'There are no stones there. Remember, we travelled in the truck for a few hours to reach the place where they were collecting the stones.'

'Is there a place to stay near the rocks?'

'No.'

'That's why they're all going to Tranomaro,' said Jack. 'It must be the nearest place to stay.'

They reached Tranomaro by nightfall. Since there were no hotels, visitors would stay as paying guests in local homes or rented shacks. The boys found out about a Chinese buyer who was staying nearby and decided to take a chance and try to meet him. The man told them he was looking for a stone called sapphire. The boys had never heard of sapphire but didn't want to show their ignorance.

'Do you have a photo of the stone?' asked Tony.

When the Chinese man showed them a photo of a rough sapphire in a gemstone book he was carrying, the two were shocked. It was the same small stone Jack had lovingly collected on their last trip. They both looked at each other and told the man they'd seen the stone and fixed to meet him the next day.

'I knew there was something special about that stone,' said Jack as soon as they left the inn.

'Those construction workers knew nothing.'

'You collected so many of them,' said Tony. 'You didn't keep any?'

'No. I used them all to shoot the birds. Arrrgghh! I'm so stupid,' said Jack, kicking a plastic bucket lying nearby.

'No, you're smart, Jack,' said Tony. 'You even asked those men about the stones. We'll leave early tomorrow and look for more, OK?'

Every muscle and joint in Jack's body ached after the treacherous road trip from Fort Dauphin, but he couldn't sleep. He was haunted by images of the stones in his slingshot, and his pockets and hands full of sapphires. *I had them in my hand. A treasure, and I threw it away.* His body finally overtook his tortured mind, and he fell into a deep slumber.

The next morning, Jack woke early and started searching for sapphire in an area four to five hours' walk from Tranomaro. It was the nearest place he remembered shooting down the birds. Maybe the stones are still lying on the ground, he thought. He found a few pieces of blue agate, which the Chinese customer rejected.

'I return in one week,' said the man. 'You keep stone ready, OK?'

Jack and Tony nodded, realising their only option was to return to Andranondambo. They left early the next day.

Last time, they'd hitched a ride with the truck and reached Andranondambo in a few hours. This time, they had no choice but to walk. Because of the limp in his leg, it took Jack most of the day to get there. Unlike last time, Jack couldn't find enough sapphires to fill his pockets. He found only eight stones, which they brought back to Tranomaro. As promised, the Chinese buyer returned and paid US$50 for the sapphires, which seemed like a fortune to Jack. He went back to Andranondambo, and this time found a single piece weighing two grams, for which a week later the Chinese buyer paid US$70.

The price was going up as more Chinese arrived in Tranomaro, seeking sapphires. Jack couldn't understand how the small sapphire was fetching more money than the heavier rocks. The cost of living in Tranomaro also went up with a surging population putting pressure on the limited resources. After another week to ten days of trying to find and sell sapphires, Jack realised he'd spent more money on food and shelter than he'd made from the stones. He made the hard decision to return to Fort Dauphin.

By that time, the boys had learnt the buyers were not Chinese, but gem cutters and dealers from Thailand. Three months after Jack returned to Fort Dauphin, the price of rough sapphire jumped to US$1,000 per piece. Over the months that followed, Jack kept hearing news of people striking it rich by finding sapphires and selling them for an even higher price. Jack tried to drown out the sapphire noise he was hearing in the market by focusing on being a good tourist guide and finishing his studies. But one day, after seeing one of his friends drive a brand new four-by-four jeep, he decided to return to Andranondambo. Jack was shocked to discover over a thousand people digging everywhere. He didn't stand a chance.

The number of fortune hunters kept growing, reaching a peak of more than 10,000 people who were living in the village of Andranondambo under primitive hygiene conditions[1] (Schwarz, Petsch, and Kanis. *Gems & Gemology* 1996).

After observing the impact of a small blue stone and the opportunity he'd lost due to his lack of knowledge, Jack Mampihao decided to go head-long into the gem mining business. It took him a few years to find a job mining tourmaline in Tranomaro. Tony started working as a translator for a Thai group in Andranondambo. Still feeling burned by his bad luck with sapphires, Jack later joined a mining company in Andranondambo and leveraged that opportunity to learn about geology, gemmology, and mining. His passion for gems and hard work got him promoted to team leader.

The company switched gears and spent a few years on gold exploration and mining. In 1995, a new sapphire rush ensued in Ambondromifehy, province of Diego Suarez. The price was incredibly low, US$10 per gram with one lot equalling a bucket load; although there was quantity, the grade was average. Three months later, the price shot up when higher-quality stones were discovered.

After six months, the mine owner asked Jack to accompany him on a journey to look for sapphires in northern Madagascar. Most good mines were already taken, and Jack spent months prospecting the Diego province, especially the western part in Bobakilandy, Bobasakoa, and Mangaoka. He found tiny indications of mineralisation, which were unsatisfactory. During this time (1996), Jack discovered small green stones, which he had never seen before. When he showed them to the mine owner, the man rejected them because they weren't sapphires.

Jack followed his intuition and held onto the stones. In 2008, a gem rush in the area revealed them to be rare and highly prized demantoid garnets. When the time was right, Jack sold the ones he'd collected in 1996 and was able to build a house and buy a car with the sale proceeds.

1   https://www.gia.edu/doc/Sapphires-from-Andranondambo-Region-Madagascar.pdf

Author's Note

This story is based on actual events as experienced by Jack Mampihao. Minor fictional elements have been included for scene setting and dialogue. Special thanks to notable gemmologist, Ken Scarratt, for sharing his valuable insights over many Sunday morning phone calls on the challenges related to origin determination for sapphires.

Around the time of the sapphire discovery in 1990, gem labs misidentified top-quality blue sapphires from Andranondambo, Madagascar as Kashmir sapphires from India due to the similarity of their inclusions. Despite increased awareness of Madagascar sapphires within the industry, multiple factors continue to cause origin-related confusion between Sri Lanka and Madagascar for sapphires.

To better understand the reasons behind these mistakes in origin determination, I sought answers in geology, seeking a correlation between the history of Sri Lanka and Madagascar before the split of the supercontinent Gondwana.

An article by Claudio C. Milisenda and U. Henn[1] explains that 'the Tranomaro Belt, in which new sapphire deposits have been located, closely resembles the supracrustal sequence of the Highland Complex of Sri Lanka'. A subsequent paper, published in the *Journal of Geology*[2] details the geological association between Sri Lanka and Madagascar. But, despite similarities, that link between origin determination and geological similarities is tenuous because diverse factors contribute towards the formation of gemstones.

The first ingredient for gem formation is the element responsible for the colour of the stone, such as chromium for rubies, and titanium and iron for blue sapphires. Second, the host rocks at various locations across the length and breadth of the planet contain a distinctive set of elements. The third and most important factor are the tectonic plates, whose movement creates the heat and pressure, which causes a chemical reaction, leading to the formation of gemstones.

For example, gems formed in marble, such as rubies in Myanmar (Burma), have a completely different chemistry to gems formed in the Mozambique Belt of Africa. A gem lab has to correlate trace element chemistry, optical data, inclusions, and infrared data, along with observation, to provide an expert opinion on origin.

1   https://gem-a.com/images/Documents/JoG/Archive/1956-97/JoG1996_25_3.pdf
2   https://www.researchgate.net/publication/249182785_Sri_Lanka-Madagascar_Gondwana_Linkage_Evidence_for_a_Pan-African_Mineral_Belt

Now that we better understand how the complexity of gem formation causes errors in origin determination, let's consider the rarity factor. Beauty, durability, and rarity are the three most important qualities that assign value to a gemstone. Even though Madagascar rates high on beauty and durability, since the probability of finding top-grade sapphires from Kashmir and Sri Lanka is low (Kashmir is not producing, and Sri Lanka has been mining for centuries), the rarity factor of good-quality sapphires (rich, saturated blue colour, large sizes, excellent crystal) from these two origins is high.

This brings us to the human angle. The brand name of Ceylon or Sri Lanka is well-established, recognisable, and easier to sell compared to Madagascar. Because of this, it attracts a premium price in the marketplace, sometimes almost double that of a similar-looking, top-quality sapphire from Madagascar. For this reason, industry sources inform us that it's not uncommon for sapphires from Madagascar to be cut and sold as Sri Lankan sapphires. The complex nature of origin determination may sometimes aid the deception. For this reason, most labs will not undertake origin determination, leaving that task to specialised gemmological laboratories around the world.

Over the years, Jack experienced his fair share of difficulties in the gem business as a miner, merchant, and consultant. From 1999 until 2002, he was working in the fishing sector. After the company stopped operations, Jack found himself out of a job and with no business prospects. He learnt carpentry and started selling furniture, which allowed him to earn enough of an income to buy a second-hand computer and establish his gem-trading company called Jack Boom Gem.

Jack hired two staff to run the carpentry business under his supervision, and then returned to the bush, where he found 15 grams of good-quality rough aquamarine, re-establishing his position in the gem industry. In 2004, Jack was hired by the Jewelry Television (JTV) network company as their resident buyer in Madagascar. Despite his small successes, Jack has experienced his fair share of betrayals and losses. He views each as a learning experience to do better in the future. Currently, Jack is working as a carpenter, welder, and a gemstone cutter. He is a single parent of five children—three sons and two daughters—between the ages of five and 22. Jack's contributions in the past have been noted in industry journals[1], and he continues to stay in close contact with the gem community.

1   https://www.gia.edu/gems-gemology/
winter-2015-gemnews-grandidierite-madagascar

To quote Jack: 'I always enjoy life. Without problems, your life becomes tasteless. KEEP smiling!'

Recommended Reading

https://www.gia.edu/doc/Sapphires-from-Andranondambo-Region-Madagascar.pdf

The Mineral Sun

1991
Windhoek, Namibia

'LET'S MAKE one quick stop before we reach the airport,' said Hans-Jürgen Henn to his son, Axel. After two weeks of buying gems in Namibia, the father and son were going to the airport to catch their return flight to Idar-Oberstein in Germany.

'Are you sure we have time, Dad?'

'Yes. Yes. Always time to see some stones. I'll be quick.'

Axel smiled. He could never associate the words 'quick' and 'gemstones' with his father. Jürgen's unadulterated love for coloured stones knew no limits.

They walked into an office of a local dealer Jürgen knew well. After the initial pleasantries were exchanged, the dealer pulled a small, clear plastic pouch from his desk drawer. He switched on the overhead lamp and removed a folded white paper from the pouch.

'This is something very special,' he said, as he ceremoniously opened each fold. When he unveiled the material, Jürgen leaned forward. Although his expression remained unchanged, Axel could sense his excitement. The dealer, however, unable to read Jürgen's poker face, asked gingerly, 'Have you seen these before?'

'No; where are they from?' asked Jürgen.

'From a remote part of Namibia in the north called Marienfluss, a deposit at the Kunene River, near the border with Angola.' He then ventured, 'What do you think?'

Jürgen took out his tweezers from his pocket and started inspecting the small stones that lay on the table. After a few minutes of negotiation, he told the dealer he would buy them all. They spent the next few minutes discussing the possibility of future supply.

Fifteen minutes later, Jürgen and Axel were back in their car on their way to the airport. This time, true to his word, Jürgen had not taken long.

'Dad, you told me you don't want to work with tweezer stones anymore. Why did you buy these?' asked Axel.

'Axel, I have never in my life seen such spectacular electric fireball orange garnets. You saw them. Amazing! There must be more.'

'They were sensational, Dad, but like you I was trying my best to not show any emotion,' said Axel.

At the airport, after they had checked in and cleared security, Jürgen went to make a phone call, leaving Axel with their handbags in the Lufthansa business class lounge.

'Is everything fine?' asked Axel when his dad returned.

'Yes. I called Lothar and told him about the stones,' said Jürgen, referring to his longtime friend, Lothar Klein who lived in Windhoek and had a successful salt business in Namibia. 'He said he's going to start making enquiries to find the source.'

'So, we come back in a few months?' asked Axel.

'Months! It'll all be over in months, Axel. No, no, I am planning to return in a week, or sooner.'

'I don't understand. These small orange garnets are beautiful but why the urgency to return, Dad?'

'These orange garnets are like holding a bright sunset in your hands, son. They are a wonder of nature. With stones—'

Before Jürgen could finish his sentence, the Lufthansa ground staff made the boarding announcement. As they walked towards the departure gate, Jürgen said, 'I'll tell you a story about rubies when we're on board.'

Three hours into the flight, most of the passengers had finished their dinner. The cabin lights were dim, and Jürgen was enjoying a glass of red wine when Axel reminded him, 'You were going to tell me a story about rubies.'

'Oh, yes. Like I was saying before, if you want to be successful in the gem business, you need to be at the right place but also at the right time. This story is from 1984,' said Jürgen. 'My very good friend, Colin Curtis, came to visit me in Idar. He was living in Tanzania and Kenya at that time and was fluent in Swahili.'

'I remember him. An Englishman, right?'

'A Bermudian with an old-fashioned English manner. One of the things he would often say, "I am willing to give my life for the Queen".'

'He used to entertain us by speaking a funny type of English,' recalled Axel.

'Old English. When we travelled together, he would switch to old English, which I could never understand,' said Jürgen a little wistfully. Sharing the tale with his son was bringing back old memories.

'So, what about Colin?' Axel prompted his dad.

'I dropped him at the airport for his flight to Nairobi. And I said to him, "Colin, if you run into something special, you let me know".'

'Why did you say that?'

'Because he's close to the source, and miners and local dealers would keep bringing him stones. Anyway, I said this to him, and I forgot about it. We had a big order from an international jewellery firm in the US, and I got busy with the job. After a few days, I got a call from the airport, and it was Colin. He had returned to Idar and wanted me to pick him up.'

'Why?'

'That's what I wondered. When I met him at the airport, I asked him why he was back, and he said, "I came across something important." He asked me to take him straight to the lapidary. Once we were there, he showed me what he'd brought. It was the most beautiful rough ruby from the John Saul Mine in Kenya.'

'Why is it called the John Saul Mine?' asked Axel.

'The mine is named after the man who, in 1974, became the first person to stake a claim to this ruby deposit in Kenya's Tsavo National Park. The name stuck.'

'Are the rubies from this mine very beautiful?' asked Axel.

'With every mine, there is good-quality, medium, and low or commercial-quality material. The rubies from the John Saul Mine were known to be of excellent colour, but many of the rough stones I came across were opaque, not very transparent crystal. But still good for cutting into a domed cabochon shape. Colin showed me this ruby, and it looked fantastic, but it was important to see what the rough would become after cutting. Very important for future decision-making.'

'What was the result?' asked Axel.

'We spent a few days cutting it and the result was unbelievable. When we assessed the finished stone, we knew the quality was good. Colin left the very next day for Kenya to make sure the stones were reserved for us. In those days, you could reserve stones by providing verbal assurances, no paperwork, no deposit needed.'

'I think I remember now,' said Axel. 'You left for Africa the day after Ingo's confirmation ceremony in the church.'

'Ha! You have a good memory. I had to wait for the function because your mother gave me an ultimatum. Colin advised me to join him in Nairobi, two days before, but your mother said, "If you leave now, and miss the last big family party, don't bother coming back".'

Axel started laughing. 'That sounds like Mother.'

'How could I leave after that? I had to stay. Anyway, I'm happy I was there but listen to what happened next. The party was over, I'd packed my bags, and I was all set for my flight to Nairobi the next morning. Around midnight, the house phone rang. And I was thinking, "Who's calling so late?"'

'Was it Colin?' asked Axel.

'No, it was another lapidary owner from Idar.'

'Who? Do I know him?'

'Wait; that's not the point of the story. The man, he said to me, "I heard that you fly to Africa tomorrow to buy some rubies".'

'How did he know?'

'Exactly! How, when we had kept everything so secret? This is the second thing to keep in mind, that however much you try, there can always be a leak, so you must be ready to act fast.'

'What did you say?'

'Nothing. I was shocked. He said, "I make you an offer. Before I also go to Africa and we bid against each other, making the African rich, I offer you a partnership." I thought about it, and even though I didn't like that my secret was out, I agreed because I realised, this is the better way, safer, less risky. We had a verbal agreement over the phone.'

'It was just the two of you?'

'No, there were two companies from Idar-Oberstein, plus our company, and Colin brought an American company on board. But I was leading the negotiations and taking all the decisions on behalf of the group. I'd never done that before. Big responsibility.'

'What happened in Nairobi?' asked Axel.

'I arrived two days later than I was supposed to, and Colin picked me up from the airport. He had booked a lovely suite at this historic hotel called the Norfolk. But there was no time to wash or change. We went straight to see the rubies. The dealer had a licence and a decent office where he showed us the parcel. It was several kilos of selected material worth a fortune.'

'Was it all as amazing as the one you had cut, Dad?'

'If a normal person had seen that lot, Axel, they may not have paid even US$10,000 for it, because it had a thick outer skin, and to the untrained eye, it may as well have been pebbles from the pavement because the rough rubies had a dark layer you had to remove during the cutting to unveil the lovely red hue of the stone underneath.'

'So you were not late. The dealer still had the stones for you.'

'Ah! But I was. After sitting for maybe 45 minutes and chatting with the dealer about everything except the rubies, the man told me his asking price for the parcel on the table in front of me. And then, everything was quiet.

And in that silence, from the room next door, I could hear someone speaking in Hebrew. When I heard that, I knew all was lost.'

'I don't understand,' said Axel.

'There was a group of Israeli buyers in the next room, waiting to buy the parcel if I refused.'

'Could you hear what they were saying?' asked Axel.

'I didn't need to. The fact they were in the next room meant if I said no, the dealer would sell the parcel to them. If I had arrived two days before, I may have been the only buyer, and I could have negotiated the price down by a few hundred thousand dollars.'

'What did you do?'

'There was only one thing I could do. Say yes. No negotiation, nothing. I just agreed to the asking price.'

'You got the rubies then?'

'I did, but I felt terrible. I knew I had no choice. It was such a rare opportunity to get this large quantity of rubies. When you do a big deal, you should feel good, like you achieved something. I felt the opposite.'

'How did your partners react?'

'We'll come to that later. First, let me tell you about another surprise I got the next morning. I was at breakfast with Colin at the Norfolk hotel, when a local Kenyan dealer who knew Colin approached our table. He started congratulating me. When I asked why, he said, "For the rubies you purchased yesterday." The man knew how much I had bought and for what price. The information was out in the market.'

'How?'

'I don't know, and this is third thing for you to remember. Like in Idar, in Africa also, information was leaked. You must be prepared for it.'

'Were you upset?' asked Axel.

'Surprised and a bit concerned but not upset. Colin and I didn't like the attention, and we decided to leave. He had a place in Mombasa and suggested we go there.'

'That's an incredible story,' said Axel.

'Wait. It's not over yet. We drove through the coast, and it was during this drive, I first saw Mt Kilimanjaro—so majestic. I said to the mountain, "Give me a little time, I'll come and visit you." Which I did. I returned a few years later and climbed Kilimanjaro.'

Jürgen was an avid mountaineer, and Axel wanted to keep his father focused on the story. He could see that the mention of Kilimanjaro had brought a dreamy smile to his face. 'I don't know what you love more,

Dad, faceting gems or climbing mountains. Come back to the rubies; what happened next?' said Axel.

'Don't worry; I won't start another mountain story. OK, back to the rubies. We were driving towards Mombasa and Colin said, "We have to fill the jeep with gas." We stopped at this very primitive gas station. Colin knew the Kenyan lady who owned the place. She was tall, heavy set, well educated. You saw her and you knew this was someone you don't mess with. Everyone called her "Mumma". After we filled the tank, she said to us, "Boys, come in. I have something to show you." We followed her inside. And she showed me one rough ruby, a large one.'

'Was it good?'

'It was spectacular. Better than anything I had seen in the parcel I bought in Nairobi. But I had no money. I said to her, "Mumma, we don't have any money; we spent it all in Nairobi".'

'What did she say?' asked Axel.

'She just kept bringing the price down because she wanted to get rid of the stone. It reached a stage where we just couldn't say no. We agree to buy but told her that we'd buy the stone through the licenced dealer in Nairobi because he could make all the paperwork for export, etc.'

'But you had no money. How did you buy it?'

'We had a little money left, which we used to buy this last stone, and then all the money was finished. I came back to Idar, and we started cutting the rubies. The stone I bought from Mumma was unbelievable, like blood, rich, ruby red colour. And I had bought it so cheaply. The others I'd bought in Nairobi, most of the pieces had this greyish tinge in the colour.'

'How is this story connected to the orange garnet we saw in Namibia?'

'You see, the ruby I bought from Mumma made the whole deal profitable. If I didn't have that stone, we'd be in trouble. Why did I tell you this story? To show you that in the gem business, skill is not enough. Like I said before, to be successful, you must be at the right place, at the right time, have luck on your side, and be willing to take big risks. Coming back to the orange garnets, in the international market, no one knows about this stone yet. We know. We have an advantage for a short time. We must move fast.'

'So, when will you return to Namibia?' asked Axel.

'I'd go back tomorrow if I could, but I must make some preparations. Let's get some sleep; we have a lot to do when we arrive home.'

In less than a week, Jürgen was back in Windhoek, Namibia. His friend, Lothar, had discovered the name and contact of the Namibian man who owned the orange garnet mine. They were on their way to a small town in the northern part of the country, where the man had arranged to meet them at a guest house.

'How did you find him?' Jürgen asked Lothar.

'I have my sources. I may be in the salt business, but you know I love gemstones. I called a few people,' said Lothar. 'Your son Axel didn't join you this time?'

'No. We have some pending orders that needed supervision.'

'Axel would be the fourth generation in your gem business, right?' asked Lothar.

'Indeed. Coming from Idar, and given your love of gemstones, I am surprised you're not in the business yourself,' said Jürgen.

'I thought about it but decided it was more of a hobby for me,' said Lothar. 'But funny how we are both sitting in Namibia, huh? The stark beauty of the desert with its incredibly breathtaking vistas as far as the eye can see, something out of a sci-fi movie, versus the fertile mountains, river, and lush green valleys dotted with traditional cottages in Idar, like a picture-perfect storybook.'

'I think that's why I love coming to Namibia,' said Jürgen. 'It's so different, but because of the German influence, there's also a familiarity.'

'Gem-cutting started in Idar in the late 15th century, right? I'm trying to remember what we learnt in school,' said Lothar.

'Yes. Riverside mills with water wheels used to power huge stones that were used to grind and shape minerals. But that was when Idar had gem deposits: jasper, agate, amethyst.'

'When did the gem deposits finish?' asked Lothar.

'I think around the 18th century. I remember my granddad used to tell me how he would travel to other countries and bring back rough gems to cut.'

'Speaking of gems, I think we're almost there,' said Lothar.

* * *

Three days later, the men were at Lothar Klein's residence in Windhoek.

'Don't you have enough of this garnet?' Lothar asked Jürgen. 'We found the man who had the mine. You purchased everything he had. Why are you going on this crazy trip across Namibia?'

'Like you said, he had the mine. He sold the mining rights to a South African company.'

'How does that matter? They aren't mining.'

'But they will eventually, Lothar,' said Jürgen.

'Hans, you must have 10 to 15 kilos of this garnet; surely that's enough?'

'You don't understand. I have never seen this intense orange, vibrant garnet before in my life. This is something important. I must try my best to buy whatever is on the market.'

'What's your plan?' asked Lothar.

'I'm going to travel around Namibia, visiting every single dealer—big ones, small ones, jewellers, goldsmiths, anyone who has these stones—and buy every single one of them.'

'You're crazy, my friend,' said Lothar.

'Yes. I'm crazy about gemstones,' replied Jürgen, with a big grin on his face.

Lothar looked at his friend. He had a wild look in his eye. The same look he got when he made up his mind to climb a mountain. Nothing could stop him.

* * *

Six months had passed, but, true to his word, Jürgen had chased down almost every single piece of rough orange garnet in Namibia and brought them to his atelier in Idar-Oberstein. He'd paid top dollar and didn't bargain with any of the sellers. His only focus was to amass the largest collection of Namibian orange garnets.

Once the stones were cut, polished, graded and sorted into layouts, Jürgen launched them at all the international gem trade shows around the world. He named them Kunene garnets, after the Kunene River, which flowed near the deposit. Since it was the first time this type of intense orange garnet had been presented to the market, there was no other garnet against which he could benchmark the price. The gem's brilliance after cutting, and exceptional saturation and colour, made the task even more difficult. As the date of the trade shows came closer, Jürgen priced the Kunene garnet based on his experience and instinct and started promoting the material.

* * *

'Why won't they sell?!' said Jürgen, as he banged his fist on the office table in his atelier. 'It's been almost a year, and we haven't sold a single stone. I've done everything possible to promote the stone: written articles, given interviews and talks, showcased the goods at every international trade show. It's spectacular, rare, durable, and untreated. What are we missing?'

'Maybe we just need to wait, Dad,' said Axel. 'There's a lot going on in the world right now. The US economy is just coming out of this recessionary period, the European Union was formed last year, and the Soviet Union has collapsed.'

'Perhaps,' said Jürgen, as he paced up and down his office. 'What else can we do? I'm missing something?'

'What about the price?' said Axel.

Author's Note

This story is based on actual events as narrated to the author by Hans-Jürgen Henn. Jürgen and his team reduced the price of the Namibian orange garnets by 30 per cent and, to their surprise, the gem started selling. Before Jürgen named the stones Kunene garnets, a few dealers used to call them Hollandite garnets as orange is the colour of the Dutch royal family. When the market for the gem picked up in Asia, customers found it difficult to pronounce Kunene, and dealers started offering the precious gems under the name of mandarin garnet.

In 1998, similar garnet varieties were discovered in Nigeria and, in 2007, in Tanzania. However, none have come close to the exceptional colour, rarity, and beauty of the Namibian Kunene garnets. Garnets of an orange hue are also known as spessartite or spessartine garnets which, according to industry sources, is based on the Spessart Mountains in the Aschaffenburg District of Bavaria, Germany, which many believe were the first to produce this variety of orange-coloured garnets.

Axel and his brother Ingo Henn have both joined their father in the business as the fourth generation. An avid mountaineer, Jürgen has climbed many of the well-known mountainous regions around the world. Some of the notable ones being the Alps, Andes, Himalayas, Karakoram in northern Pakistan, and Mount Kilimanjaro.

With more than 50 years of experience and having travelled to some of the most remote locations (and mountains) in the world in search of gemstones, Jürgen is one of the most respected professionals in the industry. His counsel and expert opinion is frequently sought by connoisseurs, museums, auction houses, and international jewellery companies. The family offer their rare and exceptional collection of gemstones, jewellery, and one-of-a-kind works of mineral art through their two brands: Henn, and Henn of London.

Trained as a master goldsmith, Jürgen's lifelong motto is: 'That which is rendered great by nature should not be diminished by man.' A sentiment that perfectly reflects the profound respect he has for gemstones and the natural world in which they are found.

In the last 20 years, the price of top-quality orange garnets has significantly multiplied.

Neu Schwaben

'Mining is like falling in love with someone. You don't realise how complicated they are till you climb in.'—CHRIS JOHNSTON

August 1996
Neu Schwaben, Namibia

LOOKS LIKE a piece of crystalised lagoon, Chris Johnston said to himself, as he turned over the hexagonal blue-green tourmaline crystal in his hand. A quiet moment with a beautiful stone at the Neu Schwaben tourmaline mine in Namibia reignited that rush he'd first experienced when he was eight years old, standing in the hall of gems at the American Museum of Natural History in New York City.

'He's following me,' he'd whispered to his mother, walking around the pedestal case of the 562-carat star sapphire. The six lines forming a star on the sapphire's domed surface hypnotised young Chris as the precious stone cast its spell on him, rotating on its little turntable. Many years later, sharing his childhood memory with his friend, Charlie Key, he'd said, 'In that moment, I became certain of two things: that magic existed, and I had just seen the face of God.'

Chris spent the better part of his adult life in pursuit of that heady feeling. In 1975, he enrolled in the College of Mines at the University of Idaho in the US and got his Bachelor of Science degree in geology with minors in finance, marketing, and accounting. This was followed by a course in diamond grading with the Gemological Institute of America (GIA), and a return to the College of Mines to study optical mineralogy.

He was admiring a beautiful tourmaline, which the workers at his mine had just extracted from the ground. For the last minute he'd been diligently rubbing off the final speck of Namibian soil stuck on one end of the rough gemstone. 'There you go, buddy, squeaky clean,' he said out loud to the stone.

'Mister,' said Sam, the mine superintendent, interrupting Chris's mineral moment. 'Look there; someone coming.'

Chris looked up. What now? He thought, gazing in the distance to where Sam had pointed. Despite the merciless light of the midday sun, Chris could see a convoy of three trucks, led by a police jeep, their approach raising an angry cloud of dust across the arid mining concession. The trucks were bursting with protestors, shouting, and waving sticks.

'Sam,' said Chris. 'Go call security.'

* * *

Three years earlier (1993)
On the road to Windhoek, Namibia

Within minutes of entering Namibia, Chris felt as if he were home. The majesty of the parched landscape with vistas stretching almost 100 kilometres in all directions was slowing his heart rate. Vast, open spaces were punctuated by occasional rolling hills, mountain ranges, sometimes far, sometimes near, interspersed with ravines cut sharp by ancient desert rivers. And the colours took his breath away. Shades of tan, gold, brown, and red framed by a sky that looked like a double blue aquamarine. He turned towards his friend and mentor, Charlie Key, and said, 'This reminds me of the Great Basin without humanity.'

Charlie responded with a chuckle. 'I knew you'd love Namibia,' he said. 'The country is around 825,000 square kilometres, bigger than Alaska and Texas combined, but the population is only a million. You don't see a soul for days.'

'My brain is still processing what my senses are experiencing.'

'Well,' said Charlie, 'you'd better prep your brain for some serious stargazing at night.'

'Looking forward to it,' said Chris. 'When I first heard about Namibia, it just blew my mind. To see not only the arch of the Milky Way as it stretches across the horizon, but also planets like Venus, Jupiter, and star formations all with the naked eye, it's just unbelievable.'

'There is virtually no light pollution, which is why the sky is one of the darkest in the world. Can you see that?' said Charlie, pointing towards a white speck in the distance.

'Yeah, I see it. What is it?'

'It's a farm located almost 15 kilometres away. Water vapour absorbs light, and the air is so dry here, it enables visibility as far as the human eye can see.'

'Thank you for bringing me here, Charlie,' said Chris.

'Hey, it's the least I could do after the disastrous few weeks you've had in South Africa.'

'Please don't say that, Charlie. I'm grateful for the experience,' he said, adding, 'Did I tell you that when I was a geology student, my roommate's grandmother got us in to see the chairman of Newmont Mining and he offered us jobs on a diamond exploration project in Namibia?'

'No way.'

'I turned it down.'

'Why?'

'I was in love, and my fiancée didn't want me to leave. And in the last ten years, I've caught myself wondering on more than a few occasions what my life might have been like had I taken the job and moved to Namibia in 1985.'

'We all have those moments, man. But you're here now,' said Charlie. 'And you're gonna love meeting Sid Peters when we reach Windhoek. He has two tourmaline mining operations, one in Usakos and another in Neu Schwaben, and a fantastic collection of minerals and gems he sells from his store, House of Gems.'

'Sounds amazing,' said Chris.

'Peters is a legend in these parts, a character. He looks more like a pirate than a miner, wearing a black eye patch and with a raspy voice that forces you to pay attention.'

The duo carried on discussing the natural wonders of the planet and Namibia's treasured position. The raw, untamed splendour of the landscape had Chris hooked. Everything he'd been worrying about a few days ago seemed unimportant and small in Namibia. The land had been washed anew by rainfall, and the lush, knee-high green grass swayed carelessly as the wind rushed through it from the right to the left side of the road. The sole sign of humanity's imprint was the good road that cut through the dusty ravines, and their jeep as they flew towards Windhoek. Charlie loved to drive fast, very fast.

The next morning the two friends arrived at the House of Gems store in Windhoek.

'Sid, I'd like you to meet a dear friend of mine, Chris Johnston,' said Charlie Key.

'Welcome to Namibia, and to the House of Gems,' said Sid Peters, shaking Chris's hand. 'What brings you to our remote corner of the world?'

'I'm a geologist, and I also sell gemstones,' said Chris.

'Geologist, eh? Did you see the minerals in the window outside?'

'Some of them. Didn't get a chance to look in detail.'

'Don't bother; that's for the tourists. I have some serious collectibles inside my safe. They're all for sale,' Sid added.

Chris looked around the shop, which was a mishmash of minerals scattered across dusty shelves that lined the walls. He wondered if there was a method to the madness as touristy trinkets sat next to rare specimens. 'Happy to look,' he said. 'Not sure I have the budget to buy one of them yet. I see you also have gemstones. Where are they cut?'

'In-house. We have a small gem-cutting setup in the back room. Our cutter has been with us for years. Let me introduce you,' said Sid, taking them through a back door to a well-lit space where an old man was sitting hunched over a faceting machine. Not used to receiving visitors, it took him a few moments to look up.

'Meet Igon,' said Sid. 'He comes from a long line of cutters from the historic lapidary centre of Idar-Oberstein. After the war, the Germans left Namibia, but like many others Igon and his family stayed behind.'

Igon acknowledged Sid's words with a half-nod before returning to the stone in his hand. He was using a classic jamb peg faceting machine with a flat horizontal wheel and diamond powder coating, which Igon kept applying through the cutting process. To cut a stone, he would first secure it with warm wax on the tip of a stick called a 'dop', before placing it against the moving wheel. For stability during cutting, there was a vertical column next to the wheel drilled with small holes at various heights. Igon would place the other end of the dop against one of the holes and keep changing the resting position of the stick as he worked his way across the length and breadth of the gem.

His cutting station was placed alongside a long table, which contained a variety of plastic trays with an assortment of rough gems, awaiting their fate. Chris noticed Sid tossing a few small stones inside a metal container at the far end of the table. 'What are those?' he asked, pointing towards the box.

'Anything less than a gram or too flawed gets chucked in this box. Honestly, I don't know what to do with them. They're either odd shapes or too small.'

'Do you mind if I rummage around?' asked Chris.

'Rummage away,' said Sid, opening the container and pushing it towards Chris. 'Help yourself to whatever you like.'

Delighted, Chris spent the next hour picking from an array of multi-coloured rough tourmalines, while Charlie made his mineral selections for his inventory. Chris had never seen such diversity in fine quality and colour with tourmalines. The sizes were small, but he knew cutters in Sri Lanka and Thailand who worked with small rough for the watch industry. *They'd transform these into amazing gems*, he thought.

'Why don't you come and see my mining operation in Usakos?' said Sid. 'My son-in-law David will be here soon; we can all go together.'

After a quick working lunch, the four men set off for the mines. The tourmaline deposit at Usakos looked more like a hillside quarry than a mine. It overlooked its namesake town and was a typical pegmatite deposit, meaning the miners had to keep drilling and removing hard igneous rock until they hit a tourmaline pocket. Straightaway, Chris could spot a few issues with the way the mine had been engineered. Since he'd just met Sid, he stayed silent.

Sid explained how the uneven distribution of the tourmaline-laden pegmatite pockets in the area, combined with the lack of geological clues, made the operation challenging. 'I can't tell you how many times the miners have had their drills—'

'Just drop in the middle of a gem pocket?' said Chris, completing Sid's sentence.

'Yes. How'd you know?'

'I've had some experience using 120-pound rock drills in the US. You can't daydream for even a second; otherwise, the machine itself will start spinning, instead of the drill bit. If that happens, it can break your wrist. I remember we could feel how the drill was reacting to the rock, when it was getting into something soft, indicating we were near a gem pocket. Sometimes, if luck was on our side, we'd hit the edges of the pocket. The worst was when the drill would just drop a foot or more right in the middle, damaging the crystals. Comes with the territory when you're mining pegmatite.'

Sid smiled. 'You said it. Pegmatite mining is so unpredictable. Tests your financial and mental limits. Sometimes we mine for a year and get nothing. But when you find that pristine pocket, it makes it all worthwhile. Come. Let's go to Neu Schwaben while we still have the light. It's my second tourmaline mine.'

As they drove, Sid shared some historical details related to the Usakos deposit. 'Until the Second World War, the area was home to a mine owned by the Brusius Brothers. For years, they stockpiled tourmalines they'd found while mining for tin. They would keep them in wooden barrels. As the story goes, after the war, one or maybe two lapidary owners from Idar-Oberstein in Germany came over and bought the entire lot of tourmalines. From what I heard, they cut and sold those stones for years without revealing they got them from Namibia. The location was their trade secret. At most, they would say the stones were from Africa, which is something that went on for decades.'

The rest of the drive continued similarly, discussing the diversity of Namibian gem deposits. Chris was surprised to learn about historic discoveries of red and pink tourmalines displaying top colour and crystal form. Sid suggested Chris may have seen them at gem shows in the US, but they were probably labelled 'Brazil' or 'Africa' and mixed with goods from other countries on the continent. It seemed most of the discoveries were sporadic and the pockets were quickly mined out, not uncommon with gemstones.

Within an hour, Sid announced they had arrived. The magnitude of the expanse was overwhelming. The entire flat land bank was approximately two or three square kilometres. Towards the back was a small ridge of hills that ran perpendicular to the long axis of the field. From their vantage point, Sid pointed towards the middle of the field. 'You see that hump?'

'You mean the one with those buildings on top?' asked Chris.

'Yes. We're digging in the hump. Hard-rock mining again. Drill and shoot,' said Sid, as he stuck his hands in his jeans and puffed his chest out.

Leaving Charlie with Sid, Chris started exploring the flat area surrounding the elevated mining mound. On the drive over, Sid had explained to Chris that bedrock in Namibia was only half a metre down. 'We don't have soil horizons here,' he'd said. 'We got dirt, sand and rock.'

Chris marvelled at the grandeur of the mountains overlooking the plains around him and stumbled as he took his next step. What was that? He sat down on his haunches to examine the ground. An ordinary-looking rock had saved him from falling into a small dugout pit. A few minutes later, he discovered another coarse pit and found a stick, which he started using to poke the ground as he began pacing the concession.

To prepare for his mining job in South Africa, Chris had been revising his geological knowledge related to the region, which included Namibia. He recalled reading that over the course of nearly a billion years since the continent had split, pretty much everything in this part of Namibia had been flushed into the sea. Could it be? He wondered.

Moving quickly towards the edge of the flat basin, he climbed on a boulder, hoping the elevated position would enable him to get a better understanding of the topography. From his vantage point, he spotted a few more holes and noticed that the land was slightly inclined. From his observations, he realised that in Neu Schwaben, instead of dipping towards the sea, the land was tilting away from it[1].

---

1   Chris Johnston later determined that the land was tilting away from the sea by three degrees.

This meant that each time there was a torrential downpour, the rainwater probably loosened things up and weathered the ground and rocks, but never enough to overcome that incline and send the stones down to the sea. The textbook definition of what was called a restrictive outflow basin lay in front of Chris. *Holy shit! This whole thing is a giant alluvial deposit[1], probably sitting on top of a pegmatite swarm. It's all still here and they missed it.*

'There you are. Where did you go off to?' asked Sid, as Chris returned to the group a good hour after he had gone for a walk.

'Just wandering around, taking in this incredible landscape,' said Chris.

'Chris is also a fantastic photographer,' said Charlie. 'Unfortunately, he's not carrying his camera with him this time.'

'You are welcome to return with your camera any time. Did your geologist eyes spot anything interesting out there?' asked Sid.

'Not really. Next time,' said Chris.

* * *

Three years later (April 1996)
Windhoek, Namibia

After his first visit, Chris returned to Namibia on 12 separate occasions. Besides buying rough gemstones from multiple sources, he would go down to Neu Schwaben to stay updated on the developments with the alluvial deposit. With each visit, he'd find more holes created by diggers.

He began paying attention to what was being offered for sale on the streets of Karibib and realised that the quality of stones from the alluvial deposit was seriously good, superior to any he'd seen from Africa. His attention to detail and his tenacity in correlating the stones he bought with locations in Namibia (through frequent visits) brought him to a point where he could look at a rough tourmaline and identify that it was from Neu Schwaben.

While Chris's research on the Neu Schwaben deposit continued, he and Charlie developed an active working relationship with Le Roux van Schalkwyk who was mining spessartine garnets of an intense orange hue in the far north of Namibia, within spitting distance of the Angolan border. Visiting

---

1   Alluvial deposit: a term used to describe gem deposits that have, due to weathering, broken from their host rock (where they were formed) and been carried by rivers to another location. Alluvial deposits, also known as secondary deposits, tend to be of higher quality than primary deposits (found in the rock where they were formed) because of the natural tumbling, polishing, and concentrating process they have endured.

Le Roux's mine was like travelling to the moon. It would take three days to drive up.

'If we break a 20-cent part on one of our machines,' Le Roux had once explained, 'and we don't have a spare, we'll be out of business because it takes a week to get the part from the nearest town.'

Chris had a business arrangement with Le Roux to process all the spessartine that weighed less than one gram out of his mine. There was a factory in Sri Lanka that specialised in cutting highly calibrated, extremely small gems, typically used in watches, which Chris began using to cut 250,000 to 300,000 garnets, most of which went to Japan.

In late 1995, a group of investors approached the Namibian Ministry of Mines. They were interested in establishing a value-adding gem-mining and processing company in the country. The ministry recommended Le Roux, who passed them on to Chris, giving him the perfect opportunity to set his plan in motion.

Sid Peters and his family owned the claim on the ridge down the middle of the field in Neu Schwaben. Already in his seventies, Sid was getting tired of running both the Usakos and Neu Schwaben operations. The tourmaline they were getting from Neu Schwaben was green with a black C axis[1]. To make matters worse, the material wouldn't heat, so they couldn't improve its appearance.

In comparison, the material from Usakos was significantly better, providing greater returns. But the area surrounding the ridge, which was home to the alluvial deposit, was owned by a man called Hannes Kleynhans. Chris had heard unpleasant stories about the man's ruthless nature and wasn't sure he'd be able to pull off acquiring both concessions in Neu Schwaben: the primary deposit under the ridge owned by Sid Peters, and the secondary deposit surrounding Sid's claim, which was owned by Hannes Kleynhans.

After closing the deal with his investors, Chris moved to Namibia in early 1996 and hired Charlie Key. By now, a steady flow of tourmaline from Neu Schwaben was available in the gem market. Most of the good-quality rough was sold by a South African man, Alastair McTavish, who would buy them from a variety of sources, asking no questions. The material was top grade and 85 per cent could be heated.

---

1   C axis of a gem: the long axis of a gem crystal (when viewed from the top). It runs parallel to the length of the rough gem crystal. With tourmalines, a C axis can be open (light colour) or closed (dark colour). Gem cutters prefer an open C axis, which displays a lighter hue when viewed from the top, down the length of the trigonal crystal. This tends to yield a much better final product versus a closed or dark C axis.

'Charlie, we need to stop buying from Alastair,' said Chris. 'Let's make Sid Peters an offer for his mining claims in Neu Schwaben.'

'Why Sid,' asked Charlie, 'when what you really want is Hannes' alluvial tourmaline deposit?'

'Let me explain,' said Chris. 'Imagine the field is my arm. Down the middle of the arm is Sid's ridge, and on the sides of that is the Hannes' alluvial tourmaline deposit. The plan is to transect or cut across the dyke swarm and the alluvial field with a trench, and as we mine, we'll backfill the open pit, moving from one end to the other. To mine in this way, we need both claims.'

'Understood,' said Charlie, 'let's first focus on the low-hanging fruit: buy Sid's deposit, then go after Hannes.'

* * *

Four months later
August 1996
Neu Schwaben, Namibia

'Mister Chris,' said Sam, rushing into the sort house where Chris and Charlie were preparing a large shipment bound for Hong Kong. 'Please come quick, there's been a collapse.'

'Shit, this is what I was worried about,' said Chris, as he and Charlie followed Sam out of the building.

Alastair McTavish had taken serious offence at a bunch of Americans entering his stomping ground and vowed to teach them a lesson. Three months after Chris Johnston had established the new mining company and started operations in Neu Schwaben, a few hundred individuals raided his concession, set up camp, and started illegally mining the alluvial deposit. They sold their tourmaline finds to Alastair and other rough-gem dealers who were perpetually stationed just outside the concession boundaries.

The police refused to get involved in what they called a private dispute. With his company's maiden participation in two international trade fairs only a few weeks away, Chris had no choice but to focus on first getting the mined rough tourmaline cut and polished in time for the sales events. Follow up with the Ministry of Mines to help resolve the illegal invasion would have to wait.

Sam jumped behind the steering wheel of the company jeep and said, 'I'll drive, Mister. I know where it happened.'

They raced towards the site of the accident, piercing a dusty path through the beige landscape. As they got closer, Chris could see 50 to 60 miners gathered around a depression in the ground, shouting instructions. His heart sank as the jeep stopped. A woman was trapped underneath the soil. Luckily, her head was above ground, so she could breathe. The diggers surrounding her were trying to grab her arms to pull her out. It took Chris a few seconds to realise what had happened, and what could happen if he didn't intervene.

'Stop, stop,' said Chris, raising both his hands and running towards the woman. Sam and Charlie ran close behind. With Sam acting as translator, Chris explained to the concerned group of onlookers that the ground beneath their feet was four to six metres of unstable dirt and rock. It didn't have any solid support like a hard rock.

From the angle of the trapped woman's head and arms, it seemed to Chris that she may have been digging beneath the topsoil in a cavity. The roof of that hole probably collapsed on her and may have broken her back. Chris explained how they needed to extract her from the soil to avoid further injury. After the diggers had started the extraction process, Chris stepped aside to speak with Charlie. 'Listen, you need to take the jeep and go back to my house and unhinge the kitchen door.'

'Why?' said Charlie. 'What's the plan?'

'We'll need to strap her to the door to keep her spine in a stable position,' said Chris. 'You also need to radio for a medivac helicopter that can take her to Windhoek.'

'Are you sure, Chris? A medivac chopper will be crazy expensive, man. We haven't even begun mining.'

'She won't survive the drive, Charlie. We must do whatever we can to make sure she lives.'

'Of course,' said Charlie. 'I'll go now and get it all organised.'

* * *

It had been a week since Chris and Charlie had saved the life of the female digger by getting her timely medical aid and paying for her surgery and medical costs. Chris had finally got an appointment to discuss the illegal encroachment on his mining concession.

'What did they say?' Charlie asked Chris as he walked into the sort house and flung his hat on the table. He'd just returned from a meeting with the Ministry of Mines in Windhoek, where he met 15 officials, including the minister.

'What do you think they said?' Chris retorted. 'Bloody bureaucrats don't want to do anything; they said it's a civil dispute and the ministry does not intervene in civil disputes.'

'Now what?' asked Charlie.

'Our company is the legal claim holder,' said Chris. 'We need to exercise our right as per the law of the land. Let's get security and give everyone 72 hours to get off the mine.'

* * *

Four days later
Neu Schwaben, Namibia

'Mister Chris,' called out Sam, as he jogged across the concession towards Chris, who was busy examining a rough tourmaline crystal they had just pulled out of the ground. By the time Sam reached him, Chris had put the crystal in his mouth and was swirling it around, spitting out the dirt as it dislodged itself from the stone.

'Mister, we have water at the mine. You don't need to keep putting stones in your mouth to clean them,' said Sam.

After another round of swirling, spitting, and wiping, Chris took the now clean tourmaline out of his mouth, held it against the morning light, and said, 'I know we got water, but it's fun.' The stone glistened, displaying its deep blue-green colour and clean interior.

Despite Chris's efforts, illegal mining had resumed on his company's alluvial deposit. Chris had now reported the breach to his investor, a notorious European businessman called Jack Rackam. Chris was hoping Jack's connections in the region may help in getting the attention of the Namibian government. Jack's people had asked Chris and Charlie to join them at the Windhoek Country Club for a meeting next week.

Until then, Chris had enough to keep him busy preparing for two of the most important trade shows in the world, the Hong Kong show in September, followed by the gem show in Munich. He was getting rough tourmaline from Sid Peters' hard-rock mine on the ridge and the open market where he was competing with other local and international dealers.

The new mining infrastructure was still under construction. Given the small size of the rough tourmaline, the low cost of cutting combined with top-notch skills, made Sri Lanka one of the best locations to send the stones for processing. But the important pieces from the mine were cut in the

United States by Martin Key, an internationally regarded gem cutter, and Charlie's son.

'Mister,' said Sam, softly this time. 'I think we have a problem.'

'What's happened now?' asked Chris. He continued playing with the crystal, wishing Sam away so he could go back to what he loved most - mining.

'Not happened but happening,' said Sam.

'Is this really important, Sam?' said Chris. 'I got a million things to do. There's a problem with the booth at the show in Hong Kong. The Germans are making my life difficult getting my advertisements kicked off their jewellery magazines. And I gotta prepare for a meeting with my investor next week!'

'Mister Chris, there is a man who has come onto the concession. They say he's the secretary general of the Mine Workers Union. He is giving a talk to all the illegal diggers. Say bad things about you. I think you come and see, please.'

'Shit. OK, let's go.'

Fifteen minutes later, Chris was positioned behind a group of illegal diggers listening to the union leader who was standing on top of a flat rock outcrop. The man had a megaphone in his hand that he was using to address the gathering of 500 to 600 people, mostly men and a few women.

'What's he saying?' Chris asked Sam.

'He says that they have to get rid of the American.'

'Surprise, surprise. But what's that word he keeps repeating?'

'What word?'

'He keeps saying "foreign moffie". What does that mean?' asked Chris.

'I cannot tell you, Mister,' said Sam.

'What do you mean, Sam? You gotta tell me.'

'I can't.'

'Sam. Stop it. Just tell me. It's OK.'

Cornered, Sam hung his head down and said, 'He is saying that you are a homosexual, Mister.'

Sam had seen Chris upset, but he could have never imagined what happened next. It was as if someone had waved a red flag in front of Chris as he bulldozed his way through the crowd towards the speaker. Sam stood petrified for a few seconds, not sure whether he should follow or abandon his boss. He chose to move closer to their Land Cruiser in case they had to make a quick getaway. The speaker saw something moving towards him but didn't realise what or who it was until Chris jumped on the boulder and grabbed the megaphone right from his hands.

Two days later
Neu Schwaben, Namibia

'Mister Chris was angry when I told him what moffie meant. He go crazy. Like a bull going through the crowd towards the speaker,' said Sam. He was sharing the story of Chris's encounter with the secretary general of the Mine Workers Union to a few of the mine's staff over their lunch break.

'Then what happen?' asked Adolf, one of the chisel men.

'Then, Mister Chris grab the megaphone from the speaker. And the man is shocked because he never thinks that the American he is shouting about will come to the centre of the group and face him.'

'What did Mister Chris say?' asked another miner.

'He shouted, "I am not moffie!" And then he told everyone they had no legal right to be there and to get off his property.'

'Then? What they say?'

'What they gonna say? Nothing. Everyone was shocked. I get worried that they attack Mister Chris, so I start waving at him to come down.'

'Did he listen?'

'Yeah. He dropped the megaphone and moved quickly through the crowd shouting, "Get the fuck out of my way!" I never seen him this angry before.'

'That's it?' asked Adolf. 'Then why they call Mister Chris the crazy Englishman with six invisible knives?'

'Because they think he is possessed and they are terrified of him,' said Sam, rolling his eyes at the term.

'What you think is gonna happen, Sam?' asked Adolf.

'I think everything will be fine. I drove Mister Chris to Windhoek the next day to meet with Mr Rackam and then they go together in Mr Rackam's car, they ask me to follow. You know who they meet?' said Sam. He was relishing the attention of his peers, who were hanging onto every word. They shook their heads. Sam gestured for his colleagues to come closer, lowered his voice and said, 'They met with the president, for lunch.' As soon as he said the words out loud, he placed a finger on his lips to show the confidential nature of the information.

'Did you see him?'

'No, but they were in there for a long time. Then when Mister Chris gets in the car, he and Mister Charlie start talking. There is a big delegation from the government coming today to the mines. Someone that the president sent, a lady, and with her, the minister of mines.'

Just as soon as the words were out of Sam's mouth, one of the miners pointed towards a cloud of dust in the distance. Sam shoved the last bite of his lunch in his mouth and ran towards the sort house.

'They are here, Mister Chris,' said Sam, bursting into the room.

'Right. This is it, Charlie; let's go,' said Chris.

The duo followed Sam outside, just as the convoy of cars was pulling up. The first person to step out was the minister of mines. He was accompanied by the mining commissioner, a representative from the president's office, and a slew of government officials and security personnel. After a few minutes of introductions and pleasantries, the group made their way towards the illegal encampment that had mushroomed on the outskirts of the mining concession.

By the time the group arrived at the camp, a thousand diggers had assembled. As soon as the minister got out of the vehicle, he was surrounded. It took the security personnel a few minutes to create a path for the minister to climb on top of his truck and address the gathering. He started by introducing himself and the rest of the delegation, and then launched into a speech about the economic benefits of investors in the country.

After five minutes, he said, 'You are all here illegally.'

Chris breathed a sigh of relief. Finally, someone upholding the law of the land, he thought.

The minister looked at Chris for a brief second, and then turned towards the crowd and said, 'But we're going to make a plan for you with the mining company.'

Chris couldn't believe what he had just heard. There was nothing he could do but stare, dumbfounded, at the minister.

When they all returned to the mine office, the minister said, 'Mister Chris, I am here to resolve the matter, that does not mean the resolution is all in your favour. But we will not leave you hanging. It will be something beneficial to both parties. To maintain peace and harmony.'

And votes, thought Chris.

* * *

August 1996
Neu Schwaben, Namibia

The government had mediated a settlement between Chris's mining company and the diggers. The terms included the company issuing 500 photo identity cards, which would allow the diggers to continue working in the alluvial section of the concession with the caveat that by nightfall they would move out of the camp, leaving no litter or personal items behind. Any stones found on the concession by the diggers would be first offered to the mining company, and only if they refused were the diggers free to sell the gems in the open market.

Once the settlement was concluded, Chris got to work organising support facilities for the diggers. He and his team cleared out 5,000 kilograms of garbage from the concession, organised daily fresh bread delivery for the diggers, and made sure they had access to clean water. Tempers cooled down and everyone retreated to focus on their jobs. For Charlie and Chris, that meant buying tourmalines and getting them shipped to their cutting centres in time for the upcoming trade shows.

A few days later, Charlie was preparing a large shipment bound for Sri Lanka when Chris burst into the sort house and said, 'They have to go. I can't take it anymore, Charlie!'

'What are you talking about?' asked Charlie.

'The chickens! Those 20 chickens that have been left behind.'

'Chris, what chickens? I can't understand what you're saying.'

Chris sat on the chair behind his desk, leaned back, and stared at the ceiling for a few seconds to compose himself before straightening up. He looked at Charlie, who sat opposite Chris's workstation, and said, in a calmer tone, 'When the diggers were living on our concession, there was a poultry farmer who had a stock of 20 chickens and a rooster. The birds would supply him with eggs, which he would sell to the diggers. It was a small business.'

'OK. So, what's going on now?' asked Charlie, as he tried his best to control a grin that was threatening to surface.

'Remember how, as part of our agreement, we told them that anything that is not removed from our concession will be dumped?'

'Yes. And?'

'Well, isn't it obvious, Charlie?'

'I am afraid it's not. Get to the point.'

'They left the chickens behind! Those bloody birds have been creating havoc in our camp. Yesterday, I went to the latrine to take a dump, and there were three chickens there. They had pooped all over the seat.'

Unable to control himself, Charlie started laughing, and said, 'Well, give them credit for being in the right place.'

'Right place to get me mad. I went to the pantry to grab a few biscuits just now. They've broken into my biscuit tin and wrecked the pantry. It's going to take the rest of the day to clean their mess.'

'Why don't you tell the owner to remove them?'

'I have! Sam told him last month. Nothing. Then, ten days ago, I spoke to the man. He kept saying "yes, yes", but they are still here.'

'There's nothing you can do, Chris, so no point in getting worked up.'

* * *

One week later
August 1996
Neu Schwaben, Namibia

As the convoy of trucks piloted by the police jeep got closer, Chris and Sam could hear them shouting.

'Sam, go call security,' said Chris.

As Sam turned to go, he saw their security guards running towards them.

'I don't understand. I thought we had a settlement,' said Chris. 'Everyone's been happily mining.'

The trucks stopped and hundreds of diggers poured out, screaming for Chris's blood. He couldn't understand what they were saying. But the crowd were angry, pointing their fingers at him, and shouting at the top of their lungs.

Chris looked at his security head and said, 'Festus, what's going on? Tell them we have a legal settlement supervised by the minister of mines.'

Festus stepped forward to speak with the police officers. A few minutes later he turned to Chris and said, 'Mister, this is about the chickens.'

'You're kidding right?' said Chris.

'The man wants his chickens back.'

'Well, tell him we ate 'em.'

'We still have ten chickens, Mister,' said Festus, eager to diffuse the situation.

At that point, the local police chief accompanying the convoy approached Chris and asked whether Chris ordered the man's chickens to be killed. Chris tried explaining that the chicken owner was given enough time to come and get his chickens, but he didn't, so Chris figured he didn't want them.

The policeman said, 'We don't care. You took his chickens. You had no right to do that.'

'I didn't take them. He abandoned the chickens. If this was America and the chickens were people, they'd be suing him for abandonment.'

'Mister Chris, this is not America,' said the police officer. 'This is Namibia, and we are taking you to jail.'

'Look, fellas,' said Chris. 'Let's figure something out here. I'm too busy to go to jail right now.'

After an hour of shouting and negotiating, the entourage left after Chris promised to buy the man 20 chickens, which meant he would now have 30 chickens, along with paying the police something for fuel and their wasted time because they had other, more important, matters to handle.

Chris returned to the sort house. As he entered the room, Charlie looked up from his desk and said, 'What was all that commotion about?'

'Hell, Charlie, you didn't even come outside to help. I was getting arrested over those damn chickens.'

'I figured you had things under control and if they were really arresting you, someone would come and get me. The Hong Kong show is less than two weeks away. We have a lot of work to do.'

After Chris shared the details of the saga with Charlie, he said, 'Chris, you realise that you almost lost one of the world's greatest tourmaline deposits because of ten chickens.'

* * *

December 1996
Neu Schwaben, Namibia

'We're in trouble, Charlie,' said Chris, as he sat down next to his friend. They had finished dinner and were sitting in their outdoor lounge, created using two car seats from an old Mercedes.

'I think you're overreacting,' said Charlie.

'I wish I was. Rackam isn't happy.'

'But why? We've started generating income. You sold goods at both the Hong Kong and Munich shows, and now we have enough stock for the world's biggest gem show in Tucson. What's the problem?'

Chris took another sip of his cold drink, leaned back, and said, 'Hong Kong, we just about broke even.'

'We would have sold more,' said Charlie, 'but that booth number screwed things up.'

Chris slapped his forehead and said, 'I thought we were getting a good deal when they offered us that big booth with the 4444 number. I didn't know that the number four sounds like "death" in Cantonese.'

Charlie laughed softly. 'Remember how that guy came and told you, "Mister Johnston",' he said, trying to mimic the visitor's accent, '"your booth means death, death, death, and death".'

'Two culturally insensitive Americans in Hong Kong: perfect,' said Chris, looking glum.

'Speaking of America, we have a massive booth at GJX. We're gonna kill it in Tucson. And then Rackam will call you personally to thank you for making it rain.'

'You think so?' asked Chris.

'You know why the Germans bullied that magazine to pull our ads for the Munich show?'

'Why?'

'Because for years they kept Namibia a secret, selling goods at a premium. When we land in Tucson at the Gem & Jewelry Exchange with our stock, it's gonna blow everyone's socks off, and the Germans know that. They're freaked out.'

'It does feel good to hear you say it, Charlie, but time will tell.'

'What do you mean?'

'It can't just be about one season,' said Chris. 'To really make a mark, we must consistently show up every year. That's when we'll start moving the needle.'

'Sure, but you gotta start with step one, right?'

'Right.' They continued drinking in silence, and then Chris looked up at the starry sight of the moonless night. A million stars looked back at them. 'Man, look at that, Charlie,' he said. 'We gotta be the luckiest guys in the world to have this view.' It was close to midnight, and the arc of the Milky Way looked like a tear in the diamond-studded velvety fabric of space. The air was clear and quiet.

'See that?' said Charlie, pointing towards a shining object in the sky. 'That's Jupiter.'

The two friends spent the next 30 minutes star spotting before they turned in for the night.

* * *

January 1997
Gem & Jewelry Exchange (GJX)
Tucson, Arizona, USA

Chris Johnston had a good feeling about the show. He scored a superb booth at the GJX Gem & Jewelry Show where they had a 14-foot by two-foot showcase in a 10-foot by eight-foot booth. Every square inch was stuffed with the finest quality tourmaline, perfectly cut to maximise optics.

'It's got snap, Chris,' said Charlie, as he placed the last tourmaline layout in the case. 'It's impossible for anyone to walk by without stopping. The cutting just brings out the best in the material; it's sparkle grabs you from a distance.'

'Are they lining up for us?' asked Chris, looking at the cluster of people who had started hovering and pointing towards various stones.

'Looks like it,' said Charlie.

'Right. Let's get this show on the road, then, shall we?'

As soon as the duo, along with their staff, began making eye contact with the visitors on the other side of the showcase, all hell broke loose. The next couple of hours were spent selling goods nonstop. Buyers patiently waited for their turn and snapped up the tourmalines as soon as the prices were quoted. Seasoned merchants from other pavilions, like the American Gem Trade Association (AGTA), heard about the commotion and hopped over to check what the fuss was about. There was simply no precedent for what Chris and his team had brought to Tucson, period.

Occasionally, both Charlie and Chris would step back to marvel at what they had accomplished. Then the mindful moment would pass, and it was time to climb back into the fray. On the morning of the second day, a man enquired about a single tourmaline in the showcase. When Chris quoted him the price, he frowned. In a thick New York accent, with thinly veiled disdain, he asked, 'Why so much?'

Forcing down his prodigious temper, Chris told himself, *Stay cool*. 'Listen, pal,' he said, 'you go anywhere in this show and find me a stone like this for less, and I'll buy it from you. Deal?'

Chris's ultimatum irritated the New Yorker even more. He looked at him and said, 'You from Boston?'

'Right now, I'm from Namibia,' said Chris.

'I'll be back.'

'I'll be here,' said Chris.

The New Yorker came back after two hours and said, 'Write it up.'

The days flew by, and before they knew it, there were only a few hours left before the show closed.

'Hey, Charlie,' said Chris. 'How did we do? What's the final sales number?'

'It ain't over till the fat lady sings,' said Charlie. 'We still got two hours left. Be patient.'

With 30 minutes left for the show to close, Chris and Charlie started packing up as they had finished selling their last box of tourmalines.

'We have one last customer, Chris,' said Charlie, pointing towards a man who was standing on the other side of the now empty showcase.

Chris approached him. His visitor badge stated he was from Brazil. 'You have any rough gemstones to sell?' the man asked.

'Nope,' said Chris. 'We don't have any rough, and we don't have any plans of selling rough in the future.'

Undeterred, the visitor asked, 'Do you have any pre-forms[1]?'

'Yeah,' said Chris. 'I got a kilo of pre-form tourmaline.'

'How much do you want for it?' asked the visitor.

'I want 50,000 US dollars.'

'OK. I'll be back.'

With five minutes left before the show was to close, the Brazilian buyer returned with US$50,000 in cash and cleaned them out.

'Well done,' said Charlie.

'You know,' said Chris. 'I was just thinking. That Brazilian will probably cut those tourmalines and sell them in Brazil as Brazilian.'

'Wanna know our total sales figure, Chris?'

'Hit me.'

'After this last sale, we brought in US$425,000. What do you think about that?'

'Holy moly!' said Chris. 'We did that with tourmalines?!'

* * *

---

1 Pre-form: during the cutting process, the first step involves giving the gem material an initial shape. It's a vital step before the cutting and polishing process as it determines the final shape of the stone.

Three months later
April 1997
5.30 pm
Neu Schwaben

'It's over, Charlie,' said Chris, as he grabbed a Fanta from the nearby cooler and sat down on the beat-up Mercedes seat in their outdoor lounge.

'Meeting didn't go well?' asked Charlie, referring to the appointment Chris had with their principal investor, Jack Rackam.

'There was no meeting. He just sat me down and mumbled some nonsense about landing in hot water with some business ventures in Africa, and that he couldn't afford this mining operation anymore.'

'What?! Did you tell him how well we did in Tucson?'

'I did, but no use. It's not a money issue. Seems he doesn't want any political heat.'

'But we already settled with the diggers. And the wash plant testing is also done. We just have to flip the switch to start mining,' said Charlie.

Both men were seriously pissed off.

'I know, Charlie,' said Chris. He was sitting with his shoulders slumped, feeling like his entire world had just fallen apart.

'What about all the orders we've been getting from customers?' asked Charlie.

'Jack wants us to track down every single stone from wherever we've shipped them and bring everything back. He's sending a team of auditors in two weeks to reconcile stock and payments.'

'I'm so sorry, Chris,' said Charlie. He stopped pacing and sat down next to his friend, sensing his disappointment. As the seconds stretched into minutes, the two sat and watched the departing sun paint the sky in hues of pink, orange, and flaming red before switching off like a mercurial mood swing.

'I wouldn't trade a minute of what I've done for something else,' said Chris. 'For every guy who strikes it rich, who finds the big ruby or diamond, for every guy like that, Charlie, there's probably 100,000 who never get close, and there's a few who get close but not quite, and it's OK. We had a good run. It's OK.'

Author's Note

This story is based on true events and the experiences of Chris Johnston. Minor fictional elements have been included to aid narration.

After Chris and his investor group shut down their mining operation, the government of Namibia cancelled all mining claims on Neu Schwaben and declared the concession open for independent diggers. Currently, the property produces the occasional pocket of gem material, but looks like a battlefield with craters merging across the area. Many of the original 500 miners live at the roadside just outside the fence.

At the end of my interviews with Chris, I asked him, given how difficult Neu Schwaben had been, why did he persist? He said, 'I was driven by pure blind ego, the overwhelming desire to prove myself right as a geologist and to be seen by the industry as a force to be reckoned with. In the end, I was Captain Ahab, and Neu Schwaben will forever be my white whale.'

After Neu Schwaben, Chris Johnston undertook two notable mining ventures. The first was to rediscover a rare mineral called jeremejevite (Mile 72 Project), and the second was for the coveted demantoid garnet (Green Dragon Mine).

Both operations were built by Chris from the ground up. The jeremejevite mine, known to all in the mineral world as Mile 72, was backed by Bryan Lees of the Collector's Edge Minerals and lay within 600 metres of the Atlantic Ocean. The Namibian coastline is called the Skeleton Coast because of its inhumane weather, the remains of rusty shipwrecks and bleached whale bones littering the coastline for a thousand miles. Chris battled harsh elements here for more than two years in search of this highly valuable mineral. 'We hit the sea with the first drill hole at 70 centimetres and battled the ocean the entire time,' he said.

A Namibian woman originally discovered jeremejevite, which garnered her the nickname "Tannie Klippe" or "Aunty Stone" because she would walk behind her husband who drove a road grader, looking for interesting crystals to sell. As the story goes, one day she brought a bag of blue prisms, thinking they were aquamarine, to Sid Peters, who sent a piece to John Samson White, curator of gems at the Smithsonian Museum. It came back as jeremejevite, causing quite a stir because up until this point it was only found in sizes of one- to three-millimetre grains in Eastern Russia.

On Chris's recommendation to Bryan, the jeremejevite (Mile 72) project was closed. After exposing the original discovery outcrop, it became clear the jeremejevite pocket had formed at the intersection of seven discrete rock units, a circumstance that had not repeated. After moving 4,000 tonnes of rock, it was time to put the shovel down. 'It's damn hard to mine anomalies,' said Chris.

Chris's second mining project was the Green Dragon Mine. He spent five years in this venture and was successful in building the first ever mechanised gem-mining operation in Namibia. To circumvent the lack of water (essential for processing mineral ore), he pioneered non-aqueous extraction of garnet. He used local suppliers in Southern Africa, and a shoestring budget, to build an operation, which yielded half a million dollars in revenue at their first sales event in Tucson, eventually cutting nearly 500,000 garnets. The venture put Namibian demantoid garnet in front of the gem world for the first time.

Due to medical reasons, with a heavy heart, Chris gave up mining after 30 years at the end of 2010. He continues to live in Namibia and deals in mineral specimens and gems and is considered an authority on the subject. Chris wanted me to acknowledge, Martin Paul Key and Charles Stuart for their heroic efforts at getting the Neu Schwaben tourmalines cut to the highest standards in a ridiculously short period, Janet Vogenthaler for her able assistance, and Graham Sutton and Bryan Lees for Mile 72.

A few words of advice from Chris to miners:

> You are not doing this to get rich. That's not the point. If you are lucky, you'll cover your running costs. And if you stay at it long enough, once or twice in your life, you'll find something important. And if you are smart when you do, you'll stop and really enjoy the moment; it is very much like catching lightning in a bottle. Never forget, if it was easy, it would already be done!

Christopher Lyn Johnston at the Green Dragon, demantoid garnet mine, Usakos district, Erongo region, Namibia (2006). Photo credit: Chris Johnston.

Charles Locke Key and Christopher Lyn Johnston, Gathemans Restaurant Windhoek Namibia, (Nov. 1994). Photo credit: Chris Johnston.

Paraíba-Like

1998
Nampula, Mozambique

IT WAS time to leave Mozambique. Moussa Konate had been buying rough gems from local diggers and dealers for a few months and had accumulated 80 kilograms of rough multicoloured tourmalines. He was a seasoned merchant who specialised in sourcing rough gemstones from Africa. His clients were some of the world's top gem cutters, and only purchased the best quality material. *They'll like this assortment*, he thought as he closed his slender order book and placed it inside his jacket pocket.

Guinean by birth, Moussa's present business interests were in Mozambique. He'd first arrived there towards the end of the civil war in 1989. The country's pristine beaches with sunlight glimmering off its warm turquoise waters reminded Moussa of the home he'd left behind.

He felt invigorated not only by Mozambique's natural beauty and fresh seafood, but the plethora of mineral opportunities his entrepreneurial instinct anticipated. In 1992, the signing of the Rome General Peace Accord had brought an end to 15 years of civil war in Mozambique. Moussa registered a local company called Mozambique Gems Limitada in the same year and acquired a concession to mine aquamarine.

In the mine's first year of operation, it hit a rich aquamarine pocket. A large percentage of the crystals displayed the coveted deep blue shade, known as Santa Maria after the famous mine near the municipality of Santa Maria de Itabira in Brazil, which first produced aquamarine with that distinct blue. Once news of the mine's good fortune spread, Moussa started receiving offers for outright purchase. But he was keen to develop the deposit without external involvement. Lack of funds, however, forced him to temporarily stop mining and fall back on gem trading. He was determined to earn and save enough so he could reopen the mine.

But that created a new problem. Miners were supposed to sell their production to a government department under Mozambique's Ministry of Mines, which purchased the rough gems well below market value. As a veteran gem exporter to international markets, Moussa understood the real worth of the material and, like others in the industry, resorted to physically carrying the goods out of Mozambique. In this case, 80 kilos of uncut tourmalines.

'Boss, is this OK?' asked Moussa's houseboy, who was helping him pack.

Moussa was standing by the window of his apartment in Nampula, using the morning light to examine a package of high-quality rough tourmalines. He turned around and replied, 'Yes. Good', as he handed the package to the boy and started examining his travel documents. He had to catch a flight to Maputo, and then an international connection to Frankfurt, Germany. From there, he would take a bus, which would bring him to his destination, the picturesque town of Idar-Oberstein.

'Boss, I pack everything? You sure you carry all them stones this time?'

Irritated at being disturbed again, and surprised at the boy's impertinence, Moussa said, 'Why you ask? You know something I don't?'

'No, boss. Just asking. If you wanna leave some stones behind, I take good care.'

What's his game? thought Moussa. He looked at him again. The boy seemed genuinely concerned. Moussa softened and said, 'You don't worry, OK? Everyone knows me in Mozambique. They take care of me. Pack all the stones nicely.'

The boy smiled. His boss in a good mood meant a nice tip. He returned to the suitcase. The last package of stones looked fragile. The boy spotted an old red metal box lying on the writing desk and went to pick it up.

'What are you doing?' asked Moussa.

'The stones in this parcel very shiny, boss. I'll pack them nice and tight inside this box.'

'No. Give me the box,' Moussa said, outstretching his hand. He grabbed the dusty container from the boy and wiped it against his spotless shirt. 'Go, tell the driver we'll leave in an hour. I'll finish packing.'

As the boy scurried away, Moussa sat on the edge of his bed and traced the grooves along the lid of the box. It had been his prized possession when he'd been forced to leave his home, at only 12 years of age.

Moussa was born and raised in Guinea. His father, a mining engineer, worked as the national director of mining. After 100 years of colonial rule, Guinea had gained independence from France in 1958 following a referendum organised by politician Ahmed Sékou-Touré, in which most of the country's population had rejected French President Charles de Gaulle's offer to join a new federal community. Ahmed Sékou-Touré became the country's first president, embraced communism, and ruled with an iron fist.

Communism had crippled Guinea's economy and increased the country's dependence on the Soviet Union for aid.

Twelve-year-old Moussa was one of seven children. His father's meagre salary as a government employee had sufficed. But one day in 1968, a few months after his twelfth birthday, Moussa's life was turned upside down when his father passed away due to heart failure. With him gone, and no savings, the burden of providing for the family fell upon his mother. A brilliant student who had excelled in school, Moussa was now forced to drop out. His maternal aunt in Liberia offered to take him in and find him a suitable job so he could send money back home.

'We'll take care of him like he's our son,' he'd heard his uncle say to his mother, when they had come to pick him up. She was sitting in a chair, with her head cast down, shoulders slumped, clutching a tear-stained handkerchief.

The red metal box had been a farewell gift from his mother, which Moussa had used to store treasured trinkets from his friends at that time: a blue-green marble, a few seashells, crayons, a stamp with a picture of a boxer, and a wrinkled pull-out magazine poster of the soccer legend Pelé.

That moment when he'd hugged his mother before leaving had been one of the most painful memories of his life. The tightness in his chest had given way to tears. She'd held him close and whispered, 'You so smart, Moussa. Be good and listen to your aunty. We will be together again. I love you so much.' He'd buried his head in her shoulder and clutched her tighter till his uncle gently pulled him away.

After moving to Liberia, Moussa's aunt had found him an apprenticeship with an ivory carving workshop where he'd learnt how to transform elephant ivory tusks into exquisite works of art. Within a few months, he was sending US$300 to US$400 every month to his mother. His teenage years were spent under the care of his aunt. But once he was of age, he moved to Lagos, Nigeria. Years of hard work and dedication brought Moussa success. At 28 years of age, he was a young entrepreneur who owned an ivory atelier and showroom in the heart of the most prestigious neighbourhood in Lagos.

Through the years, Moussa became a reliable and accomplished supplier of exquisite ivory art objects, earning a solid reputation in Nigeria's corporate and government circles.

Embassy databases listed his company, constantly directing international guests to his showroom. During VIP delegation visits to Lagos, Moussa was invited to prepare exhibits on the embassy campus. He often travelled to London, Paris, and other cities to deliver his creations, taking advantage of cheap Lagos-Europe airline tickets.

By 1982, aquamarine and tourmaline had been discovered in Nigeria. The find triggered an influx of Guinean merchants. Moussa's connections in Lagos drew gem dealers from his home country to his workshop. He helped them buy airline tickets, change money, and provided a slice of home thanks to traditional meals prepared by his wife.

He would occasionally drive them to gemstone digs located 1,000 kilometres north of Lagos to purchase raw gems from villagers. As an exporter, Moussa was familiar with Nigerian customs procedures. Dealers relied on him for shipping assistance. In return, they shared their gemmological knowledge, teaching Moussa the nuances of gem value and selection criteria.

As more countries banned ivory imports, Moussa's customer base shrunk. Completing an ivory sculpture and obtaining payments could take weeks, sometimes months. In contrast, his Guinean friends could earn more than him in a few days by trading their colourful pebbles. Moussa saw many opportunities in the world of gems. He noted what Guinean merchants bought and sold, and at what prices.

In 1989, the Convention on International Trade in Endangered Species of Wild Fauna and Flora (CITES) decided to end international ivory trade, which prompted Moussa to put his plan in motion. He started visiting mining locations and markets in Kenya, Nigeria, Tanzania, Zambia, and Madagascar with his gem-dealer friends who helped him negotiate with miners, diggers, local traders and verified his purchases. To sell his wares, Moussa travelled to Idar-Oberstein in Germany, one of the top centres for coloured stone cutting in the world.

Back in Nigeria, blue and yellow sapphires from the Kaduna district were being freely traded. Moussa learnt that due to their expertise in gem-cutting and treatments, Thai gem-manufacturing firms were the chief buyers of sapphires and rubies. That knowledge prompted him to visit Thailand and build contacts in the markets of Chanthaburi and Bangkok. He moved his family to South Africa and shuttled between Madagascar and Germany with tourmaline, and sourced other gems from Nigeria, Congo, and Zambia for his clients across Europe and Asia.

Rattling around on the plane from Nampula to Maputo, Moussa opened his order book to prepare his sales plan for Idar-Oberstein. It was a path he had trudged for many years. The same routine each time he landed in Idar-Oberstein: declare the goods at customs and pay the import duty. Depending on the volume of gem material, Moussa would stay in Idar for a week or more, visiting lapidaries from dawn till dusk. At each location, the lapidary owner checked his stones, made his selections, and paid via cheque.

There was no monetary control in Germany when Moussa first started his sales trips. After concluding a sale, he would cash the cheques at a local German bank and physically carry the dollars back to Nigeria, occasionally amounting to US$200,000 or higher. As his business developed and controls tightened, his clients started wiring payments to his bank account. He liked the no-nonsense, professional approach of the Germans. They understood and appreciated quality goods and paid accordingly.

The captain announced they were approaching Maputo. Moussa had checked his luggage all the way to Frankfurt, so the only thing left to do was cross airport security with his hand baggage. Another 14 hours and he'd be in Idar, enjoying the brisk winter air. Maybe this time I'll go see their mineral museum, he thought.

As he lugged his duffle bag through Maputo airport, he spotted a familiar face. One he was not thrilled to see. It was a Mozambican gem dealer who'd been trying to buy Moussa's aquamarine mine for the past few years. After failing to yet again cajole Moussa to sell eight months ago, he recently sent a veiled threat through a common acquaintance.

'Mr Konate, what a lucky coincidence to bump into you, sir. I will now have a good day.'

Moussa smiled and shook the dealer's clammy hand. Forcing a warm tone, he said, 'Good day to you, my friend. How are you doing?'

'Scraping by; I don't have your luck, Mr Konate,' he replied shrugging his shoulders. 'You are like a pot of honey in Mozambique. You arrive, and all the miners and dealers start buzzing around you, bringing you their best stones. We are forced to survive on your leftovers.'

'I pay a fair price. You pay them good money, they'll come to you. No mystery there.'

'Yes, but we don't have your deep pockets, Mr Konate. I admire you so much. I pray to Allah that he makes me successful like you, sir.'

'I wish you the best, my friend. I must go catch my flight now. Take care.'

'You too, Mr Konate. You too.'

Two-faced rascal, thought Moussa as he took out his handkerchief to wipe his hands clean of the encounter. The chance meeting reminded him of something his father used to say: The lower the bow, the longer the blade. An hour later, Moussa was back to making plans for his sales appointments as he watched his hand luggage enter the X-ray machine at the security check.

'What's in the bag?' asked the security officer.

'Just clothes. I'm going to Germany. It's winter there. Carrying woollens and a big coat.'

'Open the bag, please.'

Stay calm, Moussa told himself as he moved to unzip his weathered brown leather bag. *Don't be in a rush*, his mind coached him. After opening, he stepped back so the officer could search his luggage.

Giving Moussa a dirty look, the officer grabbed his bag and within seconds had dumped all its contents on the table. He diligently felt the inner lining and leather handle, as if looking for bumps. Finding nothing suspicious, he stepped aside to speak into his walkie-talkie, asking Moussa to wait.

Moussa started packing his things, trying not to smile.

A few minutes later, the man returned exuding confidence.

'You need to come with us, please.'

* * *

1999
New York, USA

'Ladies and gentlemen, this is your captain speaking. We will begin our descent to New York's JFK airport in 30 minutes...'

Moussa peered outside the plane's window with mixed emotions. The episode at Maputo airport two years ago had dealt him a severe financial blow. Although his handbag was empty, on a tip-off, Mozambique customs had inspected his checked baggage, and found 80 kilos of rough tourmaline. Moussa was arrested. The authorities confiscated his entire shipment and levied a US$7,000 fine. The material was later auctioned by the government.

Moussa tried rebuilding his business, but it was tough. With no capital, he could not renew his mining licence and struggled to buy rough gems in the open market. His aquamarine concession was acquired by the dealer who had tipped off the authorities. To make matters worse, he was now separated from his wife, who had left their four children in his care. He'd hit rock bottom. There was nothing left to do but start from scratch. Moussa left his children with his brother in South Africa, and started working as a gem broker for other miners and merchants.

Rubellite (red tourmaline) had recently been found in Nigeria, which Guinean merchants sold to manufacturers in Thailand and Germany. Of the two locations, Thailand had emerged as a leading hub for rubellite, but African merchants were unable to sell their goods for the prices they desired. This is where Moussa came in. He took unsold gem material to the US and was successful in selling it at higher prices to international manufacturers.

Within a few months, a prominent New York-based gem merchant, Yaya Danang, invited Moussa to join his gem business.

I hope this is a smart move, thought Moussa. With all his travel between Africa, Europe, and Thailand, he hardly saw his children. They were still living in South Africa with his brother. who took good care of them, but they missed their father, and he missed them. Now he was moving to New York. Yaya Danang told him to get a green card or permanent residency in the US, but that would mean Moussa couldn't leave the country without special permission till his application was approved.

I should put on my shoes, he thought, seeing the boroughs of New York appear below his plane window. But he didn't move, frozen by waves of self-doubt that were increasing the heaviness in his chest. At that moment, sunlight filtered through the ominous grey clouds, brightening the cityscape below. Moussa straightened up and peered through his window. The rectangular green outline of Central Park came into view, followed by the masculine skyscrapers of midtown Manhattan.

This is America, he told himself, *the land of opportunity*. As the aircraft floated towards JFK, Moussa leaned back in his seat. *The largest gem show in the world is a few months away in Tucson, Arizona. Rough-gem dealers from Africa will be coming to sell their goods. They'll need someone they can trust. I can help them.* A rough plan started percolating in Moussa's mind, his thoughts emerging from the gloom of insecurity towards the warmth of ambition.

* * *

2001
Yaya Danang's office
New York

Since his move to the US in 1999, Moussa had made inroads in the gem community, developing an extensive network of sellers from Africa and buyers from Brazil, Germany, and Thailand. His fluency in French, Portuguese, and English, along with his experience in dealing with diplomats and entrepreneurs from his ivory days in Nigeria, gave him a competitive edge. He'd married an American woman and was awaiting his green card so he could return to Africa.

'Moussa, come see this parcel of tourmalines from your country,' Yaya called out from his office.

Moussa knew Yaya was with a gem manufacturer from Brazil. He'd observed the man visiting Yaya before, but never had the chance to meet him. Moussa joined the men, who were sitting across from each other at a white table. A parcel of rough tourmalines lay before them, which the Brazilian was examining with a jeweller's loupe.

'Ah, Moussa! Come, meet my friend, Fonseca Saint Claire,' said Yaya.

The man looked up at Moussa. He didn't smile but offered his hand in greeting. He had a firm handshake, neither too strong as if he was trying to dominate, nor limp like someone was forcing him to be nice. 'Call me Keke,' he said.

'My name is Moussa. In English, my friends call me Moses.'

Yaya jumped in. 'Moussa has experience with gemstones in Africa. He used to own an aquamarine mine near Nampula in Mozambique, and he speaks your language, Keke.'

Keke nodded and went back to the stones.

'What do you think of this tourmaline?' Yaya asked Keke.

The Brazilian grunted in response. The parcel being discussed was a mixed assortment of rough tourmalines from Nigeria. Yaya started briefing Moussa.

'Keke knows everything about paraíba tourmaline, Moussa. Do you know that neon blue stone from Brazil? It's the most expensive tourmaline in the world. As expensive as a ruby or an emerald, maybe more,' Yaya explained.

Moussa nodded in reverence. He knew about the stone but kept quiet.

'You know, Moussa, these electric blue-green tourmalines were first found in 1987 in the State of Paraíba in Brazil. Then, they found them in Rio Grande de Norte, a different place in Brazil, but the name "paraíba" stuck. It's the same with all stones. The first location where people find that type of gem always becomes famous and prices keep going up.'

Moussa nodded in agreement but kept his eyes on Keke, who was now taking the stones one by one to the window to inspect them again under natural light.

Yaya went on, 'You have to heat them to get this electric colour, Moussa. Eighty per cent of tourmalines are heated. Do you know why they change colour when we heat them?'

'Because they have copper inside?'

'Yes!' responded Yaya, grinning. 'But with copper, they should also have manganese; both are important to change the stone's colour from green-ish-blue and sometimes violet-blue to this crazy paraíba colour.'

'How is the production of paraíba tourmalines in Brazil now?' Moussa asked Keke, who was now checking the stones with a higher-magnification loupe.

'OK,' Keke responded, shrugging his shoulders. 'The peak mining period is over. That was from '89 till maybe early nineties. The miners still find stones but few and small sizes, not clean.'

'That's why you must buy this parcel, Keke,' piped up Yaya. He looked at Moussa and said, 'This will be the first time Keke will buy Nigerian tourmaline.' He turned towards Keke. 'What do you think? Can you heat and change them to paraíba?'

'Don't know,' replied Keke. 'See this one,' he said handing over his loupe and a large piece of rough tourmaline to Yaya for inspection. 'It has thin yellow-brown tubes inside?'

'Hmm,' Yaya responded, handing the gem back to Keke.

'The tubes are there in almost all the rough. I don't know how the stones will respond to the heating,' he said, scratching his chin. 'It will be an experiment. I've never heated African tourmaline.'

'That's why I give you good price, my friend,' said Yaya. 'They've just started coming out of Nigeria. You should get them before they disappear. Supply is so unreliable.'

* * *

12th August 2002
Nampula, Mozambique

Moussa Konate was back in Mozambique. Since his chance meeting with Keke in New York a year before, the two had become good friends. Moussa's dream of acquiring a mine remained unfulfilled, but he was happy to return to Africa. His success in the US enabled him to purchase a bungalow in Nampula: a place from where he could resume gem trading, receiving local miners, independent diggers, and dealers who brought him uncut gems for sale.

'I placed some councada with a pot of tea for you on the veranda, sir,' said Moussa's housekeeper as she cleared away his breakfast, freshly baked fufu bread with leftover crab curry from dinner. The West-African woman was a skilled cook. She made her curry with tomatoes, onion, ginger, garlic, and a generous helping of thin okra slices. Her secret ingredient was a homemade blend of spices. The fragrance of roasted cumin and coriander seeds wafting through the house every weekend reminded Moussa of how his mother would prepare spices back home.

As he stepped onto his outdoor patio, he paused for a moment to stretch, letting the morning sounds wash over him. The rooster was still crowing, drowning the singing of the birds. A bicycle's tring-a-ling joined them as it ambled past the front gate. Two steps below the patio was an open square courtyard, with the front gate towards the left and a palm tree on the right. Moussa could smell the dust as the sweeper disturbed the dried leaves on the courtyard floor, his twig broom keeping beat like a metal brush on a snare drum. He relished these morning moments in Mozambique. Taking a bite of the homemade peanut-caramel treat, he leaned back in his lounge chair, licked his fingers, and got snug with his newspapers, awaiting gem miners and merchants.

Moussa had just finished reading the sports section when the squeak of the gate handle caught his attention. The first arrival was a young lad. As he walked inside the courtyard, Moussa's staff waved him over. The outdoor patio was divided into two sections. Opposite the palm tree was Moussa's lounge area, and on the other side of the rectangular space was a long table covered with a white tablecloth. This was where Moussa assessed gemstones. While the boy prepared his goods for inspection, spreading them out in piles on the table, Moussa finished his tea and asked his house-keeper to bring a plate of fresh pao (savoury bread), butter, and tea for the young dealer.

This will take time, thought Moussa, approaching the table, and acknowl-edging the boy's presence with a nod. There seemed to be more than a kilo of rough tourmalines in various shades and sizes staring back at him. They reminded him of the Pop Rocks candy his kids begged him to bring from America. *But these are much nicer*, he thought, holding a rough sea-green stone against the morning sun.

There was something unusual in the colour of the gem in Moussa's hand. Playing it cool, he picked up another rock of a similar shade, but this time, he walked away from the table. Leaning against the stone railing surround-ing the patio, he used the jeweller's loupe hanging from his neck to check the stone. *Could it be?* he wondered.

A few hours later, Moussa made a phone call.

'Hello! Keke, can you hear me?' asked Moussa in a loud voice.

'Yes, Moses. I hear you, my friend. How are you? How's Mozambique?'

'Good. I call you because I saw a parcel of rough tourmaline here. I think it can be heated and made paraíba.'

'Similar to the Nigerian tourmaline?' asked Keke.

'Better because these are bigger and clean. Colour very nice.'

'How you find them? I never heard of this tourmaline from Mozambique.'

'One of my sellers bring them this morning. I told him, "I buy this from you and give you more money. You go back to this mine and buy every single stone you find and bring to me".'

'You show him which tourmaline he has to buy?' said Keke.

'Of course not. If I do that, he'll bring only that type and charge more money!'

Keke burst out laughing and said, 'You're a smart man, Moses. Why you call me?'

Ignoring the compliment, Moussa continued, 'Once I have enough, I bring them to Brazil. Maybe in two weeks. I want you to heat them.'

'I was planning to travel to New York, but I'll change my plans now. OK, I wait for you, Moses. But it's a risk; they may not turn into paraíba. I can only try.'

'Yes, I know. I call you again when I have enough. See you soon.'

* * *

3rd September 2003
The lapidary of Fonseca Saint Claire (Keke)
Brazil

'What do you think?' Moussa asked Keke.

'Looks promising, Moses, but I can't say the stones will turn until I heat them,' Keke replied as he continued examining the rough tourmalines Moussa had brought from Mozambique.

'You buy them from me, heat them, and see,' Moussa suggested.

'What if they don't turn into paraíba tourmaline?'

'Look, Keke. I invested US$35,000 in this parcel. I sell to you for US$25,000, but one condition: you heat the stones to see if they turn into paraíba. At US$25,000, you won't lose any money if they don't change. If they change colour and become paraíba, you keep the profit, I don't want it. But I want you to tell me—so I know.'

Keke put his loupe down and stared at his friend. 'You do that for me? How you gonna cover your loss?'

'The week I was going to leave Mozambique, a morganite mine broke out. No one knew about it. I bought 85 kilograms of morganite, which I will sell to cover my loss. Don't worry; you just try to change the stone to paraíba tourmaline.'

'OK, I try my best, Moses.'

* * *

14th September 2003
Nampula, Mozambique

'Moses, can you hear me?' shouted Keke.

'Ya, I hear you, my friend. What happened with the tourmaline?'

'Moses, any more blue-green type tourmaline you find in Mozambique, you buy them all. The entire parcel you brought from Mozambique changed! The colour is just like the ones from Brazil.'

'I knew it! Ha! That's wonderful news.'

'Moses, I want to make you a proposal.'

'I'm listening.'

'US$35,000 I give to you for the parcel. That's for you to keep. The stones you sold to me here belong to you and me. We sell them together. And the tourmalines you'll now buy in Mozambique, let's do a 50-50 partnership for those gems, OK?'

Moussa smiled. 'Agreed.'

Author's Note

This story is based on several interviews conducted by the author with Moussa Konate. Information shared by Moussa was further enhanced via secondary research. Fictional elements have been included in scene setting, characters, and dialogue.

The parcel Moussa brought to Fonseca Saint Claire (Keke) sold at the 2004 Tucson Gem Show in Arizona for US$375,000. Both Keke and Moussa decided that instead of sharing the profit they would acquire a gem-mining licence in Mozambique.

With the help of his local contacts in Nampula, Moussa identified the tourmaline-producing area but encountered another hurdle. The deposit was crawling with informal diggers who were funded by rough-gem-dealer groups. Moussa realised claiming the land area where the diggers were operating could cause conflict.

In July 2004, he sought the help of geologists working in the Mozambique government's mineralogical department to identify 300 hectares of land, away from the ongoing tourmaline rush, and filed his claim. As per Moussa, the Mozambique government helped him at every step because they saw in him a formal miner, keen to develop the deposit, who would abide by mining regulations, and contribute revenue via taxes. At that time, Moussa explained, many individuals were filing mining claims across vast areas. Most did not develop into professional mining operations.

After identifying his mining concession, Moussa visited the local village and explained his intentions to the chief and community members who were informally digging for tourmalines, away from his concession. He brought them over to his claim and showed them the boundary of his future mine, requesting them to respect his jurisdiction. To garner their support, Moussa offered to help wash their gem gravel at his concession. He offered to close his operation on a pre-designated day, once a week, to allow the community to wash the ore they had mined. Once washed, his team would evaluate any gemstones found and make them an offer. If the diggers didn't like Moussa's offer, they were free to sell to other dealers in the market.

To foster a harmonious environment, Moussa also offered to assist in organising the local community of diggers into a cooperative and teach them how to restore the soil after mining to maintain the agricultural integrity of the land. Although the informal miners never took Moussa up on his offer, the government officials appreciated his sincere efforts and his inclusive approach.

Due to restricted funds, it took Moussa and Fonseca (Keke) five years to build a proper wash plant and start production. While they were developing their mine, news about the tourmalines spread far and wide. International manufacturers and merchants started aggressively buying the stones. Some would mix the tourmalines from Mozambique with those from Brazil, labelling the entire lot paraíba tourmaline. Others would keep them separate, demanding a higher price for tourmalines from Brazil and positioning them as the superior variety.

The price difference was frustrating for Moussa. He couldn't understand why a gemstone that was larger, cleaner, and looked the same should fetch a lower price solely because of its origin. Dealers who were sitting on old stock of paraíba tourmalines from Brazil didn't want to see any dilution in the value of their inventory. Moussa stayed his course. He was determined to market the tourmalines as Mozambican and close the gap in the price difference.

His efforts resulted in a detailed article by the *Gems & Gemology* journal of the Gemological Institute of America (GIA) titled 'Copper-Bearing

(Paraíba-Type) Tourmaline from Mozambique' [1]. The article was based on a visit to Moussa and Fonseca's mine by the then editor of the publication, Brendan Laurs. The rough tourmaline samples collected by Laurs were subjected to extensive testing in the GIA lab with the findings reported in the article.

In December 2012, members of the Laboratory Manual Harmonisation Committee (LMHC), comprised of representatives of the top gem labs in the world, defined paraíba tourmaline as, 'A blue (electric blue, neon blue, violet-blue), bluish-green to greenish-blue, green (or yellowish-green) tourmaline, of medium-light to high saturation and tone (relative to this variety of tourmaline), <u>mainly because of the presence of copper (Cu) and manganese (Mn) of whatever geographical origin</u>[2].' The note further explained, 'This copper (Cu) and manganese (Mn) bearing tourmaline may also be called "paraíba tourmaline" in the trade.'

Mozambique has emerged as the primary source of paraíba tourmalines, attracting several mining ventures in the region. Informal gem digs supported by dealers continues on a parallel track. The beauty of the material from Mozambique, combined with the availability of larger sizes, has ensured the ongoing appreciation of the stone. Due to the rarity of paraíba tourmalines from Brazil, that origin continues to attract a premium price.

1   https://www.gia.edu/gems-gemology/
spring-2008-copper-bearing-tourmaline-mozambique-laurs
2   https://static1.squarespace.com/static/5bfbb7e6cc8fed3bb9293bf3/t/
641427f9a639361dd80d95bc/1679042553961/LMHC+Information+Sheet_6_V8_2023.pdf

The Tanzanite Chase

29th July 2000
Block C
Afgem's tanzanite mine
Merelani, Tanzania

'HOW MUCH are we exporting tomorrow, Mike?' asked Gordon.

'Seventy thousand carats,' said Mike Nunn, founder and CEO of Afgem. Mike had acquired a tanzanite mining concession, also known as Block C, from the government last year and had hired Gordon as the mine's manager seven months ago.

Gordon whistled. 'How much do you reckon it's worth?'

'Around four million US dollars.'

'So how many you want in the convoy?'

'Let's keep a low profile,' said Mike. 'Single-vehicle convoy. Take the four-by-four, and, Neels, I'll drive. OK?'

'You sure?'

'Yeah. I don't want people to realise we're moving product,' said Mike.

'You're the boss. Let me start the preparations,' said Gordon.

'I'll leave you to it.'

Gordon watched Mike leave. He picked up one of the rough tanzanite crystals from the sort house table and held it against the sunlight streaming in through the window. The gemmologists who worked in Afgem had explained to Gordon that tanzanite was a trichroic gemstone. Depending on the angle, it displayed three different colours. Some described the colours as blue, violet and red-bronze, whereas others said the colour ranged from blue or purple-red to green-yellow.

The colour in demand, though, was deep blue, which mirrored the intensity of a blue sapphire. Gordon smiled as he turned a particularly mesmerising rough tanzanite in his hand. Mike often said, 'Tanzanite is what sapphire wishes it could be.' When heated and properly cut and polished, tanzanite in large sizes delivered a rich blue gemstone with a hint of purple, displaying an incredible depth of colour combined with its excellent crystal quality.

Interestingly, the larger the stone, the stronger (more saturated) the blue-violet colour.

Tanzanite was first discovered in 1967. Industry folks, who had visited the mine recently, credited a prospector named Manuel De Souza[1] with its discovery on 7th July 1967, near the village of Mtakuja in Tanzania. As the story goes, Manuel had initially thought he'd found sapphires, but after testing, his stones were correctly identified as the gem variety of the mineral zoisite. Until then, most in the trade had only come across green zoisite, making the find especially attractive. The stone gained attention when the vice president of Tiffany & Co, Henry B. Platt, named the blue zoisite 'tanzanite' after its host nation and included it in the company's fine- and high-jewellery collections.

The government of Tanzania nationalised the mines in 1971 to regulate mining, production, and export, and generate much-needed income via licence fees and taxes. By the late 1980s, however, the government had lost control of the mining area to thousands of informal diggers; some believe that figure to be around 30,000 diggers. In the resulting chaos, tanzanite flooded the international marketplace. Consumer interest was reawakened, but there was little control over supply. Prices plunged.

In 1990, the government curbed informal mining and divided the area into four blocks: A, B, C, and D. Block A was awarded to Kilimanjaro Mines Ltd and Blocks B and D to small-scale miners via the Arusha Regional Miners Association (AREMA). A graphite-mining company, Graphtan, picked up Block C and started developing the concession. They built a DMS[2] and a wash plant and were focused on obtaining high-quality graphite, mining tanzanite as a by-product.

Mike had a gem-cutting facility in South Africa and had been dealing in Zambian emeralds when he first came across tanzanite in the mid-nineties. Awareness levels regarding the rare gemstone were low in South Africa, but Mike strongly believed tanzanite had tremendous potential waiting to be unlocked.

He began travelling to Dar es Salaam and, later, Arusha to purchase rough tanzanite. By this time, Graphtan had gone bankrupt, and the government was auctioning their concession. Mike was successful in acquiring Block C in the late nineties. He established African Gems (Afgem) as a marketing company that mined, pioneered a proprietary grading system for tanzanite, and established sales and distribution networks. The company had plans

---

1   Manuel De Souza was of Indian origin from the former Portuguese colony of Goa, now a state within India.
2   Dense Medium Separator.

to create a tanzanite foundation, which would focus on marketing the gem globally and work with local communities to develop charitable projects in the field of education, health, and livelihood.

During Gordon's interview for the job, Mike said to him: '500 million years ago, a geological event led to the creation of this exceptional gemstone. It's not found anywhere else on the planet, except a five-kilometre stretch in the foothills of Mount Kilimanjaro in Tanzania. How insane is that?'

Afgem's neighbouring concessions (Blocks B and D) were in the hands of informal and small-scale miners who were not pleased to learn of the company's arrival. Initially, Mike had a local partner, but they had a disagreement when the man was caught trying to bribe Neels, Afgem's head of security, with US$15,000 to steal stones from the operation. Since his departure, tensions were running high due to increased animosity from small-scale miners working in neighbouring concessions who would 'accidentally' burrow into Afgem's underground tunnels, as well as death threats directed at Mike. As a result, the concession was looking more like a military camp than a gemstone mine.

Mike wanted to get to Kilimanjaro airport by 7.30 am, which meant an early departure so they could complete all the export formalities for the shipment. Gordon was used to early mornings, having served in the South African Defence Force. He returned the rough tanzanite to the pile on the table and moved to the artillery room to inspect the weapons they would carry. As he was examining a Smith & Wesson revolver, Neels walked into the room. 'Hey, heard we have an early one tomorrow,' he said.

'Yeah. Mike wants to export a big shipment to South Africa,' said Gordon. He placed the revolver in its holster and picked up a Bruno shotgun.

'Sensible to get as much out as possible. I believe he got another death threat last week,' said Neel.

'Yup. Becoming quite frequent. You think these guys mean business?' asked Gordon.

'Dunno, and don't want to find out. Best to be prepared for the worst. Is that what you're planning to carry?' asked Neels, referring to the shotgun Gordon was holding.

'Yeah. I think the first time I used one of these was when I was 16 years old.'

'Where was that?'

'At the Sandawana Emerald Mine. My dad was the production manager. We were 30 families living on campus along with a few hundred Rhodesian workers. My brother and I were in a boarding school like all the other kids, but for three months of summer holidays we'd live at the mine.'

'It probably was 50 years ago, since you're so old,' said Neels, as he gave Gordon a friendly shove.

'Very funny. Late seventies, actually.'

'Seventies? During the conflict. Place must have been like a battle zone,' commented Neels.

'Don't I know it. My brother almost died when our school transport detonated a land mine.'

'Christ!'

'On the 4th of July 1979.'

'You remember the exact date?'

'Yeah. It's the Independence Day in America when they have all these fireworks. Our version was detonating a land mine. That whole area was a hot zone at that time. As kids of mineworkers, we were given weapons training, everything from handguns and rifles to grenades and mortars. And when the war started, we were instructed not to leave the campus. Tough times all around. The liberation war was at its peak, and they were after economic targets. The mine was eventually overrun later that year and shut down. I don't think it ever recovered.'

'But what happened after your jeep—'

'It was a Puma armoured personnel carrier. Holidays were over and we were being taken back to school. My brother was almost 18. He was planning to join the army and wanted to sit with the guards. We could see Belingwe town so we thought we were in the clear, and then the detonation happened. Our vehicle was overturned. Four of the mine staff instantly killed. It was a boosted mine. I remember we found one guy's body 100 feet from the detonation site in a tree.

'My brother and some of the older students were sitting in the back on their school trunks. The force of the explosion threw my brother from the vehicle, and he ended up with fractured legs, pelvis, skull, and arms. Because I was one of the younger boys, I sat in front, and was strapped in with a safety belt, which saved me. The shots started ringing out and we began firing back. We all had guns. I remember firing like crazy; the adrenaline just took over. It was quite a frightening experience as a young schoolboy.'

'What type of gun did you have?' asked Neels.

'A Heckler & Koch G3.'

'That's a battle rifle. How the devil did a 16-year-old know how to use that?'

'It was standard issue to the Portuguese army who sold it to the Rhodesians after they left Mozambique. The private security company protecting the mine were using them, and I was trained along with the rest of the boys. We all had guns in our hands when we left the mine campus in case of trouble en route to school. The 7.62 HKG3 rifle: I remember it well. When the attack happened, the guards formed an armed perimeter around us. We had to keep fighting till the army came and rescued us.'

Gordon continued, 'They evacuated the injured, including my brother, via helicopter to a hospital in Fort Victoria. He spent the next three months in rehabilitation and recovery. The rest of us were examined by the army medic. Once they declared us to be fine, we carried on back to school. Those early years living at the mine in the middle of a war zone is what motivated me to study mining as a profession and serve in the South African Defence Force.'

'That's crazy. I've had my fair share of close calls but nothing like what you experienced,' said Neels. 'Your brother recovered?'

Gordon nodded. 'Recovered, enlisted in the South African Army as he'd planned. Was killed in action three years later, in 1982.'

'Sorry to hear, man.'

'Yeah. Was tough for the family,' said Gordon. 'Right. Enough of the past. I'm going to go check on the product in the sort house.'

'I just came from there. They were packing it in wooden crates,' said Neels. 'What vehicle are we taking tomorrow?'

'The Land Cruiser. Mike wants to keep things on the downlow.'

'Just 70,000 carats of tanzanite and three guys. Nice,' said Neels. Like Gordon, Neels had also served with the South African Army, Special Forces Unit.

The next morning, Gordon did a final inspection of the sealed wooden containers, the vehicle, and their weapons before departing for Kilimanjaro airport. 'Keep monitoring our radio system in case of any incidents,' Gordon told his team.

They hadn't run into any trouble in the past but given that they were travelling through bandit territory with four-million-dollars' worth of gemstones, he didn't want to get caught unaware. Mike sat behind the wheel of the four-by-four, with Gordon next to him in front with his two weapons. Neels sat in the back with a shotgun.

'What's that?' asked Mike, as they heard a crackling sound on the radio.

They paused to listen, but nothing came through. Dismissing the noise as random frequency play, the trio left the safety of the concession. Anyone who crossed them on the road would see three guys in a Toyota Land Cruiser exuding a nonchalant vibe, but beneath that cool exterior were sharp, observant eyes.

The path was just a track in the bush until they got near the airport where some semblance of a road appeared. Although the sun had risen, improving visibility, avoiding the undulations on their path was a bit like navigating obstacles in a video game. As they traversed down the dusty track, Gordon looked towards Mount Kilimanjaro in the distance. At 5,895 metres (19,340 feet), the majestic snow-capped volcano is the world's largest free-standing mountain, and Africa's tallest. On most days clouds inhibit a clear view of the peak but today, the gods had bestowed upon the miners a spectacular sunrise against the majestic wonder of nature.

Pulling his attention away from Kilimanjaro, Gordon scanned the surrounding bush. One of the first hurdles coming up was a narrow bridge. The rudimentary structure was made from tree trunks, branches, and organic material, and overran a small stream with a gully. Given the weight of their vehicle and the makeshift nature of the bridge, Mike slowed down to the bare minimum to make the crossing.

'What's that?' said Gordon once they had sight of the bridge. He could make out a silhouette on the other side blocking their way.

Mike peered through the misty morning light. 'Looks like a car,' he said. 'Corolla.'

Gordon unclipped his gun and checked the side mirror just as a fast-moving vehicle appeared out of nowhere and rammed them from behind. 'Ambush!' he yelled.

Two men jumped out of the Toyota Corolla in front of them. They had their faces covered with black-and-white-chequered keffiyeh (traditional headdress/square scarf worn by certain communities in the middle east). The attackers had AK-47 assault rifles and started firing on them from the sedan. They were sandwiched between two hostile groups.

Gordon immediately grabbed Mike and pushed him down. 'Mike, keep your head down and just keep driving away from here.'

Neels smashed out the back window and started firing at the car behind them. Gordon opened his window and with his left hand took six shots till his revolver was empty. He radioed the mine: 'Contact, contact, contact, we've been attacked.'

Mike made a sharp right turn into the gully, the four-by-four jolted violently in response, causing the vehicle's suspension to collapse under the impact. Gordon and Neels maintained their defence by continuously firing shots, causing the air to be filled with the acrid smell of gunpowder. Thanks to the dry season, the gully, which would normally be filled with rushing water, was now a dusty path with only a few stagnant pools. The attackers' vehicles were ill-suited for the challenging terrain, putting them at a disadvantage. The Corolla struggled to maintain pace, its engine roaring as it fell further behind, while the relentless pursuit of the car that had crashed into them grew more intense. Eventually, it retreated, unable to withstand the continuous barrage of defensive gunfire from Gordon and Neels.

For a good 15 to 20 minutes after the firing had ceased, the tanzanite trio continued navigating through the gully, their eyes scanning the surroundings for any signs of danger. They managed to get out via a shallow section that led them back onto the main path. Gordon asked Mike to stop. He and Neels got out and formed a circular perimeter around their ride to reconfirm their attackers were not following. They had a satellite phone, but there was no signal. Their four-by-four resembled a block of Swiss cheese, with bullet holes pockmarking its surface.

Mike's white-knuckled hands were still tightly gripping the steering wheel. The brazen manner of the attack had shaken him. No one except their inner circle of team members knew of the shipment, which meant the attackers had an inside track. Death threats in ink were one thing, but to be under fire with an intention to kill quite another. The reality of what they had just survived suddenly dawned on Mike and he started trembling.

'Let's get to the airport, Mike,' said Gordon. 'You can call the police commissioner from there.' The trio and their now battered vehicle continued towards the scenic Kilimanjaro mountain and airport. They were quite a sight as they pulled into the cargo terminal, their bullet-ridden vehicle clanking to a stop. Once the processing of the tanzanite containers had begun, Mike stepped away to call the police commissioner. The man had assured Mike on several occasions that he'd support him 24/7 any day of the year. *He'll find the perpetrators*, thought Mike as he dialled the number.

'Hello,' said the commissioner.

'Commissioner, it's me, Mike Nunn.'

'Ah! Mr Mike. You're still alive then?'

Author's Note

The story is based on actual events as experienced (and relayed to the author) by Gordon in the year 2000 when he was working with Afgem in Tanzania. The attack was one of several that occurred as Afgem continued mining for tanzanite in Block C of the Merelani Hills in Tanzania. The incident confirmed the team's suspicion of collusion between law enforcement agents and the attackers. Gordon believes the aim may have been to murder Mike or scare him into abandoning the mine, both of which were unsuccessful.

Gordon left Afgem in October 2001 to pursue other interests, which eventually led him to the diamond mining industry. On 16th November 2001, just as Afgem was preparing to participate in the world's largest gem show in Tucson, Arizona, the *Wall Street Journal* published an article[1] claiming links between the tanzanite trade and Al-Qaeda. Overnight, tanzanite was dropped by every retail outfit in the US from Tiffany & Co to stand-alone boutiques.

The Afgem team that pioneered a clean mine-to-market model for tanzanite (never seen before in the coloured gemstone industry), worked closely with the Tanzanian government and trade stakeholders to establish the Tucson Tanzanite Protocol at the Tucson Gem Show on 22nd February, 2002[2]. The protocol confirmed there were no links between any terrorist organisation and the tanzanite trade and outlined steps by the Tanzanian government and industry to protect the integrity of the business.

In a separate interview, Adrian Banks, a former senior employee of Afgem and TanzaniteOne explained how in 2003 the company created a trading entity and started buying rough tanzanite from miners in Blocks B and D, and more than 50 registered traders in Arusha. 'The Maasai tribe which is native to the Simanjaro district, where the tanzanite mines are located, largely controlled the supply of rough tanzanite to the traders in Arusha town, some 60 kilometres away from the mine. 'We would buy[3], rough tanzanite crystals, then if required the gems were cobbed[4], so they were clean and could be graded in accordance with the TanzaniteOne grading system. The graded rough from the trading operation was then blended with the mined production and sold,' said Banks. The trading company achieved three objectives: fill any gaps in the mine's production, recover stolen product, and help stabilise prices[5]. Tanzanite customers were happy because they were able to buy consistently graded parcels instead of mixed quality in the open market.

From 2003 to 2004 tanzanite attained the highest prices ever achieved since its discovery in 1967. It became a favourite of the cruise industry.

1   https://www.wsj.com/articles/SB1005860635600904840
2   https://www.jckonline.com/editorial-article/the-tucson-tanzanite-protocols/
3   After undertaking a "know your client" on every supplier.
4   Separating with handheld tools, like pliers, gem-quality crystals or minerals from less valuable minerals also called "host rock", in which the gem crystal may have formed, e.g., extracting Zambian emeralds from Schist rock.
5   If small-scale miners had a large production and TanzaniteOne lacked a buying office, the price could drop due to weak market conditions or customer issues in Jaipur.

Industry sources estimate that more than 70 per cent of tanzanite was sold through retail shops catering to cruise ships in the Caribbean, and jewellery stores on cruise liners.

Through port lectures, cruise companies were able to effectively communicate the story of tanzanite. The gem's natural beauty, mirroring the colours of the ocean, along with its rarity as a single-source stone proved to be a winning formula. Afgem further supported the industry via marketing campaigns like, 'Be Born to Tanzanite' and traceability initiatives such as engraving unique identification numbers on the girdle of the faceted tanzanite.

TanzaniteOne

By 2004, while the players remained the same, Afgem was acquired by TanzaniteOne, which was listed on the London Stock Exchange (AIM) in August 2004 with Mike Nunn as its CEO. As per the company's 2005 Annual Report[1], prices of US$11 per carat were achieved across all grades of mined rough tanzanite, up 22 per cent on 2004's prices of US$9 per carat, supporting improved gross margins of 61 per cent or US$9 per carat. Ongoing cost control and enhanced economies of scale contributed to a net profit before tax of US$13 million.

Worried tanzanite prices may have peaked, Afgem selected their top six customers and established a direct supply system. However, tanzanite pricing declined as manufacturers with similar quality competed against each other.

Mike Nunn handed over the baton to Ian Harebottle who took over as CEO in 2005. Mike continued to hold shares in TanzaniteOne.

Multiple factors, such as change in board members, market forces, and Mike and Ian's departure from the firm, contributed towards the company's decline and the devaluation of tanzanite. Notable among them was the 2008 financial crisis. At that stage, TanzaniteOne's trading operation in Arusha was buying more than $1 million US dollars' worth of tanzanite every month. Faced with liquidity issues and a substantial drop in demand, the company couldn't sustain their buying operation, which led to about a

---

1   https://lexingtongold.co.uk/wp-content/uploads/2015/03/TanzaniteOneAnnualReport2005.pdf

50 per cent drop in the price of tanzanite. By the time the gem industry emerged from the crisis, many of TanzaniteOne's senior team had left.

On 5th March 2013, the government of Tanzania instructed the new sponsors of TanzaniteOne, Richland Resources, to surrender a 50 per cent stake to the State Mining Company (STAMICO) as a condition to renew its mining licence[1].

On 7th December 2014, Richland Resources sold the tanzanite mining business for US$5.1 million to Sky Associates Group Limited[2].

Since the TanzaniteOne era, various factors, such as a ban on the export of rough-gem material[3], lack of marketing initiatives, and unstable supply have caused a tumultuous trajectory for tanzanite in terms of value appreciation and price stability.

The accomplishments of the TanzaniteOne team exemplify that a proficient operation that offers the industry a steady supply, supported by marketing efforts directed at consumers, and charitable initiatives (like those by the Tanzanite Foundation) can, with time, establish, safeguard, and increase the worth of a gemstone.

Key members of the TanzaniteOne team continue to achieve success in the coloured gemstone and diamond industry.

Left: Adrian Banks demonstrating TanzaniteOne's grading process for rough tanzanite stones to a group of miners from the Maasai tribe. This photo was taken at the TanzaniteOne office in Arusha in 2003. Photo credit: Adrian Banks.

Right: A miner from the Maasai tribe, assessing a rough tanzanite at the TanzaniteOne trading office in Arusha, Tanzania. Photo credit: Adrian Banks.

1 https://www.miningreview.com/top-stories/
tanzania-to-acquire-50-stake-in-tanzanite-one/
2 Lexingtongold.co.uk (2014). "Proposed sale of Tanzanian mining operations'.
3 Above 1 gram.

A Land Called Kagem

1972
Johannesburg International Airport
South Africa

'WHO YOU picking up?' asked John, biting down on his Wilson's Champion toffee. The first couple of bites were always a fight till the treacle flavour kicked in.

'New mine owner,' said Peter.

'What's he like?'

Peter leaned towards John, pulled down his sunglasses to make eye contact, and whispered, 'He's Indian. They call him SS Gupta.'

'What?! You work for a coolie[1]?'

Peter winced at the derogatory term and said, 'Must be someone important if he's bought the mine.'

'And how can they enter the country on Indian passports?' asked John.

'I think they get those paper visas. They know Senator Getz who arranges everything. Immigration just stamps their paper visa. No record of their entry or exit on the passport.'

'Don't you have an airstrip at the mine?'

'Ja. GM[2] always takes them from the tarmac straight to Gravelotte, but there's a mechanical issue with the small plane today, so he sent me with the car.'

'Careful on the road,' said John, unwrapping his second toffee.

'I will, broer [brother], but everyone knows he's Mr Money, so no SAP[3] gonna trouble him.'

'Mr Money, eh?'

'Ja. Heard some of the big boys call him the emerald king of India. They say he was buying emeralds in Colombia in the fifties. Real cowboy. Also has something in Brazil. Owns a mine, or maybe just trading.'

---

1   An unskilled native labourer in India, China, and some other Asian countries. An offensive term to denote people of South Asian origin.

2   General manager.

3   South African Police.

'What happen to Mr Roberts? Didn't he own the mine?'

'Mr Roberts old now, broer. He got no son, and son-in-law not interested, so he sold the mine to Mr Gupta.' As he finished the sentence, he spotted his guest walking into the terminal building. Peter straightened his tie, slapped John on the back, and said, 'They've arrived, totsiens [bye].'

John saw him approach a man who drew attention upon entering the terminal building. Almost six feet tall, he exuded an air of importance with his well-groomed moustache and white safari suit.

'Good afternoon, Mr Gupta,' said Peter, shaking Shiv Shankar (SS) Gupta's hand.

'Afternoon. Peter? From Gravelotte?'

'Ja. Mr Gupta, I think the GM already informed you that we can't take the plane this time. Some technical issue. The drive to the mine won't be long. Maybe four or five hours. There's a small restaurant on the way where we can grab a bite to eat.'

'Then we better get going. This is my son, Govind. His first visit to Gravelotte.'

'Hallo! Welcome to South Africa,' said Peter, warmly shaking the young man's hand.

'Your first time driving to the mine?' Peter asked SS Gupta as they made their way towards the exit.

'Yes.'

'It'll be fine. Nothing to worry about,' said Peter.

SS stopped walking. Pulling his shoulders back, he looked down at Peter, smiled and said, 'Peter, I am never worried.'

'Right,' said Peter as he rushed ahead to open the door, feeling a bead of perspiration trickling down his forehead.

Ram would have loved this, thought SS. They'd been driving for two hours, and he was mesmerised by the South African landscape. 'What do you call these trees?' he asked Peter.

'They're red bushwillow trees, Mr Gupta. You'll find them everywhere. Village women use their roots to make colourful waterproof baskets.'

'Waterproof baskets?'

'They apply a special paste to the baskets so they can carry water from rivers and wells to their homes,' explained Peter.

Govind saw his father scribbling notes in his pocket diary. He leaned forward and said, 'Peter, my father was telling me that Gravelotte is one of the most beautiful places I will ever see.'

'I haven't travelled much, but it's one of the most gorgeous spots in this neck of the woods. The entire land area is almost 100 square kilometres, with lush green hills and valleys as far as you can see, like the stones we mine. We are less than an hour's drive from Kruger National Park, so you'll see plenty of animals at Gravelotte. Can't go walking about after dark.'

'Really?' said Govind. 'I didn't realise we were so close.'

'O ja [oh yes]. Place is more like a private game reserve than a mine. We have a few houses. Two big ones, each on top of a hill. One is the general manager's home, and the other our clubhouse.'

'Clubhouse?' Govind enquired.

'It's grand. That's where you'll be staying. Mr Roberts brought a fancy architect from America to design the building. Very modern. Has five large bedrooms, all have glass sliding doors that bring you to the front patio, where we have an enormous swimming pool surrounded by gardens that slope down from the clubhouse.'

'Wow, sounds like a resort.'

'Suppose so. The clubhouse is where all the managers hang. One room overlooking the pool is a lounge with a billiards table and a bar. You'll love it.'

'What else do you have?' asked Govind.

'Got a medical centre, private landing strip for the aircraft, offices, homes for the managers, living quarters for the miners, a stable for all the horses...'

'Horses?'

'Security is all on horseback at Gravelotte, like cowboys, hee-haw! And just like the Wild West, we got a prison, too.'

'A prison? I don't understand.'

'If GM thinks one of the staff has done something wrong, stealing, or causing trouble, he'll just jail 'em.'

'Don't the police have to do that?' asked Govind.

'Oh no. GM just sends a notice to the local police chief to inform them. May sound strange to you, but we're in the middle of nowhere and being GM of Gravelotte is like being mayor of a small town.'

Govind leaned back in his seat, absorbing what he'd just heard.

'You have other mines nearby?' asked SS.

'Copper. Massive copper-mining operation in the area, maybe the largest in the world. There's a mining town nearby called Phalaborwa. They say, thousands of years ago, there were many volcanoes in this region. All that volcanic activity created many minerals, like phosphates, vermiculite, mica, and gold, but the most important is copper.'

'Sounds like an interesting setup to visit,' said SS.

168

'We go to Phalaborwa to buy groceries once a week. GM could easily arrange for you to tag along and visit one or two of these operations. Speaking of food, let's stop for a bite. There's a restaurant coming up.'

'Govind, you want to eat something?' said SS.

Peter stopped their car by the side of the road, across from the restaurant.

'Yeah, OK,' Govind said, opening the car door.

'Best if you give me your order, and we eat in the car,' Peter said, jumping in front of Govind as he started walking towards the joint.

'Govind, come back; ander nahin ja sakte [can't go inside],' SS called out.

Puzzled, Govind looked up and saw the sign next to the entrance door that stated, 'No coloured and no blacks allowed.'

Before Govind could react, Peter interrupted his thoughts. 'How about a chicken sandwich, slice of chocolate cake, lemonade, and some chips?'

'Fine. No lemonade, just a Coke,' Govind replied, returning to the car.

As he closed the door, his father said, 'We'll leave soon. Should reach the mine in less than two hours.'

'Isn't it strange, Papa?'

'What?'

'We are investors in this country but can't go inside that restaurant and have lunch.'

SS grunted in response, opened his briefcase, and said, 'I have some papers to study.'

* * *

1977
6.45 am
Jaipur, India

The Broker

Soni Pandit worked as a rough-gem broker in the historical Johri Bazaar (jeweller's market) of Jaipur, India. Established in the mid-18th century, the market was part of a city development project by Maharaja Sawai Jai Singh II. The king invited notable artisans and other tradespeople to settle in the new city, offering his patronage and protection. Soni Pandit's forefathers were goldsmiths and migrated from Agra to Jaipur in the late 18th century.

169

While his brothers remained in the family trade, Soni began working as a rough-emerald broker for Shiv Shankar 'SS' Gupta eight years ago.

The sun will be up soon, thought Soni as he looked outside his bedroom window. He'd set his alarm to go off an hour earlier than his usual 8 am. Throwing his quilt off, he jumped out of bed and went over to his cupboard to pull out his favourite blue and white check shirt and black trousers. *The entire market will talk about me today*, he thought as he performed his morning ablutions.

Thirty minutes later, Soni was sitting at the dining table, nose buried in a newspaper article about Morarji Desai, the man who many said would defeat Indira Gandhi, the current prime minister of India.

'Yeh lo [here], brakefast [breakfast],' said Soni's wife, placing a plate of fruits in front of him.

'What's this?'

'Your new diet.'

Soni stared at the assortment of apples, papaya, and pear on the stainless-steel plate, then looked across at his son devouring aloo paratha (pan-fried Indian bread stuffed with potatoes and spices). With a heavy sigh he said, 'Get some kala-namak [black salt].'

'Doctor said salt not good for your heart.'

Before Soni could protest, his wife asked, 'Accha [OK], why is Gupta Ji coming to your shop? Don't buyers always go to meet him at his bungalow?'

She's trying to change the subject, thought Soni as he resigned himself to his gastronomic fate and picked up an apple slice. 'Yes, he rarely visits any broker's office, which is why I have to leave early.'

'Wah, kya baat hai [wow, how cool].'

'Namak toh de do, devi ji [At least give me some salt, oh goddess],' Soni implored again.

'Chalo, khao aapna brakefast aur office jao [C'mon, eat your breakfast and go to the office],' his wife said, suddenly getting up from the table and marching into the kitchen.

Soni's job was straightforward: to find and manage customers for the rough emeralds SS Gupta imported from Brazil. For centuries, emerald sourcing, cutting, and polishing had remained in the hands of the Oswal and Shrimal families of Jaipur. They were the elite and had enjoyed royal patronage for centuries, honing their skills in gem and jewellery manufacturing. SS was an outsider from the Khandelwal community, whose members had only ever worked as grain merchants and confectioners.

But SS knew his destiny lay elsewhere. He started travelling to Colombia in the early fifties and to Brazil in the sixties. Emerald production was robust

170

in the state of Bahia in Brazil, but Indian lapidaries had no direct access to the material. SS identified a gem dealer, Inez Balassa Silveria, appointed her as his agent, and set up a buying operation in Campo Formoso, Bahia. SS brought his younger twin brothers, Ram and Lakshman, into the business, posting Ram in Brazil to oversee their gem-trading and mining interests and Lakshman in Geneva. The uncut emeralds they bought in Brazil were first exported to Geneva, which was a free port, then shipped to Jaipur.

As the operation's scale increased, SS realised he couldn't depend solely on the aristocracy of emerald manufacturing establishments to absorb his stock. He had to expand the market.

He was a disruptor who democratised access to rough emeralds and encouraged new entrants by offering credit facilities and importing machines to improve the cutting, grinding, and polishing of gemstones in Jaipur supporting the overall development of the sector. Brokers like Soni became SS's gatekeepers, who dealt with buyers not only from the Khandelwal community but also from the minority Muslim community in Jaipur.

In 1972, SS purchased the Gravelotte emerald mine in South Africa. Soni's workload surged as hundreds of kilos of rough emeralds were imported from Gravelotte to Jaipur. There were two categories of rough-emerald buyers. First, the big boys, who SS directly handled with members of his family. These large-scale manufacturers would get premium goods on a priority basis before the rest of the market. Second, the new entrants, who Soni managed, mostly home-based, small-scale lapidaries with limited experience in gem-manufacturing.

When SS's emerald shipments arrived, Jaipur would become abuzz with sometimes 200 buyers standing in line outside his residence to receive their quota of stones, like respectable Hindus waiting at the temple for the priest to dole out prasad (offerings of devotional sweets).

'Saab, chai? [Sir, tea],' asked Chotu, the office errand boy, as Soni took off his slippers, getting ready to sit cross-legged on the traditional divan seating. He operated from a shophouse in the heart of Johri Bazaar. The ground floor was used as a waiting area for buyers and sellers. His private space was on the first floor. Large windows surrounded the rectangular room, providing essential light for assessing gemstones. Two sides of the room were lined with a low-level divan covered with plain white cotton bed sheets that were neatly tucked under the hard mattress. White cotton bolsters divided the long seating area.

'Chai?' the boy asked again.

Soni rubbed his stomach in response, pulled out two coins from his white kurta (knee-length cotton shirt) pocket, a 50 cent and a 10 cent, and instructed Chotu to bring a plate of kachori (deep-fried flour balls stuffed with onions, chillies, and spices) with his morning tea. The boy grinned, pocketing the 10-cent coin, his tip for not informing Soni's wife about the kachori.

Once Chotu left, Soni was all business. He sent his runners with a list of instructions to all corners of Johri Bazaar informing a select group of emerald manufacturers of SS Gupta's rare visit to his office.

* * *

The Seller

It had been five years since Shiv Shankar (SS) Gupta had purchased the Gravelotte emerald mine in South Africa from Ian Roberts for around 900,000 English pounds. At the time of acquisition, the area had numerous dumps, or mounds, of processed mineral ore, from which Roberts' team had already extracted emeralds. Conscious that it was his first mining venture, SS enlisted the help of Bob Laurence Contat, a Rhodesian gentleman who had discovered the famed Sandawana emeralds in 1955 in Southern Rhodesia (now Zimbabwe) with Cornelius Oosthuizen.

Bob started working as the mine's chief geologist. Under his guidance, the Gravelotte team spent the first two years extracting remaining emeralds from the dumps before tackling the primary deposit, which lay buried inside a hill. In year three, they began developing the mine, which was an open-pit operation (no underground tunnels). There were 11 levels cut into the central part of the hill, forming a concave shape, each level around 15 to 20 metres high.

'Instead of terrace farming, we're doing terrace mining, SS,' Bob had explained.

The highest point was designated Level 1, with the ore body one to two metres wide. The emerald vein kept widening as it moved from Level 1 to Level 10, which was at the base. Towards the central section, deep within the hill, the ore body was five metres wide, stretching to eight to ten metres in width at Level 10. Although certain parts (like Level 6) had a higher concentration of emeralds, the mineralisation was homogenous (spread evenly throughout the rock). The Gravelotte team would simply blast and drop the ore body and transport it to the wash plant for further processing.

Most emeralds had a dark tone rendering them commercial-grade, which meant vast quantities had to be sold to break even, let alone generate a profit. A smaller percentage displayed good clarity, colour, and had less iron, rendering them a superior grade. Another positive feature of Gravelotte emeralds was their inherent strength and clarity, because of which they needed little oiling for clarity enhancement, especially when compared to the emeralds SS imported from Brazil, which contained a higher number of fissures. Out of all the operational pits at the mine (like North Face, Midnight), the Cobra pit generated the best and largest volume of emeralds, resulting in Jaipur merchants calling Gravelotte the 'Cobra Mine'.

* * *

The Buyer

'Rahim! Soni Ji just sent a message that Gupta Ji is coming to his office today. Get ready. Quick. This could be the opportunity we've been waiting for,' said Ikram Ullah, Rahim's older brother, shouting instructions in all directions.

Rahim grabbed his clean kurta from the hook behind the door and rushed out of his room. After graduating from college, he'd recently joined his father and older brother in their lapidary business, which involved gem carving, cutting, and polishing. They had been cutting rough emeralds brought to Jaipur by SS for a few years, but their financial limits confined them to processing commercial-quality stones. Rahim's brother, Ikram, had been trying to get a direct meeting with SS for a few months to gain access to better material.

'Just remember,' called out their father as the brothers were leaving, 'don't give him your hand until you are sure of the goods and payment terms.'

Thirty minutes later, as both brothers turned a corner towards Soni's office, they saw an entourage of 30 people moving as a swarm ahead of them, a common sight when SS visited Johri Bazaar.

'See, we're late,' lamented Ikram. 'Let's rush ahead of them.'

* * *

The Market

Chotu entered the room holding an aluminium tray upon which he was balancing a V-shaped ribbed glass of milky masala chai, and a stainless-steel plate containing two golden spheres of kachori.

Soni was speaking to a potential emerald buyer on the phone, but the aroma of the snack made him look up. Seeing Chotu's big grin, he said, 'Accha, mein aap ko baadme phone karta hoon, koi guest aa gaye hain [OK, I'll call you later; a guest has just arrived].'

As Chotu moved to place the tray in front of Soni, his assistant burst into the room and said, 'Sar [Sir], Gupta Ji aa gaye hain! Pachaas logo ne unko ghera hain neeche. Jaldi neeche aao [Mr Gupta has arrived. He's surrounded by 50 people downstairs. You better hurry and come down].'

Soni left his beloved kachori, asked Chotu to straighten the room for the fifth time that day, and followed his assistant downstairs.

It was a common sight to see SS Gupta surrounded by merchants, emerald cutters, and jewellers. He was a much-loved figure in Jaipur. Soni took one look at the swarm of admirers and plunged into the crowd. Within a few seconds, he was facing the man of the hour. Hands folded in supplication, he said, 'Gupta Ji, meri dukaan mein agar aap kadam rakhenge toh mandir ban jayeegee, aap hamare leeye bhagwan ho [Respected Mr Gupta, if you set foot in my humble shop, it will become a temple. You are like a god to us].'

SS smiled, placed his hand on Soni's shoulder and said, 'Aree kya bol raha hai yaar, chal mein chai peeta hoon tere saath [What are you saying, my friend? Come, let's have tea together].'

As Soni led SS to his office, he spotted Rahim and Ikram in the crowd and, with a quick nod, asked them to follow him.

* * *

The Deal

On entering Soni's office, Rahim saw him whispering something to SS. When Soni saw them, he paused and said, 'Come, come. Gupta Ji, these are the two brothers I was telling you about.'

SS smiled and invited them to sit across from him on the divan. Right on cue, Chotu entered, carrying four plates of piping hot kachoris. SS turned towards Soni and said, 'Mein aaj morning mein soch raha tha, ki bahut din ho gaye kachori nahin khayee [Only this morning I was thinking, it's been ages since I had a good kachori].'

'Gupta Ji, abhi garam garam mangaayee hai [just got it fresh] from brand new Rawat Sweet Shop.'

After 15 minutes of indulging in hot masala tea and kachoris, the men got down to business.

Ikram started the conversation. 'Gupta Ji, you have changed the market for gem lapidaries like ours. We could never get our hands on rough emeralds till you started bringing them from all corners of the world. My family has been buying from your team for a few years. But we would like to buy better grade.'

SS looked at Soni and said, 'Did you have a parcel in mind for them?'

Soni responded, 'Sir, I was thinking that 80-kilo one. That should be good grade for them.'

'No. The 60-kilo bori [jute bag] is better. Let them have that. Have they seen it?'

Soni asked Rahim, 'You remember the three parcels of rough emeralds I show you at Gupta Ji's home two weeks ago?'

The brothers nodded, recalling the mountain of green hexagonal uncut emeralds they had inspected with Soni.

'Bhai [brother], the last one you saw, number three, that's from Gupta Ji's Cobra Mine in Africa. Deal is you must buy the entire lot of 60 kilos.'

The brothers looked at each other, not sure what to say. They were hoping to get maybe 10 or 20 kilos. They didn't have the capital to buy the entire lot. Before either could react, SS clasped Ikram's hand, and Soni quickly covered both their hands with a white cotton handkerchief. Rahim's entire body stiffened. This was how deals were done in the industry.

The buyer and seller would clasp hands under a cloth to maintain the confidentiality of the price. If the seller pressed one finger, it meant he wanted 100,000 rupees for his goods. Squeezing two fingers equalled an asking price of 200,000 rupees and so on. Rahim couldn't discern the movement of SS's hand under the hanky, but he saw the bead of sweat trickling down his brother's forehead.

When SS fixed his gaze, it was difficult to look away. Both men kept staring at each other. Soni was quiet. He knew when to retreat. Finally, SS broke free, stood up, and put on his leather slippers, an indication the meeting was over. He turned towards the three men and said, 'I will reduce

30,000 rupees for labour and the deal is done for 570,000.' Without waiting for a reaction, he walked out of the room, leaving Soni to finalise the details.

Rahim was horrified. Where would they find the money for the emeralds? His brother had doomed their entire family.

'Congrats, bhai,' said Soni, slapping Ikram on his back. 'Finally, you got an emerald packet directly from Gupta Ji.'

'Soniji,' said Ikram, '60 kilos toh bahut zyada hai [Soniji, 60 kilos is a lot]. Hum afford nahin kar sakte [We can't afford it].'

'Kya baat kar rahe ho? [What are you saying?] You wanted to meet Gupta Ji, na? I did what you asked. Can't back out now. Chalo [Go], take possession of your emeralds. You'll thank me one day.'

* * *

The Delivery

The brothers were enroute to the Gupta residence to take delivery of their goods. Rahim was behind the steering wheel. Ikram was staring out of the window. Sensing his distress, Rahim asked, 'Kya soch rahe ho, bhai-jaan? [What are you thinking, dear brother?]'

'Rahim, what if we can't sell the emeralds after cutting? It's a lot of money—570,000 rupees—and we don't even have jewellery we can pawn to pay SS back. If we default on his payment, we'll be finished,' said Ikram.

Rahim stayed silent. He wasn't sure what he could say to reassure his brother and chose instead to focus on the road ahead. Within a few minutes, their '64 Fiat was making its way up the imposing red gravel driveway of the Gupta residence, which was lined with vibrant hues of bougainvillea flowers in full bloom.

As they walked into the front room of the bungalow, they encountered Muneem, SS's right-hand man. He was busy making notes in a ledger.

'Gupta Ji not home,' said Muneem without looking up as one of the junior staff placed an emerald-laden jute bag in front of them. The bulge in the man's cheek and his red-stained lips showed he was munching on paan (fresh betel leaf lined with areca nut, slaked lime, and catechu). They could smell the aromatic preparation of rosewater, aniseed, cardamom, clove, and mint as Muneem continued ravaging the caffeine-like stimulant.

Rahim pointed towards the emeralds and said, 'Yaar, check kar lein? [Buddy, should we check?]'

Muneem stopped his writing, looked up, frowned at them, spat a generous helping of his brick-red saliva at a nearby plant, and said, 'Check? Check kya karna? Ab toh sauda ho gaya [Why check? Now the deal is done]. Berry [very] good emeralds. Go, go. Joo [You] is berry lucky.'

* * *

The Emeralds

The next morning, Rahim woke with a heavy head. He hadn't been able to sleep all night and resolved to return the emeralds to SS Gupta.

After waiting for two hours, he got an audience with SS and explained their situation. SS stood up, placed his hand on Rahim's shoulder and said, 'Beta, toone maal leeya hai kaam karne ke leeye [Son, you've taken goods to work]. Koi chori toh nahi kee hai [You haven't stolen anything]. Payment ki fikar mat kar, bus kaam pe dhyan rakh [Don't worry about payment, just focus on your work].'

Rahim stopped on his way home and purchased a packet of baking soda, determined to get started on processing the goods. Emeralds are softer than rubies and sapphires, so special care must be taken during the cutting process. Materials from SS Gupta's Gravelotte mine were called batli panna, or bottle emeralds, in Jaipur because of their rich bottle-green colour. But the stones in Rahim's hand looked more like chunks of black and dull-green rocks than precious emeralds, in an assortment of odd shapes. The black-grey coating, which felt like tough skin, was the host rock and concealed underneath was the emerald crystal, which formed 2.9 billion years ago in a rare geological event.

First, the brothers soaked all the emeralds in a solution of warm water, soap, and baking soda. They left the stones in the mixture overnight to remove dirt and grime stuck to the surface.

The next morning, they hand-washed the stones with toothbrushes and clean lukewarm water, careful to ensure they didn't loosen any small breakaway bits. By lunchtime they had washed all 60 kilos of rough emeralds and placed them on durries in their home's open courtyard under the Jaipur sun. As they sat watching some of the green emerald crystals glisten, they felt hopeful.

'Badhiya maal pehle kaat lete hein [Let's cut the good-quality stones first],' suggested Rahim. His brother nodded in response. The burden of Gupta's debt hung over them like a heavy blanket.

* * *

The Sale

Rahim had been waiting in the anteroom of prominent gem merchant, Mukesh Gandhi[1], for almost three hours. In less than a month, the brothers had cut the best quality from the 60 kilos of rough emeralds, which amounted to less than 25 carats of cut and polished emeralds. Rahim had been tasked to sell the stones as soon as possible. Gandhi had an American buyer in town, and since Rahim was a recent college graduate, he was dispatched for the viewing to optimise the chances of success.

It was nearing lunchtime and Rahim's stomach started rumbling, but he didn't want to miss the opportunity to show his wares. Gandhi stepped out of his office. Rahim stood up, thinking his turn had come. But Gandhi ignored him and left. The security guard, taking pity on Rahim, explained that his boss had stepped out for some work and would return soon. Rahim sat down. Just as he was contemplating whether he should use the opportunity to grab a quick lunch, the American buyer emerged from the restroom. They made eye contact, and the buyer asked, 'Are you here to show me emeralds?'

Rahim said, 'Yes, sir. I've been waiting since ten this morning. I have a fantastic parcel of top-quality material.'

'Come on in. Let's see what you've got.'

Delighted at getting unsupervised face time with the international buyer, Rahim followed him inside Gandhi's office. They owed almost 600,000 Indian rupees to SS Gupta. Rahim was hoping to sell the stock he was carrying for 400,000.

By the time Gandhi returned, the deal was done.

'Kaun ho tum? [Who are you?]' asked Gandhi as he entered the room, surprised to see a dealer with his client.

---

1   This name has been changed.

'All good, Mukesh,' the American replied. 'I invited this young man inside, he'd been waiting a long time. Just look at this marvellous parcel of emeralds I just purchased from him.'

Gandhi threw his hands up and said, 'Well, you're buying at your own risk, my friend. I don't know this boy and I cannot take any responsibility for these goods.'

Turning to face Rahim, Gandhi said, 'Beta, mere customer ke saath mere peeth peeche deal karte ho [Son, you did a deal behind my back with my customer].'

Cornered but desperate to close the sale, Rahim said, 'Sir, the gentleman asked me to come inside your office and show him my goods. What was I supposed to do?'

'Yes, he's right, Mukesh. It's my fault. Don't worry; I'll wire the payment to you.'

Rahim left the office with the transaction details written on the back of the buyer's business card. He had a big smile on his face because he had sold the small collection of emeralds for 600,000 Indian rupees. SS typically offered buyers three to six months of credit but with an incentive of a one per cent discount for every month of early settlement. They could now pay SS back within one month of picking up the goods and further improve their profit margin. But he still had to extract the payment from Gandhi, whose parting words to Rahim had been that he should never set foot inside his establishment again.

The next day, Rahim managed to get the cash payment from Gandhi by offering him a two per cent commission.

It was a bold move. But it paid off. A few minutes later, Rahim was on his way to SS's house with a bag full of cash. SS honoured the discount, which totalled 20,000 rupees, and congratulated him on the deal.

As he was leaving, Muneem called out to him. 'See, told joo [you] that joo is very lucky. Good deal, na?'

Rahim turned around, went up to Muneem and said, 'Very good deal, Muneem Ji; thank you for your support.'

'Koi baat nahin [No big deal]; I see it every day, bhai [brother],' said Muneem, walking Rahim towards his car. 'Gupta Ji has made many lakh-pati [millionaires]. Just last week, a guy came to thank him. He used to be a halwai [confectioner] and today he has a lapidary employing 20 cutters. OK, best of luck to joo.'

Rahim smiled. He had one foot in his car as he was getting in. He stopped and, leaning on the open car door, looked at Muneem and said, 'Luck only helps those who work hard, Muneem Ji. Aap ki dua rahee toh firse deal karenge, adaab. [Should your good wishes continue, we'll do business again. Goodbye].'

* * *

1977
Miku Emerald Mine
Kafubu emerald fields
Zambia

'Amon, wake up!'

'What happen?' asked Amon as he opened the door of his shed. It was 2.15 am. Standing before him were two of the Miku Emerald Mine's security officers. They looked frightened.

'Some illegals; they came into the emerald pit, Amon. We run away.'

'Where is Shishiva?' Amon asked, referring to the head of security.

'Amon, he in a big problem. They catch him.'

'You left him there?!'

'They were ten. We only three people. We dash here to get help.'

Amon grabbed his pickaxe, which was resting against the mud wall of his dwelling, and said, 'Wake, everyone. We have to go to him.'

In under two minutes, the entire staff had gathered, their faces filled with fear. They stood with axes and shovels, ready for battle. Amon took the lead. He was just 22 years old, but, as the mine supervisor, they all looked to him for guidance.

'We are only six,' he said. 'They are more than ten. But we'll make a noise like we are 20, OK? Quick, let's go.'

They began running towards the pit, shouting, 'We'll kill you. We cut you alive.'

As they got closer to the emerald deposit, under the full moonlight, Amon saw the bandits take flight.

'Shishiva!' Amon's shriek pierced the air, filled with dread that they had arrived too late.

'Nooooo,' a miner let out a wail of despair.

Shishiva's body—or parts of it—was lying in a pool of blood. The gang had hacked him to pieces. Amon had seen nothing so gruesome in his life. He felt nauseous, but there was no time to waste. Ripples of rage intermingled with heartache were coursing through his body.

'Find them!' he shouted to his companions. 'They kill one of us. We take the fight to them.'

The group spent the next three hours seeking the attackers, but to no avail. At five in the morning, they gave up their search. Amon instructed someone to fetch a few blankets to cover Shishiva's body and severed head.

'What we do now, Amon?'

'We have to tell the police. I'll go to Kalulushi. You all guard Shishiva—and be alert.'

'Amon, go to Mr Audrik's house first. Take him with you to the police.'

'OK. I go now.'

Amon got on his bicycle and rode through the surrounding wilderness like a man possessed. He knew it would take him at least an hour and a half to get to Kalulushi. The image of Shishiva's mutilated corpse flashed before his eyes. His mind started playing scenes from the past. He remembered the day Shishiva had invited him to meet his family in the nearby village. 'I bring you to my home, boss. My wife is a wonderful cook. She will make us a nice dinner and I'll introduce you to my parents.'

Amon's eyes welled up with tears and he momentarily squeezed them shut. He increased his speed. The luxury of stopping for a cry was one he couldn't afford. Another scene flashed before him. 'Boss, I made chicken for everyone's dinner today. Let's eat.' All seven of them would huddle together in one hut and have dinner. The mining company didn't provide any meals. They had to buy or hunt for their meat, and then cook their food. An arduous task after a long day spent mining, but it brought them closer. They were like a band of brothers. The tears returned. *I can't stop*, thought Amon.

The dry branches from the bushes in his path scraped his arms and legs as he leaned down, tearing through them towards his destination. He whispered, 'God, help me, please.' The rays of the morning sun began colouring the sky, bringing light and life. Finally, Amon saw Audrik's house, the general manager of the Miku Mine. The man visited the operation once a week, leaving his instructions for Amon to carry out.

Twenty minutes later, Amon and Audrik were sitting in front of the police captain, outlining the gruesome events of the night.

'This is outrageous, sir,' said Audrik after the captain had written down Amon's statement. 'The police need to provide us protection. And these murderers must be arrested.'

'Mr Audrik, you're from England. Everything is straightforward there. This is Zambia. The situation here is more complicated. These fellows you call illegal miners are not miners from Zambia. They are diggers who come from Congo. I assure you, we'll try our best. But they must have already crossed the border and escaped. We cannot go after them in their country.'

'But how do we function in this environment?' asked Audrik. 'What about our man who was killed? Our staff cannot work in fear.'

'I understand, but you must also take some responsibility. How can you expect three men to safeguard a deposit where anyone can come with a pickaxe and dig out emeralds lying only three metres below the surface?'

Audrik's shoulders slumped, listening to the precarious nature of their circumstances. 'I'll speak to my boss and request more security. It's a vast area, Captain. Our security's not armed. We need your assistance.'

'I'm here for you, Mr Audrik, but you must prepare your people for more raids. They'll keep coming back for emeralds. You want police protection? The order must come from the top, OK?'

* * *

1983
The road to Kitwe
Zambia

Amon Kadichi was sitting in the front seat of the jeep listening intently to the conversation between the two VIPs he was escorting to Kitwe. One was a Zambian bureaucrat, John Mulenga, from Zambian Consolidated Copper Mines Ltd (ZCCM), and the other was SS Gupta. Since Amon was the only employee left in service from the government's Miku emerald mine, he'd been chosen to join them as a guide.

The group was headed to the Kafubu emerald fields of Zambia in the heart of the country's Copperbelt region in the north, not too far from the border with the Democratic Republic of Congo (DRC). From what Amon had been told, the Indian man, SS Gupta, owned a large emerald mine in South Africa and was looking for a similar venture in Zambia.

They'd been on the road for a few hours. Mr Mulenga was talking about the wealth of Zambia and the president's plans to transform the country into one of the strongest economies in Africa.

'Mr Mulenga, your government wants me to invest in emerald mining in Zambia, but the same government has been on an aggressive nationalisation campaign,' said SS.

'What do you mean, Mr Gupta?'

'I read a report that Zambia has one of the richest copper deposits in the world.'

'That's correct; copper mining began in the 1920s in Zambia.'

'And because of it, there has been considerable infrastructure development, giving Zambia an advantage when the country gained independence.'

'True. Some may say we had an edge compared to other newly independent African nations.'

'But despite copper production peaking in 1969, producing 769,000 tonnes, your government nationalised the mines in 1973.'

'It's part of our president's policy of Zambian Humanism. There were multiple reasons for nationalisation.'

SS continued, 'India also nationalised certain industries after independence, but in the last ten years in Zambia, almost 20,000 jobs have been lost in the copper industry due to declining production, which experts say is because of mismanagement of your government-controlled enterprises. Maybe your government will nationalise this emerald venture after a few years? What guarantee is there that I'll get an adequate return on my investment?'

'Mr Gupta, I must congratulate you on doing your homework. But I don't think you have the complete picture. When the government nationalised the mines, we also undertook an extensive skill-development drive and used the income from the mines to promote more projects benefitting the nation.'

'But that caused a drain on income from the mines,' argued SS, 'because of which the government cannot invest in maintaining equipment and so production is dropping.'

'These are challenges the government is aware of and we will soon take corrective steps.'

'Let's come back to emeralds. You haven't answered my question.'

'Mr Gupta, there are no guarantees in life, but perhaps I can answer your question by sharing some historical information about the Kafubu emerald fields.'

After pausing for effect, John Mulenga continued, 'Zambia gained independence in 1964. Two years before that, in 1962, the mining company Rio Tinto, registered an emerald deposit in the Kafubu area. They later handed over this deposit to a private company called Miku Enterprises Ltd, named after the river that runs near the location. This company continued the exploration work Rio Tinto had been doing and started small-scale emerald mining in 1967. Four years later, the Mining Development Corporation of Zambia (MINDECO) took over the mine. The government has been mining emeralds now for more than ten years.'

'So why do you need me? Your team must have a lot of experience.'

'We need you, Mr Gupta, because in ten years we haven't generated any serious income. In fact, in 1978, the government had to close the entire 100-square-kilometre area and stop all private and government operations.'

'Why?'

'Because we were losing control of the area. There were so many people mining there, but no sales were reported. Most were just digging around in informal groups. No one was paying any taxes. We believe the emeralds were being smuggled out of the country. Despite us closing emerald mining in the area, illegal mining and smuggling continues even today. Our security chief at the Miku Mine was killed by a gang of illegal miners. It's been six years since that incident and the police still haven't caught the perpetrators. Amon, who is sitting in front, will confirm this; he was there that night.'

'Yes, sir,' said Amon, turning around to face the back seat. 'It was the most terrible night of my life.'

Ignoring Amon's participation, SS continued questioning Mr Mulenga. 'If the government can't control the situation, then what do you expect from me?'

'We'll bring you into the company as our partner. You bring all your experts, and we can claim a new area for exploration and mining. It will be a fresh operation. I've heard many good things about your mine in South Africa. And the most important part for us is that you have a manufacturing setup in India so you can establish a route to market. We need to start seeing income for the country from our mineral resource.'

'Let's have a look at the deposit first.'

'One more thing, Mr Gupta. There are other interested parties who want to partner with us.'

'Oh?'

'There is a group of emerald dealers and manufacturers from Israel. Have you heard of the Kamakanga Mine?'

'Yes. Small operation. Owned by an Indian?'

'Exactly. Mr Bhagwati Rao. I can introduce you to all of them. Perhaps you can pool your resources and work together.'

'Mmm, let's see. I've always worked alone.'

* * *

Six months had gone by since SS Gupta's first visit to the Kafubu emerald fields with John Mulenga. Instead of competing with other interested parties, SS decided to partner with them to form a company called Hagura, registered in the United Kingdom (UK). The name was derived from the first two letters of Harel, Gupta, and Rao. Benzion (Ben) Harel was the representative for a consortium of emerald manufacturing firms from Israel, who were interested in gaining access to a regular supply of rough emeralds.

Bhagwati Rao was in the right place at the right time and, although he already had an emerald mine in the area (Kamakanga), it was clear from the start that SS Gupta and his team would lead the mining operation. Their experience and domain knowledge were well known, and despite its typically commercial-grade production, Gravelotte was the largest emerald mine in the world, with almost 400 sorters per shift dealing with stone volumes that could fill Olympic-size swimming pools.

SS was standing at an elevated spot that overlooked a vast green expanse known as the Kafubu emerald fields, named after the river that snaked across the area contributing to its lush green vegetation and healthy fish and crocodile population. SS was there with his son Govind, Ben Harel, Bhagwati Rao, and one of the most powerful men in Zambia, Francis Kaunda. Although Francis's official position was chair and chief executive of Zambia Consolidated Copper Mine Ltd (ZCCM), many believed he was also the right-hand man of Kenneth Kaunda (no relation), the president of Zambia.

Francis was representing the government's interest, and the purpose of this visit was to identify the emerald concession for the newly formed joint venture company, Kagem Mining Ltd. Hagura UK had 45 per cent of the shares in Kagem, with the Zambian government holding the 55 per cent majority. However, Hagura UK provided start-up capital and had management control of the mine.

'I love this name, "Kagem",' said Francis. 'The gem of Kafubu; so musical.'

'Or the gem of Kaunda?' said SS.

Francis burst out laughing. 'You are very charming, Mr Gupta. By Kaunda, I'm sure you mean our president, Kenneth Kaunda?'

'Of course,' replied SS with a smile.

'You see those guys over there?' said Francis, handing over his binoculars to SS.

'Yes. Miners?'

'All digging with no licence or permission. They're all over this area. There are two large land banks divided by the Kafubu River. On the west of the river, we have our old Miku Mine and Mr Rao's Kamakanga Mine.'

'Kamakanga has produced fantastic emeralds,' mused Gupta.

'Yes, but so has the Fwaya-Fwaya belt, which lies east of the Kafubu River. That's the most active area right now.'

'What does Fwaya-Fwaya mean?'

'It means "searching, searching". All these emerald pits were first discovered by the local people living in the area. In the seventies, you didn't even have to dig much and you'd get emeralds. So many stones were smuggled from Zambia. Even today, most of the sellers don't know the true value of the emeralds. Imagine how much of our country's wealth has already been stolen and is still being taken away. This is why we're joining hands with you, Mr Gupta. We need to turn this situation around and start generating income from our mineral wealth. There is so much work ahead of us. So, when will your geologist arrive?'

'He'll be here soon.'

'And you think he's the man for the job?'

'He's one of the most experienced persons I know. He discovered the Sandawana emerald deposit in Rhodesia (Zimbabwe) and is currently serving as CEO and chief geologist at my mine in South Africa.'

'Can he fulfil both roles? How will he manage operations in both countries?'

'Our production at Gravelotte is declining and becoming unviable, the quality of the material is commercial, the cost of hard-rock mining high. When I'd purchased the mine, we were moving three tonnes of waste to get one tonne of emerald ore. Now, we must move 20 tonnes of waste to extract one tonne. I'll be selling Gravelotte soon, which is why I am planning to move Bob to Kagem. There he is now.'

Bob (Lawrence) Contat joined the waiting group. He was holding large rolls of geological maps, and trailing him were two staff members who were carrying a table for Bob to spread his papers on.

'Good afternoon. Hope I haven't kept everyone waiting too long?'

'We're happy to wait, Mr Contat,' said Francis Kaunda. 'You're vital to our mining operation.'

'No pressure, Bob,' chimed SS.

'Gentlemen, I've been closely studying the mineralisation zones and correlating my findings with the geological information Mr Kaunda's team has supplied,' said Bob, spreading out one of the large geological maps. The group gathered around the table.

Bob continued, 'In our story, we have two heroes. First is an ancient rock that we geologists call talc magnetite schist or TMS for short. This shaded area on the map marks the location of the TMS, which contains the colouring agent for emeralds, which could be chromium or vanadium. Do you see these thick lines shaded differently? This depicts the location of the second hero in our geological story, pegmatite, which contains the beryllium. Emeralds in the Kafubu area formed 500 million years ago when the pegmatites flowed up from deep in the Earth and intersected with the TMS. The point of intersection is what we call a contact or reaction zone, and this is where we look for emeralds.'

'How many contact zones do we have in this area?' asked Francis.

'We currently know of ten emerald prospects. Five are east of the Kafubu River, which are Libwente, Dabwisa, Fibolele, Fwaya-Fwaya East, and Fwaya-Fwaya West. On the other side of the river, towards the west, we have the Miku deposit at the northernmost point, and, as we move down towards the central section, we hit Mr Rao's Kamakanga Mine, then Pirala to its right, and, further south, are Nikabashila and Mitondo.'

'So, we have five emerald areas to the east of the river and five to the west,' said Francis. 'What do you think? East or west?' he asked SS Gupta.

'Difficult to say,' SS responded. 'Bob, we need to take a decision today. What's your expert opinion? Which area should we focus on for our new mining operation?'

Diagram Description automatically generated

Source: Geological Setting of Zambian Emerald Deposits, A.S. Sliwa and C.A. Nguluwe;

Zimco Limited, Minex Department, P.O. Box 30090, Lusaka (Zambia).

* * *

1985
Jaipur, India

February was SS Gupta's favourite time of the year. Mornings in Jaipur were cool, averaging 13 degrees Celsius. The garden was lush with bright bougainvillea flowers in vibrant hues of magenta, interspersed with orange and white blooms. Despite it only being 7.30 am, the garden was a symphony of sounds. A peacock had perched himself on top of the garden wall and his intermittent calls for a mate were punctuating the gurgling sounds of the water fountain and the musical notes of the Indian mynah bird.

SS enjoyed his morning tea and breakfast in the front garden of his bungalow with a pile of newspapers, a routine he savoured until the merciless summer months drove him indoors. His son, Govind, joined him around 8 am. It was their quiet time to catch up with each other before the brutal routine of the day pulled them apart.

'What's wrong, Papa?' asked Govind as he grabbed a newspaper from the pile on the wooden stool. He'd noticed his father pensively staring into space as he approached their table.

'I don't know how long we can sustain this mining operation in Zambia,' said SS. 'We've been pumping money into that deposit for two years, and other than the odd emerald pocket, we haven't found anything substantial.'

'Did you get another call from Mr Kaunda?'

'No, from Ben, last week. The Israelis are fed up. They've called for a meeting in Geneva to take stock of the situation and decide once and for all.'

'What was he saying?'

'The usual. We've all invested millions and no emeralds have been discovered. Meanwhile, the informal miners are finding something every day.'

'How do they know what the informals are getting?'

'Who do you think is buying from them? It's only these guys. The diggers who infiltrate our concession, or the informal miners in other locations, they sell the rough emeralds in the open market, which the Israelis and other merchants buy,' said SS.

'What's Bob saying?'

'They're mainly concentrating on the Fwaya-Fwaya belt. There are multiple contact zones, and Bob's explored almost all of them. He said the Gravelotte hill was like a chocolate cake with emeralds being the chocolate. All they had to do was slice off large pieces of the hill and crush the ore to extract the emeralds. At Kagem, the emeralds are like chocolate chips hidden inside a big vanilla cake. He needs more equipment, more men, but that would mean drawing down even more funds.'

'Hmm.'

'I told Bob he should finish exploring all the pits. Give this another two to three months.'

'And then?'

'We'll have to talk to the others and cut our losses.'

'We should have picked the area west of the river,' said Govind. 'You think we made a mistake?'

'Kya faida ab aise sochne ka? [What's the point of thinking like that?] Let's see in a few months.'

Govind opened his mouth to say something about visiting Zambia but decided to wait when he saw his mother purposefully marching towards them with two of their house staff carrying trays bearing their breakfast of poha (savoury rice flakes), a plate of sandwiches, and hot jalebis (spiral-shaped traditional deep-fried sugary confectionary). Govind knew he would have to wait till they were in the office to continue the discussion. His father's attention would now be on his breakfast.

Four weeks later Bob was walking Benzvi through the exploration work they had done so far. Benzvi had been employed by the consortium of investors from Israel to assess the potential of emerald production at Kagem. They were both poring over geological maps of the area at Bob's desk when a soft knock at his office door interrupted their discussion.

'Come in,' said Bob.

The mining superintendent, Nicholas Banda, entered. 'Sorry to disturb, bwana [boss],' he said, 'but what's the plan for tomorrow?'

'Nicholas! Just the man I wanted to see. Come and look at this map with us.'

'What are we looking at?'

'This is a geological map of our mining concession. These triangles show all the potential emerald areas, and the crosses next to them show the ones we have already explored.'

'All of them are crossed.'

'Yes, but I was looking at this section, which I hadn't marked. Following the pegmatite and TMS, it looks like a suitable spot to explore.'

'We can't dig there, bwana.'

'Why?' asked Benzvi.

'Is it because it's underwater?' Bob asked Nicholas.

Before Nicholas could reply, Benzvi jumped in and said, 'So? We have water pumps. Your team can start pumping the water out tomorrow. How many days do—?'

Ignoring Benzvi, Nicholas looked at Bob and said, 'We can't, bwana.'

Embarrassed by how Nicholas had interrupted Benzvi, Bob glared at him. The man was sweating and seemed visibly agitated. 'Nicholas, Mr Benzvi was trying to say something when you interrupted him. Please apologise.' After Nicholas apologised, Bob said, in a softer tone, 'What's the real problem?'

'How to say, bwana? That area is cursed. None of the workers will dig there.'

The last thing I need right now, thought Bob. Having worked all his life as a geologist and miner in Africa, he knew this was a delicate matter that had to be taken seriously.

'Can you explain to me why it's cursed?'

'Before Kagem and even before the Miku Mine, people stop digging there. Anyone who dig there, something terrible happens to him or to someone in his family.'

'Are there emeralds there?'

'Nobody know, boss, because no digging long time.'

'Can't we get someone to lift the curse?' Benzvi offered.

'I heard that some diggers, long time ago, try, boss. One of them, his grandmother, was a sangoma [traditional healer]. But it don't work. That guy he was bitten by a deadly snake the next day! He die instantly. The other guy he was eaten by a crocodile.'

'But that could easily happen whether or not we dig there,' continued Bob.

'It's the curse I tell you! That area is possessed by an evil spirit.'

'Nicholas, you're a Christian man, like me. How can you believe in this?'

'Jesus Christ is good, boss, but we live in Zambia. We're surrounded by spirits of the land, animals, everything around us, and spirits of our ancestors. They guide our lives. We have to live in harmony with everyone.'

'Nicholas, I'm going to be honest with you. Mr Benzvi is in Kagem representing the investors because we have exhausted all options. We need a miracle—or the mine will close. I've been studying these maps and the chemical analysis from the soil samples. Everything in my gut is telling me we need to drain that reservoir and dig. It's our last option. What should we do?'

Both men stared at each other in silence. Then Nicholas said, 'One idea, boss. I talk to the village chief.'

'What will he do?' asked Benzvi.

'He'll drive away the evil spirit.'

'How will he do that?' Benzvi asked.

Bob was familiar with traditional rituals he had seen conducted at mines across Southern Africa, especially when miners were about to start work on a new pocket. He started explaining, 'The village chief is like royalty. The belief is that he carries within him the knowledge of his ancestors. Through a special ceremony, he will speak on our behalf to his ancestors. The healer accompanies him in the ritual, gives offerings, and conducts the ceremony.'

'What offerings?' Benzvi asked Bob, looking a bit worried.

Nicholas jumped in, 'Locally brewed beer, water, blood of—'

'Blood?! I don't think—' said Benzvi.

'No, boss. I explain everything. Then, you decide.'

'OK, go on then.'

'The chief will come to the pit with the healer. They start by first singing some praises to the spirit. Then, the healer will spread limestone powder around the area we going to mine. Next, a white chicken is slaughtered, and its blood is spread around the pit, like an offering.'

'Chicken?'

'Yes! Only chicken, boss. You eat chicken every day. How you think he come to your plate?'

'Fair enough. Go on.'

'After the chicken, he offers locally brewed beer in a dried-up gourd cup. Finally, an offering of water is done to the spirits. Sometimes they mix the water with the beer, sometimes they carry water in a clay pot. Can change a bit.'

'That's fine, Nicholas. I think Mr Benzvi has understood.'

'Wait! You didn't hear the most important part.'

Bob could see Nicholas was really enjoying relaying the ceremony. He let him carry on.

'They will do traditional chanting and beat their drums, singing praises of the spirits and requesting the chief's ancestors to help drive away any evil from the land and bring prosperity.'

'How long will this take?' asked Benzvi.

'At least an hour or an hour and a half. We also have to arrange food and drinks for some of the community members who will join in, and our mine staff who attend.'

'Fine. Get going on this ritual, immediately. I want your team to start mining the pit within the next 48 to 72 hours.'

* * *

Later that week
Gupta residence
Jaipur, India

'Any news from Bob?' Govind asked his father at breakfast.

'Only to tell me they did some traditional ceremony to drive away evil spirits from a reservoir he wanted to drain and mine.'

'Oh God. He's resorted to spiritual healers now?' asked Govind.

'We also worship Lord Ganesh [Hindu elephant god] before starting a new venture. They have their own way. A little divine intervention doesn't hurt.'

'Whatever you say, Papa. I just find it terribly worrying that someone like Bob, a geologist, a man of science, is organising cleansing ceremonies.'

The housekeeper, running towards the duo from the bungalow, stopped SS from defending his friend.

'Saab. Jambia se fone aya hai [Sir, call from Zambia].'

SS discarded his newspaper and stood up.

'I'm coming with you,' announced Govind, dashing indoors after his father.

'Hello? Bob?' said SS.

'We found them, SS,' said Bob.

'Found what?'

'What else? Emeralds! Come here and see the treasure we've uncovered.'

'How's the colour?'

'I've never seen rough emeralds like this in Africa. Perfect hexagonal form. Well saturated deep green colour. Many are three inches long, and others are two inches and less, but all hexagonal.'

'And what about the crystal quality?'

'Top-notch, SS. Like you guys say, paanidaar.'

SS laughed at Bob's use of the traditional term merchants used in Jaipur to describe translucent emeralds that exhibited superb crystal quality radiating light, as if full of water.

'In your estimation, what would be the value?'

'I'm a geologist, not a merchant. Here, talk to Benzvi. He's been inspecting the stones since they came out of the ground.'

'SS! Bloody brilliant lot of stones we found,' said Benzvi, grabbing the phone from Bob.

'Well done. Govind and I are getting on the next flight to be with you all at the mine.'

'Great. I'm going to call Harel and the others. We need to celebrate!'

'What's the rough estimate of value?' asked SS.

'By the time you get here, I can give you a better idea, but based on what I've seen in my hands, and what's still embedded in the host rock, perhaps four million US dollars on the conservative side and five million on the higher end.'

'Fantastic.'

'But we have a problem,' Benzvi said as he lowered his voice.

'What?'

'Security. Even when we weren't finding emeralds, the security team was dealing with incursions daily. I don't know what's going to happen now. News must have already spread about this discovery.'

'What about the Zambian police protection?'

'Not enough. Our security team here are all local staff who are not well trained.'

'What do you suggest?'

'A friend of mine owns a private security firm in Israel. Let's hire them to secure the area. They can also train our team. I already spoke to the others, and they all agree.'

'Hmm. They'll carry weapons. We'll need special permission from the government.'

'I'm here for a few weeks. I'll go meet Rao. He'll agree if he doesn't have to put in any more money. You must speak with Francis.'

Author's Note

This story is based on actual events as relayed to the author by the late Shiv Shankar Gupta in 2020, his son, Govind Gupta in 2021, and his grandson, Akshat Gupta in 2021. Additional interviews were also conducted with Mr Rahim Ullah in 2021, and Dr Sixtus Mulenga, Chairman Kagem Mining Ltd. Fictional elements, characters, scenes, and dialogue have been included to aid narration.

When Shiv Shankar Gupta first started bringing rough emeralds to Jaipur in the early sixties, the city had 20 emerald manufacturing firms and 200 emerald cutters. Many lapidaries still used manually operated faceting wheels. His efforts in importing faceting machines, supporting buyers like Rahim Ullah, and providing goods on consignment, played a pivotal role in expanding the emerald manufacturing sector in India. It is estimated that approximately 90 per cent of Zambian emeralds are now cut and polished in Jaipur.

As per industry sources, there are approximately 200 companies involved in organised manufacturing and trading of emeralds on a regular basis. Jaipur is also home to a large cottage industry of lapidaries that have mush-roomed because of a regular supply of rough emeralds from the Gravelotte and Kagem mines. According to the Gem and Jewellery Export Promotion Council (GJEPC), around 200,000 to 250,000 individuals are working in the emerald manufacturing and trading industry in Jaipur. A reduced figure because of demonetisation of the Indian currency in 2016, followed by the Covid-19 pandemic.

The discovery of the emerald pocket in 1985 at Kagem led to further development of the deposit by Hagura. By 1986-87, when an influx of capital was required, BD Rao opted to sell his shares to his partners and exit the venture.

When Kagem Mining Limited was formed, management control had been with Hagura UK. In 1990, the government of Zambia assumed control. This ushered in an era of operational and financial difficulties, including 12 months of frozen production. In 1996, Hagura UK regained management control, which gave it the authority to expand the team, invest in equipment, and hire geologists and mining engineers. Bob Contat had retired, but the Gupta family recruited Dr García, an experienced Spanish geologist, to lead the operation. By this time, the consortium from Israel had sold its shares to the Gupta family. Govind Gupta was now the executive director of Kagem Mining Limited and committed to rebuilding the mine.

Rough emerald sorters at the Gravelotte emerald mine in South Africa (1970s). Photo credit: Akshat Gupta.

Shiv Shankar (SS) Gupta relaxing in his garden in Jaipur, India (1970s). Photo credit: Akshat Gupta.

The Emerald Theft

**April 2000
Tuesday, 6.00 pm
Conference office
Kagem emerald mine
Zambia**

'ZAMBIAN EMERALDS are formed because of a chemical reaction between two rock types, pegmatite, and TMS or talc magnetite schist,' said Jawahar Dey at a meeting his boss, Dr Santos García, chief geologist of the Kagem emerald mine, had organised.

Superintendents, geologists, and managers from various departments gathered in front of Dey. The mine's last emerald auction had taken place four months ago, and the dwindling revenue from that sale was causing concern. With the next auction only weeks away, and dismal emerald production, stress levels at the mine were high. Dr García was hoping a better understanding of emerald geology may help improve morale.

Dey continued, 'The pegmatite contains beryllium and the TMS has trace elements like chromium or vanadium, which are responsible for an emerald's green colour. Five hundred million years ago, hydrothermal activity underneath the Earth's surface pushed the pegmatites up and caused chromium to go into beryl, giving birth to a rough-emerald crystal. Where that pegmatite rock intrudes into the TMS rock is what we call a reaction zone, where the emeralds might grow as crystals. Any questions?'

'Bwana [boss],' said one of the mine superintendents, raising his hand. 'I don't understand. We're mining in all these reaction zones you and Dr García have marked. If these are the places where this reaction happen like you say, where emeralds grow, why can't we find any emeralds?'

'Excellent question. A contact or reaction zone is no guarantee of emeralds. It also depends on the nature of the interaction between these ancient rocks. If it's too quick with sudden heating and cooling, then it's unproductive. No emeralds.' He paused and looked around the room. Blank faces stared back. 'Imagine TMS and pegmatite are husband and wife,' he stated, and after a second of silence, everyone burst out laughing. Dey waited for them to quiet down and continued. 'Let me explain. Each time a husband and wife are intimate, there is a chemical reaction, but the act alone doesn't mean they will produce children, similarly—'

'I have opposite problem, bwana,' said the wash plant superintendent, interrupting Dey's lecture. 'I produce children every time.' More laughter and hooting ensued.

'You saying you only been with your wife five times?!' a voice echoed from the back, causing another round of teasing and shouting.

Dey exchanged a smile with Dr García. The energy in the room seemed lighter. The harsh reality of possibly being unemployed in a few months was momentarily forgotten. Stepping forward, Dey raised his voice to regain control of the gathering.

'Similarly with emeralds, there are no guarantees. We can observe the mineralisation zones, follow the science, but till we mine, we don't really know whether we'll find emeralds. Another example, sometimes we see thick clouds but no rain. Like this, in certain sections of the mine we can see the pegmatite and the TMS but may find emeralds further away from that reaction zone.'

'Is this why we dig in many places, bwana?'

'Exactly. If we operate at 10 to 12 potential locations, we may hit one or two rich emerald pockets.' After making a few more points, Dey handed over to Dr García to explain further and outline the plan for the next day.

He went and sat next to Navin Thorgalmath, a senior geologist and an integral member of his team. The Kagem emerald mine was a joint venture between the Zambian government and a consortium of industry professionals under a company called Hagura. Most of the staff were Zambian with a few expatriates. Dey and his team of geologists had been recruited by Hagura in 1997 as part of a larger plan to overhaul the mine, which was stagnating because of pilferage, low production, lack of adequate funds, and operational issues. Three years had now passed.

Kagem was an open-pit operation where miners had to remove overburden waste rock to access the emerald ore. 'Only one out of 100 trucks carrying waste may contain material from the reaction zone or run-of-mine (ROM), Navin,' Dey had explained, 'after washing, sorting, and grading, maybe 35 to 40 kilograms could be commercial-quality emeralds with only 1,000 grams of premium quality.'

When Dey joined, the mine had been in a state of disarray, with the crew working under dangerously high walls. The mining pits looked more like large wells, which flooded during the rainy season. Informal staff alliances were undermining management control, and waste management and exploration were practically non-existent.

'They're just digging holes without planning,' Dey had explained during Navin's induction training. 'The pit crew keep shifting the same waste ore from one place to another, duplicating their work and increasing the cost of operations.'

Under Dr García's guidance, Dey and his group of geologists refined procedures to improve exploration, production, and plug leakages. They created a team template for every active mining point, which comprised a geologist, four to five chisel men, two to three shovel men, and one unarmed Kagem security officer.

Dey would rearrange the mining crew into new teams every Monday morning. This way, no one knew which part of the concession they would mine and with whom; Dey hoped this tactic would inhibit collusion between miners and security personnel. Each geologist on the mining team had a dual role—documenting emerald ore production and monitoring the extraction process. Dr García conducted a daily debriefing session to review the geology team's observations and plan work for the next day.

* * *

Wednesday, 2.00 pm
Fwaya-Fwaya mine pit
Kagem emerald mine
Zambia

Weather's perfect, thought Navin, as he took a deep breath. An earthy fragrance filled the air as water from the rocks in the reaction zone[1] intermingled with the mineral-rich soil. After last night's presentation, the team felt energised. With the next auction only three weeks away, pressure was high. Navin was busy making notes when he sensed the energy shift in the mining pit. He looked up. The chisel men had stopped working. *Something's happening*, he thought as he put aside his notepad and approached the miners.

'Bwana, see what we find!' exclaimed one miner.

The man held out a rough emerald, two inches long. Navin took it from his hand and began wiping away dirt stuck to the surface of the stone. He

1   Zambian emeralds were formed 500 million years ago when two rocks – pegmatite (containing beryl) and talc magnetite schist (TMS) containing chromium/vanadium – intersected.

197

scooped water from a nearby puddle to further clean the emerald and held it up for closer inspection. The stone had a perfect hexagonal form, uncommon with most Zambian emeralds. A layer of black-grey schist rock blanketed the emerald, which some miners called its outer skin.

'Show me where you found it,' said Navin, handing over the gem to the security officer for safekeeping as he moved towards the chisel men.

The uneven hard rocks gave way to soft mica-laden soil that sparkled as Navin approached the reaction zone.

'We find big emerald pocket, bwana,' said a chisel man.

Navin saw green gems peeking from the broken grey floor. He turned around and saw that the miners were celebrating with an impromptu dance, all smiles and laughter. Their enthusiasm was infectious, and Navin allowed himself a quick smile. But he had to maintain a sense of decorum. 'Back to work,' he said, waving the chisel men to the emerald pocket. 'More emeralds waiting to be taken out.'

'That emerald looked good,' said the security officer.

'We'll only know once we've cleaned it in the D-Zone,' said Navin, taking the crystal back.

Dey and his team would wrap exceptional emerald crystals in paper, for extra protection, before depositing them in a secure red metal box. The red containers bearing a single-use security number tag would go directly to the D-Zone (sort house) where the emerald crystals would be cleaned and sorted to prepare them for auction. After Navin had secured the stone, he radioed for more production, or run-of-mine (ROM), boxes. A few seconds later, he noticed miners from the neighbouring pit looking over. They'd heard the request over the radio. News of their find rippled through the concession. Navin and his team would have to undergo an extra security check.

By 5.30 pm, the emerald pocket was mined out. Navin watched the last truck take ore surrounding the production point, the run-of-mine (ROM) ore, to the wash plant where another group would crush, clean, and hand-pick more emeralds from the broken rocks, placing them in red ROM boxes for onward transport to the D-Zone. Navin instructed the team to close the production point for the day. He was eager to report the discovery to his supervisors.

* * *

Dr García and Jawahar Dey stood at a small white table in the sort house. They were watching the supervisor unlock the red ROM box containing the prized emerald crystal. Only a select few had access to the secure location where the final sorting and grading of rough emeralds was done. With caution Dr García reached inside the metal box and began unwrapping the precious stone, close to the centre of the table.

'What a perfectly formed hexagonal emerald,' said Dey, commenting on the stone's shape.

'Dey, let's get all this schist covering removed; only then will we know what we have,' said Dr García.

Dey spent the next hour watching the sort house team chip away the black schist from the rough emerald, using various handheld tools such as pliers and knives. They worked slowly to ensure they didn't apply too much pressure, which might break or crack the crystal.

Once the stone was clean, Dey brought it back to Dr García. 'It looks like a fine specimen,' he said, placing it in the geologist's hands.

Dr García observed aloud, while feeling the emerald, 'Beautiful hexagonal crystal with soft edges and natural termination.' He brought the gem near the table lamp and pointed out the sharp edges on the other end. Picking up a magnifying glass, he took a closer look. 'It looks like someone broke it here.'

'Broke it? You mean on purpose?' said Dey, taking the stone from Dr García.

The emerald was eye clean, extremely rare as most emeralds contained inclusions which looked like moss or soil trapped inside, which the trade called the garden inside an emerald. Lapidaries would either cut away the included parts or treat the emerald crystal with oil or resin to improve its clarity and lustre. Dey couldn't spot a single inclusion inside the rough Zambian emerald. The glass-like crystal glistened in the afternoon sun, displaying a deep green hue. Dey's hands trembled as his senses awakened to the treasure he was holding. One end of the hexagonal crystal looked broken.

'Maybe the other half's in the ROM coming from the wash plant?' said Dey handing the stone back to Dr García.

'Could be.' Dr García placed the emerald crystal on a sheet of paper and started tracing its shape. Once he was done, he handed the sheet to Dey. 'We need to recover the other half, which may be a small emerald crystal that fits this broken end.'

'Like a puzzle?'

'Exactly.'

'I'll go outside and find Navin. He must have sent the remaining ore to the wash plant. We'll start our search there and then expand to the rest of the material.'

'Dey, also alert security. Extra dogs in the pit tonight, and no one leaves camp tomorrow without a physical security check.'

* * *

8.00 pm
Dr García's bungalow
Mukuba village
Kitwe, Zambia

Jawahar Dey was sitting in the drawing room and flipping through a book of minerals. Dr García was cooking their dinner in the kitchen, assisted by Tembo, the housekeeper. When Dey joined Kagem three years ago, Dr García had suggested he stay with him in the 6,000-square-foot, five-bedroom bungalow provided by the company. The house came with vast gardens, which Dr García put to good use growing fruits and vegetables such as avocado, blueberries, tomatoes, bananas, guava, and mangoes. The plan from the start had been that Dey would eventually replace him as chief geologist and move his family to the bungalow.

'What do you make of this missing emerald business?' said Dr García, as he joined Dey in the drawing room and poured himself a glass of wine.

'I was just thinking about that. If there is another piece, is it still at the mine or has it already been taken out?'

'Million-dollar question. Were you satisfied with the security check?'

'Absolutely. The GM and I supervised the exit search. Plus, every single box and drawer was checked at the wash plant. Nothing.'

Both men sat in silence until Tembo came over and announced supper.

Dr García and Dey had a fixed routine. Like the rest of the crew, they stayed at the mine during the week. On Friday, they would leave camp around 1 pm and Dr García would unwind by preparing dinner, which was usually soup, roast chicken, fish, vegetables from the garden, potatoes, and freshly baked bread, with his signature caramel custard for dessert. The next morning, they would visit the supermarket, pick up supplies for the days ahead, and return to Kagem. Saturday and Sunday would be dedicated to exploration activities, which they undertook with a small team of geologists, miners, and a drilling team.

They were halfway through their meal when the house phone rang in the drawing room. A few seconds later, Tembo entered the dining room and informed Dr García that he had an urgent call. The doctor got up from his seat, grumbling at being interrupted during dinner.

He returned soon after and said, 'Dey, you carry on. I need to step out for a few minutes.'

'Should I join you?'

'No, it's OK. Short drive. I'll be back soon.'

Dey went back to his dinner, but, with only the ticking of the wall clock to keep him company, he finished quickly.

'Who was that on the phone?' Dey asked Tembo as he cleared the table.

'Don't know, bwana. A Zambian man wanted to speak with Doctor. He said it was urgent.'

'Hmm, please put some chicken and vegetables in the oven for Doctor. I'll have my dessert in the drawing room.'

An hour had gone by. Dey had polished off his portion of the caramel custard. His plate lay discarded on the side table by the sofa where he had dozed off reading the morning paper. The sound of the car door closing awoke him.

'You're back, I was just—' Dey said but stopped when he noticed Dr García's expression.

'Should I heat your dinner, bwana?' Tembo enquired as he took Dr García's coat.

'I've lost my appetite,' responded Dr García. He walked past them to the bar trolley, where he helped himself to a generous pour of whiskey.

Dey gestured for the housekeeper to leave and closed the drawing room door. 'What's wrong?' he asked.

Dr García took another sip of his drink and sat down in his favourite lounge chair. 'I saw the other half of our emerald.'

'What!' said Dey, sitting down next to him. 'Are you sure?'

'Unfortunately, I am. It's been stolen from our mine. My contact showed it to me as a courtesy. The men who took it, I don't know who they are, want to sell it in the open market this weekend.'

'But how—'

'It's smaller than our half of the stone but the exact same colour. On one side the edges are soft. On the other, sharp like it's been broken off. It's the missing piece.'

'We checked every single person who left the mine today. Even if they stole the other half of the emerald crystal, how did they get it out of the mine?' said Dey. He stood up and started pacing the room, going over the events of the day in his mind. 'We must have missed something.'

Dr García pounded his left fist on the side table in anger.

'We need to find the culprits, Dey. They are taking money from our pocket.'

* * *

One week later
Friday, 10.30 am
Fwaya-Fwaya pit
Kagem emerald mine

Navin pretended to take notes as he had been instructed by Dr García, who had said, 'Navin, the best way to discover the leak is to act normal.'

Dey purposely reported late to work on Monday, so Dr García could repeat the crew assignments of the previous week. Four days passed with no unusual sightings.

'The theft may happen tomorrow because everyone returns to Kitwe for the weekend,' Dey had suggested at the debrief meeting the previous evening.

How did they do it? thought Navin, observing the crew's movements from behind his sunglasses.

Miners needed to constantly de-water the aquiferous reaction zone to extract emeralds. The water pump was clearing the pit for the chisel men, its motor rattling as the inlet pipe sucked the water out. Miners shovelled ore for the excavator to collect. Security was watching both groups. Navin's ears perked up as he heard a metallic clanking sound, distinct from the surrounding noise. His eyes sought the noise. The water pump operator had tripped on a rock and dropped the inlet pipe he was carrying.

'Stop!' yelled Navin. In three large strides, he'd reached the man.

'Sorry, bwana; I'll be more careful with the equipment.'

Navin pointed to where one joint had given way. 'What's this?' he asked, kneeling to touch the black ooze dripping out.

'Dirty water from the pit, bwana,' the man explained.

'Search the pipe. Take all the water out,' Navin instructed security.

* * *

Two months later
GM's office
Kagem emerald mine

Dey couldn't believe what he was hearing. When he'd reported for work that morning, the security team had informed him that Mittal, the general manager, had asked to see him in his office. On entering, Dey had been surprised to see Bhattacharya, Kagem's admin officer also waiting for him.

'You're firing Navin?' exclaimed Dey.

'I don't have a choice. Security found emerald fragments in his gumboot,' said Bhattacharya.

'It's a setup. The mine workers have been gunning for him since he caught that group stealing emeralds. Navin's the one who discovered how the pump man was scooping small emerald crystals from the floor of the mining pit and stuffing them in the inlet pipe once he had finished de-watering the area,' Dey said, throwing his hands up in the air. 'We upgraded our security procedures because of his efforts.'

Mittal said, 'Why didn't he empty his boots like we've instructed everyone to do before the security checkpoint?'

'He told me he forgot,' said Dey. 'He wasn't even supposed to be working. It was his rest day.'

'Then why was he at the wash plant?'

'It's my fault,' said Dey. 'I asked him to work because we were short-staffed.'

In the last two months Navin had thwarted many attempts to steal emeralds from the mining pit, each time leaving the would-be thieves frustrated and empty-handed. But the current situation was a web of complexities. Dey looked at Bhattacharya, and said, 'The value of the emerald fragments found in Navin's boot is probably less than a dollar. Can't we let him off with a warning?'

'You all know that company policy is clear in such matters,' said Bhattacharya. 'If anyone is found with emeralds on their person, it's immediate termination. The workers saw the emerald grains fall out of Navin's boot. How can we ignore this?'

'But this was more accidental than intentional,' said Dey.

'Dey, in the last two months we've dismissed more than six people for the same reason. Immediate termination. No appeals. We can't prove Navin's intentions.'

For a few seconds, Dey and Bhattacharya just glared at each other. Dey broke the silence. 'If it's not accidental, then Navin's being framed. He's responsible for catching almost all of the recent pilferage attempts. Whoever's behind these is clearly worried. They want him out.' Dey looked at Mittal. 'He's innocent.'

'I understand your frustration, Dey. We don't want to fire him, but our hands are tied. I'll request the board let him resign and give him a good recommendation letter.'

Rough Zambian emerald crystal embedded in the host rock. Photo credit: Gemfields.

A rough Zambian emerald crystal still embedded in the host rock. Photo credit: Gemfields.

A typical Zambian emerald production point inside one of the mining pits at the Kagem emerald mine. Photo credit: Gemfields.

Author's Note

This story is based on actual events as relayed to the author by Jawahar Dey, who worked at Kagem Mining Limited for more than 11 years. Minor fictional elements have been included for scene setting, and dialogue.

Even though the emerald grains found in Navin Thorgalmath's gumboot had insignificant value in the market, he was forced to resign from the Kagem mine. Navin was one of Kagem's most vigilant geologists. Dey was extremely upset that he was unable to help him stay.

The incident was one of many where stakeholders in the Kagem emerald mine disagreed. Investors represented by Hagura felt they had no control over an operation in which they had invested millions. Increased incidents of pilferage and deteriorating conditions at the mine led Hagura to file a case against the Zambian government in the UK courts. Both parties eventually came to a settlement, which resulted in the government divesting 30 per cent of their stake, giving Hagura the controlling interest of 75 per cent in 2005.

After leaving Kagem, Navin joined a tourmaline mining operation located near Zambia's border with the Democratic Republic of Congo (DRC). Dey and Navin remained good friends, with Navin seeking his advice and blessings when he got married. In a tragic turn of events, Navin died of malaria six months after his marriage.

Dey was further disheartened to hear of Dr García's death in 2001 as he held him in high regard and considered Dr García as a father figure.

During Dey's tenure, he and his team introduced new procedures, which are still in use today. He fondly recalls Sen, Shekhawat, Terni, Navin, Sunil, Dadich, Aron, Alex, and others who built systematic exploration and production plans to meet auction targets every quarter. Dey's plan of an 80:20 production ratio varied with seasons: shallow-level production areas for the rainy season and deeper levels for the dry seasons.

During his more than 11 years at Kagem, the mine conducted 33 rough-emerald auctions. He worked closely with a team of Indian and Zambian professionals, some of whom are still with Kagem. Their greatest achievement was the opening of the F10 pit, which generated 31 truckloads of reaction zone material in one week, feeding multiple auctions held by Kagem. Over time, Dey was promoted to manager and later deputy general manager for Kagem.

Following his departure from Kagem in 2007, Dey worked on projects involving rubellite, gold, and sapphires in Madagascar. He then moved north to work in Kenya for a year at a ruby mine. After working on a feasibility study in Zimbabwe on the Sandawana emerald deposit, Dey moved to Brazil to undertake projects related to manganese, gold, and emeralds. He works as an independent consultant and, in recent years, has executed feasibility studies and projects in Ethiopia, Rwanda, Zambia, and Angola.

New Heat

30th May 2002
American Gem Trade Association (AGTA)
Gem Testing Centre (GTC)
New York, USA

KEN SCARRATT couldn't believe the words he was reading. *Is this a prank?* he wondered. *Should I report it to the police?* Only moments before, he'd congratulated himself for clearing most of his unread emails. The one in front of him had arrived seconds before his planned return to the lab. 'If only I'd left my desk a few moments earlier,' he lamented, 'I'd have been in the lab right now, happy as a clam, lost in the microscopic world of minerals instead of reading these horrible words.'

As director of AGTA's Gem Testing Centre (GTC) in New York, his duties extended beyond the scientific to the managerial. But there was nothing in Ken's job description about dealing with something of this sort. The email was blunt—three sentences, direct and to the point. *May need something stronger than coffee*, he thought as he placed his empty espresso cup on the table and picked up the telephone receiver to call his friend and industry colleague Tom Moses at the Gemological Institute of America (GIA).

'Tom, I just got an email, which I think is a death threat.'

'Are you serious? What does it say? Who sent it?'

'The email address is gibberish. Probably fake. Grammar's terrible. Basically says we're ruining the gem business, and if we return to Bangkok, we'll be shot in the head by a motorcycle assassin.' Not hearing a sound from the other end of the receiver, Ken said, 'Hello? Tom? You heard that, right?'

'I'm here, yes. Heard that. Can't believe it, Ken. They must be desperate.'

'Maybe they found out about our meeting next week in Bangkok. What do you want to do now? Should we still go?'

* * *

Six months earlier
2001
Bangkok, Thailand

Sitting in the gem and jewellery district of Bangkok, Lorenzo[1] felt like a king. Sapphires in every imaginable colour glimmered on the large, white desk in front of him. He'd known Tai[2], the owner of Vault Gems[3], for years. They'd both started out in the industry around the same time and met at a trade show. Despite numerous buying trips to Vault Gems, and Thailand, each time Tai's staff disappeared inside the stainless-steel safe room to find more gems, Lorenzo felt a familiar sense of delight.

The end-to-end transparent glass wall towards his left flooded the office with natural light from the December sun. *This moment, right now, is just perfect*, he thought, watching the sun and the fast-moving clouds play peek-a-boo with the mineral confections in front of him.

With one swift twist of his wrist, Tai opened and placed yet another mangosteen on Lorenzo's plate. The white flesh of the exotic fruit seemed to have been poured into a voluptuous mould of dark purplish-pink fibres and soft skin. *I need to stop eating these*, Lorenzo thought, biting into his fifth one. As the sweet and sour juice awakened his jet-lagged taste buds, Lorenzo's eyes travelled to the carved wooden bookshelf behind Tai's enormous desk that extended from one end of the wall to the other.

Besides an impressive collection of books on gems and minerals, a double-dragon ruby carving sat in the middle of the shelf, flanked by a jade sculpture of a goddess, and a gold-plated Thai wooden barge studded with colourful stones. The room was an exclusive space reserved for Tai's top customers and close industry friends. The levels below housed the company's lapidary and a large showroom for tourists. Wiping his mangosteen-stained fingertips on the cool wet towel Tai offered, Lorenzo leaned over and asked in a hushed tone, 'Tai, who's the guy sitting towards the back of the room inspecting stones? May I look at those after he's done?'

'Sure, sure. That's Ken Scarratt; he's the director of AGTA's Gem Testing Centre in New York.'

'Wow,' said Lorenzo, looking impressed. 'What's he doing here?'

'Selecting sapphires for his research. I got a few pastel-coloured ones from Burma.'

---

1 This name has been changed.
2 This name has been changed.
3 This name has been changed.

'Nice. Are they heated? Is his research related to treatments?'

'No, they're untreated. Ken's been studying colour distribution in natural padparadscha sapphires for more than nine months,' said Tai, referring to the rare orange-pink sapphires.

'Really? You know, I've always been fascinated by that range of colour. Tell me, what according to you is the ideal padparadscha hue?'

'Ha! Now that's a million-dollar question. Did you know that over 43 different articles have been published, each with differing views on what's a pure padparadscha colour? Mostly the industry follows the GIA definition, which limits the colour range from light to medium tones of pinkish-orange to orangey-pink hues. Globally, one of the top, if not the largest, market for these goods right now is Japan. They're crazy for padparadscha sapphires—can't get enough.'

'Hmm, that's probably why the stones are so pricey now. The last time I tried buying a padparadscha, the guy quoted me eight times the price of a fancy orange sapphire!'

'He should have asked for more,' teased Tai. 'It's the most difficult stone to cut. First, we have to find the right colour combination in a rough sapphire crystal. Then, we must cut it to deliver the perfect blend of pink and orange while making sure you don't remove too much weight. Remember, a slight slip of the hand could cause a dramatic colour shift, rendering a report of "fancy orange sapphire" instead of a "padparadscha". Poof! the premium value is gone.'

'On my last buying trip to Sri Lanka, a dealer told me padparadscha means "lotus" in Singhalese and only sapphires from Sri Lanka should be termed as padparadscha,' said Lorenzo.

'This is a never-ending debate. Same story with paraíba tourmaline,' said Tai. 'When they were first discovered in Nigeria, followed by Mozambique, the Brazilians didn't want them to be called paraíba,' explained Tai.

'I prefer to focus on the beauty of the stone,' he continued. 'As you know, that's what will hold value. Tell you what: a trader's waiting downstairs to show me heated padparadscha sapphires from Madagascar,' he said, asking his staff to invite the trader up. 'Why don't we have a look? It'll give you a good sense of my explanation on colour.'

The man entered, greeting them in the traditional Thai style with folded hands. Tai reciprocated, asking him in Thai to show them what he'd brought. The trader swung into action, pulling out boxes and plastic pouches. Within minutes Vault Gem's sapphire stock had been set aside, and the table was covered by hundreds of gems that looked like sunset candies ranging from soft to intense pinkish-orange hues. Turning over one of the boxes, Lorenzo read the description—PS (NH)—and asked Tai what NH meant. He knew PS stood for padparadscha sapphire, but the heated stones were usually denoted as (H).

After conferring with the trader, Tai replied, 'He says NH means "new heat". It's a new way to heat treat sapphires in Chanthaburi to improve the gem's clarity, lustre, and intensify its colour. To be honest, I've never heard of it.'

Turning over another box, Lorenzo gestured towards the back of the room and whispered to Tai, 'Why don't we check with the expert?'

Tai nodded and called out, 'Hey, Ken! What do you make of these padparadscha sapphires?'

Ken looked up from his post by the window. It took him a few seconds to pull his concentration away from his work and focus on the gems Tai was holding up. 'Hmm, that's interesting. Quite a lot of them.' Not wanting to leave the treasure he was evaluating; he asked the dealer to bring a few stones over to him. Accepting a strip of gems from his hand, Ken observed, 'They're packed in PVC blister strips, like chewing gum. Is that normal?'

* * *

5th December 2001
Gemmological Association of All Japan (GAAJ)
Tokyo
Japan

The chaos of Bangkok was worlds apart from the glass fishbowl that was Director Junko Shida's office at the Gemmological Association of All Japan (GAAJ) in Tokyo. Akito looked up from his microscope at his workstation on the lab floor and watched her pace up and down in deep thought. *She's worried about these sapphires*, he thought.

In the last two months, the lab had issued more than 30,000 reports for heated padparadscha sapphires worth millions of dollars, which given the rarity of the colour was an unusually high number. During an internal discussion, Akito, along with other gemmologists, had described the inclusions inside the gems as looking somewhat pulverised, as if they had undergone heating at extremely high temperatures. The lab handled over a thousand gem submissions daily, with staff working under immense pressure for speedy turnarounds. There was nothing else of note in the brief observation time.

210

Director Shida had emailed the Chanthaburi Gem and Jewellery Association (CGJA) in Thailand asking for a clarification on the seemingly new treatment. That was more than a week ago. Still no reply. Meanwhile the sapphires were pouring in for testing. Japanese dealers reported buying them directly from treaters in Chanthaburi who, they claimed, were only heating the material.

Why is she worried? pondered Akito. *Over 90 per cent of sapphires are heated.* Maybe this was a new technique developed by the Thai. Sapphires from various worldwide deposits were traded in Chanthaburi, where they were treated, cut, polished, and transformed from rough stones into jewellery-worthy gems. The Thai dominated the business.

He looked up again. Director Shida was now standing with her back to the glass wall that separated them, staring out at the Tokyo skyline. It felt strange not seeing her busy behind her microscope or at her desk, fielding calls and emails. He recalled the first time he'd met her a few years ago at his job interview. Entering the director's office, he'd been surprised to see a woman behind the desk. She was wearing a pantsuit with a blouse that perfectly matched the only decoration on her desk: a stately pink Cymbidium kanran orchid.

Despite the formal nature of the meeting, there was something about the way she listened when he spoke that put him at ease. After joining GAAJ, his respect and admiration for her had only grown. A diligent boss, she was strict but very generous in sharing her knowledge with her team. He had learnt a great deal working with her and could see why she was the only woman in Japan leading an organisation of this scale. *I hope there's nothing wrong*, Akito thought as he went back to his microscope.

A few minutes later, his telephone rang. It was Director Shida. 'Akito, please come to my office. I have finally received a reply from Chanthaburi.'

* * *

27th December 2001
American Gem Trade Association (AGTA)
Gem Testing Centre (GTC)
New York, USA

'Mr Scarratt, that package from Tai has arrived from Bangkok,' said Susan, the new lab intern. Ken grabbed the parcel like a child waiting for a new puzzle and got to work. The sapphires he'd seen in Bangkok had been troubling him on his return flight to New York. He couldn't put his finger on it, but his gut told him something was wrong. Upon arrival, he called Tai from the airport and requested samples to be shipped to the Gem Testing Centre.

His ruminations were interrupted by Susan. 'Do you mind if I help you with your experiments today, Mr Scarratt? I'd love to learn more about padparadscha sapphires.'

Not looking up as he carefully opened the package, Ken replied, 'Sure, why don't you grab that writing pad and take the seat next to mine? You can document the examination process. Feel free to ask questions.'

'What should I write is the aim of our examination?' she asked.

'To study the colour distribution in these natural padparadscha sapphires. The first step we'll follow is to immerse them in a methylene iodide solution.'

'Wouldn't water achieve the same purpose?'

'No, it won't. Why do we immerse gems in water?' asked Ken, looking directly at Susan for the first time.

Crap! Didn't think he'd ask me questions, she thought. 'To reduce the light reflection, so we can better see the inclusions inside the stone?'

'Exactly. Rubies and sapphires are varieties of corundum, an allochromatic mineral, meaning it is coloured by impurities embedded inside the stone called "trace elements". Titanium and iron are the dominant ones responsible for the blue in sapphires, and chromium the red in rubies. By observing how included a stone is, rough-gem buyers can better understand how much they need to heat the material to get rid of the impurities inside, what percentage of the rough needs to be cut, carat weight of the gem after cutting, and it's final shape. One technique rough-gem buyers use to get a better sense of inclusions inside sapphire and ruby crystals is to rub some baby oil on them or immerse them in water.'

Susan nodded, concentrating on every single word. 'Answers to these questions influence how much they're willing to pay. Coming back to your question, I am immersing these sapphires in methylene iodide and not water because the solution's refractive index is close to corundum, which means upon immersion the gems essentially disappear, so all we see are the stone's internal characteristics. Water is good, but this is significantly better. Got it?'

'Yes, sir,' responded Susan furiously scribbling on the notepad.

Her enthusiasm made Ken smile as he returned to the microscope to study the first sample. 'I knew it!' he congratulated himself. He picked up and read the accompanying lab report Tai had sent, which stated the sapphires were heated. Ken selected a different shape, a larger square-cushion sapphire weighing more than three carats and repeated his steps. *This is not simple heating.*

'Mr. Scarratt, what should I write under observations?' asked Susan.

'Ken. Just call me Ken. First, I want you to take these samples to the lab technicians. Ask them to follow their standard examination protocol, but don't mention the methylene iodide. Then, report their findings back to me. We'll resume after you have their results,' said Ken.

In less than two hours, Susan came back with lab notes declaring the 11 sapphires as heated.

This is wrong, thought Ken. *Clearly a foreign element is at play.* 'Susan, come and have a look at this sample from the horizontal microscope. What do you see?' he asked.

'I can see a light orange border on the stone and the central section is pale pink.'

'Correct. Here's the weird part: that orange border is following the shape of the faceted or cut gem, instead of the rough crystal. We call this surface-conformal colouring. It's not something natural.'

'Why?' she asked.

'Imagine you have a rough sapphire: any colour zoning in that rough is going to be relative to the sapphire's original rough crystal form. When a cutter creates a sapphire gem by cutting the rough crystal, he must work around the colour bands to achieve the best possible outcome face up. Got it?'

'I think so,' said Susan. 'For this outer colour rim to follow the shape of the faceted stone makes no sense because the shape was created during cutting, whereas the original colour zoning was created by nature before the stone was cut, yes?' After getting a nod of approval from Ken, she said, 'Incredible. So how do we document this?'

Ken closed his eyes and started dictating: 'Upon immersion of the samples in methylene iodide, we observed surface-conformal colouring. The stones displayed unusual yellow-to-orange rims surrounding pink cores, which suggests a yellow colourant is being diffused into pink sapphires. Significant overgrowths of synthetic corundum are also noted. This indicates the stones have probably undergone a diffusion treatment. At this stage, the element causing the colour shift is unclear.'

'How do the synthetic overgrowths impact the gemstone, Ken?' asked Susan.

'First, any synthetic overgrowth we see is an artificial additive to the stone. Second, it increases the weight of the stone and presents a larger gem than what the original rough crystal would have yielded.'

There was a moment of silence after Susan finished writing. 'But the lab said they were heated.'

'Yes,' said Ken, taking off his glasses and rubbing his eyes. 'If you could, please insert the notes in our lab template and email them ASAP, thanks.'

Once Susan had left, Ken walked over to his office, closed the door, and called his friend and industry colleague, Tom Moses at GIA. 'Tom, is it possible for you to come over to the lab today? I need to show you this lot of sapphires we just got from Bangkok. They display surface-conformal colouring.' Tom had one question, to which Ken answered, 'Yes, like the blue sapphires.' Then he hung up after they agreed to meet at 4 pm.

Ken went back to his routine but couldn't get the visual of the magnified sapphires out of his mind. In the early eighties, he and others in the industry had seen similar patterns in blue sapphires under magnification. Those had been surface-diffused using titanium, but this was different. The tools and techniques in the lab could not detect anything foreign, yet the visual cue was compelling.

What's causing this pattern? he ruminated. *Why can't we detect the element?* Ken's thoughts drifted towards the world's largest gem show, which was only a few weeks away. AGTA members and other dealers must be buying this material thinking it's only heated. *We need to warn them.*

* * *

14th January 2002
Office of the Editor
Bangkok Post
Thailand

Pichai Chuensuksawadi didn't like being disturbed when he was on deadline. The editor-in-chief of the Bangkok Post was reading the 14th January 2002 issue when a knock at the door demanded his attention. *This better be something good*, he thought, frowning.

Joe, who covered gems and jewellery for the newspaper, stuck his head through the doorway. 'Sorry, boss. Urgent.'

Pichai waved him in the room, gesturing for him to take a seat.

'The Chanthaburi Gem and Jewellery Association have issued a press release.'

'So?' grunted Pichai.

'The American Gem Trade Association has issued an urgent gemstone alert warning its members about a new treatment carried out on sapphires in Thailand and being traded undetected in the market.'

'They do treatments to those stones all the time. What's so special this time?'

'The CGJA denies it. They've issued a detailed press release.'

Pichai stood up, taking the opportunity to stretch his back as his doctor had advised. 'Don't read the whole thing. Just give me a summary,' he said as he began a slow trek around his office.

Relieved he'd crossed the first hurdle, Joe commenced reading from his notes, 'They are basically expressing disappointment that AGTA issued this "Urgent Gemstone Alert" after what they say was inconclusive and non-thorough testing of only 11 stones. They claim that the colour change in Madagascar sapphires from pink to the pinkish-orange padparadscha hue is only because of high-temperature heat treatment.' He kept reading from his notepad and Pichai kept pacing.

'Further, they vehemently state that no additives have been used, that the colour is 100 per cent stable up to 1,000 degrees Celsius and, while certain heaters are using oxygen to increase the temperature, that's normal. Finally, the note confirms that no "surface-diffusion" treatment is being used. They are offering samples to international labs and anyone who wishes to independently check the sapphires.' Joe looked up from his notepad and waited for his boss's reaction.

'Anything else?'

'Yes. The world's largest gem show is going to start in Tucson, Arizona, in the US. The members of the association say that this whole thing is a way for the Americans to bring the sapphire price down so they can make a bigger profit.'

'That's in the release?' asked Pichai, raising an eyebrow.

'No, just conjecture. Not official.'

'We don't deal in conjecture. And let's not make this about the Thais versus the Americans, please? That's just sensational nonsense. Stay focused on the facts. Stay focused on the science. You know what's the most important part of this story?'

'What?' asked Joe, wondering what he had missed.

'The consumer. If you can send me your piece in the next 40 minutes, we can run it once I've read it. Now please go, I have a lot to finish.'

* * *

215

15th January 2002
American Gem Trade Association (AGTA)
Gem Testing Centre (GTC)
New York
USA

Jeff Bilgore, chair of the lab committee for AGTA started the 15th January 2002, meeting by sharing highlights from a press release issued by the Chanthaburi Gem and Jewellery Association (CGJA) of Thailand. Besides his role with AGTA, in New York, Jeff worked with the celebrated jewellery house of Oscar Heyman as their lead buyer for coloured gemstones and diamonds.

'Before I hand over to Ken, you'll be glad to learn that since the AGTA alert, many industry stakeholders have called and emailed our offices to thank us for the notification. In fact, one AGTA member was about to spend a quarter of a million dollars on a significant collection of padparadscha sapphires when he saw our email. This is a fantastic example of how the work of the lab protects our members and their customers. Now, over to Ken.'

'Thanks, Jeff. As you all know, I've been in touch with Tom Moses at GIA. We are working closely with them and speaking with other experts such as Dr George Rossman, professor at the California Institute of Technology, and the eminent physicist John L. Emmett, who is an AGTA board member. New information has emerged since we issued the alert. The CGJA are correct in stating that this is not a surface-diffusion treatment like we saw in the early eighties. At that time, treaters were diffusing titanium in blue sapphires. Since titanium is a heavier element, it remained underneath the surface of the stone and was easily identifiable using X-ray fluorescence, a tool most gem labs have,' said Ken.

'Further, during recutting and polishing, the superficial layer of colour gets eroded. The treatment we are dealing with now is not surface but lattice diffusion. Here, a foreign element is being introduced from outside and can penetrate deeper into the stone, sometimes throughout the gem. John Emmett believes it may be beryllium, magnesium, or lithium as they are lighter than, and have an electrical charge or valence less than, aluminium— sapphire's chemical composition being aluminium oxide. This explains why our standard gemmological tools cannot detect them. Questions?'

'So, when you are testing these stones, what's the result?' asked one of the committee members.

'Our gemmological equipment doesn't show anything abnormal, but when we examine the stones under magnification, we know there's a problem,' explained Ken. 'It's important for us to find the element responsible for this treatment for multiple reasons: we need to counter this denial by the Chanthaburi association with scientific fact, and we need to work backwards from identification of the chemical culprit to create mechanisms and upgrade our equipment so we can recognise this treatment in corundum going forward.'

Jeff leaned forward in his chair and said, 'Ken, we have less than three weeks before the world's largest gem show in Tucson. Is that enough time?'

'Not sure, to be honest. John Emmett has recommended we use SIMS— secondary ion mass spectrometry—to measure the trace element concentrations in the samples as the equipment can measure down to ppm, or part per million levels—'

'Never heard of that in gemmology,' interrupted a committee member.

'That's because the SIMS instrument was first developed to analyse moon rocks brought back by the Apollo astronauts in 1969,' said Ken. 'The machine costs almost a million dollars and this investigation will be expensive, so it's great that we can collaborate with GIA.'

'Are you suggesting we spend a million dollars on this investigation?!" asked another participant.

'We can't; we don't have the funds,' responded Ken. 'John Emmett is connecting the GIA team with a research lab in New Jersey, which has the SIMS equipment. They'll analyse the samples for us at a lower cost. It's not a sustainable solution but will suffice for this investigation. To respond to your question, John, we are trying our best to make sure we have the SIMS analysis in time for Tucson, but it also depends on the current workload of the lab in Jersey.'

The committee members sat in silence, looking pensive as they absorbed what Ken had explained. *They already look worried. Should I tell them the other part?* wondered Ken. 'There's one more thing,' he said, biting the bullet. They turned towards him. He cleared his throat and said, 'We believe this treatment goes beyond padparadscha sapphires.'

'What do you mean?' asked an attendee.

'If treaters have discovered a way to diffuse a light element in corundum that escapes market and lab detection, they may be treating corundum of all colours. This foreign element could be in rubies, and blue, pink, and yellow sapphires. We have also observed overgrowths of synthetic corundum on these samples. Both these aspects—an element being diffused from outside along with synthetic material—significantly impacts the nature of the material. How many have already been traded? How many will continue to be sold as natural rubies and sapphires without disclosure of their treatment? And what will happen when this all comes out?'

* * *

11th June 2002
Don Mueang International Airport
Bangkok, Thailand

'You booked an airport pickup from the hotel?' asked Ken as he spotted a representative from the Four Seasons hotel holding a placard with Tom's name at Don Mueang International Airport in Bangkok.

'Yeah. With our new celebrity status as targeted men, I figured it didn't hurt to take precautions.' It was the first week of June, seven days after Ken had received the email threat.

'Agree. Did you tell Anne about the email?'

'No way! She would have freaked out. Did you tell your wife?'

'Nope. Would have been difficult to make this trip to Bangkok if she knew.'

'Then, we better make sure we get back in one piece!' Tom said, smiling.

As they both settled in for the long drive to their hotel, Ken's thoughts drifted back towards the Tucson show a few months ago where Shane from GIA, supported by their group of gemmologists and scientists, had presented the results of the SIMS analysis. They had confirmed to the gathering of industry stakeholders that the element being diffused in the sapphires was beryllium.

Ken remembered every chair around the horseshoe seating formation had been full, with another 50 standing towards the back of the room. A lively discussion had followed with many questions, like how beryllium got into the sapphires? And, going forward, how would gem labs worldwide detect this element?

'Are you thinking about that article?' said Tom, interrupting Ken's recollections. 'No one believes what that guy wrote about you. Simple case of character assassination.'

'I know. It's nonsense. My mind just drifted to Tucson and the discussions we had after our presentation.'

'Yeah. It took forever to leave the room,' said Tom. 'People had so many questions. Some were congratulating us, but most were concerned about how this discovery would impact their business.'

'This American gem dealer stood out for me,' said Ken. 'I remember I was packing my papers when he approached me. I wasn't sure how he would react to what we'd just presented. Anyway, he appreciated our presentation and then he told me we'd saved him a few hundred thousand dollars.'

'Really? How?'

'Seems he was about to buy a large parcel of padparadscha sapphires when he saw our alert.'

'What did you say?'

'You know me, I never know how to respond in these situations. I think I said that we just did, and are doing, our job. I remember telling him that the SIMS data confirms it's beryllium being diffused. Now the big task ahead is to find a solution we can use in the lab going forward.'

'Yeah. And getting the Chanthaburi Gem and Jewellery Association to confirm that some of their members are doing this treatment,' said Tom.

'I recall, he also said that the price of the padparadscha sapphires was in freefall. Goods that were going for US$4,000 a carat or even $3,000 a carat were now down by 70 per cent. I was surprised to hear that because it meant people were still buying these stones. This is just a mess, Tom; this guy was lucky but how many may have already purchased these sapphires? And now, they've lost 70 per cent of their value! It's just terrible.'

'Since we're about to reach our hotel,' said Tom, 'and have a long day of work ahead of us, may I suggest you dump that glass of self-deprecation you're swirling and get a good night's rest?'

'Will do, Mom,' said Ken rolling his eyes.

'Where were you?' said Tom the next morning as he spotted Ken walking towards him in the Four Seasons hotel lobby, balancing an oatmeal cookie on the hotel takeaway coffee cup. 'You missed breakfast, and we need to leave for our first meeting. Here, let me take your bag before you drop that coffee.'

'Thanks,' Ken said, handing over his weathered leather case stuffed with a large notebook, pens in different colours, and a travel kit of gemmological equipment. 'You won't believe this, but despite our efforts, word is out that we're in Bangkok. I've been on the phone for the past 30 minutes speaking with the president of the Thai Gem and Jewellery Traders Association. They've organised a meeting this evening, which they'd like us to attend.'

'Are you serious? And what's the purpose of this meeting?'

'To explain certain aspects about this "new heat" treatment that we may have missed during our research.'

'Ken, are we seriously going to walk into a room full of people who've been denying this diffusion treatment when we're the ones proving them wrong?' asked Tom.

'I don't think we have a choice. Let's just hear them out. International jewellery brands aren't buying these goods. Trading of sapphires between the US and Thailand is practically at a standstill. If we are to move forward as an industry, we need to communicate.'

'I agree but don't hold your breath.'

The duo spent the rest of the day in back-to-back meetings, studying and collecting samples for their research projects, gaining market insights, and gathering data. By five, despite the espresso shots, both were struggling with jet lag but knew they had to stay sharp for their final meeting with the Thai association. Although the distance to the Jewellery Trade Centre (JTC) was short, they opted to take the hotel car.

'How many people did they say were going to be there?' asked Tom on the quick elevator ride to the ninth floor of the JTC.

'They didn't say. I reckon ten, maybe?'

A few minutes later, Tom and Ken were surprised when they walked into a boardroom that was bursting with people. Every seat had been taken and, like the Corundum Conference in Tucson a few months ago, there were many people standing towards the back of the large space.

As soon as they walked in, all eyes turned towards them. It seemed as if they had arrived amidst a discussion. There were no smiles, just a gruff acknowledgement of their presence. To diffuse the tension in the room, the president of the association walked over to shake their hands, welcoming and introducing them to the key board members. 'Perfect timing,' he said. 'We just finished our routine matters.'

Once the new arrivals had taken their seats, the association president stood up to make brief opening remarks, welcoming them officially to the session and introducing a Thai gentleman who he claimed had invented the "new heat" treatment. A young team member took his position next to the gem treater to play the role of tech support and translator. They both started taking the audience through a series of images and videos involving the treatment of pink sapphires.

The process being shown was nothing more than a standard high-temperature heat treatment, one Tom and Ken understood well. They played along, quietly watching. Looking around the room, Ken saw some of the senior members nodding, focused on the screen while others were just staring at them. It was intimidating. They were in the minority, a point they understood well. When the presentation ended, the attendees once again turned towards Tom and Ken, their silence demanding a reaction. The duo looked at each other, uncertain of what to say.

To hell with it, thought Ken. He decided to break the silence. 'Very interesting,' he said. 'Now can you explain where the beryllium comes from?' The room froze. You could hear a pin drop. After waiting for an answer that Ken knew was not coming, he and Tom got up, thanked the president for their hospitality and left.

* * *

7th February 2003
Panel Discussion on Beryllium Treatment
Corundum Conference
AGTA Gem Show
Tucson, Arizona, USA

'I can't believe we're here again, a year later, and they're still denying this treatment,' said Ken, throwing his hands up in frustration.

He was in Tucson again for the AGTA, standing in a conference room with Tom Moses, Jeff Bilgore, peers from other gem labs, and representatives from two international jewellery houses. They were getting ready to present the results of their year-long research on beryllium diffusion in corundum (sapphires).

'Hopefully, the scientific data we present today will motivate them to admit to the treatment,' said Tom.

It had been a tough year. Trust and reliability were the brick and mortar of the gem industry. The concealment of treatments that changed the nature of gems like sapphires and rubies combined with the inability of labs to detect the deception had sown seeds of mistrust. Stakeholders in Thailand and around the world were all deeply concerned at how this saga could cause irreparable damage to the industry.

Within minutes, the room was full, and the presentations were underway. Since the last meeting, a year ago, the consortium of scientists had managed to reverse-engineer the beryllium diffusion treatment and establish that crushed chrysoberyl (commonly found with sapphires in Madagascar) was being introduced in furnaces to naturally supply the beryllium during heat treatment. It seemed the inventive Thai gem treaters, despite having no formal gemmological training, had figured out that chrysoberyl was having a positive impact on sapphires. Once beryllium was identified as the cause, Thai gem treaters began experimenting with the toxic element, resulting in numerous accidents, many fatal.

Besides successfully replicating the treatment, the gemmological investigators had conducted tests on 898 corundum samples. The range of mineral colour bands included yellow, pink to orange leading to red rubies, blue, purple, green, and colourless sapphires. They discovered that only one part per million atoms (ppma) of beryllium was required to shift the colour significantly, greatly improving the appearance of the gems. In samples which had been diffused over longer periods, the varying colour rims disappeared, making detection via microscopic examination impossible.

This was especially noticed in yellow and orange sapphires where less than ten per cent showed a layer of surface-conformal colour, the abnormality Ken had first spotted in the AGTA lab with the initial 11 samples. On the positive side, by comparing samples that had undergone normal heating versus stones that were beryllium-diffused, scientists made an important discovery. The transparent, rounded, grain-like zircon crystal inclusions (typically found in sapphires from Madagascar), which remained unchanged during standard heat treatment, were transformed into opaque white irregular shapes under beryllium diffusion. The condition of the zircon inclusions, in certain cases, had been identified as an indicator of whether the host gem had undergone beryllium diffusion.

The most helpful segment of the meeting was the presentation of practical tips that gemmologists could use in further examinations. The group also shared their detailed work on gemmological instruments, which stakeholders could use for future detection of beryllium-diffused corundum.

After the presentations and panel discussions were done, the presenters invited questions and comments from the audience. A gem dealer stood up and said, 'Thank you for the work you all have done. I have one question. What does the representative of the Chanthaburi Gem and Jewellery Association have to say on this?'

Everyone looked towards the gentleman in question. He didn't bother standing up and simply said, 'I'm not a scientist. I can only say what I know—that treaters in Chanthaburi are simply heating the sapphires with nothing added in the crucibles.'

The room erupted, some standing up and expressing their outrage by saying, 'How can you keep denying this? It's crazy.' Others opted to stay silent but were shaking their heads in disbelief.

After a few minutes of disruption, when some order had been restored, the lead buyer from one of the top international jewellery brands stood up. In a calm tone, she looked at the Thai gentleman and said, 'I would like to place on record that we have absolutely no need to buy any sapphires or rubies if we don't have clarity and full disclosure on how they are being treated. We cannot and will not sell these goods to our customers.'

While the room quietened down after her statement, still processing the ripple effect this may have on the industry, the CGJA representative, feeling the need to pacify, stood up and said, 'I understand there are concerns. As a dealer I share them but please believe me when I say that we are equally confused by all this data. As per our understanding, nothing is being added to the stones. Yes, treaters are secretive about their methods because this is like our Coca-Cola formula. That's it, there is nothing—'

'Enough!' shouted Ken, standing up and interrupting the man's statement. The gathering was shocked as he was known for being a reserved and emotionally restrained man. 'We've had death threats. I've had my name dragged through the mud thanks to sponsored articles. This needs to stop. This denial is getting ridiculous! The science is compelling, you can't keep refuting it. People have lost millions of dollars and here's the crazy part: 90 per cent of the gem industry in Thailand is not involved and don't want to have anything to do with these goods, so why, why is your association carrying on with this charade?!'

* * *

21st February 2003
AGTA Gem Testing Centre
New York, USA

I'm going to unplug this damn phone next time I'm working on something, thought Ken as he pulled himself away from his microscope at the AGTA Gem Testing Centre and reached out to pick up the telephone receiver.

'Have you seen Jeff's email?' asked Tom.

'Oh God! What's happened now?' said Ken, taking off his glasses and rubbing his closed eyes, bracing himself for more bad news.

'The Chanthaburi Gem and Jewellery Traders Association has issued a press release admitting to the beryllium treatment. Hello? Ken, you there?' asked Tom.

'I'm looking for Jeff's email. I can't find it in my inbox,' said Ken.

'I'll forward my copy.'

'Just read it out to me and put me out of my misery,' said Ken.

'It says and I quote:

During the animated three-hour-meeting at the Maneechan Resort in Chanthaburi, Thailand, influential members of the Thai heating community earnestly discussed the outcome of meetings held during the Tucson Gem Show including the Gemstone Industry and Laboratory Conference (GILC). In a landmark decision, the 60 association members present unanimously agreed that:

Chrysoberyl is being intentionally added to the crucible during the new heat treatment to enhance colour in corundum.

All association members are obligated to disclose and to differentiate the new treatment when selling to customers.

'The release states that all members will strictly follow this directive. They have also opened a new office in the gem centre next to the KP Grand Hotel to increase awareness, transparency, and accountability. According to the new disclosure system, natural unheated corundum will be marked as "N", thermal enhancement will be "E", and all goods subjected to 'thermal enhancement of corundum together with other minerals in an environment that allows inducing of beryllium and other elements into corundum will be marked as "A".' Tom added, 'I can't believe they finally admitted this.'

'Gosh! That's amazing to hear. Should have happened ages ago, but this is fantastic. Thanks for calling me,' said Ken.

'My phone hasn't stopped ringing. Surprised you've received no calls,' said Tom.

'I've switched off my mobile. Just picked up the lab phone. By the way, what are you doing around five this evening?' asked Ken.

'Usual lab work, nothing monumental. Why?' said Tom.

'I spotted something odd in a parcel of emeralds submitted for testing. Would love to get your thoughts. Can you swing by the lab?'

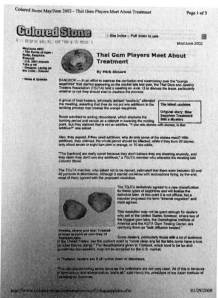

Left: Bangkok Post *article* (April 2002). *Photo credit: Jeffrey Bilgore.*

Right: Article in Colored Stone, *which appeared after the meeting Tom Moses and Kenneth (Ken) Scarratt attended in Bangkok* (2002). *Photo credit: Jeffrey Bilgore.*

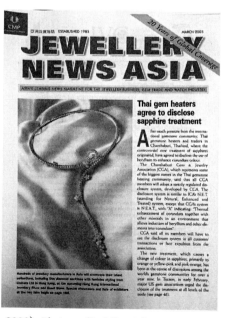

Left: Bangkok Post *article* (September 2002). *Photo credit: Jeffrey Bilgore.*

Right: Article in Jewellery News Asia *on the disclosure statement* (March 2003). *Photo credit: Jeffrey Bilgore.*

Author's Note

This story is based on actual events that occurred between late 2001 and 2003, as relayed to the author by Ken Scarratt, Tom Moses, Jeff Bilgore, Ahmadjan Abduriyim, Chris Smith, Daniel Nyfeler and Lore Kiefert. Secondary research was also conducted, and many technical articles and documents studied. Certain aspects have been fictionalised to aid narration. Some names have also been changed to protect the identity of the contributors. The dates represent the general time period when events and meetings took place.

Kenneth Scarratt was the first to reveal the diffusion treatment in sapphires globally via the AGTA gemstone alert in early 2002. As the story states, he reached out to Tom Moses at the GIA, and they worked together on the investigation along with other members of the industry and scientific community.

This tumultuous period in the industry's history, caused by the undisclosed diffusion of beryllium into corundum, significantly changed the modus operandi of gem labs worldwide. The initial research published by John L. Emmett, Kenneth Scarratt, Shane F. McClure, Thomas Moses, Troy R. Douthit, Richard Hughes, Steven Novak, James E. Shigley, Wuyi Wang, Owen Bordelon, and Robert E. Kane led to further investigations and experiments by other gemmologists around the world.

Japan suffered the most. Japanese traders had invested millions of dollars in buying padparadscha sapphires. After the AGTA gemstone alert in early January 2002, the director of the Gemmological Association of All Japan (GAAJ), Junko Shida, sent a team to Chanthaburi to conduct on-the-ground investigations, but gem treaters continued to deny diffusing beryllium, claiming that the vibrant colours were caused by high temperatures in an oxidising environment inside the crucible.

After the Tucson show in 2002, the GAAJ lab in Tokyo stopped issuing reports for padparadscha sapphires. Without the proper equipment required to detect beryllium diffusion in sapphires, labs were struggling to identify and agree on acceptable terminology for their reports. The industry was divided with some pushing to include the words 'treated' in lab reports, while others wanted to keep the term 'natural'. By summer 2002, AGTA and the GIA had started using the term 'bulk diffusion' on their reports (instead of treated).

On 1st April 2002, Junko Shida brought on board Ahmadjan Abduriyim, a graduate geologist from Kyoto University, to conduct research to find a solution that would empower the GAAJ lab to detect beryllium diffusion treatment going forward. On 11th July 2002, Ahmadjan successfully completed his research and the lab started using laser ablation-inductively coupled plasma-mass spectrometry[1] (LA-ICP-MS) for gemmological testing. Although ICP-MS had been used for decades to chemically characterise materials, it usually required dissolving solid samples in strong acids.

'Combined with the development of extremely sensitive mass spectrometers, laser ablation allowed ICP-MS to be used on gemstones with minimal damage, since the laser vaporizes only a microscopic amount of the sample for analysis[2]. Towards the end of 2002, the GAAJ lab recalled all 30,000 padparadscha sapphires for retesting without charge. They discovered 80 per cent of the recalled stones were beryllium-diffused and only 20 per cent were simply heated.

Unfortunately, given the scale of losses in Japan, despite her vast knowledge and years of exemplary work, Junko Shida was left with no other option but to resign in August 2003 from her position as director of the Gemmological Association of All Japan (GAAJ). Her industry peers and juniors were saddened to hear the news. Later that year, they learnt she had been diagnosed with cancer. She tragically passed away in 2006. She and Ken remained good friends until the end.

In the past, gemmologists depended on observation of inclusions to 'clinically diagnose' gem treatments or a stone's origin. The discovery of new deposits, especially in Africa, led to the development of new treatments to improve gem material. While each new treatment expanded the market, it also created opportunities for misrepresentation by certain unscrupulous individuals looking to make a quick buck. The market needed in-depth chemical analysis and origin determination solutions, and gem labs responded by adapting scientific tools being used in research universities and other sectors to enable gemmological analysis without destruction of the subject matter (such as LA-ICP-MS).

Today, beryllium-diffused gemstones are widely circulated in the industry with proper disclosure. Kenneth Scarratt and Tom Moses are considered among the most formidable gemmologists in the industry.

Kenneth currently lives in Thailand. His past work experience has included leadership roles at the Gemological Institute of America (GIA), AGTA's Gemological Testing Centre (GTC) in New York, the Asian Institute of Gemological Sciences (AIGS), Bangkok, and the Gemmological

1   https://www.gia.edu/doc/SU06A1.pdf
2   https://www.gia.edu/doc/Summer-2003-Gems-Gemology-Beryllium-Diffusion-Ruby-Sapphire.pdf

Association and Gem Testing Laboratory of Great Britain. He is also considered a leading authority on pearls and was approached by Bahrain's crown prince, HRH Prince Salman bin Hamad Al Khalifa, to revive his kingdom's pearling industry and launch the Bahrain Institute for Pearls and Gemstones (DANAT).

Tom Moses joined GIA in 1977 and moved to the GIA New York Laboratory in 1986 to understudy with Mr Robert Crowningshield. In 1988, Tom was appointed vice president of Identification Services and, in 2003, named vice president of Identification and Research Services. During his career, he headed the institute's more critical research projects and co-authored many articles for GIA's *Gems & Gemology*. He is the recipient of the Richard T. Liddicoat Award for Distinguished Achievement, GIA's highest honour. In 2005, Tom was named Senior Vice President of the GIA Laboratory and Research. Tom currently holds the title of Executive Vice President and Chief Laboratory and Research Officer and now oversees all GIA Laboratory and Research operations worldwide.

For more information related to this story and the subject, please search for the following articles:

https://www.gia.edu/doc/Summer-2003-Gems-Gemology-Beryllium-Diffusion-Ruby-Sapphire.pdf

https://www.gia.edu/doc/Fall-2010-Gems-Gemology-Developments-Gemstone-Analysis-Techniques-Instrumentation-2000s.pdf

https://www.gia.edu/doc/sp20-corundum-chromophores.pdf

Mr 10%

Tony Brooke
September 2003
Bangkok, Thailand

TONY LOOKED over at Brad as the traffic light turned red. *Why am I helping him? I hardly know the guy. What if he's a fraud? KJ*[1] *will never forgive me. Or worse, he'll decide to teach me a lesson I'll never forget.*

Tony's mind was spinning out of control. Two hours ago, Brad had walked into his store at the Jewellery Trade Centre in Bangkok with five kilos of rough sapphires from his mine in Songea, Tanzania, that he seemed desperate to sell. The stones were beautiful, good crystal quality, and clean, unlike their fractured sapphire cousins from Garba Tula in Kenya that Tony had recently burnt his fingers trying to sell. Some 70 per cent of the lot Brad had brought was bluish-green, 25 per cent brownish-red, and the rest exhibited an unusual purplish-red hue. The purple should burn well into a rich orange red, Tony had thought at the time.

'Thanks again for doing this. I appreciate your help,' said Brad, as if reading Tony's mind. They were both on their way to see a senior gem buyer called KJ.

If Tony was successful in facilitating a sale of Brad's rough sapphires, he'd get a ten per cent commission. Tony smiled and said, 'No worries. As I was saying, don't be too hard on yourself. Heating corundum[2] is no mean feat. Every specialist has his or her recipe for improving the appearance of their gems.'

Tony was referring to a failed project Brad and his fellow Australian partner Alan had set up in Bangkok six months ago: a heat treatment and gem-cutting facility. Their experiments were yielding brownish-red-coloured sapphires, which were proving difficult to market. Brad was now in

1   This name has been changed.
2   Sapphires and rubies are both part of the corundum mineral family with trace elements like iron and chromium impacting their colours, which give them their identity of blue sapphires (iron), and red rubies (chromium).

229

the market to sell untreated mine-run[1], hoping to generate cash their operation desperately needed.

'Have you heard of this new heat treatment with beryllium?' asked Tony.

'Yes. I believe it does wonders. But isn't it controversial?'

The sapphire industry had recently been in the middle of a scandal involving a select group of individuals[2] who'd sold beryllium-treated sapphires from Madagascar without disclosure. Beryllium's presence in the crucible during heat treatment transformed the colour of sapphires into a rare pinkish-orange hue, which the trade call padparadscha. The treatment had gone undetected for almost a year, and many gem labs had unknowingly issued in-correct reports declaring the stones as only 'heated' instead of 'heated in flux'. A difference that would significantly impact the price. When the story broke, it had cost many in the industry millions of dollars and almost brought the sapphire business to its knees.

'The treatment was controversial when it was discovered, but mainly because it was undetected,' said Tony. 'Now, gem labs have the technological infrastructure and know-how required to detect beryllium in sapphires. And the Chanthaburi Gem and Jewellery Traders Association has made a statement confirming its presence. It's all out in the open; should be fine to use. With any treatment, full disclosure is vital to build trust and a solid foundation for future sales.'

Fifteen minutes later, Tony's BMW pulled up in front of a building in the Bangkok jewellery district. Brad watched as he waved at the security guard who, recognising Tony's vehicle, opened the reserved section of the car park. 'You never explained who this KJ person is exactly. Is he a gem manufacturer?' asked Brad.

'Mmm, he's a problem solver,' said Tony.

'Does he own this building?' Brad enquired, as the guard at the entrance saluted Tony.

'Yeah. Owns the building and we are going to the top floor, which is his hallowed sanctuary. Very few have access to his office.'

'So, how is he a problem solver?' Brad wasn't sure how he felt about the VIP attention.

'I'll be straight with you,' said Tony, as they stood in line waiting for the elevator. 'KJ is a financier across industries. He's Thai, but his family came from China. He buys and sells cheques. People take goods to him when they cannot sell. He purchases inventory, no questions asked, and further hands

---

1   "Mine-run" is a term used to describe mixed quality of goods presenting a mine's standard production run.

2   See Story 14.

the stones over to a bunch of gem-cutting factories. They cut and sell the stones and give him a share of the profit. But you gotta be straight with the guy, Brad. You don't mess with KJ, OK? He was at the centre of the beryllium diffusion scandal. Some say he was close to the group of 16.'

'Group of 16?'

'This group of 16 politicians who defrauded one of the top Thai banks out of millions. Some of them were seen in and out of KJ's office.'

'Holy shit,' said Brad.

The elevator doors opened, and they both stepped in. Tony leaned towards Brad and whispered, 'The man always has an armed bodyguard with him. He's legit.'

'Maybe this isn't a good idea,' said Brad.

'Relax,' said Tony. 'KJ loves me. He'll help you out. You'll see. He's a great guy. Just don't mess with him.'

Before Brad could respond, the doors opened, and they stepped into a room flooded with light. A short man stood up from behind a large wooden desk and came around to give Tony a hug. He had sparse shoulder-length hair with a receding hairline. He wore a well-fitted T-shirt, which showed off his muscular frame. 'KJ, I want to introduce you to a friend of mine, Brad. He's mining sapphires in Songea, Tanzania.'

'Nice to meet you,' said KJ, as he warmly shook Brad's hand. The room reeked of cigarette smoke, and Brad spotted a pack of Marlboro Reds on the table, which explained KJ's raspy voice.

'How are things at the plantation?' asked Tony.

'Can't complain. I have a batch of your favourite snack coming in from Chanthaburi next week,' said KJ

'Oooo, I can't resist those,' said Tony. He looked at Brad and explained. 'KJ and I share a mutual love of these delicious roasted cockchafers and crickets. He has fruit plantations in Chanthaburi and is kind enough to get his staff to collect them and bring them to Bangkok, where his cook does a wonderful job of deep frying them. Delicious!'

'Are they like the fried grasshoppers sold at food stalls?'

'No. No. These are rare. They come out only for a few weeks at a certain time of the year. Not easily found,' explained Tony. He looked at KJ and said, 'I'll be waiting for your call when they arrive. And this time, I'll be careful to not eat too many. I was physically sick last time.'

KJ laughed out loud. The small talk carried on for a few minutes till KJ leaned back in his chair and said, 'So, how can I help your friend, Tony?'

'Like I said, KJ, Brad and his partner have been mining in Tanzania. He's got a batch of rough sapphires to sell.'

Brad pulled out the bags from his backpack and placed them on the table. KJ spent a few minutes inspecting the stones in silence while Brad and Tony were treated to a platter of dragon fruit and mangosteen. Once KJ was satisfied, he asked his staff to bring a scale. They weighed the stones, which totalled two kilos, and offered Brad US$30,000 for the goods. Thrilled with the outcome, Brad took the cash, and the duo left the building.

'That was amazing, Tony,' Brad said as soon as they got back in the car. 'I've been trying to offload those stones for almost two months without success.'

'No worries. Remember my cut. We still have three kilos left to sell, right?'

'Yeah. What do you suggest?' asked Brad.

'I'm tied up with appointments till Thursday. Why don't we drive down to Chanthaburi friday early morning? I have some contacts there who may be interested in your goods.'

* * *

Friday afternoon
Thirty minutes from Chanthaburi
Thailand

'Are we nearly there?' asked Brad. They'd been driving southeast for more than four hours on the highway from Bangkok, only stopping to use restrooms at gas stations.

'Almost in Chanthaburi,' replied Tony. 'You OK?'

'Yeah. Sleep deprived.'

'Hopefully, the four cups of coffee you've consumed helps,' teased Tony.

Brad chuckled. He didn't want to tell Tony the real reason he hadn't been able to sleep all night. His mine manager, Matt[1], had woken him up around three in the morning. There had been a shooting at his mine in Songea, involving the security staff. During his nightly patrol, one of their guards had stumbled across more than a hundred men digging illegally in their concession. Instead of reporting back to Matt, he engaged with the mob, which led to them chasing him with their pickaxes and shovels. Outnumbered and scared for his life, he'd opened fire, badly injuring one of the men in the leg. The gunshot had frightened away the crowd and woken the mine staff who rushed to the scene.

---

1   This name has been changed.

232

When Matt reported the incident to Brad, he instructed him to rush the injured digger and security guard to the hospital. Matt's mistake was stopping en route to report the incident at the local police station. Once the officers heard the guard's statement, they threw the digger in jail. Through the night, Matt begged the police to let the digger receive medical attention, but they wouldn't listen. The poor man bled to death in a few hours, and the police then arrested the mine's security guard, registering a case of murder. 'Those bastards didn't let me take him to the hospital. They watched him die,' Matt told Brad on their last call around six in the morning Thai time.

'I'm taking you to meet one of my closest associates,' said Tony.

His voice brought Brad back to reality, and he took another sip of the cold coffee in his hand. They'd arrived at the ancient town of Chanthaburi, located an hour away from the Cambodian border.

'Is he a gem manufacturer?' asked Brad.

'He's a lot of things. A dealer, farmer, owns a gem treatment and cutting operation. People leave their rough stones with him and commission him to treat them. Basically, a contract burner.'

'I can't afford to treat and cut[1] right now. Just need to keep the lights on,' said Brad. The mine was running out of cash, and after last night's events, they would need to hire professional security to keep the place from being overrun.

'I know. He also buys untreated rough. Name's Sanan but I call him Pi Tung, which shows respect for an elder in the Thai language. He has an office just off the main gem street. Every Friday and Saturday, you'll find him there buying stones. I called ahead; he knows we're coming.'

Brad nodded. To reach Sanan's office, they had to walk through the main gem market. 'When was the last time you visited Chanthaburi?' asked Tony.

'I'd been meaning to, but never found the time.'

'What?! You wanna sell rough sapphires, but you haven't been to Chanthaburi?'

'I know. Embarrassed to admit.'

'You know, in the early eighties, around 70 per cent of the world's top rubies were from Thailand. Of these, 85 to 90 per cent came from the Chanthaburi-Trat district[2],' said Tony, as the two began walking towards their destination.

'Wow! I knew they mined rubies and sapphires in Thailand. Didn't realise the country was such an important source.'

---

1   Treat the rough sapphires and facet/cut and polish them in order to make them marketable.

2   https://www.gia.edu/doc/The-Chanthaburi-Trat-Gem-Field.pdf

'The quality wasn't the same as Burma [Myanmar], but respectable. Many say Chanthaburi became an important centre for gems only in the sixties, but the region's mining history goes back hundreds of years. I think it was in 1850 when gem-mining was first reported at Khao Ploi Waen, also known as Pagoda Hill.'

'Why the sixties?'

'It's when the government of Burma nationalised their mines, effectively stopping the free flow of stones from Burma to Thailand. Faced with difficulties to access Burmese gems, the industry shifted its focus to deposits in Thailand. By the eighties, the Chanthaburi-Trat region had maybe 20,000 to 30,000 miners working across all deposits. And that was just on the Thai side of the border. Many sapphires and rubies were coming from Cambodia, which were mixed with Thai stones, the more well-known origin, and sold as Thai rubies and sapphires.'

'Fascinating history,' remarked Brad.

'I also had a ruby-mining operation in Trat in the late eighties.'

'Really? Who were your buyers?'

'The Japanese. They fell in love with the quintessential purplish-red hue of Thai rubies. Their love of that shade was vital to the success of Thai rubies during that period.'

'I heard a term,' said Brad. 'Not sure what it means.'

'What's that?'

'Light Thai. I hear dealers use it all the time in Bangkok.'

'Means the stone has inclusions,' said Tony. 'Again, in the eighties, two qualities of Thai rubies were being sold. One had this purplish-red hue, and the second was more included, but exhibited a vibrant red. That second shade was referred to as "light Thai". By the late nineties, most of the mines in Thailand had stopped operating as the deposits were depleted or became too expensive to mine, but the term stuck. Now, when a dealer says a stone is "light Thai", it means that it's a more included stone.'

'Amazing. I guess every community has their distinctive language. Another question, I thought Chanthaburi was more of a domestic gem market. Why am I seeing traders from India, Afghanistan, and Africa roaming around?'

'Chanthaburi is a melting pot in more ways than one. Merchants bring rough gems from all over seeking buyers. Like any ecosystem, there's a hierarchy. You have seasoned traders, international buyers and sellers, expats who live in Thailand, tourists, and local brokers, many of whom are women.'

'I noticed that. In other markets, like Sri Lanka, you don't see women anywhere. How is it in Chanthaburi there are so many of them selling gems?' asked Brad.

'Not just Chanthaburi, but across Thailand and Burma. Culturally, Thai and Burmese societies are more matriarchal. Female merchants are hardworking. They have more patience than men, which is why they are excellent in sales. You'll also see them in lapidaries faceting hundreds of small-sized gemstones. What we call melee or calibrated goods in the industry.'

Tony and Brad continued past air-conditioned offices that belonged to seasoned traders to reach a busy junction that was surrounded by open trading floors. Tony took the opportunity to educate Brad on the differences between the various platforms. 'You see that one there?' said Tony, as he pointed towards a hall, which was open on two sides and contained an assortment of desks with plastic chairs. 'The people occupying the tables are buyers.'

'I can see that some tables have sheets of paper hanging from the front with Thai lettering. What do they say?' asked Brad.

'Names of various gems that those buyers are interested in acquiring. For example, that guy in the green T-shirt is only interested in buying spinels. So only people who have spinels will approach that table. Simple and effective.'

'Who's the chap sitting towards the back of the room?'

'That's the boss of the trading floor. He owns the space and earns a commission on every transaction that happens in his marketplace. Each floor has a reputation to maintain. The buyer may also ask him to first get the stones checked from a gem lab before he agrees to buy. Across the street is a slightly different trading floor where the owner rents table space to sellers by the hour. The signs hanging from those tables communicate the type of stones the seller is offering. Whenever any new gem deposit is found, especially these days in Africa, you'll find the rough being sold first in Chanthaburi.'

'But not emeralds, right? Those would go to Jaipur in India?'

'Correct.'

They continued making their way past the market, dodging food and drink carts. As they turned a corner, the din of the vendors faded away. Tony stopped in front of a small shophouse.

'Is this it?' asked Brad.

The place didn't look like much, but Tony explained that the serious buyers always had the humblest establishments, as they liked to keep a low profile. 'It's the fancy and loud ones you have to be careful of around here,' he said.

They crossed a small room to reach a wooden staircase that brought them to the first floor of the building. The waiting area below was full of dealers waiting to show Sanan their parcels of rough gems.

'I always feel like we're entering a gem doctor's clinic,' said Tony as he knocked on the office door. Sanan's face broke into a big smile when he saw them, and he shooed the man sitting across from him out of the room.

'Tony! Come in. Come in. Long time. Where you been?'

Despite speaking English, the two old friends greeted each other in the traditional Thai style with hands folded. It was interesting for Brad to observe that Tony folded his hands first, which Sanan reciprocated, that micro difference in the timing of the greeting cementing Sanan's position of authority as the buyer and elder in the proceedings.

'Good to see you again, Pi Tung,' said Tony. 'I've been in Thailand, hustling to make ends meet.'

'Ah! You so dramatic, Tony,' said Sanan, inviting the visitors to sit across from him.

It took Tony a few minutes of friendly banter before he could introduce Brad to Sanan and explain the purpose of their visit. As soon as the Songea sapphires hit Sanan's desk, his smile vanished, replaced by a deadpan expression that revealed nothing. Brad watched as Sanan inspected the stones, sometimes scraping the rough surface with his fingers or holding a few of the larger pieces against the expansive, clear glass wall facing the street. He stopped to ask Tony a question and then returned to the stones.

In the ensuing calm, Brad observed Sanan. One couldn't call the man overweight, as he had a toned upper body, but he was pudgy around the waist. Something his loose, Thai-style denim shirt failed to camouflage. His farming antecedents were evident in the rich tan and deep-set wrinkles around his eyes and mouth, and how he wore a bright orange and white check scarf around his waist that hung over his trousers. He sat on the sidelines watching Tony and Sanan converse in Thai.

After a few minutes, Tony turned towards Brad and translated as Sanan continued examining the material, 'He was reminiscing about the sapphires from Hainan he used to heat.'

'Hainan? Like Hainan, China?'

'Yes. He would buy tonnes of Penglai sapphires from the deposit on the island. The material was dark blue and dark blue-green, which he would heat with beryllium for ten months in these giant two- to three-metre-high furnaces to transform the dark blue into yellow.'

'Looks interesting, Tony,' said Sanan. 'What's the price?'

'We sold two kilos yesterday for US$30,000.'

236

'Hmm. Let's have a closer look at my factory.'

Sanan got in his pickup truck and asked Tony and Brad to follow. As their convoy drove past the market and over the bridge at the river, crossing the Gothic-style Cathedral of the Immaculate Conception, Brad realised they were leaving Chanthaburi. Tony explained that Sanan owned a durian plantation in the nearby town of Klaeng, which was also the location of his heating and gem-cutting facility.

'This part of Thailand is known for its top-notch produce courtesy of vast farming estates,' said Tony, as they drove down a road surrounded by green plots of cultivated land on both sides. Most of the big guys have investments in farming. A side hustle, if you will. It's good. The gem business can be a mercurial mistress.'

An hour later, just before the town, they took a right turn and started traversing down a dirt road flanked by tall durian trees. It took 15 minutes to reach what Brad assumed was the heart of the plantation as they pulled up in front of a traditional Thai house.

'The lapidary and treatment facility is behind the building,' said Tony.

A short walk brought them to their destination, two large garage-like workshops where gem cutters were busy transforming rough stones into gems. Sanan's staff had laid out a table in the open, covered with a white cloth, and plastic chairs on both sides. The rhythmic whirring sound of the faceting machines from the lapidary dominated the space as the stones touched the abrasive wheels[1]. As soon as they sat down, they were served cold towels to refresh themselves from the journey and small plastic bottles of mineral water. Brad could see numerous rows of jute bags on the floor of the lapidary, bursting with rough gemstones, but no sign of security.

As if reading Brad's mind, Tony said, 'The only way to enter is through the front gates, and visitors are announced by the cacophony of barking security dogs. Plus, everyone has a gun around here.'

Sanan took the Songea sapphire parcels and got to work. Brad watched as Sanan, aided by one of his trusted employees, started sorting and grading the stones based on colour, size, and clarity. After two hours, Brad and Tony left the plantation with a trunk full of durian and US$35,000 for the balance three kilos of rough Songea sapphires.

'You're awfully quiet for a man who just sold five kilos of rough sapphires in less than a week,' said Tony as they drove back to Bangkok.

---

1   Typically coated with diamond paste/powder.

'Sorry, Tony. Believe me, I'm thrilled and grateful for your help. It's just that my partner, Alan, sent me a text earlier saying he wants to sell his stake in our company.'

'Why?'

'He's going through some personal hardships. The mine needs more investment, which he's unable to provide. Plus, theft from illegal diggers is a constant headache. It's not his cup of tea.'

They drove in silence for the next 30 minutes. Africa was on everyone's radar as new gem discoveries were being reported every couple of months. Tony was seeking a gem venture that would take his business in Bangkok to new heights and elevate his standing in the industry.

'If I'm not being too presumptuous,' said Tony. 'Why don't we start working together? You close your treatment and cutting operation in Bangkok. I'll become your sales and marketing agent. Meanwhile, I'll keep a lookout for an investor and together we could buy Alan's share in the coming months? I'll need to visit the operation in Songea, though, and conduct my due diligence.'

'I'll have to discuss it with Alan before I can confirm, but it sounds promising, Tony. I'd love to work together.'

'Excellent,' said Tony. 'To quote a cliché, I think this is the beginning of a beautiful friendship.'

Author's Note

This story is based on actual events, as relayed to the author by Tony Brooke. Minor fictional elements have been included for narrative purposes. Tony became the sales agent for Brad and Alan's Songea sapphire mine. Brad would visit Bangkok every two months with rough sapphires or send shipments, which Tony would sell to gem dealers and manufacturers. After a year of representing their interests, Tony picked up Alan's share of the mining venture with the support of a silent partner who had connections with a large e-commerce player, Thai Gems.

The plan was to sell Songea sapphires to Thai Gems, who had a vertically integrated large-scale operation with 900 workers for gem-cutting and jewellery manufacturing. Three months after Tony invested in the mine, Thai Gems changed their business strategy and closed their gem-cutting facility.

In Tanzania, the number of illegal diggers encroaching on their concession increased. The mine had both primary[1] and secondary[2] deposits. The primary deposit required heavier investment for hard-rock mining, whereas the secondary deposit, being gem gravel embedded in an old riverbed, was easier and cheaper to mine.

But extracting sapphires from the secondary deposit became a race between the mining company and the informal diggers. The diggers would work the riverbed at night, careful to stay away from the section where the miners were operating. After a few years of mining, the company reached a section of the riverbed that had already been cleaned out by the diggers.

Illegally mined Songea sapphires flooded the Chanthaburi gem market, driving the price down. Despite disclosure, beryllium-treated stones were considered tainted goods because of the scandal, and the market didn't want to touch them. Ironically, Brad and Tony's mine produced stunning teal sapphires, which are now in high demand, but there was no market for them back then.

Tony remembers visiting KJ with US$100,000 worth of untreated sapphires, and he had to accept US$60,000 for the stones because there was no other buyer.

One of Tony's regrets is heating an 8.5-carat top-grade teal sapphire from Songea into a beryllium-treated yellow gem. The mine was getting a higher price selling the sapphires in their rough, untreated state in Tanzania than selling cut and treated versions of the same goods in Thailand.

To quote Tony, 'When buyers go to a mine to buy, they have a bag of cash. Back in the day, a lot of it was unofficial. They needed to buy to cover the cost of their trip. The desire is much higher. I learnt this the hard way. Going down to Chanthaburi—it's more difficult to sell because the buyers know a visitor must sell versus a buyer going to Tanzania who needs to buy.'

After seven years of continuous investment and mining, the team ran out of steam. They couldn't cover their overheads and had dipped into their capital. More than 3,000 illegal diggers had established a camp on their tenement. Their presence made operations significantly challenging. In a particularly gruesome incident, a mob of 800 illegal diggers killed a man, brought and dumped his body on the sorting table of the mine, claiming he'd

---

1   This refers to where a gem is formed. Primary deposits are tougher to mine, as the gems are usually embedded in the host rock.

2   A secondary deposit is usually located away from where a gem was formed. This refers to a location where gems have accumulated after being weathered by natural forces of nature, usually ancient rivers. Gems found in secondary deposits tend to be of better quality and are easier and less expensive to extract.

been killed by one of the security guards. Luckily, a staff member outside the mine was able to get the police to disperse the perpetrators.

Eventually, the mining company was closed. Tony lost around US$250,000, but he gained valuable experience and industry insights. No longer just a gem and jewellery retailer, his enriched domain knowledge provided him many business opportunities.

He soon became director of liaison for the Thai Gem and Jewellery Traders Association and subsequently became the vice president and chairperson of overseas development for the prestigious industry body. The position enabled him to build a stellar network of global contacts. He became CEO of Richland Resources, which owned several mining ventures globally.

When I asked Tony what the moral of the story was, he said, 'Only get involved in gem-mining if you are fully funded. This is a common ailment in many businesses, but particularly in the gem industry. People go in without adequate funding, with hope in their pocket and a prayer on their lips. It never works.'

Brad and Tony lost touch after the mine shut down. The guard who'd been arrested for murder was eventually released after six months when the mine hired a lawyer to fight the court case.

The value of the five kilos of rough Songea sapphires Brad initially sold with Tony for US$65,000 would probably be worth approximately US$1,500,000 today after cutting and polishing.

Precision-Cut Dreams

2003
9.45 am
Antananarivo, Madagascar

'DON'T WORRY, Sara, there's plenty of time. I know a shortcut, we won't be late,' said Zo as she half-jogged down the narrow alley. *Thank God I wore my sensible heels*, she thought, dodging the determined Koba vendors, fruit-sellers and cyclists.

Zo had grown up playing in the gardens and streets of Antananarivo. She knew which neighbourhoods had the best food stalls, the areas with the cobbled pathways versus the dusty roads, and she could navigate through them all, saving precious time. The aroma of freshly roasted coffee beans at a cart overpowered the stench from a drain, as Zo skipped over a muddy puddle.

'Are you sure you know where you're going?' asked Sara, trying to keep pace.

'It should be just around this corner,' said Zo, as she took a right turn.

Sara followed.

They found themselves on a wide, less crowded road. The serenity of the peaceful street they'd entered versus the chaos of the narrow lane instinctively made them slow down.

'I think this is the lapidary,' said Zo, pointing towards a sign next to a metal gate.

Even out on the street, they could hear the purr of the gem faceting wheels emanating through the open windows of the small two-storey building.

Sara looked at her watch and said, 'I can't believe it. We're early.'

'Told you,' said Zo.

She had recently joined the Institut de Gemmologie de Madagascar (IGM) [Gemmological Institute of Madagascar] as the head of the lapidary department, after obtaining her engineering degree in geology and mining. Her mother was a primary school teacher and had raised her as a single parent since her father passed away when she was only five years old.

During her studies, she learnt about the immense mineral wealth of Madagascar, and the distinctive nature of the land, which motivated her to apply for the lapidary head position at the gemmology institute.

Armed with her degree and experience in cutting and polishing gems, along with gemmological knowledge and a recommendation from the association of jewellers, Zo had cleared the selection process with flying colours. The Institut de Gemmologie de Madagascar was established in collaboration with the Gemmological Institute of Great Britain (Gem-A) and supported by the government of Madagascar. Its mission was to connect with local lapidaries, understand their challenges, and provide training, which would enable them to command higher prices for their gemstones.

The newly-opened centre was equipped with the latest machines to teach the modern style of precision cutting and domed cabochon cuts. Sara was working with Zo on the community outreach programme. Their destination this morning was one of the oldest gem-cutting and polishing workshops in the capital, founded by a gentleman known in the industry as Mr Lolo. Zo was hoping to convince the industry veteran to send some of his staff to the institute for a training programme.

'Good morning,' said Zo, addressing a man who was leaning against the metal gate of the lapidary entrance, with his arms crossed against his chest. He wore a frown and his eyes seemed to question Zo and Sara's presence at the workshop. 'We are from the Institut de Gemmologie de Madagascar and have an appointment to meet the owner, Mr Lolo.'

Convinced of their legitimacy, the man opened the gate and gestured for them to follow. A wooden staircase facing the entry doorway brought them to a brightly lit room on the first floor. There were four workstations where cutters were busy shaping and polishing coloured stones in a variety of forms. Finished gems, mineral specimens, and works of decorative art lay scattered across the room.

The man they met at the gate pointed out Mr Lolo who was sitting at the far end of the workshop, polishing a stone. As Zo and Sara walked towards him, they passed a stunning geode of amethyst in one corner. Next to the geode was a long table on which Zo spotted a polished jasper with an unusual green colour, a tall vase made from a single piece of rose quartz, and other decorative items such as ashtrays and different-sized luminous crystal balls in a rainbow of hues.

On closer inspection, Zo saw that Mr Lolo was applying facets on an oval-shaped green beryl[1]. After the initial greetings, Mr Lolo invited them to occupy the stools in front of his faceting machine and stopped working.

'Mr Lolo, as you may have heard, the government of Madagascar has established this institute to support the industry and provide training and gem-grading facilities,' said Zo. 'But we can't help until we understand the challenges you face. We would also like to invite your cutters to the institute to learn precision-cutting techniques on brand-new equipment we have imported with the support of the World Bank.'

Lolo was beaming at Zo. 'I'm pleased to hear you speak with so much passion, and I feel proud that we finally have an institute in Madagascar to teach gem-cutting. It's great.'

'Thank you,' said Zo. 'You'll be happy to learn that, in collaboration with the Gemmological Institute of Great Britain, the institute also has a gemmology department and a lab. But enough about us. We want to learn more about you.'

Over the next 30 minutes, Lolo recounted his decades-long experience in the industry and how he and his siblings inherited their love for gems from their father. Like most in the trade, they never had any formal training and learnt on the job. The challenges Lolo highlighted were not related to cutting skills but lack of technology and consumable items at affordable prices, like good-quality polishing powder for the machines.

'You see this machine I'm working on,' said Lolo. 'It's ancient. I bought it second-hand from one of my business associates. If you want to support the trade, help make it easier for us to buy consumables and equipment, or teach us how to make our own machines.'

Zo and Sara made notes and promised to report everything to their seniors. They assured him again that the overall goal of the ministry was to support the sector from multiple perspectives. Lolo continued to share his wealth of knowledge on Malagasy gems. He moved around the room, picking up stones, and sharing stories related to each.

'We are so blessed to be in a country so rich in mineral resources,' he said. After a few minutes, the grumpy man they had encountered at the main gate came over to whisper something in Lolo's ear. 'I'm sorry,' said Lolo. 'My customer has arrived downstairs, and I need to attend to him.'

'No problem,' said Zo. 'Thank you so much for your time. Do you mind if we look around and see your amazing collection of stones?'

---

1   Higher levels of colour saturation courtesy of the elements chromium or vanadium would designate the same stone as an emerald.

'Please, go ahead,' said Lolo. He pointed towards the grumpy young man and said, 'My staff, Louis, will take care of you.'

Zo and Sara spent the next 15 minutes examining the stones being cut in the lapidary. They were amazed at the variety, from large rock crystals and quartz, to tiny sapphires, all in a myriad of colours. Zo loved being immersed in the activity of the workshop. She recognised most of the gemstones and delighted in discussing their origins and characteristics with the cutters. One of her tasks was to observe the gem types being brought into the lapidaries to gain a better understanding of the local marketplace. With that in mind, she kept asking Louis questions related to the source and clientele of the stones.

After a few minutes of answering Zo's questions, Louis said, 'So, who are you people?'

Despite his boss's instructions, his sour manner hadn't changed. Zo smiled, and once again introduced herself and her colleague. He grunted in response. She picked up a multicoloured tourmaline and asked why the cutter was polishing the stone into an oval shape. And what final colour was he hoping to get face up?

Instead of answering her question, Louis said, 'How you got your job at the institute if you know nothing about cutting gemstones, eh?'

Zo continued to examine the stone in her hand, staying cool under the provocative question. She was used to men who were surprised to encounter an educated woman in a professional position. Irritated that she wasn't taking his bait to engage in an argument. Louis said, 'Given all the fancy stuff you were saying to the boss, I thought you should know, just looking at a rough, what colour a cutter would get after cutting.'

His tone was taunting, and he had an arrogant smirk on his face. After another second, she placed the stone back in the tray, looked up to make eye contact with Louis, and said, 'I have an engineering degree in geology and mining and was trained by an international lapidary expert. The stone here is a tourmaline, which is doubly refractive of light, so when light enters the stone, it splits, and we see two different colours. Any expert would have to examine the rough before they could suggest which way to cut it to extract the best colour. And again, what is the best colour depends on who the customer is and what they are looking for, so it's not a simple answer.' She made sure to smile at the end of the explanation and kept her demeanour warm and friendly.

Louis remained unimpressed, ignored her detailed explanation, and carried on in his contemptuous tone. 'You said you're both instructors? Look too young to be instructors. I've been in this business for years. I'm sure if I attend any of your training sessions, it will be me who will teach you and not the other way.'

Undeterred by this open hostility, Sara said, 'So, come and attend our classes, we can share our experiences, exchange ideas.'

'Ha!' said Louis. 'You could never afford for me to attend such a time-wasting session.'

As Sara opened her mouth to respond, Lolo returned to the workshop. Zo diffused the situation by thanking Louis for his time. They both went over to Lolo and invited him to visit the institute and send a few of his cutters for the training programme. He promised to select two to three cutters and assured them that he would also send his daughter for training once she had finished school.

'The future is in the hands of young professionals like you,' said Lolo. 'Never give up on your dreams, even if other people don't see things the way you do.'

As soon as they were out of earshot, a still-seething Sara said, 'Mr Lolo was so nice, but that Louis was so rude. He made me feel like what we're doing is silly and not effective.'

'Yes, Mr Lolo was kind and is so passionate about his work. That's the secret to his success,' said Zo.

'How can he have someone so negative working for him?' asked Sara. 'Ugh! I wanted to punch that stupid frown off his face.'

'And this worries me,' said Zo. 'The support of the lapidary owner is vital, but if we are to succeed, we also need cooperation from the cutters. If someone like him, who is supposed to be our ally, doesn't trust our abilities, then who will?'

'And Louis must have years of experience,' said Sara.

Realising that the man was not alone—and there were hundreds like him out there—they both walked back in silence under a cloud of self-doubt, nervous about the task ahead.

The next day, a group of international gem merchants were visiting the institute, and the director asked Zo to show them the facilities.

'Madagascar is one of the most important sources of coloured gems in the world today,' said Zo, as she walked ahead of the small group. 'We are especially known for our rich, velvety blue sapphires, which were mistaken for Kashmir sapphires at the time of their discovery. Most of our gems are cut in countries such as Thailand, China, Germany, Sri Lanka, and India. It's our hope that with an institute like this, we can have more cutting in the country.'

'Zo,' asked one of the delegates, 'the countries you mentioned have centuries of experience in gem-cutting and multi-generational talent. Do you think Madagascar can replace these world-renowned hubs?'

'The idea is not to replace but to do more in our country than merely supply the rough. It is our government's hope that by teaching these vital skills to local gem cutters, they can improve their cutting technique and deliver gems of an internationally acceptable standard.'

'But what about economies of scale and investment in marketing?' asked another delegate who owned a gem-cutting facility in Sri Lanka.

'What do you mean?' asked Zo. As soon as she had asked the question, she knew what he was going to say, but she wanted him to say it explicitly in front of the group as it provided greater insight into industry views.

'There are two things to consider,' said the delegate. 'The technical side or skill of gem-cutting and polishing, and the business side. Let's first talk business: as a gem polishing and trading company, when we buy rough stones, we pay cash. But our customers expect credit and goods on consignment, which means we need to have deep financial pockets to sell. Plus, we travel all over the world, take part in trade shows, and need to keep a large volume of stones. This is the way gem business is done. The margin on cutting is so little that you need the volume and constant trading to stay afloat. Can Madagascar compete at this level?'

For a second, Zo wasn't sure how to respond. She took a deep breath and said, 'Sir, what you say is true. Despite the skills, we cannot compete with the grand scale of the larger hubs. But by upgrading our craft and our knowledge of gemstones, we can extract more value from our natural resource. We can sell our rough for higher prices and develop special cuts and niche markets, working with specialised designers who may only be interested in a few pieces. We want to take our place on the global stage, recognised not only for the mineral wealth but also our distinctive talents.'

'This is not how the business works, my dear,' said the delegate. 'My master gem cutter is the fourth generation in his family doing this work. Cutting a gemstone is not only about angles. You need to learn how to bring out the soul of a stone, the most valuable colour. These are secrets of the trade that are passed from father to son or daughter. And most of the material we cut in Sri Lanka and Thailand first needs to be treated before cutting and polishing.'

'Yes,' said Zo, ignoring the man's patronising tone. 'A lot to think about. I may not have answers to your questions, but I know that taking a step towards better understanding, improved skills, and learning can only be good.' *At least have the decency to look at me when I'm speaking*, thought

Zo, trying to camouflage her irritation beneath a smile. She knew he had succeeded in getting under her skin, but it was too late. She needed to say something to make her point.

'In fact, you'll be surprised to learn we recently had a young man from Jaipur, India, enrol in our lapidary programme. Jaipur is one of the most important hubs of coloured gemstones in the world, yet this individual has applied to study in our school.'

The Sri Lankan gentleman didn't reply. He simply smiled. It seemed like he wanted to say something but had decided there was no point.

Zo wasn't sure what was bothering her more, his indifference to her answer or his condescending smile, which seemed to convey he knew something she didn't. But she was playing host and there were other delegates in the group who started asking questions. *It's not worth it*, she thought, as she guided the group to the next room.

* * *

Two months later
Institut de Gemmologie de Madagascar (IGM)

'Good morning, Ms Zo, do you have a minute?' said Raj[1], the Indian student who had recently enrolled in the faceting programme at the institute.

'Good morning, Raj,' said Zo. 'How may I help you?'

'I just wanted to come over and inform you I won't be taking the exam next week.'

'What?! Why?'

'I'm quitting the programme,' said Raj.

'Is there a problem?' asked Zo. 'Has something happened that upset you?'

'Zo, you've been a great instructor, so I want to be straight with you.'

'Go on,' said Zo. 'You can speak freely.'

'Actually, I applied for your lapidary course because I needed a visa for Madagascar. Registering with IGM was a sure-shot way to get a visa.'

'I see.'

'In the last two months, I've made excellent contacts in Antananarivo, and have learnt a lot. Being part of IGM has enabled me to get my visa and I can now work as a gem dealer in Madagascar and travel to the mine with confidence.'

'I don't know what to say,' said Zo.

---

1   This name has been changed.

In some ways, Raj had been her model student. She would give his example frequently to show that the institute's work was valued not only in the country but also among international gem-cutting hubs like Jaipur. Was this why the Sri Lankan delegate was smiling? she thought. But how could he have known?

'I'm sorry, Zo,' said Raj. His words breaking her internal musings. 'I've really enjoyed my time at the institute, and you'll be pleased to learn that I'm establishing a proper business in Tana[1] and getting a licence.'

'Raj, it's OK to invest in our country, and I'm happy to hear you're doing it legally, but I must insist you finish your course.'

'Honestly, Zo, there are many good gem cutters back home in Jaipur, and I wasn't really expecting to get any value-add from your course. My goal was to just get an entry visa in Madagascar.'

A knock on the door interrupted their conversation. It was Zo's colleague Sara, telling her that the two cutters from Lolo's lapidary had arrived for their training programme. Zo told Raj that she'd speak with the director of the institute and get back to him.

'What was that about?' asked Sara, as she and Zo were walking towards the lapidary department.

'Raj wants to quit,' said Zo. 'It seems he was never interested in the training but just using the institute to get a visa.'

'Oh, no!' said Sara. 'What are you going to do?'

'What can I do? He's decided.'

Sara could sense Zo's disappointment in the way she spoke. She felt bad for her friend and colleague. They continued walking in silence.

'Forget him,' said Sara. 'The room is full of new students who have come to learn. Let's focus on them. And we helped Raj, even if it was in a way we never intended.'

'Yes,' said Zo. She pushed her glasses back, brushed a bit of fluff from the lapel of her jacket, and entered the room with a bright smile on her face.

Author's Note

This story is based on Zo Harimalala's experiences in Madagascar. Fictional elements, characters, and scenes have been included to enhance the

---

1 Antananarivo.

narration. Many thanks to Georgette Barnes, President—Association of Women in Mining in Africa (Non-Profit), for introducing me to Zo.

Many years later, when Zo was on her way to a meeting in Antananarivo, she heard someone shout her name. It was Raj, sitting behind the steering wheel of a beautiful red car. She congratulated him on his new vehicle, and he explained it was necessary for his image in the industry. He'd married a Malagasy woman and proudly showed Zo a few photos from the wedding on his mobile.

Raj confessed that being an alumnus of IGM had opened many doors for him in Madagascar and abroad. His company specialised in exporting rough tourmaline from Madagascar to India. Despite what he had said to Zo earlier, the knowledge he gained regarding gem-cutting helped him immensely in understanding the potential of each raw gemstone, enabling him to negotiate and get the best possible price.

Zo was happy to see that Raj had used the opportunity to study at the institute to build a life for himself in Madagascar. Since his departure, she had experienced many difficult situations with other students who chose to stay in the country illegally after finishing their course. She'd been dealing with multiple incidents involving students from their institute who had got caught trying to smuggle gemstones from Madagascar. Students had also been caught for having sex with underage girls, or possession and consumption of illegal drugs.

Lolo's brothers learnt precision-cutting from the institute. One of them benefitted from a post-training programme by receiving a donation of equipment for precision-cutting and free participation in international and local gem fairs, so they could promote their gem collections. As per Lolo's suggestion, IGM started facilitating the import of lapidary equipment and good-quality consumables. The Institut de Gemmologie de Madagascar also partnered with the university of Madagascar to produce locally made tools, more affordable for local lapidaries.

A few years later, as promised, Mr Lolo sent his daughter to train at the institute. During a casual conversation, Sara and Zo asked her about Louis and what role he played at the lapidary. She informed them he didn't have any experience and was working as a trainee when they'd met him. Lolo's brothers later trained him on precision-cutting after they had completed the course at the institute. Zo and Sara were pleased to learn that Lolo's clients now asked only for precision-cut style in gems, which is why they had to train the entire team on the new cutting technique.

Once they had completed the intensive training session, Mr Lolo's brothers shared their expertise with new recruits in their lapidary business. Some of them later found jobs in lapidaries abroad, and others established their own small workshops, employing and training new entrants in the industry.

After working for more than a decade in the mining sector, Zo was frustrated with the institute's lack of impact on the overall development of the gem-mining sector. Most of the small-scale miners were reluctant to learn more than their empirical knowledge. Some wanted to study but didn't have the financial means. Others were operating in the industry illegally and wouldn't risk registering their name and activities, especially with a government institute.

According to Zo, gem-mining in Madagascar has a strict hierarchy: men, women, children, and patrons have their respective positions and roles in the supply chain. The mining locations are dominated by men. Women are reduced to deal with low-value materials or put in charge of sorting stones. Children handle tailings, transportation, babysitting, or domestic chores.

Even though Madagascar is one of the most important sources of gemstones in the world, and many in the business benefit from the gems they buy from the country, the contribution of the mining sector to the country's development is not tangible. In 2017, Zo received a scholarship and left Madagascar to study development in Australia, hoping to learn from the successful mining culture of the country, and apply some of her learning in Madagascar.

When she returned to Madagascar, IGM could not hire her. The institute is currently undergoing a restructuring process, and Zo is working in Madagascar as an independent geology and mining consultant. She is trying her best to promote a fairer distribution of revenue through her work in the industry so individuals on the lowest rung of the mine-to-market ladder are not exploited.

The Panidars of Kagem

'If you come across a pegmatite deposit, run for the hills and never look back.'—Professor Morris Viljoen, Geology, Wits University, South Africa

16th September 2008

SEAN GILBERTSON touched the belt around his waist to check that he had the battery for his miner's hat, and his drager, a small device that produces enough oxygen to breathe for five to 15 minutes in case of emergencies. It was 3.30 in the morning, the start of a 12-hour shift for Sean at an underground gold mine in Klerksdorp, South Africa.

As he descended in a cage-like elevator with a few hundred miners, he began experiencing something he'd never felt before: dread. In a flash, Sean found himself crawling on his stomach along a narrow stope, or tunnel. *How did I get here?* he wondered. Pressure from the surrounding walls was restricting the movement of his limbs as he struggled to propel his body forward. The roof and the floor of the tunnel were pressing on him like a sandwich maker.

And then it happened, every underground mine worker's nightmare. He was stuck. With his fingers, he tried to shift the battery on his belt to wiggle himself free, but it didn't work. The realisation that he was trapped beneath two kilometres of hard rock was making it difficult to breathe. His co-workers were a few paces ahead, but they couldn't hear him shouting for help. *Don't panic. You have the drager*, he told himself, but when he reached to pull it out, it was missing. And then, he heard someone call out to him, 'Sean.' It was faint but getting louder. 'Sean!' He started shaking.

'Sean, my love, wake up.'

Sean opened his eyes. He was at his home in London, and his wife, Daniella, was by his side. He was drenched in sweat. 'Are you OK?' she asked, as he sat up in bed. 'You were shouting in your sleep. It was just a dream.'

Still disoriented from his nightmare, Sean said, 'Felt real. What's the time?'

'Five in the morning. When did you come to bed?'

'Around three, I think.' Sean pulled his wet T-shirt off and threw it on the floor.

'Let me get you a fresh one,' said Daniella, as she stepped away to grab a shirt from the nearby cupboard.

'Thanks, my love,' he said, as he let the soft warmth of the dry shirt cover his cold, wet body.

She stood by his bedside, watching him against the pale moonlight filtering in through the curtains. He looked weary and vulnerable. Taking a step closer to the edge of the bed, she pulled him towards her, enveloping his head in the folds of her cotton nightgown.

'I'm fine. Just need some sleep,' said Sean.

'What did you dream?'

'Something silly. I was stuck between two stopes in an underground mine.' The words were uttered in a plain, factual manner, as if it was normal to have dreams about being stuck inside a mine.

She leaned down and kissed his forehead. The sound of their ten-month-old son crying on the baby monitor pierced the hush of their bedroom. 'Go back to sleep,' said Daniella. 'I'll take care of him.'

'Will you wake me up around seven, please?' Sean asked. Daniella nodded and left the bedroom.

Sean lay back on his pillow. It was damp from his sweat. He turned it over and closed his eyes trying to keep his thoughts from wandering towards the exigencies of work. Eight weeks ago, he had taken over as interim chief executive officer of Gemfields. Although his past experiences involved corporate finance, investment banking, and the establishment of a trading platform for the coal industry[1], his current role as CEO was his first leadership position in an operational role, that too in a listed[2] company. It was his opportunity to step out of his father, mining magnate Brian Gilbertson's shadow.

After graduating as a mining engineer from Wits University in Johannesburg, Sean had interned at two of the country's underground gold and platinum mining operations. His nightmare was related to an incident that had occurred during his apprenticeship at a gold mine in Klerksdorp. The moment remained one of the most frightful of his 35-year life. But, contrary to his dream, Sean had been able to wriggle free by breathing out

1   Global Coal.
2   LSE:AIM.

and adjusting the battery pack that had gotten caught on the roof as he leopard-crawled.

He took a deep breath and closed his eyes. As the aftermath of his nightmare dissipated, the musty odour of newsprint by his bedside started infiltrating his thoughts. The papers all screamed the same story: Stock Market Crash. Lehman Brothers Files for Bankruptcy. Dow Industrials take a 504.48-Point Dive. Mounting Fears Shake World Markets as Banking Giants Rush to Raise Capital.

Sean propped himself up, switched on the lamp, and grabbed his water bottle, hoping the hydration would appease his parched throat and lull his mind back to sleep. A children's picture book peered up at him. Sean had been using it as a coaster. He smiled and picked it up. It was a toddler's version of *The Wizard of Oz*. He'd been reading it to his three-year-old daughter for the past two weeks. Unlike the Street's analysts, she wanted the same story every time. *The markets are definitely melting like the wicked witch of the west*, he mused.

Sean put the bottle and book away, switched off the light, and lay back in bed. But it was too late. His mind mercilessly began replaying pivotal moments from the past 12 months that had led to his current state of stress.

In November 2007, after two years of discussions, number crunching, research, and negotiations, Pallinghurst, an investment firm Sean founded in 2005 with his father and three other partners[1], had purchased 75 per cent of Kagem Mining Limited in Zambia. The idea of acquiring Kagem had come from a coloured gemstone entrepreneur called Rajiv Gupta. He had first contacted Pallinghurst in 2005, seeking an investment into his recently listed company, Gemfields Resources plc (Gemfields), which owned emerald mining licences in Zambia.

Gemfields' mines were a few kilometres away from the globally renowned Kagem emerald mine, which Rajiv's uncle, Shiv Shankar 'SS' Gupta, had established[2] as a joint venture operation with the Zambian government in 1983. Rajiv was involved in the family business with his uncle but decided to establish Gemfields as his own independent company in 2004.

Despite a successful listing on the London Stock Exchange (AIM), and an infusion of funds, investment in equipment and on-site expertise, Gemfields had failed to produce high-quality emeralds. The company's last two sales events had resulted in revenues of US$770,000 in November 2006,

---

1   Priyank Thapliyal (former right-hand-man to Anil Agarwal of Vedanta), former banker Arne Frandsen, and Kiwi Andrew Willis.

2   Along with BD Rao and a consortium of eight gemstone specialists from Israel led by Mr Harel.

and US$1 million in March 2007[1], not enough to sustain a hard-rock mining operation that had already chewed up more than US$20 million.

Unable to convince Pallinghurst to invest in his company, Rajiv had suggested they buy Kagem first and then merge their purchase with Gemfields to extract the much-needed economies of scale and knowledge that would make the consolidated operation compellingly profitable.

'Kagem has the emeralds, Gemfields brings the management and expertise, and Pallinghurst supplies the funding required for this venture,' Sean had explained to the Pallinghurst investment committee in 2007, seeking their approval for the deal. 'Gentlemen, the coloured gemstone market has been overlooked. De Beers did a wonderful job marketing diamonds and took everyone's attention away from coloured gemstones.

'It's a fragmented and undercapitalised sector. It does not have scale, it does not have the equipment, it does not have the skills. But if you walk up and down Bond Street in London and look inside the display windows of the top jewellery brands, you'll see fabulous rubies, emeralds, and sapphires. The market is there. We believe there is a solid opportunity for our combined venture to bring structure, consolidation, and growth, resulting in an overall expansion of the entire coloured gemstone sector. My favourite saying is, "Once you've had a colour television, you never go back to black and white".'

'But aren't gemstones typically found in small pockets?' one of the committee members had asked.

'True,' said Sean. 'But this is exactly why the Kagem emerald mine is a fantastic buy. That entire area, designated by the Zambian government as the Ndola Rural Emerald Restricted Area, contains bands of potentially emerald-bearing ore. As per our research and Kagem's historic performance, we could be looking at one of the largest emerald deposits in the world. The problem is that most of it is going to be low quality. We estimate that only five to maybe seven per cent of emeralds produced from this massive operation will provide the bulk of the mine's revenue. And to obtain that handful of precious emerald, which is scattered across this vast concession, we'll need to move many million tonnes of hard rock.'

Sean went on to share detailed technical and financial information related to the investment opportunity with the committee. He finished his presentation by citing the positive attributes of Zambian emeralds. 'Finally, all emeralds contain fissures inside. Manufacturers and merchants improve the appearance of such emeralds by oiling them or inserting soft and hard

1   https://www.diamonds.net/News/NewsItem.aspx?ArticleID=17086

resin, which sinks into the fissures. Since the refractive index of these oils and resins is close to that of an emerald, they aren't visible to the naked eye, making the emerald look cleaner, or improving its clarity. Industry sources and our independent research informs us that top-quality emeralds from Zambia contain fewer fissures, which means the rough may yield a larger gemstone during the cutting process and the final emerald may need significantly less clarity enhancement relative to Colombian emeralds. This has a direct impact on the price that an emerald can fetch in the marketplace, and its value appreciation over time.'

The committee had approved the deal.

To set their plan in motion, after acquiring Kagem, Pallinghurst completed a reverse takeover of Gemfields by exchanging their Kagem shares for a controlling interest of 55 per cent in Gemfields. Sean had championed the deal and was appointed interim CEO of Gemfields Plc in July 2008 after the firm was relisted on the London Stock Exchange (AIM). Rajiv Gupta continued to serve on the board as a director.

There was a lot to be done. Kagem had accumulated US$13.8 million dollars of debt, spread across ten different loan facilities from the Finance Bank of Zambia. After the acquisition, Sean spent considerable time restructuring Kagem's debt, settling US$7.5 million of the debt in the months that followed the deal, and accepting a payment plan for the remainder.

Thanks to the investment from Pallinghurst, Gemfields spent around US$52 million to upgrade infrastructure and equipment, expand the mine's operation, and start a gem-cutting factory in Jaipur in August 2009.

The gem-cutting factory had raised a few eyebrows among Kagem's old customers. They saw it as a potential threat to their business model, fearing the facility would get the best emerald rough from the mine. The initiative was in line with Rajiv Gupta's vision of a vertically integrated coloured gemstone company. There was another US$13 million budgeted for capital expenditure in 2009.

But Kagem wasn't the only jewel in the Pallinghurst crown. In January 2007, the private equity fund had purchased the Fabergé brand name from the multinational conglomerate Unilever for US$38 million.

Peter Carl Fabergé was a renowned master jeweller during the late 19th and early 20th century. From his workshop in Saint Petersburg, Russia, Peter Carl and his team of artisans crafted a range of jewels and decorative art objects.. They used diamonds, coloured gems, and his signature guilloché enamel technique in a variety of hues unique to his workshop.

Bejewelled items from the House of Fabergé were especially popular for gifting among royals and aristocrats. Peter Carl gained global fame, acquiring cult status, for his one-of-a-kind jewelled Easter eggs made annually for the Russian imperial family from 1885 until the Russian Revolution in 1917. Each egg exemplified the pinnacle of artisanship, design, and engineering, and featured techniques that transformed coloured gemstones, diamonds, and enamel into superlative works of jewelled art.

The father-son duo of Brian and Sean Gilbertson believed Fabergé would be the perfect vehicle to further fuel the resurgence of coloured gemstones in fine and high-jewellery segments. Their plan was to replicate De Beers' success with diamonds in the field of coloured gemstones. Fabergé's relaunch was slated for September 2009.

Giving up on the idea of sleeping, Sean decided to go for a quick run. By 8 am, he was at his desk in the office going through Kagem's emerald-production numbers. The mine was producing an average of 2.4 million carats of emeralds and beryl[1] per month, a significant increase compared to the average of 0.9 million in 2006.

The transformed company's first emerald auction was scheduled for November 2008, less than two months away. The auction would be a litmus test, tangible proof of whether Sean's recommendation that Pallinghurst invest in the combination of Kagem and Gemfields was on solid ground. For more than a year Sean had been speaking with industry stakeholders, researching auction formats, and trying to better understand what made the market tick.

Unlike diamonds, there was no established connection between specified quality categories and expected pricing. The coloured gemstone market was unorganised, and transactions were executed purely on what someone was willing to pay for a parcel or gemstone. The only visible marketplace where Sean could see price benchmarks for emeralds was results published by auction houses like Christie's and Sotheby's but those were for cut and polished emeralds, already set in jewellery, and mainly from Colombia.

He had access to Kagem's sales records from previous years, but the data was often skewed since the mine had on occasion sold its entire production run to a single buyer; Sean wasn't sure whether the prices he was seeing were truly a reflection of the real value of rough Zambian emeralds.

More than 90 per cent of Kagem's emeralds were purchased by 12 to 15 companies, all from Jaipur, and many from the same community. Almost all the bidders, Sean learnt, had familial, social, or cultural connections.

---

1 Every emerald is a beryl mineral. The difference between the two is the saturation of green colour. Only beryl gemstones with a high saturation of green hue (coloured by either chromium or vanadium) are designated as emeralds.

Thoughts of possible past collusion to drive down the price of rough emeralds started germinating in Sean's mind. Taking a sip of his second espresso, he opened a new document on his laptop and started hammering away, outlining the new terms and conditions the bidders would have to sign to participate in Gemfields' maiden auction for the Kagem emerald mine.

* * *

A year earlier
15th October 2007
Gemfields' emerald mine
Ndola Rural Emerald Restricted Area (NRERA)
Kafubu emerald fields

CV Suresh sat behind his desk reflecting on the conversation he'd just had with his boss, Alok Sood. Eighteen months ago, CV had answered a newspaper ad in the Times of India for a general manager position at an emerald mine in Zambia. At that time, he'd been working as deputy GM for the National Mineral Development Corporation of India, overseeing two massive iron ore mines, with combined total rock handling of about 12 million tonnes per annum.

He was well versed and trained in managing big mines, but unfamiliar with coloured gemstones. On his arrival in Zambia, he'd been dumbfounded when Alok had shown him one of the flooded mining pits, which looked more like a small pond because of a recent thunderstorm. It was a far cry from the colossal operations he used to manage in India. *This is what I am GM of, a pond?* His attraction to an international posting now seemed foolish. But there was no turning back.

Gemfields' emerald story began in May 2004, when the company's founder, Rajiv Gupta, purchased a 51 per cent interest in the Mbuva Mine, located within the Ndola Rural Emerald Restricted Area (NRERA). The region had a long history of copper mining, which overshadowed the discovery and exploration of emeralds that had been underway since 1962[1]. A year later, the company acquired the neighbouring Chibolele deposit, and a legendary emerald mine called Kamakanga[2], famous for producing some

---

1 Please refer to the story, "A Land called Kagem," for further information.
2 Rajiv Gupta purchased the mine from BD Rao, who used to own the Kagem emerald mine, and his last name's initials are the "RA" in the acronym HAGURA (see below). He had owned Kamakanga before the establishment of Kagem.

of the finest Zambian emeralds. The three deposits were merged under the Gemfields umbrella.

By the time CV joined as the mine's GM in June 2006, there was already a group of Gemfields professionals conducting exploration and mining operations in the shadow of the magnificent Kagem emerald mine that lay across the Kafubu River, around ten kilometres from their location.

'Kagem,' CV said the name out loud. Occupying 43 square kilometres in the heart of the government's 863-square-kilometre protected emerald zone, Kagem was the most prolific emerald mine in Zambia. CV and his colleagues had often discussed what it would be like to manage such a vast operation. And today, the gem gods had granted his wish.

'We've taken a controlling interest in Kagem[1] and are deputing you to take charge of the newly merged operations, CV,' Alok had said during their call a few minutes earlier. 'This will include our current mining operations at Gemfields and now the Kagem emerald mine.'

As the reality of the responsibility set in, CV was unsure how he felt. *Will things be different now that we have Kagem?* he wondered. The Gemfields mining operation had yielded more quantity than quality and the results of its recent emerald auction had been dismal. In contrast, Kagem had an established reputation for producing top-quality Zambian emeralds. Some believed the mine was geologically gifted with almost 30 per cent of the mineral-bearing area on the prolific Pirala Fwaya-Fwaya belt falling inside its licence boundary. But it was a vast operation that had also suffered from continuous pilferage, high mining costs, and the bugbear of emerald mining: inconsistent production.

Emeralds in the Kafubu region formed 455 to 500 million years ago and were buried deep beneath the Earth's surface. Instead of an underground mine with tunnels, Kagem was an open-pit operation, which required heavy investment in equipment and infrastructure for the removal of millions of tonnes of hard rock and soil to reach a few handfuls of emeralds.

CV had heard murmurings among the Gemfields staff that Kagem's glory days were over. While some believed the best emerald pockets were already mined out, occasionally, a superb, hexagonal, green, emerald crystal would appear in the markets of Kitwe, which would restore Kagem's mythical status. CV could not help but think of Kagem as both magical and monstrous.

---

1 HAGURA (an acronym for the three partner names: Harel, Gupta, and Rao) owned 75 per cent of Kagem with the remaining 25 per cent held by the government. Pallinghurst had purchased HAGURA and sold it to Gemfields in exchange for a controlling interest (55 per cent) in Gemfields (reverse takeover).

I'll have to call Unmukta and let her know I won't be able to come home for Diwali[1] again, thought CV, contemplating the difficult conversation he'd need to have with his wife. He'd missed celebrating the festival last year with his family and had planned to attend this year. CV gazed at the trees outside. The rainy season had started in Zambia and the air felt damp and heavy. His office was a simple prefabricated structure with cut-out windows. There was no cooler or fan, making the hot and wet months in Zambia especially difficult.

A soft knock on the door dragged him away from his ruminations. It was Exilda, one of CV's early hires. Some of the staff had raised an eyebrow when he had hired a woman to work at a mining company, but her smart responses in the interview had given CV the confidence to bring her on board. In the last eight months, she had proven indispensable, and he'd promoted her from security to her current position as an emerald-grading officer. In addition to her work in the sort house, she frequently spent time with the miners and geologists in the pit, recording emerald production and preparing reports for government departments and senior management.

'I hope this is a good time?' said Exilda, as she poked her head through the half-open door. 'I've brought last month's production report for your review.'

'But that wasn't due for another week.'

'I'd already finished the work. Thought it best to submit now so I have time to make any changes.'

CV smiled at her. 'If you keep this up, in a few years, you'll be sitting in my chair.'

She smiled back, beaming at the compliment.

'I also have good news to share,' said CV 'Our company is now the majority owner of the neighbouring Kagem emerald mine.'

'Kagem? Really?' exclaimed Exilda. 'That's wonderful, sir.'

'It's a step towards a bigger operation, which will bring its unique challenges. But keep this to yourself right now, Exilda. I'm going to make a formal announcement tomorrow,' CV said before sending her on her way.

He opened the first page of the document. Production levels hadn't improved, and it seemed like most of the material in the sort house was of commercial, rather than good, quality. He grabbed the small hand towel

---

1   Diwali is the Hindu New Year. For people of Indian origin globally, it's considered a combination of Christmas and New Year, a time to spend time with family and friends and offer prayers to the Hindu deity Lord Ganesha and Goddess Lakshmi, for good luck and prosperity.

that was hanging from the armrest of his chair, wiped off the sweat from the back of his neck, and started editing the report.

* * *

**One week later
22nd October 2007
Kagem emerald mine
Kafubu emerald fields
Zambia**

Aaron Nyangu had finished another long day and was walking towards the senior mess (dining room) for his dinner. He'd been working as a mine surveyor at the Kagem emerald mine since October 1996. Aaron entered the small room, grabbed a bowl, spoon, and tray, and got in line behind his friend and colleague, Peter[1], who worked as a mining engineer at Kagem.

'What's for dinner?' he asked, trying to peek above Peter's shoulder to where the kitchen staff were serving up at the food station.

'You really asking?!' responded Peter, as he turned around to give Aaron an incredulous look. 'It's either chicken or beef stew, as always.'

Aaron chuckled. As the cook poured the stew into their bowls, the duo looked at each other and said, 'Chicken!' They started laughing and made their way towards the communal table.

'Hopefully, we get better food with these new owners,' said Peter, amidst a spoonful of the watery stew. 'When does the new GM arrive?'

'I think next week,' said Aaron. 'His name is CV Suresh, Indian man. Same who runs the Gemfields mine across the river.'

'You know, I spoke with one of them during their last visit,' said Peter. 'They sound sharp. It looks like we're going to have people who may turn the company around. They were saying we'll have more machines and a large push back of the mine pit to open new production areas.'

'Aaron,' said one of the mine superintendents, who was sitting across from him at the table. 'You think we'll get a raise?'

'I can't answer that, but the investors seem like big money people,' said Aaron.

'Why do you say that?' asked Peter.

'The tall South African one among them—they say his family has a long history of mining.'

---

1   This name has been changed.

'What's his name?' asked Peter.

'Sam or Sean Gilbertson. Something like that,' said Aaron.

'Maybe they'll make a better road so we can bring our vehicles straight to the mine. Then, after we knock off at the end of our shift, we just drive back home,' said one diner.

'Or regular electricity, so we're not in darkness at ten every night,' said another.

'Maybe security will get better,' said Aaron.

The surrounding diners murmured their approval at this statement. Tensions between the miners and the security guards had been high. The staff was tired of the guards waking them up in the middle of the night to conduct surprise searches for emeralds in their quarters.

'What about internet?' asked a diner.

'You talk like you a got a fancy computer in your room! What you need internet for, eh?' said another from across the table, which caused a round of laughter.

The miners sat chatting long after their dinner was done, excitedly sharing their wish list of what they longed to get in terms of an improved work environment and better living conditions. An air of hope permeated the room. They went to bed content in their belief of better days ahead.

* * *

Three weeks later
12th November 2007
7.00 am
Kagem emerald mine
Kafubu emerald fields
Zambia

'Whenever an opportunity presents itself to you, take it, otherwise you'll live to regret.'—Jackson Mtonga

The sun was up, and large pillowy white clouds had started marking their territory against the clear blue sky. A cool breeze accompanied Exilda and her two female colleagues as they entered the all-male Kagem mining camp.

'Wait!' said one of the security officers at the gate. 'Who've you come to meet?'

'We're the staff from the Gemfields mine,' said Exilda. 'We have an appointment with the GM.'

261

'Appointment?' he laughed out loud. 'Don't you know women cannot enter the mine?'

'We were told to report at this time by the new GM, Mr CV Suresh,' responded Exilda. She pulled her shoulders back, gave the guard a polite but firm stare, and said, 'Please call his office to check before you turn us away.'

The man grunted and asked one of his men to run over to the GM's office to verify Exilda's claim. 'You wait outside the gate,' he said.

The abrasive attitude of the security guard didn't surprise Exilda. She knew of the superstitions in the community surrounding female presence at mines. When she had joined Gemfields in 2006, her family and friends had been surprised. 'But you're a woman,' her uncle had said. 'They say, the emerald is a woman and when she sees other women at a mine, she becomes jealous and goes back in the ground. A mine is no place for a woman.'

Exilda had scolded him. 'If I have to continue to live here, the only jobs are in mining, Uncle.' She was 29 years old, armed with a college degree, and needed to work to support her four younger siblings. It was a job in mining or nothing at all.

At Gemfields, she'd been relieved to find an inclusive environment. Women could work in the mining pit, the wash plant, and in the sort house. Although she had congratulated CV on the Kagem acquisition, she'd started feeling insecure because she knew there were no women at the Kagem mine. Now, the GM had summoned them to his office. She and her female colleagues feared their families were about to lose their source of income.

The man returned after 15 minutes and whispered something in the ear of the main security-in-charge who had stopped them. He opened the gate, and said, 'Nicholas[1] will take you to see the GM.'

When they reached the GM's office, Exilda took the lead and knocked on the door. 'Come in,' said CV.

'Good morning, sir,' said the three women in unison, as they entered the cabin.

'Morning, morning. Please, take a seat. As you all know, only a small percentage of employees from our Gemfields mine have crossed over to Kagem,' said CV, getting straight to the point. 'The good news is that you three are part of that small percentage.'

The women looked visibly relieved and thanked CV for the company's trust in them. He raised his hand, interrupting their expression of gratitude, and said, 'No need to thank me. You work hard. You all deserve it. But there's a catch.' The women fell silent. He leaned forward, and in a softer

---

1   This name has been changed.

tone said, 'We can't give you the same positions you had at Gemfields as those are already filled by experienced, highly qualified staff here at Kagem.'

Ignoring the disappointment on their faces, CV continued. 'We tried to find you jobs in the same departments, but it wasn't possible for various reasons. One of them being that this is the first time women are entering Kagem, and it's making the men nervous.'

'Nervous?' asked Exilda. 'What do you mean, sir?'

'You're Zambian. I'm sure you know very well this ridiculous superstition about women bringing bad luck to a mine. The company doesn't believe this, which is why you're here. But the problem is your Zambian colleagues at Kagem have this belief stuck in their heads.'

'What jobs would we have?' asked Exilda.

'You would work in the kitchen,' said CV, point-blank. He felt sick in his stomach as he said the words.

Exilda looked especially shocked, as if he'd slapped her across her face. 'Sir,' she said. 'I was a grading officer at Gemfields. How can I go from that to the kitchen?'

'Exilda,' said CV, 'I really tried with every single department supervisor. They all refused to have women in their team. I can't force them, otherwise the Mine Workers Union gets involved. And even if I somehow push them to find a job for you in their departments, they'll make life tough for all three of you.'

Exilda could hear the words CV was saying, but the tightness in her chest was making it difficult to breathe.

CV continued, 'The only department supervisor who agreed to absorb you was the head of catering. This was acceptable to the union.'

He didn't want to further dishearten the women by sharing what the male staff had said to him during their discussion: 'The fact that you are bringing women into the mine, Mr Suresh, this alone is a big problem for us. Women are bad luck. Because you had them in the Gemfields mine, your emerald production was not good. We don't want the same bad luck at Kagem.'

'The good part is that your salary will remain unchanged. No pay cut,' said CV.

Exilda knew she had no choice; she needed the job. CV explained they'd have to continue sleeping in their current quarters across the river and commute to the Kagem mine every day. After accepting the new positions, the women stepped out of the office. Nicholas, duly instructed, was waiting to escort them to the catering department. As they began walking, Exilda noticed how Nicholas kept his distance from them, staying a few paces ahead.

The cool morning breeze had vanished, replaced by the heat of the sun as it breathed down their necks. The trio spotted a group of around 30 mine workers in the distance walking towards them. They were headed in the opposite direction. Their bright blue safety hats and Fanta-orange overalls contrasted with the patch of green grass in front of a new block of buildings under construction. When they noticed the women, their demeanour changed. The laughter and conversation stopped, and they stared first in shock, and then a few started whispering to each other.

The distance between the two groups kept getting shorter. Exilda's palms became moist and her throat felt dry as she realised the men would pass right by them. Nicholas increased his pace, distancing himself even more. One miner called out to him, asking why the women were at the mine. He informed them they were new employees, and he was taking them to the kitchen.

The proximity of the approaching group allowed Exilda to see their faces, which were previously obscured beneath their hats. Most were glaring at the women. Others looked away as if a woman's gaze alone would bring them bad luck. As the two groups got closer, a miner spat in disgust on the ground towards the women. Another miner slapped the spitter on his back as a congratulatory gesture, sniggering in delight. Exilda took a deep breath and kept walking.

* * *

Three months later
12th February 2008
Kagem emerald mine
Zambia

Aaron Nyangu was looking forward to his dinner. Since the arrival of the new GM and the female staff in the kitchen, the quality of food had improved. Previously, a single vendor would supply the beef and chicken to the mine. Now, CV Suresh had opened the supply contract to multiple vendors, increasing competition, bringing better meat and vegetables at lower prices.

The aroma of fish curry greeted Aaron as he entered the mess. He picked up a tray and made his way over to the food station and was pleased to see stir-fried okra with rice and curry for dinner. Once he had loaded his metal plate, he looked around for a place to sit.

'Aaron!' called out Peter, waving his friend over to join them for dinner.

As soon as Aaron was seated, Peter said, 'We were just talking about this situation with the emeralds.'

'What situation?' said Aaron between mouthfuls of curry.

'That there is no emerald production.'

'And how are you guys going to solve that problem?' said Aaron to the group of miners sitting around him who seemed to be part of the conversation.

Peter leaned in, as did the others. 'We all know what the real problem is.'

'Peter,' he said, 'maybe I spent too much time in the sun today, but I can't understand what you're trying to say.'

'The women,' hissed Peter. 'They've brought bad luck to our mine. And now, the emerald production is almost zero.'

'That's nonsense,' said Aaron. 'I'm a superstitious man, but even I know the reason we don't have production is because the company must first catch up in removing all the waste rock so we can access production areas.'

'What do you mean?' asked a miner who was sitting to his left.

'They are removing the overburden and the soil above the emerald-bearing zone,' said Aaron.

'Yes,' said Peter, jumping in on the conversation. 'So what?'

'You all know the company was struggling with money before, so they only mined where they would find emeralds, what we call production mining. But all the waste rock had to also be removed and there's a backlog. In the last few years, because money was tight, the previous management did waste mining only if the waste was blocking an emerald-bearing section that they wanted to access right away.'

'But now we have an outside contractor for waste mining, Aaron,' said Peter. 'We're only mining the reaction zones. So why are there no emeralds, huh? I'll tell you why. First, they allow women to enter the mine, then they let them sleep in the camp.'

'Because the women were on weekend duty in the kitchen. That's why they had to stay on campus. Unlike the old system, the new owners don't let the expats live outside the mine. Someone must cook for them during the weekend,' said Aaron.

'Special weekend duty, eh?' said one of the miners, giving the others a conspiratorial wink. The men started laughing.

'And what about the auction bonus?' said Peter. 'Before, we'd get it every auction. Now there are no auctions and no bonus.'

'Maybe they are waiting till we have a good number of emeralds.'

'This is what I'm saying. They're waiting and waiting, but for how long? Think about it, Aaron. The same women were working at the Gemfields mine and I heard they sold very few emeralds at their last auction. Now, they are here. No auctions. No emeralds. How long you think they gonna keep paying us, huh?'

Aaron kept quiet. Despite an influx of new geologists at the mine, who were spending numerous hours analysing various segments of the mine's concession, and heavy investment in new equipment, there was hardly any emerald production.

In the absence of a clear response from Aaron, Peter looked over to Jackson, who worked in the sort house where they graded the mine's emerald production. 'What do you think, Jackson?'

Jackson looked up from his plate and said, 'I think you should try the fried okra with the fish curry. It's delicious.'

Irritated by Jackson's response, Peter said, 'We're having a serious discussion and you're making jokes about okra.'

Jackson put his spoon down. He leaned back from his dinner plate, looked Peter in the eye, and said, 'I joined Kagem before you, in 1995. I've seen a lot. We all know why the company did auctions every month. It was necessary to pay salaries. Emerald production had been challenging for a while, and I heard that the old Kagem owners owed a huge sum of money to the bank. If they didn't sell to new owners, maybe the mine would be closed.'

Turning towards Aaron, Jackson continued, 'You remember how much time it would take for the dump truck to deliver the emerald ore from the Chama mining pit to the wash plant?'

Aaron smiled and nodded.

Jackson turned to the rest and said, 'It would take two to three days to cover only a kilometre distance. Why?' he asked.

'I'll tell you why,' continued Jackson, 'Because the truck would start, next thing, tyre puncture. Fix that and move, engine overheated. Next thing, the steering wheel has broken. We had one excavator to cover all the production points: Chama, Fibolele, Fwaya-Fwaya. Out of seven excavators, only two worked, and sometimes only one, which would go turn by turn to each mining pit. I remember, one day, my team was waiting for it, and it broke down. We lost the day and had to wait for the excavator to finish the full route before it would be available for us again. Now, we have excavators in multiple locations, better equipment. I think we should be patient and see what happens.'

'All this is good, Aaron,' said Peter. 'But, if there are no emeralds and no auctions, this will all be over in a few months. Mark my words.'

* * *

14th February 2008
Kagem emerald mine
Zambia

Exilda had been assigned lunch duty at the worker's mess located near the main mining pit. This would be her first time outside the kitchen serving food to the mine staff. The meal service had been underway for 15 minutes when a mining supervisor approached the food station. He stood half a step away from the table, staring at her and the food. Thinking he may be confused about what to eat, Exilda asked, 'What can I offer you, sir?'

'I don't want anything from you!' he said, raising his voice. The other workers turned to look at the ensuing commotion. 'Because of you, we have no emerald production. You're not supposed to be at the mine.'

'Sir,' said Exilda, as she tried her best to keep her cool, 'we work hard from morning till night, like all of you. We are just trying to do our job.'

'We don't need hard workers, we need men. You have no place here,' the man continued.

'We have been selected by the GM to cross over from the Gemfields mine. Our supervisor is satisfied by our work,' said Exilda.

She was used to the mine workers returning every evening and openly blaming the women for the day's poor production. She could hear them talk while working in the kitchen. But the vicious manner of this attack made her uncomfortable, especially as the only woman in the room .

He took a step towards her, leaned over the food counter, and said, 'We all know why you are here. We talk about it. You are here because of these white men. You are here to service them. No one wants you at the mine, you should leave.'

Her lips started trembling and she ran out of the mess. Tears were flowing freely as she made her way to the shelter of her room. Twenty minutes later, there was a knock on the door. It was one of her female colleagues. 'Exilda,' she said. 'I heard about what happened. Are you OK?'

'I don't know how long I can take these insults. Did you hear what that man said about us?'

'I heard. They have a sick mind. You should go to Mr Suresh and complain.'

'I'm fed up. I'm going to go and quit. I'm not strong,' she said.

* * *

15th February 2008
Viewing platform
Kagem emerald mine
Zambia

CV Suresh stood on the newly constructed viewing terrace, overlooking open-cast mining pits at Kagem, approximately 50 to 60 metres below the platform. The structure, rested on a shipping container and was further supported by iron pillars dug into the ground. Wooden boards formed the floor with a metal roof above. Being elevated provided a better view of the mining operations.

Most of the prevalent emerald contact zones[1] had been mined out. The old Kagem team had conducted one last auction in October 2007 at which approximately two million carats were sold for around US$1.4 million. This left little emerald in stock when Gemfields took over. CV and his team had two options before them. A short-term income generation strategy to extract and sell as many emeralds as possible in the next two to three months, or, invest in mine development. Guided by the Gemfields board, the team focused on the long haul.

The cacophony of excavators, dump trucks, and chisel men working across the massive expanse would have motivated a normal person to reach for noise-cancellation headsets. To CV, the din of the earth-moving vehicles and tinkering tools was like listening to a divine opera. He could stand on that platform from dawn till dusk.

Amidst the noise, CV thought he heard his name being called. He turned towards the sound and saw a tall Zambian man holding a file. CV approached him, and said, 'Jackson, right?' as he took the file.

'Yes, sir.'

'Thank you.'

Jackson was going to hand over the file and leave, but there was something on his mind.. He spun around and said, 'Mr Suresh, I was very ashamed to hear about the way one of my colleagues shouted at Exilda yesterday. I heard she is quitting. Is that true?'

'She was,' said CV, 'but I convinced her to stay. You know, I hired her in Gemfields. She is a smart woman and a hard worker and didn't deserve the treatment she received.'

---

1   The point of intersection between talc magnetite schist (TMS) and pegmatite rock. The contact between these two rock types is responsible for the formation of emeralds in the Kafubu emerald fields.

'Yes. I agree with you, sir.'

'When did you join the mine, Jackson?' asked CV.

'Oh, I joined in 1995, Mr Suresh,' said Jackson. 'This entire area was very different, then.'

'This means you are probably one of the longest-serving employees.'

'One of them. Yes. There are others like Amon and Aaron.'

'So, tell me. Why is that pit called Chama?' asked CV, pointing downwards, diagonally across from the platform.

'Actually, Chama is the name of the digger who first found emeralds in that location.'

'Really? 'When was that?'

'Long time ago. Before the government created the protection zone and started issuing mining licences. In those days, people didn't have to dig too deep to find emeralds. The way they were mining would be considered illegal today but at that time it was OK.'

'It was very interesting how they extracted the emeralds,' continued Jackson. 'When they find a hard rock like the white quartz, these diggers, they would set fire to it, make it become, what we can call red hot. Then, they would come with water and pour it on the stone, and the stone would crack. And that's how they were getting through these big rocks.'

'How interesting,' said CV. 'But wouldn't that create a lot of smoke?'

'Oh yes. Sure. When they would set the fire, they would be out of the trenches or the tunnel for two or three days because of the smoke,' said Jackson. 'Once they saw that the fire was almost gone, they'd come with big buckets, pour that water on the rocks—not cold water like from the fridge, but just normal water—and get some cracks. Then, they'd have big levers, big hammers. You know they had muscle. They were very strong. They used the hammer to break and carry away the rocks. You'll be very surprised that they were moving big rocks from the trenches in this manner.'

Listening to Jackson tell the story, CV couldn't help but smile. Jackson was waving his hands and had a big smile on his face. He was enjoying the opportunity to share historical insights about the deposit, exuding a positive energy that was infectious.

'Then what happened?' asked CV. He had fallen under Jackson's storytelling spell, temporarily forgetting about the file he'd just received.

'Then the government came to these guys and said, "OK, guys, whatever you've been doing in the past, we'd like to legalise, you know, in the NRERA zone." They told them like this, "If you can get a licence, you can mine here".'

'Did any of them get a mining licence?'

269

'No. Sorry to say they had not gone to school, so they were illiterate. What they were told was that the people who were going to buy this mine, they will employ you. It does not mean that we are chasing you out of this area completely. So, you can continue to mine the emeralds in a more mechanised way, but in a legal way.'

'Then the Gupta family formed this company, Hagura, with BD Rao and the Israelis, correct?' asked CV Suresh.

'Exactly. Together with the government, they established Kagem in 1983.'

'What about the history of the Kamakanga Mine? The one that's part of the Gemfields operation on the other side of the Kafubu River,' asked CV. 'Gemfields purchased that from BD Rao and when I joined, I heard so many stories about the fantastic emeralds that came out of the mine.'

'Did you know that BD Rao used to be a cutter for one of our customers?' said Jackson, setting the scene for his next story.

'Really? I wasn't aware,' said CV.

'Oh yes. I heard that in the late seventies he would travel to Rhodesia to buy rough emeralds from the Sandawana Mine for RM Shah of London. He would come to Zambia to buy amethyst from Kariba.'

'How did he land up as the owner of the Kamakanga Mine?' asked CV.

'He heard there were emeralds being found in that place. You know what Kamakanga means?' asked Jackson with an impish grin.

'Tell me.'

'In our Bemba language, makanga means "guinea fowl". If someone wanted to eat guinea fowl, they would go across the river to that area. Then, when the people started digging there, and they find emeralds, they talk to each other and start calling the place Kamakanga, the place where you get guinea fowl. So, BD found out about the emeralds, and he got a licence and bought half of the mine around 1980. The other half was with a Zambian man called Bodwin Kambala who had some political ambitions.'

'Did you ever see emeralds from Kamakanga?' asked CV.

'I didn't but I heard from our customers that they were the most beautiful emeralds ever to come out of Zambia.'

'Is that so?'

'Sure. Rich blue-green colour. Our customers said that Kagem never produced anything like those early emeralds from Kamakanga. But BD ran into some trouble with the government. He sold his interest in Kagem also very early because he didn't have the funds, but he kept Kamakanga. The government deported BD from Zambia and then a few years later they invited him back. He purchased the other half of the mine from Mr Kambala

270

and started producing good emeralds. It was a productive time for him. Finally, he sold the mine to Rajiv Gupta and Gemfields.'

'Do all the names of the mining pits have stories?' said CV.

'Oh sure,' said Jackson.

'What about Fibolele?'

'That one is funny,' said Jackson, sniggering. 'It means "rotten stones"!'

'Rotten? Like bad?' asked CV.

'Yes.'

'Oh God. Why?'

'Because that pit always produces low to medium quality emeralds. A lot of quantity but quality? Not so much. I remember once we had so much production that for one week, we were filling dump trucks with emeralds. When emerald production in Chama or Fwaya-Fwaya would be low, the company would start mining Fibolele so at least they have something to bring to auction.'

CV looked at his watch. He had a meeting of the department heads in 30 minutes, but he didn't want to interrupt Jackson's stories. Embedded inside his anecdotes could be helpful insights related to the history of the mine's geology. 'What about the one in the corner called Dabwisa?' asked CV.

'Dabwisa means "surprise". The pit would be dormant for a long time, and then one day, surprise! We'd find emeralds.'

'You work in the sort house, yes?' asked CV

'Sure, but I started with mining in the pit. Then, I was transferred to the wash plant. Then, it is very interesting how I came to the sort house. Should I tell you the story?' said Jackson. There was a twinkle in his eye.

CV started laughing, and said, 'Maybe next time. We both need to get back to work.'

As Jackson left, CV took a quick glance at the papers Jackson had brought and walked towards the edge of the viewing platform to observe the operations beneath in the mining pit. *Fifteen more minutes and then I should leave for the meeting*, thought CV, glancing at his watch. He could see three teams working in the pit.

'What's happening there?' CV said out loud to himself. He had a pair of binoculars hanging from his neck, which he now used to inspect a scene unfolding at one of the production zones. A chisel man had walked up to a mining team and started working alongside them in the pit. One of the mine workers then asked him to leave. It looked like they were arguing. The intruder kept putting his finger on his lip as if asking his colleague to keep quiet.

CV picked up the walkie-talkie on the nearby table, calling on the security chief to further investigate. *Time to leave*, he said to himself, as he grabbed his papers from the table and headed for the meeting.

CV reached their prefabricated office just in time. Once everyone had taken their seats, CV began. 'Good morning.' He turned towards the head of security, Adit Kumar[1], and said, 'Adit, I spotted some unusual activity at one of the production points. I radioed your team and asked them to investigate and report back to us here.'

'Sounds good.'

'Right, KP, why don't we begin with a geology update,' said CV, addressing Kartikeya Parikshya the head geologist at Kagem[2]. 'And before you begin, may I request everyone first summarise their strategy for the benefit of some fresh faces in our team and then delve into last week's report.'

'Sure,' said KP. 'As you know, Kagem is an open-pit mining operation. On the geology side, we have two priorities. Number one, to accelerate emerald production. To that end, Gemfields will invest about US$33 million over the next two years, the bulk of it in the upgrading and expansion of Kagem. Second, we must think beyond the immediate future and determine the sustainability of this operation.

'What is the life of the mine?' he asked his colleagues. 'Ten years, or more than 20? Our goal is not just to restore this deposit but to see it achieve its full potential. How do we do this? Our concession is 43 square kilometres. We can't just start digging everywhere. Not good for the environment and too costly. To narrow our focus, we must first conduct geophysical studies of the land, which will help us identify potential sectors for emerald production. We'll then commence trenching and drilling, to extract samples from the ground, and study them. All of this will help the mining team plan their operations. Any questions before I continue?'

'Will you need a security detail when you're conducting these surveys of the concession?' asked Adit.

'We won't because geophysical studies are done without puncturing the ground. To share further details, we'll be doing two types of studies: magnetic and radiometric. Magnetic because our main ore body is talc magnetite schist, or TMS, which contains the valuable chromium or vanadium that's responsible for emerald's green colour, and its magnetic nature will react to geomagnetic tools. This helps us figure out the orientation of the TMS band underground. But TMS alone is meaningless. We'll only find

1   This name has been changed.
2   Before Kagem, KP was in charge of geology at the Gemfields mine. He'd worked on the Kagem acquisition with Rajiv Gupta and Sean Gilbertson.

emeralds where the TMS interacted with the pegmatite rock around 450 to 500 million years ago. For this, we conduct radiometric surveys for pegmatitic dyke identification, which leads us to the contact zones with the TMS. This is where, if we're lucky, we'll find beryl. And if we're really lucky, out of that beryl, some will have enough green colour in them to be designated emeralds. And if we are really, really lucky, then a few will be top quality, which will make this operation worthwhile.'

KP paused and expectantly looked at Adit Kumar, waiting for a counter-question. Adit raised his hands in surrender, and said, 'No questions, boss.' The occupants in the room started laughing at the sheepish expression on Adit's face.

KP smiled and continued with his weekly report. 'The correctional work to fix the high walls is progressing well. We hope to resume production mining in the Chama pit within the next month.'

'Great,' said CV. 'Let me share a quick mining summary. Before our arrival, emerald mining at Kagem was basically what we call rat-hole mining, which created very high walls and dangerously deep pits. Some pits were ten metres deep and mine workers would sit inside the bucket of excavators to be lowered in the pit. Waste mining was done on an ad hoc, when-really-needed basis. To speed up the correction work, we have hired a third-party contractor for waste mining. Since they began in November last year, the quantity of monthly ore removal has jumped from 150,000 tonnes to 600,000 tonnes per month, an increase of 300 per cent in mining capacity.' CV glanced around the room. All eyes were still on him. He continued his report.

'Right now, the waste to (emerald) ore ratio is 50:1, which means for every part of ore, we need to move 50 parts of waste rock and soil. As we go deeper and push back the walls of the open pit, that ratio will increase. We'll need to do more waste mining to access the emeralds, increasing the cost of operations,' CV continued, noticing one of the security supervisors enter the room and slip a handwritten note to Adit as he spoke. Once finished, CV turned towards the security chief, and said, 'Over to you.'

'Thanks,' said Adit. 'Security has been a long-standing issue with Kagem. We know from auction records that around 70 per cent of the mine's revenue has come from only five to ten per cent of emeralds that were sold. That's the nature of the deposit—the really good stuff has all the value. Because of this, if mine workers collude with security and steal even a few stones, it can cause a huge revenue loss, impacting the profitability of the entire operation. The previous management tried various initiatives to control pilfer-age: hired Israeli security personnel, recruited Manyengo chisel men from

Western Zambia to create a language barrier, and outsourced to local security firms. Despite all these measures, the collusion and theft continued.'

He went on, 'When Gemfields took over, the priority was to secure the investment on behalf of our shareholders, which includes the Zambian government, 25 per cent shareholders of Kagem. We instituted a three-tier security system, which included local Kagem security personnel, foreign security staff, Zambia Police mobile units and established standard operating procedures. Most of the expat security officers are Gurkhas who are globally renowned for their high level of discipline, resilience, courage, and endurance. So far, it looks like our strategy is effective as the recovery rate of emeralds during searches by expat security has been much higher.'

'Any recent developments?' asked CV, keen to discover more about what he observed earlier in the mining pit.

'Yes,' said Adit. He looked at the rest of the attendees and said, 'CV noticed a squabble between two mine workers before this meeting and immediately reported it to the security supervisor.' He looked at CV and said, 'You were right. There was something odd about that argument. As you all know, the Zambian mine workers stay on campus from Monday to Friday. They return to their families for the weekend. Under previous management, the chisel men would be shuffled every Monday across different mining teams in the pit to control pilferage. We stopped this weekly shuffling and created groups to foster healthy competition and provide incentives. Having permanent teams also helps us notice patterns in case of security breaches. Turns out, Bwalya[1] from HR is still distributing weekly assignment sheets to the workers as per the old process.'

'What?' said CV. He wasn't expecting such blatant insubordination.

'Not only that,' Adit continued, 'it seems when the chisel men arrive Monday morning, some of them don't even report to their team leaders but go straight to the pit that Bwalya has assigned them. The squabble CV witnessed occurred because a worker who didn't belong in a particular group was trying to mine in the pit on the sly as per Bwalya's instructions.'

'I don't understand,' said CV. 'How do they know where they have to work? Workers must report to their assigned locations as soon as they arrive. There is no time to interact with HR.'

'He informs them on Sunday from his home in Kitwe.'

'That's ridiculous!" said CV. 'Why haven't the foreign security team or the expat geologists reported this?'

1 This name has been changed.

'I think they're all new and unfamiliar with the staff. Plus, in uniform and with their mining hats, it's easy for someone to go unnoticed.'

* * *

Three months later
15th May 2008
Mine worker's mess
Kagem emerald mine
Zambia

Aaron Nyangu could smell the aroma of dinner as he approached the entrance of the staff mess. His mouth started watering, and his stomach rumbled in anticipation. Exilda was serving the staff at the food station. When his turn came, he smiled at her and asked, 'What's smelling so good?'

She laughed and said, 'We've made chicken curry, sir.'

'This looks very different from the chicken curry I had before. What's the secret?' Aaron asked as he piled his plate with rice and curry.

'Ah! That's our special ingredient. Why don't you have a taste and let's see if you can guess what it is?'

Aaron took a spoonful in his mouth while still standing in front of Exilda and said, 'Mmmm... delicious. I will need to eat a lot to figure out the secret.'

Delighted with the compliment, Exilda laughed and said, 'We have plenty. You're welcome to return for a second helping, sir.'

Aaron gave her a thumbs up and moved on to find a spot with his regular companions at the community table.

'Have you heard what's happened, Aaron?' asked Peter, just as he'd taken his seat.

'What?' Aaron said, taking a large spoonful of the juicy chicken curry. He started deconstructing the recipe in his mind. *There's tomato, maybe some cumin powder, chilli, but what's this sharp flavour?*

'Aaron!' said Peter. 'You're not listening to me.'

'Can you not let me enjoy my meal in peace for one minute?' said Aaron. 'I'm trying to identify the spices in the curry.'

'Bwalya has been fired.'

'I heard.'

'That doesn't bother you? They're firing our fellow workers every day. What are we going to do about it?'

'Do you know why he was fired?'

'He was just doing his job, and one day he's out.'

275

'No. He was disobeying the bosses. He was disrupting the new system. And they had already given him many warnings. But he wouldn't listen.'

'It's not about him alone. There is too much change.'

'You were the one who first said these new people are very smart. What happened? You wanna go back to the old ways?' asked Aaron. He was getting irritated with the constant whining from Peter and some of his other colleagues.

'I know things are better,' said Peter. 'Electricity, good food. They say the company will put fans in all the rooms, but so many new foreign workers coming. A lot of the old people leaving. I also feel nervous.'

'Listen. Bwalya was working here for a long time,' said Aaron. He leaned closer to Peter and lowered his voice. 'But you and I both know he was up to no good. Why, on a Sunday, was he informing mine workers which pit they will be at?'

Peter didn't respond. He knew what Aaron was implying. They'd both managed to keep away from some of the unscrupulous emerald traders in the Kitwe market who were perpetually targeting workers at the various emerald mines in the Kafubu area. Both were aware of small groupings that had formed over the years involving local security personnel, chisel men, and workers in the wash plant and sort house.

Jobs were scarce. Like Peter, Aaron also felt bad when someone they'd known for years lost their livelihood. 'I don't know what the future holds, Peter,' he said. 'All we can do is keep our heads down, do the best work we can, and the rest is up to God. The old company is gone. This is a new company. New bosses. New rules. The work they have been doing for the last six months, that we have all been doing, has resulted in emerald production. We all got a bonus from the company. I think better days are coming. You think about that while I get more food.'

Aaron got up and walked back to the food station. He noticed one of the mining supervisors saying something to Exilda. The conversation looked serious. *Was this the same guy who shouted at her?* he wondered.

'Back so soon?' Exilda said as Aaron approached the food station.

'I hope that man was not bothering you. He the same one who shout at you, yes?'

Exilda smiled. She served Aaron with a generous helping and said, 'Yes. Same one. But today he came to apologise.'

'Really? What he say?'

'He said, "I'm sorry for the way I behaved. It was because of our belief that women would bring bad luck. Now we understand we can produce, so I am sorry for what I said and what I did".'

'Good,' said Aaron, smiling. 'More importantly, I think I know the secret ingredient in the curry.' He could see that reminding Exilda of the shouting incident had dimmed her cheerful demeanour, and he wanted to change the subject.

'Really? OK, let's hear it.'

'Roasted cumin!'

'Yes, but that's not the special one. It's fenugreek leaves,' Exilda said, laughing at the look of dramatic shock on Aaron's face.

* * *

16th October 2008
Kagem emerald mine
Zambia

'Relax. We have time,' CV said to his wife, Unmukta. Since he once again couldn't return to India for Diwali, she'd decided to join him at Kagem for a few weeks. The trip tied in nicely with an invitation they had received to attend a family friend's wedding in Ballito, South Africa. After attending the festivities, Unmukta would return to India and CV would head back to Kagem.

'Bas ho gaya [Almost done]. I must be careful with my sarees,' said Unmukta.

'I don't know why you decided to bring all these expensive sarees.'

'Why not? What's the point of having things if you're not going to use them. See this one,' she said, as she held up a silk burgundy saree with gold thread embroidery. 'It was a gift from your mother when we got married.'

'Accha [OK], they're all very beautiful and you will look great when you wear them.'

'But only if we don't miss our flight!' said Unmukta. 'There. Done. You can take the suitcase now.'

As the couple made their way to the company's Toyota Hilux, Unmukta said, 'Two to three hours' drive to reach Ndola airport, flight to Lusaka and then another one to Johannesburg, correct?'

'Yes,' confirmed CV. 'Plenty of time. Don't worry. I'm waiting for some printouts from the office that I need to study.'

'Didn't you say there'll be security check posts on our drive? Won't that take time?'

'So, you were listening to me!' teased CV. The last two weeks in Kagem with his wife had been a welcome change from his usual routine. 'The security checks don't take time. Our driver will show our papers, and they'll have a quick look inside the boot.'

As CV finished the sentence, Kagem's head of security, Adit, joined them, and handed over a folder. 'Latest report of recovered emeralds.'

'Great. I'll have a look and call you.'

'I also included recoveries under previous management.'

'Thanks, Adit.'

'Happy journey.'

An hour later their vehicle approached the first checkpoint. As CV had predicted, the guards checked their papers, asked the driver a few questions, and sent them on their way. He turned to his wife and said, 'See, I told you. We'll probably reach the airport early. I'm going to study these papers while you enjoy the view.'

'What are they?' asked Unmukta.

'It's a report by the security team.' CV recognised that look in his wife's eye. She wanted to know more. He took out the first sheet and said, 'Look at this table. This shows a comparison of emerald recoveries in 2007 before we took over the operation and what they look like now.'

'What do you mean by emerald recoveries?'

'When the staff finish their shift, whether it's in the mining pit, wash plant, sort house, anywhere, they go through a security check. A physical search.'

'To see whether they've stolen any emeralds?'

'Unfortunately, yes.'

'And does security find any?'

CV pulled out the first sheet from the folder and read out loud, 'In 2007, the previous management recovered 790 emeralds.'

'Wow. Actual emerald pieces.'

'In 2008,' CV continued, 'our team, since they took over in November 2007, have recovered 3,400 emeralds.'

'My God. And this is because of your foreign security team? The Gurkhas?'

'Yes. The other amazing thing our team has done is reduce the cost associated with the mine closure plan from US$5 million to around US$450,000.

'I don't understand. What do you mean by mine closure?'

'See, when you're operating a mine, if you must close it for any reason— maybe you ran out of money, or the regulation changed, or it's not cost effective anymore to mine, whatever—you need to return the land to a reasonable state. That's the responsible thing to do and it's also the law.'

'OK. But you're not closing the mine, so what's this US$5 million?'

'The five million US dollars is what it would have cost us to restore the mine if we'd decided to close it immediately after purchasing Kagem.'

Unmukta gave her husband a puzzled look.

'Let me share what we did, then you'll understand.'

'Go on.'

'Now, Kagem is an open-pit mining operation. No underground tunnels, which means we're moving a few hundred thousand tonnes of rock every month, digging a big hole in the ground. If we have to refill that hole, we need topsoil.'

'Why?'

'Because without topsoil, we can't grow any trees. We started preserving the topsoil in a separate location to use when we must refill any segments of the mine.'

'Fascinating,' said Unmukta. 'What do you do with all the rocks and soil you dig out of the pit?'

'We dump it in the pit. The technical term is called in-pit dumping or backfilling.'

'I'm confused. Isn't that what the previous management was doing?'

'No. Imagine you have a kidney-bean-shaped bowl, which is mostly full of rice and just a few peas, which are hidden beneath the rice. Let's say the peas are emeralds. To extract the peas, we need to meticulously move through the rice bowl. As we remove the peas, we keep piling the rice on one side of the dish. The way a child would squish all their food in one corner of the plate to make it look like they ate a lot.'

'What's the point of doing that?'

'If we don't do that, then we have an empty kidney-bean-shaped bowl, lots of rice outside it, and the cost of filling it with rice later, at the time of mine closure, is higher than just shuffling the rice in the bowl as we move from right to left, extracting the peas.'

'What were the miners doing before?'

'They were extracting the peas and, while they had money, they were taking the rice all the way out of the bowl. By the end, they were just taking out the peas and not moving any of rice, which was making conditions in the bowl downright dangerous, as the rice could collapse at any time.'

'I think I understand. Only problem is I'm craving a good biryani[1]!'

CV burst out laughing. 'This is nice.'

'What is?'

---

1 An Indian rice dish cooked over a long period with vegetables, meat, herbs, onions, and fragrant spices.

'Sitting here and explaining all this mining stuff to you. It's fun. Thank you.'

Unmukta smiled and said, 'One more question, and then I promise I'll let you work. I noticed a water body. What's that for?'

'Water is vital for us because we use it to wash the ore. I won't get into technical details but due to rain and groundwater, mining pits must be frequently drained of water. Where should this water go?'

'In the Kafubu River?' asked Unmukta.

'Yes. But it needs to be discharged in a responsible way. We take the mine water to another special pond, and let the sediments settle to the bottom first. Once that's happened we take the clean water and discharge that into the Kafubu River.'

CV was so engrossed in the conversation that he didn't realise the car had stopped for another security check. It was only when the guard reached inside and confiscated the car keys that CV looked outside. 'What's going on?' he asked their driver.

'Bwana,' he replied. 'They take away the car keys. Never happen before. They ask everyone to come out of the car.'

CV had gone through innumerable security checks in over two years, first working at Gemfields and now the Kagem mine. He'd never been asked to step out of the car.

'Out. Out,' said the police officer. His demeanour was hostile, uncommon with Zambians.

'Open your bags,' the man said to CV.

The checkpoint was guarded by three uniformed policemen. CV's explanations were futile, and he soon realised that there was no choice but to quietly follow their instructions.

After opening their suitcases, CV went and stood next to his wife. He noticed her hands were shaking as she wiped a bead of sweat trickling down her forehead. The couple watched helplessly as the policemen threw their clothes and belongings out of the suitcases. CV spotted four plain-clothed individuals watching from a distance. One of them was on his mobile, as if giving a report. They looked intimidating.

When the officer flung Unmukta's sarees on the dry and dusty ground, she grabbed CV's arm and lamented, 'Meri sarees [My sarees]. Kya dhoond rahe hain? [What are they looking for?]'

CV covered her hand with his and whispered, 'Emeralds.'

'Humare paas? [With us?]'

'Don't worry. Just stay calm,' said CV. Underneath his cool exterior he was trying not to panic. If they were caught with emeralds and no accompanying papers, they might be treated as thieves and arrested on sight. Their foreigner status could result in immediate deportation, possibly planned by someone. Though CV was confident of their innocence, the enthusiastic actions of the officer made him wonder if someone had planted emeralds in their luggage.

After every single item from their suitcases lay on the road, one of the police officers said, 'Pack your things and go.'

CV witnessed the senior officer make eye contact with the waiting group and shake his head once.

Rage and shame filled him as he and his wife gathered their now dirty clothes. Once they had safely crossed the checkpoint, Unmukta burst into tears. CV pulled her close, cradling her head on his shoulder. 'It's over.'

Once she had run out of tears, Unmukta pulled away and said, 'How can you carry on working here after being treated like a common criminal? Bhaad mein jaye aise naukri [To hell with this job]. We don't see you for months. The children miss you all the time and for what? To be insulted and mistreated.'

CV didn't know what to say. He felt humiliated. His years in Zambia had been some of the most difficult in his career. Besides harsh living conditions, CV and his team had endured insubordination, union issues, pilferage, low production, political interference, and long hours working in an unfamiliar country. His introduction of more effective expat security had also led to death threats. It was clear he was not welcome in Zambia and the situation would only get worse.

'Nothing is more important to me than your well-being,' Unmukta said. 'This time we were lucky. You were lucky. What about the next time, huh? Can you guarantee something like this won't happen again?'

* * *

2nd October 2008
Tank Fine Gems
Jaipur, India

Dharmendra Tank burned the tip of his tongue drinking his morning cup of tea as he read Gemfields' invite for its maiden emerald auction for Kagem. He'd slept for only three hours the previous night because his 67-year-old mother had an anxiety attack around 2.30 am—a regular occurrence since her second stroke. Dharmendra's father had passed away at 69 due to heart failure. Since then, his mother had become his number one priority.

Dharmendra came from one of the most respected families in the coloured gemstone business. Contrary to the secretive nature of most in the industry, Dharmendra's grandfather, Rajroop Tank, believed in sharing his learnings. A successful gem merchant and manufacturer, he was highly respected for his free apprenticeship programme, in-depth gemmological knowledge, and renowned expertise in cutting and polishing stones.

He wrote a detailed book on gemmology in 1960 titled *Ratna Prakās*, which was later translated into English and published as *Indian Gemmology*. In the book, scientific information related to gemstones intermingled with ancient beliefs and historic references from sacred Indian texts[1].

Dharmendra looked at his watch and called his childhood friend and business associate Nilesh Shah, in London. It had been a while he'd visited Zambia, and wanted to check if Nilesh was planning to go for the Gemfields auction.

Nilesh Shah was a gem specialist based out of London's iconic Hatton Garden, which was considered UK's hub for diamonds, coloured gemstones and jewellery. He'd inherited the business from his father, Ramanlal Shah, who was a vital link between gemstone miners and the manufacturing sector in Jaipur. After joining the firm, Nilesh expanded their portfolio and started bidding for rough Zambian emeralds at the Kagem auctions with Dharmendra Tank.

A sleepy voice answered on the other side. 'Hello?' said Nilesh Shah.

'Nilesh. It's me,' said Dharmendra. 'Time to wake up.'

'You know it's 7.30 in the morning here.'

'So? Were you sleeping?'

'Just making my morning coffee. How are things?'

'You got the invite from Gemfields for the Kagem auction?' asked Dharmendra. He and Nilesh had grown up watching their fathers work together. Now, it was their turn.

'Yeah. Have you applied for your Zambian visa?' asked Nilesh. 'The auction's in a few weeks.'

'I don't think I'll come. You can represent us,' said Dharmendra.

Nilesh closed his eyes. In the last six years, his childhood friend had travelled on maybe five or six occasions, a far cry from his usual twice or thrice a month routine. Even for those rare journeys, Nilesh had spent hours convincing Dharmendra to leave Jaipur. 'How's Aunty?' he asked.

---

1   Vedas.

'The same.' There was silence between the two friends. And then Dharmendra said, 'I can't leave her, Nilesh. What if something happens while I'm away?'

'It's been years since Kagem had a proper auction. Our emerald stock is ridiculously low, Dharmendra. We must attend together, in full force. I need you with me,' said Nilesh. 'Did you tell Aunty about the auction?'

'Yes.'

'What did she say?'

Tank let out a long sigh and said, 'That I should go. She said, "Don't worry; you'll find me healthy when you return".'

'Why don't you give Aunty a mobile phone. If she feels anxious, she can call you.'

'She already has one,' said Dharmendra. The friends were silent again. 'OK. I'll attend.'

'Excellent.'

'Have you learnt anything about these new owners?' asked Dharmendra.

'Only that the CEO is a chap called Sean Gilbertson, whose father is this big shot in the mining industry, Brian Gilbertson. From what I've read in the news, Brian Gilbertson was responsible for one of the most significant deals in mining: the merger of BHP and Billiton. They're from South Africa. And Rajiv Gupta is involved with them.'

'Gupta? As in Shiv Shankar Gupta's nephew?'

'Yeah. Same.'

'Hmm. Interesting.'

Nilesh started laughing. 'Please stop thinking about the back story, Dharmendra. Let's stay focused on the emeralds.'

* * *

Day 1 of the Kagem Mine's emerald auction by Gemfields.
3rd November 2008
InterContinental Hotel
Lusaka, Zambia

Sean Gilbertson had exactly 15 minutes for breakfast before leaving for the auction venue, a floor inside Finance Bank Zambia's building. Natural, un-tinted light was vital to help bidders assess rough emeralds, and the space they were temporarily renting from the bank was surrounded by large floor-to-ceiling windows.

As Sean shovelled spoons of his daily nutrition fix—fruit, granola and yogurt—into his mouth, he thought about the terms and conditions he'd written up for the bidders to sign before they could view the emeralds. Mining alone was not enough. The key to unlocking Kagem's true potential would be a new way of auctioning the goods to extract the highest price for the rough emeralds. 'We are going to publish auction results and show the world the true worth of Zambian emeralds,' he'd written in a recent email to the Kagem team.

'May I trouble you for a double espresso in a takeaway cup, please?' Sean asked the server. He checked his watch. Two minutes to spare. Sean preferred sitting outside. The open expanse of the veranda seating, with birdsong in the background, softened the cacophony of silverware and live food stations.

He picked up his BlackBerry to check if it was working, but the screen was blank. 'Thanks a lot, Vodafone,' Sean muttered under his breath. His team had secured a local mobile for him to stay connected with their head office in London. Between launch preparations for Fabergé, a failed take-over attempt of another mining company, TanzaniteOne, and a possible licensing deal worth millions for a Fabergé hotel in Dubai, the last thing Sean needed was to be incommunicado.

* * *

Same day
Taj Pamodzi Hotel
Lusaka, Zambia

Manoj Dhandia waved to Dharmendra Tank and Nilesh Shah as they walked into the breakfast room. He was with his son, Vaibhav, the fifth generation in their family's gem-manufacturing and trading firm.

All three men (Manoj, Dharmendra, Nilesh) had grown up watching their fathers' business dealings.

'Is that your son?' asked Nilesh. Since he was based in London, he only caught up with the tight-knit Jaipur emerald community at international trade shows or the Kagem auctions.

Manoj's son, Vaibhav, stood up to greet the new arrivals. 'My word! How he's grown,' said Nilesh. 'How old are you, Vaibhav?' he asked, taking a seat at their table.

'Eighteen, Uncle,' said Vaibhav.

Nilesh raised his eyebrows at Vaibhav and said, 'Wow. You know, your father was about the same age when he attended his first emerald auction.' He turned to Manoj and said, 'Isn't that right?'

'I was younger,' said Manoj. 'Seventeen when Dad brought me with him to Lusaka in 1983.'

'My first auction was in 1982,' said Dharmendra, jumping into the conversation. 'It was hosted by the Zambian government's Reserve Mineral Corporation.'

'You have it easy, my boy,' said Nilesh. 'Now we're staying in this nice hotel. No problem with vegetarian food.'

'In those days, we used to struggle to get decent veg food. Dharmendra, what was that temple where we'd go for dinner?'

'Swami Narayan Temple,' Sunil Mittal answered on Dharmendra's behalf as he pulled a chair from a nearby table and joined the group. Sunil was Manoj's business partner.

'Why don't you both go and grab your breakfast. We need to get going soon,' said Sunil.

The 17 invited companies were the world's top emerald manufacturers. Except for two, all were from Jaipur, India. Among the non-Indians were buyers from Israel, Hong Kong, New York, and Germany. The room was evenly divided between the older generation, who had been buying Zambian emeralds since the seventies, and the younger bunch, which included Manoj, his partner Sunil, Nilesh, and Dharmendra. For them the Kagem auction had been an essential rite of passage with their fathers. It cemented their position as the heirs apparent. And now, they were at the auction in a leadership role, carrying the flag for the next generation to follow.

Previously, brokers brought rough emeralds to Jaipur, or international buyers would travel to Zambia to purchase rough in informal marketplaces near Kitwe. Kagem's establishment, in 1983, led to organised trading, with regular emerald auctions by the Zambian government.

'Nilesh,' Manoj called out as his friend returned to the table with his omelette. 'Dharmendra mentioned you'd done some homework on these new Kagem owners. What do you make of them?'

'They have the right background,' said Nilesh. 'Hopefully, a professional company can bring some stability to the industry in terms of supply. We'll know more at the auction.' He turned towards Vaibhav and said, 'You're in for a real treat today. The quantity of rough emeralds you're going to see in one room—it's an incredible experience.'

'We'll have to see how this new company conducts the auction,' said Nilesh. 'But in the old days, there used to be one long table full of rough emeralds and we would all sit around it, taking turns to view the green mineral mounds. It was like an emerald feast.'

'Accha [OK],' said Dharmendra to the breakfast group. 'You wanna stay here and reminisce, or go buy some emeralds?'

'Vaibhav, don't pay any attention to Dharmendra,' said Nilesh, winking at the young boy. 'He's always got ants in his pants on the first day of auction. Chalo, chalo [Go, go].' Nilesh placed his hands on Dharmendra's shoulders and playfully pushed him out of the breakfast room.

They continued chatting in the taxi, exuberant in their anticipation of the day ahead. 'Finance Bank Zambia,' Sunil read the sign outside the building. 'This is the place. I want to get the first slot for viewing.' He stepped out of the elevator, wrinkling his nose at the pungent smell of fresh paint.

'Not if we register before you,' teased Nilesh, jumping ahead of them as they walked towards the waiting Kagem team.

'Good morning,' said Sean Gilbertson, stepping forward to shake hands with the early arrivals. He exchanged pleasantries and made introductions. 'Let's get started on the viewing. If you could make your way to our registration desk, Kagem's COO, Alok Sood, will share the terms and conditions of our auction process, and the contract you'll need to sign to receive the bid book.'

'Contract?' said Dharmendra. 'Why are we signing a contract when we haven't even seen the goods?'

'The contract is to participate in the auction,' said Sean. 'To confirm you accept our terms.'

'This is new,' said Nilesh. 'Why didn't we receive this in advance?'

Sean was puzzled by the question. He'd assumed the bidders had seen the terms beforehand. *This is not good*, Sean thought. Nilesh's remark had snuffed out the friendly energy in the room. 'Why don't I provide a quick overview?' he suggested, to diffuse the tension.

'Sounds good,' said Nilesh. They were still standing in the foyer outside the elevator.

'Towards our right,' Sean began, 'is the main emerald viewing room. Let's go in.'

The bidders followed Sean.

'We've created individual booths, which are strategically lined alongside tall windows. Plenty of natural light, perfect for assessing emeralds. Across from the booths there are additional cubicles, where you can comfortably check larger emerald parcels. There is no restriction on viewing time.'

'How many times can we see a parcel?' asked Nilesh.

'Once, before you cast your bid,' replied Sean.

'Sorry, that's not enough,' said Dharmendra. 'We need to inspect the emeralds under different lighting conditions. How can we do that by just seeing them once?'

The others echoed Dharmendra's views, which sparked a discussion. After some back and forth, Sean agreed. 'Given the volume, the maximum number of viewings we can accommodate would be twice in one day.'

The bidders agreed, happy to have won their point.

'What is that shiny, electric green box?' asked Nilesh, pointing towards a container on a table at the far end of the rectangular room.

'It's where you'll deposit your sealed bids at the end of each day—' said Sean.

'Hang on a minute,' interrupted Nilesh. 'You mean end of the week, right?'

'I am afraid I mean end of the day, Mr Shah. You'll have to place your bids today on whatever emerald parcels you view. You can revise your offer upwards during the week by placing a second bid, but the first one needs to be deposited before you leave the venue.'

'But we used to check emeralds on day one,' said Dharmendra, 'and again on day two, and three, before submitting our bids on the last day of the auction.'

'That's the old way of conducting the auction, Mr Tank,' said Sean. 'We've created a new process, similar to De Beers and the DTC's[1] diamond auctions.'

'But this is not the same system as De Beers,' Nilesh countered. 'They have sight holders.'

'Exactly,' said Sean. 'The buyers don't have a choice. They must accept the parcels the company allocates, which is not the case with Gemfields. We believe that market forces should reign supreme. Like I said before, you have the option to revise your offer before the last day.'

He could sense the customers were a bit annoyed, but he didn't want to give them any opportunity to potentially collude with other bidders and undercut Kagem's reserve pricing. He'd heard enough stories of low bids being cast to force the mine to sell the entire production at the end of the auction to whoever was the last one still in the room. Keen to get things going, Sean said, 'Let's step outside, I'll show you the rest.'

The group followed him into a waiting area outside the room.

1   Diamond Trading Corporation.

'You'll notice clusters of sofa seats arranged at a distance. Each lounge area is alphabetically marked and will be assigned to individual companies or registered bidding consortiums.'

'Why?' asked Dharmendra.

'Sorry?' said Sean.

'Why this assigned seating?'

'We would like bidder groups to not interact with each other during the viewing. When you're not viewing the goods, you must wait for your turn in the lounge area designated for your company.'

'So, we can't speak to our industry colleagues?' asked Dharmendra. His pitch was getting higher with each question, a telltale sign he was getting upset.

'Why don't I take you to the registration desk and we'll get going,' said Sean, avoiding the question.

After registration, Sean said, 'Now that you have signed the contract, please hand over your mobile phones to security. They will provide you with a token, which you can use to collect your phone when you're leaving.'

'Sorry, what?!' said Dharmendra, as he raised both hands in protest. 'I can't surrender my mobile.'

'Mr Tank,' said Sean. 'I'm sorry, but mobile phones are not permitted inside the viewing room. New rules for the auction.'

'Why weren't we informed of all these rules when you sent us the invite?' asked Nilesh.

'Whether you knew in advance or not, the process would have remained unchanged. We're trying to make everything more organised.'

'What would have changed is our attendance,' said Dharmendra.

'No one is forcing you to stay,' said Sean in a polite but firm manner. As he said the words he stood before them with his arms crossed against his six-foot-one frame. He could sense a rebellion brewing and wanted to nip it in the bud.

'Fine,' said Nilesh. 'Refund our airline ticket and hotel and we'll leave.'

'I am afraid we can't do that.'

'Look here, I'm not trying to be difficult,' said Dharmendra, softening his tone. 'My mother is genuinely not well, and I need to be available in case she calls. That's non-negotiable.'

'This is true,' chimed Manoj from the back. 'We're all aware of how gravely ill Dharmendra's mother has been. In fact, he wasn't coming for the auction.'

Sean suggested Dharmendra hand over his mobile to a designated security personnel in the viewing room. 'As soon as your phone rings, he'll bring it to you,' said Sean.

Dharmendra agreed and he and Nilesh proceeded to the first viewing booth.

'Sorry Mr Dhandia,' said Sean, turning his attention to the next group. 'Only two persons allowed inside from each company.'

'But this is my son,' protested Manoj. 'It's his first auction—he's come all the way from India. What's the big deal?'

'We weren't informed he would be attending. Our records only have you and Mr Sunil Mittal registered under Dhandia Gems Corporation.'

'We didn't inform you in advance because we never thought you'd have an issue. Why does it matter whether we are two in the booth or three?'

'We can only allow those who are registered, I'm afraid.'

'We'll register him now.'

'Mr Dhandia,' said Sean. 'If we start making exceptions for you, then other customers will protest. I'm afraid my hands are tied. Your son must wait outside.'

'What if he attends for an hour, and then swaps with my partner, Sunil?'

'That won't be possible,' said Sean. 'You need to decide now who will be the second person for the entire duration of the auction.'

While Manoj and Sunil verbally wrestled with Sean outside the viewing room, a new issue began brewing inside between Dharmendra Tank and Jackson Mtonga.

'Look here, Jackson,' said Dharmendra. 'This isn't my first emerald auction, or yours. I can't check the goods like this.' He was referring to a tray of emeralds before him. The rough stones were covered by a transparent plastic, and Jackson had just finished explaining to Dharmendra that he would have to inspect the stones without removing the protective sheet.

'I understand, sir. But this is a new system.'

'But it's nonsense. Why can't we take the emeralds out?' Dharmendra continued. 'Are we thieves who are going to steal these stones and run away? I must check each piece against the light and see how I am going to cut it, what yield I can get after cutting? What quality? Price? Only after I assess it properly can I bid for the stone. Please go and talk to your bosses and sort it out; otherwise, we're leaving right now.'

'OK, Mr Tank. Please don't leave. I'll go and talk to them.'

A few minutes later, Jackson returned. 'Mr Tank,' he said. 'As per your request, we're changing the process.' He looked at the security staff manning the booth, and said, 'You can remove the plastic covering. Customers are allowed to inspect the goods in their hands. However, you will weigh the stones before and after inspection and reconcile against the carat weight in the bid book.' Jackson then looked at Dharmendra and Nilesh, and said, 'Hope this works for you, gentlemen?'

* * *

Last day of the Kagem emerald auction
7th November 2008
8.30 am
InterContinental Hotel
Lusaka, Zambia

'Did I wake you?' said Daniella.

'I should be up. Need to leave for the auction anyway,' replied Sean.

'How's it going? I haven't heard from you all week.'

'I know. Sorry, my love. It's been an insane roller-coaster ride, without seatbelts or sleep!'

'Why?'

'I don't know where to begin. Day one, buyers showed up, and when we presented them with the new terms and conditions, they were shocked. Turns out they hadn't received them in advance.'

'Shouldn't someone have emailed those across?'

'Yes. It's a reasonable ask, and I need to investigate why it didn't happen and who dropped the ball. Meanwhile, throughout the auction, a big chunk of my time was spent apologising to bidders for our failure to advise the correct viewing dates and the terms and conditions. To make matters worse, a few customers arrived late, in the middle of the auction week, because they weren't aware they had to register on day one. Since they'd travelled all the way from India, we had to allow them to see the goods. This upset the ones who'd arrived on time. They felt it wasn't fair to them. Just one thing after another.'

'I am sure it wasn't all bad.'

'Well, many shared positive comments on the way our team had graded and sorted the emeralds. They also liked the privacy our booths provided, but overall, there was a lot of pushback.'

'Have you opened the bids?'

'Yup. And it ain't pretty.'

'Not enough bids?'

'We had the bids but not the prices we need. It took all my willpower to keep a straight face as we made note of the values bidders were assigning to our emeralds.'

'What's the difference?'

'Half of the minimum reserve. Some of the bids were one-third of our MRP[1].'

'How could there be such a huge difference?'

'It's baffling. Maybe this new process I've created has thrown the customers into a tailspin, or—' Sean paused.

'Or what?'

'I don't even wanna say it out loud. Or we've led investors into an asset where the revenues are never going to justify what we're spending.'

'That sounds extreme. Could be temporary. Because of the financial crisis. The low numbers reflecting market sentiment.'

'I hope so.'

'Sean, you're sounding so low.'

'There's just so much going on, my love. We launched a hostile bid a few days ago to take over TanzaniteOne. And since that grenade was lobbed, it's just been nonstop emails and calls between advisors and lawyers, and announcements to shareholders, because both TanzaniteOne and Gemfields are listed.'

'Hostile? I thought you'd gotten the support of the shareholders.'

'We'd won shareholder support, yes, but the TanzaniteOne board or Tanzanite One Ltd simply issued 83,739,976 million new 'B' shares in Tanzanite One Mining, a wholly owned subsidiary of Tanzanite One SA, itself a wholly owned subsidiary of Tanzanite One Ltd. This meant that 50.2 per cent of the company belonged to its own subsidiary, giving the board control over the company, diluting Tanzanite One, and, effectively rendering our position worthless. So, that ship has officially sailed. It's a goddamn shit show.'

'That's the company named after the gemstone, tanzanite, right?'

'Yeah.'

'I still don't understand why you were keen to acquire them. Tanzanite isn't as valuable as emerald, right?'

'No, it isn't. In fact, when it comes out of the ground, it doesn't look like much. Imagine a dull stone, which ranges from light beige to darkish brown. But after it's heated, it transforms into this marvellous electric purple-blue colour. The thing is, this company, TanzaniteOne, took a gemstone like that

1   Minimum reserve price.

and, based on good old-fashioned marketing, professional mining, grading and distribution, built a business that is probably the best up-and-coming coloured gemstone company in the world.'

'I see the attraction.'

'Anyway, no point in discussing it. It's not happening.'

'You still have today to turn around the emerald bids, right?'

'It'll be all hands on deck to conduct a live second-round auction among the top three bidders for every single parcel. We're going to try our best to extract maximum revenue for each one.'

'I am sure you'll pull through. You always do,' said Daniella. The situation Sean was describing sounded grim, but she knew she couldn't let that realisation reflect in the tone of her voice.

'I honestly don't know. Bottom line. If the bids don't meet our MRP, we won't sell the emeralds. Unless I can pull a bunny out of a hat, it looks like we'll be returning to the mine with most of our production. That's a whole year's worth of hard work, investment, planning, and for what?'

'I think you're being too hard on yourself, my love.'

'At the end of the day, I'm the CEO of Gemfields. An unsuccessful takeover attempt of TanzaniteOne, followed by a failed first auction on my watch. It doesn't reflect well to say the least.'

'Sean, stop. You're beating yourself up and going into this negative spiral. Remember, you're only one guy. All you can do is put in your best effort, deploying your judgement. You've been working nonstop, hardly sleeping, and so you're probably not seeing straight. There's only so much you can do.'

'You're right.' Sean took a deep breath. 'More importantly, how are our babies?'

'Bouncing along,' replied Daniella. 'Max kept me up for most of the night.'

'Is he OK?'

'He's fine. A bit of colic. Nothing serious.'

'I miss you guys.'

'We miss you, too.'

'Jeepers! It's almost nine. I must dash.'

'Love you.'

'Love you, too.'

* * *

11.00 am
Kagem emerald auction
Finance Bank Zambia
Lusaka, Zambia

The atmosphere in the viewing room was drab. Throughout the week, the Gemfields team and bidders had many arguments on the new auction rules. Unpleasantness permeated the air. 'Gentlemen,' said Sean, addressing the bidders in the room. 'Today is our last day, and we shall now begin round two of our emerald auction.' Noting the quizzical looks, Sean continued, 'If you may recall, in the terms and conditions document you signed on day one, there was a section which explained how, on the last day, we shall have a second round of bidding, with the top three bidders for each emerald parcel from round one.' Blank expressions and pin-drop silence ensued. 'It'll become clear when we begin.'

Dharmendra turned to Nilesh and said, 'Ab yeh kya bakwaas hai? [Now what is this nonsense?]'

'Let's see what happens,' responded Nilesh.

Dharmendra and Nilesh were among the top two bidders for Lot 1. Another room had been setup for the live auction. The two bidding teams were seated inside separate booths. They could see the auctioneer, but not the individuals they were bidding against.

'You are both the highest bidders on this lot,' said Sean addressing Dharmendra and Nilesh in one booth and a second bidding team in the other. 'To facilitate the final round of bidding without revealing your identity to other bidders, you have two plastic cups. Cup A represents an incremental bid of ten per cent, and Cup B is equal to an increase of 20 per cent. Please raise the relevant cup depending on the amount you'd like to bid.'

'Why can't we just write down the amount we want to bid?' Dharmendra whispered to Nilesh who just shrugged his shoulders in response.

Within five minutes of the bidding, with plastic cups being waved around, Nilesh looked at Dharmendra and said, 'I can't do this. As far as I'm concerned, this is the last straw. We should leave.'

Nilesh and Dharmendra stood up and walked out of the enclosure, catching Sean off guard.

'I am sorry,' Nilesh said to Sean. 'This is not the way to conduct an auction. We put our bid, which as you just said was one of the highest, and now you want us to play this game with these cups, which we can't understand. We're not interested in the auction and we're leaving.'

Sean stood shell-shocked for a few seconds, and then followed them outside the room where he encountered Manoj and Sunil in a heated argument with other Gemfields team members.

'Mr Shah, this is the last day. Your bid is already one of the top ones,' said Sean in an effort to re-engage Dharmendra and Nilesh.

'Your system makes no sense,' said Nilesh. 'It was fun to play along at the start when the amounts were not large, but I'm not laughing anymore. This entire auction is ridiculous.'

'There's no need to get upset, Mr Shah,' said Sean. 'All we've been doing this week is apologising. Yes, this is a new way of auctioning the Zambian emeralds. And we're not going to apologise for it anymore. We're trying our best to make things more streamlined.'

As the volume levels went up, Manoj joined Dharmendra and said, 'I know we're small traders in comparison to your big company, but we're all here to do business respectfully. Nobody is gifting us anything and we are not looking for any favours from anyone. If we're buying rough emeralds from you, we're paying in advance. You don't ship me the goods unless my money is in your bank account. We're used to competing for emeralds at the Kagem auctions. And we understand that's the nature of the business. But this is not the way business is conducted.'

By the time he had finished speaking, a group of bidders and Gemfields staff had gathered around them.

'This is our business,' said one of the Gemfields staff. 'We'll conduct it whichever way we like. Who are you to tell us how to run things?'

'We are the buyers,' shouted someone from the bidding group.

'Look, if we as your buyers can't understand this system, then what's the point?' said Nilesh. 'We put in a bid, we had the highest bid, now you want to make us compete with the next highest bidder. When does the bidding stop?'

'The bidding stops when people stop bidding,' said a senior Gemfields staff member. 'If there is a demand for a certain parcel, the bidding will continue. We want the market forces to determine the price. And this is our system. Our emeralds. Our company.'

'You watch your tone, OK?' said Dharmendra. 'This whole week we've been putting up with all the disrespect you guys have been throwing our way. Not saying anything. But enough's enough.'

'Disrespect?' asked Sean.

'Yes! This nonsense that we can't interact with each other. We can't have our mobile phones. We must sit like school children in designated corners. Take turns to eat cold pizza that you put out. What do you think? We have nothing better to do than sit around and plot how to undercut your prices? We're all running professional companies, and guess what? We are competitors. This is too much!' Dharmendra turned to face the crowd of bidders and said, 'Nilesh and I are walking out, and our company is going to boycott this auction. Who's with me?'

Others of the same generation as Dharmendra and Manoj immediately joined the boycott. But the older folks refused to leave. The room was divided.

Dharmendra said to them in Hindi, 'Hum yeh sab apne business ke leye nahin kar rahe [We are not doing this only for our business]. If we don't take a stand today, these people will continue to walk over us. Please support this. We need to be united as an industry.'

* * *

5.30 pm
Kagem emerald auction
Finance Bank Zambia

Dr Godwin Muyoba looked at his wristwatch. Thirty minutes left before the auction ended. Dr Muyoba had long served on the Kagem board representing the government's 25 per cent interest share in the venture. After the morning boycott, involving more than 50 per cent of Kagem's customers, the bidding continued with the ones who had stayed.

Some were still examining the rough emeralds. *What's going on over there?* He spotted two customers approaching Sean. From Dr Muyoba's vantage point, they seemed to be making a proposal. The conversation looked serious as the three remained huddled for a good 15 minutes, after which Sean escorted them to the elevator. He turned around, spotted Dr Muyoba and walked straight towards him.

'That was interesting,' said Sean.

'What do you mean?' asked Dr Muyoba.

'Did you see those two bidders? They offered to buy Kagem's entire emerald production at this auction.'

'Really? But what about the people who've cast their bids?'

'They think we won't sell much, so this is their way of helping us out.'

'Interesting indeed. What price?'

'That's the best part,' said Sean, as he shook his head. 'They offered one-fifth of our reserve price.'

'I'm assuming you said no?'

295

'Absolutely. The goods have been valued by an external expert, we've established our minimum reserve price, and that's that.'

Dr Muyoba nodded. While he appreciated Sean's transparent approach and commitment to the auction rules, he worried about the outcome. The restrictions imposed by the new system had put a dampener on the usual jovial atmosphere Dr Muyoba was used to seeing at Kagem auctions. There were many political and commercial eyes watching the new Kagem management. The bids hadn't been opened, but from what he'd observed, it would be a miracle if the mine sold their emerald production at the minimum reserve price.

* * *

February 2009
11.30 pm
The Business Centre
Trident Hotel, Nariman Point
Mumbai, India

This is the right move, Sean told himself as he stood staring at the twinkling lights of Mumbai. Kagem's maiden emerald auction four months ago was unsuccessful. The bids were ridiculously low compared to the value assigned to the mine's emerald production and, as feared, the team had returned to Kagem with most of the lots unsold.

The bidders who had boycotted the auction, attended the Gemfields dinner for a few minutes only to hand over a protest letter to Sean. On returning to Jaipur, they reported their experience to *Gem World* magazine[1], which published a scathing review of the Gemfields auction.

Sean had always known that his position as CEO of Gemfields was temporary while he, along with the rest of the board, sought a suitable individual. The auction results and its aftermath brought home the importance of industry experience. A change had to be made, and fast. The sound of the nearby printer choking on paper interrupted Sean's ruminations.

'All OK?' Sean asked the business centre executive.

'I am afraid not, sir. The paper's stuck inside the printer.'

In two swift strides, Sean was by his side. He stood watching the man wrestle with the machine, to no avail. 'Perhaps we can use another printer?' he suggested.

---

1 A trade publication.

'Sir, just give me ten minutes. I'll have it sorted.'

As Sean watched the man scurry away, he returned to his view of Mumbai by night. The business centre was on the top floor of the hotel. The space was surrounded by floor-to-ceiling clear glass windows that offered an expansive view of the urban jungle beneath. Despite the late hour, Mumbai heaved with action.

'There's a crazy energy to this place, isn't there?' said Ian Harebottle, as he joined Sean by the window.

'I love it,' replied Sean. He looked over at Ian and smiled. In the last seven months, the two had gotten to know each other well. Ian was the former CEO of TanzaniteOne. He'd been part of the company's incredible climb from a start-up to one of the world's largest coloured gem-mining and marketing firms, listed on the Johannesburg Stock Exchange. But a year ago, he resigned, after the departure of its founder, Mike Nunn.

When Ian learnt from Sean of Gemfields' interest in taking over TanzaniteOne, he'd volunteered his insights and help, knowing the new owners may reinstall him as CEO. It had been Sean's idea to bring Ian on board as the CEO of Gemfields after the failed emerald auction in Lusaka. Barring one voice of dissent, the rest of the Gemfields board had approved Sean's proposal.

Sean was scheduled to give a talk at a gem and jewellery show in Mumbai, and to present the first Gemfields emerald collection to have been cut and polished in the company's new Jaipur lapidary. Keen to not waste time, Sean suggested Ian join him in India, sign his new employment contract as CEO of Gemfields, and visit their offices in Jaipur and Mumbai, before a trip to the mine in Zambia.

'I'm going to step outside to check on the printout, Ian,' said Sean. 'It seems the printer has gobbled up your contract.'

'Maybe the machine knows something we don't!' said Ian in jest.

Before Sean could leave, the hotel executive returned with the documents. 'All done, Mr Gilbertson.'

'Great,' said Sean. The two sat down and began applying their signatures to Ian's employment contract. As they got to the last page, Sean stopped. 'One problem.'

'What's that?' asked Ian.

'We need a witness.' He turned towards the hotel executive and, offering him his pen, said, 'Would you mind?'

A collection of rough Zambian emeralds from the Kagem emerald mine. Photo credit: Gemfields.

Manoj Dhandia and Sunil Mittal inspecting rough emeralds at the first
Gemfields emerald auction (2008). Photo credit: Gemfields.

View of the vast expanse of the Chama pit in March 2019. On the right, example of in-pit dumping. On the left, white vertical bands of pegmatite visible in the distance against the wall of the open mining pit. Photo credit: Richa Goyal Sikri.

Bidders assessing rough emeralds at the Lusaka auction (2008). Photo credit: Gemfields.

Emerald sort house team at Kagem Mining Ltd (February 2009). Standing (left to right): SPSO – Krishna Bura, Jackson Mtonga, Ian Harebottle (former CEO), PSO – Sydney Changwe. Seated (left to right): Oswal Kapusa (retired), Nelson Ngambi, Mbalandako (left), Late Raymond Chola. Photo credit: Gemfields.

Gemfields team at Kagem. Left to right, KL Verma, Alok Sood, CV Suresh, Sumit Upreti, Kartikeya Parikshya, Arvind Mathur, the late Marlon Zimba (27th August 2008). Photo credit: Gemfields.

From left to right: Alok Sood, the late Marlon Zimba,
Sean Gilbertson, CV Suresh. Photo credit: Gemfields.

White bands of pegmatite rock visible against the wall of the mining pit at
the Kagem emerald mine (March 2009). Photo credit: Gemfields.

Gotam Jain, Julius Petsch, and Sean Gilbertson. Photo taken on 27th August 2008 when Petsch along with his long-standing business associate (Jain), visited the Kagem emerald mine. Photo credit: Gemfields.

Two emerald production points inside one of the Kagem mining pits. Photo credit: Gemfields.

Author's Note

This story is based on experiences as narrated to the author by Sean Gilbertson, CV Suresh, Dharmendra Tank, Nilesh Shah, Manoj Dhandia, Jackson Mtonga, Aaron Nyangu, Exilda, and Kartikeya Parikshya. Special thanks to Anirudh Sharma, Adrian Banks, Prahalad Kumar Singh, Govind Gupta, and Dr Sixtus Mulenga for answering my questions related to geology, gemmology, emerald-grading, and Kagem's history.

I would like to convey my gratitude to Sean Gilbertson for wholeheartedly supporting the documentation of the incidents surrounding Kagem's 2008 emerald auction. I would also like to thank Dharmendra Tank, Nilesh Shah, and Manoj Dhandia for agreeing to share their experiences. Mr Tank, and Mr Shah would like to clarify that while it may seem from the story that they were in the minority with respect to the boycott in 2008, they did have the support of many bidders at the auction, and the dissent was expressed by a fair number of Kagem bidders at that time.

Barring characters that have been identified as fictitious, the story is based on actual events, individuals and experiences. Certain scenes, dialogues, and incidents have been fictionalised to aid the narrative process. Geological and gemmological insights are based on conversations with the contributors and independent research conducted by the author.

Sean Gilbertson's decision in late 2008 to appoint someone with more experience of the coloured gemstone sector as CEO of Gemfields paid off. After joining, Ian Harebottle attracted other talent from TanzaniteOne. A pivotal hire among them was Adrian Banks who significantly recalibrated Kagem's sorting, grading, and auctioning system for rough emeralds, transforming the company's prospects. Within a few months, the new Gemfields team scheduled an emerald auction in London in July 2009.

Rough-emerald parcels were available for inspection in booths, affording bidders the privacy they had appreciated at the Lusaka auction. However, the format was relaxed. Buyers could keep their mobile phones and interact freely with all attendees at the auction.

Rough emeralds were cleaned by manually removing dark biotite schist and exposing the emerald crystals embedded in the host rock[1]. The mine's production was graded according to colour, clarity, and size. This improved rough-emerald assessment by bidders, and reduced post-purchase cutting and polishing time.

---

1   The rock type within which an emerald is formed.

Impressed with the quality of the goods and the reconfigured format, almost all the rough-emerald lots were sold (99.8 per cent sold by weight) generating US$5.9 million in auction revenue. The company doubled down on its investment in developing the Kagem emerald mine, with an aggressive waste mining programme to open more (emerald) ore-bearing contact zones for production mining.

Between 2010 and 2011, 26.9 million tonnes of rock was moved to push back the walls of the mining pit by more than 100 metres. On a parallel track, public relations and marketing programmes were initiated to increase the global awareness, visibility, and demand for Zambian emeralds. Auction revenues grew substantially. By May 2013, the company had generated a total of US$123.2 million across seven high-quality emerald auctions and US$52.4 million across five auctions, which contained mostly low- to medium-grade rough emeralds, also known as 'commercial-grade material'[1].

The July 2011 Kagem auction for high-quality emeralds witnessed the company set a record for auction revenue, generating US$31.6 million with an average per-carat sales value of US$42.71, an increase of 870 per cent in less than three years. In its 2012 annual report, the company reported US$161.7 million as profit after tax, with average monthly operating costs of US$1.34 million.

But with success came operational challenges, especially related to security and political interference. The incident with CV Suresh and his wife at the security check occurred in May 2013 (not in 2008) when they were travelling to South Africa to attend Adrian Banks's wedding. It was a period of tremendous growth for the mine, which attracted both positive and negative attention. On 15th October 2013, the mining company became the first in Zambia to receive a certificate of achievement by the Mines Safety Department for achieving 2,885,120 injury-free shifts (a feat that has since been regularly repeated by the Kagem team).

A few months later, the mine presented the government of Zambia with a dividend cheque of 10.94 million Zambian Kwacha, (then US$4 million), the first time ever that the government had received a dividend payment in the mine's history, and the first such payment to the government of Zambia from any gemstone operation in the country.

Political interference and constant requests for donations and support from government departments and special interest groups[2] continued.

1   All auction figures have been taken from Gemfields auction reports that are published on its website under 'Auction Update' on www.gemfieldsgroup.com.

2   Which as per Gemfields often turned out to be deliberately misinformed by those involved in the illegal emerald trade.

The de-politicisation of Kagem began when Dr Sixtus Mulenga was appointed as the government representative on Kagem's board. He instructed that all requests for special favours be directed to his office for review, allowing the Kagem team to focus their energy on the mining of emeralds.

The Kagem emerald mine is considered the largest of its kind in the world and has pioneered many initiatives in the coloured gem mining sector. The mine moves one million tonnes of rock every month and 65 per cent of the total revenue comes from only the top four per cent of production! To put the rarity factor of emerald discovery in perspective, in metal (copper) mining, four tonnes of waste brings one tonne of ore, of which you are relatively confident of one per cent of copper (or 10,000 grams). In emerald mining, 87 tonnes of waste are required to get the one tonne of ore which, if things go well, will generate perhaps 50 grams, or 0.005 per cent of emerald and beryl.

In 2022, the company generated a total of US$149 million in auction sales and hit a high of US$155.90 as an average per-carat sales value: an increase of 3,797.5 per cent since the July 2009 auction. The 45 auctions of Kagem gemstones held since July 2009 have generated US$964 million in total revenue[1].

CV Suresh is currently Gemfields' managing director for Zambia, and a member of Gemfields' executive board based at the company's headquarters in London. Kartikeya Parikshya (KP) is the managing director for Mozambique and Ethiopia, and also a member of the executive board. Exilda is still working at Kagem and was recently promoted to Head Chef. In August 2002, the mine employed the first four women to operate heavy earth-moving machinery in the mine. The mine has a total of 52 female employees as at August 2023, who work and live at a dedicated women's residential block on the campus.

Jackson Mtonga is working at Kagem as the sort house manager, and in the last two decades has represented the company as a speaker at various events, one of them being the first ever Zambian Emerald Summit, in Lusaka in 2013. Aaron Nyangu will be completing 27 years at Kagem and is currently the Senior Manager, Planning and Survey.

Rajiv Gupta left Gemfields in 2009. Alok Sood left Gemfields in 2010.

Dr Muyoba was removed by the government as their director on the Kagem board on 1st July 2013 after eight years. Like any great boxer, he went out on top, with Kagem's auction revenues in the 12 months preceding

1   Updated as of 02 June 2023.

31st July 2013 reaching a then-all-time high of US$73.5 million, a legacy of which he was rightly proud. He passed away in April 2020.

Dharmendra Tank, Nilesh Shah, Sunil Mittal, and Manoj Dhandia are respected and valued Gemfields customers who attend every auction. Almost all the companies that attended the Lusaka emerald auction in November 2008 are still buying emeralds from the mine and have a great working relationship with the Gemfields team.

Ian Harebottle was CEO of Gemfields from 2009 until 2017. Under his leadership, Gemfields became the all-time number one mining and marketing company for coloured gemstones.

In 2017, Gemfields was at the centre of a competitive takeover pitting Pallinghurst, then its largest shareholder with a 41 per cent stake, against the Chinese firm Fosun Gold. In the end, Pallinghurst was successful in taking over Gemfields. Subsequently, Ian Harebottle resigned as CEO in July 2017. In a comment to the author, he said, 'I left because I was unhappy with the offer Pallinghurst made to acquire Gemfields. I felt it was too low and undervalued the company.'

Sean Gilbertson who first joined the Kagem board in January 2008 and the Gemfields board in May 2008, returned as CEO of Gemfields in July 2017. At that time Gemfields' gross debt was peaking at more than US$90 million against auction revenues in 2017 of US$168 million. By the end of 2022, gross debt had been reduced to US$14 million with 2022 auction revenues reaching US$316 million. In 2019, recognising how undervalued they were, Gemfields bought back approximately ten per cent of its own shares on the stock market at an average price of just ZAR1.50 per share. In 2022, Gemfields paid its first ever dividends, sending US$35 million in cash to shareholders that year. In 2023, Gemfields repeated the payout, sending a further US$35 million to shareholders. By the end of 2022, cumulative payments to the governments of Mozambique and Zambia stood at approximately US$204 and US$152 million respectively.

Beyond the appropriate payment of taxes, Gemfields directs funding towards health, education, and livelihood projects in the communities near the mine sites, as well as funding conservation efforts. To date, the company has constructed and rehabilitated three primary schools, providing education to nearly 2,000 students, funded the Nkana Health Clinic serving a population of 10,000, and established four farming associations. There are further farming associations in the process of establishment and a vocational training centre in progress.

Industry sources estimate that the emeralds Gemfields sold in July 2009 for US$5.9 million are probably worth more than US$50 million today.

Ruby Land

'If you are not strong-hearted, you can't be in gem-mining. You need a pinch of insanity and a strong appetite for risk to be in this business'—Kartikeya Parikshya, Managing Director for Gemfields, Mozambique and Ethiopia

2002
The Boardwalk
Ibo Island Fishing Complex
Cabo Delgado district, Mozambique

ASGHAR FAKHRALEALI read the government notice for a third time and pursed his lips in anger. 'I knew they would do this,' he murmured to himself. 'We should have never trusted them.' The cigarette held between his fingers continued to burn, a miniature representation of his current circumstance. He cursed as the heat reached his skin. Stomping on the burnt butt, he lit another and gazed in the distance at the dhows[1] bobbing in the sea, their triangular lateen sails billowing in tune with the wind.

Despite the island's remote location, Asghar enjoyed living in what he considered one of the most beautiful places in Mozambique. He would finish each day with a barefoot stroll on the pristine white-sand beach, letting the limpid beauty of the aquamarine waters wash away any worries. Ibo was home to an array of land and sea creatures that Asghar had never seen. He especially loved the fiddler crabs with their bright turquoise shells and one enlarged neon orange pincer. They looked like boxers ready for a fight. 'Why would I sit inside a stuffy office when I could have this incredible view?' he'd say to visitors who were surprised to see him work from a plastic chair and a rickety stool on the boardwalk.

The Mozambique chapter of Asghar's life story started in 1995, when he met Raimundo Domingos Pachinuapa and established a fishing business. Raimundo belonged to a class of Mozambican veterans who had fought

---

1   A traditional sailing vessel made of wood.

against Portuguese colonial rule as a general in the Mozambican army, attaining independence for Mozambique in 1975. After serving as the governor of Cabo Delgado from 1975 to 1979, he became Mozambique's Inspector General from 1979 to 1994, after which his entrepreneurial interest saw him seeking ways to contribute to the economic progress of his nation.

The firm's maiden venture was a commercial fishing business on Ibo Island, which was inhabited by a few hundred locals and 125 expatriates. Their only connection with the outside world was the regular arrival of a two-week old newspaper and a radio at the island's administrative outpost.

The primary watering hole for most international residents was The Beach Hotel, and that's where Asghar was headed to have dinner with his friend Alberto, who was the director of the Quirimbas National Park, an extensive coastal nature reserve lying north of the port city of Pemba. With Asghar's family in Spain and Alberto a widower, the two had become friends over many glasses of frequently warm beer.

'What about this business, Alberto?!' asked Asghar, throwing the gazette he'd received from the Environment Ministry on their dinner table.

'What about it?' said Alberto, pretending to study the limited food menu.

'This article says they're extending the boundary of the Quirimbas National Park to the water.'

'So?'

'So?! This means our fishing business is finished,' said Asghar as he pulled in his dining chair.

Alberto flinched at the scraping of the chair's wooden legs against the floor. He wasn't sure how to respond. Over the last three years, he'd continuously reassured Asghar that the delegations of environmentalists surveying the island would never extend the protective zone to the waters. Having recently learnt of the ministry's decision, he was expecting, in fact dreading, the moment when Asghar received the notice. Alberto put away the menu and looked at his friend, who was sulkily staring outside the restaurant's window.

'You have every right to be upset,' said Alberto. 'I'm sorry. I didn't know they'd extend the reserve into the waters.'

'I will fight this, Alberto. We are one of the largest employers on Ibo Island. What about our investment? Our staff? This is not right,' said Asghar, as he grabbed the table napkin and slapped it on his lap moments before the server placed two plates of grilled fish in front of them. 'All this time, these ministry people borrowed our boats for their inspections. They never paid us a dime. Not one dime for any of our boats or the help from our staff. Nothing.'

Asghar was ranting now. 'And what did you tell me? "It's OK, Asghar. Please help them out." I helped them, alright. I helped them put us out of business. How do you expect growth when you treat investors like mud? I'm going to prepare a detailed account of all the money we have invested in this venture and claim compensation,' said Asghar, jabbing the fish with his fork and knife. 'Just because we are friends doesn't mean I won't act. We shall sue the government of Mozambique!'

'First,' said Alberto, as he meticulously folded his napkin in half and placed it on his lap, 'that fish you're attacking is already dead.' Asghar grunted in response. 'Second, the government has no money. You can hire the best lawyers, but even your grandchildren won't get any compensation.'

Asghar grunted again. Alberto continued. 'Look, you have every right to be upset. I would be too, but I may have a solution.'

'What's that?' asked Asghar. He was treating his dinner with greater care, but, in protest, refused to make eye contact with Alberto.

'Spain is famous for professional hunters. The country has a history of hunting and good relations with Germany and the United States. Why don't you take a piece of land in the protection zone of the park for hunting?'

'This is your solution?' Asghar responded, looking up. 'A hunting estate? More investment from us in a new business. Great! You must really think we're stupid.'

'It's more than 260,000 hectares of land,' said Alberto.

'Land is worthless unless we can do something on it. We know nothing about hunting.'

'Take your time, hire professionals, and come back to us with your decision. But I seriously urge you to consider this solution. It's the only option on the table.'

* * *

Seven years later
March 2009
Nacala, Nampula Province
Mozambique

Raime Raimundo Pachinuapa put the receiver down and leaned back in his office chair. He'd just received a phone call from a man from Mali who'd shared bizarre details related to the hunting concession his father's company, Mwiriti, had in Cabo Delgado. Raime had tried to explain to the man that he was not involved with Mwiriti and instead worked with a private firm managing the Nacala port. But the man insisted Raime pass on the message to his father, Raimundo Domingos Pachinuapa. *What if he's right?* Raime said to himself, contemplating the conversation he'd just finished. He picked up the phone and called Asghar, who had established Mwiriti in partnership with his father a few years ago[1].

'Hello,' Asghar's voice boomed on the other side of the telephone line.

'Asghar, Rai here.'

'Ya. Hi, Rai. How are you?'

'Good,' said Raime. 'I'm calling because I just received a strange phone call.'

'What about?' asked Asghar.

'From a gem dealer. He's from Mali but called me apparently from Montepuez. Not sure how he got my number. He said there are rubies on our hunting concession in Montepuez.'

'Rubies? Like precious stones?'

'Yes. He said many people are digging and taking away the rubies, and we should investigate the matter. Have you head of rubies on our concession?'

'When we were first offered the land for the hunting concession by the government, they also gave a report by a Norway agency, which mentioned the presence of aluminium oxide, corundum[2] in Namahaca. But honestly Raime, I didn't take that seriously because this is not our expertise.'

'But rubies sound serious, Asghar. And the concession is under Mwiriti's jurisdiction.'

'Raime, this precious stone business, it's for smugglers and mafia people, not for businessmen like us. We are involved in hunting, tourism, fishery. We don't want to be linked to this business.'

Raime stayed silent. Asghar continued, 'And why is this guy contacting you to tell you this? He wants something, I'm sure. Did he give a name?'

'His name's Samba. He said he just wanted us to be aware.'

'Nonsense. There must be an angle here. Just forget it.'

But Raime couldn't forget. Samba called him nonstop. 'Once in a century, God knocks on someone's door, Mr Raime. He's knocking on Mwiriti's door. Are you going to answer?' the man had said on the last call.

Frustrated with the situation, Raime called his father. 'Asghar's right, Rai,' Pachinuapa said. 'Leave it alone. We don't want to be mixed up with this ruby business.'

---

1   2005, as informed by Asghar Fakhraleali.

2   Corundum is the mineral. The blue variant of corundum is sapphire and the red is ruby.

After a month of repeated calls by Samba, sometimes four or five in a day, Raime went back to the Mwiriti board and got their support for Asghar to investigate Samba's claims.

* * *

May 2009
6.00 am
Pemba, Mozambique

Asghar had asked his housekeeper to pack some supplies for the day. Boiled egg and tomato sandwiches, a flask of coffee, water, and small packets of homemade biscuits wrapped in paper for Asghar to distribute to any children he encountered on his journey. He had arranged to meet Samba outside the local post office in Montepuez. 'It's going to take me three to four hours to get there, so best if you come by ten in the morning,' he'd said.

As Asghar drove down the dirt road, passing mud huts and green fields, he felt he was chasing yet another rabbit down a hole, which would yield nothing for his troubles. They had lost their commercial fishing licence 12 years ago. Since then, Asghar had been trying to develop the hunting concession the government had provided as compensation.

He'd hired professionals from South Africa to conduct aerial and ground surveys of their 260,000-hectares. The entire process took longer than expected because they had to wait for the dry season before they could start work. Animal movements had to be studied over multiple seasons to prepare a blueprint for the new hunting venture. Asghar spent many nights camping with the surveyors next to the Megaruma River. The plan was to apply to CITES in Switzerland for second premium quotas of elephant and lion. After the application was filed in 2006, Asghar was informed that their newly established company, Mwiriti, could not hunt south of the Montepuez River because of human activity related to fishing and firewood collection.

'This is a joke,' Asghar had lamented to Alberto. 'You take away our fishing business. Instead of refunding our investment, you give us this land. We again invest money, bring experts, file paperwork, and now, now you tell us about this restriction. Why did you offer us this land when you knew we couldn't use it?'

Alberto had no concrete answer except to encourage Asghar to stay the course. Mwiriti registered a hunting concession in 2007 with the camp inside the stipulated zone. A few months later, a Cuban architect approached Asghar with a business proposition. 'We are building the

Montepuez Secondary School. A project funded by the World Bank,' the architect explained. 'I've been tasked to find local sources for building material, as it's expensive to bring material from outside the province.'

'How can we help?' said Asghar.

'There is a hill in the southern part of your concession, near Namanhumbir.'

'What about it?' asked Asghar.

'We can use the stone from that hill for our construction.'

'But we are running a hunting estate. We know nothing of cutting stone from a hill.'

'It's not complicated. Apply for a quarry licence. We'll help you figure out the rest and buy all the stone you take out.'

'And what happens after your project is done?' asked Asghar.

'There are many new ventures now in Mozambique. The demand for reliable sources of building material is only going to increase.'

This opportunity seemed perfect for Mwiriti to utilise the area south of the Montepuez River. They had the land. They had the buyers. It all fitted. After another round of visiting government departments, hiring specialists and workers, Mwiriti was in the stone for construction business. Between the hunting and stone quarry ventures, Asghar had his hands full.

The last 12 years had been a continuous uphill climb to create a new revenue stream. He wanted to sink his teeth into their current investments before chasing yet another opportunity. But here he was, driving towards Montepuez to meet with Samba, the gem merchant from Mali. Asghar hoped it was a false alarm and he could get back to what was important.

* * *

**The same day
7.00 pm
Nacala, Nampula Province,
Mozambique**

Raime would typically be done with work by six in the evening, but a last-minute meeting had him stuck in office when Asghar called. The shrill sound of the telephone ringing amidst the serenity in his office startled Raime. He let it ring for a moment, hoping it wasn't his wife displeased with his delayed departure. Raime looked at his watch, groaned, and picked up the telephone receiver. 'Hello.'

'Rai. It's Asghar.'

'Asghar. Hi. Is this urgent? I'm late to meet my wife and some friends for dinner.'

'No problem. I was just calling to update you. I met that ruby man, Samba.'

'How was it?' asked Raime.

'We met at Montepuez. He said to me, "Let's go in your pickup truck. I'll show you where they're digging for rubies." I drove while he gave directions. We reached a spot and he said, "From here, better to walk".'

'Why?'

'Maybe he didn't want to attract attention. Two men approaching in a Toyota Hilux might raise a few eyebrows. I don't know. I didn't really ask.'

'Then?' *Five more*, Raime told himself. *I'll give him five more minutes to finish the story.*

'We start walking. I was keeping track of our whereabouts on the GPS.'

'Did you see anyone?'

'Yes. There were many people walking with shovels and pickaxes in groups. We followed them. Samba advised me to stay quiet and not reveal my identity as the concession holder. As we got closer to the location, the path in the bush became a highway of people. I could hear the commotion before I saw anything.'

'What did you see?'

'People. Just thousands of men all over.'

'Thousands?'

'There must have been, all together, maybe ten thousand.'

'Are you serious?!' asked Raime. The dinner engagement momentarily forgotten. 'What were they doing?'

'Digging for rubies. The entire land was full of holes. Like small burrows. Reminded me of my backyard in Madrid, where these rabbits would come and dig, dig, dig, and destroy my garden with their holes. Once I got over the initial shock, I noticed there were people around each hole, waiting for the diggers to bring gravel from underground. This gravel had the rubies inside. There must have been four to five thousand men digging across the area. They kept disappearing underground and, after some time, would come up covered in dust.'

'And how many buyers?'

'Many buyers. I estimate, five to six thousand people standing around waiting to buy the rubies. They've created a market inside our concession. I saw women cooking and selling food. Samba said the buyers were rough-gem traders from Tanzania and Kenya, but also from other parts of Africa.

To me, some faces looked West-African. We spoke to a few of them, and it seems they are basically smuggling these rubies out of Mozambique.'

'You weren't afraid, surrounded by all these people?'

'More shocked than afraid. No one knew me. They were busy digging and trading, and I kept my distance.'

'You told my dad?'

'I'm going to call him now. I wanted to update you first.'

'What do you think Mwiriti should do?' asked Raime.

'Dunno, Rai. I am planning to speak to the administrative chief of the district and get some information. Let's take it a step at a time.'

'Yeah. Sorry, Asghar, I really need to go now but keep me posted.'

'Sure. Sure. Enjoy your dinner. Bye.'

Raime disconnected, grabbed his jacket and car keys, and rushed out of his office. As he drove to his friend's home, he kept thinking about the scene Asghar had described. *Rubies. The discovery of a treasure. Is it a blessing or a burden?* The presence of international dealers was troubling him. *If they've already tasted money, it'll be difficult, even dangerous, to keep them away.*

* * *

June 2009
Maputo, Mozambique

The last month had been intense for Asghar. When he'd approached the local administration in Montepuez, they'd directed him towards the Ministry of Mines in Maputo. Days rolled into weeks without a response from the ministry, and Asghar felt helpless as the number of people inside the concession grew exponentially. Even the staff at Mwiriti's stone quarry abandoned their posts and joined the informal diggers. The local police commandant informed Asghar that they could only help remove the trespassers once Asghar obtained the mining permits.

'Rai, I think it's a conspiracy,' Asghar said when he called again. 'I've been going back to the deposit to identify the ruby area on the map, take photos. I recognised a few faces. They're police from the local station. Why will they help us when they are part of it?'

'It may not be safe for you to enter the ruby area alone, Asghar,' said Raime.

'I'm not afraid. It's our jurisdiction—we must protect it. But maybe you're right. Anyway, I'm flying to Maputo tomorrow to meet some senior people at the Ministry of Mines. That's the only way.'

In Maputo, Asghar explained the situation to the officials. He showed photos of the digging and trading inside their concession and shared the paper trail concerning their concession rights. Under the guidance of the ministry, Mwiriti applied for two prospecting licences and three mining certificates. The next step was to post an announcement of their plans in the local villages as per government regulation. The public notice had to stay up for a month to give the local population adequate time to express their displeasure or file counter claims. There was nothing left to do but wait.

During those 30 days, news of Mwiriti's moves spread like wildfire. A fresh group of traders would approach Asghar daily with offers of partnership. On 11th September 2009, Asghar returned to the police commandant with the requisite licences to remove the trespassers. Mwiriti had secured their ruby deposit, but to maintain custody, they had to begin prospecting and mining activities. Asghar engaged a Thai-Mozambican firm called Gems Ten[1], which had prior experience with tourmaline deposits. The minister of mines conducted an inspection on 6th October 2009 to ensure that Mwiriti was fully committed to the laborious task ahead. To get formal validation of their ruby deposit's value, Mwiriti engaged the services of Dr Lawrence, a geology professor from NASA.

'Dr Lawrence's report says that this deposit will change the history of the gemstone industry,' Asghar exclaimed to Raime over a call. It was the encouragement the Mwiriti shareholders needed to keep going.

* * *

March 2011
Nacala, Mozambique

Raime was examining the list of cargo ships due to berth at the Nacala port in the coming months when his desk phone rang.

'Hello.'

'Rai. It's me. Asghar.'

'Hi. Anything urgent? In the middle of something at work.'

'I just need a moment. We need to end the Gems Ten contract.'

'Why? What happened?'

'They've been stealing from us, Rai.'

'Stealing?! Are you sure?'

---

1   This name has been changed.

'Let me tell you what happened. You remember I was escorting the minister of mines to Montepuez?'

'Yes. To get an update on the work we'd done in the last year.'

'Exactly. When we arrived at the deposit, there were only two junior staff on location. That one Burmese boy and the Thai one—and that's it. No senior person available to take us around. Nothing.'

'Oh God. Then?'

'I stay calm in front of the minister. We walk around. I explain everything. Then, we go to the stockroom. I want to show her our system of keeping track of all the rubies we're finding in the concession. In the stockroom I pick up a small parcel containing four rubies and open the register to look for the entry. Nothing. Can't find it.'

'What?'

'There was no entry in the register, Rai. I covered up by saying maybe it was some mistake. I gave some instructions to the staff, and we went on with the rest of the visit.'

'You said nothing to the staff?'

'I went back after the minister left and started checking every single parcel. There were many like this, Rai. Many.'

'What did the staff say? Maybe it's a genuine mistake?'

'No. It's not. The staff started behaving like they didn't understand my English. Think about it. Their boss has been travelling a lot to Thailand from Mozambique. Whenever I call or visit, he's not there; he's in Thailand. Why all the time? I'm telling you; they are stealing our rubies.'

'We don't have any proof.'

'Unnecessary. The inconsistencies I found in the stockroom and their travels to Thailand—the writing's on the wall.'

'But we need help, Asghar. We can't do this alone. From what I'm hearing, it sounds like we're losing control. Thousands of people are pouring into our concession, looking for rubies.'

'It's because of that GIA[1] article that the whole world knows. We should have never given them access.'

'No point now. If it hadn't been GIA, it would have been someone else,' said Raime. 'Maybe the coverage will bring foreign investors, proper partners.'

* * *

---

1   Gemmological Institute of America.

316

April 2011
Arusha, Tanzania

Ian Harebottle was no stranger to gemstones. He'd spent the last decade developing what many considered one of the world's largest coloured gemstone companies, TanzaniteOne[1]. Ian subsequently joined Gemfields in 2009 as its CEO. The company owned and operated an emerald mine in Zambia and planned to become the leading player in the coloured gemstone sector.

Ian's switch triggered other key personnel from TanzaniteOne to move to Gemfields. The domain knowledge and experience of these fresh arrivals mingled well with the mining, financial and management skills already in place at Gemfields. Thanks to the combined efforts of the new team, the price per carat of high-grade rough Zambian emeralds rose at Gemfields' emerald auctions from US$4.40 in July 2009 to US$26.20 per carat by December 2010, an increase of 495 per cent. The company had plans to expand. Although Ian had relocated to Gemfields' headquarters in London, he would travel extensively across Africa, and enjoyed returning to Tanzania, a country that had been his home during his years with TanzaniteOne. On one such visit, an opportunity came knocking in the form of Ian's old friend, a well-known gem merchant, Mark Saul, who lived in Tanzania.

'I think this ruby deposit in Mozambique could be great for Gemfields, Ian,' said Mark. 'This company, Mwiriti, they're out of their depth. They don't have any mining experience or gemmological knowledge. To make matters worse, they've accumulated a mountain of debt working in a haphazard manner.'

'What do you mean?' asked Ian.

They've been shelling out cash for geological studies and prospecting, and it's all adding up now. To be fair, given their inexperience, they've done a great job of at least securing their concession. They even hired a company to prospect and mine, but that partnership has fallen apart.'

'Why?'

'Mwiriti suspected them of stealing the rubies from their concession.'

'Ah! A tale as old as time.'

'Exactly. They're looking for a company that will work with them to develop the deposit.'

---

1   Alongside the founder and CEO, Mike Nunn.

'And who is Mwiriti? As you know, Gemfields is a listed company. We do things above board, Mark. No hidden figures or games behind shell corporations.'

'I am sure you'll do your own due diligence if it gets to that stage. Here's what I know: Mwiriti was formed in 2005. The partners are a Mozambican citizen called Raimundo Domingos Pachinuapa who holds 60 per cent, and a Spanish man of Iranian decent, Asghar Fakhraleali, who owns the remaining 40 per cent[1].'

'Tell me more about the majority shareholder,' said Ian.

'A prominent individual in Mozambique. Veteran freedom fighter, and a senior figure in the ruling FRELIMO party. Pachinuapa worked alongside Mozambique's first president, Samora Machel. He was the first governor of Cabo Delgado,' said Mark.

'And the minority partner, Asghar?'

'I first met him in Bangkok. He told me many have proposed an alliance for the ruby mine.'

'Like?'

'Didn't share names but said they were industry stakeholders from India, Hong Kong, and a British gem hunter. But he refused them because, in his words, Mwiriti is interested in a serious company, not individuals looking for an adventure.'

'Sounds sensible enough.'

'Asghar's a character,' said Mark. 'He's been living on the concession with only a handful of security people for over a year. I've been there. It's basic, a small hut made of bamboo with a cot inside. Honestly, it's a miracle he's still alive.'

'Why is he there himself? Don't they have security?' asked Ian.

'I think they're stretched.'

'And this Asghar is a Spanish resident?'

'Yes. He arrived in Mozambique in the mid-nineties after the civil war on some sort of business trip. Married, has kids who are all grown up and working in Spain. He's the key man on the ground.'

'Got it. Now, Mark, you must decide which side you're on,' said Ian.

'What do you mean?' asked Saul.

'Are you working for the buyer or the seller? You need to choose because you can't play on both sides. It never works. You're either with me trying to get us a great deal, or you're with them.'

---

1   https://landmatrix.org/investor/42369/

***

13th April 2011
Namanhumbir Hill
Mwiriti concession
Montepuez, Mozambique

It's probably too early in Madrid, thought Asghar as he picked up the telephone receiver to call his daughter in Spain. 'Hello, Soraya? Can you hear me?'

'I can hear you. Happy birthday, papá.'

'Thank you, my dear. How are you?'

'I'm fine. Forget about me. How are you? I miss you.'

'Miss you too. I'm OK. Every day is the same. It feels like I'm in an endless cycle with no escape.'

'You sound especially low today, papá. Has something happened?'

'Nothing monumental. But I can't see the light at the end of the tunnel.'

'Why?' enquired Soraya.

'The company has run out of money. We can't pay salaries. Our debt is over a million dollars. We could lose our house in Spain. This whole situation has been a nightmare from the beginning. I'm sorry. I am so sorry.'

'Why are you apologising?'

'For this mess. For burdening you with my problems today. This should be a happy phone call. Parents aren't supposed to trouble their children with their problems.'

'Your problems are my problems, papá. Please don't be sad. Listen, I have around five thousand euros in my account. It's not much—'

'Absolutely not. I cannot take your money.'

'Whatever I am and whatever I have is because of you, papá. Let's call it a loan. You can pay me back. Don't let your pride come in the way of me temporarily helping you out.'

Asghar reluctantly agreed. He had no choice. Every single one of his assets was tied up as collateral against loans. He'd lost track of how many partnerships and outright sale proposals he'd received since their mining licence application in 2009. Acutely aware of their lack of knowledge in the sector, each time Mwiriti got a proposal, Asghar would share the details of shortlisted potential partners or investors with the Ministry of Mines in Maputo.

Most would receive negative reviews from the authorities. They were now down to three, which the ministry had endorsed: a Chinese group, a

319

consortium of gem dealers from India and Germany, and an international gem-mining company. Asghar felt trapped by the ticking clock that was Mwiriti's deadline to pay their debtors. *Finding a partner is one thing, but how do we complete the paperwork on time?* he mused.

* * *

9th May 2011
Gemfields Headquarters
London, UK

Gemfields' CEO, Ian Harebottle, read the email he was about to send to Graham Mascall, the company's chairman:

> Mark Saul is an old acquaintance of mine with whom we have signed a due diligence agreement to evaluate the potential of possibly incorporating their pink spinel deposit (in Tanzania) into our group portfolio. This is an ongoing process and will be presented to the board in due course and after some initial geological work being done in the area.
>
> Mark has also introduced us to Raimundo Domingos Pachinu-apa in Mozambique who owns the title and licence over an area covering approximately 100 square kilometres and which is recognised as one of the best-known ruby deposits worldwide. I have been informed by a reliable source (other than Mark) that an Indian delegation are also keen to acquire this licence, as well as a Chinese one, but that the general is keen to work with a reputable company that has a proven track record and is committed to mining, marketing, social and environmental matters—i.e., only Gemfields fills these requirements.
>
> We have thus instructed Mark to continue his discussions with Pachinuapa and update him of your Ncondezi Project, etc., so that he can have some added comfort. Given the above, and the fact that Pachinuapa will likely prefer the initial agreements (due diligence, etc.) to be in his own language and drafted in and by a Mozambican, Mark has requested your input below. Your kind assistance in this regard is much appreciated.

Ian hit the Send button and started typing a second email to Gemfields' executive director, Sean Gilbertson, and CFO, Dev Shetty. The race was on for possibly the largest ruby deposit the world had ever seen, and Ian was concerned Gemfields may not move as swiftly as others in the game.

* * *

May 2011
Asghar's home
Pemba, Mozambique

For the first time in a very long time, Asghar slept well. After weeks of nonstop negotiations, Mwiriti finally had a buyer. Asghar was planning to have a leisurely breakfast before he started reviewing the draft agreements Mwiriti's lawyers had sent over.

'Senhor, some people here to meet with you,' said Asghar's housekeeper.

'I have no meetings. Who is it?' asked Asghar.

'I don't know, senhor. Three gentlemen. They didn't give any names. Just asked me to inform you they have come on a private plane from South Africa and have important business with you.'

Asghar was both irritated and intrigued. He put on his dressing gown and slippers and stepped into his living room, where three men sat awaiting his arrival. Wasting no time, they came straight to the point, explaining they were representing a consortium keen to partner with Mwiriti for the rubies. They knew about the million dollars of debt Mwiriti had accumulated and were aware that Asghar was in talks with Ian Harebottle from Gemfields and someone from China. Asghar recognised the team. It was the consortium of Indian and German gem dealers with whom he'd been exchanging emails. Without hesitation, an individual from the group placed two briefcases on the coffee table in front of Asghar.

'What's this?' asked Asghar.

'This is the beginning,' the man said. 'US$2 million in cash.'

'I don't understand. We never had any conversation about a deal. Why this money?' said Asghar.

'The money is to pay Mwiriti's outstanding debt and settle all the court cases you're fighting with your former vendors.'

Asghar stayed silent. Two million would solve all their problems. They could be debt-free by the end of the week.

The man continued. 'We heard Gemfields has also approached you. Whatever they're offering, we'll double it.'

* * *

9th May 2011
Gemfields Headquarters
London, UK

Ian was finally ready to send his email to Sean and Dev. *Hopefully, this additional information motivates them to move faster*, he thought.

> FYI and input. As per the mail below and our earlier discussions in this regard:
>
> Copy of signed due diligence over the pink spinel licence.
>
> Draft services level agreement attached—your urgent input and suggestions would be much appreciated.
>
> As background to the two projects:
>
> I managed to have a few chats with the field gemmologist from GIA, Vincent Pardieu, and some others, during the past two weeks, all of whom know nothing about our recent moves but know both projects quite well and are fans of what Gemfields is doing to revitalise the coloured gemstone sector. Vincent's input is as follows:
>
> He says that he knows Pachinuapa who owns the ruby licence area and that he is old school, a good guy, and is very keen to make sure that the project goes ahead in the right way, with the right partners, and caters for social and environmental needs in the area—Vincent thinks that Gemfields would be a perfect fit for this project and that we must do our best to get in touch with Pachinuapa. So, should the points above be true, then this is great news for us, as we are the only ones who can tick all these boxes.
>
> He also told me that two other parties are talking to Pachinuapa (which is 100 per cent aligned to what you told me before) but he added these insights:
>
> The Chinese delegation has offered US$1.7 million to acquire the licence.
>
> The second group, which is a German and Indian consortium, has offered US$2 million cash on the spot if Pachinuapa signs now.
>
> On our part, we have agreed to no set amount yet, but have suggested that Pachinuapa signs a DD with us so that we can

investigate the resource and licences, etc. and that we will make him a fair and realistic offer after that.

* * *

29th May 2011
Kagem emerald mine
Zambia

Kartikeya Parikshya (KP) was in a good mood. After seven years at the Kagem emerald mine in Zambia, which meant spending months away from his family at a time, thanks to a promotion, KP and his family were moving to London. He entered the GM's office to sign the paperwork where the CEO and CFO of Gemfields, Ian Harebottle and Dev Shetty, were waiting for him. After a few minutes of congratulatory small talk, Ian said, 'KP, now that the paperwork is done, we must tell you about a secret project that the team has been working on for the past few months.'

'Secret project? In Zambia?'

'No, Mozambique. Gemfields is going to buy a majority stake in a company that holds the licence for mining and exploration of a massive ruby deposit. I'm flying to Maputo tomorrow to sign the documents, and I'd like you to come with me.'

'I don't understand. You're flying to Maputo to sign the documents? So the deal is closed?' asked KP.

'The plan is to visit the asset with the Mwiriti team, do an assessment, and then complete the paperwork. With Kagem, you did the geological modelling and projections, which served as the basis for that acquisition. With Mozambique, we are so far depending on limited information from the ground and senior industry stakeholders who have seen some of the gems. Your role continues to be that of a geologist, and I'll need your input on the documents Mwiriti shares and what we see when we visit the site.'

'Does this mean I'm moving to Mozambique? I thought I was going to be based at the headquarters in London?'

'And that continues to be the case. You'll be with your family in London. But your immediate focus in your new role must be Mozambique. C'mon! Pack a small bag and let's begin our new adventure. Wheels up before sunrise tomorrow. We'll catch a flight from Ndola to Maputo via Johannesburg.'

'Ian, I don't have a Mozambique visa.'

'No worries. We have an invitation letter and that should suffice. Time is of the essence here, KP,' said Ian. 'We have a verbal agreement, but we're

323

still in a race with other competing parties. Can't waste even a minute. It's vital for us to reach Maputo at the earliest.'

* * *

31st May 2011
Departure gate of LAM-Mozambique Airlines
Johannesburg International Airport
South Africa

'Can you step aside, sir?' the airline ground staff said to KP.

'Is there a problem?' he asked.

'You don't have a visa for Mozambique. We can't let you board.'

'He has an invitation letter,' said Ian. 'We were told that would be enough.'

'I'm afraid it's not,' said the LAM ground staff. 'We've already given instructions for his luggage to be offloaded.' The airline staff looked at KP and said, 'Sir, you can collect your bags from the baggage belt.'

Before KP could respond, Ian said, 'He can't. He doesn't have a South African visa. To fetch his bags, he'll have to cross immigration. This whole thing is a misunderstanding. I guarantee there won't be any issues at all if you just let us board the flight.'

* * *

1st June 2011
11.00 am
Maputo, Mozambique

'Aren't they late?' Pachinuapa asked Asghar.

Asghar looked at his wristwatch and said, 'Thirty minutes late. Maybe more.'

'Not a good sign,' said Pachinuapa. He got up and started walking around the curved rectangular table of the hotel boardroom they had blocked for the day.

'I am sure they'll be here soon,' said Asghar.

He was trying to stay calm and not let his anxiety about Ian's delayed arrival surface. After the trio of gem merchants had unceremoniously been asked to leave Asghar's home, they had flown to Maputo to try to convince Pachinuapa to get him to sell the licence. After many unsuccessful attempts to meet him, they'd managed to convey their offer to Pachinuapa via his third son. Pachinuapa had promptly called Asghar to check if they had a deal with Gemfields.

'We have a deal,' said Asghar. 'It's not signed yet, but we have a gentleman's agreement. Are you thinking of taking the cash offer?'

'Absolutely not,' Pachinuapa replied. 'I told them that Mwiriti's headquarters is in Pemba, and the GM of the company is Asghar. If I take their money, Asghar, it's the last time we'll ever get what's due to us. I am not looking to make a quick profit. We must develop this deposit into something we can be proud of in the future.'

A soft knock interrupted Asghar's walk down memory lane. The mood in the room changed as Ian and KP entered the space.

4.00 pm

Ian Harebottle took a deep breath as he waited for Sean Gilbertson and the rest of the Gemfields board to pick up the telephone. The situation in Mozambique was more desperate than he had imagined. The Mwiriti team had shown him documents that confirmed the company owed more than US$1 million to the market, which included financial institutions. They were days away from losing everything, and desperate for a deal that would provide them with an infusion of funds to settle their debts.

Ian had also learnt that a consortium of gem dealers, one of whom he knew from his TanzaniteOne days, had shown up at Asghar's doorstep offering Mwiriti US$2 million and double whatever Gemfields offered. Time was running out.

'Sean, hi, it's Ian. Is everyone there?'

'Good evening, Ian. We're assembled in the conference room, and you are on speaker. Please go ahead.'

'Right. Gentlemen, what I'm about to suggest is not how I usually do business but if we don't close this deal with Mwiriti, we may miss an opportunity of a lifetime. They're desperate, and I'm worried they'll go ahead with someone else.'

'What are you suggesting?' asked Sean.

'We must, of course, inspect the paperwork related to the concession, the licences. I've engaged a law firm in Maputo, which is checking everything as we speak. But we need to do our due diligence in the next 24 to 48 hours, which won't allow us time to visit the asset.'

'What are the numbers?' said Sean.

'I think we should offer US$2.5 million for our proposed 75 per cent stake. They keep 25 per cent of the new company. This would settle their debt and give them around a million and a half in their pocket.'

'I don't know, Ian. We're a listed company and have a fiduciary responsibility to our shareholders to follow due process. Signing without visiting the asset is not unheard of, but I'm not sure it's advisable.'

'Trust me, I hear you. All I can say is that I know Mark Saul well. He's a seasoned player in the industry and he's telling me there are literally millions and millions of dollars' worth of rubies coming out of this licence every week.'

'You mean millions being smuggled and illegally traded every day,' said Sean.

'Exactly. I've also spoken with Vincent,' said Ian.

'That's the field gemmologist from the Gemological Institute of America?' asked Sean.

'Yes. And he's a more conservative chap. When I called him, I said, "Vincent, you know we're under pressure to make a deal. What do you think?"'

'What did he say?'

'In his estimation, he's getting around a hundred thousand dollars' worth of Mozambique rubies across his desk at the GIA gem lab in Bangkok for certification on a weekly basis.'

'So, which is it? Millions of dollars' worth of rubies per week or hundred thousand dollars' worth?' asked Sean.

'Only the better-quality rubies will go to an international gem lab like GIA for inspection. Most rubies will be treated and traded without lab reports, and a whole bunch will go to other labs operating in Thailand. When I take what Vincent's told me, and Mark's insights, it seems like an easy decision. I trust both these professionals. And, as CEO, this would be my recommendation. We just need to go for it.'

Author's Note

This story is based on actual events as relayed to the author by Asghar Fakhraleali, Ian Harebottle, Raime Raimundo, Sean Gilbertson and Kartikeya Parikshya (KP). Fictional elements have been introduced for scene setting and embellishment of dialogue to enhance the narrative quality of the story.

Secondary research has also been conducted along with interviews with former MRM employees and other industry sources.

Ian got the board's approval and, in less than a week, Gemfields was a 75 per cent shareholder of the newly formed Montepuez Ruby Mining Limitada (MRM), with Mwiriti holding 25 per cent of the new company. Gemfields' statement on 8th June 2011 explained:

> The total consideration payable to the Vendor under the Agreement is US$2.5 million and is paid in stages with a first tranche payable five days from the signature of the Agreement; a second tranche payable within five days of the date on which conforming applications for the transfer of the Mining Titles to the New Company have been submitted to the Ministry of Mineral Resources; and the bulk of the consideration to be paid on completion, which is expected to take a few months.

The local press was polarised in their assessment of the deal. Some claimed that Mr Pachinuapa had sold cheap while others heralded him as a million-aire, overlooking the ~US$1 million debt that threatened to bankrupt Mwiriti, and the numerous cases filed against the company by their credi-tors, which would have eventually led them to lose the concession and the opportunity to monetise the ruby deposit.

Unlike Zambia, where Gemfields had taken over a functioning mine, it seemed as though they had entered a hornet's nest of conflict, crime, corruption, and income disparity in Mozambique. Rival gangs of smugglers had divided the area around the ruby deposit, and the situation was further complicated by the presence of government forces. Groups, some backed by corrupt police, often fought for control, evidenced by charred vehicles near the deposit when Gemfields first arrived.

Recalling those first few visits, KP detailed his amazement at discovering lentil plants (Pigeon Pea plant/arhar dal), cashew, papaya, and mango trees growing wild in the bush, a testament to the land's fertility. 'But the people there were fixated on the rubies,' said KP. 'The land resembled a wire mesh from the indiscriminate burrowing. We knew about the informal digging but had underestimated the magnitude. Around ten thousand diggers and dealers were operating in and around the core ruby area within the larger MRM concession.'

With MRM, Gemfields took the unconventional route, first refurbishing the Namanhumbir school before being properly established on the licence in order to start on a positive note with the community. Gemfields then proceeded to create the basic mining infrastructure for exploring the ruby deposit. As Gemfields built roads, laid foundations for staff housing, and began mining, the swarms of illegal miners shifted to other parts of the vast 33,600 hectare concession.

For over ten years, the MRM and Gemfields teams have accumulated a wealth of knowledge through various experiences, including lessons learnt, discoveries made, mistakes corrected, successes achieved, and failures overcome, all culminating in a cutting-edge ruby-mining operation in Mozambique. Montepuez Ruby Mining Limitada (MRM) is believed to be the world's largest mining operation for rubies and industry sources estimate it accounts for ~60 per cent of the gem's global production.

The expanse of the ruby concessions makes security and governance a challenge. Mozambican law (since 2015) prohibits mining on a licence held by another party, making unlicensed informal/artisanal mining a punishable offense. As per industry sources, when Mwiriti obtained its mining licences, it surrendered land on either side of its area to the government for artisanal mining. Over time, due to lack of usage, segments of that land were allocated for mining to various other companies who entered the sector after MRM. Designated areas are still available for small-scale artisanal miners in the Montepuez ruby region. Notwithstanding the law, thousands of informal miners continue to infiltrate company concessions, mostly during the rainy season when there is water with which to wash the ruby bearing gravels. Many believe this is ongoing only because of systemic corruption failing the well-founded mining rights regime.

Rubies inside the MRM licence are generally found in old river-bed gravels (paleo channels), anywhere from 1.0 to 10 metres below the surface and are easily extracted with hand tools. Once informal miners dig down and reach the gravel bed, which may contain rubies, they start digging laterally, collecting maximum possible gravel. This creates an upside-down 'mushroom' with a long, square stem leading to the surface. The 8 or so metres of overburden can't be readily supported because it comprises gravels and soils. This often leads to ground collapses that cause severe injuries and fatalities, particularly during the wet season. The ease of extraction, rich nature of the deposit, abject poverty in the region, and high levels of corruption make the environment ideal for ruby smuggling syndicates to thrive. These parameters also create conflict between law enforcement agents, informal unlicensed miners, and competing smuggling syndicates[1].

---

1   From an article by Richa Goyal Sikri - https://gjepc.org/solitaire/
action-shifts-to-mozambique-for-rubies/

Gemfields points to the sheer magnitude of the value lost by the citizens of Mozambique, vividly demonstrated by the Bank of Mozambique's balance-of-payments data (published on its website at https://www.bancomoc.mz/). The data shows that MRM alone accounts for 94 per cent of all of Mozambique's collective monetary inflows from emeralds, rubies, and sapphires in the decade since January 2011. According to Gemfields' CEO, Sean Gilbertson, 'Rather than an indicator of MRM's market share, this figure demonstrates the extent to which the value of Mozambique's other rubies, emeralds and sapphires have simply evaporated from Mozambique and brought zero benefit not only to local communities but to the nation. This is a function of rampant smuggling and flagrant under-declaration of gemstone value at the point of export. The Montepuez ruby deposits were both artisanally and illegally mined from 2009-2012 by thousands of miners, yet no monetary inflows show in the Bank of Mozambique's data.'

In February of 2018, a UK-based law firm filed a claim involving allegations of human rights abuses against Gemfields and MRM, initially on behalf of 29 individuals living on or around the MRM ruby mining licence in northern Mozambique. A statement made proactively by Gemfields at that time noted that, inter alia, the claim sought to hold Gemfields and MRM liable for allegations involving the Mozambican police and/or other Mozambican government forces. It also recognised that instances of violence had occurred on and off the MRM licence area both before and after the company's arrival in Montepuez. The UK legal system makes provision for individuals deemed impecunious and consequently, defendant companies remain liable for all the associated legal fees regardless of the verdict, providing considerable motivation to settle. The allegations were never tested in court, and a year later, the law firm agreed to a settlement of GBP 5.8 million on behalf of the 273 individuals it was then representing, with no-admission-of-liability from Gemfields and MRM. In a statement at that time, Sean Gilbertson, CEO Gemfields said, "Given a complex array of considerations and the likely protracted nature of the mooted litigation, we believe today's settlement best balances the interests and futures of the assorted stakeholders. Vitally, we wish to ensure that we are regarded as trusted and transparent partners to members of our local communities, rather than legal adversaries."

By December 2023, the 21 MRM ruby auctions held since June 2014 had generated over one billion dollars (USD 1,049 million) in total revenue[1],

---

1   https://gemfields.s3.amazonaws.com/News%20and%20Announcements/2023/December/20231206%20-%20GGL%20Announcement%20-%20Ruby%20Auction%20Results%20-%20Mixed-Quality%20Dec%202023%20-%20FINAL.pdf

and the government of Mozambique had received around 23 per cent of MRM's revenue as taxes and royalty payments[1]. According to the Gemfields team, no other coloured gemstone project in the history of humanity has delivered more value in absolute terms, or as large a proportion of true resource value (whether in the form of revenue or taxation) to the host nation as MRM has. While he continues to attract negative commentary from some quarters, Pachinuapa's decision to shun early and easy cash from other suitors has yielded in-country value for his country which will likely only be fully understood in years to come.

MRM ranks fourth in the CPI transparency index within the extractive sector of Mozambique (as of October 2020) and provides employment (both direct and via contractors) to ~1,400 people, 95 per cent of whom are Mozambican nationals. In 2017, MRM was awarded the Best Social Responsibility Practices prize by the government of Cabo Delgado. Notwithstanding the presence of the large gas projects, MRM has been the largest tax payer in Cabo Delgado for nearly a decade.

The company continues to navigate a challenging relationship with individuals living in the vicinity of the mine and says it is dedicated to nurturing a trust-based relationship with local community members. It has established schools, healthcare facilities and livelihood projects including a vocational training centre, as well as an operational grievance mechanism to improve community relations. Well aware that there is always more to be done in the poorest province in one of the world's poorest countries, the teams at Gemfields, Mwiriti and MRM recognise that the real work may have only just begun.

1   https://gemfields.com/wp-content/uploads/2023/02/20230215-GGL-announce-ment-Gemfields-releases-updated-G-Factor-for-Natural-Resources-figures-FINAL.pdf

Left: A typical illegal ruby mining pit (2011-12). Photo credit: Gemfields.
Right: MRM's first residential (tent) camp in Mozambique (2012). Photo credit: Gemfields

A photo of an area inside Mwriti's hunting concession that was being illegally mined for rubies.
The ground was pockmarked by artisanally dug pits (2011). Photo credit: Gemfields.

Asghar (partially visible in the white shirt between the tree trunks) at one of the illegal ruby mining and trading areas inside the Mwriti concession (2009). Photo credit: Asghar.

Asghar interrupting illegal ruby mining on the Mwriti concession (2009). Photo credit: Asghar.

Asghar pointing towards the hill on the Mwriti concession, which was converted into a stone quarry (2009). Photo credit: Asghar.

Burnt carcass of a vehicle found by Asghar at the Mwriti concession. A remnant of gang fights between competing ruby smuggling syndicates (2009). Photo credit: Asghar.

Mamaroni Goes to Mozambique

September 2008
Bank of the Ruvuma River
Tanzania

MAMARONI STOOD by the expansive Ruvuma River, waiting for the ferry to bring her from Tanzania to Mozambique. It had taken her four days to reach the second border crossing. She'd left her two small children with her husband in Nairobi and travelled to Arusha in Tanzania by bus. After spending the night in Arusha, a 13-hour bus journey had brought her to Dar es Salaam.

There, she'd bumped into a family friend, Abdul[1] who was travelling to Nampula in Mozambique and offered to be her guide and companion until Montepuez. He was an electrician and not involved with the gem business. But he knew many people in his community who traded stones. From the movement of traders, he was aware that something important was happening in and around Montepuez. From Dar es Salaam, the duo hopped on a transport, which would bring them to the Tanzanian town of Mtwara.

'Make sure you get a window seat on the left side of the bus,' advised Abdul. 'As we get closer to Mtwara, you can see and smell the ocean.'

Mamaroni and Abdul stayed a night in Mtwara, had grilled fish by the beach for breakfast, then found a ride to the border by the Ruvuma River.

Stretching for a total of 760 kilometres (475 miles), about 85 per cent of the Ruvuma River forms a natural border between the two countries, and construction was underway for the Unity Bridge to ease movement between them. Mamaroni spotted a few familiar faces, Tanzanian gem dealers who were all headed towards Montepuez. As they waited with the rest of the travellers for their ferry, Abdul asked Mamaroni, 'When did you start in the gem business?'

'It was in 2000. Most in the business had a family connection. A cousin, an uncle, but for me it was just a coincidence,' said Mamaroni.

'What you mean?'

---

1 This name has been changed.

'I had a small restaurant, but I was always trying to improve my family's life. I'd just had my second son. A friend of mine was trading gems, and asked if I'd come with her to the bush. I said yes.'

'Where you both go?' asked Abdul.

'Lemshuko. To buy the green garnet—tsavorite. I remember, we left before sunrise to reach Arusha in time to catch a Landy[1] going to the Komolo shopping centre.'

'How you know Landy going to be there?'

'Because we went on market day. My friend had gone there before so she knew the way. The Maasai who mine the garnet in Lemshuko and the nearby villages, they come to Komolo on market day for their food, beer, everything. Because of that we knew there would be at least one Landy going to Komolo. Difficult journey it was. My son was a year old, so I was still overweight. We had to sit on top of the provision crates. More than ten people stuffed in one vehicle. Those days I did it. Cannot even think about it now.'

'Smart to go on market day. Otherwise, must hire a cycle or just walk.'

'We did hire cycles. But only after we reached the Komolo shopping centre. There was no road, just a dirt track to Lemshuko. More than half the journey we were walking. The funny part was every time the cycle would go over a pothole, I would fall off.' Mamaroni burst out laughing recalling the memory. 'I was sitting behind the guy whose cycle it was. We both kept falling. Luckily, on the way back we got a lift from a broker who had his own car.'

'Your friend had knowledge about gemstones?'

'No. She was like me, trying her luck. We reach Lemshuko and start looking at the tsavorite. The first person to sell me a parcel was a Maasai. The first time I see these gems, they look like pieces of broken green glass. You know I like to express myself honestly. I told him, I know nothing, and in fact it's my first time to see gemstones.'

'What?! You said that to him?'

'Yes. I said, "I don't know the buying or selling price so when you're selling to me try to make it reasonable so I can make something out of it." So, he's the first person to give me courage because if I made nothing from the stone he sold to me, I could have lost my money, it may have been the end of story for me.'

'He give you a fair price?'

1   Land Rover.

335

'I came to Nairobi and sold the tsavorite for double price. I was so happy. Like a crazy person. It was a parcel of small sizes. Big one I wouldn't dare because I didn't know how to pick that time.'

'You were meant to be in this business. That's why you got lucky and found an honest person.'

'But I also failed,' said Mamaroni. 'In December of the same year I went to the bush. One trip can take seven to ten days from Nairobi to Lemshuko and back. But I left my family thinking maybe I can buy the stones and come back in time for Christmas. I took the chance because I knew this one digger. Our parents were friends; I'd known him since primary school.'

'You trusted him,' said Abdul.

Mamaroni nodded. 'I reach Lemshuko and this guy tells me he has special gemstones, but is waiting till Christmas to sell because not all the pieces belong to him; he has his partners in the stones. He ask me to wait if I want to buy.'

'You abandoned Christmas with your family?'

'Yes. I felt very bad about that, but he had me convinced he had good material. Some other people came over and talked to me confirming he's got stones. I didn't realise they were his friends who were helping him fool me.'

'Did he sell you fake stones?'

'The way it works in our business, if we brokers want to see nice stones, sometimes, we must spend money on these diggers and pay for their beer and food. When I reached him, I saw this digger was already spending money like crazy. I also started buying him beer and food to please him.'

'How much were you spending on him?' asked Abdul.

'In a day, he could spend 100 shillings, which was a lot at that time. If it was today, I'd tell the digger that before you spend any of my coin you show me what you have. But at that time, I was not having all that experience. I took him at face value. I didn't think that someone who I had known since we were children could spend my money like this without feeling any guilt. Anyway, all these days I was there, he was not working, just eating my money. Then Christmas came. And he starts coming with this fishy-fishy excuse like, "Oh one of my partners, he's still working; let us push the sale to new year".'

'And still spending your money?'

'Yes. To cut it short, they finished all my capital. New Year came and there were no stones. I told my story to this other broker working in the area, and he says, "My dear, forget about it. What has happened has happened. Go back to your family, get more capital, come back and try again. This time be smarter." So, I leave the bush with no stones and no money.'

'Sorry to hear, sister,' said Abdul.

'Don't be. You learn more from the times you fail than when you succeed. Good people like that man who guided me are also there. Look, the ferry is here.'

Once on board, Mamaroni and Abdul found a comfortable spot. Abdul started telling her about the situation in Mozambique. 'Once we reach the other side, we'll have to go through an immigration checkpoint. Because now many people are going to Mozambique, there will be a few Land Cruisers waiting to take us to this coastal city, Mocímboa da Praia. I know a place where we can rest for the night before we continue to Montepuez via bus.'

'I've never been to Mozambique. How is the place?' asked Mamaroni.

'It's one of the most beautiful, virgin lands. The people are so innocent and nice, and it has some of the most beautiful waters and beach you will ever see. There is a lot of fishing there, so always we can eat very nice grilled fish, which they catch fresh.'

'Sounds like paradise.'

'Ruby paradise now. I see many dealers going there.'

'Yes. I'm hoping to make good money,' said Mamaroni. 'What about you? You will also stop in Montepuez?'

'No, sister; I must travel on to Nampula. I have a job there. My boss is waiting for me. But you must be careful. Around the ruby deposit I hear people are not nice, and police make everything very difficult. They are like sharks.'

'I have another Tanzanian friend who has a small restaurant in Montepuez. I will seek his help.'

'Good. I feel better knowing you have some contacts there. Insha'Allah; all will be well with you. But take care, and trust no one.'

* * *

Three months later
Mocímboa da Praia, Mozambique

'Mamaroni!' shouted Abdul. It had been three months since he'd last seen his friend. 'How are you? How was the ruby hunting?'

'Abdul. So good to see a friendly face again. I'm well. Finally, heading back home.'

'You've been in Mozambique for three months? Must have been a productive visit,' said Abdul.

Should I tell him what really happened? she wondered. 'Got a few stones. But time will tell how productive. It was like you said, very difficult. I never experienced so much hostility before.'

'I told you. That ruby area is very dangerous. Did you go to where they are digging?'

'Abdul, that place is very tough. Bad people all around. I met my Tanzanian friend in Montepuez. Through him made some connections. They explain to me that there are two ways to get the rubies. I can go to where they are digging for rubies but for that I must bribe the askaris[1] and hire diggers. The askaris will guide us to a place where we can dig for the rubies.'

'And how much money they said to bribe?' asked Abdul.

'Starting price was US$500, going up to US$2,000 for one night to take the diggers and go in the mining area to dig for rubies.'

'What is this place where the askaris take diggers?' asked Abdul.

'It's a small place called M'Sewe. You won't even find it on a map.'

'Is it near a village?' asked Abdul. He'd never heard of the name before and was curious to understand its location.

'No. It's no place like that. I didn't go there myself so I cannot describe it to you. But they told me that the diggers stay in M'Sewe. Just rough shelter with bamboo and grass. From what they told me, when you are coming from Montepuez and going to Pemba, on the way you cross all these places near the main road, like Namanhumbir, Nanyupu, and this place where they go to dig is around 20 to 30 minutes inside the bush, away from the main road.'

'So why they have to bribe the askari to go there?' asked Abdul.

'Because it is an area which belong to someone. Some say it's a hunting concession, so there are wild animals. That's why they must bribe to gain access to the area. It's protected by the askari.'

'So they ask you to bribe US$2,000 to take your diggers?'

'Yes. Some traders told me the price has gone up. Used to be less but as more people coming. Price from askari going up. Many people there already, Abdul. Many from Tanzania. And many rubies in the ground. I heard that if you dig for three or four hours continuously, and you pay US$10,000 to the askari, you will still make profit. But it was like a race. Who will reach these officials first in the mining area because they cannot put everyone on to dig in one night. If you are late, you must wait for another day. Also, no guarantee that if you pay, you'll be digging smoothly. No. When the senior askari come from Montepuez, they chase everyone away.'

'My God. Sounds very tough,' said Abdul. 'Good you didn't go.'

---

1 Askari means "soldier" or "police".

'It wasn't just about bribing the askaris, Abdul. There was something else,' said Mamaroni. She hesitated, feeling embarrassed. 'The people there said that if you are a woman, you don't have to pay.'

Abdul stayed silent.

Mamaroni continued. 'Instead of money, you must give your body to the askaris. Then you can put your diggers there.'

Abdul wasn't sure how to respond. He'd heard the stories from other travellers but never paid attention. To hear a woman he knew, someone he respected, share her experience was disturbing.

'I asked them, "What if I want to pay?"'

'What did they say?'

'It don't matter. If a woman go there but she don't want to sleep with them, then they wait for her diggers to go in the ground and while she is waiting above the ground, they will use force to rape. After I heard that I said, "No, I came here to buy stones. I didn't come here to sacrifice my body over money or stone." That was the reason I never went to the mining area, Abdul. The second way to get rubies was to stay in Montepuez or Nanyupu and buy like normal.'

'Nanyupu? I never heard of the place. Where's that?'

'When you are coming from Montepuez, you come to Namanhumbir, near that is Nanyupu. It's from Nanyupu you go to the mining area near M'Sewe. I stayed in Nanyupu with other traders who could not afford to pay the guards.'

'You made the right decision.'

'But it was not easy in Nanyupu also, Abdul. All shelters near the main road were taken. I rented one of the three rooms in a mud hut away from the road, behind the village.'

'Who was living in the other two rooms?' asked Abdul.

'The owner had one, and in the second, some guys sleep there from the mine area. My first night there, it started raining. I was so tired but couldn't sleep. The rainwater kept dripping inside through the thatch roof. But it was worth it because after staying there for two months, in these very rough conditions, I bought two rubies.'

'After all this time only two? I thought you said there were many rubies there?' asked Abdul.

'Yes. I was also buying everyday small rubies for US$500, which I would sell to other traders for US$800. This way I was covering my expenses. But most of my money I spent on these two stones. Beautiful red colour, and when you held them against the sun, they glowed like hot coal in the fire.'

'You were successful then. Congratulations.'

'Not really. Like I said, people there very bad. I was not worried when I arrived because I had not heard anything bad happen to anyone. But they were watching me. One morning, I wake up and see that my handbag is gone. It had everything. My money, my rubies, all my papers. Gone.'

'Stolen?!'

'Yes. Luckily, I had two mobile phones. Where I was staying, there was no electricity. I would leave one mobile in the shop to charge. The other was under my pillow because it had a strong flashlight. At night, when I had to go in the bush to relieve myself, I would use the flashlight. It was only in the morning I found out they had stolen my purse and locked me inside the shelter. Maybe they drugged me while I was sleeping. I was suspecting one guy, but I had no proof. We searched him, found nothing.'

'How will you enter Tanzania without papers, sister?'

'I have them now. A man found my bag. They had thrown it by the side of the road. He looked inside and saw my picture in my passport and thought I looked familiar. We'd met in the village once. He brought my bag to the local police station. I was going there every day to check if they found anything. God bless him. At least I got my passport back.'

'You very lucky. Imagine if that man don't find your bag. Wait a minute. You said this happened two months after you arrived. Where were you last 20 days?'

'I stayed on.'

'How? You had no money?'

'Luckily, I reserved some of my money with my restaurant friend in Montepuez, left $3,500 with him. Enough for me to keep buying.'

'How you make sure they don't steal again?'

'I just risked it, Abdul. I had already paid to stay in the shelter for three months. I couldn't leave the place without any stones. The stones they stole from me I had purchased for $4,000.'

'Uff. A fortune. You found more rubies?'

'Yes. Spent the rest of my money buying more stock. But I couldn't find anything like the ones I lost, Abdul.'

'They all have to be red to be ruby, right?' enquired Abdul.

'All mixed type I see, Abdul. It depends on the haul. Not all are red. Some are more pink. Some, very dark maroon, but I also saw some nice ones, which had softer edges, more red colour. All depending on the haul, which part of the land they find them, and who has what.'

'The Land Cruiser is here,' said Abdul. 'Come, quick, so we can find a place to sit.' He helped Mamaroni with her belongings.

The short drive to the bank of the Ruvuma River was in silence. With Abdul's help, Mamaroni was able to climb on top of the vehicle and sit on the carrier. As they left the coastal city behind, the landscape changed. Mamaroni was sitting towards the front and could see the dusty beige path cut through the green on both sides. She was looking forward to seeing her children and her husband. Abdul and other gem traders she'd met kept telling her that being a woman she was lucky to be returning to Tanzania with stones and in one piece. Although grateful to have survived, she wasn't sure how she felt about the whole experience.

As if sensing her melancholy thoughts, to encourage her, Abdul said, 'You did good. I'm sure in Nairobi your purchases will fetch a good price.'

'I'm not going to sell them now, Abdul.'

'Why? You spent so much money on this journey.'

Mamaroni kept looking ahead. They were now driving past a small village. A few children came out from the huts and decided to run behind their Land Cruiser. Soon, their vehicle would leave them behind, moving closer towards its destination. 'With gemstones, you cannot buy today and sell tomorrow. That's not the way. You buy and keep until the market needs it. That's the only way you can succeed.'

Author's Note

This story is based on interviews with Mamaroni about her experiences. After her adventures in Mozambique, she continued to work as a gem merchant. By 2009, new ruby deposits had been discovered in Namanhumbir and Namahaca. The owners of the land, Mwiriti, were now alert to the presence of the ruby deposit on their hunting concession and in September of 2009 had filed for three mining certificates and two prospecting licences.

In 2010, Mamaroni returned to Mozambique, this time with a male gem dealer who was also a family friend. They found the ruby-mining areas sparsely populated and security tight. The price of gaining access to the ruby deposit had jumped from US$2,000 to US$20,000. The shelters were temporary, made from bamboo and thatch. In Montepuez the story was different. The town was flooded with buyers from Thailand and Sri Lanka, and the local dealers, who had been there since 2008, were running well-established gem businesses. During her brief three-week stay in Montepuez, Mamaroni did not see a single ruby. The foreign buyers had priority access

341

to any rubies that were extracted, and since they had deeper pockets than local merchants, they dominated the market.

Industry sources reported an escalation of violence between 2009 and 2011 in the larger Montepuez region due to the ruby deposit, which became a magnet for thousands of individuals looking to become rich by informally digging and smuggling rubies from Mozambique.

Mamaroni travelled to Thailand in 2012 seeking a buyer for the parcel of rough Mozambique rubies she had purchased for US$3,500 in 2008. She sold the parcel for US$5,500 and estimates that the two rough rubies stolen from her would have fetched over US$20,000.

Breakfast with Major Akpuaka

2012
Abuja, Nigeria

'YOU KNOW all these stories about diamonds and princesses wearing tiaras? All nonsense. It gives people the wrong idea that there is so much money in the gemstone business,' said Major Akpuaka, as he took another sip of his coffee.

He was having breakfast with Lotanna Amina, a young Nigerian jewellery designer who had contacted him a few weeks ago to request a meeting. When he'd enquired as to the purpose of the appointment, she'd explained she was championing an initiative to bring key stakeholders in the Nigerian gem and jewellery trade together for an exhibition. He had reluctantly agreed to meet.

'But aren't these glamorous stories important? It's marketing. Selling this beautiful dream. Why people buy jewels,' said Lotanna.

She was keen to have him on board with the initiative she was planning, but many had warned her that although he was helpful and knowledgeable, he preferred a low profile. Within the first five minutes of the meeting, he had categorically refused to be part of any committee or board. Lotanna hoped to change his mind before breakfast ended.

'Yes. Patronage is vital to the business, but the problem is that the glamour can be misleading,' he said.

'This is why we need someone like you with your decades of experience to participate in this initiative,' said Lotanna.

'I can tell you what I know, but you also must travel to mines, manufacturing hubs, and trade yourself. That's the best education.'

'I understand. If you don't mind me asking, how did you get into the gemstone business?'

'When I was in the army, I travelled to Pakistan in the early seventies to do a military course on telecom engineering. It was a three-year programme. During my break, I decided to hop across the border to Afghanistan. There I saw the most amazing lapis lazuli stones, deep electric blue colour. It's the type of colour you cannot imagine in real life. When you see raw lapis, you feel nervous touching it for fear the colour will come off on your hand, like chalk.'

'I love lapis, and it looks lovely set with yellow gold. So, it was because of Afghanistan that you fell in love with gemstones?' asked Lotanna.

'Yes, but also because most of the embassy people in Pakistan spent their money buying stones. And the discussions in the parties were all about gemstones. I would listen carefully. Once my course was done, I returned to Nigeria with a deep appreciation for gems—and a beautiful wife.'

'Really? You got married there?'

'Indeed. I first saw my wife Azra during a church service in Rawalpindi in December 1973. I found out about her family and went to call on them. You know, they'd never seen an African man before. And her mother got upset with her. She was asking her, "Why this man come and ask for you? Is he your boyfriend? Have you been seeing him?" And, poor thing, she had no idea I'd noticed her in church.'

'So, you got her in trouble with her family?' asked Mina, giving a conspiratorial wink.

'A little bit,' said Major Akpuaka, as he laughed out loud. 'I was smart. I didn't go alone. I took with me this Irish priest.'

'So, you proposed marriage? Just like that?'

'Yes. She was beautiful. Still is beautiful. Her mother then asked the church to find out if I had a wife maybe in Nigeria that I was hiding, and what was my reputation?'

'Then what happened?'

'It took a month for the church to get all the information about me through their network. It was all good, and we were married in February of 1974.'

'Your mother-in-law was happy obviously.'

'Of course! Hardworking woman, God bless her. She worked as a matron in a railway hospital. Her Muslim husband had divorced her, and she had to support three daughters in Pakistan. Not an easy life. Azra was the middle child. I remember my mother-in-law told me that she used all the money she earned to give her girls the best education and training she could afford. She passed away in 2009 on the 25th of November.'

'Sounds like an incredible woman,' said Mina. 'Coming back to gemstones. What did you do after returning to Nigeria?'

'By the time I returned, I had a small collection of gems. But I was still working in the army. Then, I retired in 1979. And that's when I decided to visit Bangkok to sell my gems. It didn't go well because my selection wasn't the best, you see.'

'What did you do?'

'I realised I had to educate myself. So, I enrolled in a gemmology course with the Asian Institute of Gemmological Studies (AIGS). I was in the first batch of students. The institute was established by a young Thai man, Henry Ho. I did the full course with them and also learnt how to cut stones.'

'But you were a merchant. Why did you learn gem-cutting?' asked Lotanna.

'Because to understand the value of a rough gemstone it's important to know everything about it. What will you get after cutting? How does a stone respond to treatment? Take the Nigerian blue sapphires. Depending on where they're from, they'll react differently to heat treatment. For example, the ones from Gombe and Kaduna don't respond well to heat, whereas I have seen blue sapphires from Mambilla and Bauchi turn a beautiful open shade of blue when heated. It's important to know all this to realise the true worth of a stone you want to buy.'

'What happened after your course?'

'I came back and started practising. And this is when I encountered this problem with money in Nigeria.'

'What do you mean?'

'This oil boom Nigeria experienced. Money was just floating around like balloons. All these people who got the contracts to work in Nigeria. At the end of their time, they went into these villages with naira[1] and just bought whatever gems they could find. They overpaid. The gem sellers stopped coming to me because they could sell their stock for silly money to people who weren't in the industry. It was better for me to travel to Kenya and buy than in Nigeria.'

'Why do you say that?'

'In Nairobi, I would go to the shops there and buy yellow tourmaline. If I buy for three dollars, I could make five dollars when I sell. But there is nothing you can buy in Nigeria and make profit. To make money, you must buy the right quality at the right price.'

'The Nigerian miners must have made money with all this demand?'

'Not really. You know, only five to ten per cent of stones that are mined are good enough to export. The miners spent a lot of money excavating because of their expectations coming from all this oil money floating around. For them to break even from just ten per cent of their production was impossible. At the end, the miners got less and less interested and when they abandoned their mines, the cattle herders would come and pick up

1   Local Nigerian currency.

the stones from riverbeds and abandoned mines. The gemstone business has never been properly developed in Nigeria because of the high cost of mining. And when a miner hits a gem pocket, they lose control of the mine because people go in at night to dig illegally.'

'So, how did you start making money in the business?'

'It was difficult. We didn't have any Nigerian practitioners based in Manhattan, you see.'

'Practitioners? Manhattan? I don't understand' asked Lotanna.

'Everyone wants to go and sell their stones in the US. It's a top market. But it's not easy. You need local contacts, local support. There was no Nigerian network of merchants or brokers in New York. The Thai sapphires are as dark as the Nigerian blue sapphires, but they sold for much higher prices in the US than Nigerian ones because the sellers had Thai Americans living there who helped with the marketing and distribution of gems, same as Brazilians.'

'I see.'

'Not only marketing but when these merchants would arrive in Manhattan, they could stay with their local contacts in their homes. For Nigerians, the hotel bill would cost more than whatever money they would get selling their gemstones.'

'But from what I heard, you have an international network of buyers in the US. May I ask how you managed?' asked Lotanna.

'Don't believe everything you hear about me. I was lucky. I'd made some money. Enough to get me to Manhattan. And there, I visited a Jewish gem merchant originally from Brazil called Mr Ary. I had with me a bag full of rough amethyst. Maybe, half a kilo or more.'

'And did he buy them?'

'I went to his office for the first time. And I showed him my goods. He asked me how long I'd been in the business. So, I tell him my story. He says, "I can do two things today. Make you an offer right now based on what's on my table, which would mean you may not make enough money to cover the cost of your trip. Alternatively, if you're willing, I can show you how you can clean these rough amethysts and grade them, which may help you get a better price".'

'Really? That was very kind of him. What did you do?' asked Lotanna.

'Of course, I took him up on his offer. So, we go to this other room. And there, he brings out this special hammer and chisel and shows me how to remove all the white part that was stuck to the purple amethyst. It wasn't easy, because the stone is sharp, and I cut my hands in many places.'

'And then?'

'After he cleaned two pieces of rough amethyst in front of me, he loaned me his tools to go back to my hotel room and clean the rest. He said, "When you clean it, you come back, and we value it together and you know what's what." I returned the next day. Both my hands were badly cut but I had managed to chip away all the extra bits, which were not purple. We sat in his office, and he taught me how to grade my goods. I understood why a particular crystal was one dollar and the other was 50 cents. By the time we finished, I had sorted my rough amethyst pieces into three categories: graded as per the intensity of the colour, the clarity, and the crystal quality. It was a great learning experience. Sorting and cleaning your gemstones is vital to extracting the maximum value.'

'And the price?'

'Now, it wouldn't be right for me to share the price with you, but I can tell you, before, I would have lost money on the trip to the US. Now, the price Mr Ary offered enabled me to cover my cost and make a little profit.'

'Why do you think he did that? He had to pay more to you.'

'I asked him the same question and he said, it was an investment in future supply. When I returned to Nigeria, I tried teaching other sellers of amethyst what Mr Ary taught me. I even learnt from him how to make that special chisel and hammer he was using for the stones. But back home, sellers were not interested. They were OK to just smash the rough amethyst to reveal the purple inside, damaging their goods in the process. They didn't have the patience.'

'Did you go back to Mr Ary after that first time?'

'Yes. Many times. Once, I found emeralds in Nigeria. You know Nigerian emeralds are around 213 to 141 million years old?[1]. I bought a lot of them and of course, I informed Mr Ary that I was coming with some kilos of emeralds. He organised these big buyers and a meeting was set up. And then my parcel was opened. They were emeralds but no colour.'

'I don't understand. How can they be emeralds but no green colour?'

'The green was there but very pale. Mr Ary said we call them beryl and not emeralds. The crystals were beautiful. There was a big expectation and it came to nothing. The gem business is funny like that. It's the same stone, but when it's a pale green, it's called beryl, when it has no colour that same beryl is called goshenite, or white beryl. Only when it is a more saturated green can we call it an emerald and expect a higher price. But you learn the

1   Gaston Giuliani 1, Lee A. Groat 2, Dan Marshall 3, Anthony E. Fallick 4 and a. Y. B. 5 (2019). "Emerald Deposits: A Review and Enhanced Classification". https://www.mdpi.com/2075-163X/9/2/105

most from your mistakes. This is where the Senegalese have an advantage over us Nigerians.'

'How do you mean?'

'Because a lot of them now are third generation in the business. They've learnt from the mistakes of their fathers and grandfathers. They have one brother in Zimbabwe, one in Zurich, one in Namibia. They don't have to go somewhere and find buyers and start selling. They just go and drop the stones to their cousin and come back to Africa. And they can stay in the bush for six months and keep buying till they get exactly what they want.'

'I heard this about the Senegalese,' said Lotanna. 'But I don't understand how they can sustain themselves for six months in the bush in a foreign country. It can't be easy?'

Major Akpuaka smiled at her and stayed silent. Instead of clarifying, he started eating his omelette. She felt that maybe she'd said something ignorant but wasn't sure what else she could ask. *Best to keep quiet*, she thought.

After a minute or two of eating in silence, Major Akpuaka said, 'This is my understanding. The Senegalese comes into Nigeria, he gets a lot of money from Zurich or wherever his buyers are based. He arrives in Nigeria with around 50,000 US dollars, for example, and changes the money into Naira. Straight away, he's made money in the conversion. Then, he moves down to the village, and gets friendly with the village chief. Rents a room from the chief and starts living in the village. The people start bringing him stones and he starts buying big. This is what they do. They buy the whole lot. Everything. Keep the one or two pieces that are good and resell the balance to local Nigerians. Once he has enough of the good-quality pieces, he returns to Zurich. The Nigerians don't have the patience.'

'What you just explained. I've never heard this from anyone else.'

'People know. But it's not normal to talk like this. You're asking questions, which I'm just answering. Nothing more,' said Major Akpuaka.

'What would you suggest to someone new in the business?' asked Lotanna.

'In what way?'

'Anything. If you had to maybe give some advice related to understanding the worth of your goods. Like what you said before about cutting. Is there something else?'

'There is nothing like experience. I'll share one story with you about this time in 1987 when I was exhibiting at the Tucson Gem Show in the United States of America. In the booth next to me was this young man from Afghanistan. Nice boy. We had drinks and became friends. He had a booth but there was nothing in it. He said his goods were delayed. I had some tourmalines from Nigeria, which were basically very average. The second day, the Afghani's goods arrived. I've never seen such sizes of tourmalines. The red was so bright. And green gems, their colours were like emeralds. The size was amazing. Clean and big. Some up to 100 grams. And crystal clear.

'The man didn't stay even 30 minutes in his booth before the big guys came and took him away for negotiations. If I hadn't seen these tourmalines from Afghanistan, I would have thought the Nigerian ones I had were the best in the world and I would have put the highest price. This is something you cannot learn in the books. Enough about me,' said Major Akpuaka. 'Tell me more about what you are doing these days. What are your plans?'

'Right now, I'm preparing to travel to a few small-scale mines in Nigeria,' responded Lotanna.

'Really? And what is the purpose?'

'I want to learn more about the challenges they're facing and see if there's a way I could help.'

'How do you see yourself helping?'

'I don't know right now. I think I need to educate myself first. In the last year since I set up my business, I get many people coming to my office to sell me stones. I've been curious from day one about what stones we have in Nigeria and why our gem-mining industry is not more developed. I've learnt a lot from you today. But I also realise, like you said, if I want to have a deeper appreciation and understanding of the industry, I need to travel to the source and speak to the people.'

'Always a good idea.'

'Coming back to your story. May I ask what happened with that Afghani boy and his beautiful tourmalines?'

'He had a good night. Sold everything in less than an hour. Even paid my hotel bill and put some money in my pocket. Big guys immediately swooped down on him. They didn't want him to display the goods. When you have the best it's not a problem to sell. It takes a lot of travelling and a lot of mistakes and a lot of comparisons. I've never seen such sizes of tourmalines. I was afraid to bring out mine after seeing his collection.'

Lotanna started laughing. 'I've heard you have a beautiful collection.'

'It's OK. Pays the bills. Go to the mines, see what you need to see, and then contact me.'

'Does this mean you'll support our initiative?'

'I'm always available to support anything good for the industry. But I suggest you first gather information. Observe. Absorb. Then, we talk again. You travelling alone?'

'No. I have a family friend coming from the US. I'm going with him. And I have some trustworthy contacts helping with the trip.'

'Boy from the US, eh? Should be fun. I wish you a happy and safe journey.'

Author's Note

This story is based on an interview conducted with Major A. I. Akpuaka (retired). His early struggle to understand the worth of his goods is one that is common with most miners and gem merchants who are based at or near the source. Lack of knowledge is one challenge. Another is being forced to sell at whatever price they are getting from the traders who travel to mines and buy from the source. Miners and merchants work with a constant fear of being taken for a ride. This can lead to mistakes in under and overvaluing their rough gemstones. Most lose money, and only the steadfast and smart win in the long run.

Major Akpuaka did support Lotanna in the Nigeria Gemstone and Jewellery Exhibition (NGJE), which was held from 14th to 15th October in 2015. He officiated as the chair of the opening ceremony, and subsequently participated in other initiatives. After working in the industry for four decades, Major Akpuaka has now retired from the industry. He owns and operates a prawn farm in Nigeria.

.

Nigerian Dreams

11.00 am
Lotanna Amina's home
Abuja, Nigeria

'HAS THE new car come?' Lotanna asked, as she entered the living room.

'Not as yet,' said her mother. 'Weren't you and James supposed to leave after breakfast?'

'Yes,' said Lotanna. 'That was the original plan, but Abu[1] called to say there was a problem with the car. He's arranged a new one, a Toyota Hilux I think, but it's cost us precious time.'

'Relax,' said James[2]. 'It'll be here soon. Why are you so anxious?'

'Because,' said Lotanna. 'We have a long way to go, James. This isn't like the US, where you just get on the freeway. We're visiting two different gemstone mines in Nasarawa state. There'll be a border check to enter the state. We can only go up till a certain point in the car, after which we'll have to switch to motorbikes. A delay gives us less time with the miners.'

'Easy,' said Lotanna's mother, as she frowned at her daughter. 'It's been a long time since James was last in Nigeria. You must look after him on your journey today.'

'Don't worry, Auntie, I'll be fine,' said James, as he puffed his chest out. Lotanna and James had known each other since they were children. His parents had migrated to the US before he was born but had stayed in close contact with their friends and family in Nigeria. James was in Abuja for two weeks to visit his ailing grandmother and catch up with family friends like Lotanna's parents.

'He's a grown man, Mumma,' said Lotanna, playfully throwing a cushion at James who was quick to dodge. 'He'll be fine.'

'You didn't say anything about motorbikes before, though,' said James.

'How else do you think—wait, they're finally here. Let's go.'

---

1   This name has been changed.
2   This name has been changed.

Lotanna grabbed her small backpack, gave her mother a quick kiss, and rushed out. Trained as an engineer, gems and jewellery had not been part of her original life plan. After obtaining her engineering degree from Covenant University, Nigeria, Lotanna was studying business and innovation, in the UK, when she decided to pursue her interest in gemstones. She enrolled with the Gemological Institute of America (GIA).

In 2011, she established Mina Stones in Nigeria after becoming a graduate gemmologist. Her mission was to revive the country's ancient techniques in crafting jewellery, through her contemporary interpretations. Old Nigerian motifs and coloured gemstones became the two pillars of Lotanna's design style. She positioned Mina Stones as a socially conscious, vertically integrated gemstone and jewellery brand involved in the value chain from mine to market.

Vertical integration was more of a necessity than a choice because of a lack of professional gem and jewellery workshops in Nigeria. Her love of coloured gems, adventure, and a desire to learn more about their origin led her to connect with small-scale miners in Nigeria. They all shared a common problem: lack of resources and knowledge. One in particular had been chasing Lotanna to visit his aquamarine and tourmaline mines. Unable to put him off any longer, she'd decided to take him up on his offer to be her guide. It had been her mother's idea to bring James.

'Mumma, I don't need James,' Lotanna had said. 'I'll be fine. There's nothing to worry about. Abu's coming with me. He's a gem dealer and travels frequently to the mining areas.'

'You want to go to these remote places where it's dangerous for men, let alone a woman. And you expect me not to worry?'

Lotanna's mother had worn her down, and she'd agreed to include James in their group.

The roads from Abuja to the first border checkpoint had taken more than two hours. As they drove away from the city, the potholes increased. In certain sections the road disappeared, challenging the suspension of the vehicle as it tumbled towards the meeting point the mine owner had suggested.

'Nigeria is an oil-rich country. Why can't they build good roads?' asked James, as they drove through an especially tough patch.

'Corruption, my friend,' said Abu. 'The money's there, but for a politician or bureaucrat to spend it on infrastructure, they must first stop lining their pockets. They're too busy to do their job. That's the sad truth.'

After they crossed the state boundary, James pointed towards a group of men and a police jeep waiting by the side of the road. The tallest among them raised his hand when he spotted their SUV, hailing them to stop.

'Uh-oh. Is that a problem?' James asked Lotanna.

The men looked like vigilantes, and some of them bore arms. Policemen were never a welcome sight in Nigeria. James leaned forward on high alert.

'You see that man, waving us to stop,' said Lotanna. 'That's the mine owner. This is the group that's escorting us to the mines. We need to leave our car behind.' James felt his shoulders relax as Lotanna stepped out of their vehicle and started shaking hands and making introductions.

After the policeman had checked the identification documents of the visitors, the convoy of around 15 motorcycles began their journey to the first mine. Lotanna had insisted James ride ahead of her so she could keep an eye on him. They had only ridden for ten minutes when James fell off his bike.

'You, OK?' Lotanna asked as Abu helped him get back on the Yamaha bike.

'I should have told you at the house. I don't know how to ride a motorcycle,' James confessed.

'What?! You're telling me this now,' said Lotanna. 'The first time you decide to ride a bike is in the middle of the bush in Nigeria. Why didn't you say anything?'

'I can ride a cycle. Figured, how hard could it be?'

Over the course of the hour-long journey to the aquamarine mine, which involved riding uphill, traversing valleys, and crossing rivers, James continued to fall off his motorcycle almost every 15 minutes. Each stumble was met with loud hooting and laughter by the men in the group. They had never known a man who couldn't ride a bike. When James slipped for the tenth time, the policeman accompanying their group couldn't resist saying, 'This lady who looks so delicate is able to ride the bike. She is not even budging, and this macho man keeps falling off his bike. Are you sure you Nigerian, my friend?'

As James spent more time riding and less falling, the group settled into a rhythm. One of the locals, who was on a bike next to Lotanna, started telling her about the security problems their community had been dealing with for years. He belonged to a task force set up by the Nigerian government to curb the theft and kidnappings that had become rampant in the area. Although he was technically a government employee, his pay was not enough to support his family and, like others in his squad, he supplemented his meagre income by doing odd jobs such as working as a guide.

'They look to first kidnap foreigners, so they can demand a handsome ransom,' he explained. 'Eventually everyone is released, but not before their family and friends must pay tens of thousands of dollars.'

'You better keep your voice low,' said Lotanna, as she pointed towards James, 'otherwise you may scare my friend.'

'The situation is much better now. Our task force was able to curb the problem. Cannot stop completely. The thieves, they keep returning, but it's safer now.'

'What are they stealing?' asked Lotanna.

'Anything of value they can find. This is why we must travel in a convoy under police protection, because they are always targeting visitors to the mines.'

'What about at the mine?'

'They attack the mines also. Steal the stones. But more than stones they prefer to take food or other valuable commodities, which they can easily sell or consume.'

By the time they reached the aquamarine mine it was lunchtime. The mine owner had arranged a simple meal of boiled rice with a vegetable and meat stew for the group. The owner explained how they sometimes used explosives to clear the land before they could reach the aqua-bearing quartz vein. The actual extraction was manual, with the miners using pickaxes and their bare hands to extract the rough aquamarine crystals.

As the group toured the operation, the mine owner showed them a gem pocket that his team had exposed where pale blue, hexagonal aquamarine crystals were seen embedded in quartz. Having recently purchased a parcel of rough Nigerian aquamarine that displayed a deeper shade of sky blue, good clarity, and perfect hexagonal form, Lotanna was disappointed with the pale colour of the aqua at the mine. She was working on a pendant design that would allow her to set the aqua in its rough state with minor polish.

The next stop was a tourmaline mine, but to reach the location the group had to return on motorbike to their car and then proceed further. In comparison to the aquamarine operation, the tourmaline mine was less developed.

'If I didn't know this was a mine, I would have thought it was a farm,' commented James, once they reached.

'You're right,' said Lotanna. 'It is a farm; you can see some of the staff working in the distance. Looks like corn. Both mines are owned by the same group of three families.'

'I saw you speaking with the mine owner,' said James.

'He was telling me how the state government had promised them a lot. Better roads, for one, but as you can see there's been no infrastructure development here at all. He'd decided to start mining himself because a few years ago, his father entered into a verbal agreement with a man who promised that in exchange for permission to mine for gems on their farmland, he would share a percentage of the income from the sale of the gemstones.'

'I'm afraid to ask what happened,' said James.

'The man mined for six months, and then disappeared. He took the stones, and they never saw or heard from him again. In the absence of a written contract, there was nothing they could do to claim what was rightfully their property. They didn't realise they should have involved a lawyer.'

'Not just the paperwork,' said James, 'To know what to do if someone violates the agreement, and how to enforce it.'

'Exactly! If they don't know the next recourse that's available, the agreement's just a piece of paper.'

'The other thing I found especially painful to see,' said James, 'was the children. Two- and three-year-olds running around with no clothes on or tattered fabric hanging off their bony bodies. I've never seen poverty like this, Lotanna. You remember that lorry that was in front of our SUV in the afternoon?'

Lotanna nodded.

'I was so ashamed to see it. I couldn't look those people in the eye. Those poor children shoved in there with cows, goats, pigs. I just wanted the driver to overtake the truck, so I didn't have to make eye contact.'

'The problem is that poverty and family don't work together. The men, even if they have no money, marry, keep procreating, and don't take any responsibility for the children they produce. The women are left to fend for themselves and the children,' Lotanna explained.

'What happens to these kids?' asked James.

'They become beggars. They always bring problems back to society. It's a vicious cycle that keeps repeating itself. And the government just looks the other way.'

On the way back to Abuja, Lotanna spotted a truck. On further enquiry, her local guide informed her it was a company that was mining in the area. He couldn't recall whether it was for tin or tantalite. 'Haven't they built a school or some infrastructure as part of their CSR[1] efforts?' Lotanna asked the guide.

---

1   Corporate social responsibility.

'Nothing. Not even one borehole for water supply. The government allows this to happen. They only recognise this area and these people when it's election time, and they need votes.'

As the lights of Abuja became visible, Lotanna and the driver were the only ones still awake in the vehicle. By the time they reached her home, it was past nine in the evening.

'How was it?' asked Lotanna's mother, as the duo walked into the living room.

'It was a proper adventure,' replied James.

'We'll chat over dinner. C'mon, you two, wash up. You both look terrible.'

Once dinner was over, James left for his grandmother's house. Lotanna's father suggested they go for a post-dinner walk to digest the indulgent meal. 'All OK, Lotanna?' he asked.

Throughout dinner, Lotanna had hardly engaged in any small talk. When the topic of their day's adventures came up, James did most of the storytelling. Her father could tell something was bothering his daughter.

'What do you mean, Dad?'

'You hardly said anything at dinner.'

'I'm feeling so angry.'

'Why? Did someone say something to you?'

'No. I'm angry at the government. The places we visited today. There were no roads, no clean water, no taps, no electricity. The worst part is that there are probably funds allocated for infrastructure development on paper—some fake report in a file talking about how the money was spent—but on the ground, nothing. Children roaming around with no clothes, hungry, crying.'

'It's the real world. And these realities of the world we live in are not easy to accept.'

'Why should we accept it? You know, we came across a company truck on our way back. They are mining there, taking the natural resources from this community, and they cannot even provide one borehole for clean water. I'm just feeling so much anger. Also, at the parents of these children who are littering all over the road because they don't have access to a clean toilet. Why produce children when you can't take care of them? When you can't feed them, clothe them, give them the necessities of life? It's such a pathetic situation.'

'Anger is good, provided you're able to channel it towards something productive.'

'What can I do, Dad? I can't even think clearly.'

'When you get a cut on your finger, and you see all that blood, for a second your brain panics, till you realise what you need to do to heal the wound. It's the same thing. You are agitated right now because you have experienced something that impacted your mind and your heart. Once you calm down, the solution will present itself. Remember, Lotanna, you cannot change everything in the world. All you can try to do is help improve things that are in your reach. Aren't you working on some event?'

'Yes. It's a gem and jewellery show at the Hilton hotel in Abuja. We have so many gemstones in Nigeria, but people are not aware, Dad. If I can do this event, it'll be the first of its kind in West Africa.'

'Maybe, you can give these miners a platform at your show?' asked her father.

'That's what I was also thinking.' For the first time that evening, Lotanna smiled.

Her father patted her back and said, 'That's the spirit. Don't let your frustrations at everything wrong you are seeing cloud your thinking. Rise above that cloud of emotions and look for a path to move forward.'

'I'll try my best, Dad.'

Author's Note

Lotanna Amina was successful in organising the Nigeria Gemstone and Jewellery Exhibition (NGJE) from 14th to 15th October in 2015. The event was organised by Raw Materials Research and Development Council (RMRDC) in collaboration with her company, Mina Stones. The show featured numerous gemstone suppliers from across Nigeria, including places such as Kaduna, Bauchi, Zamfara, Nasarawa, Jos, Lagos, Oyo, and Abuja.

Over two days, approximately 800 people (Including participators, exhibitors, and visitors) attended the exhibition. The majority were from the region, but the show attracted international visitors from China, Indonesia, Sri Lanka, South Africa, and the United States. The opening ceremony was chaired by Major AI Akpuaka (Retd), and Dr Yau, honourable commissioner, Environment and Natural Resources of Kaduna State, inaugurated the exhibition. The show was attended by several senior dignitaries from state and central government departments and ministries.

In the years leading up to the show, Lotanna began helping small-scale miners through various initiatives, such as providing soft-skills training on communication, how to conduct themselves in a business setting, administrative functions—applying for a mining licence, maintaining paperwork, drafting community agreements, establishing a legal entity, opening a bank account, and paying taxes. Her office became a help centre for small-scale and informal miners.

The success of the first gem and jewellery show organised by Lotanna led to its transformation into the African Gem and Jewellery Exhibition and Seminar (AGJES). The number of small-scale miners exhibiting at the show kept increasing. Some found new buyers. Others were lucky to connect with investors who started supporting their mining operations. One of Lotanna's fondest memories from the event was when a group of miners gifted her a bag full of rough gemstones. When she protested, they said, 'We never imagined that we could be in a place like the Hilton hotel selling our gemstones in a respectable manner.'

Lotanna married an American citizen of Nigerian descent. She now splits her time between the US and Nigeria and continues to support the mining sector via her non-profit foundation: SGJES Sparkle Foundation. She is a member of the Society of Women Engineers, Technologists, and Scientists (SWETS) Africa, where she is actively involved in mentorship and community service. She is on the advisory board of Black In Jewelry Coalition (BIJC), and is also a member of Women in Mining in Nigeria (WIMIN), and the Women's Jewelry Association (WJA) USA.

Lotanna's work for miners covers education and training, grouping miners into cooperatives, providing administrative and operational support, sourcing tools and equipment, and helping miners find a route to market so they may get fair value of their production. During the years of the global pandemic, her team also provided Covid-19 relief to 30 mining operations across 12 states.

Never Drop a Ruby

2018
Austria

'NO, YOU don't understand the situation,' said the officer at security control in Vienna International Airport. 'As per our policy, I must check every gemstone. You need to hand over that pouch of rubies right now,' he added, folding his muscular arms.

Brandishing his boarding card again, Stephan Reif pleaded, 'Officer, please, there are more than 50,000 stones here across 15 Ziploc bags. My flight for Hong Kong leaves in 30 minutes. There isn't enough time. I am a gem merchant, my papers are in order, I am registered to attend one of the largest trade exhibitions in Hong Kong, and I have a very important meeting tomorrow at the show. I must catch this flight.'

Unmoved, the officer took a step closer to Stephan. 'Sir, first, your carry-on stroller is too heavy with these stones, so even if you reach the aircraft, the airline will probably ask you to check it. Second, like I explained, we need to put every single stone through the X-ray machine and then check for traces of explosives. If you want to catch your flight, you better let go of that plastic bag. Furthermore—'

Stephan could hear his heart pounding in his chest. Given that most gem-mining employed explosives for blasting hard rock, his probability of getting arrested seemed high. The bag containing the rubies felt heavier as he stood stupefied. He realised he couldn't talk his way out of this one and decided to concede. His shoulders slumped as he indicated his consent through a half-nod, which spurred the officer to reach for the open packet of rough rubies in Stephan's hands. They miscalculated the timing of the transfer. The bag dropped, and the precious red gems scattered across the dull grey airport floor.

* * *

2016
Tanzania

This may be a complete waste of time but there's only one way to find out, thought Stephan as he approached the immigration counter at Julius Nyerere International Airport in Dar es Salaam. The officer started flipping through his documents. Pointing to the accommodation details on his arrival form, she inquired, 'You staying here?'

When he confirmed, she chuckled. Shaking her head, she stamped his passport and said, 'OK, enjoy! And welcome to Tanzania.'

Stephan made his way to the exit, wondering what she'd found funny about his accommodation. Three weeks ago, he'd received a phone call that led him to Tanzania. A common friend had connected him with a man called Richard[1], an erstwhile member of the elite Special Air Service (SAS) unit of the British Army. He was now working in private security. During a hiatus between contracts, Richard and his friend Joe, a Tanzanian citizen, had started exploring a ruby deposit in the remote Handeni district of the country.

It had been an interesting call during which Richard had invited Stephan to visit their ruby mine with a view to buy some of their production and possibly form a marketing alliance. Curious about Richard's background, Stephan did a quick online search to understand what being part of the SAS meant. He was impressed to discover that it had one of the most stringent training programmes in the world, with only ten per cent of recruits able to finish the course.

Clearly, Richard had what it took to operate a ruby mine in an obscure border territory of Tanzania. But he was not a gemmologist. Stephan had gone down enough rabbit holes in the past to be sceptical. He also knew how difficult it was to estimate the economic worth of a gem deposit. His own family had invested in and still owned the first demantoid garnet mine in Namibia. Typically, by the time a miner realised the deposit wasn't worth much, he or she had already spent considerable funds. Still, there was something intriguing about Richard's story.

After messaging his wife to let her know he'd landed safely, Stephan took a taxi to the guest house Richard had recommended. As the white Toyota whizzed past palm trees, dusty pavements, buildings, and billboards, Stephan took a deep breath. Although he'd travelled extensively in Africa

---

1   This name has been changed.

and had many adventures worthy of movie scripts, he never got tired of this feeling on arrival, when the journey ahead was full of possibilities.

Stephan reached the guest house and was pleased to notice a lively atmosphere in the lobby. The resto-bar adjoining the front desk was promoting a 'Fajita Special' with beer on tap, and he spotted some activity around a pool table next to the bar.

He had a large room on the top floor of the guest house. The room had a four-poster bed with wispy mosquito nets. There was a writing desk next to double glass doors, which opened onto a small veranda. Next to the entrance was a floral-patterned sofa and a modest wooden table, with a metal vase containing bright pink bougainvillea blossoms.

Stephan calculated he had ample time for a nap and a quick shower before his dinner with Richard. Hot fajitas with cold beer sounded good.

'Did you manage some rest after your long flight?' asked Richard.

'Not really,' Stephan replied. 'There was a romantic couple next door, which made sleep challenging, but hopefully they've worn each other out and the night will be peaceful.'

As they sat devouring their fajitas and sipping beer, Stephan took the opportunity to listen and observe, forcing Richard to fill the awkward gaps in their conversation. The man was at least six feet tall, late thirties, sat straight on the cushioned beer-barrel stool, fit like a bodybuilder with intense eyes that seemed to notice everyone in the room.

Richard explained how his partner's family had agricultural land in the Handeni District of Tanzania, where they were operating a cashew nut farm. A farm hand had brought pinkish pebbles from one of their remote concessions to show the foreman, who'd brought the find to the family's attention. They'd started mining with basic tools. After Richard joined, three months ago, he'd managed to get earth-moving equipment to the location and increase the scale of the operation.

A recent sale in Arusha of moderate-quality rubies from the concession enabled the team to generate cash. But they'd kept the higher-grade material for international clients, hoping to fetch a better price. Stephan's visit was well timed, as they seemed eager to recover some of their original investment. Richard suggested they leave early the next day as the drive to the mine could take nine hours. 'We need to reach the camp before sunset as there are no roads and the neighbourhood has security issues,' he said.

* * *

The early morning light was faint as they rode through the lanes of Dar es Salaam. Stephan slowly sipped the watery coffee from his flask, waiting for the caffeine to kick in. He'd crashed straight after dinner and, given his exhausted state, decided not to take a sleeping aid to knock him out. Bad idea. Things had started falling apart around 2 am. The moaning, the grunting, the creaking of the beds. Echoes of lust wafted through the walls of the guest house and continued till Stephan's alarm went off. It all made sense now: the sniggering immigration agent, the popularity of the resto-bar, friendly ladies, eager men. The guest house Richard had suggested was a trendy spot for working girls and travelling boys.

Stephan leaned back and closed his eyes, letting the tempo of the rugged road lull him to sleep. An hour later, the lack of movement awoke him. After a quick stop for essentials, they continued their long journey, traversing down muddy paths, their Toyota Land Cruiser smelling of fruits, vegetables, and dusty cartons full of rice, coffee, beans, and biscuits. With eight hours of driving ahead, Richard started sharing his story.

After completing his term in Iraq, under the British Special Air Service (SAS), he'd found himself in Congo (DRC) as security-in-charge for a mining company that was prospecting for gold and diamonds. Like others before him, he was captivated by the beauty and opportunities of Africa and decided to take a break in Tanzania between contracts. A common friend in Arusha introduced Richard to his current business partner, a Tanzanian citizen. Their friendship, combined skills, resources, and domain knowl-edge led to the formation of a partnership they hoped would result in riches beyond their reach today.

'What about you?' Richard asked, glancing at Stephan. 'I believe you've been in the gem business all your life.'

Stephan smiled and replied, 'It certainly feels like it. I come from a family of gem merchants. My grandfather was an adventurous traveller. During one of his gem-buying trips in Namibia, he met a half-German half-Namibian prospector in a bar who had just purchased a mining concession producing beautiful emerald-like gems. Long story short, the stones were not emeralds but rare demantoid garnets. My family decided to invest in the venture with the gentleman.'

Richard's tame reaction on hearing 'demantoid garnets' made Stephan realise that he wasn't aware of the rarity and high value of the gems. He took out his mobile and started showing Richard photos and videos of the elec-tric green gems. 'Till this discovery in Namibia,' Stephan explained, 'Russia was the primary source for demantoid garnets. When I turned 18, my family sent me on an internship to our mine in Namibia.'

Enjoying the walk down memory lane, Stephan continued, 'I remember, our resident gemmologist, Eric[1], and I would travel together for days across the arid Namibian landscape. He would make me sleep on a camp bed next to our jeep, while he slept on the roof of the vehicle. One night, we were in the middle of nowhere and I kept hearing these clicking noises, which progressively got louder. To me it sounded like an animal, but I couldn't see a thing. Namibia has the darkest night sky because the air is so clear and there is no light pollution,' he added.

'Suddenly, something big and heavy landed on me. I started yelling. Eric got up and flashed a light from his spot on the jeep's roof. What I thought was an animal turned out to be two tribesmen who were drunk out of their minds. Between Eric's light in their eye, my shouting, and their intoxicated brain cells, they didn't know what the hell was going on. Luckily, Eric spoke their language and was able to calm their nerves. In less than a minute, they were on their way, stumbling home in the dark.'

The lightness of the moment was disrupted by the sight of a police officer flagging their car to stop. Stephan smiled, familiar with the mysterious 'on-the-spot-fine', levied by the traffic police, especially when there was a mzungu [white man] in the vehicle. It was a ritual performed to supplement the meagre salaries of law enforcement. The fine was usually equivalent to a dollar, but the duration of the delay depended on the skill of the performers in the charade. Richard was an experienced player, ready with small currency notes, and they were soon on their way to the mine.

Stephan regaled Richard with another tale from his early travels in Namibia. 'This particular evening,' said Stephan with a glint in his eye, 'Eric had been trying to scare me by saying he'd heard there were lions in the area. This was our third trip together, so I didn't take him seriously and was too exhausted to care. The next morning, during breakfast, we noticed paw marks in the ground near my camp bed. It seemed I'd spent the night a few feet away from a pride of lions who visited during the night—fortunately on a full stomach!'

Richard and Stephan continued sharing battle stories during their nine-hour-long journey. Despite 18 police stops, the duo arrived at the mine just before sunset, extremely tired but with a newfound understanding and respect for their distinct life experiences.

Richard's army background was evident in the mining camp's layout. There were several tents, large and small, neatly arranged in an L-shape. They stretched in a long row, intersecting at 90 degrees, with another

---

1   This name has been changed.

363

cluster arranged perpendicular, facing the main entrance. Richard's partner, Joe[1], was waiting for them with a cold beer and a warm smile. Together, the friends took Stephan on a quick tour.

The first large tent they entered on the right side of the camp was an office with maps and papers scattered on a long table. All tents had their boundaries marked by pebbles in classic army-style. The next one was a dining area with space for storing provisions and an outdoor cooking section, followed by individual tents, which were the private sleeping quarters for Richard, his partner, and their supervisor, with the last one for Stephan.

The large canvas enclosure towards the back of the camp was the main living area/dormitory for the workers. They had only 20 employees, but they'd built the mining camp with a view for possible future expansion.

Their attention to detail and safety impressed Stephan. He noticed the heavily armed security personnel carrying machine guns. During the drive over, Richard had explained how the security situation near their location had deteriorated in the last month because of terrorist groups in the neighbouring valley who had recently clashed with government forces.

'We're responsible for our people and on our own here, we can't afford to take any chances,' Richard explained.

After a simple meal of rice and beans, they retired for the night, exhausted but hopeful.

The next morning, a staff member awoke Stephan with coffee in an army-style metal mug covered with a steel plate containing biscuits. He pointed out the shower area Stephan could use before joining the rest of the crew for breakfast. As Stephan sipped his coffee, he started making a mental checklist of questions. So far, the only rubies Richard had shown him had been cabochon-grade[2], which would need heat treatment to enhance their clarity, lustre, and colour. For this venture to be successful, they required better-quality stones.

The shower turned out to be an upside-down metal drum with holes in the bottom. There was a lever one had to pull to release water from a tank outside the cramped enclosure. The cold temperature encouraged a quick shower. Stephan's eagerness to leave almost resulted in a nasty bite from a black spider the size of his palm, which had crawled under the towel. Breathing a sigh of relief that it wasn't a snake, he made his way to the dining tent.

They spent the morning surveying the area. As Stephan observed Richard and Joe share their mining adventures, and seeing the average quality of

---

1   This name has been changed.
2   Medium quality, only good enough to be cut into a dome shape or converted into beads.

rubies they'd produced in their last four months, he worried this may be another case of 'gembola'[1], where a gem explorer's perception of reality is clouded by his ambition and romantic notions of potential wealth.

Richard and Joe had plenty of hunting and military experience, but they didn't understand geology or gemmology (let alone how the gem market worked). They asked Stephan if he'd be interested in establishing a marketing alliance to help them get the best price for their rubies. He replied, 'Look, I don't want to give you any false hope. We can try, but let's first see how the day goes. Honestly, it depends on the quality of the production and your price expectation.'

Stephan spent the afternoon giving them a basic geology lesson. He explained how when gems are mined from the rock in which they form (host rock), it's called a primary deposit. To extract such gems requires more work, and miners must be careful to not damage the rubies during the extraction process. He then explained secondary deposits as a location where the gems accumulated after they'd been carried through erosion, and water, away from where they formed. 'Imagine a geological race with the strongest rubies collecting in smaller but more concentrated deposits: easier to mine, offering a quick return, and delivering gems of better quality as natural forces had already curated the material for the miner.'

Stephan's audience was devouring every nugget of knowledge he served. Each helping would trigger a series of questions. He patiently answered every single query. Around four in the afternoon, he suggested they return to the mine, where he showed them how their deposit was mainly primary, interspersed with several alluvial groups, which were secondary deposits. The group spent their time learning how to clean the surface and open up the area, the cheapest way to seek alluvial goods.

Stephan further advised them not to touch the primary hard rock underneath but to first focus on the secondary deposit. The last lesson involved teaching the miners an efficient way to wash ruby gravel. They were quick learners.

'OK, that's enough for today; tomorrow we'll sort and grade. That should give us a better idea of what we have,' said Stephan, as he looked up at the fading evening light. Over dinner, he continued to answer questions.

'Do you typically ship the stones or prefer hand-carrying them for safety?' Joe asked.

'First, I make sure my paperwork is legit and then, honestly, I prefer to hand-carry my goods as much as possible. Sometimes you can't depend on

---

1   A portmanteau of "gem" and "Ebola".

the courier service, or the value of the stones may be less than the cost of shipment,' Stephan said.

Despite his experience, if he went ahead with this alliance, it would be his first time processing and marketing rubies. He had contacts in Thailand and Sri Lanka who could do the heat treatment and cutting. But would there be enough good-quality material to cover expenses and provide a return for all stakeholders? He wasn't sure.

* * *

After another encounter with Mr Spider in the shower the following morning, Stephan recommended the team focus on washing, sorting, and grading the gemstones while they had light. 'If I'm to market the mine's output, I can't be in Tanzania all the time,' he explained. 'You must accumulate the production and do some pre-sorting and basic grading. I'll need to know if it's worth coming down here.'

He still hadn't seen enough nice-quality rubies to take a decision. As the morning rolled into the afternoon, the miners continued working hard. They knew this was Stephan's last day; they wanted to make the most of it. By lunchtime, they'd washed most of the ruby gravel stored in buckets and sorted the material according to size and colour.

'Let's break for a quick lunch and use the afternoon to finish grading,' Stephan suggested.

As he shovelled rice and meat stew made of some mysterious creature down his throat, Stephan contemplated how he would teach them a complicated topic like grading in hours. There were various factors that made evaluation of rough rubies tough. First, the density of the material, making inclusion identification a long and painful task. Then, the market expectation in terms of colour and clarity, which meant more wastage during cutting and polishing to deliver cleaner gems with good colour saturation. Sometimes a lapidary had to cut away almost 60 to 70 per cent of the rough.

By one in the afternoon, they'd started grading. Stephan showed them how to use the sunlight and a jeweller's loupe to identify inclusions like inky blue spots inside the rubies. 'Depending on the location of the inclusion, whether it's located towards the centre of the stone, on the side, closer to the surface or embedded deeper,' he explained, 'a lapidary would either heat the ruby or just cut away the blemish.'

By sunset, Stephan had agreed to join hands with Richard and Joe to market their rubies. He cautioned them that from what he'd seen; only two per cent of the mine's production could be cut into good-quality gems. The rest would require intense treatment and even after, would only be good for beads and cabochons, fetching lower prices. They would need to continue mining, washing, sorting, and grading to find the top material. The best would be offered collectively, to fetch the strongest price.

'Periodic sales of medium- and lower-grade rubies,' he said, 'should keep funds flowing, but you must keep this location a secret, and not discuss your work with anyone.'

* * *

2018
Vienna

As the rubies fell from the open pouch onto the floor in Vienna International Airport, Stephan's heart sank. They had spent two years accumulating the rough rubies, which represented the mine's best material. Richard and Joe were operating on their last dollar, as most of the production from the deposit had turned out to be of lower grade. They were depending on Stephan selling this parcel to a buyer in Hong Kong, so they could break even. Horrified, Stephan started shouting at the airport security.

'Oh, my God! What have you done?! Nobody move; I need to secure the parcel!'

The security team stepped back, realising the gravity of the situation, and making sure the awaiting crowd of passengers didn't step into the ruby zone. The pouch that fell contained around 150 rough rubies, each one the size of a peanut weighing a total of 72 grams. Luckily, the grooves on the floor helped contain the gems, and after five minutes of crawling on his hands and knees, Stephan was able to retrieve what he hoped was the entire stock.

The commotion attracted the security superintendent. He approached Stephan, who by now was drenched in sweat and close to a nervous breakdown. After hearing Stephan's plea and examining the paperwork, he instructed his officers to randomly select only a few rubies for the secondary check and leave the rest. Ten minutes later, a dishevelled Stephan was running through the international terminal dragging his worn out stroller bag.

As he turned a sharp corner, he crashed headlong into the luggage trolley of a newly arrived family who were walking towards the arrival hall. The accident broke one of the wheels of the heavy stroller. Staring at the bag's broken body, Stephan wanted to scream out loud in frustration, and then, he heard his name: 'Passenger Stephan Rief, Stephan Rief for Cathay Pacific flight 538 to Hong Kong. Your flight is ready for departure. Please make your way to gate 24 for immediate boarding,' boomed the voice, snapping him out of his self-pity mode.

He took a deep breath, knelt and, channelling his inner hulk, lifted and placed the carcass of his bag on a nearby trolley to restart his sprint. Ten minutes later, as he neared the finish line of his marathon run, he saw the airline crew waving at him from the boarding gate.

Stephan entered the aircraft looking and smelling like the last person anyone would want to sit next to in the luxurious business class cabin.

'Sir, let me help you place your bags in the overhead bin. We need to secure the cabin for take-off,' said the efficient flight attendant.

'I can manage, don't worry,' Stephan responded but it was too late.

As soon as the attendant tried to lift the case, she said, 'Oh my! This is too heavy. Regulations don't permit us to place something so weighty in the overhead bin.'

Physically and mentally shattered, Stephan collapsed on the armrest of his seat and said, 'I can't check it in. What about the closet?'

The flight attendant shook her head informing him that the closets were full. Taking pity on Stephan, she said, 'The only solution, sir, is for you to remove your items from the suitcase and distribute the weight across multiple overhead bins.' Stephan didn't move, staring dumbfounded at the bag. His risk-averse brain was struggling to process the cabin crew's suggestion. Sensing his reluctance, the flight attendant said, 'Let's do it together, so you can sit back, relax, and enjoy your flight.'

Stephan opened the case, revealing the 15 vulnerable, clear, Ziploc pouches of rough rubies. Pretending like she handled such cargo all the time, the professional cabin attendant guided Stephan as they rushed around the business class cabin, placing the crystals in multiple overhead bins. Stephan ignored the various scenarios of doom playing like a C-grade movie in his mind, finally taking his seat and fastening his seatbelt.

The cabin attendant returned with a cold towel. As Stephan started to relax, his thoughts drifted to Tanzania. For the past few months, he'd been telling Richard to wind up the operation. A mine owner himself, he recognised the symptoms. They'd started dipping into their savings, which Stephan had warned against. *That's the trouble with coloured gem mining; it's like gambling*, Stephan thought. *Most think, I'll just dig a little this way and become a millionaire. For a handful, that may be the case, but for most, the story ends differently.*

Although hoping for a different outcome, deep down, Stephan knew the probability of striking it rich was ridiculously low when he'd agreed to the partnership. The problem was, he too was a gem addict. While he understood the risks and the rewards better than Richard and Joe, his decades in the industry had enabled the gem fever to gain a stronger hold over his heart and mind. There was no escape. Perhaps he should have walked away from the venture after that first visit, but that's not how addicts think.

The buzzing of his mobile interrupted his ruminations. It was his wife.

'You didn't message me like you promised, Stephan!' she complained. Not waiting for a response, she admonished further, 'I still don't understand why you couldn't skip the September show. They just reported on the news that this typhoon Hong Kong is expecting may be the strongest in the city's history.'

Considering whether he should tell her about his airport adventures of the last hour, Stephan instead chose to assure her the airline wouldn't fly if it wasn't safe.

'By the way,' his wife said, 'the shipping company called for you; they tried reaching you on your mobile, but you didn't pick up. They wanted me to tell you that if you still want to ship those rubies to Hong Kong, they can combine it with another parcel leaving today. It will cost less, and the goods will arrive sooner than their previous one-week estimate. They have an office at the airport; that's why they were trying to reach you.'

Stephan closed his eyes on hearing that he could have easily avoided what had been one of the most stressful airport experiences of his life.

'Hello? Stephan? Are you still there?' his wife asked.

The cabin attendant returned with a tray of champagne and a smile. Stephan opened his eyes, looked at the cabin crew and said, 'I'm going to need something stronger.'

Author's Note

This story is based on actual events as relayed to the author by Stephan Reif. Fictional elements have been included to aid narration. Stephan Reif managed to sell the parcel of rough rubies to a buyer in Hong Kong. The sale generated enough revenue to enable Richard and Joe to pay their final bills. But it wasn't enough to keep the operation running. Stephan returned to the ruby deposit six months after they had closed the operation and was pleasantly surprised to see that nature had reclaimed the area.

After an extensive career in the gem industry, many of which were spent promoting demantoid garnets from his family's mine in Namibia (the Green Dragon Mine), in 2020 Stephan left the industry to become CEO of a leading international packaging manufacturer for the cosmetics, pharmaceutical, chemical and food industries.

The ruby mine Stephan visited in Tanzania (2016). Photo credit: Stephan Reif.

A section of the path to the ruby mine (2016). Photo credit: Stephan Reif.

Emeralds, Not Coffee!

October 2017
Jeffery Bergman
Paris, France

JEFFERY BERGMAN put down his glass of Margaux, as the server placed a medium-rare steak on the table. *I hope they haven't overdone it*, he thought. *I don't care if this is France; I'm going to send it back if it's not right.* He cut into the beef, pulling away a slice with his fork and smiled at the perfect shade of pink inside. *Thank God; otherwise I would have been another American earning the wrath of a French chef.*

His moment of pleasure was interrupted by the buzzing sound of the mobile phone in his pocket. It was an email from a man named Aynalem Hailu, an American of Ethiopian origin. He put his fork down to read the email. Hailu explained that he had found Jeffery's contact online, he was in Bangkok with his boss, Wodessa Bululta, and wanted to show him half a kilo of rough emeralds from Shakiso, a town in the Oromia region in Ethiopia.

This is interesting, thought Jeffery, as he took another sip of his wine and typed back a reply, explaining that he was in France and could only see them next week. By the time Bergman had finished his dinner, there was another email from Aynalem confirming that the Ethiopians had changed their flights and were looking forward to meeting him.

Easy tiger, Jeffery told himself, as his gem-addicted soul started whispering possibilities of an emerald treasure. Emeralds from Ethiopia had surfaced in the market a year ago, and Jeffery had been on the lookout for a lot he could purchase after seeing spectacular examples seven months ago at the Tucson Gem Show, in the US.

Aynalem explained in the email that his boss, Wodessa, was a successful coffee grower and had been mining gold and tantalum for several years under the Bua Obsa Gold and Tantalum Mining Ltd Cooperative Society in the Seba Boru district of Ethiopia. In August 2016, they'd found emeralds on their land. Since they were already organised as a cooperative, it didn't take them long to start mining. They'd exported their first production of rough emeralds in October 2016, exactly a year ago.

Aynalem said he wasn't interested in selling the rough emeralds but wanted to meet Jeffery to explore other business opportunities. Jeffery shot them a quick reply confirming a date and time for a meeting in his office in Bangkok.

A week later, both Aynalem and Wodessa were sitting across the table from Jeffery with the emerald parcel. Even in their rough state, the emeralds exuded a compelling green glow, drawing Jeffery towards them. An initial grading had already been done by the Bua Obsa cooperative members. Jeffery could see the obvious similarities between the rough Ethiopian emeralds on his table and Zambian emeralds.

Both were formed around 500 to 600 million years ago during the African orogeny, or mountain-building period. The tectonic movements of the land masses had created a mineral-rich band that extended from East Antarctica through East Africa up to the Arabian-Nubian Shield, also referred to as the Mozambique Belt. The mineral zone was responsible for the formation of most of the prolific gem deposits in Africa: Mozambican rubies, Zambian emeralds, tsavorite in Kenya and Tanzania, spinels, sapphires, and Ethiopian emeralds, to name a few.

Zambian and Ethiopian emeralds resulted from a chemical reaction between two rock types: talc-magnetite schist, which contained emerald's colouring agents, chromium and vanadium, and pegmatite rock, which brought the precious beryllium. Unlike Zambian, Ethiopian emeralds had a distinctive appearance comparable to Colombian emeralds, despite their geological differences. Their colour seemed more intense, exhibiting a vivid green hue. And in top-quality, they did a great job competing against the best Colombian emeralds.

'What do you think of our emeralds, Mr Bergman?' asked Aynalem. For the last 20 minutes, he'd been intently watching Jeffery as he examined the parcel on the table.

'You mentioned in your email that you didn't want to sell them? May I ask, what's the purpose of this meeting?'

Aynalem smiled. After he took a minute to translate to Wodessa, he said, 'Mr Bergman, you're one of five people we were planning on meeting during our visit to Bangkok. In fact, you are the last one we've met.'

'May I ask who were the other four?'

'Doesn't matter. Why I said we don't want to sell is because for the last year we've sold many of our rough emeralds to a variety of buyers, Japanese, Indian, European. They all come, pay good money for our production, and go.'

'That's usually how trading works,' commented Jeffery. He wasn't sure where the conversation was going but coached himself to be patient.

'If these buyers are paying us a few hundred thousand US dollars, they're probably selling our emeralds for a lot more after they cut and polish them, correct?'

'Yes. True. Everyone's in the business to make money.'

'We want a piece of that action.'

'Excuse me?'

'I think you understand what I mean, Mr Bergman.'

'Please call me Jeffery. And yes, I do.'

'Is there a way we could do it? Together?'

Jeffery wasn't prepared to go down this path. He'd thought all the gentlemen wanted was to sell the rough like most miners and traders. Feeling unprepared, he returned to examine the emeralds again. The stone he selected looked just like a Colombian emerald with a segment of black-grey schist rock still stuck on the surface.

'Have you heard of a mining company called Gemfields?' Jeffery asked.

'Not really. Should we have?' asked Aynalem.

'Gemfields owns possibly the world's largest emerald mine in Zambia. It's a joint venture where they own 75 per cent of the company, and the Zambian government owns 25 per cent.'

Aynalem and Wodessa looked blankly at Jeffery.

'What if we do the opposite?' said Jeffery. 'We form a company in Bangkok. You continue mining the emeralds in Ethiopia. I'll get them cut and polished and then market them internationally. Your mining costs are yours. I'll absorb all expenses on my side, and whatever revenue we get from the emeralds, we split. 75 per cent for your cooperative, and 25 per cent for my company. What do you think?'

Jeffery watched with bated breath as Aynalem translated his proposal to Wodessa. The man spoke English, but his repertoire was limited. After a few minutes of discussion, the duo looked at Jeffery and gave him a thumbs up.

* * *

Eight months later
Bangkok, Thailand

'Listen, this oil versus resin business is just nonsense. What do you think cedarwood oil is, my friend?' said Jeffery. He was arguing with a wholesaler who was pushing back on a parcel of emeralds because it was enhanced using liquid resin and not cedarwood oil.

'Cedarwood oil is a highly industrialised product,' continued Jeffery. 'You don't walk up to a cedar tree, put a tap in it, and have the oil drip out like with maple.' The voice on the other side pushed back. 'Listen. Here are the facts. If you want cedarwood oil refined so you can use it to enhance emeralds, it needs to undergo, like I said, a highly industrialised process. To call it natural is kinda like calling heroin natural. Yeah. It's a derivative but highly refined, so this snobbery about calling cedarwood oil superior is stupid. I gotta go. Getting a call from a buyer in the US. You pick the date, and I'll make the reservation. We'll go to that Lebanese place. OK. Bye.'

'Hello,' said Jeffery, as he disconnected his mobile and pressed the speakerphone button of the telephone on his desk. 'Hey! Chris[1]. How's my favourite customer?'

'Not happy, Jeff.'

'Why? How can I turn your frown upside down?'

'I hope you can, Jeff, because it's not good. Those emeralds you sold me. The Ethiopian stuff. Well, I sold them to my retail customer as "no oil", just like you sold 'em to me. My customer sent them to GIA[2] for testing. And guess what?'

'What?'

'Thirty per cent came back as oiled.'

'That's impossible, Chris. I'm sourcing directly from the miners. I have a chain of custody from mine to market. It's secure. There must be some mistake.'

'I wish there was, but I'm looking at the lab report from GIA right now. Can send you a copy. My customer returned the emeralds. The entire lot. And I'm afraid I'm gonna have to send 'em back to you. Assuming that's not a problem?'

'Of course not. I'll get them tested again,' said Jeffery. His throat felt dry as he struggled to respond. He started worrying about other parcels he'd sold in the last two months.

'You do that. Look, Jeff, I'm sure what you're saying is true, but science doesn't lie. Humans do. I reckon you need to have a chat with your miner friends and find out what's what over there in Ethiopia.'

---

1   This name has been changed.
2   GIA is the Gemological Institute of America.

'Chris, the cooperative members don't know how to oil emeralds. They're just taking those stones out of the ground and shipping them straight to Bangkok,' said Jeffery.

'Someone's oiling for sure. You need to figure it out.'

'Absolutely. Chris, I'm terribly sorry about this, and I assure you I'm going to take this seriously.'

'Sure. But to be clear, for the foreseeable future, I don't think we'll be interested in more of these Ethiopian emeralds.'

'This will never happen again, Chris. I promise. I'll get everything tested in Bangkok if you like, before shipping.'

Chris was one of Jeffery's top customers, and they'd had a fantastic working relationship for almost 20 years. To have Chris cancel this order was one thing, but if word got around in the market that retailers were returning Ethiopian emeralds, it could jeopardise a deal with an international jewellery house Jeffery had been working on for the last four months.

'Jeff, we go way back, so I'll be straight with you. If this had just happened between us, it's still cool. But I sold the parcel as "no oil" to one of my very good customers. When the guy called me and said 30 per cent of the "no oil" emeralds are oiled, I lost face. You know how tough the market is. I can't afford to have something like this happen again. You get it, right?'

'Completely. Don't worry, Chris. Just send the parcel back. I'll wire your payment over today. But I will investigate and come back to you. I'm as shocked as you, to be honest.'

'Yeah. OK, bye now.'

Jeffery disconnected the call and took a deep breath. His palms were moist with sweat. As he reached for the jug of water on his desk, he was surprised to see his hands were shaking. *Crap. How could this happen? Where did we go wrong?*

After establishing the joint venture company in Bangkok eight months ago with the Bua Obsa cooperative, Jeffery's priority was to get the rough emeralds they'd brought to his office cut and polished, ready for buyers. Thailand was known as a global hub for processing rubies and sapphires. Approximately 90 per cent of emeralds from Zambia were purchased by gem manufacturers in Jaipur, India, given their domain knowledge, expertise, and the lowest cutting and polishing costs globally. But the export-import regulations were complicated, and he wanted to keep a close eye on the cutting process.

There were only two workshops in Bangkok Jeffery trusted to cut emeralds, one owned by a Russian who was mainly cutting demantoid garnets and emeralds from Russia, and the other owned and operated by a Thai.

He sent most of the production to the Thai workshop, reserving only a few high-grade rough emeralds for the Russian cutters whose experience cutting schist-based Russian emeralds came in handy to deliver top-quality Ethiopian emeralds. When Jeffery started showing them to buyers, they would use adjectives like 'electric', 'vivid', 'paraíba-like glow'.

Most stones didn't require any clarity enhancement. The few that needed treatment were marked and packaged separately. Jeffery sold almost the entire consignment to customers in the US, Hong Kong, and Europe generating a few hundred thousand dollars in sales revenue, 75 per cent of which was wired to the Bua Obsa cooperative in Ethiopia. The added attraction was that most Ethiopian emeralds (in higher grade) didn't need clarity enhancement, unlike Colombian, where only 0.5 per cent of emeralds were 'no oil'. However, because Ethiopia was not well known as a producer of emeralds, the market was pricing them roughly 50 per cent below equivalent Colombian goods.

In the weeks that followed, Jeffery threw himself headlong into preparing a sales and marketing campaign for the biggest gem show in the industry in Tucson, Arizona.

'We need to make a splash,' he told Aynalem. 'Our emeralds are better than Zambian, comparable to Colombian, but we will never get the premium pricing without quality marketing. I'll set up press interviews and meetings, but I need the next lot of rough soon. We have only a few weeks to cut the goods and be ready for the show.'

Aynalem promised him he'd have the rough emeralds in Bangkok by 3rd January, leaving Jeffery three precious weeks to turn around the production. When the shipment arrived, Jeffery was pleased to see that the total weight was slightly over a kilo, but as he started examining the goods, he noticed that most were smaller, and generally lacking the extra-fine clarity of the first parcel. *At least the colour's great*, Jeffery told himself.

He managed to cut a few layouts of top-quality stones, which were enough to make the shipment profitable. Not to the extent the first one had been, but respectable. When he shared his concerns with Aynalem, the man assured him they'd make up for it in the next one as they'd purchased new mining equipment, which would allow them to expand their operations.

The launch at Tucson was a success. Jeffery had created marketing materials in English and Mandarin, along with a website, and social media pages. He was branding the goods as 'Shakiso Emeralds: Exceptional Ethiopian Emeralds'. The product posters showed an image of a large rough Ethiopian emerald in the background with seven precision-cut emeralds in the foreground that seemed to radiate light. The market was on fire and demanding more goods.

The next parcel Jeffery received from Shakiso in April 2018 was even larger, weighing around two kilos, but the quality was deteriorating. This time, the stones lacked clarity, size and the intense green colour that had become the origin's signature.

'We can't make any money with this quality, Aynalem,' Jeffery had explained over a stressful phone call. 'Our cutting costs are high in Bangkok. This type of material needs to be cut in Jaipur, India, to make ends meet.'

Jeffery was keeping the lights on by selling the few top-quality stones in their inventory leftover from the previous parcels, hoping they would last till the next shipment from Ethiopia. Throughout, the one thing he'd been insisting on was maintaining the integrity of the Shakiso brand.

'We are selling a story here, Aynalem,' he'd said. 'Your story, of your cooperative society, the families that will benefit directly from the sale of these emeralds. A mine-to-market story, and for it to be successful, it's imperative we only market the highest quality emeralds mined on your land.'

'Jeff, the new shipment from Ethiopia has arrived,' said his assistant, Opal, bringing him back to the harsh reality of the day and Chris's phone call.

'Set it up in the conference room. I'll be right there,' he said. *Maybe someone made a mistake at the lapidary*, he mused. *Yes, that's what must have happened. This is the problem with outsourcing the cutting. You can never have 100 per cent control over the manufacturing process.*

Jeffery walked into the conference room and took a seat at the head of the table as his staff started opening the packages from Ethiopia. He was preoccupied, trying to solve the mystery of the oiled emeralds in his head, not paying attention to the plastic pouches that were being weighed and arranged on the large wooden table. Once his staff had finished unpacking, they announced that the total weight of the shipment was seven kilos. Jeffery stood up from his seat and approached the goods. Without breaking eye contact with the emeralds, he said, 'Opal, will you please get Aynalem on the phone? I need to speak with him urgently.'

A few minutes later, Jeffery was back at his desk, staring at the telephone, waiting for Opal to connect the call to Aynalem. Within half a second of the ring, Jeffery pressed the speakerphone button.

'Aynalem, hi,' said Jeffery.

'Jeffery! How are you? Did you receive our shipment?'

'Yes. Opal and the team just finished unpacking it in the conference room. We'll talk about that later. We have another problem on our hands right now.'

'What's that?'

'I received a call from one of my top customers in the US who said that 30 per cent of the "no oil" emerald lots I sold him came back as oiled when they sent them for testing to the gem lab. I told him that's impossible because everything is sourced directly from the cooperative and the mine they operate.' Jeffery paused to catch his breath. He was expecting Aynalem to respond immediately, but there was silence on the other side.

'Hello? Aynalem? Did you hear what I said?'

'Yeah. I heard you, Jeff.'

'You guys aren't treating the emeralds at the mine, are you? Look, we're partners. We must be honest with each other.'

'No, Jeff; we're not treating the emeralds at the mine. We don't even know how to treat emeralds.'

'That's what I told him!' said Jeffery. He leaned back in his chair. A wave of relief washed over him.

'But there's something you should know,' said Aynalem. 'We've been buying rough emeralds from the open market and mixing them with the stones from our mining operation.'

Jeffery felt as if the ground underneath his feet had given way. 'Why?'

'Because for the last three months, the mine didn't produce any emeralds. And you did such a wonderful job in marketing our stones. Now, there's so much demand, we didn't want to disappoint you.'

'But, Aynalem. I thought we had a clear understanding that we would only sell emeralds from the cooperative's concession. The problem with buying from the open market is you don't know exactly what they're selling, or even where it's from, and what treatment they might be using on the emeralds.' There were a million questions pounding Jeffery's head. For how long had they been mixing the emeralds? How many had Jeffery sold as 'no oil'?

'I don't understand why you sound so stressed, Jeff. In the grain and coffee business, it's common to buy from third-party vendors and mix with your production. We must do the QC[1] and sort and grade the material, but it's perfectly acceptable. This is the same thing,' said Aynalem, who exported grain from the US to Ethiopia, outside of his involvement with the gold, tantalum, and emerald mining operations of the cooperative.

1   Quality control.

'But this isn't the grain business, Aynalem. This is a luxury product. The look of the stone alone isn't enough. A gem's value, the price it will fetch in the market, and how that stone will appreciate over time depends not only on its beauty but also on key factors like the rarity of that emerald, the assurance of where it was mined, and the confidence that it's untreated.'

'But our emeralds are so rare, Jeff.'

'Yes, but even more rare are the ones that are beautiful and untreated. That's what the market values. And we have the third element as well.'

'What's that?'

'The story of your cooperative society. That the revenue is going back to your community who are involved in the mining operation.'

'So, what's the problem?' asked Aynalem.

'The problem is that when you start buying from outside and, without checking, we mix it with our emeralds, the integrity of what we are selling comes into question. We can't sell them as "no oil" because we don't know what treatment has been done on those stones. Plus, we can no longer say the revenue is benefitting your community because now the money's also going to these outside people you're buying from. God knows who they are. Are they miners? Did they steal the stones they're selling to you? Are they from Tanzania, Zambia, or elsewhere? How can you know?'

'I think you are overthinking this, Jeff. Have you seen the shipment? Seven kilos! We've never been able to export so many emeralds.'

Jeffery stood up from his chair. 'Aynalem. I'm sorry to say this, but it's you who isn't realising how serious this is. The weight of the shipment doesn't matter when the integrity's compromised. I've seen the shipment. They're all low-grade material. You'll make more money selling them as they are in Jaipur than you will cutting them in Bangkok. For the last eight months, I've been working day and night, chasing every single potential sale to where we have one of the top jewellery houses in the world ready to sign a contract with us worth millions. But now, it's over. Poof. Gone. Finished.'

'Over? What do you mean?'

'I can't risk my name, my reputation, my life's work. Our partnership is over. I'm out.'

Author's Note

This story is based on interviews with Jeffery Bergman and his experiences. Fictional elements have been included for dialogue and scene setting.

Aynalem Hailu and Wodessa were both shocked at Jeffery Bergman's decision to dissolve their partnership agreement and close the company. They tried to dissuade him by providing assurances they would not buy again from third-party brokers.

To quote Jeffery, 'The main reason that I withdrew from the project was because I was trying to build an ethically sourced, traceable, mine-to-market supply chain. Their misrepresenting of the emerald's origin from the Halo Mine destroyed the integrity of that supply chain. Whatever profit I could make short term to keep the illusion going that we had a secure mine-to-market supply chain was not worth the permanent damage to my reputation.'

In the short period Jeffery was marketing Shakiso emeralds from Ethiopia, the pricing of fine quality stones went up by 30 per cent to 50 per cent in the wholesale market. Since 2018, Jeffery estimates that emeralds from Ethiopia that were selling for US$10,000 per carat are probably selling now for over US$20,000 per carat. For super fine, 'no oil' emeralds, the price appreciation may be higher because the customer segment desirous of that quality is knowledgeable and appreciates the rarity of the material.

Taking a step back from Ethiopia, with expansion of the coloured gemstone market and increased access to gemmological information, the demand for untreated stones has significantly increased. This makes it difficult to discern how much of the price appreciation seen in 'no oil' Ethiopian emeralds is because of its origin and how much is purely because of the growing demand for natural emeralds containing zero clarity enhancement.

Jeffery Bergman continues his career of more than 50 years in the gem trade. He recently sold a stunning 14-carat unheated padparadscha sapphire he named 'Chameleon Padparadscha' due to its rare tenebrescent phenomena. The colour is orangey-pink until exposed to a UV light source, such as spending several hours in direct sunlight, which changes it to a pinkish-orange hue lasting several days. The colour reverts to the original orangey-pink when exposed to a strong incandescent light for a few hours or after several days without any light exposure. This change can be repeated ad infinitum offering the owner the option to adjust the colour to their personal taste, hence its chameleonic name.

Ruby Peppercorns

November 2019
Sariaka Manjaka's Lapidary
Antananarivo, Madagascar

'WEALTH IN the world of miners can change quickly, a bit like games of chance. You can win or lose a lot in a few months.'—Sariaka Manjaka

Sunlight was streaming in through the window behind Sariaka Manjaka, as he sat hunched over the faceting[1] wheel in his two-room lapidary workshop. In his hand was a standard 15-centimetre-long dop stick, which had a pale salmon-coloured morganite stone stuck on one end. Sariaka was transforming the stone into a beautiful gem. The only sound dominating the room was the high-pitched, shrill protest of the morganite each time Sariaka pressed it against the abrasive, fast-moving faceting wheel.

Next to the machine was a small table where he'd arranged the finished gemstones on a newspaper sheet, after their arduous transformation. The one he was holding was the last of the lot before the next stage. Fifteen minutes later, he removed the gem from the dop stick and picked up his loupe to examine his work. Not bad, he told himself. Just need to apply a perfect polish. He recalled the words of his teacher from the institute, 'The final polish is crucial. It's what sets apart the good gems from the great.'

Sariaka paused for a moment, quietening the wheel and the stone. He straightened his back and rotated his neck for a stretch.

The rumbling from Sariaka's stomach made him glance at the short desk clock, perilously balanced on a wooden stool next to his workstation. It was 3.30 pm. Sariaka and his friend Andry took turns bringing each other lunch every Friday. Today, it was Andry's turn, and he was late. Sariaka grabbed his steel mug that was lying near the clock and dunked it in the clay pot on the floor, hoping the water would briefly repress his hunger. The smell of the wet mud from the water reminded him of his grandmother's kitchen. Water

---

1   Faceting: creating smooth planes on a rough gemstone by grinding it against a moving wheel laced with a layer of diamond powder. The craft is known as faceting, as the lapidary artist is applying facets on the stone according to a pattern, which will transform the gem from a rough stone into a sparkly gemstone.

stays nice and cool during the hot months, she used to explain to him when pouring a glass from the earthen pot in her kitchen.

After covering the clay container, Sariaka returned to the morganite. It had been two years since he'd graduated from the Institute of Gemmology and started a small lapidary business in the heart of Antananarivo. In the last 12 months, he had travelled to numerous remote locations in the country, seeking rough rocks he could convert through his faceting technique into profitable gems. It had been hard.

On his first buying trip to the sapphire fields of Ilakaka in southwest Madagascar, he'd been stunned to come across many prospectors who tried to sell him synthetic or fake gems. Luckily, his education at the institute ensured he emerged unscathed. High prices were another issue. He was competing for rough stones against brokers who were supported by international buyers with deep pockets. In other instances, even though Sariaka was offering a better price, he couldn't purchase gemstones because miners were duty-bound to sell their production solely to their financiers. He realised he'd have to start by acquiring lower-priced gems and slowly develop his trade.

Sariaka began polishing the morganite, hoping the task would distract his belly from the delayed lunch. He was halfway through the third stone when Andry knocked on the open door of the lapidary to announce his arrival.

'Finally!' said Sariaka to Andry. 'I'm starving. What took you so long?'

'I bumped into this beautiful woman in the market,' said Andry. 'But I'm such a good friend I left her and brought you this delicious spaghetti.'

Sariaka burst out laughing. Andry was known for being an incorrigible flirt, a handy skill for a waiter at a four-star hotel. 'That pasta better have meatballs,' said Sariaka, as he put down the stone, turned off the faceting machine, and sauntered over to give his buddy an affectionate high five. One fringe benefit of Andry's position was free food, especially on the weekends.

'What are you working on?' asked Andry between mouthfuls of pasta.

'A parcel of morganite gems,' said Sariaka. 'Keeps the lights on. But I am tired of cutting these less expensive goods that have little profit margin.'

'What do you want to cut?' asked Andry.

'I would love to buy a rough sapphire or a ruby, but it's very difficult.'

'Mmm have you travelled towards the east?' Andry asked. 'I hear there's some mining near Marolambo and Mananjary in the southeast.'

'I've mostly visited the west. Never been east.'

'Why don't you go?' suggested Andry. 'My family lives near Marolambo. You can stay with them. I'll ask my mother to meet you at the main bus stop. She was telling me when we last spoke that my cousins are involved in ruby mining. Maybe you'll get lucky.'

'That would be amazing.'

'It won't be an easy journey,' warned Andry.

'I'm used to travelling in crowded buses,' said Sariaka, boldly. 'I'll be fine.'

'You misunderstand,' responded Andry. 'It may be difficult because of the language. The region is inhabited by the Betsimisaraka people. They have a distinct style of speaking, a special accent. The same word you may already know can have another meaning in the south.'

'I didn't think about that,' said Sariaka. 'If they can't understand me, how will I buy stones?'

'Maybe my mother can help you. Our neighbour has a mobile phone. I can speak with her through him. I'll let you know what she says.'

A few days later, Andry confirmed to Sariaka that his family were happy to host him, and his mother, Fanaja, would take him to his cousins, who had many ruby parcels for Sariaka to see and possibly buy.

Sariaka couldn't believe his luck. Within a week, he delivered his pending jobs and packed his belongings for the trip. The only way to reach the bus stop closest to Andry's home was to take a bush taxi, a four-by-four pickup truck. The road conditions were dreadful, and Sariaka had to make the 45 kilometre drive crammed with 17 other travellers in the back of the vehicle. But he was still grateful to have a spot inside, unlike others who were sitting on the roof, getting drenched during the eight-hour thunderstorm that accompanied them for most of the way.

As the bush taxi approached Sariaka's destination, he spotted a lone woman waiting for him. Andry's description had given Sariaka an impression of an older lady, but Fanaja looked middle-aged. He got off the bus and approached her with a half-smile, unsure if she was his contact. She smiled back, revealing the wrinkles around her eyes, which gave away her age. But being a farmer's wife, Fanaja was physically fit, with muscular arms and a lean figure.

They exchanged pleasantries, and she informed Sariaka that to reach her home they'd have to walk for almost three kilometres. What Andry had failed to mention was that the journey from the bus stop would involve trekking through a river and two streams, dodging crocodiles and water serpents. Once they were hip deep in the river, Fanaja teased Sariaka by saying she had seen a crocodile last week in the same spot.

By the time they reached Andry's village, Sariaka was exhausted. His clothes and hair stuck to his body, and the tepid night air offered no comfort. Fanaja explained that they lived in a small community with four families in homes made from organic materials found in the surrounding region. She described the construction process of their huts as she lit a fire outside.

'First, we cut bamboo and wood to make four pillars and build a skeletal structure,' she said. 'Then, we use ravenala leaves, or traveller's palms, for thatching the roof. For the window blinds we stitch together the veins of the leaves.' Sariaka noticed the entire house was resting on stilts. The raised foundation protected the dwellers from snakes and other critters.

Fanaja wasted no time in preparing a simple meal of rice and chicken for Sariaka and the rest of the household. The flavour varied from what he had eaten before, and he licked his bowl clean. Once the family were done with dinner, she took Sariaka to a larger neighbouring hut, which she explained was a half-finished church for their community, built in the same manner as their homes. For sleeping, she gave Sariaka a blanket, and a rug made of the Lepironia plant, which they called tsihy.

'It will be safer to sleep on the tsihy,' she said. 'You'll avoid direct contact with the floor, which may not be clean because of soil, moisture, and all kinds of insects.'

Sariaka woke up with the sun, around 5.30. He felt rested. The night before, Fanaja had shown him the path to follow to a stream located a few metres from their home. Familiar with the ways of rural communities, courtesy of his travels, he got busy doing his morning ablutions. By the time he was finished, more villagers had arrived. By 6 am, the family was ready for breakfast.

Fanaja had prepared coffee by grinding and roasting fresh beans. She flavoured the thick, delicious brew with sugarcane juice, both of which were grown in the field behind their home. Leftover chicken and rice from the previous night's dinner were breakfast. Nothing was wasted. After their morning meal, Fanaja fed the remaining bones to the pigs and ground the rest to sprinkle as fertiliser for the plants.

'May I help you?' Sariaka asked Andry's mother, as she got busy with household chores.

She laughed at him, declining his offer, saying he would only slow her down. It didn't take her long to finish her morning tasks, after which she told Sariaka that they would walk over to meet her nephews in a nearby village. 'They are gold washers,' she said.

For more than two hours, Sariaka cut across the countryside along a narrow dusty path that snaked up and down the hills dotting the landscape. He counted six villages on the way, some next to rice fields. The tapered track they followed was surrounded by lush vegetation. When a villager would pass them, he or she would greet Andry's mother. Some would stop for a few minutes to chat with her, but they avoided acknowledging his presence.

'They are wary of strangers,' she explained to him.

In the distance, he could see the outline of high mountains that were covered with traveller's palms and primary forest cover. When they weren't navigating the mountainous terrain, they were dodging snakes across rivers and agricultural land.

Once they reached their destination, Andry's cousins rushed to greet their aunt and make them feel welcome. Fanaja did most of the talking, explaining the purpose of Sariaka's visit. The boys became excited when she said he was interested in buying gemstones. They started telling tales of discovering blood-red rubies, emeralds that were as green as the mountain after a heavy rainfall, and pale pink gems whose colour resembled forest flowers.

They expressed their frustration to Sariaka at the lack of buyers in the region and claimed that they were regularly forced to sell gems at throwa-way prices because of their inability to travel to the big city. To provide them comfort, Sariaka shared his collaborative way of working as a gem trader, which involved sharing the little knowledge he had to allow the miners to better understand the value of their gems so they could build a long-term relationship.

After they'd spent an hour chatting, Andry's cousins left to bring their mining associates and the rubies. They asked Sariaka to wait, promising to return with a vast collection of gemstones. The level of excitement Sariaka felt on hearing those words knew no bounds. During the journey from Anta-nanarivo, he'd wondered whether coming on such a tough trip had been a mistake. But all his aches and pains were melting away at the thought of finally buying good-quality gemstones. *I'm going to do whatever it takes to buy at least one ruby*, he told himself.

The cousins had described the rubies they'd found to be as big as a thumbnail: an incredibly rare size for a ruby. Sariaka had never seen rubies that large and of the quality they claimed to possess.

While Sariaka and Fanaja waited for the miners to return with their precious stones, the ladies of the house prepared unripe bananas cooked with a little salt, and soanambo, a fruit found only on the east coast. The village women told Sariaka that they also cooked blackberries with salt, which they ate in the morning to keep their bodies well satisfied and nourished.

The cousins returned after two hours, just as they had finished eating. They brought three miners with them. After introductions were made,

Sariaka asked, with Fanaja's help, how they found the stones. The cousins explained their method of using handwoven baskets to collect gravel from the bottom of the riverbed and, using hand gestures, showed Sariaka how they washed the gem-laden gravel in the flowing waters. Once the dirt and soil had been removed, they sorted through the stones left in the basket looking for anything that looked colourful or had a good crystal character.

The men were lean and muscular. They said they were in their forties but in better shape than most young men because they weren't afraid to work hard. Sariaka asked them how deep the river was where they mined and whether they were afraid of crocodiles. They said that river mining was difficult and risky, especially during the rainy season when the water was deep, but they still had stones to sell.

To ensure they wouldn't be disturbed during the gem viewing, the miners and Sariaka shifted to another hut that was at a distance from the rest of the village. One of them went to get a plate to display the rubies, while the others started taking out small plastic bags laden with stones.

Sariaka took out a magnifying glass and weighing scales. He opened the nearest bag of gems, and a hush fell over the small hut as all five pairs of eyes started watching his every move. He examined the first lot, and within seconds realised they were garnets. *There are nine pouches left*, Sariaka told himself, trying not to feel too disheartened.

He moved on, taking his time to scrutinise every single stone in the remaining bags. With each parcel, his disappointment grew. The miners could sense that the stones were not meeting his expectations. One of them asked him, 'How old are you?'

When Sariaka said he was 23 years old, the man snorted and shook his head in disgust.

'What are you doing with that glass?' asked another, pointing to Sariaka's magnifying lens.

'I want to see the differences between the stones of this region and those from other parts of Madagascar,' said Sariaka, 'because I am here not only to buy but also to learn.'

'Learn, eh?' said one of the other miners. 'I'll teach you something.' He inched closer and picked up one parcel, which contained some of the larger garnets, and said, 'These rubies are some of the best we've ever seen from this area. You'll miss an enormous opportunity if you don't buy them now.'

The atmosphere in the hut was getting tense. The miner who had asked Sariaka his age started murmuring to the others, 'He's just a boy. What does he know about the value of our rubies?'

Sariaka wasn't sure how the miners would react if he told them the stones they thought were rubies were actually garnets. Their open hostility was making him feel uncomfortable, but he also felt sorry for them. He understood now why they felt they'd been selling their stones cheaply in the past.

Sariaka took out a small sample ruby from his pocket and showed it to the miners. He then brought out a neodymium magnet to give them a demonstration. Sariaka placed his sample ruby next to a garnet. When he held the magnet above the two stones, the instrument's magnetic force immediately picked up the garnet, while the ruby remained on the table. Sariaka then explained how the higher concentration of iron resulted in the garnet reacting to the magnet.

His efforts at educating them about the differences between ruby and garnet caused a change in their body language. By the end of his knowledge sharing, his sincere manner had won them over. As a gesture of friendship, he bought the miners rice and dried fish from a nearby vendor for their lunch and spent the rest of the afternoon hearing their stories.

By four in the evening, Fanaja suggested they leave so they had enough time to reach home before sunset. Sariaka promised the miners he would return to buy stones from them the next time he was in the area and would send more buyers their way.

As he walked back with Fanaja, Sariaka felt a void inside. The day had begun full of promise, and now all he felt was a deeper sense of frustration. The precious ruby remained out of his reach. Fanaja, sensing his melancholy mood, started humming a folk song, the melody in sync with the rippling sounds of the river that flowed to their left. As if inspired by the song, a flutter of butterflies joined them on their walk back home. They danced in front of them, attempting to ease Sariaka's weariness.

The green hills ahead of their path in the distance looked majestic against the burgeoning orange sky. They encountered farmers who were returning home after a hard day's labour in the fields. This time, he was surprised to see them smile and acknowledge his presence. One of them stopped to chat with Fanaja and gave her a handful of peppercorns and herbs, which she carefully packed away in the folds of her colourful sarong.

'Aren't these the same farmers we met this morning?' asked Sariaka.

'Yes. They go back home now,' Andry's mother replied.

'They were frowning at me earlier. Why are they smiling now?'

'They recognise you,' she said. 'You are no longer a stranger.' They continued down the path near the rice fields. 'Let's walk fast. We're losing the light, which will make it more difficult to spot snakes.'

Sariaka followed, picking up his pace. 'I didn't find any rubies,' he blurted. And as soon as he'd uttered the words, tears filled his eyes.

Fanaja patted him on his back and said, 'Just because you didn't find the stones you wanted, doesn't mean you return empty-handed, son. You go back knowing more than you did when you came here. That's something, isn't it?'

'I suppose it is.'

'Tomorrow, you try a new place, and maybe you find your gemstones. Look,' she said, pulling out the stems the farmers had gifted them, which were laden with green and red unripe peppercorns, 'I got these peppers from the farmer. When we get home, I'll make a nice curry with them for you.'

Sariaka looked at the woman's wrinkled, weather-beaten hands cradling the vibrant spices. In the fading light, the peppercorns looked like gemstones. Sariaka smiled at Fanaja. 'I once saw a small emerald in the market,' he said.

'What's an emerald?' she asked.

'It's a beautiful green stone, like the green peppercorn in your hand.'

'Ah! But can it flavour a curry?' she said, as she playfully shoved Sariaka.

They both burst out laughing.

Author's Note

The above story is based on Sariaka's actual experiences in Madagascar. Unable to converse in English or Malagasy, we spent several months exchanging emails. Sariaka would send me emails in Malagasy, which I would translate into English. I would write my replies in English, translate them in Malagasy, and email my feedback. After almost six months of back and forth, I was able to use the information he had shared to write this story. Lack of education, inability to travel, limited resources, and the opaque nature of the coloured gemstone industry are some of the reasons it is difficult for miners to get a fair value for their production.

Sariaka is currently managing a stone company based in Antananarivo, which involves fulfilling orders from local and international firms. He used to hunt for gemstones in artisanal mining areas out of respect for the miner's hard work and because it allowed him to share his knowledge with them.

His hope in the work that he does is to have the opportunity to develop international routes to market in a transparent manner, which would allow small-scale actors to also progress. He hopes to publish his understanding and methods related to gemmology and gemstone faceting and polishing so they are accessible to his industry peers, whether artisanal miners or lapidary workers.

To quote Sariaka: 'The fortune of miners is commonly seen as a curse in Madagascar because, for many, gemstones are spiritual, whereas the business of stones is frequently accompanied by low blows and betrayal, not always, but often.'

Gratitude

ON 20 October 2017, I was on a beach in Thailand, blissfully sipping my coconut water, when I received a text from a friend asking if I'll see him in three days at the ICA Congress in Jaipur. 'What's ICA?' I messaged back. He explained that ICA stood for the International Colored Gemstone Association, a leading body for mining companies, manufacturing firms, merchants, and the industry at large. Abandoning the weighty coconut, I sat up straighter in my deck chair and typed, 'I am with my husband and in-laws at a family reunion holiday in Thailand, planned almost a year ago. I can't just get up and leave. What's the conference about?' He sent me a web link that listed the agenda. My husband, Rohan, who was next to me, sensed my energy shift and asked, 'All OK?' I looked at him, we locked eyes. 'How much do you love me?' I said.

The first person I'd like to thank is my husband, not only for supporting me that fateful day in Thailand, but every step of the way on an unbelievable journey. Rohan, you are my best friend, my knight in shining armour, the love of my life, and every other romantic cliché that exists in this universe.

I vaguely recall reading that behind every successful woman is a partner and a parent. Not sure who said it, but it's spot-on. My parents, Gursharan and Subhash, encouraged my sister and me to never measure ourselves by society's perception of a woman's capability. I walked into the ICA Congress in 2017 as a nobody. But within a year, I was invited to speak at the World Emerald Symposium in Colombia on the art of storytelling. Some may call that dumb luck. I call it 20 years of corporate training and learning from the best bosses and role models in the whole wide world—my mom and dad. Thank you for providing me with the blueprint for life, teaching me that there is no substitute for hard work, honesty is still the best policy, and for understanding and letting me go when I got infected with gem fever. Thank god my parents had another child because I can't imagine my life without my sister/grandmother, Isha, who helped me with the opening lines of my first Robb Report article in 2017, and has always taken time out to read initial story drafts, make suggestions, listen to me ramble on about gems, and cook the most delicious vegetarian, gluten-free, and dairy-free food for me! My brother-in-law, Karan, thank you for your 'Sailing Sundays', which always lifted my spirit during the two years of the pandemic spent research-ing, and writing this book without a single break.

They say you don't just marry the person; you marry the family. And in this department, I totally lucked out! Big thanks to my rockstar mom-in-law, Ranjani Sikri, who never hesitates to roll up her sleeves when I call for help, and my father-in-law, Anil, who is always ready to go with the flow. Adit and Anamika Sikri, you permanently reside in my zone 1, thank you for always checking on the book's progress, we need to plan that trip!

This book would not have been possible without the original idea, and unwavering support of Sean Gilbertson, CEO Gemfields. Thank you, Sean, not only for trusting me with this incredible project, but for wearing many hats—mentor, friend, therapist—throughout my gem journey. Your gener-ous spirit and support continue to be a tremendous motivating factor for me.

This book owes its existence to the countless individuals who contributed their stories and experiences. I'm immensely grateful to each one of them for their trust in me and for collaborating to ensure that every story was accurately portrayed—Julius Petsch, Naushad Osman, Stephan Reif, Joseph Mbiriri, Ken Scarratt, Tom Moses, Jeffery Bilgore, Ahmadjan Abduriyim, Moussa Konate, Shiv Shankar Gupta, Govind Gupta, Rahim Ullah, Jawahar Dey, Bruce Bridges, Chris Johnston, Jack Mampihao, Zo Harimalala, Hans-Jürgen Henn, Abraham Nassi, Mamaroni, Gordon, Guy Clutterbuck, Lotanna Amina, Major AI Akpuaka (retired), Sean Gilbertson, CV Suresh, Dharmendra Tank, Nilesh Shah, Manoj Dhandia, Jackson Mtonga, Exilda, Amon Kadichi, Aaron Nyangu, Kartikeya Parikshya, Sariaka Manjaka, Tony Brooke, Jeffery Bergman, Asghar Fakhraleali, Ian Harebottle and Raime Raimundo.

Many individuals supported this project by sharing their knowledge and making introductions. Thank you, Cedric Simonet, Jean Claude Michelou, Dharmendra Tank, Akshat Gupta, Suresh Hathiramani, Joe Belmont, Mike Nunn, Bryan Lees, Inam Ullah, Demetris Manolis, Ed Johnson, David Nassi, Gautam Jain, Dhiraj Soriya, Lynda Lawson, Dr Daniel Nyfeler, Chris Smith, Dr Lore Kiefert, Mario Picciani, Keshav, and Mehul Durlabhji, Randy Wema Tango, Georgette Barnes, Nevin Sher, Rashmi Sharma, Robert Weldon, Wim Vertriest, and Brendan Laurs. I am also grateful to Hardeep Sachdeva, Aneeq Karim Durrani, Nishka Crishna, Shariq Patel, and Pushpita Ghosh, for their timely help and advice.

I would like to extend my profound gratitude to the following members of the Gemfields team for sharing their insights, knowledge, and expertise, which helped me better understand some of the more technical aspects associated with the extractive and gemstone sector—Adrian Banks, Elena Basaglia, Frankie Fong, Anirudh Sharma,[1] Gopal Kumar, Jackson Mtonga, Dr Sixtus Mulenga, Prahalad Kumar Singh, CV Suresh and Kartikeya Parikshya.

Switching gears to 'friends like family', I'd like to thank my dear friend, Milind Sanghvi, for being my one-man focus group. His candid feedback, and our long conversations after each reading session, led to several rewrites. My darling friend, Sumati Nagrath, dug into her past experience to provide edits and sensible suggestions at various stages of this project. I shall forever be grateful to both Milind and Sumati for taking time out of their busy corporate lives to help. A special shout-out to Jyoti, who provided prompt feedback on the last story when I was racing against time; and Vani for her positive reinforcement when I was struggling to finish the manuscript. Lots of love to my Singapore friends who are our family on the little red dot, and my friends in India and beyond, who continuously cheered me on. Special shoutout to Prem Bhatia and Gaurav Shrinagesh for their timely introductions that led me to my fantastic publishers, Austin Macauley.

When I first started writing this book, I had a completion deadline of March 2021. As I delved into the project, I realised that to gather a truly diverse collection of stories, more time was required. Sometimes, it took six months to establish a connection with a potential contributor, a few weeks to persuade them to share their experiences, followed by several months rummaging through their memories over several phone calls so I could find enough material for a short story. In other cases, where multiple contributors were involved, each person's recollection of an event would differ, requiring verification and repeated conversations. I want to express my gratitude to Gemfields for their patience and support through this extensive research and writing journey. Special thanks to the superwomen who are the force behind Gemfields' public relations and marketing division—Emily Dungey, Helena Choudhury, Beatrice Howe, Sophie Ebbetts and Jennifer Head—thank you all for your patience, your support, and leaving no stone unturned (!) to employ your genius at various stages, including the design of the book cover and the promotion of this book.

Thank you, Janet Gyenes, for your questions, suggestions, and feedback in June 2023, which enabled me to look at the book with a fresh perspective.

---

1   Anirudh Sharma has moved on from Gemfields to a new role in the extractive industry.

The process of researching and writing articles enriched my knowledge of stones and the inner workings of the industry. I want to thank the editors who offered me opportunities to write for their respective publications. Thank you, Akshita Nahar Jain, Chumki Bharadwaj, Sitara Mulchandani, Supriya Dravid, Rochelle Pinto, Maanya Sachdeva, who commissioned some of my early works for Bazaar Bride, Robb Report, India Today, Harper's Bazaar, and Elle India. Shanoo Bijlani, thank you for always saying yes! I am grateful to the late Jean Claude Michelou, the amazing editor of *InColor* magazine, and an industry stalwart who was passionate about responsible sourcing, and Cynthia Unninayar. Sonia Esther Soltani, Editor, *Rapaport Jewelry Magazine*, it's a pleasure working with you. Rachel Beitsch-Feldman, *Rapaport Jewelry Magazine*, thank you for your edits, and for coining the book title – No Stone Unturned! Others I had the privilege to write for include: Celine Yap for *Vogue* and Robb Report Singapore, Olivia Quiniquini for Jewellery Net Asia (JNA), Jennifer-Lynn Archuleta for *Gems and Jewellery* magazine (Gem-A), the outstanding team at the Natural Diamond Council, led by the dynamic Richa Singh, Shivpriya Bajpai, and Rasna Bhasin (Editor), Harper's Bazaar India.

Thank you, Francesca Cartier for your advice when it came time to deliver my first talk on this book in Geneva for GemGenève, two years before publication!

I would like to complete this segment by thanking organisations that were a great source of information for me – the Gemological Institute of America (GIA), the Gemmological Association of Great Britain (Gem-A), International Colored Gemstone Association (ICA), auction houses Christie's and Sotheby's, the World Jewellery Confederation (CIBJO), Tiffany & Co, Cartier, Van Cleef & Arpels, and Fabergé.

I'd like to express my gratitude to individuals who, although not connected with this book, have influenced my gem journey. First, Jessie Aunty (Jasjit Sidhu) for allowing me to tag along with her and my mom as a child to the jeweller, where I spent countless hours watching her handle gems and commission jewels. I'd also like to thank my first guru, Veronique Vitte, because of whom I fell in love with gem inclusions and started travelling to mines. Nandini Singh, for her encouragement, and supporting my talk on coloured gems for the YPO (Young President's Organisation) in February 2017. Rajiv Sikri, who taught me key photography skills that remain an essential part of my storytelling style. Brenda Kang, for her friendship and for teaching me about antique jewels, Ronny Totah for his wisdom, time, and educating me about Kashmir sapphires. I am also grateful to Dr Géza von Habsburg for his early advice, and Josina von dem Bussche-Kessell for her support. The Kasliwal trinity of Sid, Samarth, and Sarthak for opening their vault, workshop and tiffin box, to feed my soul and my vegetarian + dairy-free + gluten-free appetite, Sumit and Amit Mehta, Rajiv and Tarang Arora, Shaleen, Shashwat, and Anuj Shah, Sakhil and Arun Dhaddha, Dharmendra Tank, Jay Puglia, Gagan Choudhary, Nitin Khandelwal, Milan Choksi, Dolly Choudhary, Mandira Khanna, Alex Popov, Dr Usha Balakrishnan, Bharany family, Meera Kumar, Susan Stronge, Derek J Content, Mina Hingorani, Nina Ernst, Hugh Tanner, Joe Pirapan, Maria Belmont, Nilesh Shah, Rishabh Tongya, Yoram Finkelstein, Ida Faerber, Nico Landrigan, Pia Tonna, Olga Oleksenko, Natasha Kietiene, Victor Tuzlukov, Vincent Pardieu, Chatree Khaegthoop, Michael Koh, Angela Loh, Nelson Lee, Apoorva Kothari, Philippe Ressigeac, Lauriane Pinsault, Ho Yu, Oscar Baquero, Guillermo Galvis, Gabriel Angarita, the Molina family, George Smith, Carlos Palacios, Arthur Langerman, Nadège Totah, Amedeo Scognamiglio, Marco Hadjibay, Francesca Cartier, Paolo Costagli, Henry Ho, Angharad Guy, Ashoo Sinchawala, Thomas Faerber, Manoj Godha, Craig, Josh Saltzman, Sebastian Bahri, Mikola Kukharuk, Jasmine Vidal, Vivienne Becker, Sumed Prasongpongchai, Thanong Leelawatanasuk, Reuben Khafi, the Diamond Exchange of Singapore (DES), GIA India, Dev Shetty, Rupak Sen, Gianluca Maina, Antoine Barrault, François Garaude, Sameer Lillani, Sylva Yepremian, Robert Gessner, Chaoqiu He, Claudia Hamman, Prida Tiasuwan, Shachee Shah, Hanut Singh, Alexey Burlakov, Liran Eshed, Fabio Ottaviano, Aja Raden, Feriel Zerouki, John Glajz, Maksud Agadjani, Runjeet Singh, Sara Sze Tan, Gem X Club, Alan Crown, Vinod More, Armil Sammoon, Marie-Cécile Cisamolo, Coralie Nacht, Sharon Novak, David Bennett, Daniela Mascetti, Mithun Sacheti, Dimitri Gouten, Gilles Zalulyan, Alyssa Sophia, Ming Lampson, Anastasia Kessaris, Olivier Bachet, Longo Zinsner, Adrianne Sanogo, Paula Crevoshay, Sarah Duncan, Sweta Jain, Anil Gandhi, Nirupa Bhatt, Atul Jain, Alan Hart, Khatchig Jingirian, Melanie Grant, Ronald Ringsrud, Marianne Fischer, Shu Ng, Laurent Massi, Helen Molesworth, Dr Michael S. Krzemnicki, Daniel Nyfeler, Patrick Pfannkuche, Klemens Link, Donatella Zappieri, Tay Kunming, Mathieu Dekeukelaire, Joseph Gad, Gabriel Ammar, Rashmi Sharma, Christophe Dubois, Dave Bindra, Philip M. Persson, Bernd Munsteiner, Victor Tuzlukov, Richard F. Bunomo, Kavinda De Silva, Kasun, Roshan Opatha, Nasr Khan and Simon Bruce Lockhart.

In the bustling excitement of seeing my work in print, there may be cherished friends whose names slipped through the cracks of acknowledgment.

To those, I extend my deepest gratitude. Your presence in my life has enriched every step of this gem adventure, and your absence in the acknowledgments does not diminish the significance of your role. Thank you for being the silent champions behind the scenes, cheering me on with your love and encouragement.

Last but not the least, my tribe of gem and jewellery addicts on Instagram, your unwavering support and engagement have been the fuel behind my creative endeavours. Though your names may not grace the pages of my book's acknowledgments, your presence and encouragement in the digital realm have been invaluable. Thank you for being a vital part of my journey, for your likes, comments, and shares have propelled me forward in ways I never imagined. Your support means the world to me.

ABOUT THE AUTHOR

Richa Goyal Sikri is a journalist and storyteller specialising in gemstones, diamonds and vintage and contemporary jewellery. She has a bachelor's degree in commerce, a master's degree in business administration and has completed several courses with the Gemological Institute of America (GIA) including 'Colored Stone Grading' and 'Gem Identification'.

She spent the first 20 years of her career as executive director of STIC Travel Group, Asia's leading travel and tourism organisation. In 2014, as a connoisseur of gems and jewellery, she began curating educational visits to mines and gem cutting centres globally for groups of aficionados seeking to better understand the journey of a gem from mine to market. Based on her experiences, Richa debuted her unique storytelling style on Instagram in 2017 garnering wide interest and engagement from the press and industry stakeholders.

Richa has pursued her second career in the gem and jewellery sector since 2018, delivering talks, projects, digital storytelling campaigns and articles for many notable organisations including the Art Science Museum in Singapore, the Asian Institute of Gemmological Studies (AIGS, Thailand), Buccellati, publications like *ELLE*, *Harper's Bazaar*, *Robb Report*, *India Today*, *Vogue*, Fabergé, Gemfields, the Gem and Jewellery Export Promotion Council (GJEPC) of India, GemGenève (Geneva), the Gemological Institute of America (GIA), the Global Congress of the International Colored Gemstone Association (ICA), the Gem and Jewellery Association of Sri Lanka, the Natural Diamond Council, the World Emerald Symposium (Colombia), and the World Jewellery Confederation (CIBJO).

Richa lives with her husband and son in Singapore and experiences FOMO every time someone calls her from a gemstone mine.

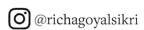 @richagoyalsikri

CARRIERS

OF THE

FIRE

The Women of the Welsh Revival 1904/05

their impact then, their challenge now...

Karen

GW00750429

Shedhead Pr
Antioch Centre
Copperworks Road
Llanelli
SA15 2NE

CARRIERS OF THE FIRE
Copyright © Karen Lowe January 2004

All rights reserved

Unless otherwise stated, all Scripture quotations are taken from
the HOLY BIBLE, NEW INTERNATIONAL VERSION.
Copyright © 1973, 1978, 1984 by the International Bible Society.

ISBN : 0-9546989-0-8

First published March 2004 by:
Shedhead Productions
Antioch Centre
Copperworks Road
Llanelli
SA15 2NE

Printed in Great Britain by :
J.D.Lewis & Sons Ltd
Gwasg Gomer
Llandysul
Ceredigion
SA44 4QL

Contents

Dedication

To my "Braveheart" Mark
and our courageous children,
Samuel, Bethany, Rhosanna and Josh

and to the fiery women of
"nations company"[1]

Acknowledgements

This book has been a team effort and friends all over Wales have been part of the team - thank you so much. Thank you also to everyone who has invested financially in this book to make it happen. Special thanks to Deb who has spent hours and holidays taking this book from dream to reality - it is the story of the women of your nation - you are a wonderful friend and one of the forerunners in this day.

Thank you Kev for provoking me to write the book, providing the research to make it possible and for being a major influence on my life.

Antioch, you are an amazing church, thank you for being patient with me whilst, in my head, I have been wearing the large black hats and long skirts of 1904 well into 2004! Thank you "eXplore"[1] for your patience in all the missed opportunities to sleep under hedges!

Thank you Helen for all the typing, proof reading and encouragement, and all the other friends who have read, re-read, corrected, encouraged, researched, advised and inspired: Steve and Jen, Zoe, Pippa, Anna, Annie and Liz. Thank you also to Elisabeth James and Gareth Huws for translating and checking the Welsh for me and Ann Wilkins for providing research material.

Tim and Ann for producing the video/DVD and for your generous friendship, Alan and Rachel for your thoughtfulness, Pete, Pip and boys for your deep investment in my life in love and friendship over many years. It is exciting to follow you to the "Global Gates" - you are an inspiration and true pioneers.

To all who have inspired us and stood with us as a family, and as a church - Rob Whillier, John Powis, Peter Leavers,

Todd Atkinson, Steve Lowton, Dave Day, Martin Scott, the leadership of "nationscompany" and many, many others, thank you so much.

Thankyou to Bob and Freda for doing so much to help us as a family, and to my parents also. There aren't enough "thank yous" for Mark; for all that you are; for believing in me and for all you have carried practically to allow this book to be written. Thank you Samuel, Bethany, Rhosanna and Josh for being such fun and for not being ashamed of your "mad" mum. Jesus, thank you for taking a wrecked life and turning it around - you are everything to me.

Endorsements

"At last, a book that majors on what they did right in 1904/05. 'Carriers of the Fire' lets history speak for itself. Through reflection on what actually happened, Karen reveals a key, long hidden, that one hundred years on is just beginning to unlock God's purposes again. It is not until we make space for the least and the last - the women! - to carry God's fire that we will see lasting revival and our communities transformed. A "must read" for anyone who is looking for what God will do in our time and for every church leader - especially those who just happen to be male!"

Steve Hallet,
Church Leader, The Gap, Cardiff

"As a woman of Welsh descent, called to lead women, tears flowed freely as I recogised the significance of this book.

In an hour when the Father is illuminating fresh revelation of His heart and call upon His daughters, and the strategic role they will play in His unfolding plans, this book is a "must read" for men and women of all ages. Get ready, for I believe there will be an impartation of revival fire that will burn within those who dare to venture into Karen Lowe's depiction of the lives of women who have journeyed before us, on a path we must yearn to experience ourselves. There are modern day Deborahs, Esthers, Ruths, Marys, waiting to be released; burning with boldness, courage, conviction and passion for Christ. There are those, like David, Joshua, Barak and Boaz who will invite them to partner in bringing in the harvest."

Sheryl Lindberg
President of Aglow, Canada

"As I started to read this book I felt the quickening of the Spirit within. It is a timely prophetic declaration, recounting history accurately but always with an eye on the present and a sense of "He who has an ear, let him hear what the Spirit says to the churches." It is a trumpet call for women and young people to live in their God-given destiny rather than be limited by man's expectations. It is also a major challenge to present day leadership. If these Holy Spirit inspired events happened today how would we respond? This is an important book by a woman with the same passion for Jesus and the lost that consumed the people she writes about."

Pete Leavers
Heart-cry for Wales/Cri O'r Galon Dros Gymru
& Advisor to the Aglow International
Regional Board for Wales

Journey

Hidden wounds
And buried anointings,
Deep in the underbelly of the earth
I am restoring the
childhood of the nation;
Breathing
On an ancient shrivelled heart"
Lost keys found
The Father returns to the Father's house
In the Father's land
A prodigal nation
Lifts its head and looks.
"This time I am not coming for a hundred
thousand, but for a nation"
Wild fire revival.
A nation transformed
For the transforming of other nations.
Glory flowing like molten gold
To the places of least resistance.
Torch the wells and run!
The message -
My presence and the poor.
Wales
A small stone set in the Bride's engagement ring
A bluestone token
A nation given before time

Introduction

"I love the Lord Jesus with all my heart"[1], in the spring of 1904 the cry of 15 year old Florrie Evans put a match to a nationwide yearning in Wales. A yearning that exploded in Revival fire through the life of Evan Roberts and went worldwide.

The 1904/05 Revival saw the nation of Wales lift its head and turn as 100,000 came to faith in a few short months. Listen to an eye witness account, just one month into the Revival outbreak:

'A great number of young people have been inspired to such an extent as to make them courageous enough to speak to sinners every chance they get...prayer meetings are held in the trains and many converts are made. The public houses and beer clubs are empty; old debts are paid, jealousy vanishes, church and family feuds are healed; great drunkards, prize fighters and gamblers pray in the services and give their testimony; the chapels throughout the populous valleys of Glamorganshire are full every night, all denominations have sunk their small differences to co-operate as one body and the huge processions along the streets send a thrill of terror through the vilest sinners. Owing to these things the attention of the whole of South Wales is entirely captivated, the revival is the topic in all spheres and amongst all sections of society; and strong people are overwhelmed by reading the newspaper accounts of it. People begin to pour in from all parts of England, Scotland, Ireland to see and judge for themselves of the nature and characteristics of the movement and most of them say - "This is truly the work of the Holy Spirit and it is wonderful"[2]

This was a Revival, different in many ways to the ones that had gone before, in a land which had experienced revival after revival.[3]

This Revival, more than ever before, was a grass roots movement where women, young people and children found their voice. It marked the beginnings of a worldwide outpouring of the Holy Spirit which would reshape the Church and reshape the nations. It sparked a revolution in which the Father took the poor, the young and the women to demonstrate in fire the counter-culture revolution initiated by the life and death and resurrection of His Son, Jesus.

Nowhere is this revolution more radical than in the role given to women. From heaven's perspective this was no surprise, but rather a necessity; an urgent "Wake up!" call. From earth's perspective, what may have looked incredibly new and different was in fact the breaking through of a quietly revolutionary stream that had been flowing underground for some time.

This book captures something of the untold story of the women of the Welsh Revival. Their story is fundamental to an understanding of the significance of the Revival then, and to an understanding of its significance now.

I was challenged to write this book by Kevin Adams[4] a contemporary historian of the 1904 Revival. He asked me to do this because I was a woman leading a church within a few miles of Loughor where the Revival broke out in 1904. He provided the majority of the research and much of the encouragement and help - although the controversial views are all mine!

I didn't want to write a book out of revival sentimentality. Yet, as I talked to women across Wales I realised that the radical women who had been forerunners of the Revival were forgotten figures, and that the involvement of the women in the Revival was now a forgotten history.

The descendants of "Plant y Diwygiad", "The Children of the Revival", the Revival converts, had been robbed of an inheritance. It was not just a robbery of inheritance in Wales, but across the world, as many of their descendants are now sown into other nations.

It was a robbery re-inforced by some of the 're-telling" of the Revival which doesn't reflect the impact of the women as displayed in the first hand accounts. The "re-telling" has, at times, become a blame shift in which the women are held responsible for the weaknesses of the Revival. This is, in itself, an example of the way in which the women were "shutdown" after the Revival. Yet, there is a spiritual inheritance open to all, waiting to be stirred up and provoked by the accounts of ordinary women who broke out of the mindsets of their age as they responded in obedience to the Holy Spirit. Their story is a revival well, waiting to be torched!

They were dangerous women to be around. Their testimony carries faith which calls out for a repeat performance! So that what happened once could happen again in fresh expressions for each New Day.

They embraced a corporate anointing which fell on women across the nation of Wales. There is now a corporate anointing falling on women across the nations. However, the story of the women of 1904 is not one of women working in isolation from men. It is a story of teams, of interdependence, of authority based on anointing and of the ebb and flow of ministry handed from one to the other. It is a story of congregations and communities finding new ways of being and relating to each other in the midst of an overwhelming outpouring of the love of God.

The women of the Welsh Revival speak to us today, into a century that is radically different from theirs. In 1904 the chapels were full but there was little fire in the house. There was a lack of personal testimony because there was scant assurance of salvation. Witness, where it happened, ran mainly along denominational lines and the baptism of the Holy Spirit was not common amongst the average church-goer.

Today this is a post-Christian nation, a land where churches, haemorrhaging children and young people, have been described as hospices for dying denominations. This is not, however, the whole story, there is a spiritual hunger in the land amongst those who don't know Him and the beginnings of a cry for change amongst those who do. We have the baptism of the Holy Spirit but few miracles and comparatively scant salvations. We need signs and wonders on the streets and even in the churches!

We dare not live in a dangerous pride over our heritage, nor in an entrenched despair over our future. The women of 1904 picked up a baton of God's purposes and ran with it. A baton which in the aftermath of the Revival was largely taken away from them; a removal which few resisted. They were back to being "abnormal" Christians in "abnormal" church. Today we have our own expressions of "abnormal" church, but we also have an opportunity to run again and embrace the radical obedience to the Holy Spirit which they embraced. We have a fresh opportunity to see nations transformed to serve the transformation of other nations.

This book reflects the words and deeds of the women of that time. Some of them were well known, others are unnamed; yet all shaped history through the yielding of their lives. They were "Carriers of His Fire". This is their story, told often in their own words. It is a provocation for us to become "Carriers of His Fire". It is a provocation for us to run with strength to see this counter-culture revolution reach its fulfillment in the return of the King. Let's do it!!

Keys

The keys are in the house
Hidden in the hearts of a nation's
people
Buried in a nation's land
Kingdom keys
Keys of heaven
Keys of heaven's sight

1

What was life like for women at that time ?

The role of women in the 1904 Revival is even more extraordinary when it is placed against the social and spiritual background of that time.

They did not allow the daily hardships and drudgery of life to excuse them from being "willing volunteers in the day of God's power"[1]. They chose not to hide behind the rigid expectations constructed for them. They didn't opt out in the face of the social and religious conventions of their day. Instead, they stepped out, in an era at the beginning of the twentieth century, when life was very difficult for women.

Homes were often overcrowded and damp - places of hard, physical work. Frequent pregnancies and poor diet meant that mothers often described their children in two sets of figures - those who had died at birth or in infancy and those who

A typical family

had lived. Evan Roberts' mother, Hannah, described herself as having 14 children, 8 living.

In the Rhondda, one of the Revival hot spots, it is recorded that, "The unremitting toil of childbirth and domestic labour killed and debilitated Rhondda women as much as accident and conditions in the mining industry killed or maimed Rhondda men."[2] It also killed the children, sometimes through the lack of pithead baths for the men.

"We had to bring a tub or a tin bath, whichever we had, into the same room that we lived in and heat the water over the living room fire in a bucket or a boiler, whichever we possessed, so you can imagine the life of a miner's wife is no bed of roses. No wonder so many children are scalded to death in Wales...A little one living close by me, 5 years old, died last week by falling in a bath of hot water."[3]

In the period from 1901-10 the mortality rate for young women in the Rhondda was significantly higher than that for men. The women needed to pay if they wanted to see a doctor (only insured workers were covered for healthcare)[4] and they would often make themselves the last priority. The high price of mining was frequently borne by these hidden workers in their homes, whose working hours were often longer than those of their menfolk. It is interesting that this is paralleled in the Revival in the Valleys as the hidden workers were at times the women - women who were undoubtedly paying a price to see the Revival come through.

In the Rhondda, as in other places bad housing was rife, this included 500 cellar homes with no natural light and no ventilation.[5] The poor quality of education for women was also a problem. The hated 'Blue Books'[6] of 1848 falsely blamed women for the low moral standards of the children.

A report on the low number and poor quality of recruits for the Boer War blamed high infant mortality rates on the ignorance of working class mothers[7]. In a broad sense women were blamed for low moral standards and poverty. In schools this made domestic skills the priority in a girl's education.

However, two ground-breaking magazines produced for women, *Y Gymraes* (The Welsh Woman), followed by *Y Frythones* (The Female Briton) championed a higher view of women and a better quality of education for them.

The fact that *Y Frythones* was edited by a woman, Sarah Jane Rees - known as Cranogwen - of whom we will hear more later, was in itself a victory. The magazines saw poor education for women as the robbery of a woman's potential, with a subsequent robbery of benefit to her family.

These magazines still, however, reflected the belief of the time that men and women should live in "separate spheres". The man's duty was in the workplace and politics, the woman's place in the home and it was felt that there should be no mixing of the spheres. Practically, on farms and in small businesses this did not always work out, but the values were still maintained.

The high ratio of men to women in the Valleys meant great marriage prospects but little chance of a job; this was reversed in rural areas where the lack of men meant few marriage prospects but no shortage of work on the farms!

In the Valleys with little work for the women outside the home it is little wonder that the archetypal "Welsh Mam" emerged - an avenger on dirt and poverty, courageous in protecting her home and family.

The notion of "separate spheres" was challenged in the Revival as men and women worked together in teams, with authority based on the anointing of the Holy Spirit rather than on a title or gender. "Spheres" shifted as God's work became the responsibilty of all; men and women working in partnership and interdependence within the move of the Holy Spirit.

The Suffrage[8] movement was not strong in Wales amongst working class women because of the lack of employment for them in the industrialised areas. This meant that they didn't join the Trade Unions which had aided the Suffrage Movement in England.

Before the First World War women did not vote, nor could they stand for election in parliament. However, The Married Women's Property Act[9] meant that married women had the same rights to own property as widows and single women.

However they didn't have equal divorce rights or any right

at all to custody of the children. The age of consent had been raised from 13 to 16, but incest wasn't made a criminal offence until 1908.

As a middle class woman you were known by your husband's title - for example, the Rev. Mrs Evans. The few single women, in teaching or medicine were defined by their profession. Newspaper reports of the Revival reflect some shift of perception as women were defined by their "revival role". Women, more generally, became "useful workers' and soloists became "Singing Evangelists"!

In fact, the chapels were the only place where "respectable" women could find a wider expression. Within certain constraints, women could benefit from education in the adult Sunday school, entertainment in the Singing Festivals and confidence building in the women's meetings.

It is not surprising, therefore, that the first large scale women's organisation, the women's section of the Temperance Movement[10] was rooted firmly in the chapels. Women were aware first hand of the power of alcohol to destroy families.

Mrs. Sarah Matthews set up the North Wales Temperance Union in 1892. Ten years later Cranogwen set up the South Wales equivalent.[11] The groups met in chapels and their Christian faith was central to the movement. Their motto being "Er mwyn Crist, cartref a chymydog" (For Christ, home and neighbour).

The number of groups grew rapidly. In these groups women were encouraged in public speaking, writing pamphlets and organising events. The Temperance Movement was linked to broader issues of 'moral purity' with a focus on "fallen women" and those at risk such as barmaids. The Wrexham and Rhondda branches set up homes for such women at risk. The latter being regarded as, "Not only exposed to moral danger but also as the victims of the brewer's greed."[12]

However, by 1896 Sarah Matthews, the founder of the

North Wales Movement, was disappointed by lack of progress amongst the women.

"We do not find that readiness to speak, either in branch or public meetings, that we expected holding 4 years of women's meetings would have produced. We are perfectly aware that it involves a considerable effort to address a mixed audience and that it is a new and untried field of influence to us as Welsh women...let me appeal to each one of you...to determine that henceforward, cost what it may, your voice will not be silent at the women's meetings, and if necessary, that you will conquer the nervousness and reserve which has hitherto overcome you when the call to battle in a more public manner reaches you".[12]

Year after year, Sarah and others would urge,"We women can do the work and do not be persuaded that you have no power or ability"[12].

The "call to battle" for many came within the Revival. The Temperance cause was "respectable" in that the wives of Liberal MPs and the wives of church ministers were very active. These women obviously had the permission of their husbands to be involved. The role of significant men in releasing the women in their lives to develop in gift and calling cannot be underestimated. It was as valid then as it is now. However, for the women of the Temperance Movement there was still a lot of prejudice to contend with - there is still a little now!

This is the view of Ceridwen Peris as she looked back from the "greater freedoms of 1931":

"A woman's action in climbing on to the stage to speak in public struck against the general idea of a woman's place in society. The hearth and home was a woman's place, and silence her virtue - that was the public's opinion at the time. The prejudice had to be faced by those women who wished to convince the nation that women had their own message and mission in the world and that their sphere of service extended beyond the four walls of their home and

in many places chapel elders feared the scowls of other members when announcing that sisters were coming there to talk about temperance."[13]

Photographs of ministers and deacons of the time give a clear impression of institutions where women and young people were not in roles of influence and leadership! Yet there are indications of small shakings. The belief in "separate spheres' and the view of the women as "The Angel *in* the House" was changing. This was partly as a result of women's involvement in social reform after the 1859 revival in areas such as temperance work and

Preacher

prisons. An acceptable view emerged of "The Angel *out of the House"*[14]. This would have been epitomised by women such as Florence Nightingale who said of herself that she went into nursing when the church refused her offer of service in mission.

These small shakings are reflected in discussions initiated by the Forward Movement.[15]

"Participation by women in the work of the churches had been the subject of discussion at the Llandudno Association of the Calvinistic Methodists in November 1897. The sending of women missionaries to foreign lands had been accepted practice for a number of years but the needs of the home missions and the Forward Movement brought the issue of the ministry of women into the open. The Association's minutes urged the need for "Our younger sisters" in such secular vocations as nursing and the hospital services. They also recorded: "We consider the time has arrived when we ...should make some arrangement for securing the services of some of these sisters who are prepared to offer themselves to the work of the Saviour's kingdom in our midst" "[15]

They were grappling with the strange logic that it was acceptable to send women to lead and die on the mission field, yet it was not acceptable for male sensibilities to be upset by women taking an active role within sight of the chapel doors. The cause of world mission may have been gloriously but "accidentally" advanced by the prejudice of the church. Yet, it also raised the question of whether the home nation was a suitable mission field for women. The Forward Movement were at least grappling with the issues when others were simply hoping that the women would go away!

It is also interesting that Seth Joshua of the Forward Movement was an initiator in the Revival with his prayer for God to raise up a young man from the mines rather than the colleges to turn the nation of Wales. In effect he was calling in prayer for someone to upset the established order.

At the same time, the Temperance Movement was facilitating an underground revolution as women were equipped for service. In many cases this happened under the rather grudging noses of the chapel elders, who saw the problems of alcohol as simply a domestic issue and, therefore, still aligned with a woman's sphere. When the Holy Spirit moved in power, many women were already prepared, however nervously, to step out and take risks in speaking and ministering in public.

It was perhaps prophetic but not surprising, therefore, that one of the earliest Revival meetings links back to the Temperance Movement. On the 16th November 1904, the six-monthly meeting of the South Wales Temperance Union was held in Pontycymer and it was suggested that they invite Evan Roberts. They did and the meeting was full of "passionate singing...supernatural stirrings and rejoicing at the Throne of Grace"[16]

Cranogwen, the "Field Marshall" of the Temperance Movement took part as did Rosina Davies, an evangelist.

Cranogwen encouraged the young people "to place their trust in Jesus". Cranogwen and Rosina, in different ways, were forerunners of the Revival and in this meeting the forerunners embraced the Revival for which they had made a way.

The climate of the time, despite the efforts of the Temperance Movement, meant that the release of women in the Revival still came as a major shock to many. However, there had been a few women, such as Rosina and Cranogwen, who had acted as ground-breakers in walking against the prevailing tide of social and church convention in the years preceding 1904. They had also walked against the "wear down" factor of the sheer physical hardship of life for many at that time; a hardship which women, because of their role in the home, experienced most keenly. These forerunners were women who blazed a trail, as individuals, for the widespread outpouring on women which was to come.

Transition

"...The process of changing from one position
to another."
Positions for transition in labour:-
This is a difficult stage in which
to find a comfortable
position.
Contractions
seem
relentless
but if you   understand that
the baby will
be born soon,
that should give
you the
confidence
to stay calm (!)

Swirling tide turning,
Caught in turbulence of currents
crossing over
from death to life.
Feel the pull, the dance and sway,
Transition, reversal intertwine,
No standing on shifting ground.
What has been meets what will be
The only fixed point,
Yielding,
Connecting with Your eyes' kind gaze.

2

Forerunners of the Revival

The forerunners of the Revival include five significant but now largely forgotten women. They were amongst those who prepared the way for an outpouring of the Spirit that empowered women across the nations. The experience of a few became the experience of many across the world as women saw the River of God flowing and jumped in.

Three of these forerunners were also closely connected with the beginnings of The Salvation Army in Wales. The Army as a movement was a major forerunner of the freedom for women to become "workers" for the gospel in Wales. Wales was also a place of "firsts" for the Salvation Army as we shall see later. The Salvation Army was born as a revivalist movement and as such had a theology which gave room for women. It is, perhaps, ironic, that it was the Salvation Army who initially had to make a way for women to fully participate in revival in the "Land of revivals" - Wales.

Mary David's life, however, was connected to the Calvinistic Methodists and to the roots of Moriah Chapel where the Revival broke out on October 31, 1904

Pamela Shepherd and principally her daughter Kate, were the key figures in the 1879 revival, the last revival before the outbreak of 1904.

Rosina Davies was saved as a young girl through the Salvation Army in the Valleys during the 1879 revival. She worked as an evangelist in Wales, England and the USA for 60 years.

Cranogwen prepared the way for women to be involved in ministry in Wales through the example of her life and through the Temperance Movement which she led.

Mary David

Mary David was an uneducated elderly lady who insisted on teaching the children of Loughor about Jesus, although she said she knew very little herself. She did this in the first years of the 19th Century. Out of this Sunday school "it became essential to have a Meeting House"[1]

This Meeting House developed to become Moriah Chapel. It was in the schoolroom of Moriah Chapel, Loughor that the Revival broke out when Evan Roberts met with a group of 17 young people including a little girl.

Mary David's story is that of an ordinary woman who took courage to act despite her "limitations" and the prejudice of others. The local vicar was surprised that she had decided to start a Sunday school. She answered his concerns by admitting,

"That my knowledge is meagre, but were not the disciples of Jesus thus? Yet you must admit that they did a great deal of good in spite of their lack of knowledge because they were obedient to Jesus...the disciples were ignorant like other Galileans, yet they did splendid work". The priest was amazed to receive such a sensible answer!"[2]

In fact the Sunday school was extremely successful, "In no other place, even when started by prominent men of the cause, no movement was more successful than the one of Mary David and her assistants"[2]

Mary David pioneered an initial beachhead that became Moriah Chapel. She also laid a foundation which welcomed the Revival to come in the century which followed hers.

I believe that her prayers and actions prepared the way for a Revival led by a self educated miner, young people and women. Her action was a realignment towards the heart of the gospel; ordinary, uneducated people transformed by the love of Jesus, confounding the wisdom of the day through sheer obedience. This was to be the story of the many ordinary women who followed. Small realignments were preparing a way for revival streams to break through.

Mother Shepherd

Pamela Morgan, later known as Mother Shepherd, was born in 1836, her story is closely entwined with the beginnings of the Salvation Army.

Her family were forced to move to London from Wales when she was a young girl. Her father had been involved with the Chartists[3] in the struggle for workers rights, this led to him being driven out of his job in the Cambrian Iron Works in Maesteg.

In London, with his dreams demolished he slid into alcoholism, leaving Margaret his wife to support the family by taking in washing.

Pamela, his daughter, became an alcoholic after marrying Bill

Mother Sheperd in 1878

Shepherd who spent time in and out of prison, deserting her and leaving her with three girls. As a deserted wife she was utterly destitute, in a worse position than a widow as the Poor Law guardians would offer no help. At this point of desperation she decided to kill herself and the children.

She sewed the irons her mother had used to "keep them alive" by taking in washing, into her clothes and took her children with her to a spot on the canal "where the suicides go". She knew she was "walking towards Judgement Day stamped suicide and murderess". She was walking towards the canal, full of torment, when through the darkness she heard a voice calling her name - it was the voice of Mrs. Evans, an old friend of her mother's. Mrs. Evans told Pamela how that very day she had been thinking of her, and of the request that Pamela's mother had made before she left London, that someone would befriend her daughter. "The thought had come "I wonder if she is befriended, why should she not come to me? "Like an answer, Pamela's face and gown passed by the window, she had hard work to open it in time before Pamela went out of sight into the darkness. Both women felt God's hand had helped to open the window for them."[4]

Sometime later Pamela became a Christian through what was to become the Salvation Army. The Salvation Army made a way for women to minister. Pamela's life, as one of the early Army pioneers is a story of "firsts", a story of suffering and a story of breakthrough against all odds.

Gypsy Smith, a well known evangelist of the time said "I love to tell the story of my little friend Kate Shepherd in the early days of the Salvation Army. Her mother was taking care of an office for General Booth, the husband and father of the girls was in gaol. The General, when the mother was converted, put her in the office rent free and she cooked his meals"[5]

After working for ten years with the Salvation Army in London, Commissioner George Scott Railton told Pamela that she was to go to Aberdare and start a work in Wales. She was horrified, she felt that at 42 she was too old, she was barely literate and she had forgotten most of her Welsh. Railton insisted she go saying "You'll manage to find people to do the writing for you, as Mr. Booth says, "Go for souls and go for the worst" Railton added "The language of heaven must be the key to the treasury of the gospel for Wales, the key to their Welsh hearts".[6] Kate, her eldest daughter at 16 was to be her helper as was Pamela 14, and Sally who was 4 years old.

Pamela took courage and refused to allow her age, past pain, her limitations, her failures and her responsibilities to disqualify her. She chose to use a rusty key she had already been given, the key of her native language. If Pamela Shepherd didn't refuse to go it leaves us with few excuses. In our more "professional" day she probably wouldn't even be allowed to go! In our more apathetic day many of us would be glad of any excuse to avoid taking the risks of faith she took!

Life became no easier for Pamela when she actually arrived in Aberdare. She had trouble getting permission from the police to hold an open air meeting on the Saturday night, a woman had never held such a meeting there before and Aberdare was a violent place. Apart from the three children she was without support as she started to preach.

"*A roar went up from the rough men standing around who made a rush for Pamela shouting in Welsh "Push her off the old English woman!". Pamela heard the Welsh and understood what they were going to do...she had seen people trampled on before, she was like a tigress at bay,*

"*The people came running in hundreds and pushed up against us, I was afraid they would hurt my children". "GWRANDEWCH (listen), CHWARAE TEG (Let's have fair play), I'm a Welsh woman born in Talywain, I am in my own country, I have a right to be heard. If you are men stand back, you'll crush my children...Shame on you, shame on you men of Aberdare, how would you like your wives, your mothers, your little children to be pushed about by big strong men who should know better! Drunk some of you are, pushing and shoving like pigs in a sty. I know what it feels like because years ago I was no better myself. Yes, a drunkard I was! Yes and I haven't always been a preaching woman - a fighting woman more like and I would have given some of you a black eye then for pushing my children about." The men fell backward open mouthed, there was a deep silence, "Now God has sent me not just to scold you but because He loves you. But you must listen, must open your hearts...must be sorry and turn to Jesus who died for you and change as I did. Come to the Temperance Hall tomorrow night, bring all your friends, there is plenty of room and hear this message of salvation".*[7]

She and the girls brought out their tambourines, and singing "Mae'n fy ngharu" (Jesus loves me) marched off through the crowds which opened up for them to pass."

The next day the Temperance Hall was packed and when the meeting was over Pamela spoke of people going away in such a condition of "heartache and wretchedness about their sins that it is next to impossible for them to eat, sleep or work until they are cured".

They were asked to move on from the Temperance Hall because they were "not nice tidy worshippers at all". They moved to a disused sawmill and in the meeting that night something happened that brought Aberdare under severe conviction.

"A heckler cried out "There is no God, if there be a God strike us dead in our seats all of us three". The man was not to be restrained and carried on. "There you are, you see nothing happens!" His scornful laughter reverberated around the walls. Pamela's voice rang out now, there was an authority, a clarity in her tone, it was like a bugle call "Infidel, God is not mocked. On your knees man, beg forgiveness while you still have time". "The man appeared to have lost all control of himself..as if possessed by some evil force...it was frightening...There was a great gasp from the hushed crowd, the man suddenly grasped at the rail of the bench in front of him with an iron hold. His friends had to prise his hands loose, then he slumped to the floor. The two men on either side tried to lift him, then one burst out in a shattered voice "he is dead!". Within a few weeks the other two men fell ill and died. The incident produced a profound impression in Aberdare, there was no further attempt to hinder the work in the town"[7]

Many were "cured" - became Christians, leaders were appointed and a strong Salvation Army Corps was planted in the town!

Kate Shepherd

Kate Shepherd was sixteen when she came to Wales. She was initially very fearful and wanted to go back home to London, until she went to a night of prayer, "A Council of War" in Merthyr led by Bramwell Booth. There she was baptised in the Holy Spirit.

"I received the blessings of a clean heart, do you know what I mean, yr Ysbryd Glan [the Holy Spirit], in your hearts...you must know God's power and not hold anything back, not shyness or unwillingness to witness, that's what I was doing. I knew I was saved, ever since a little girl but I'd never fully given myself to God"[8]

On the night Kate publicly shared what had happened nine people became Christians. Her experience in 1878 was to be the experience of many women in 1904, as the baptism of the Holy Spirit released a boldness to witness and a deep givenness to God's purposes. In the New Year of 1879 when she was 17 a letter arrived asking Kate to work in the Rhondda with Charlotte Bateson.

At that time the Rhondda was said to be one of the "blackest hells" in South Wales, full of "drunkenness, wife beating, and debauchery, gambling, dog and cock fighting". The conditions in the mines at that time were terrible - a constant threat of death underground and starvation on top, as wages were reduced to what they had been thirty years previously. One gentleman came up to Kate in the street just before she left for the Rhondda and said "It's a shame of Mr. Booth to send a young innocent girl like you to that wicked place" She looked straight at him and said "Did Jesus die for the bad or for the good?"[8]

Gypsy Smith said this of her :

"When the General wanted officers he asked Kate to go down to a station in the Rhondda valley, and told her not to tell anyone her age. Though she had a living experience she was a child in years,

she was no scholar but I knew she was Spirit filled. The General said "Remember you're not going to an easy place, don't let your age militate against your usefulness". She went down and shook that valley in the power of God and hundreds of colliers were converted under the ministry of that girl."[9]

When she arrived one of the first things she did was to go down a mine to better understand the conditions the miners faced. Her identification with the plight of the miners broke a way into their hearts that went beyond words and hundreds were converted.

This again was to be a pattern in the Revival of 1904 when women found the same boldness to go into the mines and the same boldness to go to those despised by the chapels - the destitute, the alcoholics and those on the fringes of society.

Catherine Booth said Kate's power in prayer was unique,

"It was not so much what she said as the way she said it, "Oh Lord they are mis-er-a-ble" she would begin, and the heart of every sinner in the congregation seemed to echo back almost audibly "You know we are miserable"...Then followed a simple testimony to God's saving grace, and appeal upon appeal for every sinner to decide there and then the question of his soul's salvation. "Won't you come? You'll be sorry for it someday, yes you will!" and the large dark earnest eyes brimful of tears enforced the argument"[10]

Her mother, Pamela, initially didn't want Kate to go to the Rhondda but felt happier when she could move to be closer to her. Pamela said this of her,

"Kate went to labour in the Rhondda valley full of power and the Holy Ghost, and though only 17 years old God used her in a mighty manner so that her name was ringing throughout Wales. Many chapel people said she was an ignorant girl but God used her and saved thousands of souls through her feeble instrumentality. The place was shaken, every chapel was open all the while, people were praying night and day. Such havoc was made among the men working underground that they used to say even the horses were

converted. Mr. Cory (the mine owner) said his men did better work than ever before."

Pamela's 14 year old daughter, Pam also had a role to play, taking over from Kate as her mother's main helper,

"Pam and I fought on alone, she was such a child! But Pam fought well! One night while she was speaking 42 people came out for salvation and one a minister. Porth was a straggling sort of colliery place only 8 miles from where Kate was so I could keep a motherly eye on her."[11]

Kate's age, her lack of education, her poverty and her gender were no disqualification to an outbreak of revival.

The revival was reported in the press. The publicity through the press, the salvation of miners, the role of young women and the use of processions and singing in the street, were all forerunners of what was to happen in 1904.

"Miss Shepherd has been holding revival meetings in the public hall, Pentre, Ystrad. She has been here somewhat about a month and has such influence in the locality that she draws a multitude of people after her until the hall is so crowded that scores cannot get admission and therefore go to Pentre United Colliery School where they are addressed by some other young lady missionary from Devonport who assists Miss Shepherd...On the last two Sundays the ladies took a procession from the public hall as far as the Ystrad station...There are thousands joining the procession and the singing is very effective. The ladies have been the means of drawing hundreds of the lowest class of people to hear the gospel preached. People who are undoubtedly beyond the reach of our ministers. There are to say the least 500 converts here, after they are converted she tells those not used to some place of worship that they must go wherever they have an inclination to go and that it does not matter what denomination they go to. What a happy change has taken place here, instead of drunkenness and fighting, cursing and swearing...the talk is now "How many of you were at the meeting last night and how many were converted?"[12]

Kate encouraged people to get saved even if they weren't

part of a denomination. This stood against the prevalent view of the time that a church was only really responsible for those historically affiliated to it. She was pushing for a new priority and a new unity in working together for harvest.

The woman who took over from Kate at Pentre, Louisa Lock, was 18. She was the first female Salvation Army officer to be imprisoned and she became their first martyr in Wales. She was gaoled for 3 days for kneeling to pray with 4 others in Bridgend Square. She died aged 20 as a result of an illness contracted in prison. She was regarded as a martyr "In God's fight against injustice on the spiritual battlefields of the South Wales valleys".[13]

Rosina Davies

Rosina Davies was converted in the Rhondda in 1879 through Captain and Mrs. Herbert at the same time as Kate and Pamela Shepherd were in Pentre and Aberdare. She was desperate to get to a meeting in a chapel in Blaenrhondda which was a good distance from where she lived. Her mother found her difficult to manage and locked her in her room so that she couldn't go. However a number of young men saw her crying and unbolted the window so that she could escape and go to the meeting.

She knew she would be in major trouble on her return. However she tried to escape the birch-rod by "saying her prayers more than once!" But,

"My mother waited and the birch-rod was administered across my shoulders and I took it without a murmur. She gave me another stroke thinking I was hardened and then I told her that I was not hurt because Jesus bore the strokes for me, "With His stripes we are healed". The birch-rod fell from her hands and tears filled her eyes. My beloved mother, she suffered more than I did, she feared her little girl was going astray and she wanted to save my soul. God took the matter in hand and answered her prayers, both our souls were saved."[14]

Captain and Mrs. Richardson were going to start a work in the Maesteg Valley. They didn't speak Welsh themselves so they asked Rosina to join with them; she sang and preached in Welsh. She was in her early teens at this time and her parents wanted her to go home and finish her education. Rosina refused to return home saying that she must be about her Father's business.

Rosina Davies - USA tour

At that time a girl evangelist in Wales was a phenomenon:

"For women to take part in any public capacity was unthinkable and that sentiment continued amongst ministers and laymen for a long time with some exceptions; the women mothered me, even the wives of the ministers who objected...I had no fear and prejudice failed to discourage me or break my heart with opposition. Many said in public it was only a flash that would soon pass. Women took courage, came out in temperance work and prayer meetings and found that there was a call for help in all public capacities. They realise today that God expects the hand that rocks the cradle to rule the world. No nation, tribe or country can rise higher than its womanhood."[15]

Rosina's boldness was noticeable even as a young girl. When she heard that Peter had walked on water, she decided to have a go on a nearby pond and was ashamed by her lack of faith when she fell in! As a woman evangelist she needed all the courage she was given to walk on the water of other people's expectations and disapproval, but she would not give up.

Cranogwen - Sarah Jane Rees

Cranogwen was also a woman who knew what it meant to persevere, born in Llangrannog, she was an unusual woman of her day. She was the daughter of a ship's captain and insisted on going to sea with him as she hated cooking and sewing. She later taught navigation and mathematics locally, in London and in Liverpool. She was deeply influenced by the 1859 revival and taught in Sunday school and Band of Hope. She was a writer and a poet, a lecturer and a preacher. She had a less middle class background than many other leaders in the Temperance Movement, as she had to work to support herself throughout her life.

She experienced great prejudice as a woman, her biographer Rev. D.G. Jones of Pontardawe recalls how "Some men still believed that women and wives were still things to be kept shut up in houses to wait upon the men folk, things to be at their lord's service in every respect, washing their clothes when need be, cleaning their shoes and looking after their owners as if they were omniscient and almighty beings. When they saw Cranogwen in the pulpit addressing a crowd of men they thought that the end of the world had come. They thought it excellent to suggest that she was a man in female form, or a woman in masculine form and we heard some suggest that she belonged to neither one sex nor the other." It is hardly surprising that Cranogwen suffered bouts of depression and lack of self confidence in the face of such reactions, but the important non-conformist leader, Thomas Levi, rushed to her support in an article on Cranogwen in *Trysorfa y Plant,* a denominational magazine he edited in which he addressed the whole question of women preaching in very positive terms".[15]

The issue Cranogwen faced then was an issue that women faced in the Revival and one that is still faced today. The calling on her life led to attacks on the very core of her being and personality as a woman. She was judged by how she looked and as a tall, large woman was often written off as "trying to be a man". There was no recognition by her critics that she was simply fulfilling her gifting in Christ as a woman called to lead. These attacks touched Cranogwen's deepest vulnerabilities but she would not give up despite being misunderstood and ridiculed, she found grace to keep forgiving and pressed on.

Cranogwen
(By permission of Llyfrgell Genedlaethol Cymru/National Library of Wales)

Cranogwen and the other women were ploughing up hard ground and making a way for many to come through, although those coming through would have to face the same issues.

The need to persevere and the grace to keep forgiving are needed as much now as then, the only safety is in a deep sense of God's Fathering and in a deep rooted revelation of identity in Christ. Sometimes women are complimented "on not leading like a man". Sometimes that is simply because there is little understanding of the glorious variety in what it means to lead as a woman! Loudness or quietness of leadership style often have less to do with gender and more to do with the character and gifting of the person expressing it - man or woman!

The role of the Salvation Army was crucial in Wales and Wales was also a "first" and a turning point for the Army itself. In 1878 Commissioner Railton writes

"When asked to describe the incident that I consider most important in the history of the Army before 1880 my mind turns instantly to the invasion of the Rhondda Valley by Kate and Pamela Shepherd and Lt.Bateson in 1878. The work of the Hallelujah Lassies in and around Gateshead and Newcastle attracted far more notice thanks to the newspapers, and had more to do with the future

of the Army externally, but it was the Rhondda experience more than anything else that satisfied the General as to the propriety of sending out just such lassies, although in this case he asked (them) in spite of the very great misgivings on the part of Mrs.Booth. Her sentiments were shared by most of those around her, and it is the light from the Rhondda more than from any other spot that may guide anybody to the understanding of what God could do, and would do anywhere if allowed freely to carry out His plans"[16]

The phrase that "may guide anybody to the understanding of what God could do, and would do anywhere if allowed freely to carry out His plans" could equally be applied to the role of women in the 1904 Revival.

Indeed, it is a letter from Florence Booth published in the South Wales Daily news in 1904 that clearly bridges the gap between the revival of 1879 and the Revival of 1904. Florence, a daughter of a doctor in Blaenau was another young woman around at the time when Kate Shepherd was seeing revival break out in the Valleys. Florence went on to marry William Bramwell Booth in 1882, a year before Kate herself married Charles Coole. Florence wrote this :

"As to my views on the part that women should play in the revival and in church work generally I can only say in few words that women ought always to be well to the front in things pertaining to God and His Kingdom. In nothing has the influence of the Saviour been more quickly felt by the world at large than in the new standard of womanhood which His influence has raised up.

Woman as the world knows her since Christ came and set her free is a totally different being from the woman of old. Her influence, her position, her example, her responsibilities have all changed. There is a fitness about this in view of the fact that woman was unquestionably ahead of man in her service and love when Jesus was on earth. Women played a great part in most of the important events of His life. When in His direst straits men forsook Him and fled women were faithful. So far as we know, no woman who once joined Him forsook Him or drew back. In the Salvation Army the principle is maintained that woman has an equal share with man in the service of God. There is neither male nor female in Christ Jesus. This feature is present I understand in the revival movement...I earnestly hope that women everywhere may take advantage of this opportunity, their influence can materially help to make the results permanent."[17]

This lucid, "Battle Cry" for the freedom of women to serve was the cry of a forerunner who was longing to see something permanent established. In 1904, the women picked up the baton from the Valleys Revival of 1879 in a corporate way. Many, many women were released, yet even up until this day the full freedom of women to minister and lead has not been resolved. The cry from 1904 is still being sounded in 2004. There is still a baton to be picked up and run with afresh.

The trials and triumphs of the forerunners hold the keys to the glory and the pain of the dilemma women faced then and still face now. It is a dilemma tied up in the freedom to serve, or not, in all the glorious gifting and responsibility that Jesus has made available.

These issues were to be highlighted even more clearly in the first few weeks of the Revival.

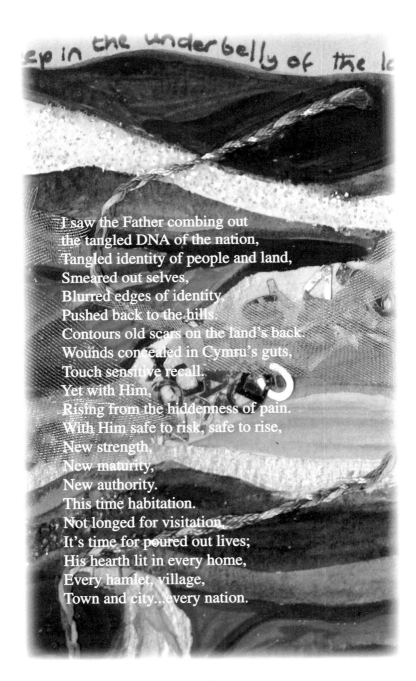

ep in the underbelly of the l

I saw the Father combing out
the tangled DNA of the nation,
Tangled identity of people and land,
Smeared out selves,
Blurred edges of identity,
Pushed back to the hills.
Contours old scars on the land's back.
Wounds concealed in Cymru's guts,
Touch sensitive recall.
Yet with Him,
Rising from the hiddenness of pain.
With Him safe to risk, safe to rise,
New strength,
New maturity,
New authority.
This time habitation.
Not longed for visitation,
It's time for poured out lives;
His hearth lit in every home,
Every hamlet, village,
Town and city...every nation.

3

It's all in the Beginnings

The early months of 1904 in Wales were marked by a growing hunger for a move of God. These months, and the first few weeks of November when the Revival finally broke out, are the crucible in which the key elements were formed. The role of women was crucial both in the breakout of Revival fire and in the shaping of its direction, much of this through their influence on Evan Roberts and other key figures.

Joseph Jenkins, the Calvinistic Methodist minister in Newquay, had been impacted by Keswick in 1903. He invited W.W. Lewis and John M. Saunders and his wife to speak at a conference in the New Year of 1904. John M. Saunders' wife had never spoken in public before except once at the Forward Movement meetings following the conference at Llandrindod. She "urged an experience of Christ".

Jenkins was desperate to see the young people in his church impacted by the truth of the gospel. In February, nearly two months after the conference, he preached on 1 John 5:4, "This is the victory that overcomes the world, even our faith." Fifteen year old Florrie Evans was deeply troubled by his message; she wanted to see him after he had preached but was too scared to talk to him. "I waited for you in the lobby hoping you would say something to me, but you did not. I went to meet you on your way home, but you took no notice of me beyond saying "Good evening". I have been walking in front of the house for half an hour and I was obliged to call. I am in a fearful state concerning my soul. I saw the World in tonight's sermon and I am under its feet. I cannot live like this."[1]

After some conversation Mr. Jenkins asked her, "Can you say "My Lord" to Jesus Christ?" "Now I understand it" she

Florrie Evans

said, "but I cannot say it. I don't know what He will ask me to do, something very difficult perhaps." "Yes, oh yes" said the minister, "He does ask difficult things. It is a narrow gate that leads to the peace and joy of the gospel."[2]

Her opportunity for the "difficult thing" came a week later in the young people's meeting which Jenkins held after the Sunday morning service. He had been holding these meetings for some months out of his concern for the lack of spiritual reality amongst the young people - that Sunday about sixty of them were present. He asked them to "relate their spiritual experience in a few words". He challenged them with a question which they found deeply embarrassing: "What does Jesus Christ mean to you?" Finally Florrie Evans, in front of all her friends, declared, "I love the Lord Jesus with all my heart".

This simple declaration of her faith had a dramatic effect. "An unaccountable power accompanied her simple testimony, and seemed to overwhelm the people. After that the meetings multiplied, and some were held in private houses wherever entrance could be got. In all the neighbouring villages and towns people were everywhere electrified by the intense passion of the meeting."[3]

The "unaccountable power" was perhaps the breaking of the silence in a nation which had gone quiet on the issue of personal faith, conversion and testimony. It was the power of radical obedience in the face of embarrassment and fear. It was the "Yes" of the Holy Spirit to the breakthroughs that were coming through young people, women and children. It was the lighting of the Revival fuse.

Teams of young people were sent out by Joseph Jenkins into neighbouring churches and the fire spread to Blaenannerch, Newcastle Emlyn, Capel Drindod and Twrgwyn. Many of the young people were between the ages of 16 and 18 and many were young girls. Joseph Jenkins had been in the Rhondda in his youth; at the very least he would have heard how the valleys had been shaken by Kate Shepherd and the women of the Salvation Army. It is possible that this made him more open to the involvement of young women in the teams that he took all over Cardiganshire and North Wales.

In September Evan Roberts and his friend Sidney Evans went to the Grammar school in Newcastle Emlyn to become educated enough to become chapel ministers. At the same time in Newcastle Emlyn, Seth Joshua was holding a mission followed by a conference in Blaenannerch.

Sidney Evans came under real conviction in the Newcastle Emlyn meetings. "I preach Christ as Saviour - do I know Him thus myself?" Although he felt compelled to pray at Joshua's meeting and had been urged by Maud Davies and Florrie Evans of Newquay to make open confession of Christ, it was only after a severe conflict that he submitted at the Wednesday night meeting... "I got up on my feet shouting "I love Jesus Christ and give myself entirely to Him". There was no sleep that night with the sheer joy and anticipation of going to Blaenannerch the following morning." [4]

The young women having been through such depth of experience themselves, were desperate that others should know salvation, the assurance of salvation and baptism in the Holy Spirit.

It was at Blaenannerch that Evan Roberts was to have the encounter with God that would turn a nation.

"The young women from Newquay tried to influence me, but nothing touched me. And they said, "We can do nothing for you?" "No," said I. "I have only to wait for the fire. I have built the altar

and laid the wood in order, and have prepared the offering. I have only to wait for the fire." About half past nine the next morning the fire fell and it is burning ever since..We started for Blaenannerch about six o'clock Thursday morning. Now joyful, now sad, now hard and cold - so my feelings varied on the journey that morning. We sang in the break and my feelings were very varied - now high, now low. The seven o'clock meeting was devoted to asking and answering questions. The Rev. W. W. Lewis conducted. At the close the Rev. Seth Joshua prayed and said during his prayer, "Lord, do this and this, and this and bend us." It was the Spirit that put the emphasis for me on "Bend us". "That is what you need" said the Spirit to me. And as I went out I prayed, "O Lord bend me". At the breakfast table at the Rev.M.P. Morgan's house Mag Phillips offered me bread and butter and the thought struck me, "Is it possible that God is offering me the Spirit and that I am unprepared to receive Him; that others are ready to receive, but are not offered?" Now my bosom was quite full-tight. On the way to the nine o'clock meeting the Rev. Seth Joshua remarked, "We are going to have a wonderful meeting today." To this I replied, "I feel myself almost bursting." The meeting, having been opened, was handed over to the Spirit. I was conscious that I would have to pray. As one and the other prayed I put the question to the Spirit, "Shall I pray now?", "Wait a while" said He. When others prayed I felt a living force come into my bosom. It held my breath and my legs shivered, and after every prayer I asked, "Shall I now?" The living force grew and grew and I was almost bursting. And instantly someone ended his prayer - my bosom boiling. I would have burst if I had not prayed. What boiled me was that verse, "God commending His love". I fell on my knees with my arms over the seat in front of me and the tears and perspiration flowed freely. I thought blood was gushing forth. Mrs. Davies, Mona, Newquay, came to wipe my face. On my right was Mag Phillips and on my left Maud Davies. For about two minutes it was fearful. I cried, "Bend me! Bend me! bend us! Then Oh! Oh! Oh!" and Mrs. Davies said, "O wonderful Grace!" "Yes" I said, "O wonderful Grace!" What bent me was God commending His love and I not seeing anything in it to commend. After I was bent a wave of peace came over me and the audience sang, "I hear

Thy welcome voice". As they sang I thought of the bending at the judgement day, and I was filled with compassion for those who would be bent on that day, and I wept...Henceforth the salvation of souls became the burden of my heart. From that time I was on fire with a desire to go through all Wales, and if it were possible I was willing to pay God for allowing me to go. A plan was agreed upon, and eight of us were to go through Wales and I was to pay all the expenses." [4]

The Newquay girls were instrumental in provoking both Sidney's encounter with God and also Evan's. It is not surprising that Evan and Sidney wanted them to be part of the team that would go around Wales sharing the gospel. They were "Carriers of the Fire" an integral part of the teams they envisaged. Apart from Sidney and Evan the rest of the team were to be women:

Maud Davies
Elsie Phillips
Mary C. Jones
Miss Davies
Mrs. Davies, Mona, Newquay
Florrie Evans
Mrs. Evans, Newquay

Evan had saved two hundred pounds, which he thought would fund ten workers for twenty eight weeks.

Releasing of teams and the place of women in those teams proved to be a major force and feature in the way the Revival spread. This planned mission around Wales didn't take place as Evan Roberts was led to go back to Loughor. However, although plans changed, which was also a feature of the Revival, the desired outcome was the same - a nation transformed by Jesus. Those listed for the original team all became workers in the Revival, with Maud Davies, Florrie

Evans and Sidney Evans taking particularly significant roles.

Evan was writing regularly at this time to Mary, his youngest sister, and the letters show his concern for her spiritual well being and his concern for the spiritual well being of the young women at Loughor.

"*Last Thursday's meeting, Blaenannerch, was the most awful and pleasant day of my life. The young women of Newquay were there - about thirty in number. And Oh! I should like such a spirit would fall on the young women of Loughor. Then they would not and could not speak lightly in church and all their frivolity would be swept away. Would you not, Mary, pray for such a spirit. Some of these young women have been reckless characters. Reading novels, flirting, never reading their Bibles. But now what a wonderful change. In truth this is a divine miracle. In concluding I wish you such a spirit, from your brother Evan.*" [5]

He encouraged Mary to change by pointing to the changed lives, the testimony, of the Newquay women. The transformed lives of women would again and again be used as a provocation to others. Mary in the next week was to experience her own miracle.

Letter to Mary Roberts, October 28th, 1904:

"*Well I can't tell you how busy the devil is at this place. I have told you before how we have met the young girls from Newquay at Newcastle and at Blaenannerch and at Twrgwyn. They, the people of this place make such stories which are downright lies. Some say we go to see the young girls and not for the cause. Others ask (but not in our faces) how it is that we three and not others have felt so? And others say it is only shaming we do as also the Newquay people. Others so make light of these spiritual things...It would be a treat for you if you could hear these young ladies from Newquay when they pray. They are so earnest, so simple and not in the least nervous. How should you like to pray in Pisgah? (A smaller chapel linked to Moriah) You and Alice and Sarah and Miss Jordan? You walking on, reading a hymn, and reading the Bible and praying - as you never heard any person pray, and fearless. But first you must feel that you are a lost sinner and then feel that Christ died for you, and last of all that you must have the baptism of the Holy Spirit and then work.. Your true and affectionate brother, Evan John Roberts."* [6]

This letter signals the beginning of the controversy that would continue throughout the Revival about the involvement of women. It was a controversy around the issue of "this isn't the way things are done" and a questioning of the motives and capabilities of those involved. He also urges Mary to do something she would have never done before, actively minister as a young woman by taking part in a meeting. He writes simply of the three steps he encouraged all to enter into in the Revival: salvation, the Baptism of the Holy Spirit and then action. He wrote to her in private, the challenges he would bring to many in public. He made it clear that as a young girl she was not exempt from any of the steps.

Mary Roberts

What happened to Evan in Blaenannerch convinced him even further of the importance of the baptism of the Holy Spirit.

"The baptism of the Holy Spirit is the essence of revival, for revival comes from a knowledge of the Holy Spirit and a way of co-working with Him which enables Him to work in revival power. The primary condition of revival is that believers should know the baptism of the Holy Ghost." [7]

His embracing of the baptism of the Holy Spirit was the primary reason for his full involvment of women in the move of God. They were included in the outpouring "on all flesh". therefore their inclusion meant responsibilities to be enjoyed and outworked.

Evan wrote to Florrie to let her know why he was leaving Newcastle Emlyn to return to Loughor.

"Dear Florrie, a word in haste. I am going home this morning to work among our young people for a week. The reason for that is - that the Spirit wants me to go. I was in the six o'clock service Sunday, and the Spirit brought the case of our young people before me so powerfully that it was impossible for me to keep my mind from it...I should be glad if you could have a meeting on our behalf for our Lord Jesus' sake...I have been asking God if it would be better for some of you to come to Loughor with me, but He did not answer in the affirmative. Yours in Christ, Evan John Roberts."[8]

Evan had obviously wanted the Newquay women to come to Loughor with him and his letters show that he viewed them as co-workers, wanting them to pray for the work, even if it wasn't right for them to join him at that point.

Evan's family were so concerned about his return home that they thought he was either ill or going mad. When he said he was planning to "go through Wales to offer Christ to sinners" his mother remarked, "If you do that you will have no money to go back to school because you will have spent it all." "Oh," replied he, "My heavenly Father has plenty."

He asked Dan and Mary to go to the meeting that night. Dan said no because of his weak eyes (Evan had prayed for them earlier and from that time they grew stronger). This is the first, and perhaps most significant, healing recorded in the Revival. Prophetically the healing of sight could also have spoken of the need to see things through clear eyes in the new landscape the Holy Spirit was defining. A landscape of freedom in the Holy Spirit, a landscape viewed through the love and goodness of God. A landscape in which all could be reached by the love of Jesus and all involved in proclaiming His love and demonstrating it to others.

"I am not coming," said Mary "because I must do my lessons." "Well" he remarked, "you will lose the blessings if you do not come." Later, relating it to D.M. Phillips, Mary said she did not know what he was going on about "when speaking about blessing and being filled with the Holy Spirit and such things". I wonder how many times homework has been used as an excuse to nearly miss a revival!

In the end, because of their concern for him, four of his family went to the first meetings; his mother and Sarah went to the seven o'clock meeting and Dan and Mary joined Evan at the eight o'clock meeting for young people. It was in this meeting that seventeen young people including a little girl were impacted. The Revival had started.

This is the account of Hannah Hughes, one of the young people involved:

"He asked us to confess Jesus Christ as our Saviour. The thing was entirely new to me. I did not understand it, but I accepted everything from him because I looked up to him as a boy out of the ordinary, and he meant everything he said. The meeting went on until 10.30pm and there was much concern in our house because I had not arrived home. "Young people or not" my mother said, "I'll be there tomorrow night." Soon the big showers came of course, with people crying out for forgiveness, making up old quarrels, paying their debts."[10]

The young people stirred the hunger, or at least the curiosity of their parents and the Revival momentum grew.

There was also dramatic change in his own family; they started to meet to pray together, his father praying out loud for the first time in front of his family. Evan said of Mary, "My sister, a girl of 16, who before was a sarcastic and peevish girl, has had a grand change and her testimony is that she is happy now and that there is some joy in living...The great feature of this work is that people are being awakened and learning to obey."[11]

The emphasis on obedience again and again gave children, young people and women the same dignity, but also the same responsibility as men in how they worked out their salvation.

Evan was close to Mary, he had spent a lot of time looking after her when she was a baby as his mother had been very ill when she was born. Mary became one of the main workers alongside him in the Revival. Her presence also made it acceptable for other women to travel with him as part of the Revival Teams - he was certainly used to having sisters around!

Hannah, his mother, was deeply troubled, then deeply changed by the Revival. The baptism in the Holy Spirit was her defining moment. His mother went to several Revival meetings and stayed in one until three o'clock but then walked out. Her son followed her out as if to shut the door and he said to her, "Are you going home now?" She pointed out rather sharply that everyone in the village was asleep because they would have to go to work at 5am, but when she went to bed she grieved over her words and could not rest until Evan came into her room at 5am and she and her son prayed together. Tudor Rees, a family friend of theirs and a recorder of the Revival, tells the sequel:

Hannah Roberts

"One day after having spent some time on his knees in his tiny room, Evan went out to his mother. Placing his hand on her shoulder he said with a tremor in his voice and a strange light in his eyes, "Mother, you have been a Christian a good many years and a good Christian mother you have been. But mother, there is one thing more that you need." Mrs. Roberts, astonished and visibly affected, looked into her son's face and wistfully queried what this one thing was. He answered, "Mam, the one thing more that you need is the baptism of the Holy Ghost." So unexpected was the message and so strangely was it uttered that the mother said little if anything to her son about what he spoke. "For eight days I pondered his words over in my heart, mentioned the incident to nobody, and prayed that He

would baptise me with His Holy Spirit. Day after day I uttered that petition. The heavens seemed as brass and there was no answer. But the eighth day the fire descended and my joy knew no bounds. Oh what a change has come over me, and not only me but the whole family since then."[12]

In the first two weeks of the Revival all the main elements came into place, including the role of prayer, and the role of children which he communicated in a letter to Florrie:

"All our children at Moriah are every night and morning praying this beautiful prayer given to me by the Holy Spirit: "Send the Spirit to Moriah for Jesus Christ's sake." Now you also teach your children to pray this prayer. Do not attempt to make it longer because it is a prayer given by the Holy Spirit."[13]

It was clear that he was discipling and instructing Florrie as to how to proceed. He regarded the women as co-workers from the first, encouraging them to take responsibility. The gospel was no longer being hindered by the false separation of "separate spheres" in the work of the Kingdom. There was a development of true partnership and co-working between men and women, young and old. All were responsible to be disciples and to disciple others. He also wrote to Sidney Evans regarding the steps to take in the Revival meetings as initially, Sidney Evans had stayed on in Newcastle Emlyn.

"Establish Revival meetings there, call the denominations together. Explain "The Four Conditions":

1.If there is past sin or sins hitherto unconfessed we cannot receive the Spirit. Therefore we must search, and ask the Spirit to search. 2.If there is anything doubtful in our lives it must be removed. Anything we are uncertain about, its rightness or wrongness, that thing must be removed. 3.An entire giving up of ourselves to the Spirit; we must speak and do all that He requires of us. 4.Public confession of Christ. And at the end of the meeting let all who have confessed Christ remain behind and initiate the round of prayer.

Take care that each one prays:
1.Send the Spirit now for Jesus Christ's sake;
2.Send the Spirit powerfully now for Jesus Christ's sake;
3.Send the Spirit more powerfully now for Jesus Christ's sake;
4.Send the Spirit still more powerfully now for Jesus Christ's sake."[14]

This form of prayer would have had its roots more in early monasticism than in the tradition within which he grew up. The simplicity of this prayer "crafted" by the Holy Spirit was dynamite when it was prayed out by those who had previously been silent witnesses in the face of the power of God.

In a letter to Sidney on November 7th he described what happened in one of the early meetings in Loughor when they prayed this prayer:

"During this time Mary Parry was on her feet, handkerchief in hand, leading the singing - the people it seems singing too slowly to please her. Before she was quiet and retired, but now she is completely changed! ..Then we added to the prayer, "Send the Spirit more powerfully for Jesus Christ's sake". The prayer begins its journey. And Oh! What effect! The Spirit was coming nearer and nearer all the while. On this journey the Spirit descended on two sisters and Oh it descended with power! They were shouting aloud - shouting as I have never heard anyone shout before. The prayer was not allowed to finish its journey around. The people were in a circle around them, there was a sight! The people looked amazed and terrified while I smiled, saying "Oh there is no danger"...and on the way out Elizabeth Rees broke out into weeping, being filled with the Spirit, and would have fallen had not some of her friends held her." [15]

The power of testimony released the beginnings of the Revival through Florrie Evans and remained a key feature. Everyone could have a testimony, including women. The emphasis on giving a verbal declaration of faith pushed women to speak rather than keep silent. There was a boldness that came in speaking out and even in shouting out as the young girls did in the previous passage. This would have been contrary to everything they would have known of chapel. Their response wasn't contrary, however, to a powerful baptism in the Holy Spirit! A new boldness in the women was there from the earliest days of the meetings in Loughor.

Evan saw this as a fulfilment of the prophecy of Joel that in the last days "God would pour out His Spirit on all flesh." His emphasis on this released women to move in radical obedience. Gender was not an excuse for disobedience. In Pentre on December 4th he said, "You must do anything and everything, anywhere and everywhere."[16]

In the beginning of the Revival people seemed to receive the gift of God regardless of who was carrying it. This meant that even those who, outside of a revival setting would have been most despised, the women and the young, were received because of the anointing they were carrying. It was as if in daring to be used, in humbling themselves and breaking barriers of convention and fear, the Father dramatically raised them up. Evan's preaching in later meetings further validated their involvement,

"In the afternoon meeting he spoke for an hour, emphasising the "idea that the members of the Christian Church were all one family...and met as one family around one hearth." The use of domestic images again gave a place for both women and children. At another time he said, "In this movement we are one happy family, and children play quite as important a part in it as they do in the home. No more sectarianism. We have been fighting each other long enough. We shall have more time to fight the devil henceforth." In Hafod on Friday December 16th he told this story..."He said that one evening while at Loughor he walked from his home down to the Post Office, and on his way passed a gypsy woman who saluted him with "Good evening, Sir". The word "Sir" went straight to his heart, and he asked himself why, in acknowledging this kindly salutation, he had not said, "Good evening Madam." From that moment he had felt his heart was full of the divine love and that

he could love the whole world, irrespective of colour or creed or nationality. The world was changed to him now." [17]

The world was "changed" not only to him but to the women who had been part of lighting the Revival fuse, to the young people who had been released, and to those who found themselves in a Revival unlike one they had heard of or seen before. A Revival with echoes of the past but one which was also creating a new landscape. A landscape where the disempowered were finding new room as they risked a bold obedience. The young, and the women had found their voice; the revolution was now visible, for those with eyes to see . The different elements formed in the crucible of the early Revival weeks would pour out in even greater strength as the teams of revivalists were released.

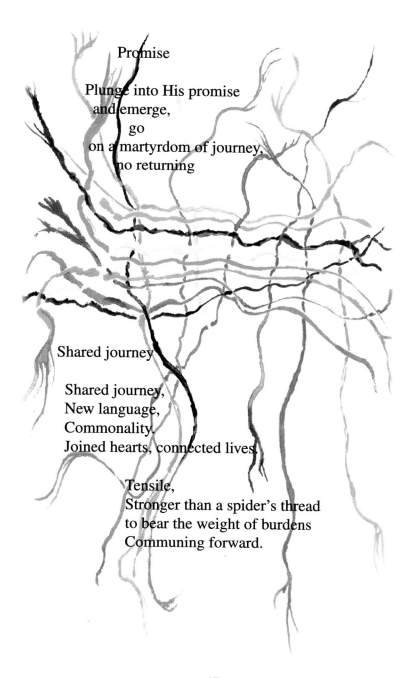

Promise

Plunge into His promise
and emerge,
        go
on a martyrdom of journey,
    no returning

Shared journey

Shared journey,
New language,
Commonality.
Joined hearts, connected lives.

Tensile,
Stronger than a spider's thread
to bear the weight of burdens
Communing forward.

4

Releasing the Teams

The release of teams in the Revival of 1904 blasted the "slate-like" quarries of religious respectability. In the twenty-first century, the release of teams and team ministry may not seem very radical, we may even be overfed and bored with the concept. At the time of the Revival it was dynamite - a blowing up of the safe religious order!

"Team" was in and, for an all too brief moment, "One man ministry" was out. Mixed teams affronted the religious propriety of the day, but didn't affront the Holy Spirit who had orchestrated them.

It was a time when the Holy Spirit played congregations like a harp, drawing worship, prayer and testimony from those who didn't have titles; drawing a sound regardless of age or gender, social standing or education. It was a sound drawn from those who found themselves in the midst of a river they didn't understand, occasionally tried to control but mostly allowed to sweep over them. A river in which many found faith and many touched destiny.

The release of teams demonstrated in a visible and unmistakable form that it was time for the Body of Christ to operate as a Body. It was a loud, clear and untidy sign of greater release to come.

Evan Roberts, himself, clearly felt comfortable with teams. When Evan was returning to Loughor he had obviously wanted Florrie and others to join him but felt no release to ask them. Teams were clearly in his thinking as a Biblical model of ministry, appropriate to a time of the Holy Spirit's outpouring. However, the initiative for teams did not rest solely with Evan. In the first two weeks of the Revival, Mary

Roberts had already become one of its main workers. Other women also started to take initiative, not only in the meetings but also out on the streets. The explosions of life in countless initiatives, many never recorded, had begun.

On Saturday 12th November a group of women revivalists went into the pubs and into the streets. Crowds quickly gathered. There was deep conviction amongst those who listened - men and women started crying like children.

"But perhaps the most remarkable service of the day was that held in the middle of a large gypsy encampment on Kingsbridge Common (near Gorseinon). The dwellers in tents received the missioners with a degree of suspicion which augered ill for the success of the service. Before the meeting had been long in progress, however, this suspicion gave way to wonderment, and later on to devout awe. Then came paroxysms of grief from female members of the encampment, some of them tearing their hair in their self-denunciations. When the meeting came to a close a collection was made on behalf of the poor gypsies and a promise was given them that another service would be held on Saturday afternoon." [1]

However, it was in a Gorseinon meeting that five young women came forward to give themselves to God's work in the Revival, as singers. It would seem that before then, Evan had no deliberate plans to use singers. Yet from that time on he was associated with "The Singing Evangelists".

The Llanelly Mercury of December 1st, 1904 gives a description of them which was also reported in the South Wales Daily News.

The five included Priscilla Watkins described as a minister's sister-in-law, Sunday school teacher, choir member and chapel organist. Her decision to give up her job as a school teacher to join the Revival missions caused quite a stir, although the school managers did seem to understand!

"At a meeting of the managers of the Gowerton group of schools on Wednesday it was reported that one of the teachers at Penyrheol

School, Gorseinon, had departed with the revivalists without tendering notice...The opinion was expressed that the action of the teacher in question was excusable, that no legal steps be taken against her and that she be paid her salary in full up to the time of leaving."[2]

Lavinia Looker was eight years old when her mother died. She was now 21 years old and a dress maker. She taught in the Sunday school and was a member of the choir, but "until lately had been too retiring to sing a solo in the chapel."

There were two named Mary Davies! The first was from the Post Office in Lower Gorseinon. She was a Sunday school teacher and a Board Teacher for a while. She was the daughter of a prominent Anglican who also got involved in the Revival. She was not very strong healthwise and soon returned from the tour, giving much time to "religious painting". In the aftermath of the Revival she took care of the converts and in the late 1920's was instrumental in the outbreak of a second, smaller revival.

The second Mary Davies was a daughter of Mr. Thomas Davies, "a mason from Penyrheol, Gorseinon". She was 23 and a member of Brynteg Chapel, Gorseinon. Her father, concerned about her involvement in the meetings in the Rhondda, went to see her to ask her to return home. "Do you compel me?" she said, "I'm going to preach the gospel." He felt he couldn't argue with that and she remained involved in the work!

Annie May Rees born in Cwmbwrla, Swansea was adopted by her grandmother when she was six months old. They moved to live in Gorseinon when she was seven. She was the daughter of the phrenologist[3] "Professor Rees" who advertised his practice in the Llanelly Mercury during the Revival years. Annie May was trained in elocution and poetry reading as well as singing. She was 15 years old when she got involved in the Revival.

The shortness of time since their conversion was no hindrance to their involvement. The raising up of teams also gave rise to new challenges and to new ways of working. It was radical for mixed teams to travel together. There were safeguards in place in that they stayed with families and in ministers' houses. However, it did raise questions. Evan's behaviour towards the women was very respectful and he was obviously used to having sisters around. The newspapers called him the "transparent man" and although there were whisperings, he gave no ground for scandal. The new landscape which gave room for women to take part in this way also led to an exploration of new ways of working. There was inevitably a fast learning curve as effective team work developed. There were of course rumours that it didn't always work smoothly between the different team members. Emphasis being placed on the fact that they were women and therefore jealousy and tension was only to be expected! This is not necessarily the case! There is no clear evidence of tension, however team ministry involving different skills and mutual submission to one another was bound to have provoked some sparks! Seasons of revival don't turn human beings into "super saints", in fact the issues often seem to become more heightened, if not also more painful!

Evan hadn't expected to have singing evangelists travelling with him, but they did, and shaped the course of the Revival alongside him.

On November 13th the pastor of the Calvinistic Methodists in Trecynon, Aberdare, asked if Evan Roberts might be available to take the services as they had been let down by someone. So on Sunday morning, after an all-night service on the Saturday, Evan caught the train for Aberdare with the five young converts. The sedate congregation were shocked when the revivalist and two young ladies stood at the front. There was a heavy sense of disapproval. They didn't announce the usual hymn. Instead, one of the young ladies started to sing a song which conveyed her new-found faith. She started sobbing and a strange stillness fell in the church "like the quiet presaging an electrical storm".[4]

Again and again it was the action of a woman that sparked breakthrough in a meeting. Why this was so I am not sure, maybe it was their abandonment to God in acts of obedience, despite their own fears.

A prominent and proud member of the congregation broke down, confessing her sins, and the Revival broke open in a storm of prayer, singing and confession of sins continuing throughout the day.

This was the beginning of "team", with an easy flow between the different team members as meetings progressed. From early November services are described as conducted by "Evan Roberts and the five young singing evangelists who accompany him."

There was a real sense of disappointment, not only if Evan Roberts didn't turn up at a meeting, but also if the "lady evangelists" were absent. As in Ogmore, "contrary to expectation, and much to the disappointment of many, neither Mr. Roberts nor the young ladies attended. The meeting nevertheless was an excellent one."[5]

Evan Roberts and the revivalists

Volume One of the Western Mail Revival Report describes the "Singing Evangelists" like this:

"The young ladies who accompany him are not professional singers; but they are manifestly touched with the spirit of singing pilgrims, and in the summing up of the strangeness of the power thus introduced, one can only be reminded of the story of the humble origin of the disciples of old, as "the fishermen of the Sea of Galilee"."

There is the well known photo of "Mr. Evan Roberts and the Group of Lady Revivalists", which is a striking statement in itself, particularly in the era in which they lived.

In the newspapers, over the course of time, there were photographs of numerous other Revival soloists. Often, frustratingly little was said about them. These include Miss May John; Madame Kate Morgan; Miss Edith Jones, Emlyn House, Ynysybwl; Miss Mattie Williams, Pontypridd; Miss C.A. Jones, Ynysybwl; and the 15 year old Miss Gwennie John. There were also photos of the more well known singers like Annie and Maggie Davies.

It would seem that there were more female than male soloists, unless the newspapers were more taken with the "pin-up" factor, or at the very least the novelty value of female revivalists! Evan Roberts himself was certainly a focus, with many people requesting his autograph. He appeared on many of the Revival souvenirs produced at that time. The first newspaper report of the Revival was on November 11th, and from that time on the newspaper reporting played a significant role in the spread of the Revival. The prominence of the women in the Revival reports must have encouraged other women that they too had a part to play.

Florrie Evans' breakthrough released teams of women, influenced Evan Roberts and released a "permissioning" in the Spirit. An underground movement that had cut a path within the Temperance Movement was now springing up all over the nation. In Wales, the women of the Salvation Army had been regarded as exceptional in leading the way. The "exceptional" was now becoming the "normal" as women all over the nation started to move into their destiny.

From the first weeks of the Revival other teams started to form. Sidney Evans returned to Gorseinon on Saturday November 12th and he and Evan ministered together in Loughor for one night, although in different buildings. Sidney had not been sure if Florrie Evans and Maud Davies would be able to join him from Newcastle Emlyn. He was starting to lead Revival meetings in his home church of Libanus, Gorseinon, as Evan left for Trecynon. To his relief, Maud and Florrie arrived on the Tuesday and took part, singing and praying.

The early influence from Newcastle Emlyn had shaped Sidney. He too allowed a real freedom to the Holy Spirit and chose to work in team with these two women and others.

"The meetings in Gorseinon were left in the hands of Sidney Evans "and a number of female assistants" after Evan Roberts left for Trecynon. Prayer meetings had been held daily in the steel works...at night between shifts a meeting was held, workmen all grimy, imploring divine pardon...One of the lady missioners raised the meetings to fever heat as she read the last chapter of Revelation with its wonderful description of "the river of the water of life, clear as crystal, proceeding out of the throne of God and of the Lamb...And there shall be no more night there, and they need no candle, neither light of the sun." The scene indeed was an impressive one. All around was the murky gloom of the works, the blackness here and there being relieved by furnace fires before which stood out, illumined, the shadowy figures of the men. Above the whir of the huge wheels and the heavy lumbering of the rolls was heard the familiar strains of a hymn."[6]

Sidney Evans is also mentioned in an article in the Llanelly Mercury, December 29th, 1904 which appears under the title, "The Maesteg Songsters at Gorseinon."

"*A meeting was held at Libanus Methodist Chapel, Gorseinon on Sunday night. The minister was away and therefore no sermon was preached. But Mr. Sidney Evans, a revivalist, was in the pulpit and read a portion of the scriptures and then said that the meeting was open. Following this Miss Maggie Davies...sang a Welsh hymn which brought tears to the eyes of nearly all in the edifice. Then a young man went to the Sêt Fawr[7] and said that he was very glad to be a Christian. He had a godly mother who used to pray for him...he used to laugh at her...he used to fight with his friends but now he prayed for them...Then a lady from Newquay prayed very earnestly on behalf of those who had not been saved...A young lady asked for prayer for her father, as did his wife. The father was weeping, and later on when Sidney Evans went to speak to him he was converted...A woman rose and said, "O I feel as if I should like to jump to heaven. I have never enjoyed my Christmas so well, but the fact is I did not know Jesus so well.*"

The initial influence of the Newquay women was profound in the way it shaped the multiplication of teams of men and women all over Wales, not only amongst the well known revivalists like Evan and Sidney and Dan Roberts, Evan's brother, but also amongst the less well known.

The team who accompanied Dan Roberts included Maggie Davies, Annie Davies' sister:

"*Miss Maggie Davies is the elder of the Maesteg sisters, whose singing in connection with the great meetings of Evan Roberts at the start formed such an important feature of the revival. Miss Maggie Davies' position in these meetings of Mr. Dan Roberts is almost as important from the vocal point of view as that of Miss Annie Davies at Mr. Evan Roberts' meetings. Miss Maggie Davies, however, does not confine herself to singing, for she is a useful all-round evangelist. Last but by no means least comes Miss S.A. Jones of Nantymoel, whose career as an evangelist dates from that extraordinary meeting at the Bridgend town hall, where the little band of workers from Pontycymer and Maesteg had been left to begin their first day's work on their own account after Mr. Evans*

S.A. Jones	Maggie Davies	Mary Davies
(Nantymoel)	(Maesteg)	(Gorseinon)

had left for Pyle. Miss Jones was a few days previously "a frivolous girl, very frivolous", as she said to me when she went over the story at that time. But she is now not only one of the most earnest, but actually the most fervent, torrential, striking speaker - practical and pithy in address and powerful in prayer - of the little band of girls who are supporting Mr. Evan Roberts, Mr. Dan Roberts and Mr. Sidney Evans in that great work."[8]

Evan Roberts was also quite specific about his guidance in taking teams with him.

"Only the previous day he had one matter on his mind concerning some who tried to come to these meetings in his shadow. He thought he had no right to stop anyone, but the Spirit told him no-one must come except the two young ladies who accompanied him, as it would otherwise be partiality on his part, and that would not do. Annie Davies and Mary Davies both spoke and gave their testimonies. Mary's was "undoubtedly interesting. She raised a hearty laugh when she declared that before her conversion she went to hear Evan Roberts simply because she had heard that he was "off his head". She had been "off her head" since then herself, and gloried in it. She was even before her conversion a very regular attendant at the services - as regular as the minister."[10]

Teams and team ministry were prominent throughout the time of the Revival, and very quickly developed to the place where women were taking meetings on their own in Wales and in other parts of Britain.

The release of the teams was spontaneous and fast moving. It was a spontaneity born in part out of a growing hunger of many within and outside of Wales to connect to the outpouring. People were desperate to connect with those who were carrying the fire so invitations came from many places and opportunities opened up. Radical obedience to the Holy Spirit was opening up new pathways and new connections for men and women alike. Open doors ignited further passion to see the lost saved as the church yielded across the nation. As the church yielded and the lost were saved, the teams provided a new shape as to how the Body of Christ might act and move.

The church was becoming more fluid and more mobile, more able to respond to the needs of the hour. More space was being created for men and women to taste something of their destiny and to work with others to see a harvest come in. More space was created for each person to know they had a part to play, and to understand the giftings and responsibilities which were theirs to fulfill within the Body of Christ.

Alongside the harvest, there was a fresh flexing of intent which, by the end of the twentieth century had led to new models of ministry and new wineskins among large sections of the church worldwide. The multiplication of teams within the Revival acted as part of the catalyst to this changed landscape. A landscape which is painfully reshaping once again for the very different century in which we now live.

It is time for a canopy of
continuous prayer and worship
to be raised over this land
so that the harvest can come safely in.
Unending Song,
Unending Harvest.
It is time for the underground streams
to be cleansed, wells of bitterness
and strife to be converted to sweet water,
immersion in clean anointings
 of generations past.
New springs rising - cleansed
land stirring.

5

Unending Song

A new sound carrying echoes of earlier times was heard in the land. It was the sound of many voices flowing as one in worship, an unending song of tears and joy.

"Out on the roads I could hear companies of people going down to Aberdare and singing. Companies going to the east and to the north and to Cwmdare. About 4 o'clock I went home and I could hear companies in the early morning singing with all their might. I went to bed but could hardly sleep, and when I did I was laughing for joy in my sleep and I got up in the morning full of joy."[1]

The joy that Grawys Jones, a minister from Aberdare felt was echoed in the hearts of many.

"In all Wales songs of praise raised in ceaseless chorus from the burning hearts of countless thousands were heard in homes and churches and even in the coal mines. There are few if any parallels with this mighty outpouring of religious fervor bringing a whole nation to its knees at the foot of the cross in adoration and praise...Such marvellous singing, quite unrehearsed, could only be created by the Holy Spirit. No choir, no conductor, no organ, just spontaneous, unctionised soul-singing. Singing, sobbing, praying intermingled with intercession."[2]

Women's voices were heard in the chapels as they sang. Yet in the Revival, as they came to Christ, trained singers and soloists became worshippers in ways they had never known before. This was certainly true of Annie Davies who is the person most identified with the worship during the Revival and with the hymn "Dyma Gariad"[3] (Here is Love). It is this hymn which captured the heartcry of the nation.

Annie Davies, from Maesteg, was eighteen when she

was converted and drawn into the move of God. She was the daughter of Richard and Hannah Davies of Nantyffyllon, Maesteg. Her father was a miner, an underground lamp man. He was musical, a conductor of singing at Zoar Congregational Chapel, which Annie attended with her sister Maggie. Annie had been trained in singing in Dowlais with Mr.H. Davies, and in Cardiff with Madame Clara Novello. The newspapers of the time noted all these details. Certainly her training helped in the techniques she sometimes used - "whispered" singing in "Flee as a Bird" and dramatic presentations of songs such as "The Dear Little Bible".

Annie Davies

In a letter to D.M. Phillips, January 10, 1906 she explained how she got involved in the Revival. She decided to go to hear Evan Roberts when he was at Pontycymer on the 17th November, and on the way there on the train the tune "Britain's Lament" came into her mind along with the words of "Dyma Gariad". She had to wait for two hours to get into the meeting because of the crowds, and when she saw her sister Maggie she realised that "Maggie's soul was in great agony, it was evident that the Spirit of God was working within her". Annie, however, was simply full of curiosity, yet indifferent to the heart of what was happening.

"Just before closing Mr. Roberts asked all those who could stand up and say in their own hearts that they loved Jesus above everything else to do so. My sister and I sat together and our first impulse was to get up and show that we were of those who could stand up and say so, but we were checked from doing so. An irresistible power

kept us from doing so. Soon after the meeting closed, but I felt very unhappy, conscience spoke very loudly to me, it told me that I had betrayed my Saviour. I had been a member for years before but had not done anything for the glory of God. I felt God could never forgive my countless sins. I tried to sleep and forget all about the meetings but found it impossible to do so. I knew things would have to get different from what they were then as everything seemed empty to me. I had to find peace or die.

I was counting every hour before the time arrived for the second meeting. At last the time came. When entering the chapel I knew there was a great power working there, my soul was moved to its depths, my tears flowed freely when the Rev. David Hughes asked me and said, "Cana rhywbeth Annie" ("Sing something Annie"). With an irresistible force I leapt from my seat and sang "Here is love vast as the ocean" to the tune "Britain's Lament". I could not finish it as I was sobbing too much, I could not refrain from weeping throughout the meeting.

After coming out, Miss S.A. Jones, Nantymoel met us. We had never met before but she felt compelled to speak to us, and in the short time she told my sister and me how she felt. It happened that she felt very similar to what we did, we three felt drawn to each other immediately. We felt a great desire to consecrate our voices to the Master. We met Mr. Roberts and told him of our desire. He told us to pray about it and ask to be led in the right path. We went again to the afternoon meeting. I felt a wonderful peace filling my soul and could not refrain from taking part. I felt convinced that God had called me to the work. I remain yours in the service, Annie Davies."[4]

Maggie Davies, S.A. John and Annie Davies

Annie Davies accompanied Evan Roberts to Abergwynfi. Indeed, from that time onwards she travelled with him throughout most of the Revival.

"The visits of Evan Roberts and his Singing Evangelists appear to be merely what he himself so aptly described them as, "opening the doors" of the revival for the work which is carried on by others. The work is becoming vast in its extent and wonderfully effective in its operations. People who attend the meetings get "fired" with the zeal of the revival and proceed to the neighbourhoods in which they live, and spread the infection wherever they go, not only in the churches but in the works, in the streets, in the trains and the subject has become, especially in the mining valleys, the principal topic of conversation among all classes of the community...The only gospel promulgated is the gospel of love, and the most effective sermon heard on Sunday beyond question was the performance of a young girl with a beautiful voice at Abercynon, singing with the most thrilling pathos:

"Dyma gariad fel y moroedd,	*Here is love, vast as the ocean,*
Tosturiaethau fel y lli;	*Loving kindness as the flood;*
T'wysog bywyd pur yn marw	*When the Prince of life, our ransom*
Marw i brynu'n bywyd ni:	*Shed for us His precious blood.*
Pwy all beidio â chofio amdano?	*Who His love will not remember?*
Pwy all beidio â thraethu'i glod?	*Who can cease to sing His praise?*
Dyma gariad nad â'n anghof	*He can never be forgotten*
Tra fo nefoedd wen yn bod."	*Throughout heaven's eternal days.*

"It was all the more effective because the words and the music expressed the thoughts of all, and because the hymn expresses in eight lines the real gist of the gospel of this revival. The second verse was equally powerful and frequently sung:

"Ar Galfaria yr ymrwygodd	*On the mount of crucifixion*
Holl ffynhonnau'r clyfnder mawr.	*Fountains opened deep and wide.*
Torrodd holl argaeau'r nefoedd	*Through the floodgates of God's mercy*
Oedd yn gyfain hyd yn awr:	*Flowed a vast and gracious tide.*
Gras a chariad megis dilyw	*Grace and love, like mighty rivers*
Yn ymdywallt yma 'nghyd;	*Poured incessant from above;*
A chyfiawnder pur a heddwch	*And heaven's peace and perfect justice*
Yn cusanu euog fyd.[5]	*Kissed a guilty world in love."*

"Dr. W. Morris said, "Calvary is the key note of the anthem. "Here is love vast as the ocean" is the rallying point of the new world. The simple gospel of the Father, the Son and the Holy Spirit as we heard it in our childhood, as we experienced it in the revivals of 1859, 1876 and 1879."[6]

In Ynysybwl in the 2 o'clock meeting some reckoned that one of the highest points of the Revival was reached when Annie sang "Dyma Gariad" whilst a man was simultaneously praying with great power. The intensity of the singing and the praying fused the meeting to a white heat.

"Later on, when in the midst of a powerful prayer, one man asked the Lord to enable them all to realise the greatness of the sacrifice of Jesus Christ, Miss Davies, very gently and with quivering voice sang, "Dyma gariad fel yr moroedd" and then she stopped, but presently added the second line, "Tosturiaethau fel y lli", and there was another pause, as if she were playing a touching accompaniment to the prayer. The same thing happened on Monday, when she punctuated with glorious music the rousing remarks of a speaker who stood in the front of the gallery. Mr. Evan Roberts himself does not object to this method of procedure, and he experienced it today when he smilingly went on with a number of exhortations to the tender accompaniment of music, which was so modified in volume as not to interfere with his voice, but seemed to come from a distance, although in one instance Miss Davies who sang was standing at his side."[7]

That in itself is a striking image of the team work and also of the sense of support he felt from her.

The sense of team and partnership flowed beyond the team of singers themselves into a partnership and flow with the congregation as a whole.

"Some of their solos are wonders of dramatic and musical appeal. Nor is the effect lessened by the fact that the singers, like the speakers, sometimes break down in sobs and tears. The meeting always breaks out into a passionate and consoling song until the soloist, having recovered her breath, rises from her knees

and resumes her song. The praying and singing are both wonderful, but more impressive than either are the breaks which occured when utterance can no more, and the sobbing in the silence, momentarily heard, is drowned in a tempest of melody. No need for an organ, the assembly was its own organ as a thousand sorrowing or rejoicing hearts in the sacred psalmody of their native hills...and all this vast quivering, throbbing, singing, praying exultant multitude intensely conscious of the all-pervading influence of some invisible reality...they called it the Spirit of God. Those who have not witnessed it may call it what they will. I am inclined to agree with those on the spot."[8]

The flow of prayer and worship has echoes of the antiphonal worship of David's tabernacle, singers reflecting back and underscoring the emphasis of the spoken words and the intercession. Such a sound would have been heard in the earliest days of Christianity in Wales at Llantwit Major, which was one of only three sites in Britain of Continuous Prayer and Worship in the early Celtic monastic era. Singing and worship were crucial then and crucial also to the Revival of 1904.

The worship seemed to echo the sound of Heaven expressed in worship before the Throne. It seemed to resonate from heaven to earth drawing out a deep longing from the land and from the people of the land: earth singing back the breath of heaven as at the heart of the Revival gatherings prayer, worship, testimony, and the prophetic flowed. The Holy Spirit leading the release of Heaven's Unending Song through ordinary people. Ordinary people who had been shaped throughout history by revival hymns deep within their being. It was a Revival where worship and prayer, mainly in Welsh, sometimes in English, were woven seamlessly together as many came to salvation. In the words of W.T. Stead,

"The revival has not strayed beyond the track of the singing people, it has followed the line of song, not of preaching. It has sung its way from one end of South Wales to the other."[9]

Teams of singing evangelists were released, each had their own styles and favourite songs which reflected their own experiences. In early meetings in London, Seth Joshua had the help of Florrie Evans and Maud Davies. One of Florrie's favourite songs was "Ar fy nhaith" (On my journey), Maud Davies' song was "Bodlon Mwy" (Now contented).

There was a team of women from Dowlais who often used to sing together. Kate Llewelyn Morgan, "A famous Welsh contralto", Maggie Davies "a noted soprano", Keturah Evans "an excellent contralto". She and Maggie used to sing duets. Some of the songs were quite dramatic, one of Kate's favourites, based on The Parable of the Lost Sheep ,was "Yr oedd cant namyn un" (There were only ninety-nine). There was always a powerful response when she sang "Trwy'r nef mae gorfoledd, y ddafod, y ddafod a gaed"(Throughout heaven there is rejoicing, the sheep have been found, the sheep have been found).

However, the singing and worship didn't simply belong to the well known soloists and singers; it was a corporate flood of thankfulness. Breakthroughs often came through ordinary women and children singing out and triggering repentance, salvations and reconciliations.

In Morriston, on January 1st, a little girl was singing while an elderly man went to the front to read from the Bible. At that same moment he was told that his brother had just come to faith. "He was overcome with joy as he and his brother hugged."[10]

Dowlais, Tuesday January 24th, "When Evan mentioned that "Victory" was written on the banner of the Cross, a Dowlais young lady struck up very appropriately, "Syrthiodd fy ngharau au wiw ond buddugoliaeth Calfari enillodd hon yn ôl i mi, mi ganaf tra fwyf byw..." (My crown of dignity fell, but the victory of Calvary won more back for me, I will sing whilst I live). Then when the "Test" for converts was made, and people rose to signify their surrender, the singing of "Diolch Iddo" (Thanks be to Him) became literally triumphant, and when the enthusiasm grew, the singers, hundreds of them, actually clapped their hands with joy, keeping time with the music by the hand clapping. Handkerchiefs were waved and the scene formed another feature of a truly wonderful meeting. "Any more to save?" asked the evangelist. "Yes, yes" were the cries, and passionate prayers followed, while some young ladies struck up singing "Come, sinner, come". A man from the gallery shouted, "Another here has surrendered. He could not speak, so he has written a note to say he accepts Jesus Christ!"[11]

Prejudices of class, gender and age melted in the same furnace that forged together the worship and the prayer.

In Clydach Vale, Tuesday December 20th, "Inside there was absolutely no distinction of class or creed, for in the "big seat" and pulpit, with ministers of various denominations, a miners' agent, a couple of colliery officials and two revivalists were women and children, and while one of the most eloquent of the young revivalists was praying, a little dot of a girl, not more than six years of age, actually sitting next to him, was singing "Gwaed y groes sy'n codi i fyny",(The Blood of the Cross raises up) and the congregation joined her. Yet that fervent prayer went on, and at last prayer triumphed even over praise.[12]"

Many times Evan refused to let people "hush" the singing. He said to one leader, "Would you stop the dawn chorus of birds and allow just a few to greet the rising sun?" He would only stop the singing if people were trying to control the meeting by showing off or taking over. He wisely said at Cwmbwrla, "If they obeyed the Spirit in singing they could obey in stopping."

In Llanelli, as in many other places, worship was used on the streets to powerful effect.

"Shortly before eleven o'clock it was decided to make a tour of the New Dock district and hundreds of people formed themselves into a procession. They marched through the streets singing hymns and gathering strength as they moved along. A number of men and women under the influence of drink approached, and all these were persuaded to return to the chapel where prayer was offered on their behalf. The converts included sailors, tin-plate workers, colliers and several women all falling on their knees and asking for forgiveness. Mr. Evans and others prayed for them, and this went on until the sabbath had been ushered in."[13]

Even when the women weren't singing, sometimes they were being sung about, and sentimental as this song is (Tell mother I'll be there), it was used to bring back numbers of sons! It also provoked other responses. In one meeting Gypsy Smith broke down as he remembered his mother dying of smallpox "Without a Saviour" or a Bible.

It was also used to stop one of the most violent, if slightly humorous incidents of the Revival:

"A gang of drunks invaded Tabernacle Baptist Chapel, Cardiff, lifting a deacon up and threatening to throw him over the edge of the balcony. The refined pastor, Charles Davies, could only send a desperate cry to the Lord and that was answered at once. Miss Annie Rees was prompted to sing, "Tell mother I'll be there", and the drunks were subdued and sober long before she ended. They sat to worship with tears in their eyes"[14]

and I am sure the deacon was also thanking God for mothers!

TELL MOTHER I'LL BE THERE

When I was but a little child, how well I recollect
How I would grieve my mother with my folly and neglect.
And now that she has gone to heaven, I miss her tender care
Saviour, tell my mother I'll be there.

Tell mother I'll be there in answer to her prayer;
This message, Blessed Saviour, to her bear;

Tell mother I'll be there, heaven's joys with her to share;
Yes, tell my darling mother I'll be there.

Though I was often wayward she was always kind and good -
So patient, gentle, loving when I acted rough and rude;
My childhood's griefs and trials she would gladly share;
Saviour, tell my mother I'll be there.

When I became a prodigal, and left the old roof-tree,
She almost broke her loving heart in mourning after me;
And day and night she prayed to God to keep me in His care;
Saviour, tell my mother I'll be there.

One day a message came to me - it bade me quickly come,
If I would see my mother ere the Saviour took her home.
I promised her, before she died, for heaven to prepare;
Saviour, tell my mother I'll be there."

Some of the actions of the mothers may not have been so appreciated. "A woman living in Rhos publicly registered her child last week with the name of "Revival Hughes" (The Sunday Companion, 1905). "This child at least will remember the revival; whether it will appreciate the name remains to be seen!"

The release of singing through the women of the Revival reflected an area of chapel life where women had previously experienced some freedom; in revival time it became a mighty flood. Many women, known and unknown, were carrying the very heart of revival in worship. Worship and prayer formed a canopy over the land; a canopy which turned people's hearts to heaven and created an environment where faith rose and salvations followed in a growing harvest. Again and again worship was the means of breakthrough as heavens glory was released afresh on the land through the "whosoevers", little girls or elderly men it didn't matter. It was worship that men and women, old and young could carry together. It was a song of the heart, the flow of heaven's grace and love, carried often by those considered, through human eyes to be the least - the women, the children, the poor and the elderly. It was "The Blood of the Cross raising up, the feeble into a mighty conqueror."[12]

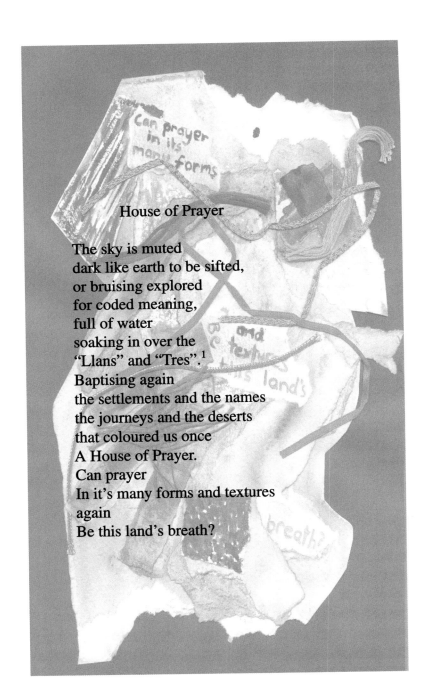

House of Prayer

The sky is muted
dark like earth to be sifted,
or bruising explored
for coded meaning,
full of water
soaking in over the
"Llans" and "Tres".[1]
Baptising again
the settlements and the names
the journeys and the deserts
that coloured us once
A House of Prayer.
Can prayer
In it's many forms and textures
again
Be this land's breath?

6

Dangerous prayers - Dangerous women

The hidden cry of prayer was suddenly being shouted from the rooftops of the nation. The women were hidden no longer, not even in prayer. There was a sense of reversal in this: of an old order being shaken under the re-alignment of the Holy Spirit. Many of them were unnamed in the Revival accounts, yet their prayers were recorded in the Welsh National Press of the day. It was probably a shock to some as they saw their deepest heartcry in print for the nation to read!

Mother Shepherd was amongst many who had been crying out for a fresh move of God in a land where the chapels were full but there was no fire in the house. She was not content with her work running rescue homes for women, nor in her work in the police courts as a missionary. She was desperate for a move of God like the one she had seen many years before through her seventeen year old daughter Kate.

Mother Shepherd was in her 70's when the Revival broke out, and she said, "It was just like Kate's Rhondda all over again!" She was also pleased that in Aberdare, where she lived and worked, there were more conversions than in any place of a similar size. It would seem that

Mother Shepherd in her 70's at the time of the Revival

her prayer, her hunger for God and her work over years had been part of the Revival preparation.

"She must have been one of the hidden ones (Psalm 83:3) who had agitated at the throne of God for a manifestation of divine power and saving grace."[1]

The Revival is full of accounts of women praying and of things happening. It seems that many of the women in their boldness and willingness to take risks of obedience were catalysts, the ignition points in many meetings and situations. When they prayed people repented and got converted, reconciled and healed, saw visions and dreamt dreams. These women, some elderly, some mothers with young children, some teenagers, some little girls, were dangerous people to be around. In the Revival itself they found a freedom in prayer they had never known before. The doors of heaven were open to them and they would not keep silent. In the words of one elderly lady they no longer needed "to use stamps" to get heaven's attention, "I thank Thee, Mighty Jesus, Thou hast cleared the bills; we no longer use stamps to send our messages to Thee."[2]

There were urgent prayers to see family members converted:

"One of the early meetings of the revival was held in Brynteg Congregational Chapel in Loughor. About 400 people were present at this Thursday night meeting. The majority of the congregation were feminine, ranging from young misses of twelve to matrons with babes in their arms...From another part of the chapel could be heard the resonant voice of a young man reading a portion of scripture. While this was in process, from the gallery came an impassioned prayer from a woman crying aloud that she had repented of her ways and was determined to live a better life henceforth...At 2.30 o'clock I took a rough note of what was then proceeding. In the gallery a woman was praying and she fainted. Water was offered her but she refused this, saying the only thing she wanted was

God's forgiveness. Prayers of repentance and cries for salvation mixed with the "anxiety of many present for the spiritual welfare of members of their families". One woman was heartbroken for her husband, who was given to drink. She implored the prayers of the congregation on his behalf."[3]

They were not ashamed to pray:

Hafod, Saturday December 17th:
"It was with a gladsome spirit and a hearty vigour that the exercises of exhorting and praying were conducted, and women and children were not ashamed in this vast congregation, and in the presence of men of cold demeanor, to bear testimony to the joys and blessings of their new experiences."[4]

Prayer was often specific:

"A young girl aged 18 was praying for her drunken father who was feared in the area. She said, "Lord, go to 65, Prospect Place and save my father." The Lord did go, and now the father and two brothers are converted and following Jesus."[5]

"There are references to fervent prayers being offered by elderly women, "Mothers in Israel", and references to the answered prayers of children.

Cwmbwrla, Monday January 2nd:
"It was stated that the prayer of the little girl - of ten years of age - at Clydach on Wednesday had been answered, her father, for whom she had been praying, having become a convert."[6]

Cwmbwrla, Wednesday January 4th:
"The evening meeting was held in Trinity Chapel, where the congregation had been gathering from the early hours of the afternoon. The most thrilling incident occurred about ten o'clock. A young, well dressed shop assistant tottered into the "Sêt Fawr", embraced a minister and asked him to pray for him. Mr. Roberts came down from the pulpit and the young man threw his arms around him. The two then went up to the pulpit and the young fellow shouted to the congregation, "Ydi mam yma?" ("Is mother here?").

A voice from the back seats announced that the mother was present. The young man then said, "Mother, I have had to give in at last. I tried to refuse but I was compelled." The mother burst into prayers, and her son shouted, "Well done Mam!"[7]

It also often involved action:

Senghenydd, Wednesday December 7th:

"A young lady from Bedwas rose in the gallery and in English said she had gone to Mr. Evan Roberts on the previous night to ask him to pray for her. "What do you want?" He asked, and she replied that she did not think she was doing enough for Jesus Christ. Ultimately he advised her to tell her neighbours in Bedwas and others about her Saviour. She went home and in the morning, when in the train, she spoke to a woman from Pentre, Rhondda Valley, who said neither she nor her husband went to any chapel, although some of the children went. She prayed with the woman, but at first without avail. She prayed again and the woman accepted Christ and promised to try and influence her husband. Then the young lady added, "I hope my brother is in this congregation. Will you pray for him?" Several prayers were offered, and ten minutes or a quarter of an hour later a shout was raised from the far end of the gallery. Her brother was converted and there was a mighty shout of "Diolch Iddo" and "Songs of praise I will ever give to Thee."[8]

Sometimes the answered prayers were ones which, prayed over many years, had seemed to come to nothing.

"Martha Howells of Bethel Chapel, Aberdare prayed every day for her rebel son Tom without result. She died in 1893. On a Saturday night in November 1904 he made his way into the revival meeting. "He hears the voice of some lady singing under the gallery opposite where he stands, it is his sister Lizzie. She leads the crowd in prayer, a prayer for her brother Tom, who she thought would be drunk as usual, wasting his money and destroying his soul. The next day, Sunday November 20th, a young people's meeting was held in Ebenezer Chapel. Who should come in with a child in each hand but Tom Howells...A cry broke out and drowned all else, and a man whose hair was beginning to grey fell almost full length on the floor.

His children were afraid and weeping, imagining something strange had possessed him. It was Tom calling for God's forgiveness." He was a changed man from that day as all his family and neighbours would testify."[9]

Caerphilly, Monday December 5th:

"Evan said that some people objected to so much singing. "But" he explained, "there are two stages to a revival: singing first and praying afterwards. The second stage will come". "[10]

The second stage did come and there were explosions of prayer and Revival all over Wales; Many without any direct connection to Evan himself.

In Ammanford, after Joseph Jenkins had been there in the early autumn of 1904,

"...At about 10 o'clock a young girl in the corner...rose to her feet and prayed with an explosive passion until a Pentecostal cloud broke over her. It poured out its contents everywhere until everyone lost control and turned to praying, yes, and shouting, some asking forgiveness, some giving thanks and some praising, everyone in the confusion doing something. Never before had we seen such a holy disorder in a religious meeting...a beautiful harmony was sensed in the confessing, praying and praising."[11]

In Morriston, in meetings being taken by Sidney Evans:

*"There were moments so intense as to be painful. A deep hush fell over the people when a beautiful girl of 15 or 16 years rose from the front of the gallery and prayed, trembling like an Aspen. The petitions came at first halting and broken, but her voice gathering strength she became passionate in her pleading. She asked that Treforus, Morriston, should be captured for Christ. That the town should have the sight of the devil in all his hideousness, that it should also see the Saviour in His glory. The silence was unbroken for min*utes, then the *"Diolch's"* (Thank You's) and *"Hallelujah's"* broke out."*[12]

In Newport:

"In the meetings in Newport at the end of December Mary Roberts had a dynamic effect in prayer. From a kneeling position she was heard pouring out very fervent prayers for a baptism of the Holy Spirit with fire. Following her example, other women began to play a more and more vital role during the afternoon meetings."[13]

In Haverfordwest:

"The Rev.O.D. Campbell invited the ladies to take the leading part in the following night's service. He said that he "felt assured that what the cold hearts and rougher tongue of men had failed to do, the warmer hearts of women would accomplish." The women responded to the invitation and "the results were such as to prove that Mr. Campbell's compliment was thoroughly well deserved." As a result of the services there are about 80 converts."[14]

North Wales:
(Llansamlet, Sunday January 8th)

"Some women, including one who had come all the way from Bala to the meeting, prayed with great eloquence. One then prayed that she might be able to go back to North Wales with some of the "fire" from South Wales."[15]

In Bethesda:

"In Bethesda the free churches joined together to meet in November for a mission because of the profound difficulties being caused by a strike in the slate quarries. The person leading the mission was Hugh Hughes, a Wesleyan minister. The prayer meetings were the most powerful times. The evening meeting was followed by a young people's prayer meeting which sometimes went on for three hours. In the afternoon some 500 women met for prayer, weeping and testimony woven together with singing. They started to see conversions and healing of the rifts and feuds in the quarries. In December Joseph Jenkins came to take some meetings accompanied by Maud Davies and Florrie Evans. One of the local ministers, John T. Job, said this: "The revival was everything. Talking about Christ's mighty work in Carmarthenshire, especially among the students in Aberystwyth; the young girls singing and

weeping; sharing experiences of the Holy Spirit; each one of us praying all the while until the early hours of the morning. I felt the Holy Spirit as a torrent of light shaking my entire nature. I feel I can pray by laughing these days."[16]

In Rhos:

"In Capel Mawr, Rhos on Monday night, as a great multitude gathered together for prayer, the normal form of the service was interrupted by a little girl, hardly 12 years old, rising to her feet in the midst of the crowd and offering one of the most striking prayers ever heard. A child's prayer it was for sure, but in its very simplicity it was overpowering. Strong men cried, and many a cheek was wet with the flood of tears, cheeks that had been dry in many a worse circumstance." For many that was the strongest impact of the revival and the one that affected them most deeply."[17]

"Wednesday a prayer meeting for the sisters was held...This meeting set the sisters on fire. By now two great forces in the communities had been stirred, namely the young people and the ladies."[18]

These are just a few of the places impacted by women who had suddenly realised that they were dangerous in prayer. Women who understood that the Father was desperate to answer their cries for their families, their communities and the nations. They were women who were willing to allow their voices to be heard by men, confronting their own fears and self consciousness, that their prayers might be answered by God.

The answers to prayer were so visible there could be no doubt that the women's voices rising all over Wales had caught the ear and heart of heaven. The prayers were also there for all to read in the newspapers of the day. The language often reflected the Biblical richness of the teaching in the Sunday schools, particularly in the more rural and Welsh speaking areas. Sometimes the language was colloquial and raw in its pain. This may have appalled the more religious but it gave permission for those not used to praying to find their voice in language which they understood and now felt that their Father in heaven could not only understand, but would even answer. Prayer had again become part of the experience and expression of ordinary people. It had been taken out of the chapels and released onto the streets of the nation. The dangerous prayers of dangerous women were giving voice to the Father's Heart for a nation He was transforming with His love.

It's time for
mobility,
standing with
others -
people and
regions -
to see them
come through.
It's time for
pilgrimage,
walking
the land and
praying,
circuit riding
for a new
day, signs and
wonders , the
good news as
the good news,
fierce raging
music in the
streets, in the
clubs, even in
the churches.
The Kingdom
of God opening
up for people,
religion
shutting down.
Poor and
broken running
- a revolution
of the cross.

7

Great was the Company...

"The Lord announced the word, and great was the company of women who proclaimed it." (Psalm 68:11 - Good News Bible)

Rosina Davies in later years

The days leading up to and during the Revival saw a new confidence rising in women as they discovered that not only were they supposed to declare the Good News of Jesus, but that wonderful things happened when they did!

Rosina Davies had been "proclaiming the word" as an evangelist since the moment she was converted in the Valleys revival of 1879. She continued as a forerunner of Revival in the build up to its outbreak in October 1904. She was someone who, born into revival, had the opportunity to prepare for and then reap in another.

This is Rosina's description of a meeting in pre-Revival 1904 - January 3rd, a mission at Bethania, Treorchy, Rhondda:

"As usual the chapel was overcrowded. The Spirit of God was manifested since early 1903. There was a revival of the Spirit in the churches, especially in North Wales. The indifference was passing and there was an earnestness, a desire for the deepening of the spiritual life. The gospel in its simplicity was eagerly listened

to. I realised at the mission in Treorchy that the awakening of the churches was spreading in North and South Wales, souls were won for Christ and His kingdom."[1]

In February she held a successful mission in Rhos near Wrexham, which later became one of the epicentres of the Revival in North Wales. She also focussed on young people in a mission she took in Dolgellau. She said they were,

"...An excellent group of young people who were earnest in prayer and made the mission a success." In Dolgellau a young girl came up to her after she had been talking about the pain of the crown of thorns and asked, *"How can I, a little servant girl, crown my Lord?"*[2]

Later many girls and many women would crown Him with the yielding of their lives. When the Revival had fully come Rosina embraced it with enthusiasm.

"During 1904 I held 256 services, and according to my diary 250 surrendered to the Lord. I spent a great part of the year in North Wales. I was filled with joy to hear when I returned at intervals of the revival in South Wales, and having so many missions and services myself, I had but few opportunities to attend meetings where Mr Evan Roberts took part....Many souls were saved by the revival from the depths of sin and corruption; many have gone rejoicing to their eternal home; many have remained to be stalwart workers in the church today, and even one soul is of greater value than the whole world."[3]

Woven into the accounts of the Revival meetings are records not only of women praying, but also of women giving testimonies. There are stories of conversions, of witnessing and of women preaching in meetings, in gypsy camps and on the streets. This was not the usual practice prior to the Revival! The desire to witness had become a burning passion in many women.

There was a fresh boldness and a willingness to risk criticism. Even to this day there is an added pressure on women who lead and preach. Comments like, "You are the first woman who has ever preached here," increase the pressure to perform! As does the knowledge that if you do badly it will often be said it is "because you are a woman". Personally, I have noticed that if a man teaches or preaches badly he is not normally criticised, "because he is a man"! It all adds to the fun, and the invitation not to take yourself too seriously. However, all of this makes the boldness of the women even more challenging for the age in which they lived. Many of them would have had biblical figures such as Miriam and Deborah as role models to follow but no living role models. They were forging new paths, that hopefully others would follow.

Jessie Penn-Lewis wrote this in her first hand account of the Revival.

"It is now no uncommon thing to see a young girl of 18 speaking under the evident control of the Holy Spirit while in the big pew sit ministers and elders, at times with tears coursing down their faces. The servants and handmaidens are prophesying as foretold by Joel. Again we find that the prophesying takes the form of witnessing - the special mark of Pentecost. In Wales for many years it has been considered too sacred a thing to speak of the inner dealings of God, yet suddenly we see it all changed, and sermons put aside for testimony and public confession of what the Lord has done for the soul."[4]

In the early stages of the Revival Evan Roberts encouraged the "Christian worker bands", many of whom were women. In the crowded chapels, where it was often hard to breathe let alone move, they would scramble over pews, balconies and people to get to the unconverted who were at a point of decision. It was exciting when they cried out, "Here's another one!", although some must have found it embarrassing when the details of their lives were shouted over the noise of the crowds!

Evan also encouraged the "witnessing bands" who went

out onto the streets and brought all sorts of people into the meetings, particularly after the pubs had closed. His cry was this:

"We must all be workers and sincere in prayer. It will not do for us to go to heaven by ourselves. Friends, we must be on fire for saving others, we cannot do so without being workers...Oh that we were filled with the Spirit of the great Lover."[5]

As women were consumed by the love of God, they found the grace to reach out in ways they would previously have been too ashamed or fearful to do so.

Ferndale, Saturday December 10th:

"Fervent and enthusiastic workers paraded the streets of Ferndale at night "sweeping in" drunkards who could be found, and endeavouring to lead them to brighter ways and better things. There were in the afternoon some striking scenes witnessed, not the least being the sight of so many local ladies quietly and unostentatiously acting as "workers" in the midst of the congregation."[6]

Some were prepared to visit the poorest of places:

"Into the lodging houses went groups to sing or pray, exhorting and encouraging the most abandoned to come to Jesus. Young women, beautifully dressed, knelt with vagabonds of the road who had casually turned in for a night's lodging. They pleaded with them "to turn from the error of their ways" to Christ, "the new and living way"...As these young people knelt on dirty, dusty floors surrounded by banana skins, orange peelings, cigarette butts, newspaper scraps, hardened toast rinds and eggshells praying for these wanderers, the unkempt room seemed to be filled with the glory of God..."[7]

"In the Aberdare area young people in teams visited homes and held cottage meetings. If there was a home where people weren't converted they asked permission to hold a service there. "In this way the influence of the Welsh revival was felt in the poorest dwellings." There was worship instead of blasphemy, and money was given to feed and dress half-starved families. This was so unusual, and had

such an impact in homes and neighbourhoods, that people were amazed at what God had done. "These things were accomplished through spiritual novices." Rent books were cleared, old debts were sorted in shops by these young people, they revelled in doing exploits...It was love work to them, and love never feels any burden when on active service for the King of Kings." [8]

In the past, one or two extraordinary women had broken through, the Kate Shepherds and the Cranogwens. The limits were now taken off. There was a corporate breakthrough in sharing the good news of Jesus. Soloists became "Singing Evangelists'. Shy housewives invaded the pubs. Middle Class women challenged prize fighters to "get converted". It was glorious chaos where no one was safe. In the enthusiasm some people were offended, particularly ministers, challenged by "in your face" young people. It was not a time when women felt disqualified because they were women - they enjoyed the freedom of being able to work and serve alongside the men - it was harvest time in Cymru!

These are stories of some of their adventures in God as recorded in the Revival reports:

Pentre, December 3rd:

A lady relates "*How she was the instrument in the hand of God to persuade a prize fighter to accept Christ.*" [9]

Pentre, Sunday December 4th:

"A young woman, sitting under the shadow of the balcony, rose and in passionate tones, but in a voice evidently almost lost by recent straining, proclaimed, "I do believe, I will believe, that Jesus died for me." [10]

"The young revivalist smilingly remarked, "She has lost her voice in telling the people about her Saviour." The lady hailed from Treherbert where, during the last nine or ten days, full of the Revival "fire", she had been so active that she alone had brought no fewer than 105 converts to the local churches. Scarcely had silence come upon the touched congregation before the young lady from Treherbert already alluded to was again on her feet, and with her face glowing with fervor she exclaimed,

"Count your blessings, name them one by one,
Count your blessings, see what God hath done;
Count your blessings, name them one by one
And it will surprise you what the Lord hath done."[11]

They were sometimes described as "militant girls" as in the title of this newspaper report in the Llanelly Mercury:

"They conducted their meeting in front of the Dynevor Arms, and finding that little attention was paid to them the Rev. Nantlais Williams walked inside and was followed by a number of young men and women. They found every room full. The young girls went to the bar and offered a fervent prayer on their knees. One man threw his beer into the fireplace, many walked out and some joined in prayer. Afterwards the meeting was resumed outside, the crowd increasing and most of the occupants of the house joining."[12]

It is again time for a new militancy in the gospel, a time to take risks, a time to be bold.

From early Revival days women led meetings without Evan Roberts or other of the main Revival figures being present.

For example, whilst Evan was leading a meeting in Cymmer, Miss Davies (Gorseinon), Miss Maggie Davies (Maesteg) and Miss Jones (Pontycymer) were at an Ynyshir chapel, a mile and a half away, conducting another service there, and a very successful one too according to the newspaper report!

Many women young and old discovered that they were preachers.

This happened from the earliest meetings, November 11th:

"A young girl shouts, "What of heaven if it is so good here!"[13]

"The story told by another young woman drew tears to all eyes. She said that her mother was dead, and that her father had given way to sin, so that she was indeed orphaned in the world...the Spirit

had come upon her, bidding her to speak. And she did speak! - her address being remarkable for one who had never spoken before in public."[14]

Tylorstown, December 13th:

"A young lady faces the huge congregation and recites a poem in Welsh dramatically showing the journeys of two trains, the one to heaven, the other to hell. Evan Roberts jumps up and asks if anyone is on the last train. One young fellow rises and acknowledges openly his lost condition."[15]

In meetings where Dan Roberts was accompanied by Maggie Davies and Miss S.A. Jones the outstanding feature was "Miss S.A.'s preaching".

"Miss S.A.Jones, taking the cue from the last speaker, made quite an eloquent appeal to all "to join this army". Instead of the King's shilling, "they would be given a crown"; instead of a small wage every day they would be given "100 per cent of the blessings of this world and eternal life in the world to come"."[16]

"On the following Sunday in Pontypridd, a man here remarked that they were styled "mad revivalists", but they were he said "mad" on the right side, and this brought Miss S.A. Jones to her feet. This lady took the man's remark as the subject of a very racy address. "Oh it is not madness" she said subsequently, "It is sanity. It was before the revival I was mad, but I am sane now," and she then went on to discourse quite eloquently on the change wrought in her character. The close of the meeting was marked by several conversions."[17]

The three women also went down a mine - the Maritime Level Colliery in Pontypridd to lead a prayer meeting:

"Accompanied by several friends they made the journey into the level in a tram and "when a halt was made in the central position some 200 workmen gathered together and a very impressive service was opened by the singing of "Lead, kindly light." Miss S.A.Jones delivered an English address in which she dwelt upon the importance of having the light of Christ in life, in and out of the colliery. Miss

Mary Davies, in the course of a Welsh address, remarked that if there was anyone in need of a Saviour more than another it was a collier, who risked his life in the dark and dangerous surroundings of the coal pit. Miss Maggie Davies fervently prayed in Welsh for the safety and salvation of all those present, and for the spread of the revival throughout the whole world...Just as the party reached the mouth of the level the young ladies rendered "Diolch Iddo".[17]

Women were talked of as having had such a baptism of power that they reminded people of Catherine Booth (co-founder of the Salvation Army). It seemed that many women were now carrying her revivalist anointing. The anointing that had rested on a few outstanding women was now being seen in women across a whole nation. Other revivalists included May John, who had been known mainly as a singer, and a Miss C.A.Jones.

May John, from the Rhondda, was described as having "a cultured soprano voice". In Newport she became an "In your face preacher" as - "decoded" from the "polite revival speak" of the newspapers - she challenged the women to speak out!

"May John earnestly entreated that God might be supplicated to give the sisters grace to speak. There were many of them who felt it deeply. They had not the strength to testify openly for Him. The men were having it all in this revival, now let the women come forward for there was much work before them that men could not do. She especially entreated the young sisters to come forward so that they might have a long and useful life in God's service."[18]

May John

May John was one of the few whom Evan kept in touch with after the Revival.

Miss C.A. Jones is described as,

"One of the three young ladies of the same surname (!) all living at Ynysybwl, whose work in connection to the revival has brought her to the fore as a revivalist. She takes part in the devotional services as well as the singing portion of the proceedings and is useful and active in talking with waverers."[19]

"She took part in revival meetings with the Rev. B. Davies at Clydach Vale a week before the explosion and pit fire at the Cambrian Vale Colliery. Some of the men who took part in those services were a week later among the victims of the explosion."[20]

The dangers of the coalmining industry acted as a backdrop to the Revival and added an urgency to the task of male and female evangelists alike.

In one-line references in newspaper reports, brief mentions in letters and writings from the time, a picture also builds up of the large number of women who travelled as revivalists to different places.

"As the church leaders and ministers ceased to go out with the converts on missions onto the streets, people tended to form unattached teams such as that in Pontypridd - Mr John and Miss M.J. Jones, Miss Lizzie Lloyd and Mr. David Daniel."[21]

Sometimes there were photographs of revivalists in the newspapers, they were named, but no explanation was given of what they had been doing - Miss Sarah Jane Hopkin and Mr Richard Jones", are one example.

A number of women who were either daughters, wives, or widows of ministers worked as revivalists. Mrs.C.K. Evans, the widow of a Wesleyan Minister was a revivalist to England. She went from place to place in London and further afield, holding revival missions. Her husband had been in charge of a large mission in Pontypridd and she had her first experience of preaching when he built a little hall in which she preached on Sunday nights! A singer called Gwen John travelled with her, Gwennie was 15 and had been converted in the Revival and baptised on New Year's Day. Many came to faith through these two radical women. Kate Morgan Llewelyn from Dowlais held a mission in Swansea following a successful mission at Beaufort Hill. There is also a record of her holding a mission in Abertillery and one in Ebbw Vale after striking out on her own from Evan Roberts' Revival teams.

Others also went on Revival teams to London, including a team from Neath, consisting of Mrs. John Davies, Melincrytha; Miss Mary Davies, Penydre, Neath and Mr. W. Rosser.

The role of significant men in releasing the women in their lives cannot be underestimated. Many seemed to take their lead from Evan Roberts, Joseph Jenkins, Sidney Evans and Dan Roberts.

Welsh revivalists also took meetings in Middlesborough. In 6 weeks hundreds were converted and the churches stirred to action. The revivalists were Mr. E. Illtyd Jones, a student at Cardiff University, Miss Davidson and Miss Roberts.

Revivalists also went to Scotland. One trip was paid for by a wealthy Glasgow businessman. The main meetings were in Glasgow, with two of the group going to Paisley. It was a very

Welsh Revivalists in London
S.A.Jones, Maggie Davies, Mary Davies

successful mission. The group was made up of 6 women and 2 men. The group included Mrs. Davies, Aberdare; Miss Rachel Thomas, Mountain Ash; Miss Mary Davies, Gorseinon; Miss Sissie Morgan, Treharris; Miss Kate Mathias, Cardiff; Miss Nelly Sutton, Cardiff; Mr. D.Thomas, Pontycymer; and Mr. C. Penrose.

Miss Mathias, had just returned from Bath, where, at the meetings in which she took part, "190 converts enrolled".[22]

In an era when it was less common for women to work outside the home, ones who did have jobs saw the workplace as a mission field.

"In Swansea the old lady at the Post Office where I called to despatch a telegram was ready to give all details as to the route to be taken and talked eagerly of the wonderful work, believing that a wave of salvation was flowing over the country"[23]

Another challenges fellow workers in this way.

"At the moment all our thoughts are turning towards Wales, doubtless many of our hearts are crying "Lord, let revival reach us"...What could not be done if every lady in the district offices were to give herself to Jesus for His work...Sisters in the GPO, the Lord is waiting and longing to send the mighty revival, shall not you and I yield unreservedly to him for what he wants to do in us and through us?"[24]

At least one woman revivalist, Miss Linton, came from England to Wales to help with the Revival.

"Miss Linton (evangelist), who has been conducting revival services at Garndiffaith, comes from a Methodist family in Dunston, Lincoln. She commenced to labour as a local preacher with the primitive Methodists and soon becoming very popular, was prevailed upon to throw herself entirely into the work of an evangelist. She is powerful in speech and well built, is nearly 5ft 11in. high, a good visitor, and has a habit of much prayer. Her services at Garndiffaith were very succesful."[25]

Many were converted in these meetings and on the streets;

converted alcoholics sharing the radical change in their lives. At times when the newspaper reports weren't lacking in detail they could sometimes be quite personal! It seems that Miss Linton may have suffered from some of the same descriptions as Cranogwen who was described as masculine looking with a deep voice!

Other revivalists, particularly Annie Davies were described in ways that made them the "babes" of their day.

"A representative of The Porcupine, a satirical Liverpool paper wrote "Seated at the back of the pulpit were Miss Davies and Miss Roberts, becomingly dressed and wearing large black hats of fashionable design. Miss Davies had a bright expression, retrousse nose, sparkly eyes and pretty dark hair. The revivalist's sister is younger than her friend and has fair hair which hangs down her back.""[26]

The novelty factor of women revivalists may have drawn some to the meetings, however, it was the powerful anointing of the Holy Spirit at work through them which brought the breakthroughs.

It raises questions which were an issue then as much as they are now. Can you be a woman in ministry and still be feminine? Do you have to behave like a man to minister? Are you a "babe" to be viewed and judged on outward appearance? Do you have to be very quiet to prove you are submissive? Do you have to work twice as hard to prove you are worthy? Do you have to be an extrovert to divert attention from your vulnerability? And if you are an extrovert will you be thought of as "loud and proud"!

Jesus is calling us to lay down our masks, to walk in the fulness of all that He has called us to be as women in Him. He is calling us to walk in the same level of vulnerability, yet authority, in which He walked. It is the same challenge now as then and it is only in Him that we find the resources to be as bold and outrageous as He wants us to be!

"I am restoring the childhood of the nation
breathing on an ancient shrivelled heart."

"It means seeing me as Jesus sees me,
Sifting through the burnt out layers
for His fingerprints in me...
The Father's Yes,
His pleasure as I run...
not being forced to be the same as you...
molten fiery love in the eyes of Jesus...
children picked out of culture's rubbish heap.
A laying down of lives
across the generations,
Fathers
and children
running together."

Teenage Revivalists

1904 was initially a young people's movement. It broke out in a youth meeting on October 31st led by a 26 year old man. It was influenced in its early days by teams of teenagers aged between 16 and 18 sent out from Newquay. Annie Davies was 18. Dan Roberts and Sidney Evans were around 20 years of age when they took a major lead in the Revival.

Annie May Rees was 15 when she took Cardiff by storm. Mary Roberts was 16 when she travelled Wales and Liverpool as a revivalist, working alongside her brother. Florrie Evans at 15 embraced the Revival she had sparked.

Annie May Rees

Annie May Rees, one of the five original singers who offered themselves to work in the Revival, was a colourful and confident figure.

Annie May Rees

A gifted speaker and singer, she received her training in the Rhondda meetings with Evan. During these meetings she became a revivalist in her own right. Yet it was in the Cardiff meetings that she came into her own, both as a revivalist and as a leader.

She wasn't afraid to do things differently to make a point. Breaking a social convention - one which needed breaking - she brought two converted gypsies into the pulpit. She was a young woman able to take risks. Maybe her background was less steeped in chapel culture; she was certainly not overawed by it. It was a season when boundaries and conventions were being tested and shifted and Annie May seemed to enjoy playing her part in this!

In a Rhondda meeting when Evan was ill she happily filled in for him, singing popular revival hymns such as "I need Thee" and "O Happy Day"[1.] As she learnt to introduce hymns, she felt confident enough to start preaching through telling stories. She started calling sinners to conversion from the pulpit.

On the 2nd of December she took a meeting by herself at Moriah Chapel, Pentre. The main team were taking meetings some miles away. She was not thrown by this, but sat in the "Sêt Fawr" and began to sing some of the songs of the Revival. The congregation were probably quite startled but joined in the singing! Next she opened "properly" in prayer and led the meeting alternating between Welsh and English. She was fifteen years old and female!

On the 8th of December in Ferndale she led an overflow meeting in English in a local school whilst Evan was leading a meeting in Welsh in the chapel. During the meeting a significant testimony was given by one of the converts from the Caerphilly Football Club.

"A young man rose in the middle of the congregation and said he had come all the way from Caerphilly to give his testimony. He was one of the converts from the Caerphilly Football Club, he was a gambler and a drinker. And he said that after his conversion he handed to Miss Rees a dance card for he added he had wasted valuable time in connection with dances..He now wanted to tell young men of his own age all he could about the love of the Saviour."[2]

The meetings in Cardiff are not so well documented as some, presumably because Evan and the other leading revivalists did not go there. However, Annie May Rees was there along with others in Llandaff Road, Canton, and then in Tabernacle Baptist Church in The Hayes in the centre of Cardiff.

This is an account of a meeting in Cardiff. It was a meeting full of drama; families were reconciled, prostitutes converted, the destitute melted by the love of Jesus - and then sent back onto the streets because there was no-one who would take them in:

"Owing to an estrangement the son had left home three years ago, and the parents and he had not since met...for a few moments the mother scarcely realised who was standing beside her husband in the aisle, then with a shriek that rang with pain through the chapel, she rushed from her pew and throwing her arms around her son's neck showered kisses on him...the two holding each others hands knelt together in prayer, the father looking on at the scene and showing that he felt it was the supreme moment of his life...A young woman who had that morning appeared in the dock at the Cardiff Police Court, and was discharged under the First Offenders Act reverently took part in the service for several minutes and prayed with others. This wonderful meeting was followed by an impromptu street mission, which produced results unexpectedly successful...many men and women were met as they left the public houses and in a very short time there began to stream into the Tabernacle a motley crowd...with many tales of despair.

One poor woman told how she had come from Breconshire to Cardiff, bringing with her an invalid husband and three children, the youngest of whom was eight months old. With her husband unable to work the burden of providing for them was thrown on her, and to gain her bread she was driven to the wretched life of the streets. Drink was no temptation to her, but her mode of life made it a necessity. "Show me" she cried "how I may earn food for my husband and little ones and I will gladly be an honest woman once more".

A fine handsome woman who had evidently fallen from a life in far better circumstances, told a still more terrible tale. She was a married woman separated from her husband and (to her greater grief) also from her child. Her despair, she avowed had driven her so far that night would have been her last had not a helping hand been held out to her. She had fully determined to seek death either under the wheels of a tramcar or in the waters of the canal. But a sympathetic word from one of the missioners had, happily, turned her from her resolve.

Another was also separated from her husband. Where he was she knew not, though she believed im to be at sea. Again destitution had been her fall.

Many more such stories were told, and the earnest inspired pleadings of the missioners turned many a lost soul towards the light. The majority of these 50 or 60 sinners were willing to seek a better life if, as all declared, the world would give them a chance.

A little before two the meeting ended and the little band of workers set about to seek a home for the sinners they had reclaimed, but the only place of refuge they could find was at the Salvation Army home in Moira Place, and there they had room for no more than half a dozen. For the rest they had no shelter, and these had to be left to drift back to the streets and to wander no-one knew whither. Principal Edwards was one of the most earnest of the missioners at this remarkable meeting, and was deeply touched by this the saddest phase of the night's work."[3]

I wonder if we would cope, or even want to cope if there was such a response today amongst the desperate in our towns and cities? Would we be prepared to have people in our homes or in our church buildings? Such challenges were heightened in the Revival but still remain the same today. The churches also found that they didn't know what to do with the teenage revivalists and women who had suddenly been mobilised.

At Christmas Annie May Rees returned to her home town of Gorseinon and was invited to speak at Bethel Chapel. She impressed everyone because she was so young and because she was "one of their own". Some of those who came to the meeting had no "sympathy for the revival". She sang some solos from the "Sêt Fawr" and "delivered an excellent address", although the report notes that there was no sermon preached. Did they differentiate between a sermon and an address because she was a woman?

"Miss Rees said " My heart is in the work and I am eagerly looking forward to the time when I shall return to Cardiff to continue the meetings"...she mentioned the name of Rev. Charles Davies, a respected pastor of Tabernacle Baptist Chapel, Cardiff who was giving her great assistance...before the meeting was finished an announcement was made that all people present had been saved."[4]

That surely can't be bad! On her return to Cardiff she took the lead in a roller coaster of a meeting in Tabernacle Baptist Chapel.

"The chapel was crowded in every part...there were almost as many nationalities as on the Day of Pentecost...soldiers in uniform, sailors, colliers, deck hands, Members of Parliament, civic dignitaries, learned professors, ministers of the Gospel, wealthy merchants, noted journalists...It is like nothing else I have ever seen...The meetings begin, proceed and end, guided by some mysterious impulse. They are chaotic with confusion, and decent though disorderly. No-one can say what the audience will do next. There is no leader, and yet there is a fresh leader every five minutes...A French pastor, Monsieur Cadot tried to speak over the noise. He asked for prayers for the struggling little French Protestant churches, then it was that Annie May Rees took over and walked calmly into the vacant pulpit. "Everybody, not one only" said Miss Rees "But let everybody pray for France. Now then come along!" M.Cadot prayed with great feeling and towards the end of his prayer Miss Rees began to sing, "I need Thee, O I need Thee" in a low crooning voice as a kind of minor accompaniment, and when she had finished it was taken up and sung again and again as I think only Welshmen can sing". The excitement was growing with two or three hymns being started at the same time. Towards the end of this meeting Miss Rees gave a brief address explaining why this meeting had been advertised as a "farewell meeting". Some of them she hoped were going to say "farewell to the devil". "Don't mind me" she went on" I am nothing, do just as the Spirit moves you. Don't be afraid of interrupting me. The only thing I beg you not to do is quench the Spirit.""[5]

The meetings in Cardiff raise a lot of questions. There was clearly a huge response amongst the poor and broken, with Principal Edwards and his wife from Tabernacle Baptist Church fully involved in the meetings.

"Principal Edwards seems to revel in rescue work, it is the joy of his life. All sorts of conditions of men and women, drunkards, gamblers, debauchers, prostitutes, prodigals, have been coming in night after night, where they have found salvation...Mrs. Edwards has taken a prominent part in this mighty movement of mercy. She has thrilled to ecstasy by her sweet singing, many hearts that were broken by sorrow and sin and has helped to feed hundreds of poor starving children who crowd daily to the Tabernacle, which is the centre of a great rescue movement into which the Cardiff revival has developed. Over 600 have been converted, many of whom saved from the lowest depths of sin."[6]

However it seems as if many ministers stood aloof from the Revival or at least didn't quite understand how to relate to it.

J.Vyrnwy Morgan [7] quotes a well known and highly respected Welsh minister who, unable to enter a full chapel, was reduced to looking through the chapel window from the garden behind. He saw groups of people all over the building praying for those not yet converted.

A common reflection on this aspect of the Revival is that the women had to act because the men and the ministers wouldn't. This may partly be the case. However, there is a wider issue, maybe the Father didn't view women as a rescue package but rather as His instruments of choice! If He only uses a woman when He can't find a man, it makes the "end justify the means" and "if it is wrong for a woman to minister, the exception cannot prove truth, for truth is unchanging and does not have exceptions..."[8] This is a dilemma which many people find themselves in. They recognise that God has gifted women in a specific area and that they could use the gifts to fulfill a role of ministry or leadership. If these roles are not open to them, then it begs the question of why God gifted them in this way in the first place. If people do take the view that God does make exceptions - then how exceptional does a woman have to be to qualify? There seems to be few agreed upon exceptions - except maybe Mary, the mother of Jesus, and Catherine Booth!

The situation with the women in Cardiff does highlight, however, a lack of understanding by the "spiritual fathers and mothers" in the land as to how to act in a situation when young people and young converts were taking the lead.

The Welsh Revival highlighted a "hanging back" by the "spiritual fathers and mothers" in the land. This was not true in every case. Mother Shepherd helped David Matthews with an issue which, if not dealt with, would have derailed him. Evan Phillips gave Evan Roberts wise advice on whether he had heard God about returning to Loughor. However, the more general dislocation of leaders in the land left a vacuum into which discouragement and much worse was to flow as time went on.

In 1906 Evan Roberts said that he still regarded Cardiff as a "festering sore of sin", "in spite of what had been done by Miss Rees and her fellow workers during the winter of 1904-5."[7]

Perhaps the most striking thing is not the sin of Cardiff but his acknowledgement that the team was led by a 15 year old girl. The pain of Cardiff still cries out even in this day and in this century.

Maybe Cardiff is still waiting for the teenage revivalists and the leaders with a deep compassion for the poor. Maybe Cardiff is still waiting for spiritual fathers and mothers who will not disengage, but who will find a way to release rather than control. Maybe the time is now for Cardiff, for Wales and for the nations.

Mary Roberts

Mary, Evan Roberts' 16 year old sister, is described by him as changing from a "peevish girl" into someone who was happy! She became one of the main workers in the Revival from its earliest meetings in Loughor, as shown in this great account by Edward Wilkins who later went out as a missionary to South Africa.

"He went to Loughor to see Evan Roberts in the revival. "Suddenly Mary Roberts, Evan Roberts' sister came in, "And O how glad we were to see her. She at once took the meeting and said "Dear brothers and sisters we were at Aberafon last night where we held two meetings in the same church. The first one was very good, but O the second meeting, the power of God came down and dozens of people were gloriously saved. That's what we need here this afternoon." It didn't come and the meeting was drawn to a close. The people began to leave and we were only a few behind when I passed Miss Roberts, I told her that when she was describing the service in Aberafon I felt that I would like to see the same here because I wanted to be saved. "O that's grand, come down on your knees here" she replied. Down I went and she began to pray that the dear Lord would save me. The people that had left returned when they heard the praying. William John, one of my friends was one of them. He asked loudly "What is going on here?" Someone said "Miss Roberts is praying for Edward Wilkins". 'And for me too Miss Roberts" he cried . And went down more in the manner of a swimmer than of a cow, just the same as the Rev. D. Morgans, Tabor, did when he fell on his face in the aisle when he showed people how to repent. By now all the people had returned and the power of God came down and the revival started. This friend of mine sang "Lord I'm coming home, coming now to Thee, wash me cleanse me in thy blood". The dear Lord listened and answered his prayer because he was wondrously saved and also the other two. They all jumped into the lifeboat, but I failed and the meeting came to a close again. We left with many rejoicing in the Lord"[9]

Edward Wilkins later understood that he needed to "believe and receive" and he was born again underground at Penygroes

Emlyn Colliery on the 16th February, 1905.

"I remember on that memorable day Jesus Christ was a real companion to me and I felt Him by my side as a living bright reality. When we came to the railway crossing...I noticed that the gate was open but not enough for two of us, and because I could not change my position at His side I did not like to go before Him or behind Him, so I asked Him "What shall we do now?" But that was nothing to Him and we went through alright."[9]

Accounts of Mary's contribution to the Revival are contained in many of the newspaper reports including this one of a meeting in Pentre on December 4th:

"It may be added that among the workers who arrived during the meeting were Mr. Evan Roberts' younger sister, seemingly only fifteen or sixteen years of age, but full of the work, and Miss Hopkins of Loughor. The two subsequently proceeding to Tonypandy to assist in a meeting that evening"[10]

"Miss Mary Roberts gave a short address during which she referred to a text on the wall of the building "Except a man be born again he cannot see the Kingdom of God", and said that two months ago she did not understand the meaning of that verse but thank God she understood it now"[11]

She spent some time on teams with Sidney Evans before travelling with Evan. Evan Roberts asked Mary and Annie Davies to go with him to Liverpool. Mary and Annie seemed to make quite a team, Annie would frequently break the way open for the spontaneous Spirit led meetings that were at the heart of the Revival, Mary praying and speaking.

"In Liverpool on March 29th Mary read 1 John chapter 4 and then delivered a "pithy address in English appealing to the unconverted to take Jesus as a friend, an appeal which roused the congregation to sing "Diolch, diolch Iddo" (Thanks be to Him). The next day she again "delivered a brief English address", "I offer you Jesus with a smile" she said "because my own heart is full of joy."[12]

In a difficult meeting in Liverpool on April 3rd she prayed

"for the removal of every hindrance to the meeting so that souls might be saved in the chapel and among the great congregation outside." The people sang and she then preached during which time the people outside could be heard singing.

On Sunday April 9th she delivered a "pithy Welsh address based on the words "For God so loved the world" and Annie sang as a solo "Y Gwr wrth Ffynon Jacob" (The Man at Jacob's Well)."[13]

Mary Roberts and Annie also went with Evan to Anglesey.

"Presently Miss Annie Davies' voice rings out in one of Sankey's hymns and every other voice in the throng becomes silent. During the brief interval of silence that followed, Miss Mary Roberts, who is becoming wonderfully proficient in Welsh reads Isaiah chapter 55, "O Come to the waters" and bases on the opening verse a winning and persuasive address...It is a custom in North Wales, not in South, to call out publicly the names of converts as they yield and this adds no little to the interest and the excitement of the proceedings. Thus tonight it was found that amongst the women converts was the wife of a man who surrendered last night at Llandeusant." "Glorious" cries the revivalist "we must save them in families"[14]

Mary worked effectively in team. She saw meetings and situations break open, again and again when she prayed, preached or gave testimony. She was truly a "Child of the Revival".

Florrie Evans

Florrie continued as a powerful force in the move of God she had triggered through raw testimony.

"Robert Ellis tells how Joseph Jenkins acknowledged that God had used Florrie to help deliver him from self and philosophy. It seems that one evening in October 1904 she interrupted his sermon and began to sing "Just as I am" until by the last verse he was on his knees, slain, singing "O Lamb of God I come". On the evening

of her public confession of Christ she told her pastor that the Holy Spirit had compelled her to testify"[15]

She continued to move powerfully in prayer and prophecy, as she worked amongst the churches of Cardiganshire, North and South. She continued to travel with Joseph Jenkins and went with him and Maud Davies on an exciting tour of North Wales. Florrie was known for her praying, her weeping and her fearless sharing of what God had shown her. At times she and Maud took meetings on their own in places such as Llangollen, Ruabon and Coedpoeth.

In Bangor one of them declared in a meeting of 1500 people at Twrgwyn Chapel "O what a hard people you are. Here has Mr. Jenkins been preaching to you for an hour and not a single Amen. You are no friends of Christ."[16] Straight talking was obviously the order of the day!

We are challenged now by the testimony of Florrie, Annie May and Mary. Can He raise up again such radical, fiery teenage revivalists? Will we let Him? If they are raised up will we find a way to partner with them without controlling or crushing? Will we release without abandoning? Many women's movements across the nations along with chapels, and churches, are dying of old age. Mentoring and discipleship must not be lost as the most natural of lifestyles. It is time to explore a fresh partnership and releasing across the generations. If we do not take risks and experiment we will surely die a lonely death.

Ash Valley

The Father
Watching
Over a valley of Ashes
and burnt stones -
His eyes searching,
singing, green shoots
out of dead land.

9

Salvations, Signs and Wonders

"I had felt for a year or two..that the storm could not be far away. Soon I felt the waters begin to cascade. Now the bed belongs to the river and Wales belongs to Christ."[1]

Evan Phillips' words speak of a nation receiving a flood tide of salvation. A cold and prodigal nation had turned and received the Father's kiss.

Evan Phillips' daughter, Magdalen, was one of the many of every age and class who came to salvation. Her story is told by her niece, Bethan Lloyd-Jones, the wife of Martin Lloyd-Jones the famous preacher and teacher.

"Magdalen was without doubt a rebel...she was distinctly uncomfortable in this atmosphere of revival, she was somewhere in her early thirties. I don't know that she ever voiced her doubts and feelings - she was too devoted to her parents to do that. But she didn't need to; her silence and aloofness spoke volumes, although she was a very great favourite with us children because she was full of fun and could think up the most lovely things to do. Now she was caught up in this tremendous visitation of God the Holy Spirit - resenting it and wishing no doubt she could get away. She went to the meetings with the others and seemed unmoved until one night the meeting was over and Sunny Side kitchen was alive with family and friends when in rushed Mag sobbing uncontrollably. She fell on her knees in the middle of the floor and poured her soul out, confessing the hardness of her heart, the rebelliousness and the coldness of her spirit, thanking God for all he had done in Christ and beseeching Him to forgive and receive her, weeping and crying aloud all the time. Suddenly in the open doorway stood my grandfather, he had realised that something unusual was happening and had come to investigate. Now he recognised that his prayers were answered. With the tears pouring down his cheeks he said, "Thank God, O

Mag's Family - Sunny Side

thank God I can die happy now that Mag is safe". Indeed Mag was safe, her experience was no flash in the pan, she was filled with an undeviating love and loyalty to the Lord who had so wonderfully broken through all her resistance and given her the joy of salvation. She later married one of the ministerial students who became minister of the Welsh Presbyterian Church at Senghenydd. It was during their time there that the terrible pit disaster occurred when over 400 miners were killed."[2]

There was an urgency about the times, as those saved became workers not simply in the heat of the Revival but in the difficult years that followed. There was also an urgency in the meetings themselves:

"There was not a cubic inch of vacant ground anywhere. People clambered up the rails of the pulpit, sat on the steps leading from one pew to another, and scores struggled in vain at the entrance to the chapel to get within hearing distance...Women fainted and had to be carried out while the revivalist was speaking, but he went along with the same smile on his face. "Don't take them out" he pleaded" Let them go on their knees and ask forgiveness. That is the sovereign remedy"."[3]

In Hafod Evan "pronounced, "the two watchwords of the present Revival were "subdue the church and save the world"...In concluding his address he suggested that the present time saw the beginning of the fulfillment of the prophecy of the prophet Joel that in the latter days God would pour forth his Spirit on all flesh" [4]

These women were living proof that the Holy Spirit "was being poured out on all flesh" and they were passionate that none should miss the opportunity to come to Him.

The story of the Revival is woven from the stories of wrecked lives turned around. May we be wrecked by the broken heart of God as we read them, not simply for their lives then but for the lives around us now. These testimonies of the past release faith for radical salvations now.

In Clydach, in 1904, there was

"A woman on whose face was indicated the agony of soul she suffered. The evangelist took in the situation at a glance and immediately saw that she was seeking. "Teach me to be good" she pleadingly besought the missioner and when he advised her to pray she despairingly replied that she could not - her sins made it impossible...The missioner was earnestly pleading with the woman, whose tears streamed down her face, the people in the mean time singing and praying for the woman. The woman and missioner were seen to kneel together, and then the people completely lost themselves and shouted, some with hands uplifted and others actually clapping their hands with joy and sang "Diolch iddo" with a fervor seldom heard in revival meetings... The woman who had never been taught to pray even in the simplest of ways had found the Saviour and promised to lead a new life henceforth"[5]

In Newport:

"On Tuesday night the service was notable because three of the conversions were as a result of prayer that had been made in the last week. "One woman after praying all night for her husband had the joy of seeing him surrender to the Lord, although up to that moment they were both unaware of each other's presence in the meeting."[6]

"There were 70 conversions and a number of notable conversions. In one case a woman was brought in under the influence of drink

and after a service which lasted several hours and during which the prayers for her were continued, she became converted and the next day became reconciled with her husband from whom she had been separated."[7]

In Barry:

"A man and his wife were quarrelling when they were both drunk and she threatened to go out and kill herself. She was on her way to the docks to commit suicide when she passed the Melrose Street chapel. She was attracted by the singing from the revival meeting and as she went in crying, asked the congregation to pray for her. They did, and she was converted that night."[8]

In Merionethshire:

"The proprietress of a pub was converted in one of the revival meetings and the first thing she did after her conversion was to get a ladder and pull down the sign board over the door at the pub. In another meeting she said she had never felt so happy in her life as when she took the sign down."[9]

At a meeting in Pwllheli with Evan Roberts in the market hall, "One woman in broken accents thanked God for the 26th of January last when she forsook her old ways for ever. She related the contrast in her appearance in that hall to that of previous occasions when she appeared before the magistrates."[10]

Whole communities of ordinary people were being transformed by a supernatural gospel. In 1978 Elizabeth Williams from Gwyddelwern was asked for her memories of the Revival,

"That was the year I went to Maesgwyn Farm as a maidservant. We were allowed to go to chapel regularly to the prayer meeting on Monday...One day we went...then Edward Hannan stood up again and said "Thomas Lloyd needs to be saved"- just like that. And out he went. Well, we knew then that something great was happening. Everyone was singing and praying. We saw the door open and we could see nothing apart from a great light. It was blinding us. The first thing I remember is that we were all on our knees..I think now

that it was the Holy Spirit who came. That was the light. It's in the Bible isn't it? It says there, "They were all with one accord in one place and suddenly there came a sound from heaven" and He came like that. "It was lovely you know we lost ourselves"...The Holy Spirit had taken hold of everyone - the young people, the sick, the children in school. He had gone to the school and they had formed little groups during the lunch hour to pray. And those who heard them said they were excellent...The Old Tavern remained closed for years with no talk of it. There is talk sometimes of some who turned away after experiencing the revival but I did not see any. Those at Gwyddelwern held anyway. After the evening of the tavern, there was a prayer meeting the following evening and who should be there but some who had been in the tavern the previous evening, praying and giving thanks for being set free from sin. I know that they remained true to the Lord."[11]

There is an urgency in the day in which we live, many endure a living hell, only to face a dying one. We cannot choose to place our personal comforts, pains and weaknesses before the cry of the lost. As a family we live in an ordinary street of terraced houses; hurting seven and eight year olds hammer on our door for help. Many all over the nations have no doors of lives, homes or churches to hammer on. Even when there are doors which would open up to the cry of the lost, the doors are sometimes so hidden as to be useless.

Then, a church that was part of the fabric of the culture suddenly became visible. Today our invisible lives and churches need to look for fresh doors into the culture itself. He is calling us to connect - the connection for many will be in a supernatural demonstration of the power of the gospel.

Evan's own emphasis on visions and the recounting of the 13 major visions he received released a freedom amongst the people to engage with a supernatural gospel. Others started moving in signs and wonders, had dreams and saw visions. Some were having them already.

In Swansea a visitor to the Revival noticed that

"There was one remarkable person present, a Mrs. Jones, who has had visions of this revival. All she said was in Welsh but it was evident that all her heart came out in what she said of God's purpose for her country. This is one of the proofs of how long God has been preparing this outpouring of blessing."[12]

Some visions were connected to salvation,

"...One of the most remarkable utterances of that remarkable night was that of a woman who gave a vivid description of a vision she had seen on the previous evening. "I saw" she said "a great expanse of beautiful land, with friendly faces peopling it. Between me and this golden country was a shining river, crossed by a plank. I was anxious to cross but feared that the plank would not support me. But at that moment I gave myself to God and there came over me a great wave of faith and I crossed in safety"[13]

Other visions were connected to His heart for a particular location,

"At another of the meetings a young woman declared that she had seen a vision of Jesus Christ with outstretched arms blessing the churches of Newport. This was several weeks before the revival came to Newport and she stated at the time "That the Lord had a mighty blessing in store for the town." From what has happened since it seems that the prophecy has been more than fulfilled".[14]

The ordinariness of women's everyday lives was being disturbed but also enriched by this incredible outpouring.

"There was an acceptance of a new freedom and role for women. Sisterhoods and guilds and women's missionary auxiliaries would have been radical before 1904. These early women's meetings had a free experimental feel about them. Although they had to have male elders of the chapel to start the service, praise and worship were central in the meetings...In the mornings in Bethesda, the wives got up with their husbands at half past four in the morning and did daily housework from five to half past eight, when they sent the children to school. Then the mothers would go into any chapel if the revival

was on there and then they'd go home to meet the children coming home at 12. And after they sent the children they'd go back again. It was throughout the whole town like that for the mothers were so interested. They would go home in the afternoon and prepare dinners for husbands and then return to the House of the Lord. It was all praise and worship and God was glorified in a wonderful way. The people were blessed and life was worth living."[15]

One otherwise ordinary woman, Mary Jones of Egryn had her life transformed in the most extraordinary way. We have seen the release of young single women or widows. There was also the release of women with families who were not free to travel. Mary Jones was a farmer's wife deeply rooted in her community. She didn't travel widely but she had a profound impact on the nation through reports of the Egryn Lights, supernatural signs in the heavens which were associated with her ministry. She lived in the small hamlet of Egryn, on the coast between Barmouth and Harlech. She had lived in the farmhouse at Islawrffordd all her life. Her life had not been easy as she had been orphaned while young and brought up by her older sister. She was brought up in the chapel and had become a member 17 years before the Revival broke out. Some years before the Revival her son died and four years after that her sister, who was more a mother to her, died as well.

"She felt the loss so severely that she hardened against God - "I do not believe that anyone had harder thoughts of Him than I did then". Though she was a member of the chapel she stayed away more and more, though her husband, who was not a member but a faithful attender, kept going. One Sunday evening he wanted her to go with him but she wouldn't go, "There was nothing in the chapel for her". After they (her husband and her 12 year old daughter) had gone something strongly moved her to ask, "Is there no book in this house that can help me?" There was a Bible but that had become a blank book. Searching among the few odd volumes in the house she found Sheldon's "In His Steps". She began to read, listlessly

at first, then with growing interest almost awe. When her husband came home he was struck by the changed face - a face which had been softened by no tears, lighted by no smiles for months and now it alternated with both. She told him how the light had come, "What would Jesus do?" was from that night her one question. "[16]

"She returned to her chapel and became a most faithful and silent helper, her only public ministry being the giving out of a hymn. But when the news of the South Wales movement came she was deeply moved and at last asked her brother who superintended the mission - or branch chapel - to announce meetings for prayer. She was full of expectation but the first meeting on a Monday evening chilled her very heart. However another was announced for the Thursday, it was better attended and people took part more readily"[17]

"Impressed by the work Evan Roberts was performing in the South, she in the privacy of her chamber prayed long, earnestly, repeatedly that she might be made the means of converting her friends and neighbours. "I did not want to go outside to the big world outside Egryn, but I longed to be the means of bringing my husband to Christ". For 17 years my example had shown him the hollowness of a mere profession of religion and my heart yearned to be allowed to undo the wrong I had thus done him. I prayed that I might convert all my friends, relations, neighbours - "I did not ask for more than that. I prayed that night whether in body I cannot tell or whether out of the body I cannot tell, but in any case in a vision of the night the Saviour appeared and told her that the mission for which she longed was not for her but reserved for another whose name for obvious reasons I suppress". In the morning she visited this friend and told her the message. "O, I can never do it, I can never do it" was the response to the proffered commission. That night, Mrs. Jones' "Star" appeared for the first time."[18]

This was the beginning of the "Egryn Lights", of signs and wonders appearing in the sky over that region. The lights took various forms including the star, a pillar of fire and lights forming over the houses. She saw these lights as signs giving her guidance as to where she should visit and as to how many people were going to be saved in particular meetings. That night

" She attended the little chapel, related her vision, told how her friend had refused the heavenly commission and added, "She has missed the one great opportunity of her life and my service is accepted". And that night, Monday, December 5, 1904 she entered upon her mission. Within a fortnight all but 4 of the inhabitants of the district she had prayed to be allowed to be the means of converting made public profession of Jesus Christ. Among the converts are her husband and immediate neighbours...Throughout the district she is held in universal esteem. Every post brings her letters from England, Scotland, Ireland for her prayers on behalf of particular prodigals."[18]

One one occasion

"She had seen the light hovering over some houses on the hilltops, and was puzzled for she thought there was no-one in those houses unconverted or at least out of church membership. But one day she was told by the Wesleyan minister at Barmouth, and another friend who visited her, that there was one old woman in one of those houses not now on Christ's side. "Ah that must be it" she said. The two friends went up and found the woman in concern for her son. Mrs. Jones visited her, she became one of the 51 in that marvellous fortnight."[19]

The Egryn Lights became one of the most startling phenomena of the Revival. They ended up being investigated in the National Press by the Mirror and the Mail - both reporters saw the lights. The lights were also seen by others, here is a description given by a local reporter.

"When after several hours friendly chat with Mrs. Jones in her own house I rose to leave, she stopped me with a remark, "You had better wait that you might see the light for yourself. It would be a pity for you to go back without seeing it." Then I waited and saw. The Rev. Llewelyn Morgan and the Rev. Roger Williams, Dyffryn and one other were there. Mrs. Jones said, "We cannot start yet, the light has not yet come", 5 minutes later she went out again and returned saying the light has come and we could go. Mrs. Jones directed our attention to the southern sky. While she yet spoke, between us and *the hills there suddenly flashed forth an enormous luminous star, flashing forth and enormously brilliant white light, and emitting from its whole circumference dazzling sparklets like flashing rays from a diamond...So far the light and star had been equally visible to and seen alike by the five who formed our company. Now it made a distincion...I suddenly saw three brilliant rays of dazzling white light stride across the road from mountain to sea throwing the stone wall into bold relief...as though a searchlight had been turned on that particular spot. There was not a living soul near, nor a house from which the light should have come. Another short half mile and a blood red light appeared to me in the centre of the village street just before us. I said nothing until we had reached the spot. The red light had disappeared as suddenly and mysteriously as it had come and there was absolutely nothing which could have been conceivable for its having been there before...I had not told Mrs. Jones what the nature of the lights I had seen was...but she described the two appearances precisely as I had described them above, thus establishing beyond question the fact that we had both seen the self-same manifestation. Those are the simple facts, I offer no comment on them, I simply state what I saw."*[20]

This is how she was interpreted in *Y Goleuad*, June 9, 1905,

"The mission of this woman evangelist is unparalleled, just as that of Evan Roberts. These are two leading figures today in Wales. Both have emerged from the ranks of the ordinary people, quite untutored. They were both nurtured in villages on the seaboard and were the products of the "seiat". They had experienced the most exacting spiritual discipline and had seen the most remarkable visions. Having received a special message from the Living God they were both moved by the Holy Spirit at about the same time to proclaim it until a whole nation has been awakened and set alight. "[21]

At one point, Mary pleaded with God, "O Lord, stay your hand until I have put on immortality" because of the extent of the power of the Holy Spirit she was experiencing.

The response to her was mixed. The *Barmouth Advertiser* maintained an objective approach to her throughout the Revival in North Wales. The last report is of her taking a service in May 1905. The *Cambrian News* responded differently.

"The worse than silly talk about revival, visions and flashes and spirit compellings goes on. The revival is being discredited and the neurotics are monopolising attention."[22]

"The individuals who begin to see visions, hear voices and rappings cannot be too carefully tended by their friends. Mr. Evan Roberts and Mrs. Mary Jones must take care of their stomachs and nerves, they may be upset...God is not reduced to conjuring tricks of a low order."[23]

The response to Mary Jones and the Egryn Lights remains mixed to this day. Fursac, a French psychologist interested in the Revival, developed a theory in line with the growing rationalism of the age. He believed that her visions resulted from her earlier difficult life. Fryer's lecture "read to the society of psychical research suggested that the lights could be the result of a mental stimulus not dissimilar to the way a sharp blow to the head causes one to see stars...For some...trained to trust anything abnormal as delusion...what they could not disprove they denied or pushed aside as mere auto-suggestion."[24]

It is interesting that in the Hebrides Revival lights were also seen over houses.

For Mary the lights were a sign that pointed to those on the verge of salvation, they were a sign that released faith and obedience. For Evan the visions released the sign and wonder of a nation turning, heaven invading earth and the Kingdom of God advancing. These signs confronted a nation with the reality of a supernatural gospel. This supernatural gospel wasn't, however, embraced by everyone. The culture then was one of a "Christianised" society resting against a backdrop of increasing rationalism and liberal theology. There was a growing suspicion towards anything which couldn't be "scientifically explained". The culture now in Western Europe is Post-modern. The emphasis now is on the highly experiential as people are mistrustful of the "over-arching" meta-narrative - *the ONE truth*. People want to see, feel and experience things for themselves. If this happens and they feel and see the power of God they may just want it explained, as at Pentecost. It is time for a fresh expectation to arise of signs and wonders on the streets and even in the churches. It is time to lay aside passivity, cynicism, unbelief and fear. In 1904 there was a brief taste of what could happen when a nation is touched with the supernatural power of God, surely it is time again for more. They experienced a controversial taste of Acts 2:17-21 surely we cannot be satisfied with the dust of history unless it challenges us to reach for more today!

Acts 2:17-21

"In the last days, God says, I will pour out my Spirit on all people, your sons and daughters will prophesy, your young men will see visions, your old men will dream dreams. Even on my servants both men and women I will pour out my Spirit in these days and they will prophesy. I will show wonders in the heaven above and signs on the earth below, blood and fire and billows of smoke. The sun will be turned to darkness and the moon to blood before the coming of the great and glorious Day of the Lord. And everyone who calls on the name of the Lord will be saved."

TRANSFORMER of the NATIONS

You lift up my head
All sorrows cast down
Filled my life with hope again
Now that You're around me

You burnt up my shame
With a flame that is wild
Gave me back my dignity
With the heart of a child

If You could do it for me,
You could do it for our Nation
Wash away the pain
And give us Your name

Your purpose lives on
For Your presence we cry
Flowing out to the nations
From wells no longer dry

If You could do it for me,
You could do it for the Nations
Wash away the pain
And give them Your name

So lift up your head
To the Transformer of the Nations
Turn and face Him with no shame
He's calling your name.

10

Women Worldwide

The cork had "popped"- the new wine could not be contained in Wales - it was destined to flood the nations and in this too women would play their part.

In the early months of the Revival Evan believed,

"That this revival has not only came to Wales, and would reach over all Wales, but that it would go over England, Scotland and Ireland as well." More than that he considered that we were on the eve of a revival that would go over the whole world. He had, he said, himself seen a vision of a candle burning brightly, and then the light of the sun shining upon all; and he took it to mean the light of the gospel, first as a candle and then as a great sun shining upon the whole world."[1]

His conviction of this grew stronger as the Revival continued.

"Let them follow God's example and give to Christ as He gave. When Wales became obedient and bent to God then all the nations of the world would bend to Wales, which would then be the Temple of God. If the Principality would not obey the devils would dance on her."[2]

These strong words contrast to one of the first lighthearted references to mission in an early Revival meeting. A missions offering was taken up and in the excitement of the moment.

"Some threw every penny in their possession into the boxes and the young ladies who took the boxes round had been so much absorbed by the mighty influence of the service that they could not count the money!"[3]

Newspaper reports encouraged the news of the Revival to spread in the UK and further afield. Letter writing meant the news spread quickly along people's networks of relationships. Jessie Penn-Lewis, a main motivator in establishing the Welsh Keswick at Llandrindod Wells in 1903, was significant in this through her many overseas connections. In fact this passing on of Revival news was possibly her most useful contribution to the Revival as a whole.

People from many nations were drawn to visit Wales to catch the Revival fire, or at least to see what all the excitement was about.

Hospitality was an important factor in the receiving of visitors from home and abroad. On February 8th, when Evan had decided not to go to Cardiff there was an influx of visitors to Nantymoel.

"With strangers who arrived from Cardiff and elsewhere there was a rush for lodging accommodation. Scottish, English, French, and North Wales ministers and laymen were numerous, so that there was ample opportunity afforded for the display of Welsh hospitality, and it was freely offered and accepted...In Nantymoel on Thursday night there were visitors from England, three ladies from Germany who did not understand even English, six French gentlemen, a lady sent from Paris by the church with which she is connected, two missionaries on a visit to the country from China, and dozens of Scottish, English and North Wales clergymen, preachers and laymen."[4]

There were visitors from overseas in many of the Revival meetings with women often prominent amongst them.

"There was a deputation of well known ladies and gentlemen from France and Switzerland. They went to see a Welsh Sunday school at two chapels and in one visited the infants department of the school. They were received by Mrs. Lewis, the wife of the pastor. Mdlle. D'Aubigne of Geneva delivered a brief address and the party sang a hymn in French. Mdlle. D'Aubigne was struck that in Welsh Sunday schools not only were children present but that "their fathers and mothers, grandfathers and grandmothers were also present." She later spoke in an International Revival Service conducted by

"Awstin"(the Western Mail Revival reporter) at Ton. Her father was historian of the Protestant Reformation in Europe, and her mother an Irishwoman who was the founder of the first Sunday school in Geneva. She spoke mainly about the spiritual darkness and plight of the miners in Belgium. "Prayers were offered for the spread of the revival to France, Switzerland and Scotland, and indeed the whole world."... To hear these people describe the scenes at a Paris meeting convened to hear the report of four French pastors who had visited the Welsh revival was touching; while to hear the same people declare that the revival had not actually broken out in France and Switzerland (notwithstanding their wonderful experiences and their own determination to come to Wales to catch some of the "fire") reminded me strongly of the early days of the revival in Monmouthshire, when my friends there, with hundreds of converts then enrolled, were "waiting for revival"."[5]

The visitors often wanted to meet the Revival figures they had heard about.

"An American deputation headed by Mr. Weaver, a rich American, visited Mrs. Jones, the Merionethshire seeress at Egryn whose remarkable spiritual experiences has deeply impressed him."[6]

Annie Davies' brother, who was 15 at the time of the Revival, obviously had mixed feelings about the visitors to his home!

"During these revival days my home was a prolonged prayer meeting or religious gathering. People came literally from all over the world to meet the parents of the famous young girl evangelist as my sister had become...they were a fanatical crowd."[7]

In Liverpool there was a special meeting arranged for the women in which a clear call to mission was given.

"Evan Roberts, "Speaking eventually with much difficulty" said there was someone who had for some time resisted and was still resisting the promptings of the Spirit to consecrate their life to the work of foreign missions."There are millions of pagans," he said, "in the world without knowledge of the gospel, and yet there is

someone in the building who refuses to carry the light to them. He or she must at once plead for forgiveness".

This announcement gave rise to a painful and extraordinary incident. A little while before the evangelist arrived a young lady, seated on the ground floor, had offered up a remarkable prayer, and now she got up and, sobbing, publicly confessed that she was guilty of the act of disobedience which had been alluded to. For three years she had felt impelled to offer herself in mission work in the hills of Khasia, Assam, but her love of home, of family and of friends had proved too potent for her. She had loved home more than Christ. Then the young woman from Blaenau Ffestiniog burst out into passionate prayer, pleading for forgiveness and strength, "O, Lord," she cried, "I yield, I yield. Do Thou with me as Thou wilt." The congregation was affected to tears."[8]

The outpouring from Wales went worldwide, with India, probably, the nation most affected. This was as a result of the strong mission links between the two countries.

"A letter is printed from a lady missionary from Machynlleth who is a worker for the Calvinistic Methodists in the Khasia Hills of India. "Only just a word by this mail to tell you the glorious news that I know you will be rejoiced to hear. The revival has broken out in great power in the Khasia Hills. Think what it means. God has had mercy on India. This great land of teeming millions, the stronghold of Hinduism and Mohammedanism, and in this far north corner of Assam the Holy Spirit has been poured out upon the native Christian church."[9]

News began to break from different parts of India. In many places it was the women who were impacted first.

"At Cherrapoonjee when a girl began to pray for her uncles, all the people began to scream and cry for pardon...while this went on the heathen came running in and then ran out, then in again, not understanding what had taken place. At first the women seemed more affected than the men, but now the men and women are similarly moved."[10]

Orphanages were transformed as children responded. In Dohnavur Amy Carmichael described what happened in her work amongst the Tamils:

"It spread to the women...soon the whole upper half of the church was on its face on the floor crying to God...oblivious of all others. The sound was like a sound of waves or strong wind in the trees...I have never heard of such a thing among Tamil people.

The results of this were that the workers were revived, all the children were converted and in the village there were several notable conversions. Amy Carmichael said, "It is as if "the powers of the world to come suddenly became intensely real"."[11]

Perhaps the greatest outpouring in India happened through the work of an extraordinary woman, Pandita Ramabai. The daughter of a Brahmin scholar, she became a Christian and started a work in Mukti in the Maharashtra area of west India. She drew together about 2,000 widows and numerous orphans. They built workshops and school houses for girls who had been rescued from immorality.

She had, out of her real hunger for God visited Keswick in England, so in January 1905 when she heard about the Welsh Revival

"She told her pupils all about it and called for volunteers to meet her daily for special prayer for a revival in India. Seventy came forward and from time to time others joined"[12].. *"Then they heard the news of the revival in Khasia. On the 30th June, 1905 the Spirit fell on all present and a number of girls were stricken under conviction of sin. They continued in prayer all night...The Bible School is full of Spirit baptised girls, only a few are left and they are seeking. I think at last 400 have received the Holy Spirit. The revival spread from Mukti to Poona, at Poona 120 girls were described as in a state of revival, they were shaking, laughing, agonising in prayer and many of them had a vision of Jesus. Miss Abrahams (an American missionary) took a group of eleven girls to Telegaon and there in the famine orphanage witnessed scenes similar to those in Mukti.*

Miss Abrahams and a small team were invited to Ratnagiri, an American Presbyterian mission station which was then shaken by the power of the Holy Spirit."[13]

Revival came in a form the missionaries didn't agree with but didn't dare quench.

There is a wonderful report of what happened through the girls in an article headed "A Band of Apostolic Girls". They didn't simply spread news of the Revival to other orphanages and mission stations they went out into the villages:

"Miss K. Steele of the Poona and Indian Village mission says, "I should like to give my testimony to the wonderful work the Holy Spirit has done in the girls from Mukti Orphanage...their lives are consistent through and through, their consciences are tender. Their Matron said "It is not very difficult to matron these girls - the Holy Spirit is so working among them it is a work of God's grace to see 75 women and girls living week after week in such love and sweet fellowship with many trials and difficulties to bear. It is one long praise meeting, they go out in bands with us to preach the gospel. They are despised, evil spoken against, have stones, dirt and all manner of things thrown at them. Rough people try to frighten them. But they stand unmoved and truly seem to love not their lives to the death. They give clear ringing testimony of what Jesus has done for themselves and of what He is willing to do for people. Their hearers are often wonderstruck and cannot understand by what power these girls can speak in such a way. Their prayers and praises are full of the name of Jesus and His precious blood. Most of them pray at times in tongues."[14]

The ongoing influence of the Revival continued through the sending of missionaries who had been impacted through 1904. India again was a particular focus.

Beatrice James' life was transformed in the Revival and found a deeper commitment to overseas mission. In the Revival she was changed from simply being a faithful member of the Baptist church in Barry to an activist prepared to go to India. The daughter of the Principal of the Baptist College, Cardiff,

Lillian Mary Edwards also went to India. William Edwards and his wife were leaders during the 1904/05 Revival. They had been very involved in the meetings in Cardiff amongst the poor and the destitute. They felt that their daughter Lillian's calling to missions was part of the fruit of Revival, Lillian herself named meeting Evan Roberts as a major influence on her life.[15]

Three of the key figures in the Revival also went to India as missionaries. Sidney Evans and Mary went in 1920. Sidney was Principal of the Cherra Theological College and influential in the CM Foreign Mission. Prior to marrying Sidney, Mary Roberts had spent 5 years in the Jamestown Girls Institute in Nigeria.

Florrie Evans also went to India. She spent a year at Doric Lodge, the Regions Beyond Missions Centre. However she returned from India after 3 years, and some denominational leaders felt that she "should not have gone, believing her to be unsuitable for work in that land".[16] Quite why they thought she was unsuitable I have not discovered!

Madagascar was also dramatically impacted by Revival. In May 1905 Thomas and Elizabeth Rowlands received Revival reports which they read to the local Christians. This stirred intense prayer borne out of a real desire for revival. On May 6th the Holy Spirit broke out in power.

"There was a scene of wildest confusion, some sobbing, some praying or singing scraps of penitential hymns...late at night they continued to praise and pray. Thus we had earnest of more to follow and no-one doubted we had our Pentecost."[17]

The next Sunday 83 converts were baptised and in meetings in May the outpouring continued.

"Elizabeth Rowlands and Rakotovao, a headmaster, went out to the villages. Nothing could dampen the zeal of Elizabeth Rowlands who itinerated untiringly over a large area.. It was a typical Welsh revival."[18]

Elizabeth Rowlands said of one journey "I will only add that in the seven divisions of our district we had evangelistic and revival services during the past months and many hundreds have decided for Christ."[19] In one district there was a mass movement for Christ. Elizabeth Rowlands was the preacher, her husband having a real ability to disciple. He spent much of his time explaining the gospel and counselling people personally. The results were changed lives, families getting rid of their idols, people getting delivered from demons and many salvations. Elizabeth noted the ministry of the women as an important feature, they were praying visiting and preaching and she regarded this as part of "the dawn of a new Madagascar"[20]

There are countless examples of the involvement of women in revival in different nations. In Japan it was sparked through girls in prayer.

"A missionary wrote of a revival outbreak in a girl's school in Japan - "Some four months ago the Christian girls asked if they might meet together once a week for prayer for they felt they were cold hearted...The meetings were quite ordinary until one Saturday they began to pray one after another. Pleading for the outpouring of the Holy Spirit, telling the Lord they could not separate until the Holy Spirit was given."[21]

In the USA Elinor Williams from Llangollen combined temperance work and preaching, encouraging revival not just amongst the Welsh churches. She was in America for an extended period whilst other preachers and evangelists were visiting more briefly. "Rows of men and women would be on their knees, and Elinor Williams described the presence of God "as the bush burning without being consumed."[22]

In Patagonia a powerful work broke out on the 16th and 17th of May, 1905, particularly amongst the young people. This outbreak again resulted from hearing reports about what was happening in Wales. Eluned Morgan, who had visited

Wales in 1903, went back to Wales after the Revival meetings in May and asked Evan for a word for Patagonia. "His word for Patagonia was that they should persevere in spite of all obstacles and disappointments. He assured the Welsh in that land that the prayer of faith and a holy life would prevail." [23]

The Pentecostal movement, with its roots in the Welsh Revival, was similarly mission minded. The Apostolic Church of Wales focussed on Argentina. A Revival convert from Skewen, Neath, Catherine Hollis, went to Argentina with her husband Joseph. In our day Argentina is still experiencing a dynamic ongoing revival.

Perhaps two of the best known missionaries to be sent were Rees Howells and his wife Elizabeth. He had been profoundly impacted by the Revival and Elizabeth had come into assurance of salvation during the course of the Revival itself. They went to South Africa with the SAGM (South Africa General Mission). Weeks after arriving in South Africa in 1915 they were experiencing revival.

"It was known that they came from the land of revival. Rees Howells told some of the stories of 1904-05 even though there was no word for revival in the language of the people. As he listened to the singing and praying "he recognised the sound he had heard in the Welsh revival."[24] *On Sunday October 10th a young lady got up in the meeting to pray because she felt she was not ready for Christ's second coming. "As she prayed she broke down crying, and within five minutes the whole congregation were on their faces crying to God. Like lightening and thunder the power came down. I had never seen this, even in the Welsh revival. I had only heard about it with Finney and others. Heaven had opened and there was no room to contain the blessing. I lost myself in the Spirit and prayed as much as they did. All I could say was, "He has come"."* [25]

The ongoing influence of the Revival was continued through witness and training across the nations and back into Wales itself. Some years later Rees Howells established the Bible College at Swansea.

The Porth Institute was also established, founded by R.B.Jones and W.S. Jones. The Institute was deeply rooted into the Revival, and came out of the conventions which were held in the latter stages of the Revival as a means of training the converts. Missionaries were sent out from the Institute. Lillian Jones broke new ground by going to Japan, Sallie Evans went to Latvia, Arianwen Jones to Poland and Miss Wood went to Spain.

Mary Ann Davies of Ogmore Vale, later known as Mair Davies of Bengal, was described as a stately figure in an Indian sari, "Always talking rapidly with a heart of gold." She said, "I was just a bitter, passionate girl brought up in a quarrelsome house which I was later forced to leave. It was at my father's grave-side that I heard a voice speaking to me. Christ was saying, "Come over into Macedonia and help us". " Rejected by her grandmother, she was almost penniless when she went to Porth to speak to R.B. Jones. He said, "If the Lord is still calling you He will take care of you, so come to Porth." She knew what she was called to do and was trained and later sent out with the Baptists as a missionary although this time it was against R.B. Jones' advice! She was awarded honours in Bengal for her famine relief work.[26]

In the aftermath of the Revival, mission giving remained a priority in some churches such as R.B. Jones' church in Ynyshir. Pit workers and others managed to give a seventh of their income to the Lord. One lady, a Mrs Evans, was sometimes heard praying, "Lord show me how much I can spare. Help me to live on a little..." R.B. Jones admired her so much that he encouraged people to visit her and learn "the secret of sacrificial devotion".[27]

The impact of the Revival was also felt through "Plant Y Diwygiad"- the Children of the Revival who went to other nations. One such amazing lady is the Rev. Catherine Hollister-Jones. Elisabeth Lloyd James (of whom we will hear more later) met her at the National Prayer Breakfast of Wales in Cardiff 2002.

"At the time I was told, "You must meet her. We sense that she's "carrying" a seed from the last revival in Wales." She came to Wales and stood on the platform in Cardiff City Hall and told of her mother relating to her tales of 1904-06, and then she sang a revival song in Welsh. I heard the words "Pan ar eraill rwyt yn galw, Paid a'm gadael"(When on others You are calling, do not pass me by). Something stirred deeply in my spirit...I discovered that Catherine's grandmother and my grandfather were brother and sister. Words failed us both!...Catherine now in her eighties is an ordained Presbyterian minister, one of the first "batch" to be ordained in New Zealand. For 35 years she worked with the poor in India as a missionary, then went back to New Zealand to be the Prayer Co-ordinator for the Presbyterian Church in New Zealand for 6 years. She is now Prayer Co-ordinator for the city of Tauranga in New Zealand...Catherine returned to Wales again to attend the 2003 Prayer Breakfast held in Bala. When all was at an end she asked me to accompany her to Brynbedwog, the old family home, still standing in the hills about 5 miles from the hotel on Bala Lake. She walked the lonely and quiet track up to the farmhouse, now unoccupied. There we both recited Salm 121 (Psalm 121) in Welsh together and prayed. I told her that I'd often heard the phrase "Cymru i Grist a Christ i'r byd" (Wales for Christ and Christ for the World)... The last time I spoke to her over the telephone she had just returned from a mission on South Island, New Zealand. At one meeting she ministered and prayed with a long line of seekers, whilst another preached! Intercessor and Evangelist working side by side. The seed of the last Welsh Revival is still good seed producing good fruit!"[28]

The ongoing effect of the Revival is still felt now in many nations.

"This outpouring of the Holy Spirit, of which the Welsh revival was only one expression, was the head waters from which flowed the modern day Pentecostal, Charismatic and Church renewal movements. Other than speaking in tongues (which broke out

roughly two years after the revival) and manifestations of healing, nearly all the current spiritual manifestations of the Charismatic movement were present in their early forms in the Welsh revival. The Azusa Street meetings of 1906, to which most historians trace the modern origins of the Pentecostal/Charismatic movements, were simply another of the many powerful manifestations and expressions of this unprecedented outpouring of the Spirit of God, the after effects of which continue on to our own day."[29]

The candle that Evan saw in a vision truely became the light of the gospel - "A great sun shining upon the whole world".

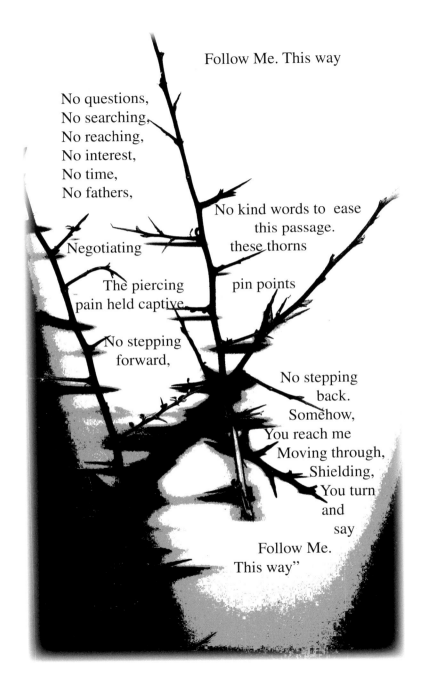

Follow Me. This way

No questions,
No searching,
No reaching,
No interest,
No time,
No fathers,

No kind words to ease
this passage.
these thorns

Negotiating

The piercing
pain held captive.

pin points

No stepping
forward,

No stepping
back.
Somehow,
You reach me
Moving through,
Shielding,
You turn
and
say
Follow Me.
This way"

11

The Glory and the Pain

The Revival outpouring was moving worldwide. However in the February of 1905 there were signs of strain amidst the blessing. However, the blessings were still enormous as Gomer Roberts writes:

"What of the debts that were paid and the enemies reconciled to one another? What of the drunkards who became sober and the prodigals who were restored? Is there a balance that can weigh the burdens of sins that was thrown at the foot of the cross?" [1]

During the 18 months of the Revival it is estimated that five per cent of the population of Wales became Christians and joined the church, that is, one person in every twenty.[2] The social impact was dramatic and often led to unusual trend. For example the Poor Law Guardians in Swansea noticed that elderly parents were being taken back from the workhouse where their children had sent them.[3]

However despite the blessings of the Revival, many have noted that it began to decline from the beginning of February 1905. This followed an attack on Evan by Peter Price which appeared in the correspondence columns of the Western Mail on January 31st. Peter Price was a Congregational minister from Dowlais, he signed his abusive letter "Peter Price (B.A.Hons) Mental and Moral Sciences Tripos, Cambridge (late of Queens College Cambridge). His pride in his intellectual achievements didn't endear him to many of the Revival converts! He believed he was involved in the "True revival" and that Evan Roberts had initiated a "False revival".

"My honest conviction is this: that the best thing that could happen to the cause of the true religious revival amongst us would be for Evan Roberts and his girl companions to withdraw into their respective homes, and there to examine themselves and learn a little more of the meaning of Christianity, if they have the capacity for this, instead of going about the country pretending to show the Way of Life to people, many of whom know a thousand times more about it than they do...Yes but he has a lovely face and a beautiful smile - so some women say - this is the last straw."[4]

Peter Price's criticisms had a sharp pharisaical edge; clothed in religion they promoted a form of godliness but denied the powerful move of the Holy Spirit at the heart of the Revival. His attack stirred a nationwide debate on the Revival, largely conducted through the correspondence columns of the Western Mail.

Some of the responses to Peter Price's criticism were made by women in letters to the Western Mail.

"We were astonished to find that a man who is a servant of the Lord could be so indiscreet as to call this wonderful revival a farce. The Rev. Peter Price should remember that even if Mr. Evan Roberts has not a university degree he has a far more desirable one, viz. "Born Again". If God were not with him Evan Roberts' mission would be a failure, but it has been blessed since the commencement, and is increasing in its fervour. If God is for us who can be against us? No-one, not even a B.A., can injure any of God's people. We heartily wish Mr. Evan Roberts and his co-workers God speed. We are & c., SCHOOLGIRLS." (Peter Price had been dismissive of Evan's lack of a university education).[5]

"Mr. Evan Roberts speaks both English and Welsh. He also sang at the close of the meeting "Never lose sight of Jesus". Mr. Price referred to women speaking of his smiling face. I am a young woman, but in his face I saw the smile of the Divine. May God bless Evan Roberts. A True Believer in Jesus Christ". (Tredegar).[6]

The criticism brought mixture to the Revival stream as did the reactions it drew out. Evan never directly responded to the criticism but it seemed to harden his responses in meetings, there seemed to be less emphasis on love and grace and more on judgement and on not grieving the Holy Spirit.

It is difficult to assess the impact of the criticism on the women who worked with him, although it must have distressed them. In the Liverpool meetings Mary Roberts and Annie Davies seemed to take more weight and were obviously covering his vulnerabilities.

Others seemed to distance themselves. Florrie Evans and Maud Davies, who travelled with Joseph Jenkins, were described in some reports as "Formerly associated with the Revivalist". It may have encouraged women like Kate Llewellyn Morgan to step out and take missions on her own. Although this is hard to assess accurately.

However, as time went on Evan's desire to work in team lessened, until in December, on his last Revival mission, he was not accompanied by any of the women.

The criticism hit in full force in February but it had been there from the very first meetings in the November of 1904. Young people and young converts were criticised for the place they were taking in meetings in which ministers felt swept aside by the corporate response and initiatives being released. There was also criticism of "emotional women".

"Veritas" of Loughor wrote this letter in the South Wales Daily Post, November 15th 1904:

"The inevitable result of the singing coupled with the late midnight hour is that young girls and women, fatigued with exertion, are strung up to a pitch of feverish excitement. Their emotions overpower them and they break out into wild cries and gesticulations. These effects are unfortunately put down as a manifestation of the Spirit. Some participants have since been confined to their homes with nervous prostration. Mr. Roberts says that he opens his mouth in obedience to divine inspiration and that the Spirit speaks through him. What need of denominational colleges? What need of universities? What need of laboriously prepared sermons by ministers if inexperienced

youth and girls can be mouthpieces of the divine intelligence? Then all our educational institutions connected with religion are superfluous."

Comments such as those made by an American evangelist at a meeting in the Rhondda wouldn't have helped any already insecure ministers!

"Some people think this revival is the fizz of a bottle of pop. No, it is the fizz of a fuse and the dynamite is at the end of it...God is going to save the masses and He must do it in His own way. He has told the ministers to stand on one side and let Him have a try."[7]

In some ways the ministers had good reason to feel insecure as an underground revolution had surfaced. A revolution that would release the Body of Christ to minister, released through the unlikely means of young people, women and children, breaking all the "rules". In many cases they didn't realise they were revolutionaries, yet it was a revolution focused on seeing Jesus enthroned in the lives of those who were desperate and hungry for Him. It was a shaking of structures, a shaking that continues to this day as the church struggles to fulfill its mandate to the lost of the nations.

Women were criticised for being emotional - in many ways they were an easy target. They were not just criticised for being emotional but in some cases for taking any part in the meetings at all, whether it was in praying publicly, preaching, testifying or even reading the Bible out loud. There was undoubtedly excess in some of the meetings. Although even that is hard to judge as much of it was the response of frail humanity to the outpoured, outrageous love of the Father. It was the exuberance of ordinary people caught up in an extraordinary move of God, rather than dying the slow death of a cold religion. I really enjoyed an account of two older ladies, caught by police as they climbed over chapel railings to get into a meeting. I think more such "excess" should be encouraged!

Many ministers however were unhappy with the attacks on the Revival. Even years later Rev. Nantlais Williams expressed his disgust towards those who disparaged this move of the Holy Spirit:

"Words often heard from the mouths of some during the first years of the revival were, "O the revival has ended now; everything has gone back to normal now." For such people the revival was nothing more than a sad misadventure which disturbed the peace and quietude of church and country...Very often the words, "O the revival is dead" were nothing but the expression of a deep desire in the speaker's heart...Some, although they saw clear evidence of the saving work of the Holy Spirit, refused to acknowledge it as His work."[8]

The attack by Peter Price gives a flavour of more general criticism of the Revival. It also heralded the beginnings of a very difficult time for Evan personally. He didn't respond to the attack directly, but it shook him and began to colour the way he ministered.

By February 3rd he had been advised by a doctor to rest "in consequence of an attack of nervous prostration". The outcome of this was Evan's decision to have "Seven Days of Silence", staying at Godre'r Coed, Neath. At a time of obvious vulnerability the only person he wanted to see was Annie Davies, whom he obviously trusted and felt safe with. Although there is no evidence for this, written or recorded, he may have also felt attracted to her, even if he spiritualised it.

"He communicated with her through written instructions. On Thursday morning the book contained the instruction to Annie: "There is no person except yourself to see me for the next seven days - not even my father and mother. I am not ill. Tell Mary to inform Dan that he need not trouble for it is the Lord's will."[9]

After the "Seven days" Evan again threw himself into the work of the Revival. The team around him were supportive, yet the one often described by leaders and journalists as "the transparent man" was deeply aware of the need to be careful in how he related to the women who travelled with him. He clearly had no desire to be "some kind of cult leader with female devotees". Even so, rumours could circulate.

"On one occasion one of the singers offered to mend his socks and the story ran like wildfire through the villages![10]

He was devastated when on a day trip to Llandudno before the Revival mission in Gwynedd he saw the newspaper headlines:

"Forthcoming wedding of Evan Roberts to Miss Annie Davies the Singer...He is going to marry Miss Annie Davies, who travels with him frequently."[11]

The story had been copied from an English newspaper, *The Christian Worker*. He knew that many would read the false rumours. This may well have contributed to his decision to "Go alone" on the last of his Revival journeys, the "Caernarvonshire Mission" (December 16th-January 14th, 1906), not even taking Mary with him. In a meeting with the Bala students some time earlier he told them that " a bad atmosphere had developed, so he gave up the singing team idea." The rumours and criticisms of others had taken their toll. At this point he was becoming even more isolated. The seven weeks of mission were to be held in the seven different parts of the county. In fact this didn't happen, and the mission finished at Brynrodyn on January 14th. He didn't return, going back instead to Loughor. In the summer, in a broken down condition, he went to live with Jessie Penn-Lewis and her husband in Leicester.

Annie Davies went with her sister Maggie to London - where they trained as nurses. Annie later married.

The glory of the Revival shone in changed lives, restored marriages and families where children had enough to eat because money wasn't being drunk. It shone in changed workplaces, renewed communities, vibrant churches and the stirring of a world-wide movement of the Holy Spirit. Yet the pain was felt through a pharisaism which silenced, and controversy which divided, bruising the young men and women who had broken through into a different place, taking a nation with them.

The challenge this presents, even now, is enormous. To work in team and face the inevitable wounding with others to affirm and support, rather than to withdraw into isolation is just one of those challenges. There is also the pain they faced in the sound, not just of criticism, but in the even more resounding sound of silence. This "silence" came from the spirtual fathers in the land. Their silence and absence left few places of shelter for those at the forefront of the Revival. The lack of connection across the generations deprived them of the wisdom and encouragement of those who had already walked through the fires of slander and criticism.

It left few places where there might have been genuine accountability; it did however leave a void which those with strong personal agendas were eager to fill. Later Evan, in breakdown, was to hand over responsibility for his life and ministry, in a seemingly irresponsible way, to someone with just such an agenda.

The crushing of hope and the grieving of the Holy Spirit left a hole in the heart of the nation which is still leaking strength. It is a strength which will only be regained in this nation and across the nations as there is true and healthy connection across the generations.

We have to learn, particularly as women, how to lay down offence and find fresh grace, in relationship with others, to run and not give up. If we back off, pain will yet again rob the fulness of the glory waiting to be released in nation after nation.

Dreams with Tread

Dreams with tread on
for rough terrain,
tough dreams?
No tough treading on
our rough dreams.

12

In the House of "Jezebel"?

The most difficult woman to write about in regard to the Welsh Revival is Jessie Penn-Lewis. She is certainly the most controversial. Her name provokes strong reactions, revered in some circles she is strongly disliked in others. Her role in the Revival is associated with its ending, through her influence on Evan Roberts.

Jessie Penn-Lewis, daughter of a Calvinistic Methodist minister in Neath, focused her ministry on a view of the cross which J.C. Pollock referred to as "rather one tracked".[1] She followed the Revival closely and usefully communicated about it to others through articles and in letters to the many influential people she knew.

In the *Life of Faith,* at the end of November 1904 Jessie Penn-Lewis wrote "We have prayed for revival; let us give thanks! The cloud as a man's hand...is now increasing. God is sweeping the southern hills and valleys of Wales with an old time revival."[2]

She felt a connection with the Revival not simply because of her Welsh roots, but because of the stirring that happened in Newquay and region through those who had attended the Llandrindod Convention which she had helped to initiate in the summer of 1903. The fuse to the Revival had been lit in the Newquay area.

Jessie was in many ways a remarkable woman for her day. Married to a supportive and fairly wealthy husband, she advocated the rights of women to minister; she taught, preached, prayed and counselled people. Despite ill health she travelled widely and connected people together from many nations. Yet, as is the case with many of us, she was a real mixture. She was determined to meet Evan, and the accounts of her pursuit of him are disturbing. She started writing in "a black notebook" the things he said that she wasn't happy about! By January of 1905 she had already written to him wanting to meet him personally, "to help him in some way",

"Will you seek the mind of the Spirit and let me know when you would be free to see me. I do not want to come for a few minutes but I have much on my heart from the Lord. I believe He means me to have time to speak to you on things of God. HE will tell you this. I only want to know what He shows you."[3]

She particularly wanted to talk to him after his week of silence in February 1905. She also pursued meetings with the other Revival figures whom she felt were behaving in unhelpful ways. She told her friends that she had met with the lady singers, Dan Roberts, Sidney Evans, and told them that "following "The Way of the Cross"[4] would keep them free from all oppressions and deceptions". We don't know what impact these meetings had on the women. It would be interesting to know how they perceived her and how they responded to her instruction. She wanted Evan to be helped by the same message; he didn't want to be helped by her at this point!

The *Cambrian News* reports of his struggles in the Newquay meeting in March 1905 made her even more concerned. In a number of letters she invited him to Leicester for "counsel and prayer before he broke down altogether or fell victim to some demonic attack". He did not reply. However, by August 1905 she seems to have met him a few times. Letters arranging these meetings fell into the hands of the press, who tried to imply that she was pursuing him for a "relationship". She was, but not for the sort of relationship they suspected!

"If you have no light for future steps yet, OUR house is YOURS for as long as He wills". It seems that she wanted to prepare him for an "even higher ministry"[5], not in Wales, but in Leicester.

Evan didn't return to North Wales to finish the mission he had left, but in the Easter of 1906 went to speak in a Keswick-style convention for church leaders. It could have been Jessie speaking and praying. It was as if he were quoting directly from some of her booklets, maybe he was!

"If I am spared, it will be my only aim to preach Christ and Him crucified, not theoretically but as living truth."[6]

He was involved in a mission at Llandrindod in August 1906. Less than a month later, broken down for the fourth time, he was taken to the Penn-Lewis house in Leicester. During the mission Jessie had been in dispute with various church leaders. She was "so hurt" that she told friends that she would in the future stay away from Wales. "Evan", she said "felt quite shattered by these quarrels and would need some kind of getaway." [7]

"Sitting by the bedside of the sick man she encouraged him to talk about all the visions and voices he had known and all the examples of his strange power to look into people's thoughts and feelings. Then she made him look frankly at the mistaken actions and the misjudgments and to ask himself how he could have been deceived. Believing he was a transparent soul, and thus open to the attacks of deceiving spirits, she both instructed him and comforted him with the following explanation.

"The more spiritual he is, the more open he is to spirit, evil or good. If any believer will seek an experience without the Cross, Satan will give him the desired thing. Then the evidence of a false leading shows up, namely doubts and agitations, and a kind of self exaltation because they have this feeling that God is going to do great things through them and they have been summoned. This is deception.

Evan Roberts would see that his recent depressions and struggles, together with the bold claims he had made in the past, were enough proof that he too had been deceived. From now on he would distrust mystical experiences and would claim that things such as tongues and prophesyings and visions were not safe until believers had far greater wisdom and experience."[8]

Her re-interpretation of the Revival is all there; the fear of emotionalism, the concern that Evan was drawing glory to himself and that the operation of the gifts of the Spirit had been demonically inspired. She interpreted much of the Revival as being the fruit of demonic deception.

During these years he was very isolated, refusing to see his family including his father and Dan. News of his mother's illness wasn't passed on, according to a neighbour, "because of his nervous condition". Later he refused to see her before she died. There is no record that any of the "Revival" women tried to contact him. I wonder if they felt betrayed by his leaving of Wales, and his rejection of family and old friends. Jessie's explanation of this kind of behaviour was that

"...He cannot open the things of God to those who are severed from him in spirit by doubt or unbelief. Those who are around him cannot get into conversation with him even if present in the same house if these laws of the Spirit are ignored."[9]

Others were also kept from contact with him. Perhaps most seriously, Alexander Boddy who, central to the Sunderland Outpouring, wasn't allowed to meet with him. Evan's life might well have been different if they had met. Boddy wrote a letter to Jessie saying that he feared that

"Satan was making people so obsessed with possible counterfeits and delusions that they had lost sight of the fact that "the Holy Spirit can and does manifest Himself more powerfully and wonderfully. They minimise the power and the care of Christ for His people, and they flee from abandonment to God..."[10]

The description applied very clearly to Jessie's own position. Alexander Boddy wanted to meet with Evan on his own so he and his wife invited Evan

"... to come and see what was happening and to hear testimony of those who had "received". They wanted him to see that what they were involved in was scriptural and that their heart was for the "pure centre of every revival". Jessie didn't want him to go there, but wanted them to meet Evan in her house, and she spoke for Evan in saying that "he has clear light on the matter and is greatly burdened about you." In the reply to their request she also said that she was praying for them "to turn to the Lord" and that "God was giving her a work to do on these dangers". Her letter brought to an end any attempt to meet."[10]

War on the Saints by "Jessie Penn-Lewis with Evan Roberts" attacked all that had happened in 1904 and condemned the emerging Pentecostal revival connected with Alexander Boddy and others as "the work of an invading host of evil spirits".

"In December 1913 in *The Overcomer* (Jessie Penn-Lewis'teaching magazine), Evan Roberts published a letter that was headed, *"An explanation of my position at Leicester'*

"Nearly eight years ago I was invited to Leicester by Mrs Penn-Lewis in conjunction with Mr. Penn-Lewis. The church of God acknowledges this servant of God, Mrs Penn-Lewis, as one sent of God. Her name sends forth no ill savour. Her work can only be understood by the faithful ones of God whose eyes are opened of God. Now during revival in Wales I, in my ignorance, did not escape the wiles of the enemy, who does not leave even the elect to escape him...Then seeing what I saw not, understanding what had not yet broken on my spiritual vision, Mrs Penn-Lewis wrote me very reasonable and spiritual letters asking me to come to stay at her home in Glen, Leicestershire. I followed God's path, came for a short period, and have stayed here nearly eight years...Those who proclaim unbelief in my work only the louder proclaim their own blindness. Have they seen my messages in 'The Overcomer'? Then why could they not see the signs of God in them? Have they not read 'War on the Saints' - my unnamed biography?...Are these truths in it an unveiling of the deep things of Satan? And who could reveal

*them without knowing them? My co-work with Mrs Penn-Lewis on
'War on the Saints' was of God, for spiritually I was too burdened
to write it myself, and apart from me neither could she write it, and
it would have been useless to search elsewhere for a pen to do so. I
know of none equal to her in understanding of spiritual things. She
is a veteran of heavenly things and why must she be persecuted for
doing God's will?"*[11]

In looking after him in breakdown there was obvious
kindness at work, yet it led to a withdrawal from his family,
from public ministry and from Wales. In the co-writing of
War on the Saints there was a disavowing of the strengths
and joys of the Revival in a fear that seemed to have a stronger
belief in the enemy's power to deceive than in the Father's
power to keep. As a book it reflects many of Jessie's beliefs
rather than the things that Evan had spoken and demonstrated
during the Revival. In processing the roots of his breakdown
in a restricted environment, it appears he came to conclusions
based solely on the beliefs of the person who was helping him.

In her fear of his having been deceived, she led him into her
deception. The kindness itself seems to taste of the misguided
fear expressed by Mary and Jesus' brothers in Mark 3:20-21
and 31-35:

*"Then Jesus entered a house, and again a crowd gathered so
that he and his disciples were not even able to eat. When his family
heard about this they went to take charge of him, for they said, "He
is out of his mind..." "Then Jesus' mother and brothers arrived.
Standing outside, they sent someone in to call him."*

Jessie seemed to have a similar desire to "Take charge"[12] of
Evan probably "For his own protection" and the "Safety of the
Revival". However, Jessie in a wrong desire to rescue helped
to shut down the very flow of the Holy Spirit that caused the
Revival to erupt through Evan's life. It is interesting that she,
like Peter Price, talked about "True and false revival". In effect
both were involved in shutting down the life at its heart.

Although there are obvious differences in the perceptions of Peter Price and Jessie, there are some surprisingly similar echoes. He took real pride in his training and intellectual capabilities. She took pride in the priority of the "special spiritual revelations" she had received. Both reacted to the emotionalism, maybe forgetting that love, as expressed in the Godhead, is not simply a decision of will, but also an emotion. They both rejected a Revival which was turning out differently from the one they believed they had, in different ways, initiated. Jessie staked her claim on the Revival through prayer and Keswick; Peter Price through rational preaching, his attack on the delusions of the age and the steady streams of conversions he was already seeing in Dowlais. Did they both have a problem with the raising up of the sort of person who Seth Joshua had prayed would turn a nation? Perhaps they had secretly hoped for a more "able", "mature", "academically" and "spiritually trained", "discerning" person - someone perhaps more like themselves!

Not everyone went along with their intolerance towards the human factor in the Revival and in their attempts to sideline the people God had chosen to raise up. A report from a minister, Rev. David Evans, Bridgend, insisted that,

"He didn't want Jessie Penn-Lewis or anyone else to go on insisting that the Lord was blessing places not visited by Evan Roberts, because he felt such reports were unintentionally doing great dishonour to the young man who had been raised up by the Lord."[13]

In the analysis of Deborah Chapman,

"Their reactions to the emotional responses and manifestations, I believe, had more to do with the prevailing cultural "norms" than any basis in scripture.

Since the Enlightenment, and the rise of Rationalism, faith and emotions - in fact any aspect of being human, other than "reason" - was confined to the private sphere; with "reason" as the accepted

authority in the public sphere. It was not acceptable to voice any deeply held religious beliefs in the public sphere. I would see that effectively society "shut down, suppressed or dissociated" the emotional and spiritual aspects of corporate life.

The Holy Spirit broke through this false separation in the Revival as people were deeply touched and messy emotions released. It is not surprising that many of the corporate gatherings were emotionally charged and spirtually dynamic - God was breaking out of the box and He was taking the women, children and anyone else who wanted to go, with Him!

The Holy Spirit gives permission and grace for people to express themselves and their pain - it is part of the healing process. This may have been outside the conceptual framework of Jessie Penn-Lewis, Peter Price and others critics of the Revival who didn't allow for something they couldn't control.

Jessie's theology seemed to have more to do with works and self effort, perhaps in an attempt to contain her own pain, than in the extravagant outpouring of love and grace seen in the Revival! In seeking to control the situation through accessing Evan, she was involved, with others, in shutting down a Revival which challenged the very foundations of her life's work."[14]

Evan's part is also clear in that he handed responsibility for his life and ministry to Jessie in a way that robbed him of the true source of his life - the intimacy of his relationship with the Father which had previously brought him such joy and freedom.

There is mixture in any revival, mixture in any manifestation, but it is tragic that in the imbalance of her doctrine, the extremity and intolerance of her viewpoint she pulled down in some measure the Revival she had prayed for. Her interpretation of Pentecost itself discounted manifestations of power, and she insisted that Pentecost could only be interpreted though Paul's writings.[15]

"Her focus is on the Spirit indwelling, sanctification, inner life - an emphasis seen in Paul's writing. But there is another aspect of life in the Spirit, as in Luke's account of Pentecost, seen through his

Gospel and Acts. The emphasis is on the Spirit outpoured, power manifestation. Neither is wrong, nor are they mutually exclusive. Both are needed and both run through scripture, Old and New."[14]

Her view of spiritual warfare was stretched to an extreme and seemed to feed on "special revelation' that was "unsuitable" for ordinary believers to handle. If knowledge "puffs up", but love "builds up" such a view could lead to self elevation, dogmatism and a critical spirit.[16] There was mixture and immaturity in the Revival, but the antidote for this was not control. In fact one of the joys of the Revival had been, in the words of W.T.Stead,

"That it seems to be going on its own. There is no commanding human genius inspiring the advance. I found the flame of Welsh religious enthusiasm as smokeless as its coal. There are no advertisements, no brass bands, no posters, huge tents, all the paraphernalia of the got-up job are conspicuous by their absence. Neither is there any organisation, nor is there a director, at least that is visible to the human eye."[17]

Her fear of the enemy gave ground to a control which ate away at the heart of the Revival. Rick Joyner, in his book *The World Aflame* considers

"Revival is essentially the release of the living waters within the believers. This is why one of the greatest enemies of every revival has been the control spirit. The control spirit enslaves believers and stops the flow of living waters that creates and maintains every revival".

Evan's withdrawal from the Revival and Wales undoubtedly did great harm to the move of God. He did not want to be a wrong focus in the Revival. Yet in removing himself he certainly discouraged and confused many of the converts. Many of the women must have been at the least dismayed and saddened by the disappearance of one who had given them permission to be fully involved with the work of God. It would have been a real blow to their confidence. Although his removal didn't destroy the lasting and ongoing fruit of the Revival worldwide, his removal and the role of Jessie Penn-Lewis did, I believe, undermine confidence in the ability of women to minister "safely".

The controversial title for this chapter *In Jezebel's House?* focuses and reflects much of the ongoing debate over the role of Jessie Penn-Lewis in the Revival.

In the end as both men and women we have fundamental choices to make as to how we live and minister. Will we control and crush a move of the Holy Spirit or will we release and empower those who are carriers of the fire? Evan Roberts, Peter Price, Jessie Penn-Lewis and the "absent" spiritual fathers and mothers in the land all made choices that in some way quenched the full force of the Revival. Our "safety" to minister is not based on gender but on many other factors including, at the very least, our willingness to embrace in partnership with others, His calling on our lives. Our "safety" to minister also depends on a refusal to be either crushed or to control.

Cry

Is yours the only path to follow across
this land, this time?
If I choose another way, different values,
Am I invalid?
If my vision doesn't fit the way you see things,
My strategy take a different form,
Am I irrelevant?
If my words are clumsy and clang around me
Will you mark me inexperienced?
If I have no image, connections or history
Will you write me off as not ready?
Will I be allowed to follow what
I hear Him saying
When the words I hear are not the ones
You've written down?
Will what is,
Always seek to shape
What is not yet?

13

What Happened to the Women?

The Revival saw women flowing in an active participation with men in the things of God. The women expressed and experienced a real freedom in calling and gifting, this finished when the Revival finished, in many instances very quickly. It is hard to even discover what happened to some of the key women following the Revival. Some, certainly, like Mary Roberts and Florrie Evans became missionaries. Others simply disappeared, like Evan Roberts, into the shadows of history. What was appropriate in the fire of revival was no longer deemed appropriate when the hearth was cold.

It seems that many of those who carried the Revival fire were rejected by the churches they saw revived. This included many women. The testimony of Dafydd Jones of Aberporth in an interview with Brynmor Pierce Jones is revealing in its starkness:

"Question: "Mr. Jones, did the women continue to take part in the mid-week meetings for long after the Revival?"

Answer: "No, the deacons stopped that."

Q: "What about the processions of the children, and what about the young witnesses and gospel singers?"

A: "I don't remember them for long after then."

Q: "What happened to all those young people, were they killed in the Great War?"

A: "No, only a few went to the War because they worked on farms. Later many of us went to work in England and I went away too."

Q: "A great many of you were young when you were converted. Did you get used by your chapels to take services?"

A: "No, only the 9.30 prayer meeting on a Sunday, and that was also conducted by the minister. I do not remember any missions.""[1]

However, women did find some avenues where they could serve.

Many of the converts of the Revival found that they couldn't stay in the established denominations, many of which were becoming increasingly liberal. In the words of one Revival convert, Edward Stenner, which reflected the feelings of many, "I can't live in the smoke after being born in the fire!"[2]

Meeting halls were planted and the beginnings of the Pentecostal movement emerged. George Jeffreys (The Elim Pentecostal Movement) and Stephen Jeffreys (Assemblies of God) and Daniel Powell Williams of Pen-y-groes were all saved in the Welsh Revival. The roots of Pentecostalism were deeply embedded in 1904 and Donald Gee felt its most significant contribution was the creation of a widespread spirit of expectation; "Faith was rising to visualise a return to apostolic Christianity in all its pristine beauty and power."[3]

There are wonderful testimonies of healings in the years following the Revival through for example the ministry of George Jeffreys. Many of the women healed, became evangelists themselves.

Miss F.M. Munday was miracuously healed in George Jeffreys revival campaign in the Wesleyan Central Hall,

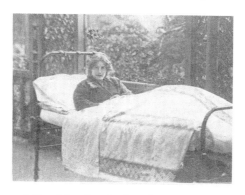

Miss Munday before her healing

Southampton in May of 1927. She walked out of her "invalid carriage" (a large wheelchair) in front of an amazed crowd. The power of God came upon her so strongly that the whole carriage shook. She had not walked or stood for 14 years after her leg had been damaged in a fall. She was in agony with the continual changing of splints on her wasted leg. She had been told that she would have to have the leg amputated and that there would be no stump left to fit an artificial limb. She was in the deepest despair.

This is her account of the healing, "Principal George Jeffreys anointed me with oil, and as he prayed my whole body vibrated with life. I was under the power of God. My leg moved up and down three times in the splint, and soon I was able to sit up. All pain was gone. I was healed. I stood up and stepped out of my bath chair without aid. I was on my feet for the first time for over fourteen years. I walked around that big building three times. My leg was like that of a frail baby's when the splint was taken off: and altogether the leg was four and a half inches shorter than the other, now they are both the same size, quite normal. You can understand how I feel when I tell you I want to sing all day : "Jesus Thou art everything to me."

Miss Munday after her healing

After her healing Miss Munday did the work of an evangelist telling others of the love of God and leading people to Jesus.

Daniel Williams of the Apostolic Church said this about the aftermath of the Revival:

152

"The weeping for mercy, the holy laughter, ecstasy of joy, the fire descending, burning its way into the hearts of men and women with sanctity and glory were manifestations still cherished and longed for in greater power. Many were heard speaking in tongues and prophesying. So great was the visitation in Pen-y-groes and the districts that nights were spent in churches. Many witnessed to God's healing power in their bodies...Confusion and extravagance undoubtedly were present but the Lord had His hand on His people and they were preserved and were taught of God to persevere and pray, and those that hankered and thirsted after God began to assemble in cottages seeking for the further manifestation of His will. The news came of God's visitation in America."[5]

In April 1906 the newspapers were talking about "The New Revival", a stirring that was happening in Pen-y-groes. Some of the key figures in this Revival were once again women. One notable woman was Sarah Jones. When Evan Roberts had been at the Llanlluon meeting on April 25th he stayed at Gors-fach heath and laid hands on Mrs.Sarah Jones, Gors-fach, Carmel. Even before that time she would be,

"Taken into a swoon, not unlike, according to the descriptions of it, that which overtook some of the mystics. Her husband Daniel was unable to go to his work for about a fortnight because of her experiences. She wouldn't become unconscious but would be swallowed up entirely by her prayers."[6]

She was soon laying hands on people praying for the Holy Spirit to come and for His gifts to be released. She would often speak in tongues and would lay hands on the sick for healing, people,

"By the hundreds crowded to see her. She held meetings beyond the vicinity of her home and jumping and dancing were seen in them."[5]

In another meeting in Maespica Farm, Cwmtwrch there was "gesticulating, shouting, praying and laughing...with shouts, wild and piercing shrieks, and the thumping of tables and chairs."[6]

There was mixed reaction to this in the Crosshands area, but there was an undoubted move of the Holy Spirit with a woman again in the centre, both of the outpouring and of the controversy!

"In the early Pentecostal movement, having the "anointing" was far more important than one's sex. As evangelistic bands carried the full gospel across the country, women who were recognised as having the anointing of the Holy Spirit shared with men in the preaching ministry...A person's call - and how other believers viewed it - was far more important than [ministerial credentials]."[7]

The story of Bethlehem Pentecost Church, Cefn Cribwr,[8] has reflected much of the journey of Welsh Pentecostalism over the last century or so. In the early days of Pentecostalism, particularly whilst meetings were happening in homes, the women played a significant role. Their role lessened as structures became more formalised. The emerging Pentecostal Church in Cefn Cribwr initially met in the home of Mrs. Jenny Phillips. Her role was central to the early group, she was the secretary and played the violin in worship, "playing in the Spirit". In 1904 an open air meeting was happening in John Street outside the home of Henry and Elizabeth Matthews who, without pre-arrangement, were being visited by Jenny Phillips and given the same message. Shortly afterwards Mrs. Matthews had a dream about a house with heavenly light around the room. When she came to a prayer meeting at Jenny Phillips' home she was amazed to see it was the room she had seen in her dream. During the meeting Jenny Phillips prophesied that as the visitors returned the following night they would receive an unforgettable experience. This was proved true when on the Sunday Mrs. Matthews was filled with the Spirit and spoke in tongues, not having any Pentecostal background or previous experience at all. Jenny Phillips also prophesied that a certain plot of land was the Lord's "chosen place for the church". The men responded to this and used to stand on the ground and pray for it, claiming it for the work. They bought the land and the first church building was eventually built and opened on September 6, 1930. No women were appointed to leadership in the new church building at that time.[8]

A new building - a Sports Hall - is being built in 2004 to meet the needs of the community in this century. They carry the same passion for Pentecostal fire now as they did in their beginnings.

"As Pentecostal denominations began to formalise their structure, women who were active in every type of ministry position were simply left out of denominational leadership roles. Up to this point, in fact, there is little to suggest that women doing the work of ministry, holding positions as pastors, teachers and evangelists, were even questioned in the validity of their function. Men and women of that day seemed to be grounded in the understanding that because God chose women to participate in the New Testament Holy Spirit baptism experience, it was only logical that they, too, should carry the message of the gospel. In the words of Mae Eleanore Frey, "God Almighty is no fool - I say it with all reverence - Would He fill a woman with the Holy Ghost - endow her with ability - give her a vision of souls and then tell her to shut her mouth?"[9]

The involvement of women in structured roles was also problematic in other post-Revival streams. W.S. Jones and R.B. Jones were deeply involved in the Revival yet kept their distance from Evan Roberts and his teams of women evangelists. Women were involved in the movement that developed around them, but the "Jones' " did not regularly appoint women to formal church leadership. However, the women were deeply involved as missionaries and in evangelistic teams. By 1909 W.S. & R.B. Jones had seen the need for "itinerant evangelists". As they were discussing and praying about the issue a letter arrived from a Mrs. Hollis of Cardiff who "had yearned to use her wealth and time for village mission in Wales or for welfare work in Ireland"- but had found all doors closed. Now a friend told her of an advert in a Christian magazine offering a "gospel van" for sale - so she bought it and offered it to the "Efengylydd" Committee. The "gospel van" was a converted gypsy caravan and used around Wales. The list of donations to fund the ongoing work of the van included money collected by a widow and a little girl who went around their area carrying a picture of the van - "Many pennies came from other widows. "[10]

The Porth Bible Institute, started in 1919, received women as well as men and prepared them for work in the UK as well as overseas. Their training included missions and open air work including "Annual Treks". The pioneers of the Annual Treks were "a quartet of girl students who walked from Llandrindod Wells to Brecon". They drew crowds to their meetings at which Miss Llywela Thomas played the violin and the rest sang.

Long term, the young women were often sent to the Mildmay Mission and Hospital, childrens' missions, orphanages, women's refuges, and city missions. Some, such as, Margaret Williams and May Thomas joined the Forward Movement. Nancy Russel was sent to Ireland. Ann Wilkins was "a locally sponsored sister of the people" at Gorseinon.

Eventually the vision of the "gospel van" was inherited by "the faith mission in Wales". Two Welsh speakers, May Owen and Margaret Francis got involved immediately, visiting from house to house in often isolated rural communities. Ceridwen and Myfanwy Jones joined the team. It wasn't until later that any men joined the work. 121 people were sent into overseas mission or home mission from the Institute, of these 57 were women.

There were 74 students who became ministers, only one, Bronwen Hale, became a "lady pastor", although several others married ministers.

The situation is still similar today in Wales as in many other nations. It would be unusual to find a woman in a senior position of leadership within the Church. There are only a handful of women even now who hold such a role in Wales. Undoubtedly there are many more who have been anointed and gifted to serve through leading.

However, R. B. Jones did allow women deaconesses in Tabernacle, Porth. "The pastor has two deaconesses; Miss Sutherland and Miss Ellis, his deacons and visitors kept a strict watch on several hundred members."[11] A deaconess was obviously a position of some authority within that regime!

On the mission field, Pandita Ramabai and Elizabeth Rowlands pressed for the freedom of women to be involved in every aspect of serving including preaching. However, they did not see women enter structured positions of leadership, the only route to this would have been through ordination.

The converts who stayed in the denominational churches were noted by Dr. Martin Lloyd-Jones as the ones "who were keeping the doors to the chapels open". They were also the ones who kept the "spiritual fervour" alive in the prayer meetings and Sunday schools.

One of the special things that happened after the Revival was the story of Mary Davies. Mary stayed at home doing painting and craftwork and taking care of the converts of the Revival. In the Autumn of 1928 she felt God was asking her to draw together a few people to pray. At the first meeting there were three people and this grew to about 30 people. The Holy Spirit started to move in the group and so they sent for Evan. When they got the telegram saying he had agreed to come back one of the sisters grabbed the telegram and ran

Mary Davies

out on to the street shouting "Evan Roberts is coming back!"

On his return he reminded them that the Holy Spirit is the only source of spiritual life, "It is not by might, nor by power, but by my Spirit saith the Lord". Even at the first meeting backsliders of the Revival of 1904 were restored. After a couple of weeks they moved to Moriah Chapel because of the numbers. Although the gifts were manifested Evan rebuked someone who tried to speak in tongues. There was a real awareness of the spiritual battle, a strong encouragement to pray and the taking of Bible classes. At one of these he said he had given up hope of an instant national revival; he told the class that "revival is not the goal, it is *a* goal, but not *the* goal"[12]

There were many conversions as a result of the prayer. Evan also prophesied, cast out evil spirits and prayed for healing. It is interesting that he found the freedom to return to Wales and minister in this way after breaking his connection with Jessie Penn-Lewis a few years previously. She, in fact, died in 1927. The work in Gorseinon continued for a few years but this time there was no outward flow of the revival to other places and other nations.

When the church is awakened and aflame with the love of Jesus, women and young people are released to run with the message and the poor are reached. The cry of the poor fell on many deaf ears in the years after the Revival, one person, however, stands out: D. S. Jones, Bridgend "was more like a Franciscan friar than a non-conformist minister. His whole life was steeped in holy compassion and redeeming love for the unloveable"[13] He welcomed the hungry and the prostitutes, disappearing from church services to meet tramps. Will Ifan tells the story of a country walk with him.

"I saw him stop suddenly by a thorn bush and a shadow passed over his face. I knew without words, what pained him - he was remembering the Crown of Thorns. Suddenly a smile of victory lit up

his face as he pulled a tract out of his pocket and put it on the thorn
bush where everyone could see - held fast by the thorn bush...he had
gained a victory over the thorns by making them sing praises to the
One who was once so marred"[14]

The thorns that grew up after the Revival marred Christ's body, as women and the young could no longer take their place alongside the men and as the cry of the poor and broken became less and less valued. These thorns still scar the Body of Christ worldwide.

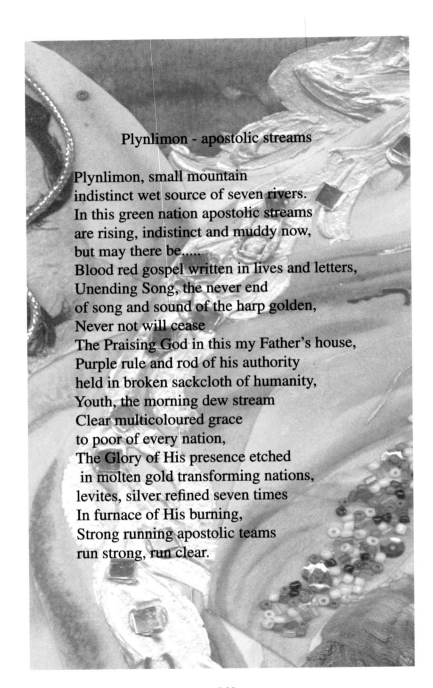

Plynlimon - apostolic streams

Plynlimon, small mountain
indistinct wet source of seven rivers.
In this green nation apostolic streams
are rising, indistinct and muddy now,
but may there be.....
Blood red gospel written in lives and letters,
Unending Song, the never end
of song and sound of the harp golden,
Never not will cease
The Praising God in this my Father's house,
Purple rule and rod of his authority
held in broken sackcloth of humanity,
Youth, the morning dew stream
Clear multicoloured grace
to poor of every nation,
The Glory of His presence etched
 in molten gold transforming nations,
levites, silver refined seven times
In furnace of His burning,
Strong running apostolic teams
run strong, run clear.

14

Forerunners of the next revival?

There were forerunners of the 1904 Revival. Are there forerunners of the revival which is to come? This book tells the stories of some ordinary yet extraordinary women at the beginning of the twentieth century. Here are the stories of a few women at the beginning of the twenty-first century who would consider themselves very ordinary, yet whose lives and words urge us to run with an extraordinary God.

Elisabeth James describes herself as a housewife, elder and a "mother in Israel". Marilyn Harry is an evangelist with the Elim Pentecostal Church, and a senior pastor in Newport. Sarah Trinder leads an Assemblies of God church in Pontllanfraith. Lucy Keys, 16, is at college and a youth leader in Llanelli.

Elisabeth James

In January 2002 in Kampala, Uganda, Suzette Hatting told me, "God wants to bring blessing to Wales in HIS way. Be released, be free, let God be God. Be a witness. Tell what you've seen and heard and experienced"

In godly humility, I'd like to *encourage* you by saying, "Come on Wales! You who are Welsh speakers, you who are non-Welsh speakers, you who are from other nations, God didn't leave Wales in 1904."

Throughout the last 100 years God has been at work in the nations. The seed of His word and His Holy Spirit has been pollinated, going out from Wales and coming into Wales.

In November 2002 a "Releasers of Life" Conference for women was held in Aberystwyth. The visiting speakers were from Toronto and British Columbia, Canada. As they were leaving they gave me a gift which they hoped would "speak to me". It was a crystal glass dove, packed in a red bag with red and silver paper. It immediately brought to my mind an article, written in Welsh by my late husband Dan Lynn James. In it he describes a vision he received whilst in Trefeca, Brecon in May 1978. It was of a dove in two colours - half of it a fiery red colour, half of it the colour of pure, crystal clear water. To me it symbolised the baptism of divine endorsement - as His people we are beloved and chosen; and the baptism of divine empowering - with His Holy Spirit we are equipped.

In 1983 in the February 15th issue of *Y Cymro*[1] there appeared a call to a whole night of prayer before St.David's Day, March 1st. Following that, Welsh language renewal meetings were held and renewal songs were translated into Welsh. The translation of Graham Kendrick's song "Shine, Jesus, Shine" was portrayed in the form of a spectacular banner, and was presented by the Sunday Schools Council for Wales/Cyngor Ysgolion Sul Cymru. The literal translation in Welsh is,

"Glorious Word of God, give your light to Wales today,
Come Holy Spirit, give us your fire;
River of grace, flood the nations with your love,
Give thy word, and there will be light."

In a time of prayer for the nations in the autumn of 2001 I found myself praying, "Lord I pray for another touch of Your hand upon my life so that I may be *one* amongst all those whom you are preparing to be *releasers* in Wales at this present time. Paradoxically, I find myself set mostly in a place of tension. But this is a good privileged position to be in. Thank You Lord. Please hold me there! Lord, I place before you the picture of a harp. The harp is an instrument, the tension and fine-tuning of its various strings creating a harmonious and pure song".

The picture then developed to be one of a harp set over a map of Wales. My prayer then continued, "Lord, master tuner and musician, please repair the broken strings of Wales. Put new ones in place, tune them all and set them in a creative tension together so that the sound of a new song of repentant worship pouring out of our lips and lives to You for Your glory will soon be heard throughout our land".

The words of the famous Welsh hymn by William Williams, Pantycelyn then came to mind which speaks of the praise to Jesus on the golden harp in heaven which will never come to an end.

Dechrau canu, dechrau canmol
Ymhen mil o oesedd maith
Iesu, bydd y bererinion
Hyfryd, draw ar ben eu taith
Ni cheir diwedd
Byth ar swn y delyn aur.

Lord let it be so! The above words were shared with a gathering of Christians in Cefnlea, Newtown during the first week in December 2001. In that same meeting I heard Arnold Muwonge (UK co-ordinator for Trumpet Mission) say the word "Push!", and I heard another Christian say to me "Go for it, girl, now or never". In less than a month, in January 2002 I was in Kampala, Uganda attending The African Prayer Convention and was also there officially representing Wales and asked to carry the Welsh flag on stage and through the streets of the city! As a teenager, like many other young persons, I had sensed a call to go to a mission field (the Annibynwyr[2], at the time mostly went to Madagascar), but I didn't go and was almost a pensioner when I arrived on African soil in Uganda.

It was a spiritually healing time for me personally. I also sensed it to be a time of spiritual breakthrough, a birthing time for God's present purposes for Wales. I prayed and interceded for Wales there in a manner and with a fervency which I had not previously experienced. I was immersed in an atmosphere of prayer for 10 days and I prayed in Welsh but in Ugandan style! On my return I read a quote from Oswald Chambers' book *My Utmost for His Highest*. The scripture verse above the quote is Ephesians 5:14,"Wake O sleeper, rise from the dead and Christ will shine on you".

"When God sends His inspiration, it comes to us with such miraculous power that we are able to "arise from the dead" and do the impossible. The remarkable thing about spiritual initiative is that the life and power comes after we "get up and get going"."

It's time for us to get up and get going!

Sarah Trinder

"The women of Wales are well used to suffering, to patiently carrying burdens, both in the natural and spiritual realms. They are also wildly passionate and fiery; it is both of these traits that are building to a culmination of purpose and destiny for the land. God is poised...the women are moving into position...the breakthrough - the pain, excitement, endurance, the cost, the women are prepared.

I see these women who have received from the depths of the earth, coming like Acsah, daughter of Caleb, to claim the land, their inheritance. What is being born out of Wales will go to the nation and the nations; a company of women, carrying an old yet new sound...the song of the Lord from the land; a company of women who "love not their lives unto death."

Lucy Keys

"I received a prophetic word just two weeks after moving from North Wales to Llanelli in South Wales, and just two weeks before going off to Thailand on mission with a team of other young people for a month during the summer of 2003. I am just sixteen years of age but felt that this was a significant word for me at a significant time.

The word given suggested the plans I was making in my

heart weren't big enough, that it was time to be repositioned and not to limit God to my own understanding because He had great expectations for me and expected me to fulfil them. That meant that God wasn't going to change His mind, so I had to change mine. God told me that I had pursued the safe place for long enough and He was calling me to the excitement of battle, to the gap on the front line, calling me from the back, the safe place to take responsibility for taking others into battle.

I was happy with a place at the back, never pushing myself forward, but now it seemed God was shifting me to a frontline position. Although a little scary, I also knew that this was God's word so I would need to be obedient.

I went to Thailand very conscious of these words and instead of taking the usual low key role, I found myself leading others who previously I thought were more confident and able than myself. During our time in Thailand we travelled to villages where the gospel had not reached and witnessed primarily to Buddhist people through worship, drama and testimony. We saw approximately 200 villagers become Christians, including 3 Buddhist monks that we know of. This time has caused me to expect greater things from God, He has enlarged my vision and perhaps I have begun to see myself as He sees me.

After moving from North Wales to Llanelli and having received the prophetic word, together with my experiences in Thailand, I am now prepared to accept that God can use me in a front line position in the battle He is calling us all into. I believe it is important that if we are to see revival in the nation of Wales again, however insignificant we feel or how young we are, we have to start to see ourselves as God sees us and allow Him to shift us into positions where we will be most effective."

Marilyn Harry

"It is with gratitude to God that we read of the women mightily used by God in the 1904 Revival. What a tremendous legacy they have left us which fills us with an incredible hope that God can move on ordinary women today to bring a lasting change to our communities and generation.

Throughout the gospels we hear how the Lord Jesus was ministered to by women and how He impacted their lives. Also down the years there have been outstanding women , like those mentioned in this book, who have served the Lord selflessly.

I remember preaching in a gospel crusade in East Africa in a mainly Muslim area when the leader of the meeting announced to the excited crowd, "Look how the God of the Bible lifts up the women".

Apparently they had never heard a woman preach before. Well! it is not about lifting up the women, but about the women lifting up the magnificent name of Jesus Christ of Nazareth.

As Wales approaches the 100 year anniversary of 1904 it does our faint hearts good to hear the adventures and escapades of ordinary men and women. In this case the women moved as the Holy Spirit came on them. These valiant women leave us with an amazing challenge to take heart, have faith and pick up the baton of the passionate, powerful preaching of the gospel; the wind of the Holy Spirit causing us to run with the greatest message on earth to every village, town and city of our nation of Wales and into the continents of the world.

Now is not the time for comfortable armchair Christianity, but radical apostolic leadership, sacrificial and anointed service to reach the lost and see the nation come to Christ.

There is no doubt the promise of the book of Acts is still applicable today. God is indeed pouring out His Holy Spirit on all flesh, igniting a fire that cannot be put out in the hearts of His people."

"Call to me and I will give you the nations as your
inheritance" Psalm 2:8"

A baton was dropped in 1904 when the women adapted
to the pressure of "abnormal" Christianity. Now is surely the
time for the baton to be picked up. Now is surely the time for
radical revivalist movements of women to emerge, desperate
to see the mercy and power of God break out once again
amongst the poor and broken of the nations.

New nets for
　　New harvests,
　placed alongside
　　established nets,
　　　visible,
multicoloured,
　　　　nets so finely woven
　into the texture of
　　　the culture
　that they are
　　　　　barely seen.

15

It Is Time

In 1904 an underground stream of molten glory broke through to the surface, the fire of women desperate to be among the "great company of those proclaiming the works of God". It is time now for a movement of women to emerge who will dare to see breakthroughs in this nation of Wales and in nations across the world. Our age, our gender, our past hurts and disappointments are no excuse.

Sometimes the obvious needs to be restated as in the words of Frederick Franson.

"Two thirds of all Bible believing Christians are women...When two thirds of the Christians are excluded from the work of evangelising, the loss for God's cause is so great that it can hardly be described"[1]

We cannot see women lost from embracing their place in the purposes of God. The cry of the lost is too great for us to retreat into a false passivity, a false humility.

There are clear parallels between what happened to women in the aftermath of the Revival and what happened to women in the aftermath of the First World War.

During the First World War, out of necessity, women became actively involved in war work, taking on roles and jobs that had hitherto been a male preserve. However, the end of the war in 1918 was a turbulent time for women. Overnight they changed from being viewed as "our gallant girls" to "women who stole men's jobs".[2]

After the Revival, women were regarded as "Surplus to requirements" in any initiating or leadership role with the churches. "Abnormal" church was back in place and women were expected to play an "abnormal" role in the system. They were expected to go back to their pre-Revival involvement rather than to take up their place in the ongoing "wartime" role of the church.

The women of the Salvation Army and the Temperance Movement had paved the way for a move of God amongst and through the girls and women of 1904. Following the Revival the freedom the women had enjoyed was lost.

Revivals throughout history have been accompanied by a fresh understanding of truth, followed by reform which has often taken long years to come to pass. The abolition of slavery is the major example. However the issues of child labour, prison reform and a renewed social conscience were also faced in the years which followed the revivals of previous centuries.

The Women's Rights Movement was born in the Christian revivals of the nineteenth century, yet the church is now regarded as an enemy by Women's Rights activists. When we understand the value that Jesus places on women we may see this as unfair, but it is an understandable perception.

The stirring of women in the Revival of 1904 and its worldwide impact hasn't yet led to the full freedom of women within the church to have "equal opportunity to serve".[3]

In the words of Martin Scott "We are not looking at who can rule (a worldly model), but who can have authority to serve".[4] The authority to serve is also about having the authority to lead if that is what we are called to do.

It is wonderful when husbands, fathers and male church leaders are affirming and releasing of the women they care for. My husband is a hero who has been misunderstood and judged for the way he has released and encouraged me. He has, at times been judged as less of a man and less of a leader for so doing.

As men and women we are asked to be obedient to the call of God on our lives, our gender is not an allowable excuse, even if we, and those around us, would like it to be so.

This is not about power games but about a humble partnering in the work of the gospel for the sake of the name of Jesus. This is about the mobilising of the whole church to reach the whole world, the most broken and powerless of whom in every culture tend to be the women and children.

This is not a cry for the rising up of strident and controlling women in the face of oppressive structures but for the emergence of women of meekness and power in Wales and in the nations. There is an urgency in our day and in our land. In the words of Evan Roberts, as we have not obeyed "the devil has danced on Wales". Yet, there is an often unnoticed spiritual hunger in the land. This is not a time to be passive but a time to act.

In the words of Loren Cunnungham, founder of YWAM, one of the world's largest mission organisations,

"I see every little girl growing up knowing she is valued, knowing she is made in the image of God and knowing she can fulfill all the potential he has put within her. I see the body of Christ recognising leaders whom the Holy Spirit indicates. The ones whom He has gifted, anointed and empowered, without regard to race, colour or gender. This generation will be one who simply asks "Who is it that God wants?"[5]

I long for the day when I won't wince when my daughters tell me they want to plant and lead churches. I long for the day when they will be received and not rejected because they are women. I long for the day when they will have a freedom to serve in whatever sphere of life or work they are called into.

Eifion Evans, an authoritative writer on 1904, said the following; I believe he is totally wrong.

"The teaching of scripture establishes clearly defined limits to the public ministry of women in the life of the church. A public exercise of ministerial and teaching duties is expressly forbidden. The reason goes back to God's created order whereby the woman's nature is such as to follow rather than to lead. Her spiritual equality

with man as a recipient of God's grace is unquestioned. But for the purpose of public worship the woman is not constitutionally equipped by God for a teaching role. Her role is one of submission rather than authority. At the time of the revival this scriptural norm was not always observed, its omission left the movement open to emotional excesses and to a related failure in providing adequate doctrinal foundations."[6]

The Holy Spirit never does anything that contradicts His word. Our traditions have often caused us to interpret the scriptures in such a way that women have been hindered from obeying God's call. However, if we look at the Bible afresh we find a very different perspective.

This is a time to seriously consider a fresh biblical perspective and come clear. At the very least we must consider Galatians 3:28 "There is neither Jew nor greek, slave nor free, male nor female, for you are all one in Christ Jesus"

In the time of the Azusa Street outpouring a magazine called *Apostolic Faith* was produced, it echoes the same heart.

"Before Jesus ascended to heaven, holy anointing oil had never been poured on a woman's head; but before He organised His church, He called them all into the upper room, both men and women, and anointed them with the oil of the Holy Ghost, thus qualifying them all to minister in this Gospel. On the day of Pentecost they all preached through the power of the Holy Ghost. In Christ Jesus there is no male nor female, all are one."[7]

God offers the same renewal and salvation to all - regardless of race, gender or class. "He also gives the same high calling, responsibility and privilege to all. Both male and female are equal ambassadors for Christ and His gospel.(2 Corinthians 5: 14-21), for both males and females are being transformed into the image of Christ (2 Corinthians 3:18 cf. Genesis 1:26-28)"[8]

We may fulfill that calling as ambassadors in many different ways; in our homes, in our workplaces, in our schools, in our churches, leading or not leading. The key - a yielding of our lives to Jesus in radical obedience.

It is time for "Carriers of the Fire" to rise up and run with fresh strength. It is time for us to pick up the baton of the passionate, powerful preaching of the gospel "and run with the greatest message on earth to every village, town and city and out into the continents of the world."

It is time for this revolutionary stream to rise again for the sake of His name and for the sake of the lost. It is time for fresh fire to herald the return of our King.

Footnotes

Abbreviations of book titles/articles

OOTS - *Out of the Shadows - A History of Women in Twentieth Century Wales* - Deirdre Beddoe.

EE - *The Welsh Revival of 1904* - Eifion Evans (1969).

WOTV - *Woman of the Valleys - Mother Shepherd* - Charles Preece.

DMP - *Evan Roberts, The Great Revivalist and His Work* - D.M. Phillips, (1923).

DM - *I Saw the Welsh Revival* - D. Matthews.

DD - *Y Diwygiad a'r Diwygwyr*, 1906.

Voices - *Voices from the Welsh Revival* - Brynmor P Jones, (1995).

TGR - *The Great Revival in Wales - An Interview with W.T.Stead* - Shaw.

WTFF - *When the Fire Fell* - R Maurice Smith, (1996).

RD - *The Story of My Life - Rosina Davies, Evangelist*.

JPL - *The Awakening in Wales* - Jessie Penn-Lewis

JVM - *The Welsh Religious Revival 1904-5*, J. Vyrnwy Morgan. (1909)

HD - *Revival in India,* Helen Dyer.

NG - *On the Wings of a Dove - The International Effects of the 1904 - 05 Revival* - Noel Gibbard. (2002)

TT - *The Trials and Triumphs of Mrs Jessie Penn-Lewis* - Brynmor Pierce Jones, 1997.

FSAT - *For Such a Time as This - The Liberation of Women to Lead in the Church.* - Martin Scott (2000)

OML - *Our Mother's Land 1991.*

WM - *Western Mail Revival Supplement.*

SWA - *South Wales Argus.*

KC - *The King's Champions* - Brynmor P.Jones, (1986).

Acknowledgements

1. eXplore is a training context that involves experimentation and risk taking. It is based at Antioch Church, Llanelli and it seeks to release a radical revivalist movement with its roots in the Celtic tradition. It provides an opportunity for us to explore together monasticism in today's culture, including: inner/outer journey, His presence, rhythm of life, spiritual disciplines of retreat, solitude and silence, walking the land, signs and wonders, ministry amongst the poor, 24 hour prayer and worship, creativity, mission, insightful teaching based on Biblical frameworks.

2. Nations company - www.nationscompany.org is an apostolic revivalist movement that is marked by -
- a movement that will affect the nation of Wales and the nations;
- an emphasis on mobilising women from all walks of life to run with the gospel;
- proclaiming the word of God with signs and wonders following;
- a commitment to release teams of women across Wales;
- a passion for God's presence and the poor;
- an emphasis on prayer, worship and evangelism;

For more information please contact :-
Marilyn Harry : tel. 01633 245911
Sarah Trinder : sarah.tab@btopenworld.com
Karen Lowe   : rising4@aol.com

Introduction
1. 'Rwy'n caru'r Arglwydd Iesu a'm holl gallon" - Florrie would have spoken this in Welsh. The Revival was largely Welsh speaking, with some meetings containing a blend of both Welsh and English. There is an attempt to express some flavour of this in the book, to be true to the richness of the Revival language itself.
2. DMP - Treorchy, November 29th - December 1st.

3.Recorded revivals :

1st : 1620 and 1630 - Vicar Pritchard's.

2nd : Calvinistic Methodist Revival.

3rd : The same revival in 1762. It was called "Y Diwygiad Mawr" (The Great Revival).

4th : 1785 - 87 - A theological Revival.

5th : 1790 - 94 - A missionary Revival.

6th : 1806 - 09 - A practical Revival.

7th : 1811 -14.

8th : 1814 -15.

9th : 1817 - 22 - The "Beddgelert" Revival.

10th : 1828 - 30.

11th : 1831 - 32.

12th : 1839 - 42.

13th : 1849 - 50 - The cholera Revival.

14th : th '59 Revival.

15th : 1876 Revival.

16th : 1879 Revival.

4. Kevin Adams for quality 1904 Revival resource - videos,DVDs, books visit www.1904-revival.com.

Chapter 1 - What was it like for women at that time?

1. Psalm 110:3.

2. OML - Counting the Cost of Coal - Dot Jones.

3. OOTS -pg17.

4. OOTS - pg19.

5. OOTS - pg15.

6."Reports of the Commissioners Enquiry into the State of Education in Wales".

7. OOTS - pg27.

8. Suffrage - "The right to vote", a suffragette wanted women to have the right to vote in elections.

9. OOTS - pg14.

10. Temperance - abstinence from alcohol. Women had been involved in mixed Temperance Societies from the 1830's - OOTS - pg37.

11. UDMGC - Undeb Dirwestol Merched Gogledd Cymru - The

North Wales Women's Temperance Union. was set up in Blaenau
Ffestiniog in 1892. UDMD - Undeb Dirwestol Merched y De
- The South Wales Temperance Union.
12. OML - From Temperance to Suffrage.
13. OML - From Temperance to Suffrage.
14. *Constrained by Zeal - Female Spirituality amongst Non-
Conformists, 1825-1875* - Linda Wilson
15. EE - p175. The Forward Movement was started by John Pugh
in 1872. It was the evangelistic and church planting movement
of the Presbyterian Church of Wales. It was full on militant
evangelism, key workers were Seth and Frank Joshua, converted at
a Salvation Army meeting.
16. *W M*

Chapter 2 - Forerunners of the Revival.

1. A small chapel was built in 1828 and it was called "Capel
y To-Gwellt" (The Thatched Roof Chapel). When this chapel
was outgrown Moriah Chapel was built in 1842. *History of the
Methodists in West Glamorgan*, a 1997 translation by Ivor
Griffiths of *Hanes Methodistiaid Gorllewin Morgannwg*
written by Rev. W. Samlet and published by Cwmni y Cyhoeddwr
Cymraeg Cyf, 1916
2. Extract from *History of the Methodists in West Glamorgan,*
a 1997 translation by Ivor Griffiths of *Hanes Methodistiaid
Gorllewin Morgannwg* written by Rev. W. Samlet and published
by Cwmni y Cyhoeddwr Cymraeg Cyf, 1916
3. Chartists stood for worker's rights - 3 leaders were sentenced to
death in Monmouth, this was changed to transportation and they
were sent to Van Diemens Land around the time the family went to
London.
"*Of those we left behind we never hear a word.
We fought for Lovett's Charter and it seems all in vain.
We fought for nothing but our rights, and though it seems
we failed,
While working men still are oppressed this struggle carries on.*"
- a haunting Chartist protest song about the three.

4. *The War Cry,* January 27, 1881.
5. WOTV - Charles Preece quoting Gypsy Smith.
6. to 8. WOTV.
9. WOTV - Charles Preece quoting Gypsy Smith.
10. Commissioner Frederick Dr. Booth-Tucker, *The Life of Catherine Booth, the Mother of the Salvation Army*.
10. *The Great Revival in the Rhondda Valley - South Wales Daily News*, Saturday March 15th, 1879
11.WOTV - Charles Preece quoting *The History of the Salvation Army* .
12. *The Great Revival in the Rhondda Valley - South Wales Daily News,* Saturday March 15, 1879 and RD.
13. WOTV - Charles Preece quoting *The History of the Salvation Army.*
14. RD - p35.
15.OML - *from Temperance to Suffrage*
16.Commissioner Railton, A Key Incident of the Salvation Army, *All the World,* 1898
17. Florence Booth, *South Wales Daily News*, 1904

Chapter 3 - It's all in the beginnings.
1. DMP - p113.
2.Voices - p89.
3. TGR.
4. to 6. DMP
7. *Great Revivals,* Whittaker - p8.
8. to 9. DMP
10. Voices - cassette No 103 - Copy Evangelical Library of Wales, Bridgend.
11. DMP.
12. LE.
13. to 15. DMP.
16. WM.
17. WM - Porth, Sunday November 27th.

Chapter 4 - Releasing the Teams.

1. WM.
2. *South Wales Daily News*,December 1, 1904.
3. Phrenology - a "dodgy" study of the conformation of the skull as a supposed indicator of mental faculties and character.
4. DM.
5. WM.
6. *Llanelly Mercury*, November 24th, 1904, Workman's Meeting at Gorseinon
7. Sêt Fawr - "The big seat", the front row of the church where the ministers and deacons sat.
8. *Llanelly Mercury*, December 29, 1904 - The Maesteg Songsters at Gorseinon
9. WM - January 18th - Gelli.
10. WM - January 3rd - Swansea.

Chapter 5 - Unending Song.

1. WTFF - p69 - M Holyoak, "The Afterglow : Gleanings from the Welsh Revival".
2. DM.
3. "*Dyma Gariad*", written by William Rees (of Liverpool), 1802 - 1883 - better known by his bardic name, Hiraethog or Gwilym Hiraethog.(Gwilym is Welsh for William). He was born near Llansannan to the west of the town of Denbigh. There is a mountain - Hiraethog - near Bala lake
4. DMP.
5. Sunday November 20th - *Western Mail* Supplement, Vol.1.
6. DMP.
7. WM - November 23 - Ynysybwl.
8. DMP quoting Mr Stead - impressions of the Revival at Maerdy - *Daily Chronicle*.
9. W T Stead - *The Revival in the West* on December 15, 1904 and DMP.
10. WM.
11. WM - This hymn by William Williams, Pantycelyn (1716 - 1791) is in the Annibynwyr (Independents) hymn book , titled *Eden a Chalfaria* -

Yn Eden, cofiaf hynny byth,
Bendithion gollais rif y gwlith;
Syrthiodd fy ngharu wiw.
Ond buddugoliaeth Calfari
Enillodd hon yn ol i mi;
Mi ganaf tra fwyf byf
In Eden, I will always remember it
Numberless blessings I lost,
My crown of dignity fell
But the victory of Calvary
Won this back for me
I will sing whilst I live.

"*Diolch Iddo*" - Thanks be to Him - This is probably the first verse of a hymn by Morgan Rhys (1716 - 1779) titled "*Teilwng yw'r Oen*" (Worthy is the Lamb).

Dyma Geidwad i'r colledig
Meddyg i'r gwywedig rai,
Dyma un sy'n caru maddau
I becharduriaid mawr en bai:
Diolch Iddo (x 2)
Byth am gofio llwch y llawr.
Here is a Saviour to the lost
A doctor for the withered ones,
Here is one who loves to forgive sinners
Great their sin:
Thanks be to Him (x 2)
For forever remembering the dust of the earth.

12. WM - A hymn by William Williams titled: "*Grym y Groes*" - The Power of the Cross.

Gwaed y groes sy'n codi i fyny
'Reiddil yn goncwerwr mawr;
Gwaed y groes sydd yn darostwng
Cewri gedyrn fyrdd i lawr
Gad i'm deimlo (x 2)
Awel o Galfaria fryn.
The Blood of the Cross raises up

The feeble into a great conqueror;
The Blood of the Cross subdues
Strong giants, many, down.
Let me feel (x 2)
A breeze from Calvary.
13. Llanelly Mercury.
14. Voices - p247.

Chapter 6 - Dangerous Prayers - Dangerous Women.
1. DM.
2. DMP - December 12 - 13th - Tylorstown.
3. to 8. WM.
9. Voices - T Williams Adgofion - pg 96 - 8.
10. WM.
11. Seren Cymru - February 26, 1904.
12. South Wales Post - November 27, 1904.
13. Voices - pg 74.
14. Haverfordwest Telegraph - January 25, 1905.
15. WM.
16. EE and DD - pg 110, 166, 178, 216, 217, 218.
17. Voices - *Y Greal (The Grail)* - November 1906, pg 291.
18. Voices - *Y Greal (The Grail)* - November 1906 - Diwygiad yn Rhos, pg 2-4.

Chapter 7 - Great was the Company...
1. to 3. RD.
4. JPL - pg85 -86.
5. LE - pg 59 - Rhondda.
6. to 8. DM.
9. to 11.WM.
12. to 14. DMP.
15. to 17. WM.
18. SWA - December 31, 1904 - Ebenezer Chapel, Newport.
19. to 20. WM.
21. WM - December 26, 1904.
22. WM.
23. Dr. M. Caig (Principal of Spurgeon's Pastor's College,

London), *The Welsh Evangelist* Vol 1, No. 1 : Revival
Atmosphere.

24. M. E. Hale, *Revival Number, The Postal, Telegraph &
Telephone association, Senior Branch. The Quarterly Mail*,
April 1905, London Branch

25. WM.

26. DMP.

Chapter 8 - Teenage Revivalists.

1. "*Mae Deisiau Di Bob Awr*"(I need Thee every hour) - A.S.
Hawks, 1835-1918.
"*O'r Hapus Awr*" (O Happy Day) - Philip Dodderidge, 1702
- 1751.

2. to 3. WM.

4. *Llanelly Mercury*, December 29, (1905).

5. *Baptist Times*, January 13, 1905 and Brynmor P Jones *Voices
from the Welsh Revival 1904-1905*, (1995).

6. *Baptist Times*, March 3rd and 10th, 1905

7. JVM.

8. FSAT - pg 168.

9. Edward Wilkins, *Memories of the Revival of 1904 and 1905*.

10. WM.

11. SWA - December 31, 1904.

12. WM.

13. WM. "Y *Gwr wrth Ffynon Jacob*" (The Man at Jacob's Well)
- A hymn by Thomas William, 1761 - 1844.

Y Gwr wrth Ffynon Jacob
Eisteddodd gynt i lawr
Tramwyodd drwg Samaria
Tramwyed yma'n awr;
Roedd syched arno yno
Am gael eu hachubhug
Mae syched arno eto
Am achub llawr murg.
The Man at Jacob's well
Sat down there once
He travelled through Samaria

May He walk here now;
He was thirsty there -
Thirsty to save them
He is still/now thirsting
To save many more.

14. *South Wales Daily News*, Llanfachreth, June 14th
15. *The Evangelical Magazine* for September/October 1949
16. *North Wales Guardian*, 27th January 1905

Chapter 9 - Salvations, Signs and Wonders.

1. J. J. Morgan, *Coviant Evan Phillips*, p 332 (1930)
2. Bethan Lloyd-Jones, *Evangelicals Now*, October 1987, My memories of the 1904-5 revival in Wales
3. WM - November 16th - Pontcymer
4. to 5. WM.
6. SWA - January 12, 1905, Revival at Newport, meeting at Corporation Road Hall (Forward Movement)
7. SWA - Malpas Road Hall.
8. *The Sunday Companion*, February 4th, 1905
9. *Esgairgeiliog Merionethshire*
10. *Welsh Farmer's Gazette,* February 8, 1905
11. *Cassette 203 in the Oral History Project Collect*, Clwyd Library, Mold.
12. DMP.
13. WM
14. SWA - during the Newport Mission
15. Voices - Tanygrisian, Blaenau Ffestiniog.John Powell Parry in a recorded interview with Paul E. G. Cook,
16. Primary Source all material re Mary Jones, Egryn - *Stars and Rumours of star: The Egryn Lights and other Mysterious Phenomena in the Welsh Religious Revival, 1904-1905* by Kevin McClore, 1980 archive. Also *The Barmouth Advertiser* February 2, 1905 - Rev. Elvet Lewis.
17. *The British Weekly Article-* Rev. Elvet Lewis, January 26, 1905.
18. *The Sunday Companion*, February 25, 1905.
19. *The British Weekly Article* - Rev. Elvet lewis, January 26,

1905.

20. *Daily News* Beriah Evans, February 9, 1905.

21. *Y Goleuad* - Hugh Ellis, June 9, 1905, pp310 - 311.

22. *Cambrian News* - Editorial, March 10, 1905.

23. *Cambrian News* - Editorial, March 17, 1905.

24. Fursac Mouvement - pp144 - 8 and Voices - pg 249.

Chapter 10 - Women Worldwide.

1. WM - December 5th - Caerphilly.

2. *Cambrian News* - December 15, 1904 - Pwllheli townhall.

3. DMP.

4. to 6. WM.

7. *"In Search of Myself"*- D.R.Davies - pg38 (with thanks to Desmond Cartwright).

8. WM - April 11th - Liverpool.

9. *The Sunday Companion* - June 3, 1905.

10. EE - J Pengwern Jones.

11. EE - Scenes of Revival - Frank Howton, Amy Carmichael of Dohnavur.

12. to 13. HD.

14. "A Band of Apostolic Girls" - *The Christian Herald and Signs of our Times,* November 21, 1907.

15.NG .

16.NG - *Outward Bound from Doric Lodge. The Regions Beyond*, July 1908.

17. to 20. NG.

21. "The Schoolgirls Saturday Meeting "- *The Christian Herald and Signs of our Times,* November 21, 1907.

22.to 25. NG.

26. KC - pg236.

27. KC - pg 119.

28. Elisabeth James - first hand account.

29. WTFF - pg17.

Chapter 11- The Glory and the Pain.

1.Sidney Evans a Gomer M.Roberts - *Cyfrol Goff a Diwyiad 1904 - 05.*

2. WTFF - Orr, The Flaming Tongue - pg 18.

3. Voices - pg 65.

4. WM - January 31, 1905 - Double Revival in Wales by Peter Price, B.A. Hons.

5.to 7. WM.

8. *Yr Efengylydd* - October 1916, pg 147.

9. WM.

10. Some notes on the personality of Evan Roberts by Brynmor Pierce.

11. LE.

Chapter 12 - In the House of "Jezebel"?

1. Keswick Story,1964, pg 121.

2. EE quoting DD, pg59.

3 - 11 TT.

12. Insight from Sue Mitchell.

13. TT.

14. Deborah Chapman - unpublished paper - Jessie Penn-Lewis.

15. *War on the Saints* - Jessie Penn-Lewis with Evan Roberts.

16. Insight from Pippa Gardner.

17. *The Revival in the West* - W.T. Stead, pg 30 and 34.

Chapter 13 - What Happened to the Women?

1. The testimony of Dafydd Jones of Aberporth in an interview with Brynmor Pierce Jones in October 1989.

2. *The Revivals Children - Early Welsh Pentecostalism in the growth of Bethlehem Pentecost Church*, pg9. (1980)

3. EE - The Pentecostal Movement, pg 88.

4. *The Miraculous Four Square Gospel* - Supernatural - George Jeffreys (founder and leader of the Elim Four Square Gospel Alliance). Vol11. London Elim Publishing Compnay Ltd, Park Crescent, Clapham, SW4.

5. EE - The prophetic Ministry (or the voice gifts) in the Church.

6. G.Brynmor Thomas (transaltion Gareth Huws) SWDN (April 13, 1906) - Revival Pandemonium.

7. FSAT - Appendix 1 - "Pentecostal women in ministry: where do we go from here?" Sheri R. Benvenuti. Edith Blumhofer, "*The*

Assemblies of God: A popular history" Springfield Gospel
Publishing House, 1985, pg 137.
8. *The Revivals Children - Early Welsh Pentecostalism in the
growth of Bethlehem Pentecost Church(1980).*
9. FSAT - Appendix 1 - "Pentecostal women in ministry: where do
we go from here?" Sheri R. Benvenuti.
10. to 11. KC.
12. LE.
13. to 14. KC.

Chapter 14 - Forerunners of the Next Revival.
1. The Welsh Language weekly newspaper.
2. Annibynwyr - "The Independents" - A Welsh speaking chapel
denomination.

Chapter 15 - It is time!
1. Frederick Franson,"Women called to preach" (Lindale:COP
Publications 1989), pg42.
2. OOTS.
3. *Equal to Serve,* Gretchen Gaebelein Hull - "Secular Feminism
centres around gaining equal rights; Biblical Feminism centres
around equal opportunities to serve."
4. *The Role and Ministry of Women* - Martin Scott, pg 44.
5. *Why Not Women?* - Loren Cunningham, David Jones Hamilton
with Janice Rogers.
6. EE
7. FSAT - appendices - from the September 1907 edition of
Apostolic Faith.
8. FSAT - pg 106.

Appendix 1

Recommended Further Reading

For Such a Time as This - The Liberation of Women to Lead in the Church, Martin Scott (2001). P.S.Promotions.

The Role and Ministry of Women, Pioneer Perspectives Series, Martin Scott (1992). Word UK Ltd.

Why Not Women - A Fresh Look at Scripture on Women in Missions, Ministry and Leadership, Loren Cunningham, David Joel Hamilton with Janice Rogers (2000). YWAM Publishing.

The Role and Ministry of Women - Small Group Bible Studies, Elizabeth Watkins (2004). Shedhead Productions.

In the Spirit We're Equal/The Spirit, Bible and Women : A Revival Perspective, Susan C.Hyatt (published 1998). Hyatt International Ministries.

Women on the Frontlines, Michal Ann Goll(published 1996). Destiny Image Publishing.

Women : God's Secret Weapon - God's Inspiring Message to Women of Power, Purpose and Destiny, Ed Silvoso (2001). Regal Books.

Index of Poems/Text and Images

Shedhead Productions

Shedhead is a creative partnership which produces design, print, photographs, enamels, poetry, reflections, meditations and video/DVD's that seek to express a different perspective on life and the experience of journey. The poems and pictures included in this book have been taken from the Destinᵧation Series - Cymru embracing destiny - a full colour series of 11 booklets of reflection in words, images, design, of a cry to see a transformed people and a transformed nation. The 11 sections of Destinᵧation are available separately or in a complete edition.

For further details please visit the website : www.shedhead.org , e-mail : shedheadproducts@aol.com.

*The song "Transformer of the nations" is available on CD from www.newidstudios.net